OXFORD WORLD'S CI

LA DÉBÂCL

Émile Zola was born in Paris in 1840, the son of a Venetian engineer and his French wife. He grew up in Aix-en-Provence where he made friends with Paul Cézanne. After an undistinguished school career and a brief period of dire poverty in Paris, Zola joined the newly founded publishing firm of Hachette which he left in 1866 to live by his pen. He had already published a novel and his first collection of short stories. Other novels and stories followed until in 1871 Zola published the first volume of his Rougon-Macquart series with the sub-title *Histoire naturelle et sociale d'une famille sous le Second Empire*, in which he sets out to illustrate the influence of heredity and environment on a wide range of characters and milieux. However, it was not until 1877 that his novel *L'Assommoir*, a study of alcoholism in the working classes, brought him wealth and fame. The last of the Rougon-Macquart series appeared in 1893 and his subsequent writing was far less successful, although he achieved fame of a different sort in his vigorous and influential intervention in the Dreyfus case. His marriage in 1870 had remained childless but his extremely happy liaison in later life with Jeanne Rozerot, initially one of his domestic servants, gave him a son and a daughter. He died in 1902.

Elinor Dorday studied French and Russian at Sidney Sussex College, Cambridge, and translation at the British Institute in Paris (University of London).

Robert Lethbridge is Professor of French Language and Literature at Royal Holloway, University of London. He has edited Zola's *L'Assommoir* for Oxford World's Classics.

OXFORD WORLD'S CLASSICS

*For almost 100 years Oxford World's Classics have brought
readers closer to the world's great literature. Now with over 700
titles—from the 4,000-year-old myths of Mesopotamia to the
twentieth century's greatest novels—the series makes available
lesser-known as well as celebrated writing.*

*The pocket-sized hardbacks of the early years contained
introductions by Virginia Woolf, T. S. Eliot, Graham Greene,
and other literary figures which enriched the experience of reading.
Today the series is recognized for its fine scholarship and
reliability in texts that span world literature, drama and poetry,
religion, philosophy and politics. Each edition includes perceptive
commentary and essential background information to meet the
changing needs of readers.*

OXFORD WORLD'S CLASSICS

——

ÉMILE ZOLA

La Débâcle

——

Translated by
ELINOR DORDAY

With an Introduction and Notes by
ROBERT LETHBRIDGE

OXFORD
UNIVERSITY PRESS

OXFORD
UNIVERSITY PRESS

Great Clarendon Street, Oxford OX2 6DP

Oxford University Press is a department of the University of Oxford.
It furthers the University's objective of excellence in research, scholarship,
and education by publishing worldwide in

Oxford New York

Athens Auckland Bangkok Bogotá Buenos Aires Calcutta
Cape Town Chennai Dar es Salaam Delhi Florence Hong Kong Istanbul
Karachi Kuala Lumpur Madrid Melbourne Mexico City Mumbai
Nairobi Paris São Paulo Singapore Taipei Tokyo Toronto Warsaw

with associated companies in Berlin Ibadan

Oxford is a registered trade mark of Oxford University Press
in the UK and in certain other countries

Published in the United States
by Oxford University Press Inc., New York

British Library Cataloguing in Publication Data

Data available

Library of Congress Cataloging in Publication Data

Zola, Emile, 1840–1902.
[Débâcle. English]
La débâcle/Emile Zola; translated by Elinor Dorday;
with an introduction and notes by Robert Lethbridge.
(Oxford world's classics)
1. Franco-Prussian War, 1870–1871—Fiction. I. Dorday, Elinor.
II. Lethbridge, Robert.
III. Title. IV. Oxford world's classics (Oxford University Press)
PQ2500.A33 2000 843'.8—dc21 99–053690

ISBN 0-19-282289-6

1 3 5 7 9 10 8 6 4 2

Typeset in Ehrhardt
by RefineCatch Limited, Bungay, Suffolk
Printed in Great Britain by
Cox and Wyman Ltd., Reading, Berkshire

CONTENTS

INTRODUCTION

The historical events transposed in Zola's great war-novel of 1892, *La Débâcle*, have had a shaping influence on modern France. For its subject is the catastrophic defeat suffered by the French at the hands of the Germans in 1870. Ever since, it can be argued, the country's national identity and foreign policies have been inseparable from the perception of the threat across the Rhine. For two world wars (and, as a consequence, the dynamic of Franco-German relations in the second half of the twentieth century) can be traced back through a causal pattern which originates in the Franco-Prussian War. As a direct result of it, by the Treaty of Frankfurt in May 1871, France lost its eastern provinces of Alsace and Lorraine, an amputation only avenged by the terms of the Treaty of Versailles (1919) which, in turn, provided Hitler with the opportunity to reverse them. Yet, in the same way as Tolstoy's *War and Peace* transcends the Napoleonic campaigns which are its own historical context, *La Débâcle* retains its power over and beyond the particular time and place which are its setting. If it enjoys, in French literary history, a reputation as 'a seminal work' for all modern depictions of war,[1] it is because of its *fictional* design. However vouchsafed its accuracy may be, Zola's novel reworks events in such a way as to continue to engage the reader at the level of the timeless conflict between vast historical forces and the human beings subject to such fatalities beyond their control.

The Franco-Prussian War and the Commune

It is nevertheless useful to be reminded of the outline of those dramatic events of 1870–1, and it is notable that *La Débâcle* skilfully inserts, even for earlier generations of readers, allusions which plot the chronological coordinates of this chapter of French history. There is room neither here nor, for that matter, in Zola's novel to explain the complex *origins* of the Franco-Prussian War. The

[1] Denis Boak, 'War and the Holocaust', in Timothy Unwin (ed.), *The Cambridge Companion to the French Novel: From 1800 to the Present* (Cambridge: Cambridge University Press, 1997), 161.

apparently unlikely *causa belli* was the Spanish throne, vacant since 1868. In supporting the candidature of King William of Prussia's obscure relative Prince Leopold of Hohenzollern, Chancellor Bismarck had found the perfect pretext to draw France into a war necessary to drive the southern German states into a powerful union with Prussia. Consternation in France, at the prospect of having to guard its Iberian frontier too, escalated into an ultimatum to the Prussian government to withdraw the Hohenzollern candidacy. In the ensuing diplomatic manœuvring, during the first two weeks of July 1870, France played into Bismarck's hands. Relying on its alliance with Italy and Austria, and supremely confident of crushing the pretensions of an incipient German Empire, France declared war on Prussia on 19 July. In its opening pages, *La Débâcle* evokes the rejoicing in Paris at the news, 'when crowds swept down the boulevards, and bands of people brandished torches crying, "To Berlin! To Berlin!"' (p. 14). And, from then on, Zola does refer us (often through rumours, the conversations of his characters, or the newspapers they come across by chance) both to significant moments in the War and to the salient features of the doomed French resistance to the invasion.

This was masterminded by Field Marshal von Moltke and spearheaded by three brilliantly led German armies: General Karl von Steinmetz's across the Moselle; that of the King's nephew, Prince Frederick Charles, from the Palatinate (the region north of Alsace on the left bank of the Rhine) heading towards Metz; and Crown Prince Frederick's from the upper Rhine towards Strasbourg. A French army advanced into the Saar and won a minor victory at Saarbrücken. But then the German 'avalanche'—to use the contemporary metaphor—began. On 4 August, the force under General Abel Douay was defeated at Wissembourg. Two days later, at Frœschwiller, Marshal MacMahon was routed (with his 35,000 men outnumbered by 140,000 Prussians) and forced to evacuate Alsace-Lorraine, as the Crown Prince surrounded Strasbourg and moved towards Nancy. The indecisive Marshal Bazaine was soon shut up in Metz. His army's final destruction was only a matter of time. Between the 14th and the 18th (in the battles of Borny, Rezonville-Gravelotte, and Saint-Privat), his attempts to break out were repulsed, and the Germans advanced on Châlons-sur-Marne. When MacMahon tried to relieve Bazaine at Metz, he found the road

closed and was decisively defeated in the battle of Sedan on
1 September. His army, with Napoleon III himself, capitulated the
following day. When the news reached Paris, on the 4th, the end of
the Second Empire was formally voted by a pressured legislature,
with responsibility for the war transferred to Léon Gambetta's
government of National Defence. But, after Sedan, the German
armies swept on. Bazaine surrendered at Metz on 27 October, with
6,000 officers and 173,000 men. Paris was besieged and its population reduced to virtual starvation before its capitulation on 28 January 1871. Before that, on the 18th, and in the very same Hall of
Mirrors, at Versailles, where revenge would only be exacted half a
century later, France was subjected to the humiliating spectacle of
William (with his new title of *Kaiser*) being proclaimed as Emperor
of Germany, thus bringing Bismarck's grand strategy to a successful
conclusion.

For the French, however, there was worse to follow. Faith in the
government's ability to prosecute the war had been progressively
undermined throughout the winter by a virtually unbroken sequence
of military reverses, most acutely felt in Paris by the abortive
attempts to break through the German encirclement of the city.
Having undergone the fruitless suffering of four months' siege, the
disaffected population felt itself betrayed by the government's nego-
tiation of an armistice and the ensuing national elections which
returned a conservative-leaning (and largely provincial) majority
pledged to end the War at any price. This included the further
humiliation of the entry of German troops into the capital within the
devastating peace terms accepted by the National Assembly, meeting
in Bordeaux, on 1 March. Paris refused to accept that authority. The
National Guard there, which the Germans had failed to disarm by
the armistice of 28 January, appointed a central committee and
seized cannon belonging to the regular army on 18 March. The
subsequent election of the Commune, both to run the city and as an
alternative government, effectively marked the beginning of a civil
war. This continued through the spring, with Paris now besieged
for a second time, this time by French forces under the orders of
Adolphe Thiers's 'official' government, now moved to Versailles.
Only between 21 and 28 May (known as the 'Bloody Week') did
these succeed in taking back control of the city, and then at a terrible
cost. On both sides there were calculated atrocities and an almost

unimaginable barbarity. The Versailles troops worked their way through the barricades in indiscriminate slaughter compounded by mass executions often carried out with terrible cruelty. Summary courts martial and deportations would continue into the months and years ahead, the last of them in 1875, with a general amnesty declared only in 1880. It is estimated that at least 25,000 French died at the hands of their countrymen during that one week in May 1871, more than in any single battle of the Franco-Prussian War. As the Communards retreated, they set fire to the city. Paris was in ruins. The Third Republic had been born in what Victor Hugo called *L'Année terrible*. *La Débâcle* is the story of that year.

Les Rougon-Macquart

Zola took no part in the war that brought about the fall of the Second Empire, a fact which critics of *La Débâcle* would later throw in his face with scorn. Of an Italian father who had died in 1847, Zola had been a naturalized French citizen since 1862. But, recently married (31 May 1870) and as the only son of a widow, he was exempted from military service and, on the outbreak of hostilities, his myopia prevented his being admitted to serve in the National Guard. He left Paris in early September, making his way first to Marseilles (where he helped found a short-lived newspaper) before moving across to Bordeaux, the seat of the provisional government, in mid-December. Having made several vain attempts to obtain a post as a regional sous-préfet, he at last solved his financial problems by becoming secretary to a member of Gambetta's government. Shortly afterwards, at the very end of the year, he was joined by his wife and mother who had accompanied him to Provence. He remained in his new position until February 1871, thereafter earning his living by writing a parliamentary chronicle for *La Cloche*. On 14 March he returned to Paris, following the National Assembly's decision to resume its sessions in Versailles. He was arrested briefly by both sides during the civil war, once in Paris on his way to Versailles, the second time during a haphazard round-up there, the very next day, of suspected rebels. As events reached their climax, Zola retreated to the Seine hamlet of Bennecourt, returning to Paris on 27 May, once the Commune had been definitively suppressed. He would continue to send his reports to *La Cloche* until 1872, infinitely bored by the parliamentary proceedings he was forced to witness, yet having no other means of support. In a private correspondence in which there are few references to the War itself, one gets the impression, above all, of an immense frustration at being unable to get going on his literary career.

For it was only shortly before this that Zola had launched the series which would become *Les Rougon-Macquart*, that massive novel-cycle which would ensure his one-time status as the greatest European writer of his generation and his permanent place in literary history. The serial-publication of its opening volume, *La Fortune des Rougon*, had been suspended in June 1870 because of the impending crisis. By the time it was finally published, in October 1871, Zola's entire project would have to be recast. This is true of both many individual novels and the thematic perspectives of the series as a whole. As far as the future *La Débâcle* is concerned, for example, his original proposal to his publisher, in 1868–9, had envisaged a novel about the Italian war of 1859 against Austria, describing the life of a soldier and the relationship of the army to the Empire. Now, the events of that campaign paled into insignificance and such a book was never written. His study of military life would in due course be inserted into *La Débâcle*, but within a novel of far greater scope and meaning. As for *Les Rougon-Macquart*, Zola would still aim to do for the Second Empire what Balzac had done for the Restoration and the July Monarchy, but the fall of the regime meant that his series would no longer be a contemporary chronicle. Instead he would be the historian of a vanished society. He could have preserved the contemporaneity of his series by modifying his plan and extending its time-scale into the early years of the Third Republic. But he decided against this on artistic grounds, for 'the crushing finality of the Franco-Prussian War was a fifth act which history itself seemed to be proposing to the dramatist'.[2] For if it was politically inevitable (one of the reasons why Napoleon III had been persuaded to undertake such a fatal foreign adventure was in an attempt to bolster his disintegrating support at home), the regime's denouement also provided Zola's series with a note of finality and completeness which the rigorous artist in him would be able to exploit.

La Débâcle is the nineteenth and penultimate volume of *Les*

---

[2] F. W. J. Hemmings, *Émile Zola* (2nd edn., Oxford: Clarendon Press, 1966), 68.

Rougon-Macquart, but it is the real conclusion of his vast historical panorama, with *Le Docteur Pascal* (1893), as the twentieth, largely functioning as an epilogue to the family chronicle. And that concluding 'débâcle' is prefigured (whether in Zola's vocabulary, the catastrophe's metaphorical staging, or its synchronization with plot-endings[3]) in many of the novels he wrote during the 1870s and 1880s, in which his evocation of a corrupt period of French history is overlaid by the dramatic irony of its apocalyptic finale. Zola was perfectly aware of *La Débâcle*'s privileged positioning in this respect. *La Fortune des Rougon* is a tale of beginnings, not least that of the Second Empire itself, in the *coup d'état* of 2 December 1851 (when the elected President Louis-Napoleon seized power and styled himself Emperor). If *La Débâcle* tells of its end, the rise and fall of Napoleon III is thereby afforded the symmetry of a classical tragedy. Founded in blood, his regime had appropriately crumbled in blood. It would make of Zola's cycle, as he had rightly foreseen in 1871, a closed circle. Many of the novels within it virtually stand alone, sometimes only tenuously connected by the hereditary branches of his Rougon-Macquart representatives of the age. But if all his theoretical and fictional texts are informed by deterministic laws of causality, the inexorable logic of History provides the overarching structural and thematic coherence to a series subtitled 'The Natural and Social History of a Family under the Second Empire'.

La Débâcle

Zola started serious work on *La Débâcle* in March 1891. He claimed to have read over a hundred books on the Franco-Prussian War. He certainly annotated a very large number, including specialist tomes on gunnery and uniforms. He got hold of French translations of German accounts of 1870–1. He exploited the file of press-cuttings he had assembled over a period of twenty years in anticipation of writing *La Débâcle* He had an interview with Émile Ollivier who had been Prime Minister when war was declared. He met former military commanders as well as reading their memoirs. He consulted eminent historians and veteran field surgeons, spoke to many survivors, and received letters from others. In April 1891, Zola visited

---

[3] Most obviously in *Nana* (1880), *La Terre* (1887), and *La Bête humaine* (1890) which end with the 1870 declaration of war.

the battlefields, returning with over a hundred pages of notes. The publicity surrounding the visit itself generated further unsolicited testimony, civilians and ex-soldiers alike bringing him their eyewitness evidence. Nearly all Zola's work-notes are preserved in the Bibliothèque Nationale, in Paris. Those for *La Débâcle* come to well over a thousand pages, more than half of them devoted to his research. The end-product of this careful preparation is the most documented of all the novels of *Les Rougon-Macquart*. Both contemporaries and historians testify to the validity of the novel's reconstruction of events. When hostile critics belaboured Zola with tedious lists of supposed inaccuracies, he clearly took a certain amount of pleasure in refuting their charges point by point. Indeed, it has been claimed that only one incident (when Goliath has his throat slit in Part III; Chapter 5) does not have some basis in fact. And readers cannot fail to be struck by the extraordinary mastery, on the part of a 'mere' creative writer, of the technicalities of war.

Yet it is also clear that, as in the case of his other novels, Zola's documentation was to some extent *preceded* by properly imaginative work on the shape of the work, its structure and major themes. In the case of *La Débâcle*, he articulates a vision of the events of 1870–1 gradually elaborated over the years prior to the research which he undertook in May and June 1891 and continued through the subsequent stages of its writing. He began drafting on 18 July 1891, complaining to friends that it was a slow business. By January 1892, however, he had finished the first two parts of this enormous novel, the longest of all *Les Rougon-Macquart*. And, astonishingly, a mere four months later, on 12 May, he penned its final words. Its serialization had begun in *La Vie populaire* back in February. *La Débâcle* appeared in volume form on 24 June 1892. The fact that it was more than twenty years since the events it recounted did nothing to assuage the critical reception focused on Zola's treatment of the French army; and that strain of hostility to this novel would be revived in the context of Zola's public stand against the military in the Dreyfus Affair in 1898.[4] For the most part, however, there was widespread acknowledgement that *La Débâcle* was one of his finest

---

[4] In 1898 Zola achieved international fame by coming out publicly (in his open letter to the President of the Republic, *J'Accuse*, on 13 January) on the side of Alfred Dreyfus, the army officer wrongly convicted of treason, and thus provoking the state to put the novelist on trial for his violent attack on the military authorities.

achievements, not merely in its own epic qualities, but also (and this is what makes it unsurprising that, during Zola's lifetime, it remained the best-selling of all his novels[5]) in providing for a whole generation a better understanding of France's national tragedy in 1870–1.

That distance from those events has major consequences for *La Débâcle*. It would have been a very different novel if it had been written in the immediate aftermath of the Franco-Prussian War. Interpretative perspective would have been subordinate to topicality and eyewitness accounts. In an 1872 review of one such collection of personal reminiscences, Zola had declared that it was still ten years too early to gain critical purchase on recent events. By the time he himself did so, the meaning and the protagonists of France's defeat would be viewed from another kind of distance, both philosophical and aesthetic. The portrait of Napoleon III we find in *La Débâcle*, to take a specific example explored below, is enhanced in ways which bear little resemblance to the caricature figured in Zola's polemical articles in the opposition press at the end of the Second Empire.

What remains invariable, however, is a fundamental anti-militarism which is characteristic of Zola's attitude at the time as well as colouring the wisdom of hindsight. Even before the formal declaration of war, Zola was one of those radical journalists exploiting the imminence of hostilities as further evidence of the regime's leading his country to disaster. In a piece in *La Cloche* of 11 July 1870, entitled simply 'The War', he recalled the Emperor's campaigns of 1854 and 1859 and aligned himself firmly in the anti-militaristic camp. A week later, in the same newspaper, Zola called for the voice of reason to recount 'the horror and madness of the slaughter' behind the promised glory. In his journalism throughout that summer, he would continue in the same vein, including recalling how, as a boy, he had watched the smartly uniformed soldiers marching to the front, only to see them eventually return 'limping and bleeding as they dragged themselves along the road'. If such recollections, whether authentic or invented, were the common currency of that section of the press which had not succumbed to the general chauvinistic frenzy, Zola's stance was by no means opportunistic. For, as long ago as 1862, he had written an anti-militaristic tale,

'Blood' (reprinted in *Contes à Ninon* two years later), in which a battlefield is evoked through the hallucinatory devices of the Gothic novel. At its close the four soldiers of the story ignore the call of duty and walk off arm in arm in search of peace, leaving behind them the blood of their nightmares and agreeing that 'our job is a filthy one'. Such pacifist idealism would not prevent Zola later calling patriotically to his countrymen to fight the Prussian invader to the death. But it does reveal, in the future author of *La Débâcle*, a deeply held revulsion for the physical realities of war. This is evident, for example, in his descriptions of the fortress at Sedan, filled by the stench of excrement and decaying corpses. There is a crucial distinction to be made, however, between Zola's consistent rejection of militarism, on the one hand, and, on the other, a philosophical conception of war gradually accommodated within a Darwinian vision of man and of the eternal conflict between the forces of Life and Death within a larger evolutionary struggle. This had not yet been arrived at, either during, or immediately after, 1870. It would receive its ultimate expression in *La Débâcle*.

Zola's long-standing anti-militarism is certainly evident in his own contribution to *Les Soirées de Médan* in 1880.[6] The collection, as a whole (including, most famously, Maupassant's *Boule-de-suif*), is consciously aimed at demystifying military glory too easily confused with admirable patriotism, not least at a time characterized by the vengeful enthusiasm for renewed conflict with Germany. Zola's *The Attack on the Mill* ends as Dominique is shot by the Prussians under the eyes of Françoise, his fiancée, for having defended his future father-in-law's mill. After the French counter-attack has driven out the enemy, the Captain's final victory-cry foregrounds the emptiness of such nationalistic triumphalism. For, as her father is killed by a stray bullet, Françoise is left imbecilic with grief amongst the smouldering ruins. This looks forward to the episode in *La Débâcle* in which Weiss defends his house against the Bavarians before being shot in front of his wife. The earlier tale is bathed in an uncomplicated sympathy for innocent victims. In *La Débâcle*, by contrast, Silvine's mournful trek amongst the dead in search of her fiancé's body, or the spectacle of the wretched prisoners-of-war

[6] This was a collection of anti-militaristic tales published by Zola and his literary circle (including Huysmans and Maupassant, the latter's *Boule-de-suif* establishing his reputation).

herded like beggars across the land, are treated with an authorial compassion not incompatible with a more dispassionate vision. Nor is that the only difference between *The Attack on the Mill* and the later novel, with which, as Zola stressed, it had no link except in so far as it originally appeared under the title of 'An Episode from the Invasion of 1870'. Both in tone and in their limited purview, Zola's tale and his polemical articles stand significantly apart from his picture of war in *La Débâcle*.

To judge that picturing is to do so with Harry Levin's dictum in mind: 'War is the test-case for realistic fiction. No other subject can be so obscured by the ivy of tradition, the crystallisation of legend, the conventions of epic and romance.'[7] Zola had many examples of the pitfalls. While admiring Hector Malot's portrayal in his *Souvenirs d'un blessé* (1872), he pointed to the danger inherent in this author's attempt to extend the technique initiated by Stendhal in his depiction of Waterloo in *La Chartreuse de Parme* (1839). For Malot's hero is made to range all over France in order to satisfy a double imperative: remaining faithful to the Stendhalian mode of approaching reality solely through the consciousness of the protagonist; but simultaneously trying to give a complete picture of the Franco-Prussian War. Zola avoids these kinds of problems by choosing to focus so centrally on Sedan. This was deliberate. For while a revised list of novels, in 1872–3, included separate studies of the Italian campaign of 1859, the end of the Second Empire, and one devoted to 'the War, the Siege and the Commune', the choice of Sedan (as he told a critic) enabled him both to close his novel-cycle and fulfil many of the intentions of the planned three distinct works.

La Débâcle falls into three parts, each of eight chapters. The first of these describes the march of the 7th Corps from Rheims to Sedan, the second the catastrophe of Sedan, and the last is a brief recapitulation of the disasters of the winter of 1870–1 followed by an epilogue-like description of the Commune and the burning of Paris. Standing at the centre of the novel, Sedan is emblematic of more than simply the military fiasco of 1870. After news of the early reverses had reached Paris, it had become clear that only a stunning military victory could save the Second Empire. Instead it suffered the most comprehensive and crushing of defeats. *La Débâcle* is not a

[7] *The Gates of Horn* (New York: Oxford University Press, 1966), 137.

neutral title. That the 80,000 prisoners taken at Sedan included Napoleon III himself underlined the extent to which, while it may not have been as important as the battles around Metz, Sedan represented *the* 'débâcle' in its multiple senses: for an army, an emperor and his empire, a government, a society, and a world. Sedan allowed Zola, as he put it, 'to show France . . . irrevocably fated to disaster'.[8] Nor was his choice of regiment fortuitous in this respect. Even before he went to Sedan on his fact-finding visit in April 1891, Zola had decided to recount the story of the 7th Corps.[9] When he got there, he retraced its steps in the minutest detail, from village to village. For historians and contemporaries alike, its experience summed up everything that had gone wrong, from the trivial to the fatally absurd; and, by placing his fictional characters in its 106th Regiment, Zola focused the novel on a microcosm of the confusion, irresolution, and incompetence of the French offensive of 1870.

He explained to Robert Sherard, his first English biographer, that the march from Rheims to Sedan, described in the opening section of the novel, 'is an epic event, pregnant with the irony of Fate'. For 'the reader follows the movements of this ill-fated Corps', Zola told him, 'knowing what a terrible shadow of defeat, disaster and death overhangs it'. As the novel begins, the lack of supplies, rifle-parts, medical and other support staff, and an uninformed commanding officer, all contribute to a general state of chaotic unreadiness. And in the incoherence of military operations preceding Sedan, the army becomes a bewildered and directionless mass, gradually overcome by paralysis. In Chapter 2, a growing and helpless panic was to be correlated, as Zola wrote in his work-notes, to the army's remorseless disintegration. When the regiment is loaded into cattle trucks, we are reminded of the last pages of *La Bête humaine* in which the idea of the herd being led to the slaughterhouse is made equally explicit. In *La Débâcle*, the peasants in the fields are aware only of cannon-fodder passing at speed, while the soldiers heading for Metz

[8] Quoted by Ernest Vizetelly in his 1892 preface to *The Downfall* (London: Chatto & Windus, 1899), p. vi, recording Zola's interview with Robert H. Sherard, editor of the *Weekly Times and Echo* of London in which the translation of *La Débâcle* was originally serialized. All further references to this interview, in the course of this Introduction, are cited from the same source. See also Michael Tilby, 'Émile Zola and his First English Biographer', *Laurels*, 59 (1988), 33–56.

[9] It was well known (and Zola read it himself) through Georges Bibesco's *Campagne de 1870. Belfort, Sedan: le 7e Corps de l'Armée du Rhin* (Paris, 1872).

scream out the grotesquely distorted echo ('Off to the slaughter', p. 44) of the chauvinistic cries for Berlin at the end of *Nana*. For so long foreseen throughout Zola's series, the shadow of Sedan now looms in its reality on the landscape of north-eastern France. When the army reaches the fated city, like a promised land, after a day of terrible marching, with the triumphant cry of 'That's Sedan' (p. 131), the tragic irony of the name needs no further commentary.

Concerned, above all, with reinforcing this sense of inexorability, Zola declared that 'each movement of troops that contributed to the final dénouement is exposed'. The text opens with the arrival of General Félix Douay in the camp of the 7th Corps outside Mulhouse. He decides that the army should retrace its steps back to Belfort. Taken back to Paris by rail, the men are then immediately dispatched to Rheims, where they learn they will be joined by the whole army of Châlons which has been retreating since morning. Through the technique of having a character come across a newspaper we learn of the disagreement in high places. One item reveals the official decision to retreat towards Paris. A Republican article provocatively states that the Empress, having forbidden her husband to return to the capital for fear of revolution, has ordered the Châlons army to advance to meet Bazaine at Metz. Having wasted the invaluable advantage of the time to effect an efficient mobilization and advance across the Rhine, the French army finally sets off for the unknown on 23 August. Three days later comes word of the decision to withdraw. Awakened by the passage of troops through Le Chesne, Zola's character learns that the retreat has been abandoned and that, after a message from Paris, the Emperor and MacMahon had made the fateful decision, politically motivated but unjustifiable from a strictly military point of view, to advance, eventually to Remilly and thence to Sedan. The first part of *La Débâcle* thus relates how the illusory prospect of a triumphal entry into Berlin is shattered by events.

To underline the inescapable defeat to come and darken the shadow of Fate hanging over the army, Zola even arranges the weather to artistic effect. The narrative opens under lowering clouds, and the howling wind expresses the anguish of the moment. As the soldiers wait for news, the portents of catastrophe are visible. During the second day of the retreat to Belfort, the landscape itself reflects their mood. As they straggle across the barren plain, the smoke which fills the sky seems to follow them as they march. And when they reach Sedan, the mists and grey dawn signal the disaster to come. Presages of the latter are visibly inserted by the novelist. A cry of suffering rings out in the night to interrupt Rochas's enumeration of the great French victories of the past, and Maurice's intoxicating evocation of Napoleonic glory is immediately followed by his coming across two soldiers who in turn recount the defeats of Frœschwiller and Wissembourg.

This kind of interpolation of fictional and historical narratives is part of Zola's solution to the problem of conveying to the reader both the partial experiences of individuals and the wider angle in which they are set. Much as he admired Stendhal and had recognized the brilliance of the Waterloo episode in *La Chartreuse de Parme*, Zola adopted a rather different standpoint. There are instances in *La Débâcle* when characters do suffer a disorientation akin to that of Stendhal's Fabrice. This is particularly the case where the temporal rhythm (a week in Part I; hour by hour in the single day recounted in Part II) allows a variety of viewpoints, interspersing that of the humble soldier at Sedan with an authorial cross-referencing between simultaneous narratives located in different sectors of the battle. More generally, however, Zola is less interested in exploring the psychology of the individual soldier than in creating the larger backdrop against which the destiny of human beings is played out.

This all-embracing view is arrived at in a number of ways. One of these is through a properly historical narrative abbreviated to form an extraordinarily allusive texture (to which the Explanatory Notes at the end of this edition bear witness) and shaped into a rhythm marked by stylistic repetitions and modulations given the authority of omniscience. Secondly, Zola shifts his focus so that those who assume a literally panoptic overview of the battlefield become his privileged observers; and these are not limited to active participants: Delaherche, as a civilian, has the freedom of movement to witness key events within the narrative whose coherence he assures. By a process of accretion, the more restricted views of other characters also add up to authorial elucidation, not least through the artifice whereby soldiers repeatedly overhear the plan of action decided upon by their superiors. In Part III, in which Zola's own historical perspective is most evident, Henriette does the job for him by sitting down next to the wounded Maurice and reading out to him (and to us) a chronological synopsis, drawn from a newspaper, of events in

France during the preceding months. Earlier, two of the protagonists, in particular, are responsible for alerting the reader to the inevitability of disaster. Weiss, the Alsatian thoroughly familiar with the
terrain around Sedan, serves Zola as an expert in military strategy.
Having watched the developing situation for days, he warns the
unheeding French generals that Sedan is a death-trap surrounded by
hills, and his earlier prediction is realized as he points out to Jean the
German armies making their encircling movement on the high
ground. Zola also took full advantage of the Prussian King's presence on the heights of La Marfée overlooking the battlefield, where
he is seen on three occasions between dawn and sunset. Each of them
takes to a further stage the remorseless closing of an iron set of jaws
strangling the life out of the French army.

   Zola's art of characterization is partly a consequence of such
explanatory positionings. As in much of his work, there is an
emphasis here on vast impersonal forces at the expense of individu-
ated inner lives. So too, his remark, in an 1892 article in *Le Figaro*
(responding to *La Débâcle's* critical reception) that the Châlons
army was itself the one major 'character' of *La Débâcle* can be juxta-
posed to Zola's reputation for his powerful crowd-scenes, like those
in *Germinal* (1885). If the stages of the army's disintegration are as
identifiable as those of an individual like Gervaise in *L'Assommoir*
(1877), its emotions of fear, suffering, and humiliation are those of
the mass, and he acutely registers its changes of mood, from contagious hope to renewed despair. But, as he had chosen the one
episode of Sedan as emblematic of the War as a whole, so Zola's
characters within the doomed army are essentially representative of
a larger group. Thus the ignorant general Bourgain-Desfeuilles
exemplifies the incompetence responsible for France's defeat. The
veteran Napoleonic sergeant Rochas incarnates the legend of
French military invincibility born at Marengo and Austerlitz. There
is a deliberate effort, on Zola's part, to show the backgrounds and
political views of different kinds of soldier. On the enemy side,
Zola's work-notes also make it clear that he conceived Otto Gunther
as the personification of the Prussian mentality, hard, cautious, and
disciplined. During the retreat to Belfort, the peasant woman who
stands accusingly at her door is a symbol of the French national
conscience. It was an incident which Zola found in his reading, but
he dramatically embellishes it to make of her a figure larger than life.

The whole question of artistic licence is brought into sharper relief by Zola's treatment of the most important of all the novel's historical models, namely Napoleon III himself. He makes an oblique entrance in many of *Les Rougon-Macquart*. Nowhere is this as extensive as in *La Débâcle*, where his character is sketched with the same brief repeated strokes found in earlier novels. His watery eyes, especially, suggest weakness and vacillation. And throughout the campaign, Zola portrays him as he was, in excruciating pain from kidney stones, and physically and mentally incapable of dominating the situation. In sharp contrast to King William, the embodiment of German confidence as he watches the mathematical encirclement of the French, Napoleon III is seen as a man sick, helpless, and vulnerable. One particular detail, however, provoked intense controversy after the publication of the novel. Critics were quick to question the authenticity of sightings of the Emperor with rouge on his cheeks in order to disguise his pallor and keep up the appearance of courage. Zola could point to his source in Gabriel Monod's *Allemands et Français* (1871), but he was perfectly aware that it was not a version which had ever secured complete assent. In his 1892 *Figaro* article he made the point that, faced with uncertain evidence of this kind, it remained the novelist's prerogative to sacrifice absolute veracity in the interests of artistic necessity. It was poetically right, above all, that the man who had dictated the theatrical sham of the Second Empire should make his exit made up as an actor. Zola's portrait of him seldom loses sight of the dynastic stakes at risk in his imminent fall. There is a patently Hugolian echo in *La Débâcle*'s retracing of a Bonapartist destiny whose criminal origins are finally atoned for at Sedan. As he flees guiltily, he is pictured alone in an inn on the Belgian border, where two engravings meet his weary eyes (and which were still there when Zola visited the room in April 1891): the first, of the 'Marseillaise' being sung, symbolizes the people's revenge on the despotic seizure of power, from Napoleon Bonaparte's 'Dix-Huit Brumaire' to his nephew's own *coup d'état*; the second shows the Last Judgement, the appropriately divine retribution for that criminal 'Deux-Décembre' of 1851. More generally, the recurring appearances of the phantom-like figure of the Emperor give a unity to the novel by drawing the intensifying curve of his Empire's demise.

Zola denied, however, degrading the memory of Napoleon III by insisting on his physical discomfort and personal inadequacies. To a Dutch admirer, Zola explained that it was also for effect that he had included the possibly apocryphal episode in which he was jeered by his troops as they were being driven into captivity. It is significant that, the best part of a decade earlier, Zola had told another correspondent that he was intending to exploit this scene. The forlorn figure of the Emperor, thrown down from the pinnacles of power to be abused by the rabble, summoned up, in Zola's view, a tragic intensity of Shakespearian proportions. And, indeed, *La Débâcle* confirms the sincerity of Zola's 1895 statement that he had modified his conception of Napoleon III since the embittered 1860s. For although we are never allowed to forget that he is ultimately responsible for the chaos around him, we are left above all with the impression of a victim of Fate. He is also, more prosaically, a victim of Parisian machinations; and, left helpless and bewildered among the scattered trappings of his Empire, he becomes a spectacle of undeniable pathos. The soldiers' diagnosis is a brutal 'Done for' (p. 66), as the former glories of his reign are embodied in the shiny ambulatory kitchen which accompanies him and which, like himself, clutters the roads. Its uselessness is underlined by the fact that the Emperor can hardly get through a paltry and solitary dinner, yet another marker of the end of a period characterized throughout *Les Rougon-Macquart* as one of orgiastic excess and sated appetites. No longer the brilliant sovereign of the Tuileries or of Compiègne, and rejected by the capital, the sinister bandit of Hugo's *Napoléon-le-Petit* becomes, in Zola's novel, a figure of suffering and distress. He advances to Sedan in the certain knowledge of defeat, and searches for death among the hail of bullets, awaiting the working-out of an interlocking set of fatalities. The die had been cast, as Zola alerts us, in the meeting with MacMahon at Le Chesne. By having Maurice see Napoleon III through a window after the decision to advance to meet Bazaine, the novelist could (as he put it in his work-notes) 'enlarge its meaning', the silhouette against the window-pane outlining the empty shadow of divested power and authority.

This is an entirely different perspective from the one found in Zola's earlier writing. In *La Cloche* of 18 February 1872, he had vigorously denounced a brochure attempting to rehabilitate the Emperor's memory and give him credit, as historians now tend to do, for his humanity at Sedan in capitulating rather than prolong the slaughter of his men. Twenty years later, after immersing himself in the documentary evidence, Zola could leave behind his polemical invective. And Napoleon III's efforts to stop the massacre by ordering the hoisting of the white flag are seen in the novel as a restoration of his humanity. In the 1870s, he was universally found guilty, even to the point of the National Assembly declaring that he alone was responsible for all of France's misfortunes. Only in our own time is his reputation gradually being revised. It is to Zola's credit that, while seeing the Emperor's downfall as inevitable, his treatment of Napoleon III at Sedan is a noble one. It remains true that it was not merely the wisdom of hindsight which prompted this modified portrait. When he cited Shakespeare, Zola underlined his own aspirations for *La Débâcle*. Tragedy requires that even the merited fall of a tyrant should evoke our pity.

It was also only from twenty years' distance that Zola could finally bring the Commune into the same interpretative frame as the Franco-Prussian War. His attitude towards this revolutionary uprising has been much criticized, often by those wedded to the tradition of the resistance, on the part of French intellectuals, to oppressive establishment forces. Such is Zola's selective use of his sources that he omits any mention of the idealism of the Commune or its well-intentioned social reforms. It has even been suggested that Zola's treatment of it in *La Débâcle* was distorted by his desire, at the time, to enter the Académie Française. His view of it was in fact fixed and hardening long before 1892. In 1871 he had been appalled at the carnage, but moved from a refusal to take sides to a position of increasing hostility. Although he was severely critical of the Versaillais repression, the Commune was for Zola a demented nightmare, with its leaders characterized by their self-interested mediocrity and demagogic hysteria. The swaggering Chouteau, in *La Débâcle*, is precisely the type. And here, whatever sympathy Zola displays for individuals swept blindly along in the violence of the storm, the Commune is seen as an essentially pathological phenomenon, a symptom of debilitated brains and frustrated patriotism erupting in a monstrous collective madness. While his view of the Commune is thus the one Zola had retailed in his writing through two decades, what is distinct, in *La Débâcle*, is the symbolic significance it is afforded. For it is seen as an extension to the

Franco-Prussian War in the sense of being the final purificatory ritual after which France could rise from the ashes of imperial corruption. It is clearly a moral thesis rather than a political one. And its internal logic is as problematic as ascribing military defeat to decadent values rather than inferior generalship, poorer artillery, and anachronistic tactics. Similarly, both the ideological complexities and existential contradictions of the Commune experience are subsumed in a mythical scenario of elemental forces and historical progression. Within this, the themes of punishment, expiation, and rebirth hold a central place. For the idea of the Last Judgement is not restricted to the figure of the Emperor alone. As Otto Gunther watches a burning Paris from its northern suburbs, Zola makes explicit the comparison between the Second Empire and imperial Rome laid waste by the barbarians from the north. And Maurice has a hallucination of a ball going on in the Tuileries, implicitly conjuring up 'Nero's fiddling' at the same time as, inevitably, Sodom and Gomorrah. These had already been the tropes of opposition polemics in the 1860s as well as thematically informing European artistic practice from Wagner's *Götterdämmerung* to the lamentations of Paul Verlaine. Their development in *La Débâcle* makes of this novel both a contribution to, and a reflection of, the cultural landscape of the *fin-de-siècle*.

That properly terminal mythology is integral to a biological conception of history. Zola shares with the majority of his contemporaries the notion of society as a collective body, with a life-cycle organically plotted through growth and maturation, and decline and fall. If the Second Empire is viewed as a period of convulsive and dissipated energies, the medical analogy is extended through feverish decomposition to the necessary bloodletting of the Commune. *La Débâcle* foregrounds this idea of ridding a sick France of her impurities. The last thirty pages of it are punctuated by the reiteration of 'Paris is burning'. The Seine becomes a ribbon of fire and the horizon a blood-red sea. The entire novel leads to this climax. As Zola told Sherard, it was to end with 'the flames which clear away not only an old régime, but a whole psychological state, and prepare a fresh field for a new and regenerated people'. Maurice is Zola's mouthpiece as he recognizes, in the symbolic consumation of the accursed imperial city, the cauterizing and purgatorial fire of the Commune itself.

What distinguishes Zola's from many other *fin-de-siècle* discourses, however, is its ultimately positive thrust. In the midst of the sunset of destruction, Jean experiences the sensation of an equally red dawn. Beyond the conflagration of an imperial past *La Débâcle* ends with an underlying hope in the future, reinscribing the death of the old France within the myth of Eternal Return guaranteeing the birth of the new. That myth, most literally rehearsed in the germinations of rural life in *La Terre*, is all-pervasive in Zola's work: from the cemetery bursting with fecundity in *La Fortune des Rougon* to the very title of *Germinal*. In *La Débâcle*, it finds expression in the overlaid imagery of the Crucifixion, prefaced by the 'biblical stories' (p. 193) in which Judas is evoked. The 'passion of the Châlons army' (p. 379) expiates the sins of the Empire, and its supreme hour of suffering in the Camp of Misery at Iges is 'without glory, spat upon', that of the Cross, evoked as paganized symbol of the agony of France preceding its resurrection. Maurice explains that, with the Commune, 'the calvary had been climbed right to the top, to the most terrifying of agonies, the crucified nation was expiating its sins and was about to be reborn' (p. 509).

Even more explicitly, Zola endows the two central characters of the novel with allegorical significance. It is not by chance that Jean, serving with the army of National Defence, should kill Maurice, the Communard, on the barricades. For as they each represent one part of France, and as their friendship underlines national unity faced with the Prussian invasion, so the fact that they subsequently find themselves on opposite sides images a country divided within itself by a fratricidal civil war (underlined by Henriette as Maurice's twin sister and the alternative face of the nation). Maurice, who joins the army after a debauched existence in Paris, is the decadent and sickly element. As Zola told Sherard, with his chauvinistic enthusiasm and vague liberal idealism, Maurice is 'the type of the France of the Empire, embodying her grace and her faults. He is the type of the France that, sated with pleasure, rushed to disaster.' As the national disease reaches its climax in the Commune, so the fever of the wounded Maurice follows the course of the raging inferno. If Zola makes it abundantly clear that his expiatory death is the necessary condition for France's renewal, Maurice goes so far as to see himself as the gangrenous limb that must be amputated from the social body so that the nation will not die. His own death at Jean's hands completes the allegory. For Jean, by contrast, represents the soul of a

France more eternal than an ephemeral regime. Not concerned with ideology or politics, his is a more practical commitment, beyond Maurice's delirious vision of the Commune as a cosmic catastrophe. The reader is never in the slightest doubt where Zola's sympathies lie, as Jean looks to the task ahead. In the next and final novel of the series, *Le Docteur Pascal*, that fertile future is confirmed as Jean is seen ploughing and sowing his native soil, thus confirming his 'confused vision' (p. 416) of it in *La Débâcle*. After his barren marriage during the Second Empire, his new wife gives him three children, and it is they who are Pascal's hope for the renewal of the country. Zola hardly needed to spell out for Sherard that Jean was 'emblematic of the France of the future'. In this respect, *La Débâcle* comes dangerously near to a *roman-à-thèse*, putting at risk the integrity of its fictional achievement.

Such a conclusion to the novel also surprised a good number of its first readers. For Jean Macquart comes to it from *La Terre*, where his own terrible suffering is equalled only by the primitive savagery of the very peasantry in whom Zola now seemed to be putting an irrational faith. The latter is certainly more poetic than political. Indeed, it could be argued that *La Débâcle* is irremediably flawed by the paradox of its regressive ideology (a Rousseauistic return to the non-cerebral purity of rural France) and Zola's discursive embrace of the scientific advances which (by contrast with Germany) the country had ignored at its peril. Such contradictions can only be reconciled within the binary thematic grid which enabled the four soldiers of 'Blood', mentioned earlier, to go off to plough. For pastoral fecundity and the destruction of war are so often antithetically aligned in Zola's work that he even told one critic that the subjects of *La Terre* and *La Débâcle* had originally been conceived to be incorporated within a single novel. He was certainly never in doubt that Jean should be the hero of both texts. And, in his preparatory notes for *La Débâcle*, Zola made a résumé of Jean's career in the earlier novel, in the course of which he quoted several of his characteristic speeches, and reinforced the bridge between the two novels by referring to passages from *La Terre* at the beginning of the later book. Thus Jean, the sower of seeds in *La Terre*, moves to sow death and destruction. But the closing vision of *La Débâcle* completes the cycle with the triumph of the forces of Life.

This recourse to the reassuringly timeless patterns of Mother

Nature effects a 'naturalization' of history and politics to which not every reader will subscribe. It lays Zola open to the charge of an aesthetic distance synonymous with a more invidious detachment. For his is a vision in which eternal laws make of the battle of Sedan or the fall of an empire a minor episode. Thus, in *La Débâcle*, the fields are seen beyond the battle in a shift of focus from the mortality of man to the perenniality of the earth. Both before and after it, Maurice sees a peasant in the background calmly following his plough, putting the carnage into perspective (p. 270). More generally, men are repeatedly seen from a distance or a height, and the lines of troops become no more than figures on a 'chessboard' (p. 228), insignificant dots on the landscape, unable to intervene in their own history. While Tolstoy's heroes revolt against the absurdity of their suffering, Zola's soldiers accept death on the battlefield as their share in the terrible necessity of the struggle which is part of a greater and unknowable evolutionary scheme of things. 'I want to show war as it really is', Zola wrote in his notes, 'the essential struggle for life, Darwin's grand and distressing idea to which the individual is subordinate, crushed like an insect by the imperatives of a vast and sombre nature.' It is a conception of war very different from that of his polemical writing in 1870. In an article on the twentieth anniversary of the battle, 1 September 1891, and entitled simply 'Sedan', he stressed those Darwinian fatalities of 'Eat or be eaten' which *La Débâcle* explores. It is within such perspectives that Zola's insistence on the certainty of France's defeat has to be seen, not just in terms of military inferiority, but also within the biological necessity of the strong and the young devouring the old and the weak. Prussia's application of modern technology to the science of war is part of this scheme, but largely incidental in providing the catalyst for France's recognition of its own fatal decline. As much as by longer-range artillery, the French are destroyed, in *La Débâcle*, by what is repeatedly described as 'an invincible and logical force' out of sight.

The reader is more likely to be moved by the novel's awesome sense of tragedy, by the way in which the novelist makes us *feel* both the stupidity and bravery of men fighting for their country in an age of increasingly advanced military technology. Zola's gift for detail provides us with haunting images of the terror, hunger, and cold suffered by individual human beings heading towards a terrible end.

And there is a visceral power in his descriptions of amputations in field hospitals, human flesh grotesquely smashed by artillery batteries beyond the field of vision, and the bravest of cavalry charges cut down by the precision of breech-loading rifles. For his French contemporaries, on the other hand, Zola's novel provided an almost therapeutic liquidation of one of the most disastrous chapters in their history, opening out on to a more optimistic future grounded in the lessons of the past. The modern reader may well sidestep some of this rhetoric, or at least question those of the novel's philosophical assumptions which reduce the inhumanity of war to a Darwinian necessity observed from afar. It is not beside the point, however, that the first English translation of the novel was published with the subtitle *A Story of the Horrors of War* and was partly motivated by that inscription. For if *La Débâcle* retains its value as a work of art, it is not merely as the finest depiction of the Franco–Prussian War, but also because, in spite of its debatable conclusions and almost undermining their distancing perspectives, it does push the reader up almost unbearably close to the human realities of suffering and useless courage, to what a later poet would call 'the Pity of War' and the 'Old Lie: *dulce et decorum est | Pro patria mori.*'

R. L.

NOTE ON THE TRANSLATION

The text on which this translation is based is the Pléiade edition, published by the Editions Fasquelle et Gallimard, 1967.

Having been interested in Zola during my studies, I often felt that the 'purists', the fans of Flaubert, Balzac, and Stendhal, for example, looked down upon him as someone who only really wrote 'pot-boilers', and whose Naturalist pretensions were something of a gimmick to give him literary status, that he was an author more concerned with content than with style. Yet it is only when one looks closely at his work that one starts to appreciate the repetitions, the key phrases, the symbolism, the linguistic signposts and aides-mémoires that he includes, which on ordinary reading almost pass by unnoticed, yet all the while do their work, creating *idées reçues* and building up a sort of fictional memory bank. It is almost as if Zola is taking cues from the oral tradition of storytelling, where repeated epithets, choruses, and phrases serve to strengthen the narrative and give an underlying cohesion and rhythm to the whole, creating a legend, a song, something that will be told and retold, handed down from one generation to the next. For this novel, which puts on record events which turned a whole generation upside-down, this property seems to be particularly apt.

I would give specific examples, but I think that it is much more interesting to try to spot them. It really is not as easy as that on first reading, although once one does see them, they seem so very obvious, and it comes as a surprise to find that they do not clutter the narrative, or overload it and make it clumsy and awkward. I hope that my translation reads with some of Zola's smoothness and subtlety, so that the final result has something of the same qualities, something of what we often see as an incompatibility between what makes a gripping best-seller and a sophisticated piece of 'literature' proper, but which Zola actually combined with such skill.

The other potentially problematic area was the dialogue, and how modern to make it. In the end, I played it very much by ear, and found that I kept a very nineteenth-century style of speech, eschewing too much use of strong expletives, apart from in the mouths of the more 'worthless' characters, such as Chouteau, where Zola also seemed to adopt cruder language. Perhaps this sometimes makes the dialogue seem dated, but I hope that it merely serves to put the scenes in their historical perspective—after all, Maurice was raised an educated gentleman, and Jean was a solid, good-hearted, and clean-living peasant, neither of whom would normally, at the end of the nineteenth century, and especially not in a novel, have used the kind of vulgar 'street' talk that is now commonplace and quite acceptable. Zola certainly did not make them talk that way. Which is why 'overmodernizing' the dialogue did not feel right for Zola—not through any sense of shock or modesty on my part, but simply because here, in this particular novel, it would have been out of place.

I would like to thank Robert Lethbridge for his help with this translation, and Judith Luna at OUP for all her patience. And a heartfelt thank-you to Peter Collier, who thought I was helping him when he was translating *Germinal*, but who in fact was letting me have a go at real translation, and who believed I could actually do it. I hope this one does not disappoint him.

E. D.

SELECT BIBLIOGRAPHY

Editions

La Débâcle, in vol. v of *Les Rougon-Macquart*, 5 vols., ed. Henri Mitterand (Paris: Bibliothèque de la Pléiade, 1960–7); includes a synopsis of the novel's genesis and composition, notes on the text, and successive amendments from the manuscript to the final version of *La Débâcle* in volume form. These 200 pages of material appended to the text constitute the fullest introduction to the novel.

La Débâcle, ed. Henri Mitterand (Paris: Collection Folio, 1984); this paperback edition contains some of the documentation in the authoritative 'Pléiade' edition.

La Débâcle, ed. Robert A. Jouanny (Paris, 1975); this is another reliable paperback edition.

La Débâcle, ed. Roger Ripoll (Paris: Livre de Poche, 1986); readers buying the novel in Livre de Poche should only have recourse to this corrected version.

Biography

Brown, Frederick, *Zola: A Life* (London, 1996); a monumental American biography.

Hemmings, F. W. J., *Émile Zola* (2nd edn., London, 1966; reissued Oxford Paperbacks, 1970); this remains the best general study of Zola's life and work.

Mitterand, Henri, *Zola*, i: *Sous le regard d'Olympia, 1840–1871* (Paris, 1999); the first volume of what promises to be the definitive biography.

Walker, Philip, *Zola*, (London, 1985); a highly readable account.

Critical Studies

Baguley, David, *Naturalist Fiction: The Entropic Vision* (Cambridge, 1990); the best general study of Naturalism.

—— 'La Débâcle et le récit de guerre', in his *Zola et les genres* (Glasgow, 1993), 103–15.

Cogny, Pierre, 'Le Discours de Zola sur la Commune', *Les Cahiers naturalistes*, 4 (1980), 17–24.

Deffoux, Léon, 'Émile Zola et l'édition illustrée allemande de *La Débâcle*', *Mercure de de France*, 209 (1929), 108–17; interesting study of the German perspective on the novel.

Guedj, Aimé, 'Les Révolutionnaires de Zola', *Les Cahiers naturalistes*, 36 (1968), 123–37.

Lethbridge, Robert, and Keefe, Terry (eds.), *Zola and the Craft of Fiction* (Leicester, 1990; reissued in paperback, 1993); contains essays on Zola's techniques as a novelist.

Mitterand, Henri, *Le Discours du roman* (Paris, 1985).

—— *Le Regard et le signe* (Paris: PUF, 1987).

—— *Zola: l'histoire et la fiction* (Paris: PUF, 1990).

Petrey, Sandy, 'La République de *La Débâcle*, *Les Cahiers naturalistes*, 54 (1980), 87–95; an acute essay on the novel's themes and ideological contradictions.

Ripoll, Roger, 'Zola et les Communards', *Europe*, 468–9 (1968), 16–26.

—— *Réalité et mythe chez Zola*, 2 vols. (Paris, 1991); contains important insights on *La Débâcle* (ii. 843–56).

Rufener, Helen La Rue, *Biography of a War-Novel: Zola's 'La Débâcle'* (New York, 1946); the editions cited above supersede this pioneering work, still found in bibliographies but accessible only in some university libraries.

Saminadayar, Corinne, '*La Débâcle*, roman épique?', *Les Cahiers naturalistes*, 71 (1997), 203–19; a good essay on Zola's inversion of Homeric structures.

Historical Background

Horne, Alistair, *The Fall of Paris: The Siege and the Commune, 1870–71* (London: Macmillan, 1965; updated and reissued in paperback, 1989); a first-rate synthesis.

Howard, Michael, *The Franco-Prussian War* (London: Rupert Hart-Davis, 1961; reissued in paperback by Routledge, 1998); a magisterial study offering by far the most detailed account of the War.

Tombs, Robert, *The War against Paris, 1871* (Cambridge: Cambridge University Press, 1981); one of the finest studies of the Commune.

Further Reading in Oxford World's Classics

Zola, Émile, *L'Assommoir*, trans. Margaret Mauldon, ed. Robert Lethbridge.

—— *The Attack on the Mill and Other Stories*, trans. and ed. Douglas Parmée.

—— *La Bête humaine*, trans. and ed. Roger Pearson.

—— *Germinal*, trans. and ed. Peter Collier, with an introduction by Robert Lethbridge.

—— *The Ladies' Paradise*, trans. and ed. Brian Nelson.

—— *The Masterpiece*, trans. Thomas Walton, ed. Roger Pearson.

—— *Nana*, trans. and ed. Douglas Parmée.

—— *Pot Luck*, trans. and ed. Brian Nelson.

—— *Thérèse Raquin*, trans. and ed. Andrew Rothwell.

A CHRONOLOGY OF ÉMILE ZOLA

1840   (2 April) Born in Paris, the only child of Francesco Zola (b. 1795), an Italian engineer, and Émilie, née Aubert (b. 1819), the daughter of a glazier. The Naturalist novelist was later proud that 'zolla' in Italian means 'clod of earth'

1843   Family moves to Aix-en-Provence

1847   (27 March) Death of father from pneumonia following a chill caught while supervising work on his scheme to supply Aix-en-Provence with drinking water

1852–   Becomes a boarder at the Collège Bourbon at Aix. Friendship with Baptistin Baille and Paul Cézanne. Zola, not Cézanne, wins the school prize for drawing

1858   (February) Leaves Aix to settle in Paris with his mother (who had preceded him in December). Offered a place and bursary at the Lycée Saint-Louis. (November) Falls ill with 'brain fever' (typhoid) and convalescence is slow

1859   Fails his *baccalauréat* twice

1860   (Spring) Is found employment as a copy-clerk but abandons it after two months, preferring to eke out an existence as an impecunious writer in the Latin Quarter of Paris

1861   Cézanne follows Zola to Paris, where he meets Camille Pissarro, fails the entrance examination to the École des Beaux-Arts, and returns to Aix in September

1862   (February) Taken on by Hachette, the well-known publishing house, at first in the dispatch office and subsequently as head of the publicity department. (31 October) Naturalized as a French citizen. Cézanne returns to Paris and stays with Zola

1863   (31 January) First literary article published. (1 May) Manet's *Déjeuner sur l'herbe* exhibited at the Salon des Refusés, which Zola visits with Cézanne

1864   (October) *Tales for Ninon*

1865   *Claude's Confession. A succès de scandale* thanks to its bedroom scenes. Meets future wife Alexandrine-Gabrielle Meley (b. 1839), the illegitimate daughter of teenage parents who soon separated, and whose mother died in September 1849

1866   Resigns his position at Hachette (salary: 200 francs a month) and becomes a literary critic on the recently launched daily *L'Événement* (salary: 500 francs a month). Self-styled 'humble disciple' of Hippolyte Taine. Writes a series of provocative articles condemning the official Salon Selection Committee, expressing reservations about Courbet, and praising Manet and Monet. Begins to frequent the Café Guerbois in the Batignolles quarter of Paris, the meeting-place of the future Impressionists. Antoine Guillemet takes Zola to meet Manet. Summer months spent with Cézanne at Bennecourt on the Seine. (15 November) *L'Événement* suppressed by the authorities

1867   (November) *Thérèse Raquin*

1868   (April) Preface to second edition of *Thérèse Raquin*. (May) Manet's portrait of Zola exhibited at the Salon. (December) *Madeleine Férat*. Begins to plan for the Rougon-Macquart series of novels

1868–70   Working as journalist for a number of different newspapers

1870   (31 May) Marries Alexandrine in a registry office. (September) Moves temporarily to Marseilles because of the Franco-Prussian War

1871   Political reporter for *La Cloche* (in Paris) and *Le Sémaphore de Marseille*. (March) Returns to Paris. (October) Publishes *The Fortune of the Rougons*, the first of the twenty novels making up the Rougon-Macquart series

1872   *The Kill*

1873   (April) *The Belly of Paris*

1874   (May) *The Conquest of Plassans*. First independent Impressionist exhibition. (November) *Further Tales for Ninon*

1875   Begins to contribute articles to the Russian newspaper *Vestnik Evropy* (*European Herald*). (April) *The Sin of the Abbé Mouret*

1876   (February) *His Excellency Eugène Rougon*. Second Impressionist exhibition

1877   (February) *L'Assommoir*

1878   Buys a house at Médan on the Seine, 40 kilometres west of Paris. (June) *A Page of Love*

1880   (March) *Nana*. (May) *Les Soirées de Médan* (an anthology of short stories by Zola and some of his Naturalist 'disciples', including Maupassant). (8 May) Death of Flaubert. (September) First of a series of articles for *Le Figaro*. (17 October) Death of his mother. (December) *The Experimental Novel*

1882 (April) *Pot-Bouille*. (3 September) Death of Turgenev

1883 (13 February) Death of Wagner. (March) *The Ladies' Paradise* (*Au Bonheur des Dames*). (30 April) Death of Manet

1884 (March) *La Joie de vivre*. Preface to catalogue of Manet exhibition

1885 (March) *Germinal*. (12 May) Begins writing *The Masterpiece* (*L'Œuvre*). (22 May) Death of Victor Hugo. (23 December) First instalment of *The Masterpiece* appears in *Le Gil Blas*

1886 (27 March) Final instalment of *The Masterpiece*, which is published in book form in April

1887 (18 August) Denounced as an onanistic pornographer in the *Manifesto of the Five* in *Le Figaro*. (November) *Earth*

1888 (October) *The Dream*. Jeanne Rozerot becomes his mistress

1889 (20 September) Birth of Denise, daughter of Zola and Jeanne

1890 (March) *The Beast in Man*

1891 (March) *Money*. (April) Elected President of the Société des Gens de Lettres. (25 September) Birth of Jacques, son of Zola and Jeanne

1892 (June) *La Débâcle*

1893 (July) *Doctor Pascal*, the last of the Rougon-Macquart novels. Fêted on a visit to London

1894 (August) *Lourdes*, the first novel of the trilogy *Three Cities*. (22 December) Dreyfus found guilty by a court martial

1896 (May) *Rome*

1898 (13 January) 'J'accuse', his article in defence of Dreyfus, published in *L'Aurore*. (21 February) Found guilty of libelling the Minister of War and given the maximum sentence of one year's imprisonment and a fine of 3,000 francs. Appeal for retrial granted on a technicality. (March) *Paris*. (23 May) Retrial delayed. (18 July) Leaves for England instead of attending court

1899 (4 June) Returns to France. (October) *Fecundity*, the first of his *Four Gospels*

1901 (May) *Toil*, the second 'Gospel'

1902 (29 September) Dies of fumes from his bedroom fire, the chimney having been capped either by accident or anti-Dreyfusard design. Wife survives. (5 October) Public funeral

1903 (March) *Truth*, the third 'Gospel', published posthumously. *Justice* was to be the fourth

1908 (4 June) Remains transferred to the Panthéon

THE FRANCO-PRUSSIAN WAR
AND THE COMMUNE

A summary chronology, 1870–1

July

19	declaration of war
26	Napoléon III leaves for the front; Empress Eugénie becomes Regent

August

2	French occupy Saarbrücken
3–4	battle of Wissembourg
6	battles of Frœschwiller and Spickeren
9	Strasbourg besieged; Ollivier government falls
14	battle of Borny
16	battle of Rezonville-Gravelotte
18	battle of Saint-Privat
19	Metz besieged
30	battle of Beaumont

September

1	battle of Sedan
4	fall of the Second Empire; declaration of the Republic under government of National Defence
7	Germans begin advance on Paris
15	first meeting between Jules Favre and Bismark to agree an armistice
19–20	siege of Paris begins
28	Strasbourg capitulates

October

27	Metz capitulates; French breakout at Le Bourget
30	Germans recapture La Bourget
31	aborted revolutionary uprising in Paris

November

6	armistice negotiations broken off
8–9	battle of Coulmiers; French retake Orléans
29	battle of Champigny

December

3   Germans reoccupy Orléans
5   fall of Rouen
6   provisional government moves from Tours to Bordeaux

January

5   bombardment of Paris begins
18   German Empire proclaimed at Versailles
19   attempted French breakout from Paris; they take Montretout but are repulsed at the battle of Saint-Quentin
23   armistice negotiations reopened
28   Paris capitulates; Favre and Bismarck sign three-week armistice

February

1   retreat into Switzerland of French army trying to relieve Belfort
6   Gambetta resigns
8   elections for a new National Assembly to negotiate peace
13   new Assembly first sitting in Bordeaux
17   Adolphe Thiers heads French government
26   Thiers government agrees to German terms for peace

March

1   peace treaty ratified by Assembly in Bordeaux; German troops enter Paris
18   government troops try to seize cannon at Montmartre; murder of Generals Lecomte and Thomas; ministers leave Paris
20   National Assembly moves to Versailles
21   National Guard open fire on anti-revolutionary demonstrators
26   election of members of the Central Committee of the National Guard
28   Commune proclaimed

April

2   Versailles troops seize Courbevoie
6   Versailles troops occupy Neuilly
17   Versailles troops take Château de Bécon
19   Versailles troops capture Asnières
30   creation of the Commune's *Comité du Salut Public*

May

10   formal signature of the Treaty of Frankfurt ending Franco-Prussian War

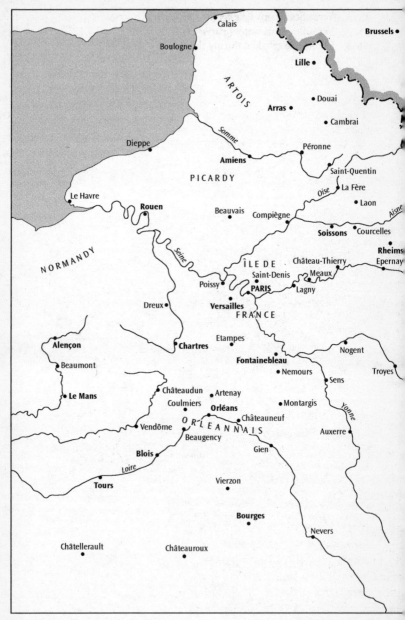

1. *Northern France*

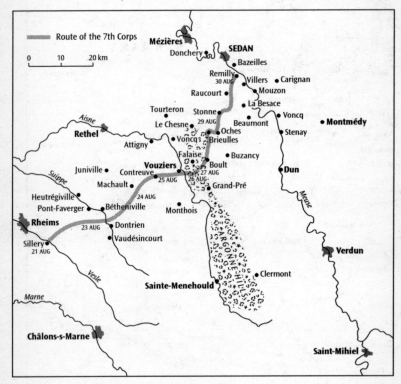

Route of the 7th Corps

0   10   20 km

Mézières

Donchery

SEDAN

Bazeilles

Remilly
30 AUG

Villers

Carignan

Raucourt

Mouzon

La Besace

Tourteron

Stonne

Voncq

Montmédy

Le Chesne
29 AUG

Beaumont

Oches

Stenay

Rethel

Voncq

Brieulles

Attigny

Falaise

Buzancy

Vouziers

Boult
27 AUG

Dun

Juniville

Contreuve
25 AUG

26 AUG

Aisne

Suippe

Machault

Grand-Pré

Meuse

24 AUG

Heutrégiville

Béthéniville

Monthois

Pont-Faverger

Rheims
23 AUG

Dontrien

Verdun

Sillery
21 AUG

Vaudésincourt

ARGONNE HILLS

Vesle

Clermont

Marne

Sainte-Menehould

Châlons-s-Marne

Saint-Mihiel

II. *Route of the 7th Corps, 23–30 August 1870*

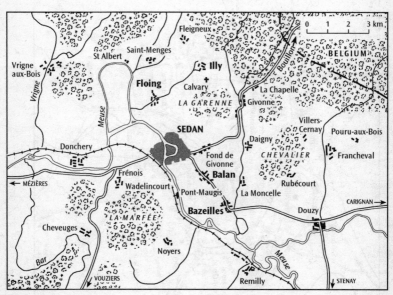

III. *Sedan battlefield*

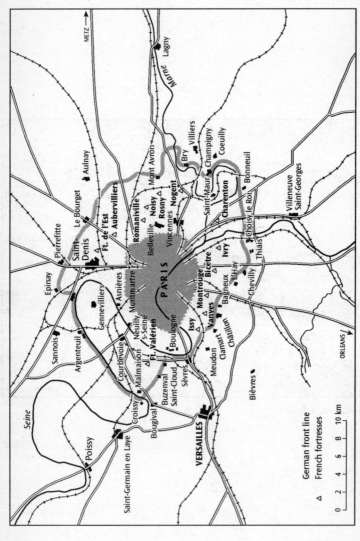

IV. *The siege of Paris*

German front line

△ French fortresses

0 2 4 6 8 10 km

LA DÉBÂCLE

THE FICTIONAL CHARACTERS

(Identifiable historical figures have an explanatory note where they first appear in the text)

Adolphe	driver in the fifth artillery battery under *Honoré Fouchard*
Bastian	drummer in *Capt. Beaudoin*'s 106th Regiment
Beaudoin, Capt.	captain in the 106th Regiment; lover of *Gilberte Delaherche*
Bourgain-Desfeuilles, Gen.	commander of an infantry brigade in the 7th Corps and in charge of the 106th Regiment (cf. note to p. 10)
Bouroche, Major	army surgeon in the 106th Regiment
Cabasse	guerrilla or *franc-tireur* (cf. note to p. 422)
Chouteau	soldier in the 106th Regiment, member of *Jean Macquart's* squad
Combette	pharmacist at Le Chesne-Populeux and its deputy mayor
Combette, Mme	wife of *Combette*
Coutard	infantry soldier in the 2nd Division of the 1st Corps
Dalichamp, Dr	local doctor at Raucourt and adopted godfather of *Silvine Morange*
Delaherche, Jules	textile merchant in Sedan, married to *Gilberte Delaherche*
Delaherche, Gilberte	daughter of *Gen. de Vineuil*, widow of Maginot, and second wife of *Jules Delaherche*; sleeps with *Capt. Beaudoin*
Delaherche, Mme	widowed mother of *Jules Delaherche*
Desroches, Maître	notary at Le Chesne-Populeux

Desroches, Mme	mother of *Maître Desroches*
Dubreuil	cousin of the *Levasseur* family
Ducat	former bailiff from Blainville who fights as a guerrilla with *Cabasse* and *Guillaume Sambuc*
Fernand	apprentice at *Combette*'s pharmacy
Fouchard, Uncle	peasant-farmer from Remilly, maternal uncle of *Henriette Weiss* (née Levasseur) and *Maurice Levasseur*; employer of *Silvine Morange* and *Goliath Steinberg*
Fouchard, Honoré	staff-sergeant, only son of *Uncle Fouchard* who has prevented him from marrying *Silvine Morange*
Gartlauben, Capt von	captain in the Prussian army, billeted in the home of *Jules Delaherche*
Gaude	bugler in *Capt. Beaudoin*'s company in the 106th Regiment
Gunther, Otto	captain in the Prussian army; a first cousin of *Weiss*
Gutmann	Bavarian soldier
Ladicourt, Baroness	inhabitant of Vouziers
Lagarde, Edmond	sergeant in the 5th Regiment
Lapoulle	soldier in the 106th Regiment, member of *Jean Macquart*'s squad
Laurent	apprentice gardener at Bazeilles
Lefèvre, Mme	wife of factory owner in Raucourt
Levasseur, Maurice	former lawyer, now soldier in the 106th Regiment, twin brother of *Henriette Weiss* and nephew of *Uncle Fouchard*
Loubet	soldier in the 106th Regiment, member of *Jean Macquart*'s squad
Louis	assistant gunner to *Adolphe* under the command of *Honoré Fouchard*

Macquart, Jean	corporal in 106th Regiment; related to the Rougon–Macquart family as the son of Antoine Macquart (cf. note to *Rognes*, p. 8)
Morange, Charlot	infant son of *Silvine Morange* and *Goliath Steinberg*
Morange, Silvine	orphan found a job by *Dr Dalichamp* as a servant working on *Uncle Fouchard*'s farm; seduced and abandoned by *Goliath Steinberg* after having been prevented from marrying *Honoré Fouchard*
Pache	soldier in the 106th Regiment, member of *Jean Macquart*'s squad
Picot	infantry soldier in the 1st Division of the 7th Corps
Poor Child	very young soldier in the 5th Regiment still using this nickname given to him as a baby
Quittard, Auguste	young son of *Françoise Quittard*
Quittard, Françoise	widow of a builder and supervisor of the dyeworks at Bazeilles owned by *Jules Delaherche*
Ravaud, Capt.	captain in the 106th Regiment under the command of *Col. de Vineuil*
Rochas, Lt.	lieutenant in the 106th Regiment under the command of *Capt. Beaudoin*
Rose	daughter of the concierge of the Préfecture at Sedan; she works in the factory owned by *Jules Delaherche*
Sambuc, Guillaume	leader of the band of guerrillas which includes *Cabasse* and *Ducat*
Sambuc, Prosper	cavalry-soldier under Gen. Margueritte (cf. note to p. 65); brother of *Guillaume Sambuc*

Sapin, Sgt.	sergeant in the 106th Regiment under *Capt. Beaudoin*
Simmonot	grocer in Raucourt
Steinberg, Goliath	Prussian spy; farmhand at *Uncle Fouchard*'s; lover of *Silvine Morange*
Vineuil, Col. de	brother of *Gen. de Vineuil* and uncle of *Gilberte Delaherche*; commander of the 106th Regiment in *Gen. de Bourgain-Desfeuilles*'s brigade of the 7th Corps
Vineuil, Gen. de	brother of *Col. de Vineuil* and father of *Gilberte Delaherche*; head of the customs service at Charleville
Weiss	first cousin of *Otto Gunther*, married to the twin sister of *Maurice Levasseur*; foreman in the factory owned by *Jules Delaherche*
Weiss, Henriette	twin sister of *Maurice Levasseur*; married to *Weiss*

PART ONE

CHAPTER ONE

A mile from Mulhouse, near the Rhine, in the middle of the fertile plain, the camp had been set up. In the fading light of this August evening,* beneath a troubled sky laden with heavy clouds, the tents were pitched in rows, and the stacks of arms could be seen glinting at regular intervals along the edge of the camp, with sentinels standing guard over them, rifles at the ready, motionless, eyes somewhere on the far horizon, lost in the purplish mists drifting up from the great river.

They had arrived there from Belfort at around five o'clock. It was now eight, and the men had only just got hold of their provisions. But the firewood must have got lost along the way, for none had been issued. And so it was impossible to light fires and cook the soup; they had to make do with chewing on cold biscuits, washed down with great swigs of brandy, which turned their legs, already wobbly with fatigue, to jelly. However, behind the rifle stacks, near the cookhouse, two soldiers were stubbornly trying to set light to a pile of green wood, young saplings they'd cut down with their bayonets, which obstinately refused to burn. Thick, black, lazy smoke drifted up into the evening air, infinitely sad.

There were only twelve thousand men gathered here, all that General Félix Douay* still had with him from the 7th army corps. The 1st Division, called up the day before, had left for Frœschwiller;* the third was still at Lyons; and he had decided to leave Belfort and advance just as he was, with the 2nd Division, the reserve artillery, and an incomplete division of cavalry. Fires had been spotted at Lorrach. A dispatch from the Schelestadt Sous-Préfet announced that the Prussians were set to cross the Rhine at Markolsheim. Feeling too isolated on the right flank of the other corps and out of communication, the general had made haste to push on towards the frontier, all the more so since news had arrived the previous day of the disastrous defeat at Wissembourg.* Even if he didn't have to offer direct resistance to the enemy, he risked being called on at any moment to support the 1st Corps. That day, that troubled, stormy Saturday, 6 August, battle must have been joined, over by Frœschwiller—you could see it in the anxious, overbearing sky, where great shudders filled the air and sudden gusts of wind blew, heavy with anguish. And for two whole days now, the division had thought it was marching into battle, and at the end of this forced march from Belfort to Mulhouse, the soldiers expected to find the Prussians before them.

The sun was sinking, and in a far-off corner of the camp the retreat began to sound, with drum-rolls and bugle-calls that were still faint as yet, carried on the strong breeze. Jean Macquart, crouching down, busy pushing the pegs in further to make sure that the tent was secure, got to his feet. At the first rumours of war he had left Rognes, still raw from the drama which had taken his wife Françoise from him,* together with the land she had brought to the marriage; at thirty-nine he'd signed up again, back at his old rank of corporal, and had been enlisted straight into the 106th infantry regiment, where the number of officers was being brought up to strength. It still surprised him sometimes to see this soldier's cape about his shoulders again: for he'd been so glad to leave the army after Solférino,* so glad he wasn't a sword-carrier and a killer any more. But what can you do, when you've lost your trade, your wife, and all your worldly goods, when the anger and grief are forever bringing a lump to your throat? Might as well take it out on your enemies if they're bothering you. And he remembered the cry he'd uttered: if he hadn't the heart to work the ancient soil of France any more, then by God, he'd defend it!

From where he stood, Jean took a quick look over the camp, where the sounding of the retreat had caused a final stir among the men. Some of them were running. Others, already dozing, raised their heads and stretched with an irritated, sleepy air. He waited patiently for the call, with the serenity and rational equilibrium which made him such an excellent soldier. His comrades always said that with a bit of education he could have gone far. As it was, barely able to read and write, he didn't even have his sights on sergeant's stripes. Once a peasant, always a peasant, was his motto.

But the pile of green wood, which was still giving off smoke, caught his eye, and he shouted over to Loubet and Lapoulle, both men from his squad, who were still puffing away furiously at the fire.

'Come on, leave that alone! We're all choking back here!'

Loubet, scrawny and nimble, a real wag by the looks of him, was sniggering.

'It'll catch, Corporal, honestly... Come on, you, put your back into it!'

And he egged on Lapoulle, a colossus of a man, who was wearing himself out trying to blow up a hurricane, his cheeks puffing fit to burst, his face all purple and his eyes red and streaming with tears.

Chouteau and Pache, two more from the squad, the first stretched out on his back, like a real lazybones fond of his creature comforts, the other crouching, engrossed in stitching up a rip in his trousers, both burst out laughing, cheered up by the atrocious grimace on Lapoulle's face, great animal that he was.

'Turn round, blow from the other end, that'll do it!' yelled Chouteau.

Jean let them laugh. There probably wasn't going to be much more cause for laughter from now on; in spite of appearances, this big, serious-looking fellow with the broad, regular features wasn't one for being melancholy, and he happily turned a blind eye when his men were having a bit of fun. But another group caught his attention, where yet another soldier from his squad, Maurice Levasseur, had been talking for almost an hour with a civilian, a red-haired gentleman of about thirty-six, with a face like a good-natured dog, lit up by two large, protruding blue eyes, whose short-sightedness had got him turned down for military service. A sergeant from the reserve artillery, who seemed a gallant, steady sort with his brown moustache and goatee beard, had come over to join them; and there they stood, all three of them, like a little family. Jean, obligingly, wanting to keep them out of trouble, felt it his duty to interrupt.

'You'd do well to take your leave, sir. Here comes the retreat, and if the Lieutenant sees you—'

Maurice cut him short.

'Please stay, Weiss.'

And turning to the corporal, he said curtly:

'This gentleman is my brother-in-law. He has permission from the Colonel, who is a personal acquaintance.'

What was he poking his nose in for, this peasant, whose hands still smelled of manure? He, Maurice, a qualified lawyer since the previous autumn, who had volunteered for the army and been allowed,

under the personal protection of the colonel, to be enlisted straight
into the 106th without having to go through the square-bashing, was
more than willing to carry the ordinary soldier's kitbag; but from the
very first hours of service, a sort of repugnance, a hidden revulsion
had set him against this illiterate yokel who was his commanding
officer.

'Fine,' replied Jean with his habitual calm, 'get caught, it's all the
same to me.'

Then he turned away, seeing that Maurice was telling the truth;
for just then the colonel, Monsieur de Vineuil, came past, with his
grand, noble bearing, his long, sallow face punctuated by a thick,
white moustache, and he greeted Weiss and the soldier with a smile.
He headed off briskly towards a farm which they could see some two
or three hundred metres away to their right, set among the plum
trees, where the military staff had set up for the night. Whether or
not the commander of the 7th Corps was there, nobody knew; the
death of his brother,* killed at Wissembourg, had been a bitter blow,
and plunged him deep into mourning. However, Brigadier-General
Bourgain-Desfeuilles,* under whose command the 106th lay, was
there for sure, bellowing away as usual, his fat body rolling along on
stumpy legs, with the florid complexion of a jovial sort whose lack of
brain cells never bothered him for a minute. The atmosphere around
the farmstead grew more restless as they waited anxiously for the
dispatches to arrive—they were painfully slow in bringing news of
the great battle that they'd all sensed to be critical and close at hand
since the morning. Where had it taken place? What results had it
achieved by now? By and by, as night fell, fear seemed to come
rolling like smoke through the orchards and haystacks close to the
stables, spreading outwards into a pool of shadow. And then, there
had been rumours that a Prussian spy had been arrested riding
round the camp, and taken to the farm for questioning by the general. Perhaps Colonel de Vineuil had received a telegram or something, to send him running off so fast.

Meanwhile, Maurice had gone back to chatting with his brother-
in-law Weiss and his cousin, Honoré Fouchard, the artillery sergeant. The retreat approached from afar, growing louder and louder,
until it passed close by them with bugle-calls and drum-rolls, in the
melancholy peace of twilight; they didn't even seem to hear it. The
young man, grandson of a hero in Napoleon's Grande Armée,* had

been born in Le Chesne-Populeux; his father had led a very unglori-
ous life, eking out a meagre existence as a tax collector. His mother, a
peasant, had died bringing him and his twin sister Henriette into the
world, and it was the little girl who had brought him up. If he was
here now as a volunteer, it was only after a life of shame. His was a
tale of the dissipations of a feeble, exalted temperament, which had
driven him to throw his money away on gambling, women, and all
the idiocies of voracious Paris, where he had gone to complete his
law studies; his family had bled itself dry to make a gentleman of
him. The strain of it had been the death of his father, while his sister,
after giving up everything she owned, had been fortunate enough to
find a husband, this worthy lad Weiss from Mulhouse in Alsace,
who'd long been employed as a bookkeeper at the General Refinery
in Le Chesne-Populeux, before becoming an overseer for Monsieur
Delaherche, one of the biggest clothmill owners in Sedan. And
Maurice really thought he'd learnt his lesson, his highly strung
nature making him as quick to hope for the best as he was to be
discouraged by the bad, generous and enthusiastic to a fault, yet
without a trace of steadfastness in him, easy prey to the slightest
change in the wind. He was small and fair-haired, his face delicately
featured with a wide, curved brow and slender nose and chin, while
his eyes were soft and grey and sometimes a bit crazy.

On the eve of the outbreak of hostilities, Weiss had hurried to
Mulhouse, seized by a sudden urge to see to a family matter; and
if he'd profited by the by from Colonel de Vineuil's goodwill to go
and shake his brother-in-law by the hand, it was because the colonel happened to be the uncle of young Madame Delaherche, a
pretty young widow whom the mill owner had married the year
before, and a childhood friend of Maurice and Henriette, who
happened to be neighbours. And Maurice had just discovered that
as well as the colonel, his company's captain, Captain Beaudoin,
was also an acquaintance of Gilberte, the young Madame Delaherche, a very close one too, so they said, when she'd been at
Mézières and married to Monsieur Maginot, the forestry
inspector.

'Give Henriette all my love, won't you,' the young man said again
to Weiss. He loved his sister passionately. 'Tell her she'll be pleased,
tell her I want to make her proud of me at last.'

His eyes filled with tears as he remembered all his past foolishness.

His brother-in-law, equally moved, stopped him short, turning to the artillery sergeant, Honoré Fouchard.

'And as soon as I'm up Remilly way, I'll be over to see old Uncle Fouchard, to let him know that I've seen you and you're in good health.'

Old Fouchard, a peasant who owned a bit of land and kept up a small trade as a travelling butcher, was the brother of Maurice and Henriette's mother. He lived up at Remilly, on the hillside, six kilometres from Sedan.

'Fine,' replied Honoré with equanimity, 'the old man couldn't care less, but go ahead if it makes you happy.'

At that moment there was a stir over by the farm, and out came the prowler, the man accused of being a spy; he was free to go, escorted only by an officer. Doubtless he had produced papers and told them some tale or other, for he was merely being seen off the camp. From such a distance, in the growing darkness, it was difficult to make out clearly the huge, burly figure with reddish hair.

Maurice, however, let out a cry.

'Honoré, look at him... It looks like that Prussian—you know, Goliath!'

At the sound of this name, the artillery sergeant gave a start. He stared hard at the figure, his eyes full of fire. Goliath Steinberg, the farmhand, the man who'd caused him to fall out with his father, who'd stolen Silvine from him, the man at the root of the whole abominable story, the dreadful business that still clawed at him! He wanted to run after him and throttle him. But already the man was moving away, beyond the rifle stacks, disappearing off into the night.

'Goliath? No!' he murmured. 'Impossible. He's out there, on the other side... I tell you, if I ever come across him!...'

He shook his fist angrily at the horizon, invaded now by dark shadows, all that purplish East which for him was Prussia. There was a silence, then once again they heard the sound of the retreat, but very far off, fading away at the other end of the camp, a dying moment of sweetness in a world where things had become indistinct.

'Damn!' said Honoré, 'I'm going to catch it if I'm not there for roll-call! Goodnight all, and goodbye!'

He shook Weiss by both hands one last time, then off he went, striding away over to the rise where the reserve artillery was parked, with no more mention of his father and leaving no message for Silvine, whose name was burning on his lips.

A few minutes went by and then on the left, over by the second brigade, a bugle called the roll. Another answered, closer by. And then a third sounded, far, far away. One by one, they all joined in, until Gaude, the company's bugle-boy, decided to come in too, trumpeting out a rapid, resounding stream of notes. He was a tall lad, painfully thin, not a hair on his chin, and he never uttered a word, always storming through his bugle-calls at a breathless pace.

Now Sergeant Sapin, a small, stiff-mannered man with a wide, distant gaze, began to call the roll. His shrill voice threw out names, and the soldiers who had drawn near answered in tones that ranged all the way from cello to flute. But the call came to a halt.

'Lapoulle!' repeated the sergeant loudly.

Still no one answered. And Jean had to dash over to the pile of green wood, which Fusilier Lapoulle was still stubbornly trying to ignite, cheered on by his comrades. Flat on his stomach, cheeks aflame, he had his mouth to the ground and was chasing the blackening smoke away from the fire.

'Bloody hell, man! Leave that alone!' yelled Jean. 'Answer the call!'

Lapoulle got up, stupefied, then realization seemed to dawn, and he bellowed out 'Sir!' in such a brutish voice that Loubet toppled over backwards laughing at the great clown. Pache, who had finished his sewing, gave a murmured, prayer-like reply which was scarcely audible. Chouteau scornfully spat out a response, not even bothering to get to his feet, then stretched himself out more comfortably.

Meanwhile Rochas, the lieutenant on duty, waited motionless a few steps away. When Sergeant Sapin came up to him at the end of the roll-call, to report that all were present and correct, Rochas grumbled into his whiskers and nodded towards Weiss, who was still talking with Maurice.

'Yes, we've got an extra one too—what the hell's that civilian doing here?'

'Permission from the Colonel, sir,' put in Jean, overhearing the remark and feeling it his duty to explain.

Rochas shrugged furiously, and moved off again without a word, walking along beside the rows of tents, waiting for the campfires to be put out; while Jean, his legs worn out after the day's march, sat himself down a few feet away from Maurice; at first, the latter's words reached him as a sort of vague droning, and he didn't really pay attention, so full was his head of obscure thoughts, sketchily formulated deep inside his dense, slow-working brain.

Maurice was in favour of the war, and believed it to be inevitable, essential to the very existence of nations. All this had become of the utmost importance to him since he'd given himself over to evolutionary ideas, and to the whole theory behind them which was to become the consuming passion of the young, educated generation. Wasn't life a sort of war, every second of the day? Wasn't the order of nature itself one of unceasing combat, the survival of the fittest, the force of life kept strong and rejuvenated through constant action, new life always rising fresh from the ashes of death? And he recalled how his heart had leapt when the thought had come to him of atoning for his sins by becoming a soldier and marching off to battle at the front. Maybe the France of the plebiscite,* even while putting itself into its Emperor's hands, did not actually want war. He himself, only eight days before, had declared it to be reprehensible and idiotic. People were talking about this claim to the Spanish throne by some German prince,* and amidst all the confusion which had gradually built up around the debate, everybody seemed to be in the wrong, to such an extent that no one knew any more who'd provoked whom, and in the end, all anyone could still be sure of was the inevitable, that fatal law that sets one nation on another at the appointed hour. But a great shudder had gone through Paris, and Maurice remembered that fervent evening, when crowds swept down the boulevards, and bands of people brandished torches crying 'To Berlin! To Berlin!' And he could still hear the voice of a tall, handsome woman with a majestic profile, standing on a cab-driver's box on the square in front of the Hôtel de Ville, wrapped in the folds of a tricolour and singing the 'Marseillaise'. Wasn't any of it true, then? Hadn't the heart of Paris beaten that evening? But then, as always with him, after this febrile exaltation came long hours of wrenching doubt and disgust at it all: his arrival at the barracks, the adjutant who had met him, the sergeant who had made him put on his uniform, the foul-smelling, dirt-encrusted barrack-room, the vulgar camaraderie with his new companions, the repetitive exercises which crippled his limbs and dulled his brain. Before a week had gone by, however, he'd grown accustomed to it, and no longer

found it so repugnant. And by the time the regiment finally set off
for Belfort, his enthusiasm had got the better of him once more.

From the very first days, Maurice had been absolutely certain of
victory. For him, the Emperor's plan was clear: they would throw
four hundred thousand men at the Rhine, cross the river before the
Prussians were ready, then cut the northern half of Germany off
from the south by means of a vigorous offensive; and then, thanks to
some brilliant success, they would force Austria and Italy to side
immediately with France. For hadn't the rumour gone round at one
point that the 7th army corps, to which Maurice's own regiment
belonged, was to board ship at Brest, then land in Denmark* and
create a diversion which would force Prussia to immobilize one of
her armies? She would be taken by surprise, battered from every
side, and crushed within a few weeks. A simple military walkover
from Strasbourg to Berlin. Ever since they'd had to hang around at
Belfort, he'd been racked by doubts. The 7th Corps had been sent to
Belfort with orders to guard the breach in the Black Forest, but it
had got there with large numbers of men missing, thoroughly ill-
equipped, and in a state of indescribable confusion. They were waiting for the 3rd Division to arrive from Italy; the second cavalry
brigade had stayed behind in Lyons, under threat of a popular uprising; and somewhere along the way, three batteries had got lost. In
Belfort, they'd been astounded to find that the stores which were to
have supplied them with all their equipment had been stripped bare:
not a tent or saucepan to be seen, no flannel belts, no field medical
supplies, no chains or forges for the horses. Not a single nursing
officer or administrative worker was to be found anywhere. At the
last moment, they noticed that they were short of thirty thousand
spare parts which were vital for rifle maintenance; an officer had to
be sent back to Paris, and brought back five thousand with him,
which he had only managed to get hold of with great difficulty. As
far as everything else was concerned, what worried Maurice was
their inactivity. Why had they been sitting there for two weeks without marching on? He could sense that each day they tarried was an
irreparable fault, another lost chance of victory. And so, before the
plan he'd dreamed of, rose up the practical reality, and all the facts he
was to learn of later, but of which he was at present only dimly
and anxiously aware: the seven army corps spread out, scattered
along the frontier from Metz to Bitche and from Bitche to Belfort;

numbers everywhere well below strength, the original four hundred and thirty thousand men reduced to two hundred and thirty thousand at the very most, generals vying with each other, each firmly set on winning his field marshal's baton, with no thought of assisting the next man; the most appalling lack of foresight—mobilization and concentration of troops done in one fell swoop to save time, resulting in an inextricable mess; and finally, the slow onset of paralysis, starting at the top with the ailing Emperor,* incapable of making any swift decisions, a paralysis which in the end would attack the entire army, throw it into disarray and annihilate it, tossing it into the jaws of the very worst of disasters, leaving it with no hope of defending itself. And yet, above the sense of unease that lurked as they waited there, as they shivered instinctively at what was to come, this certainty of victory prevailed.

Abruptly, on 3 August, news of the Saarbrücken victory,* won the previous day, burst upon them. No one knew whether it was a great victory or not, but the newspapers crowed with enthusiasm—Gemany had been invaded, this was the first step on the march to glory! And the legend surrounding the Prince Imperial,* who had quite calmly picked up a bullet off the battlefield, began to grow. Two days later, when they learned of the devastating surprise defeat at Wissembourg, a cry of rage erupted from their breasts. Five thousand men caught in an ambush, holding out for ten hours against thirty-five thousand Prussians! The cowardly massacre simply reeked of vengeance. Doubtless it was the chiefs who were to blame for the lack of foresight which had allowed them to be caught off guard. But all this would be put right, MacMahon* had called up the 1st division of the 7th army corps, and the 1st Corps would be backed up by the 5th. By now, the Prussians must have crossed back over the Rhine, with our infantry's bayonets hot on their heels. And swelled by the thought that, somewhere that day, furious battle had been joined, and by the long and increasingly fearful wait to receive any news, the lake of anxiety seeped out wider and wider every minute, spreading beneath the vast, paling sky.

Over and over again, Maurice kept saying to Weiss:

'Ah! We've given them a good old hiding today, you can be sure of that!'

Weiss nodded wordlessly, an anxious expression on his face. He too was looking over towards the Rhine, towards that East, where already night had cast its full shadow, dark and mysterious, like a black wall. Since the final calls of the retreat, a great silence had begun to fall over the sluggish camp, barely interrupted by the voices and footsteps of the odd latecomer. A light had appeared, like a flickering star, in the room in the farmhouse where the staff sat watching and waiting for the dispatches which arrived every hour, their message as yet unclear. And the green wood fire, abandoned at last, was still giving off a thick, mournful smoke, carried on the wind towards the farm, where it hung over the house, soiling the first stars in the sky.

'A good hiding,' repeated Weiss at length. 'God heed you.'

Jean, still sitting a few paces off, pricked up his ears; Lieutenant Rochas, chancing upon this trembling admission of doubt, stopped in his tracks, and listened.

'What!' took up Maurice. 'You mean to say that you aren't entirely confident? You think defeat possible?'

Swiftly, his brother-in-law moved to silence him, his hands shaking and his good-natured countenance suddenly pale and stricken.

'Defeat? Heaven preserve us! You know that my roots are here, both my grandparents were murdered by the Cossacks in 1814;* and when I think of an invasion, I want to strike out, I'd grab my rifle and my trench coat, like a proper trooper! Defeat? No, oh no, I don't want to believe that possible!'

He grew calm once more, and shrugged his shoulders, utterly despondent.

'But it's just that, well, I'm not happy about it... I know it well, this Alsace of mine; I've just travelled through it again, on business. And the rest of us here have seen what's been staring the generals in the face, we've seen what they've refused to see... Oh, we wanted war with Prussia, all right! We've been waiting quietly to settle the old score for a long time now. But that hasn't stopped us keeping up good, neighbourly relations with Baden and Bavaria, we've all got friends or family across the Rhine. We thought they were like us, we thought they dreamed of putting down those insufferably arrogant Prussians too... We're usually so calm, so resolute, but for the past two weeks and more we've been gripped by worry and impatience at the way things have been going from bad to worse. Ever since war was declared, enemy cavalry have been allowed to terrorize our villages, find out the lie of the land, and cut telegraph lines. Baden and

Bavaria are rising up, massive troop movements are under way in the Palatinate, information's coming to us from all over, from markets and trade fairs, we can prove that the frontier is under threat; and yet, when local people and district mayors finally run in fright to officers passing through, to tell them all this, they simply shrug it off, and say it's just cowards imagining things, that the enemy's way off... What's going on? At a moment when there isn't a single hour to lose, whole days are passing by! What on earth are they waiting for? For the whole of Germany to come down on top of us?'

His voice was low and forlorn, as if he had already said these things to himself over and over again—and mulled them over in his mind well before that.

'Germany! Oh, I know her of old, too; and the awful thing is that you lot seem to know as much about her as China... Maurice, you remember my cousin Gunther—the lad who came up to me in Sedan last spring, to shake my hand? He's a cousin on my mother's side: his mother—my aunt—got married in Berlin; and he's one of them, all right—hates France. He's serving now as a captain in the Prussian Guard. The evening I saw him back to the train station, I remember him saying in that shrill voice of his, I can hear it now: "If France declares war on us, she'll be beaten."'

At this, Lieutenant Rochas, who'd held himself back until now, leapt forward in fury. He was a tall, thin fellow, almost fifty, with a long, hollow face, weathered by smoke and sun. He had a huge, hooked nose overhanging a wide, fierce-looking mouth, bristling with rough, greying whiskers. Beside himself with rage, he thundered:

'Right, that does it! What the hell do you think you're doing here, demoralizing the men like that?'

Although he didn't get involved in the argument, Jean felt at heart that the lieutenant was right. Even though he was himself growing astonished at the long delays and the chaotic disarray they were in, he too had never for one moment doubted the splendid hiding they were going to give the Prussians. It was certain—after all, why else were they here?

'But Lieutenant,' said Weiss, taken aback, 'I don't want to demoralize anyone. Far from it—I wish everyone knew what I know, because the best method of preparation and defence is to be informed... And look, Germany now...'

He went on in his rational way, explaining his fears: Prussia had grown greater since Sadowa,* there had been a popular wave of support placing it at the head of the other German states, and this enormous empire was taking shape, rejuvenated, propelled by its enthusiasm and the irresistible momentum of its united desire to conquer. Then there was the system of compulsory military service, bringing an entire nation to its feet, bearing arms, trained and disciplined, equipped with powerful working material, already broken in by the great war, and still bearing the glory of its devastating victory over Austria; and then there was this army's intelligence and strong moral fibre, with chiefs who were nearly all young men, under a generalissimo who seemed set to reinvent the art of battle, endowed with perfect prudence, foresight, and remarkably accurate perception. And in contrast to this portrait of Germany, Weiss dared evoke France: the ageing Empire, still cheered by the people but rotten at the core, having undermined the nation's pride in itself by taking away liberty, returning to a liberal stance too late and to its own damnation, poised to crumble and fall the moment it failed to satisfy the appetite for worldly pleasures which it had itself unleashed; without doubt the army possessed an admirable pedigree for bravery, heaped with laurels from Italy and the Crimea,* but it had been marred by the practice of buying one's way out of national service, had got stuck in the old routine of the African school,* and was too confident of victory to think of trying to develop new techniques; finally you had the generals, most of them mediocre, consumed by rivalries, some of them staggeringly ignorant, with the Emperor at their head, ailing and indecisive, deceived by others, deceiving himself, in the dreadful adventure which was now beginning, where everyone was leaping in blindly, with no serious preparation, stampeding in terror like a herd of cattle being led to the slaughterhouse.

Rochas listened, wide-eyed and open-mouthed. His fearsome nose wrinkled up. Then, all of a sudden, he began to laugh, a booming laugh that stretched from ear to ear.

'What line are you spinning us there! What's all that rubbish meant to mean? There's no sense in it, it's too stupid for us even to bother ourselves with! Go and tell that to the new recruits, but don't come running to me with such tales, not me, with twenty-seven years' service behind me!'

And he struck himself proudly on the chest. Son of a bricklayer's mate from the Limousin,* he had been born in Paris, abhorred his father's trade, and signed up for the army at eighteen. Soldier of fortune, he had carried the army kitbag as a corporal in Africa, sergeant at Sebastopol,* lieutenant after Solférino; it had taken him fifteen years of hard living and heroic bravery to win that rank, and his education was so lacking that he would never make captain.

'But listen, my good sir, you may know everything, but you don't know this—oh yes, at Mazafran I was scarcely nineteen years old, and a hundred and twenty-three of us, not a single man more, held out for four days against twelve thousand Arabs... Oh, yes! For years and years it was the same, down there in Africa, at Mascara, Biskra, Dellys, later on in Great Kabylia, then at Laghouat:* and if you'd been with us, you'd have seen all those bloody darkies turn tail like a bunch of rabbits the minute we appeared. And then at Sebastopol—well, bugger me, I can't say it was too comfortable! Storms that blew fit to pull your hair out, real brass monkey weather, alerts every hour of the day, and then those savages, who ended up sending everything sky-high! Mind you, we did our fair share of that too, oh, yes, we led them a right old song and dance, we fried 'em well and good. And what about Solférino? You weren't there, were you? So why are you talking about it? And the heat! Even though more water probably came down that day than you've ever seen in your whole life! Solférino, where we gave those Austrians a rare old thrashing—you had to be there, to see them scram before our bayonets, falling over each other they were, trying to leg it. You'd have thought their backsides were on fire!'

He shook with mirth, his jubilant laughter ringing with all the old French military cheer. It was the legendary picture of the French trooper gallivanting about the globe, the conquest of the planet fitted in between his girl and a bottle of good wine, to the strains of a festive ditty. All it took was a corporal and four soldiers, and entire armies, thousands strong, just bit the dust.

Then abruptly he growled in a fierce voice:

'Beaten? France, beaten! I'd like to see those Prussian swine try and beat us lot!'

He moved nearer and seized Weiss violently by his lapel. His utter contempt for the enemy—whoever it might be—was written all over his tall, skinny body, with its roving soldier's physique, completely unconcerned by the present realities.

'Now listen here, and listen well, sir... If those Prussians dare come over here, we'll send them right back where they came from with a good old boot up the arse. Do you hear? A good old boot up the arse, all the way back to Berlin!'

And with childlike serenity, he made a superb gesture, with the candid, innocent conviction of the man who knows nothing and fears nothing at all.

'To be sure, that's the way it is, because that's just the way it is!'

Quite dizzy, and almost convinced, Weiss hastened to let it be known that there was nothing he'd like better. As for Maurice, who'd kept quiet, not daring to intervene in front of his superior officer, he ended up bursting out laughing with him: this fellow's words—however stupid Maurice might think the man in general—warmed his very heart.

Jean too had nodded approvingly at everything the lieutenant had said. He'd been there too, at Solférino, where it had rained so much. Now that's what he called talking! If only all the chiefs had been able to talk like that, they wouldn't have given a damn about being short of a few cooking pots and flannel belts!

It had long since grown completely dark, and still Rochas stood there in the shadows, waving his long arms about. He had only ever read a single volume of Napoleon's victories, at a laborious pace, after it slipped from a hawker's tray into the bottom of his bag. He just couldn't contain himself, and all the knowledge he possessed came out in one impetuous cry:

'Austria thrashed at Castiglione, Marengo, Austerlitz, Wagram! Prussia thrashed at Eylau, Jena, Lutzen! Russia thrashed* at Friedland, Smolensk, Moscow! Spain and England thrashed all over the place!* The whole world thrashed, thrashed from top to bottom, from one end to the other! And suddenly, now, you say it's us who're going to be thrashed! Why? How? Has someone changed the world or something?'

He drew himself up yet further, raising his arms like a flagpole.

'Just look! We went into battle over there today, we're waiting for news. Well, let me tell you what that news will be, let me tell you! We've thrashed the Prussians, we've thrashed the arms and legs off them, we've thrashed them to little pieces ready to be swept up and chucked away!'

At that moment a loud, agonized cry rang out beneath the sombre sky. Was it some night bird calling? Or some mysterious voice, carried from afar, thick with tears? A shudder went through the entire camp, lying there drowned in shadows as they waited for the dispatches that were so slow arriving, and the anxiety rose to fever pitch, seeping and spreading wider and wider. Far away in the farmhouse, the lamp which lit the nervous vigil of the staff burned higher, with a straight, unflickering, taper-like flame.

But it was ten o'clock; Gaude rose up from the black earth where he had disappeared, and was the first to sound the curfew. The other bugles answered, going out one by one, a dying fanfare already heavy with sleep. And Weiss, who had quite lost track of time, embraced Maurice affectionately, wishing him hope and courage, and assuring him that he'd give Henriette all his love and be sure to tell old Uncle Fouchard all the news. As he was finally taking leave of them, a rumour went round, causing a stir of restlessness and agitation. News had come of the resounding victory which Marshal MacMahon had just won: the Crown Prince* of Prussia had been taken prisoner along with twenty-five thousand men, the enemy army had been driven back, crushed, leaving all its cannon and equipment in our hands.

'By Heaven!' was all Rochas could cry, in his thundering voice.

Then, running after Weiss who was happily hurrying off back to Mulhouse, he called out:

'A good boot up the arse, sir, a good boot up the arse, all the way to Berlin!'

A quarter of an hour later, another dispatch arrived with news that the enemy had been forced to abandon Wörth* and was now beating a retreat. What a night! Dropping with exhaustion, Rochas had simply wrapped himself in his trench coat and was now asleep on the ground, unconcerned with finding cover, as was often the case with him. Maurice and Jean had slipped into the tent, where Loubet, Chouteau, Pache, and Lapoulle were already lying in a heap, heads resting on their kitbags. If they all drew their knees in, the tent could fit six. At first, Loubet had taken everyone's minds off their empty bellies by letting Lapoulle believe that tomorrow morning, when they handed out rations, there would be chicken; but they were all too worn out, and lay there snoring—let the Prussians come. For a moment, Jean lay without moving, squashed up next to Maurice. For all his weariness, he just couldn't get to sleep, because all the things that gentleman had said—Germany up in arms, overpowering and gluttonous—kept going through his mind, and he sensed that his companion couldn't sleep either, and was thinking about the same things. Then Maurice shifted impatiently, and seemed to shrink away from him, and Jean realized that he was cramping him. The instinctive enmity and repugnance of class and learning between the educated man and this peasant created an almost physical discomfort. The latter, however, felt shame and sadness deep down inside, and tried to make himself as small as possible, in an attempt to escape from the hostile contempt which he was aware of at his side. However cool the night air had grown outside the tent, inside they were so stiflingly hot among the heap of sleeping bodies, that suddenly Maurice leapt from the tent in exasperation, and stretched himself out a few paces further off. Jean tossed and turned miserably in a laboured, nightmarish half-slumber, in which regret at not being loved mingled with apprehension at some immense misfortune which he thought he could hear, galloping somewhere out there, lost in the deep unknown.

Hours must have gone by, and the whole black, motionless camp seemed to be crushed beneath the growing weight of the boundless, evil night, where that appalling, nameless thing lurked heavy in the air. Sudden noises would emerge now and then from a sea of shadows; the odd groan would come abruptly from an invisible tent. Then came unfamiliar sounds, the snorting of a horse, the clanking of a sabre, some late-night prowler hastily riding off—all ordinary noises, which suddenly seemed to ring with menacing undertones. But all at once, over by the cookhouses, there was a strong burst of light. The whole of the edge of the camp was lit up, and the rifle stacks could be seen, all lined up, their bright, regular gun-barrels threaded with streaks of red light, like freshly spilled blood; and against the sudden conflagration, the dark, upright figures of the sentinels appeared. Was it the enemy? The enemy that the chiefs had been warning of for two days, the enemy they'd come looking for, from Belfort to Mulhouse? And then the flame went out, with a great crackling of sparks. It was just the pile of green wood that Lapoulle had toiled over for so long, and which had lain smouldering for several hours, before suddenly bursting into flames like a blazing haystack.

Alarmed by the bright light, it was now Jean's turn to leap

hurriedly out of the tent; he almost stumbled right over Maurice, who was propped up on his elbow, watching. The darkness had already descended on them again, more obscure than ever, and the two men stayed outside, lying down on the bare earth a few paces away from each other. Before them, in the depths of the thick shadows, they could now see nothing but the farmhouse window, where light still shone out from the lone candle that seemed to be burning for a wake. What time was it? Two or three o'clock, maybe. The staff over there had definitely not gone to bed. The voice of General Bourgain-Desfeuilles could still be heard bellowing out, as he cursed this night of vigil that only hot toddies and cigars were seeing him through. New telegrams were arriving, things must be going badly, the shadows of messengers could been seen galloping past, blurred and terrified. There came the sound of stamping and swearing, then something resembling a muffled death-cry, followed by a dreadful silence. What was it? Had the end come? An icy air blew across the camp, as it lay prostrated by sleep and anxiety.

It was at that moment that Jean and Maurice recognized the tall, thin, shadowy figure of Colonel de Vineuil passing by. It must have been Major Bouroche with him, a large man with a head like a lion. Both were exchanging incoherent snatches of speech, like the half-finished, whispered words you hear in nightmares.

'It's from Basle... Our 1st Division destroyed... Twelve hours in battle, the whole army in retreat...'

The colonel's shadow halted, and called to a second, light, delicate, and correct, which was hurrying towards him.

'Is that you, Beaudoin?'

'Yes, Colonel.'

'Ah, my friend—MacMahon beaten at Frœschwiller, Frossard at Spickeren,* de Failly immobilized, stuck between the two, utterly useless... Only one corps against an entire army at Frœschwiller, quite extraordinary. And all swept away, our armies routed, thrown into panic, France left open to attack...'

Tears were choking him, more words were lost on the air, and the three shadows melted away, swallowed by the darkness.

Shaken to the very core, Maurice jumped to his feet.

'Oh God!' he stammered.

They were the only words he could find, while Jean, an icy chill in his heart, murmured,

'Ah! Damn it all... That gentleman, your relation, was right after all when he said they're stronger than us.'

Beside himself with rage, Maurice could have strangled him. The Prussians stronger than the French! That was what made his pride bleed. But already, the peasant was saying in his calm, stubborn way,

'Mind you, that doesn't change anything. Just because we take a knocking doesn't mean to say we ought to surrender... Still got to have at them, all the same.'

But in front of them, a lanky silhouette had risen up. They recognized Rochas, still wrapped in his trench coat; the passing noises and perhaps even the scent of defeat had drawn him from his rough slumber. He wanted to know what was happening, and asked what was going on.

When, with great difficulty, he at long last understood, a look of utter stupefaction came into his vacant, childlike eyes.

More than a dozen times, he repeated,

'Beaten! What do you mean, beaten? Why, beaten?'

Now, in the East, a pale light was beginning to appear, a murky light, infinitely sad, which fell onto the sleeping tents, where in one, the sallow faces of Loubet, Lapoulle, Chouteau and Pache could now almost be made out, still snoring away, mouths wide open. And there, among the sooty mists which had drifted up from the distant river, dawn rose in mourning.

CHAPTER TWO

At about eight o'clock, the sun dispersed the heavy clouds, and a pure, burning August Sunday shone over Mulhouse, in the middle of the vast, fertile plain. From parishes all around came the sound of church bells, their rapid peals of notes ringing out in the clear air and carrying to the camp, awake now and buzzing with life. This fine Sunday, a day of such appalling disaster, did have its own joyfulness, its own sky bursting with holiday spirit.

Abruptly, Gaude gave the call for the distribution of supplies, and Loubet was astonished. What? What was up? Was this the chicken he'd promised Lapoulle the day before? Born in Les Halles,* Rue de la Cossonnerie, illegitimate son of a woman who made a small living selling market wares, he had signed up in the army 'for the money' as he liked to put it, having turned his hand to all trades; and he was a real connoisseur, always sniffing out some titbit or other. So off he went to investigate, while Chouteau, the artist, one-time decorator in Montmartre, a handsome revolutionary who was furious that they'd called him back after his military service was up, made vicious fun of Pache, whom he'd just caught on his knees behind the tent, saying his prayers. Now there was churchy for you! Couldn't he ask that good Lord of his for a hundred thousand a year? But Pache let himself be teased, like some dumb, gentle martyr; he was newly arrived from some out-of-the-way village in Picardy,* puny, with a pointy sort of head. He was the butt of the squad's jokes, along with Lapoulle, the colossus, the great brute who had grown up in the Sologne marshes,* and who was so utterly ignorant that the day he'd arrived at the regiment, he'd asked to see the King. Now, despite the fact that the disastrous news about Frœschwiller had been going round since reveille, the four men were laughing and carrying on with their normal daily tasks in their automatic, indifferent way. However, they gave a pleased grunt of surprise on seeing Jean coming back from distribution carrying firewood, accompanied by Maurice. At last the wood the troops had waited for in vain the previous day, to cook their soup, had been handed out. Only twelve hours late.

'Bravo, quartermaster!' cried Chouteau.

'Never mind that, it's here now!' said Loubet. 'Ah! What a wonderful stew I'm going to cook for you!'

He usually took charge of kitchen duties quite willingly—something they were more than grateful for, because he cooked like a dream. But he always showered the most bizarre tasks on Lapoulle.

'Go and fetch the champagne, go and fetch the truffles...'

That particular morning, the Paris guttersnipe in him inspired him with a crazy notion for poking fun at such a helpless innocent.

'Come on, put a move on! Give me the chicken.'

'Chicken? What chicken?'

'There, look, on the ground... The chicken I promised you, the chicken the Corporal's just brought back!'

And he pointed to a huge white stone lying at their feet. Lapoulle, bewildered, eventually picked it up, and turned it over in his hands.

'Christ alive! Will you wash that chicken! Come on, wash its feet, wash its neck!... Come on lazybones, give it a splash!'

And just for the hell of it, just for fun, just because the thought of the soup had put him in mischievous high spirits, he chucked the stone into the pot of water along with the meat.

'There, now that'll give the stock some flavour! Aha, you didn't know that, did you? You don't know anything, you great sausage!... You can have the parson's nose, just you see if it isn't nice and tender!'

The rest of the squad doubled up with laughter at the sight of Lapoulle, now utterly convinced and licking his lips. Not much danger of getting bored with an animal like Loubet around! And when the fire began to crackle in the sunshine and the pot started to sing, they all gathered round devotedly, and sat in absolute bliss, watching the meat bobbing around, breathing in the wonderful aroma wafting from the pot. They had been hungry as dogs since the day before, and the thought of eating put all else from their minds. Defeated they might be—but that didn't stop them needing to fill their bellies. From one end of the camp to the other, fires blazed and pots bubbled, and a voracious, singing, joyful atmosphere mingled with the bright peal of the bells, still ringing out from every parish in Mulhouse.

However, just as it was approaching nine o'clock, a ripple of activity ran through the camp, officers ran this way and that, and Lieutenant Rochas walked alongside the tents of his section, bearing an order from Captain Beaudoin.

'Come on, everything's got to be folded up and put away, we're off!'

'But what about the soup?'

'The soup will have to be for another day! We're leaving immediately!'

Gaude's bugle sounded imperiously. There was consternation and silent anger among the men. What? Leave without eating, not even wait an hour until the soup was ready? The squad wanted to drink the stock anyway; but it was still just hot water, and the uncooked meat was leathery and unchewable. Chouteau growled, complaining bitterly. Jean had to intervene, to get his men to hurry up and pack. What was the great rush? Taking off like this, shoving people around before they'd even had time to get their strength back! And when someone said, in front of Maurice, that they were going to meet the Prussians and take their revenge, he shrugged in disbelief. In less than a quarter of an hour, camp had been struck, tents folded away and tied back up to the rucksacks, and the rifle stacks dismantled; and on the bare earth there was nothing left to see but the dying embers of the campfires.

The reasons which had made General Douay decide on immediate retreat were grave indeed. What the Schelestadt Sous-Préfet had said in his dispatch a full three days earlier had just been confirmed: news had come through on the telegraph of sightings of Prussian campfires in positions above Markolsheim; and besides this, another telegram had arrived, informing them that an enemy corps was crossing the Rhine at Huningue. Precise details came pouring in thick and fast: sightings of cavalry and artillery, troops on the march, descending from all directions to a central mustering point. If they hung on for even an hour longer, their line of retreat back to Belfort would undoubtedly be blocked. After defeats at Wissembourg and Frœschwiller, the general, finding himself isolated and quite cut off to the rear, could do nothing but beat a hasty retreat; particularly since what they had learned that morning shed an even more unfavourable light on the news that had reached them overnight.

The staff officers set off in advance of the rest, spurring on their mounts for fear that the Prussians might outpace them and be waiting for them when they got to Altkirch. Knowing that the march ahead was likely to be a tough one, General Bourgain-Desfeuilles had taken the precaution of going via Mulhouse, where he ate a hearty breakfast while grumbling about all the upheaval. And what a sorry sight Mulhouse was when the officers came through; when the retreat was announced, the townsfolk began coming out into the road, bewailing the sudden departure of the soldiers whose presence they had begged for so insistently. Were they just abandoning them, then? Were all the priceless valuables which had been piled up at the station going to be left for the enemy? And their city—was it doomed, come nightfall, to be no more than occupied territory? As they left the town and crossed the countryside, people came out from villages and remote houses, standing stricken and aghast outside their front doors. What? Retreating already? All those regiments they'd seen filing past the day before, marching into battle? Fleeing before they'd even fought? The commanding officers gloomily urged their horses on, and refused to answer any questions, as if misfortune itself were galloping at their heels. Was it true, then, that the Prussians had crushed the army and were now flooding into France from every direction, like a swollen river bursting its banks? Caught on the rising tide of panic, people thought they could already hear the distant rumble of the invasion, growing louder every minute in the lifeless air; already they were piling furniture into carts, emptying their houses, and a succession of families could be seen fleeing along the country lanes, swept along by the winds of terror.

In all the confusion of the retreat, the 106th was forced to halt before it had even gone half a mile, near the bridge, along the canal between the Rhône and the Rhine. The marching orders, which had been poorly given, and executed even worse, had resulted in the whole of the 2nd Division accumulating in this spot; and the way over was so narrow—barely five metres across—that the line began to stretch out interminably.

Two hours had gone by, and still the 106th stood waiting, watching the endless flood of men crossing before it. Standing to attention beneath the blazing sun, rucksacks on their backs, the soldiers' patience eventually ran out.

'Looks like we're the rearguard,' came Loubet's bantering tones.

But Chouteau was angry.

'They're taking the piss out of us, leaving us here to fry. We were here first, we should have hopped it.'

And over on the other side of the canal, across the vast, fertile plain, all along the flat country roads, running between fields of hops and ripened corn, as it became all too obvious that the forces were retreating and moving back over the ground they had covered the day before, sneering laughter came from all sides, mocking and furious.

'Aha! Fair speeding along, we are,' said Chouteau again. 'Well, fine march to meet the enemy this is, that they've been bending our ears with since yesterday morning... Really, it's too daft by half! We get here, and then before we've even had time to get some soup down us, we bugger off again!'

The laughter grew louder and uglier, and Maurice, standing near Chouteau, agreed with him. If they were going to have to stand there for two hours like blasted idiots, why hadn't they been allowed to finish cooking their soup and eat it in peace? Anger had hold of them again, and the thought of the soup, tipped out before it was ready, without any explanation for all the rush which they found so stupid and cowardly, filled them with dark resentment. Right bunch of scared rabbits they looked!

However, Lieutenant Rochas spoke harshly to Sergeant Sapin, accusing him of allowing sloppy discipline among his men. Captain Beaudoin had come over, to see what all the noise was about.

'Quiet in the ranks!'

Jean, silent as ever, true old veteran of the Italian campaign, broken in to the discipline, looked at Maurice, who seemed to be amused by Chouteau's poor, hot-tempered joke. He was astonished: how could a gentleman, someone who'd received so much education, possibly approve of such a thing? Fine, so maybe it was the truth—but even so, it wasn't something you said out loud. If all the soldiers began blaming their superiors and letting their own opinions be heard, they weren't going to get very far, that was for sure.

Finally, after waiting for yet another hour, the 106th got the order to advance, although the bridge was still so laden with the tail-end of the division that it caused the most appalling chaos. Several different regiments got all mixed up together, and some companies crossed anyway, swept along in the crush, while others, pushed to the side of the road, were obliged to bide their time. And as if to add the finishing touch to this chaos, a cavalry squadron insisted on barging past, driving stragglers—whom the infantry had already scattered in its wake—back into the neighbouring fields. After an hour's march, a whole collection of disbanded soldiers had become strung out behind the rest, loitering as if for their own amusement.

This was how Jean found himself at the back, lost with his squad on some track, unwilling to be separated from it. The rest of the 106th had vanished, and not a soldier or even any of the company's officers was anywhere to be seen. There were just a few isolated men left, a muddled hotch-potch of individuals he didn't know, shattered before they'd even set off, each walking at his own pace, wandering wherever the lanes led him. The sun beat down mercilessly, and it was extremely hot; the rucksacks dragged painfully at their shoulders, weighed down by the tents and the awkward equipment which took up so much room. Many soldiers were quite unused to carrying these bags, and already found the thick, regulation battle cape cumbersome enough, as heavy as a leaden cope. All of a sudden, a slight, pale-looking soldier with tear-filled eyes stopped and flung his rucksack into a ditch with a profound sigh, like a dying man turning the corner and coming back to life again.

'Now there's someone with the right idea,' muttered Chouteau.

He continued marching, though, bowed down beneath his heavy bag. But when he saw two others getting rid of their loads too, he couldn't hold out.

'Oh, to hell with it!' he cried.

And he deftly hoisted his rucksack off his shoulder and threw it onto the bank. He'd had quite enough of lugging fifty-odd pounds around, thank you very much! Anyone would think they were bleeding packhorses!

Almost immediately, Loubet followed his example, and forced Lapoulle to do likewise. Pache, who crossed himself before every stone cross they passed on the way, undid his straps and placed the bundle carefully on the ground, against a low wall, for all the world as if he'd be coming back later to pick it up. Only Maurice was still bearing his load, when Jean turned round and saw that his men were carrying nothing on their backs.

'Pick up your bags—they'll have my guts for garters, they will!'

But his men just walked on, unrebellious as yet, with ill-natured, silent expressions, driving their corporal before them along the narrow lane.

'Will you please pick up your bags, or I'll have to report you!'

These words stung like a whip across Maurice's cheeks. Report them! This ignorant peasant was going to report them because the poor sods were trying to take the weight off their exhausted muscles! In a sudden fit of blind, feverish rage, he too unhooked his straps and dropped the bag by the roadside, glaring defiantly at Jean.

'Fine, fine,' said the latter in his good-natured way, powerless to enter into a fight. 'We'll settle this this evening.'

Maurice's feet were causing him agony. The rough, hard soldier's sandals, which he wasn't used to, had rubbed his feet raw. His health was quite delicate, and even though he'd got rid of the bag, he could still feel its unbearable, excruciating weight upon his back like an open sore down his spine; his rifle was so heavy he was out of breath, and he had no idea which side to carry it on. What tortured him most of all, however, was his moral agony, which had plunged him into one of those desperate crises to which he was prone. Quite suddenly and irresistibly, here he was allowing his own will-power to crumble away, falling prey to bad instincts, letting himself go, in a way which would later have him sobbing in shame. When he was in Paris, his misdeeds had always been the doing of 'the other one' as he called it, that weak-willed lad he became in his moments of coward-ice, who was capable of all sorts of low tricks. And ever since he'd found himself dragging one foot after the other beneath the glaring sun, as part of this retreat which seemed so like that of a routed army, he'd become no better than a beast in this straggling, dallying herd, scattered along the roads. This was the shock wave after the defeat, from that far-distant crack of thunder, rumbling all those leagues away, which had sent its dying echo to beat at the heels of these men, fleeing, panic-stricken, before they'd so much as caught a glimpse of an enemy soldier. What was left to hope for? Surely it was all over; they'd been beaten, they might as well just lie down and go to sleep.

'Hey, so what!' came a loud yell from Loubet, with his barrow-boy's laugh. 'After all, we're not going to Berlin, are we!'

To Berlin! To Berlin! The savage cry from the crowds teeming through the boulevards, on that night of wild enthusiasm which had made Maurice decide to join up, rang again in his ears. The wind had just changed, whipped by a stormy breeze; and there was a terrible lurch, the whole temperament of the race was there in his over-excited confidence, which went plunging so precipitously into deep despair at the first sign of defeat, taking him off as it galloped away, among these soldiers who wandered, vanquished, scattered, without even having seen action.

'God, this bloody rifle isn't half sawing my arms off,' said Loubet, shifting his weapon over to the other side yet again. 'Fine bloody penny whistle this is to go walking with!'

Then, referring to the sum he'd been paid to serve in someone else's place, he said:

'I don't care what they say—fifteen hundred francs for doing this job is daylight robbery!... The rich old goat! I bet he's smoking a good pipe or two by the fire, while here I am about to get my head blown off in his place!'

'And I'd finished my service, too,' grumbled Chouteau. 'I was ready for the off... Oh aye, just my luck to get caught up in this sort of dirty sodding business, I tell you!'

And he swung his rifle furiously. Then he chucked it roughly aside, sending it hurtling over a hedge.

'Go on, piss off, blasted thing!'

The rifle turned two somersaults and crashed down in a furrow, where it lay, long and still, like a corpse. Other rifles were already flying through the air to join it. Soon the field was full of prostrate weapons, stiff and forlorn beneath the harsh sun. It was epidemic madness, brought on by the hunger gnawing at their bellies, the shoes chafing their feet, the punishing march and the unexpected defeat lurking menacingly over their shoulders. Nothing good left to hope for, what with those at the top giving way, supplies not even managing to feed them; what with their anger and irritation, making them want to get it over with here and now, before they'd even started. So there—the rifle could go the same way as the rucksacks. And in a sort of senseless rage, accompanied by jeers and sneers like lunatics on a jaunt, rifles went flying through the air, all along the straggling trail, stretching far back into the countryside.

Before getting rid of his own rifle, Loubet made it perform a neat twirl in mid-air, like a drum-major's baton. Lapoulle, seeing all his comrades throwing away theirs too, one after the other, must have thought it was all part of manœuvres, and followed suit. But Pache, with a confused sense of duty which he owed to his religious upbringing, refused to do likewise, and Chouteau began hurling insults at him, calling him a right vicar's son.

'What a little blackleg!... And all because his old peasant of a mother made him swallow the Good Book every Sunday! Off to Mass with you, then—it stinks, not going along with your comrades!'

Dark-faced, Maurice marched on in silence, head bowed beneath the flaming sky. Now he made his way as if through an atrocious, exhausting nightmare, phantoms dancing before his eyes, as if walking towards a chasm somewhere out in front; and all his culture and education went plunging to the depths, dragging him down, down to the baseness of these poor wretches around him.

'Yes,' he said to Chouteau suddenly, 'you're right!'

And his gun was already lying on a pile of stones when Jean, vainly striving to counter the abominable way his men were abandoning their arms, caught sight of him. He rushed forward.

'Pick up your rifle immediately! Immediately, do you hear?'

All at once, Jean's face had taken on a dreadful look of pure fury. This man, normally so calm, always ready to find an amicable solution, suddenly glared at them with eyes ablaze, and spoke in a voice of thunderous authority. His men had never seen him like this before; they stopped short in amazement.

'Pick up your rifle immediately, or it's me you'll have to answer to!'

Quivering with rage, Maurice uttered but one word, trying to make it as offensive as possible:

'Peasant!'

'Oh yes, that's it, I'm a peasant all right; but you—you're a gentleman!... And that's why you're such a filthy swine! Aye, I'll give it to you straight: you're a filthy swine!'

Hoots went up from the men, but the corporal, with extraordinary force, persisted.

'When you've had an education, you should let it show... If we're peasants, if we're ignorant brutes, then you ought to set an example to us all, because you know better than we do... For God's sake, pick up your rifle, or I'll have you shot as soon as this march is over.'

Cowed, Maurice picked up his rifle. Tears of rage blurred his eyes. He continued the march swaying like a drunkard, surrounded by his comrades who were now jeering at him for giving way. God, how he hated this Jean! He hated him with an inextinguishable hatred, wounded to the quick by this harsh lesson, which he knew had been justified. And when Chouteau, at his side, growled that corporals like that made you look forward to the day when you could quietly shoot them in the back of the head under cover of battle, Maurice saw red, and had sudden visions of himself smashing Jean's skull behind some wall.

However, there was a diversion. Loubet noticed that while this argument had been going on, Pache too had finally abandoned his rifle, quietly laying it down by the bank. Why had he done that? Pache, however, made no attempt to explain, but merely smiled to himself, like a well-behaved little boy being scolded for his first transgression, relishing it, yet at the same time a little shame-faced. Quite perked up, he walked on, merrily swinging his arms. All along the sun-drenched roads, weaving between the endless succession of ripened corn and hop-fields, the scattered chaos continued; the stragglers, free of rifles and rucksacks, were now little more than a wandering crowd, a hotch-potch of beggars and good-for-nothings tramping along, sending frightened villagers into their houses and behind bolted doors at the sight of them.

It was then that a chance encounter proved the last straw for Maurice. Far behind them came a dull rumbling; it was the front section of the reserve artillery, which had set off last of all, suddenly emerging around a bend in the road. The straggling laggards barely had time to throw themselves into the neighbouring fields to get out of its way. Marching in column-formation, it processed past them at an impressive trot, impeccably lined up and correct; a full regiment of six battalions, with the colonel leading out in front, and all the officers in their proper places. The cannon went by noisily, at regular, scrupulously observed intervals, each one accompanied by its ammunition chest, horses, and men. And when the fifth battery passed, Maurice clearly recognized his cousin Honoré's cannon. There was the battery sergeant-major, perched proudly on his horse, to the left of the forward driver, who was riding in front, a handsome, fair-haired man called Adolphe, on a solid mount, a fine chestnut mare, beautifully in step with the off-horse, which trotted along by her side; while among the six gunners, seated two by two on the cannon's casings and ammunition chest, was Louis, the gun-layer, in his proper place—he was a short man with brown hair, and Adolphe's comrade. These two made up a couple, as they called it, according to the old tradition of marrying a man on horseback to a foot soldier. To Maurice, who had got to know them in camp, they seemed to have grown in stature; and the cannon, hitched up to its four horses, followed by the ammunition chest pulled along by another six beasts, seemed as bright as a sun to him, loved, polished, and cared for by the entire little universe around it, men and horses riding in tight formation, disciplined and affectionate like some plucky little family. Above all, Maurice suffered horribly when he saw the look of disdain which his cousin Honoré cast upon the stragglers, and the sudden expression of stupefaction as he recognized Maurice among this herd of rifle-less men. The rear of the procession was already in sight, with the battery equipment, gun carriages, forges, and supply wagons. Lastly, in a final cloud of dust, came the reserve, the second team of men and horses; and the rambling clatter of cartwheels and horses' hooves gradually faded and died as they went trotting round another bend in the road.

'Goddamn it!' declared Loubet. 'It's all very well showing off like that when you've got wheels to do all the work for you!'

On their arrival, the staff officers found Altkirch not yet taken. No sign of the Prussians as yet. But General Douay, still afraid of turning round and discovering them breathing down his neck any moment now, had wanted the divisions to push on to Dannemarie, which the head of the column had only reached at five that evening. It was now eight, night was falling, and the men were only just setting up camp, so great was the confusion in the regiments, missing half their men. Totally worn out, the troops were ready to drop with hunger and exhaustion. Isolated soldiers, little groups, and the whole interminable, pitiful trail of limping, rebellious men scattered along the lanes could be seen trickling in right up until ten o'clock, trying unsuccessfully to find their companies.

As soon as Jean was able to rejoin his regiment, he set off in search of Lieutenant Rochas, in order to give him his report. He found him, and Captain Beaudoin too, conferring with the colonel, all three standing outside the door of a small inn, all very busy with the roll-call, anxious to find out where all their men were. As soon as the corporal began speaking to the lieutenant, Colonel de Vineuil overheard, and called him over, forcing him to tell him the whole story. His long, sallow face, eyes still inky black against his thick, snow-white hair and long, flowing moustache, was cloaked in mute desolation.

'Colonel!' exclaimed Captain Beaudoin, not waiting to hear what his commanding officer thought, 'we ought to shoot half a dozen of the rogues!'

Lieutenant Rochas nodded in agreement. But the colonel shrugged helplessly.

'There's too many of them—nearly seven hundred, for goodness' sake. Who on earth would we pick out from all that lot?... And anyway, wouldn't you know it, the General's against it. He's a paternal type, says he never punished a single man, back in Africa... Oh no, no, I can't do a thing. It's dreadful.'

The captain echoed him.

'Dreadful... It really is the end.'

As Jean withdrew, he heard Major Bouroche, whom he'd not seen standing there on the threshold of the inn, grumble quietly under his breath: no more discipline, no more punishment, army up the creek! Before the week was out, the commanders would be getting a good kick up the backside; whereas if they'd blown the heads off a couple of these jokers straight away, maybe the rest would think first before doing anything.

No one was punished.* Some of the officers in the rearguard, who'd been escorting the supply train, had wisely taken the precaution of having all the rifles and rucksacks collected up from where they lay strewn on each side of the road. Only a small number were missing, and the men were rearmed rather furtively at daybreak, as if to hush up the whole business. Their orders were to break camp at five o'clock, but the soldiers were woken as of four in the morning, and the retreat back to Belfort was hurried along, in the certainty that the Prussians were now only two or three leagues away. Again, the men had been forced to make do with ration biscuits, and the troops set off exhausted after this restless and all too brief night's sleep, still without a hot meal inside them. That morning, yet again, the orderly nature of the march was compromised by a hasty departure.

That day was worse than the last, infinitely sad. The landscape had changed, they were now in mountainous country, with roads clambering up and down slopes planted with pine forests; and the narrow valleys, covered in a bushy carpet of broom, lay in a flourish of gold. Ever since the previous day, however, a wind of panic had come blowing through this countryside, as it shimmered beneath the bright August sun, and it blew increasingly terror-stricken with each hour that passed. A dispatch, warning all mayors to advise their townsfolk to hide their valuables away somewhere safe, had brought widespread fear to breaking point. Had the enemy come, then, after all? And would they have enough time to get away? They began imagining that they could hear the approaching thunder of the invading army, that dull roaring of a river which has burst its banks, growing louder and louder now, as each village added its own fear to the rising tide, amid cries and wailing.

Maurice marched on as if he were sleepwalking, his feet bleeding and his shoulders crushed beneath the weight of his rucksack and rifle. He was incapable of thought, and just kept walking into the nightmare he saw before him; he was no longer conscious of the comrades trudging on around him, aware only of Jean to his left, like him worn out by the same pain and exhaustion. The sight of the villages they passed through was appalling, heart-wrenchingly piti-ful. As the retreating troops came into view, this disordered flight of shattered soldiers dragging themselves along on their weary legs, the villagers would grow restless and hurry to get out too. To think that only a fortnight earlier these people had been so calm! Their Alsace had been waiting so cheerfully for war to come, convinced that all the fighting would be done on German soil!* But now France was being invaded, the storm was about to break on their own territory, in their own backyards, over their own fields, like one of those dread-ed hurricanes which lay waste to whole regions with their hail and thunder in a matter of a couple of hours! Outside each house, in the midst of chaos and uproar, men were loading carts, recklessly heap-ing the furniture on any old how, too anxious to worry about break-ing it. At upstairs windows, women threw out a last mattress onto the carts below, and passed out the cradle that had almost got left behind. The baby was strapped into it and the whole bundle fastened to the top of the pile, surrounded by the legs of upturned tables and chairs. On the cart behind, sick old grandfather was lashed to a wardrobe and carried off like another piece of furniture. And then there were those who hadn't got carts, piling their homes up onto wheelbarrows; others made their escape carrying bundles of clothes, while some thought merely to save the parlour clock, clutching it to their breast like an infant. It was impossible to take everything, and bits of furniture and parcels of linen which had proved too burden-some lay abandoned in the gutter. Some shut up everything before they went, leaving their houses looking dead, with doors and windows tightly closed. But by far the largest number left them unlocked, hurrying to be off, convinced in their black despair that all would be destroyed anyway; doors and windows gaped wide open, revealing the emptiness of the denuded rooms within; and these houses were the saddest of all, with their desolate air of a town captured by the enemy, deserted in terror, its pitiful dwellings lying open to the winds, abandoned even by the cats, sensing a chilling premonition of what was to come. The heart-rending spectacle became more and more grim with each village they came to, and the number of people clearing out and fleeing grew larger and larger, adding to the general, swelling crush, clenched fists, curses and tears.

But it was on the open road, passing through the deserted countryside, that Maurice suffered most from the anguish which was choking him. Here, as they approached Belfort, the ragged line of refugees grew denser, until it formed an uninterrupted procession. Oh, those poor souls who thought they would find shelter within the city walls! The man urging his horse on with a stick, his wife following on behind, dragging her children along by the hand—entire families pushing on, staggering beneath their loads, headlong and straggling, the little ones unable to keep up, blinded by the white glare of the sun beating down on the road. Many had taken off their sandals and continued barefoot, to help them walk faster; and half-dressed mothers breast-fed tearful kids, still on the move, never stopping once. Terrified faces turned to look at the road behind, distraught hands waved frantically, as if trying to block out the horizon, while the wind of panic ruffled hair and set hastily buttoned garments flapping about wildly. Others went rushing off across the fields, farmers with all their domestic household in tow, letting out their flocks and driving them on ahead, sheep, cattle, horses, and oxen, forced out of stables and barns with sticks. They were heading for the valleys, high plateaux, and empty forests, kicking up clouds of dust left by other routs long ago, when the native peoples abandoned their lands to the invading hordes. They were off to live under canvas, in some natural circle of lonely stones, so far from the beaten track that not a single enemy soldier would dare risk his neck coming after them. And the swirling dust enveloping them faded away behind clumps of pine trees, accompanied by bellows and clattering hooves; while back on the road, the streams of carts and foot travellers flowed steadily past, hindering the troops' onward march. They swept along so thick and fast as they neared Belfort that it was like battling against a swollen, irresistible torrent, and more than once, the soldiers were obliged to come to a halt.

It was during one of these brief halts that Maurice witnessed an incident which scarred his memory like the stinging weal from a whip-lash across his face.

By the side of the road stood an isolated house, the dwelling of some poor peasant, whose meagre plot of land could be seen at the back. This man had refused to abandon his field; the roots binding him to this earth of his went far too deep for that. And so he stayed, because to leave would mean leaving part of himself behind with it. They could see him squatting on a bench in the low-ceilinged room, vacantly watching the soldiers file past, abandoning his ripened corn to enemy hands as they withdrew. Standing beside him was his wife, still young, one child in her arms, another hiding in her skirts; and all three stood weeping and wailing. But suddenly the front door was flung violently open, and there on the threshold stood the grandmother, a very old, tall, skinny woman, waving her bare, scrawny arms at them like a couple of lengths of gnarled rope. Her grey hair had escaped from under her cap, and blew wildly about her emaciated features, and her fury was so intense that the words she shouted stuck in her throat, choked and indistinct.

At first, the soldiers began laughing at her. Just look at the state of her, silly old bag! Then some of her words reached their ears.

'Bastards! Scoundrels! Cowards! Cowards!' she yelled.

Cowards! She spat the volley of insults at them, her voice growing shriller and shriller. And the laughter was cut dead, an icy cold spread through the ranks. The men hung their heads and looked away.

'Cowards! Cowards! Cowards!'

Abruptly, she seemed to get even taller. Drawing herself up, tragically thin, there in her raggedy dress, she swept a large arc from west to east, a gesture so expansive that it seemed to fill the whole sky.

'Cowards! The Rhine's not that way! It's over there, the Rhine, you cowards! Cowards!'

Finally, they set off again, and catching a glimpse of Jean's face,

Maurice saw that his eyes were brimming with tears. At this, he felt a sudden rush of emotion, and the grief in him bit more sharply at the thought that even these savages had felt the sting from that insult, that unmerited slur which they were forced to endure. Everything went to pieces inside his wretched, aching head, and he never did know exactly how he managed to complete the march.

It had taken the 7th Corps all day to cover the twenty-three kilometres between Dannemarie and Belfort; and once again, night was falling and it was already late by the time the troops were finally able to pitch their tents beneath the city fortifications, on the self-same spot from which they had set off four days previously, marching to meet the enemy. Despite the late hour and their extreme exhaustion, the soldiers insisted on lighting the campfires and preparing their soup. It was the first time since setting out that they were, at long last, getting a hot meal inside them. Sitting around the fires beneath the cool night air, they were just finishing licking out their mess-tins and leaning back, grunting contentedly, when they were suddenly stunned by a rumour going round the camp. Two new dispatches had arrived in quick succession: the Prussians, it seemed, had not crossed the Rhine at Markolsheim at all, and there wasn't a single Prussian left at Huningue. All the terrifying accounts—the Markolsheim crossing, the bridge of boats strung across the river, lit by huge electric lamps—were all nothing but nightmarish fancy, inexplicable hallucinations dreamed up by the Sous-Préfet at Schelestadt. And as for the army corps threatening Huningue, that notorious Black Forest Corps which had set all Alsace trembling in its boots, it was, in fact, no more than a tiny detachment of Württemberg troops*—two battalions and a squadron—whose artful tactics of repeatedly marching first in one direction and then back over its own footsteps, thus suddenly appearing unexpectedly all over the place, had led everyone to believe that a force thirty to forty thousand strong was at hand. Just imagine! That very morning, they had nearly blown up the Dannemarie viaduct! Twenty leagues of rich farmland had just suffered pointless damage and destruction, and all because of the most idiotic panic; and as they recalled all they had seen in the course of that dreadful day—all those inhabitants fleeing in terror, driving their livestock up into the mountains; the stream of carts piled high with belongings, rolling towards the city, surrounded by herds of women and children—recalling all this, the soldiers lost their tempers, and angry exclamations could be heard among the exasperated sniggers.

'No, really, this is just too ludicrous!' faltered Loubet, waving his spoon, his mouth full of food. 'What? Is that the enemy they were leading us to meet? No one there all the time!... Twelve leagues there, twelve leagues back, and not even the ghost of an enemy lying in wait! All that for nothing, just for the thrill of getting scared!'

Then Chouteau, noisily scraping out his bowl, began railing against the generals, though not saying so specifically.

'What bastards, hey? How much stupider can you get? Bunch of frightened rabbits we've been landed with there! Just think—if they bolted like that when there wasn't anyone there, imagine how they'd have hopped it if they'd found themselves staring a real army in the face!'

Another armful of wood had been thrown on the fire, purely for the pleasure of seeing the tall, bright flames which it sent up, and Lapoulle, blissfully toasting his legs in the warmth, started laughing like an idiot, without a clue as to why; Jean, who until then had turned a deaf ear, ventured in a paternal tone of voice,

'Quiet now... Things might turn nasty for you if anyone heard...'

He himself, as a simple and sensible man, was also outraged by the stupidity of his commanders. But they had to be respected, all the same; and, as Chouteau wouldn't stop his grumbling, he cut him off in mid-sentence.

'Quiet! Here comes the Lieutenant now: if you've got any grievances, take them up with him.'

Maurice, sitting apart in silence, had hung his head. This really was the end, the end of it all! They had barely started, and already it was all over. The lack of discipline, the men rebelling at the very first setback—this was already turning the army into a gang with nothing to bond them together, already demoralized and just ripe for any catastrophe that might happen to come along. Sitting there, beneath the walls of Belfort, they hadn't yet seen a single Prussian, and already they were defeated.

The days that followed bristled with apprehension and unease, such was their monotony. To keep his troops busy, General Douay set them to work on the town's fortifications, which were sorely inadequate. They shifted mounds of earth and hewed rock at a furious pace. And not a word reached them! Where was MacMahon's army? What were they doing outside Metz? The most exaggerated rumours circulated, and the odd newspapers that got through to them from Paris were so full of contradictions that they merely added to the deepening gloom and anxiety against which they struggled. The general had already written twice to ask for orders, without getting any reply. Finally, however, on 12 August, the 7th Corps's numbers were brought up to strength by the arrival of the 3rd Division, just landed from Italy; but still, that only made two divisions in all—the 1st Division, defeated at Frœschwiller, had got itself lost during the rout, and no one as yet knew where it had been carried off to. And then, after a week spent in this state of isolation, completely cut off from the rest of France, a telegram arrived, giving the order to move on. There was jubilation all round—anything rather than the life they'd been leading. As they prepared to depart, the guessing began again, no one knew where they were heading: some said they were off to defend Strasbourg, while others even talked of being part of a daring push into the Black Forest, to cut off the Prussian line of retreat.

As of the following morning, the 106th was one of the first to leave, crammed into cattle trucks. The wagon which Jean's squad found itself in was particularly crowded, so much so that Loubet claimed that he didn't even have room to sneeze. The utter chaos which, yet again, had plagued the distribution of supplies meant that the men had received in liquor what they should have been given in victuals: so nearly all of them were now drunk, victims of blind, roaring drunkenness which spilled out in a chorus of obscenities. The train rolled along, and inside the wagon it was impossible to see each other through the thick pipe-smoke which hung like fog on the air; the heat from the piles of fermenting bodies was unbearable, and yells escaped from the fleeing black wagon, drowning out the rumble of the wheels, and dying out far away in the bleak landscape. And it was only when they reached Langres that the troops realized that they were being taken back to Paris.

'Bloody hell!' said Chouteau, whose unfailing gift of the gab had already established him as undisputed leader in his own particular corner. 'That's what it is, they're going to line us up outside Charentonneau, to stop Bismarck kipping down in the Tuileries.'*

The others thought this was a hoot, although they couldn't have said why, and rolled about laughing. As it was, the slightest incident along the way brought deafening cheers, shouts and laughter from the wagons: the sight of peasants standing by the side of the track, anxious groups of people waiting at small country stations for the trains to come through, hoping for news, the whole of France trembling and terrified at the threat of invasion. And so the masses who had gathered to see the train got nothing for their pains but all this bawling cannon-fodder, as it whipped past their noses on the flying locomotive, a fleeting vision engulfed in steam and noise, being carted off at great speed. However, at one station where they stopped, three well-heeled bourgeois ladies, who had begun handing out soup to the soldiers, proved a great success. The men were so happy they cried, kissing the ladies' hands and thanking them.

Further on, though, the dreadful songs and wild hoots started up yet again. Some way after Chaumont, as they carried on as before, their train met another going the other way, packed with artillerymen who had to be transported to Metz. The train had just slowed down, and the soldiers in the two trains yelled out to each other, making an appalling racket. As it happened, the artillery won the fight, no doubt the drunkest of the two, standing in the wagons waving their fists, and bawling out, with such desperate violence that it drowned out everything else:

'Off to the slaughter! Off to the slaughter! Off to the slaughter!'

And a blast of cold, icy, graveyard air seemed to blow over them all. There was a sudden silence, above which Loubet could be heard jeering,

'Cheerful bunch!'

'Maybe, but they've got a point,' put in Chouteau, like some workers' club speaker. 'It's revolting, sending a load of brave lads off to their deaths for some rotten business they don't even know the first thing about.'

And on he went. Here was the subvert talking, the unreliable Montmartre labourer, the street painter, always dawdling and out on the town, full of half-digested odds and ends from speeches he'd caught bits of in public meetings, coming out with arrant nonsense all mixed up with the great principles of liberty and equality. He thought he knew it all, and began to indoctrinate his comrades, particularly Lapoulle, of whom he'd secretly vowed to make a fine fellow.

'Hey, lads? It's simple! If Badinguet* and Bismarck have a quarrel to settle, let them sort it out between themselves with a few fisticuffs, and stop bothering hundreds of thousands of men who don't even know each other and don't want to fight!'

The entire wagon laughed, amused and won over by him, and Lapoulle, who didn't have a clue who Badinguet was and couldn't even have said whether he was fighting for a king or for an emperor, repeated after him, like the great child he was,

'That's it, a few fisticuffs, and then off for a drink!'

Chouteau, however, had turned towards Pache, to give him the same treatment.

'It's like you, believing in God Almighty... He forbade fighting, did your God Almighty. So what are you doing here then, you great ninny?'

'Lord above!' said Pache, taken aback, 'I'm not here for the fun of it... It's just, you know, the police...'

'Police? Pah, we couldn't give a toss about the police! Listen, you lot, do you know what we'd do if we had any bloody sense? In a while, when we stop and get out, we'd bugger off, that's what we'd do! We'd bugger off home and leave that fat swine Badinguet and all his two-bit crony generals to sort out this mess with their filthy Prussians as they see fit!'

Cheers broke out, the subversion was beginning to take effect, and Chouteau was triumphant, dragging up all his theories, where the lot—the Republic, human rights and the rotting Empire which ought to be overthrown—all mixed and mingled in a murky swell, together with the treason of all their commanders, who'd each sold out for a million, as they'd seen with their own eyes. He was, he proclaimed, a revolutionary; the others didn't even know if they were Republicans or not, nor even how you got to be one: all except Loubet, the connoisseur, who knew very well what his own opinion was—he'd never been in favour of anything except soup. Yet each and every one of them, caught up in the moment, ranted all the same against the Emperor, the officers, and this unholy mess they'd leave behind them at the first sign of trouble, and double quick! And, fanning the flames of their increasing drunkenness, Chouteau kept one eye on Maurice, the gentleman he was amusing and who he was so proud to have with him. So proud, in fact, that in order to rouse his passions too, he decided to pick on Jean, who until then had been sitting motionless and almost asleep in all this din, with his eyes half-shut. Since the harsh lesson which the corporal had inflicted upon the volunteer when he'd forced him to pick up his rifle, if the latter did bear his NCO any grudge, then this was just the moment to set the two men on each other.

'Just like there's some I know who've talked of getting us shot,' he took up again, in threatening tones. 'Right bastards who treat us worse than dogs, who just don't understand that when you've had enough of your rucksack and your bloody gun, oopsadaisy! Chuck the fucking things in a field and see if they'll sprout! Hey, comrades? What do you think they'd say if we threw *them* onto the track, now we've got them cornered?... That's the ticket, hey comrades? We need to make an example of one of 'em, so they'll stop pestering us with their bloody war! Death to Badinguet's trouble-merchants! Death to all the bastards who want us to fight!'

Jean had turned bright red, as the angry blood went rushing to his cheeks in one of the rare moments when he lost his temper. Although the men around him were squeezing him in like a human vice, he stood up, put up clenched fists, and thrust his burning face at Chouteau, such a terrifying vision that the other grew pale.

'Jesus Christ! Will you shut your mouth, you swine!... I've kept quiet for hours, because there aren't any officers about and I can't just put you up against the wall. Oh yes, oh yes! I'd have been doing the regiment a real service, getting rid of a bloody reptile like you... But just you listen: the moment we start joking about punishment, you'll have me to deal with. Not a corporal—just a big bloke who's getting pissed off with you and who'll shut your gob for you! Ah, look at you, you coward! You don't want to fight, so you're trying to stop everyone else fighting, too! Just you say that again and see if I don't clout you one!'

By now, the entire wagon had turned to stare, and was won over by Jean's feisty manner, abandoning Chouteau, who could only stammer and back away from his opponent's hefty fists.

'And I couldn't give a toss about Badinguet, either, d'you hear? I've never given a toss about politics, or the Republic, or the Empire; and now, just like when I was ploughing my fields back then, all I've ever wanted is for everyone to be happy, for things to be as they should be, fair and square... Of course it's a blasted nuisance for everyone, having to fight. But that doesn't mean that the bastards who come round demoralizing us shouldn't be flung up against the wall, because it's hard enough to behave properly as it is. Christ alive!—doesn't your blood boil, my friends, when they tell you that the Prussians are on your soil, and that you've got to throw them out?'

Then, in one of those effortless mood swings so common to crowds, the soldiers cheered the corporal, who repeated his solemn oath to clout the first man from his squad who talked of not fighting. Bravo, Corporal! We'd sort out Bismarck in no time!

In the midst of this wild oration, Jean, quite calm again, said politely to Maurice, as if he hadn't been addressing one of his own men at all,

'Sir, you can't possibly be on the side of the cowards... After all, we haven't even fought yet—it'll be us thrashes those Prussians, one day!'

At that moment, Maurice felt a warm ray of sunshine penetrate right to his heart. It made him feel troubled and humiliated. What? Was this man more than just a yokel after all? He recalled the terrible hatred which had burned within him, as he picked up the rifle he'd thrown away in a moment of forgetfulness. Yet he also recalled his astonishment on seeing those two great tears in the corporal's eyes, when the old granny, grey hair flying in the wind, pointing to the Rhine, over the horizon, had insulted them. Was it some fraternal feeling born of the same weariness, the same pain, suffered together, which made his rancour disappear like this? Coming from a family which supported Bonaparte, he'd never imagined the Republic except in theory; he even felt rather affectionate towards the Emperor himself, and he was in favour of war, the very lifeblood of nations. All at once, he was filled with new hope, in one of those leaps of the imagination so familiar to him; and the enthusiasm which, one evening, had driven him to join up set his heart beating once again, swelling it with the certainty of victory.

'But it's absolutely certain, Corporal,' he said gaily, 'we're going to thrash them!'

Ever onwards, ever onwards rolled the wagon, carrying its load of men, amid the thick smoke from their pipes and the stifling heat from all the piled-up bodies, hurling its obscene verses at the anxious stations as it passed through, hurling them at the haggard peasants standing along the hedgerows with a loud, drunken, clamour. By

20 August, they were in Paris, at the station at the Porte de Pantin,*
and that very same evening they set off again, to disembark the
following day at Rheims, heading for the camp at Châlons.

CHAPTER THREE

Much to his surprise, Maurice saw that the 106th was getting off at Rheims and being given orders to set up camp there. So they weren't going on to Châlons to join up with the army after all? Two hours later, when his regiment had stacked up their arms, a league from the city, on the way to Courcelles, on the vast plain which stretched beyond the canal from the Aisne to the Marne,* his amazement grew still further on learning that the entire Châlons army had been in retreat since morning, and was coming to set up camp. In fact, tents were springing up from one edge of the horizon to the other, right over to Saint-Thierry and Neuvillette, even beyond the Laon road; and by evening, there would be the fires of four encampments flickering here. Obviously the plan which had been adopted envisaged taking up positions south of Paris, to wait for the Prussians. And he was very happy to see it. After all, wasn't it the safest thing to do?

Maurice spent the afternoon of 21 August wandering around the camp, searching for news. They were left to their own devices, and discipline seemed to have grown slack again, for the men drifted off and came back just as they pleased. In the end, Maurice ambled back to Rheims, to cash a money order for a hundred francs which he'd received from his sister Henriette. In a café, he overheard a sergeant talking about the mutinous mood of the eighteen battalions of the Garde Mobile de la Seine,* which had just been sent back to Paris: the 6th Battalion in particular had nearly murdered its officers. Back at camp, the generals suffered insults daily, and since Frœschwiller, the soldiers hadn't even bothered saluting Marshal MacMahon any more. The café filled with the sound of voices, and a violent argument broke out between two peaceable-looking gentlemen about the number of troops the Marshal would have under his command. One talked of three hundred thousand, which was absurd. The other, more reasonably, counted off the four army corps: there was the 12th, back at camp, only just brought up to full strength by the addition of foot regiments and a division of the marine infantry; the 1st, whose men had been turning up like flotsam and jetsam since 14 August, and whose units were being reconstituted, after a fashion; and finally the 5th, defeated without a battle, carried off and broken up in the rout, and the 7th, equally demoralized and minus its 1st Division, which it had only just met up with again, in some disarray, at Rheims. That came to a hundred and twenty thousand men at the most, even including the reserve cavalry and the Bonnemain and Margueritte divisions. But when the sergeant joined in and began angrily expressing his scorn for this army, this rabble, this herd of innocents being led to the slaughter by a bunch of imbeciles, the two gentlemen grew nervous and fled, afraid of putting themselves in a compromising position.

Outside, Maurice tried to get hold of some newspapers. He stuffed his pockets with every edition he could buy, reading them as he walked along beneath the tall trees which lined the magnificent promenades bordering the city. So where were the German armies? They seemed to have disappeared. No doubt two of them were somewhere over near Metz, the First under the command of General Steinmetz,* in a defensive position, while the Second, under Prince Frederick Charles,* tried to make its way back along the right bank of the Moselle, to block Bazaine's* retreat to Paris. But what of the Third Army, led to victory at Wissembourg and Frœschwiller by the Crown Prince of Prussia, now pursuing the 1st and 5th Corps: what was its true position at present, amid all the chaotic muddle and conflicting information? Was it still camped at Nancy? Or was it about to descend on Châlons—was that why they'd struck camp with such haste, setting fire to shops, equipment, fodder, and all sorts of provisions? And once again confusion reigned, as the most contradictory hypotheses resurfaced about the plans ascribed to the generals. It was only then that Maurice, cut off as he was from the rest of the world, learned of the events in Paris: defeat crashing like thunder over the heads of a people so sure of victory, the terrible feeling of shock on the streets, both Chambers recalled, the fall of the liberal minister* responsible for the plebiscite, the Emperor stripped of his title of Commander-in-Chief, and forced to hand over supreme command to Marshal Bazaine. The Emperor had been at the Châlons camp since 16 August, and all the papers talked about an important council that had been held on the 17th, attended by Prince Napoleon* and a number of generals; however, as to exactly what decisions had actually been taken, the papers couldn't agree, except on the bare, factual results: General Trochu* had been appointed Governor of Paris, and Marshal MacMahon placed at the head of the Châlons army—all of which implied that the Emperor had been completely removed from the picture. One could sense immense fear and irresolution, with the alternating plans contradicting and replacing each other from one hour to the next. And still the same old question: where were the German armies? Who were right—those who claimed that Bazaine was in the process of making an orderly retreat through the northern positions, or those who maintained that he was already cut off south of Metz? There was a persistent rumour circulating about colossal battles, heroic struggles taking place during the entire week from 14 to 20 August, although the only thing which seemed certain was a terrifying clash of arms, far away and out of sight.

Then Maurice sat down on a bench, his tired legs about to give way beneath him. All around him, the city seemed to be going about its normal, everyday life; beneath the beautiful trees, maids watched over children, and those with modest private incomes took their habitual, leisurely stroll. Taking up his papers again, he chanced upon an article he had overlooked, from a militant Republican opposition paper. Suddenly, everything became clear. The paper confirmed that at the council held at the Châlons camp on 17 August, the decision had been taken to order the Paris army to retreat, and that General Trochu had been nominated solely to prepare the ground for the Emperor's return. However, it added that, confronted by the attitude of the Empress Regent* and the new government, these resolutions had foundered. The Empress was convinced that there would be a revolution, should the Emperor return. 'He wouldn't get to the Tuileries alive,' was what she had reportedly said. She was stubbornly determined to see the army advance, and even join up with the Metz army; besides, her opinion had the support of General Palikao,* newly appointed War Minister, who had plans for a thunderous, victorious march to meet up with Bazaine. Maurice let the paper slide onto his lap, and sat staring into space; now he thought he understood it all—the two conflicting plans, Marshal MacMahon's hesitancy in carrying out this flanking movement—such a dangerous undertaking if the troops weren't really reliable; the impatient orders reaching him from Paris, each more irritated than the last, forcing him into this brave but foolhardy venture. And then, in the middle of this tragic struggle, Maurice suddenly had a clear, sharp vision of the Emperor, stripped of his imperial authority, which he'd placed in the hands of the Empress Regent, robbed of his command as Commander-in-Chief, recently relinquished to Marshal Bazaine; and now he was nothing at all, a mere shadow of an emperor, vague and insubstantial, a cumbersome, useless, nameless object that no one knew what to do with, rejected by Paris, yet with no place in the army either, now that he'd promised not even to give a single order.

The next morning, though, after a stormy night spent outside the tent, rolled up in his blanket, Maurice was relieved to learn that the order to retreat to Paris had most definitely won the day. There was talk of another council held the previous evening, attended by the former Vice-Emperor, Monsieur Rouher,* sent by the Empress to hasten the march on Verdun, and whom the Marshal seemed to have persuaded of the peril of such a manœuvre. Had there been bad news from Bazaine? No one dared confirm it. But the absence of any news was significant in itself, and officers with any sense at all came out in favour of waiting outside Paris, so as to act as the capital's reserve army. And now that he was convinced the retreat would begin the next day, since people said the order had already been given, Maurice was happy, and decided to give in to the childish fancy which had been tormenting him—just for once, he wanted to get away from the billycans and dine somewhere on a real tablecloth, with a bottle of wine, a glass, and a plate in front of him—all those things he'd been deprived of for what seemed like months. He had money, and off he went with pounding heart, as if he were up to some mischief, looking for an inn.

It was across the canal, at the entrance to the village of Courcelles, that he found the lunch he'd dreamed of. The day before, someone had told him that the Emperor had stopped at a prosperous-looking house here; so he'd wandered over to take a look, out of curiosity. He remembered seeing a tavern on the corner at a crossroads, with its latticed arch hung with fine bunches of grapes, already ripe and golden. Beneath the creeping vines stood green painted tables, and looking through the wide-open door into the vast kitchen, he caught glimpses of the great, ticking clock, with colourful Épinal engravings* hanging on the wall among the china, and the landlord's huge wife turning the spit-handle. Behind the tavern a game of boules was in progress. And it was all so happy and innocent, the perfect picture of the traditional French open-air inn.

A pretty, buxom girl came over to him, and, flashing her white teeth, asked,

'Will you be eating, sir?'

'Indeed I will!... I'd like eggs, a cutlet, and some cheese. And white wine!'

He called her back.

'Tell me, isn't the Emperor staying in one of those houses?'

'Yes, sir, that's the one, right there in front of us! You can't see the house itself, it's hidden behind that high wall with the trees showing over the top.'

So he settled in beneath the latticed arch, loosened his belt to make himself more comfortable, and chose a table, dappled with golden sunlight filtering through the vines. He kept looking back towards the high yellow wall which was sheltering the Emperor. It really was a hidden, mysterious house; even the tiled roof was invisible from where he sat. The entrance gave onto the other side, towards the village road, a narrow track winding between dismal walls, with not a shop or a window to be seen. Behind it, the little park was like an oasis of thick greenery among the few neighbouring buildings. And there, on the other side of the road, surrounded by sheds and stables, he noticed a whole courtyard full of carriages and wagons, amid a continuous coming and going of men and horses.

Intending it as a joke, he asked the serving girl, who was spreading a snowy-white cloth over the table,

'Is that all for the Emperor?'

'Why, yes indeed, just for the Emperor!' she replied, in her winsome, cheerful way, happy to show off her lovely white teeth.

And she listed everything, no doubt informed by the grooms who had been coming to drink at the tavern since the day before: there was the staff, made up of twenty-five officers, sixty household guards, and the scout platoon of the Imperial Escort, six gendarmes from the military police; then the royal household, seventy-three persons in all, chamberlains, serving valets and chamber valets, cooks and pot-boys; then four saddle horses and two carriages for the Emperor, ten horses for the equerries, eight for the grooms and bellboys, not to mention forty-seven post-horses; then a charabanc and twelve wagonloads of luggage, including two exclusively for the kitchen, which had won her admiration by the sheer quantity of utensils, bottles, and plates which could be seen, all beautifully laid out.

'Oh sir, you can't imagine the saucepans they've got! Shine like the sun, they do... And then there's all sorts of dishes and vases and contraptions, I couldn't begin to tell you what they're all used for!... And the wine, oh my! Bordeaux, Burgundy, Champagne, oh, you could give a fine old feast with that lot!'

In his delight at the snowy tablecloth and the white wine sparkling in his glass, Maurice ate two soft-boiled eggs with such an appetite that he surprised himself. Looking over to his left, through one of the lattice gates, he had a view of the vast plain, and it was full of tents, like some swarming city sprouting up amid the stubble-fields, between Rheims and the canal. The grey expanse was barely coloured here and there by a few patches of spindly green trees. Three windmills stood spreading their gangly arms. But above the jumbled rooftops of Rheims, awash with chestnut-tree crowns, the outline of the cathedral rose up like a massive ship against the blue sky, a colossus even at this distance, compared to the squat little houses. And memories of his schooldays came back to him, lessons learned and parroted off: the coronation of French kings, the holy phial,* Clovis,* Joan of Arc—all France's ancient and glorious past.

Then, as Maurice turned his gaze back towards the high yellow wall, struck again by the image of the Emperor staying in this modest but well-to-do residence, so discreetly tucked away, he was surprised to read the cry 'Long live Napoleon!' charcoaled in huge letters on the wall, alongside all the misspelt, outsized obscenities. The rain had washed the letters away, and the inscription was obviously years old. What an odd thing it was, to see this enthusiastic, bygone war-cry here upon the wall—doubtless acclaiming the uncle, the conqueror, and not the nephew! In an instant, Maurice felt his childhood coming back to him, singing in his memory, taking him back to Le Chesne-Populeux, where, even from the cradle, he would listen to stories recounted to him by his grandfather, a soldier in Napoleon's Grande Armée. His mother had died and his father been forced to accept a job collecting taxes, brought low like so many other sons of heroes in the fall from glory that followed the overthrow of the Empire; and the grandfather lived with them on his minute pension, reduced to the mediocrity of this petty clerk's dwelling, with no other consolation than to tell stories of his battle campaigns to his grandchildren, the twins, a boy and a girl, each with identical blond hair; and in some ways he was like a mother to them. He would settle Henriette on his left knee, Maurice on his right, and there would follow hours of Homeric tales of combat.

The centuries became confused in these tales of his, the story seemed to be taking place outside the realms of history, as every nation clashed in dreadful combat. The English, Austrians, Prussians, and Russians marched past one by one and all together, at the passing whim of alliances, so that sometimes it was impossible to work out why some were defeated rather than others. But in the end, they were all defeated, inevitably defeated in advance, in an upsurge of heroism and genius* which swept aside whole armies like wisps of straw. There was Marengo, the battle on the plain, its great lines cleverly deployed, its faultless retreat proceeding as neatly as a game of chess, battalion by battalion, moving silently and impassively in the hail of gunfire, the legendary battle lost at three o'clock and won at six, when the eight hundred Grenadiers of the Consular Guard stopped the entire Austrian cavalry in its tracks, when Desaix arrived only to die, but transformed the beginnings of a rout into an immortal victory. There was Austerlitz, with its beautiful sun shining glorious through the winter mists, Austerlitz, which began with the capture of the Pratzen Heights and ended with the terrifying débâcle on those frozen ponds, an entire Russian army corps sinking through the ice, men, beasts, and all, going down with a dreadful cracking sound, while Napoleon the god, who had naturally foreseen everything, helped the disaster on its way with cannonfire. Then Jena, that graveyard of Prussian might, first the infantry fire coming through the October fog, Ney's impatience nearly jeopardizing everything, then Augereau moving into the line and getting him out of trouble, then the mighty onslaught, tearing the enemy's centre ranks apart, and finally panic, as their overrated cavalry ran for its life, cut down by our hussars like ripe oats, sowing the romantic valley floor with a harvest of men and horses. Then Eylau, abominable Eylau, bloodiest of them all, where the butchery left a great pile of hideously mutilated corpses, Eylau, blood-red beneath the snowstorm, with its bleak, heroic graveyard, Eylau, still vibrating from the thundering charge of Murat's eighty squadrons, cutting swathes through the Russian army, strewing the dead bodies so thick on the ground that even Napoleon wept to see them. There was Friedland, the appalling trap that the Russians fell right into, once again, like a flock of dizzy sparrows, the strategic masterpiece of that all-seeing, all-powerful Emperor, our left flank holding out immobile, unshake-able, while Ney, having taken the city street by street, began to destroy the bridges; then our left flank rushing on the enemy's right, pushing it towards the river, squeezing it into the impasse, a mas-sacre of such Herculean proportions that they were still killing at ten o'clock that evening. There was Wagram, the Austrians trying to cut us off from the Danube, continuing to bring in reinforcements for their right flank to fight Masséna, who maintained his command, despite his wounds, from an open carriage, while Napoleon, like some crafty Titan, left them to it, and then all of a sudden a hundred cannon smashed their weaker centre ranks to pieces with fierce bom-bardments, pushing them more than a whole league back, while the right flank, terrified to find itself isolated, and giving ground to Masséna, victorious again, swept the rest of the army with it, into disaster, like water bursting through a ruptured dyke. Finally, there was Moscow, where the clear sun of Austerlitz shone out for the last time, a horrifying scramble of men, confusion caused by headstrong courage and sheer numbers, hillocks stormed by incessant volleys of fire, redoubts taken with knives alone, repeated counter-attacks, every inch of terrain fought over, and such fierce bravery from the Russian Guards that for victory, it took Murat leading furious charges, the thunder of three hundred cannon firing simultaneously, and the valour of Ney, that day's prince triumphant. And whichever battle it happened to be, the flags fluttered in the evening air with the same quiver of glory, and the same cries of 'Long live Napoleon!' rang out when the campfires were lit on conquered ground; France reigned supreme wherever she went, a conqueror parading her invincible eagles from one end of Europe to the other, needing only to set foot in foreign parts for the vanquished nation to turn and run.

Maurice was finishing up his cutlet, light-headed not so much from the white wine which sparkled in his glass as from all the reflected glory singing in his memory, when his eye happened upon two soldiers dressed in rags and covered in mud, like bandits weary of roaming the highways; and he overheard them asking the serving girl about the precise whereabouts of the regiments camped along the canal.

He called over to them.

'Hey! Comrades! Over here...! Hang on, aren't you from the 7th Corps?'

'That's right, from the 1st Division! Bloody hell, aren't I just. Aren't I just! I was at Frœschwiller, if you must know, and it was warm enough there, I can tell you! Listen, my comrade here, he's from the 1st Corps—he was at Wissembourg, another filthy hole for you!'

They told their story; how they'd been caught up in the panic and the rout, left in a ditch, half-dead with exhaustion, both of them slightly wounded, thereafter dragging themselves along behind the army, forced to stop at towns along the way because of bouts of fever which sapped their strength, falling so far behind in the end that it was only now that they were slightly less ill that they'd arrived in search of their squads.

Maurice was about to dig into a piece of Gruyère when he noticed their eyes staring ravenously at his plate, and felt a pang of anguish .

'Hey, Mademoiselle! Some more cheese over here, and bread and wine! Right, comrades? You'll join me? It's on me. Here's to you!'

They sat down, delighted. And, feeling a chill creep over him, he watched them, soldiers in the deplorable state of being without weapons, in their red trousers and capes held together by bits of string, and patched up with so many different rags and tatters that they looked like a couple of looters, or gypsies getting the last wear out of cast-offs from some battlefield.

'Bloody hell!' took up the taller one again, with his mouth full. 'It really wasn't much of a laugh, back there...! You should have seen it. Go on, Coutard, tell him.'

And the small man recounted their story, gesticulating and waving his bread in the air.

'Well, there was me, washing my shirt while they were preparing the soup. Imagine a filthy hole of a place, a real pit, with woods all the way round that let those Prussian bastards crawl up on their hands and knees without us suspecting a bloody thing. So at seven o'clock, shells start landing in the cooking-pots! Christ alive! We didn't hang around, we leapt for our guns, and I'm not joking, right until eleven o'clock we really thought we were giving them a first-class thrashing. Mind you, I've got to tell you that there were fewer than five thousand of us, and those bastards just kept on coming. There I was, on a low hillside, lying flat behind a bush, and I saw them coming from

every direction, right, left, straight ahead, like colonies of ants, great
black columns of ants, and there were plenty more where they came
from, too. Now don't go repeating this, but we thought the officers
were thick as pigshit, shoving us into a trap like that, far away from
the rest of the boys, leaving us there to get flattened without coming
to help. And then our General Douay, poor sod—hardly a wild boar
but no chicken either, for a change—goes and swallows a bullet, and
there he is, lying flat on his back with his legs in the air. Wiped out,
nobody left! But no matter—we hung on all the same. But there were
just too many of 'em, we had to get ourselves out of the trap. So we
were fighting in an enclosed space, defending the station, with such a
din ringing in our ears that it was enough to deafen you. And then I
don't know, the town must have been taken, and we found ourselves
up on some mountain, the Gisberg, I think they call it; and then, dug
into some sort of castle, by God, the number of those bastards we
killed! Blown sky-high they were, and it was a real treat to see them
coming down flat on their faces! And then, what could we do? They
just kept on coming, ten against one, and all the cannon they wanted.
When it comes to that sort of business, being brave's just the quick-
est way of getting killed. Anyway, it was such a mess in the end that
we had to get the hell out. Talk about thick, our officers ended up
looking thicker than two short planks, hey Picot?'

There was a silence. Picot, the taller of the two, swallowed down a
glass of white wine. Then, wiping his mouth on the back of his hand,
he said,

'Aye. Like at Frœschwiller, not even the daftest animal would have
fought in such conditions. That's what my captain said, and he's a
crafty old bugger. Truth is, we weren't meant to know that. A whole
army of those bastards landed right on top of us, and there weren't
even forty thousand of us. We weren't expecting to fight that day,
either—apparently the battle began bit by bit, the officers hadn't
planned it. Well, anyway, I didn't see everything myself, of course.
But what I do know is that the dance kept starting up all over again,
from morning till night, and just when we thought it had finished,
not a bit of it! The music struck up louder than ever. First, it was at
Wörth, a nice little village with a funny bell-tower that looks like a
stove because it's covered with earthenware tiles. They'd made us
leave it that morning, I'm buggered if I know why, because we fought
tooth and nail to get it back, and couldn't manage it. Oh lads! The

way we got mown down there! Stomachs ripped open, brains spilling out, you wouldn't believe it! After that, we got hit on the outskirts of another village, Elsasshausen. There's a name should be dead and buried. We got caught in a duck-shoot by a bunch of cannons, taking pot-shots at us from high up on this blasted hill—another one we'd abandoned that morning. And that's when I saw it, with my own eyes, as sure as I'm sitting here, I saw one hell of a cavalry charge. The poor sods, you should have seen the way they went down! A right shame it was, chucking horses and men onto such awful ground, so steep, and all covered in brushwood and riddled with ditches! Especially when it couldn't do any good whatsoever, for Christ's sake! But even so, it was brave, it warmed your heart to look at them. After that, well, the best thing seemed to be to back off a little and get our breath back. The village was flaring up like a match, and the Badeners, Württembergers, Prussians, the whole lot of 'em—over a hundred and twenty thousand of the bastards, from what they reckoned later—ended up surrounding us. But not a bit of it, the band strikes up louder than ever, around Frœschwiller! Because it's God's own truth, MacMahon might be stupid, but he's brave all right. You should have seen him, sitting on his great horse in the middle of all that shelling! Another man would have scarpered as soon as it started—no shame in refusing to fight when you're not evenly matched. But now it had begun, he was determined to go right to the edge and risk his neck. And he didn't half succeed... At Frœschwiller, you see, they weren't men any more—just beasts, devouring each other. For nearly two hours, the gutters ran with blood. And then, well, by God, we had to get out, all the same. And to think they came to tell us that our left flank had given the Bavarians a good shafting! Great God in Heaven! We'd have done the same, if we'd had a hundred and twenty thousand men, if we'd had enough cannon, and if the officers hadn't been so bloody stupid!'

And Coutard and Picot, still violent and exasperated, their ragged uniforms all grey and dusty, cut themselves more bread and wolfed down great lumps of cheese, blurting out their nightmarish memories, as they sat beneath the pretty lattice hung with ripe bunches of grapes, riddled by the sun's golden arrows. Now they came to the appalling rout which followed, starving and demoralized regiments fleeing in utter chaos across the countryside, the main roads teeming with a dreadful confusion of men, horses, carts, and cannon, the

entire débâcle of a crushed army, lashed by the mad winds of panic.
Seeing as they hadn't been capable of drawing back sensibly and
defending the Vosges passes, where ten thousand men could have
stopped a hundred thousand from getting through, then at the very
least they should have blown up the bridges and blocked all the
tunnels. But the generals just galloped on, caught up in the panic,
and such a storm of stupefaction blew up, carrying off both conquered and conquerors, that at one point the two armies lost each
other in this fumbling pursuit in broad daylight, with MacMahon
making for Lunéville, while the Crown Prince of Prussia was looking
for him near the Vosges. On 7 August, the remains of the 1st Corps
began crossing Saverne, like an overflowing, silt-laden river, sweeping the wreckage along. At Sarrebourg, on the 8th, the 5th Corps ran
straight into the 1st like one runaway torrent meeting another, in full
flight, defeated without a battle, dragging its poor commander—
General de Failly—down with it. He was almost out of his wits with
despair because responsibility for the defeat was being put down to
his own inertia. On the 9th and 10th, the stampede went on, a mad
rush, every man for himself, not even stopping to look back. On the
11th, in driving rain, they moved down towards Bayon to avoid
Nancy, after a false rumour reached them that the town had fallen
into enemy hands. On the 12th, they camped at Haroué, on the 13th
at Vicherey; and by the 14th they were at Neufchâteau, where at long
last the railway was there to meet this huge, rolling mass of men. It
took three days to load them up by the spadeful into trains, ready to
be transported to Châlons. Twenty-four hours after the last train had
left, the Prussians began to arrive.

'Bloody hell!' concluded Picot. 'We didn't half have to leg it! And
they'd left us in hospital!'

Coutard drained the bottle into his own and his comrade's glasses.

'Oh aye, we upped sticks and went, and we're still running... Well,
anyway, things are looking up, now that we can drink to the health of
all the ones who didn't cop it.'

And then Maurice understood. After the idiotic surprise attack at
Wissembourg, the crushing defeat at Frœschwiller was the thunderbolt, suddenly shedding a sinister light on the truth, to reveal it in all
its terrible detail. We had been ill-prepared, with mediocre artillery,
spurious estimates of numbers, and incompetent generals; the
enemy, which had been treated with such disdain, now appeared

strong and solid, in countless numbers, with flawless tactics and iron discipline. The flimsy curtain provided by our seven army corps, stretched thinly from Metz to Strasbourg, had been broken by the three German armies, driving through like powerful wedges. Suddenly, we were quite isolated, with neither Austria nor Italy offering a helping hand, and so the Emperor's plan had crumbled as a result of the slow pace of manœuvres and the incompetence of the commanders. And everything, even Fate, was conspiring against us, piling up unfortunate accidents and coincidences, bringing to fruition the Prussians' secret plan to cut our armies in two, sending one half back below Metz, and isolating it from the rest of France, while they marched on Paris, having annihilated the other half. From now on, it all seemed entirely logical: our defeat was inevitable, and the reasons for it were staring us in the face more and more clearly—the clash of mindless bravado coming up against cold logic supported by vast numbers. They would argue in vain, later on: in spite of everything they might say, defeat was a fatal inevitability, like the laws of nature which rule the world.

Suddenly, Maurice, whose dreamy eyes were wandering, read again the cry 'Long live Napoleon!' charcoaled on the high yellow wall. An unbearable uneasiness overcame him, a searing wound burning right into his heart. So it was true, then, that this France, this country crowned with such legendary victories, which had paraded across Europe with trumpets blaring, had now been toppled at the first blow by a tiny nation it despised? A mere fifty years had sufficed, the world had changed, a terrifying defeat now awaited the eternal conquerors. He remembered everything his brother-in-law Weiss had said, during that night of dread outside Mulhouse. Oh yes, he alone had seen the truth, and guessed at the slow, hidden causes of our decline, he alone had sensed the new wind of youth and strength blowing in from Germany. Wasn't this the end of one warfaring epoch, and the start of another? Beware the country that stands still amid the continuous striving of nations; victory will be hers who marches in the vanguard, she who is wisest, healthiest, strongest!

But at that moment, they heard the sound of laughter and the cries of a girl protesting good-naturedly. Lieutenant Rochas, in the old, smoke-filled kitchen, decorated with its colourful scenes, was holding the pretty serving girl in his arms like a conquering soldier.

He came out beneath the latticed arch and ordered a coffee; and hearing Coutard and Picot's last words, he interrupted cheerfully,

'Hey lads! That's nothing! The fight's only just begun—now you'll see our glorious revenge! By God, they've been five against one up until now. But that's all going to change, I'll stake my word on it! There are three hundred thousand of us here. All the manœuvres we keep making, which no one understands, they're all to draw the Prussians towards us, while Bazaine, who's got his eye on them, is going to grab them by the tail. And them we'll flatten them, splat! Just like that fly!'

With a resounding clap of his hands, he squashed a fly in mid-air; and his cheerful manner grew more boisterous. In his innocence he really believed in this effortless plan, finding his feet straight away through his faith and invincible courage. He obligingly let the two soldiers know exactly where they could find their regiments; and then he sat down happily, a cigar between his teeth, his half-cup of coffee in front of him.

'My pleasure entirely, comrades!' replied Maurice to Coutard and Picot, as they went on their way, thanking him for the cheese and the bottle of wine.

He too had had a coffee brought to him, and he looked at the lieutenant, won over by his good humour, but a little surprised by the figure of three hundred thousand men, when there were barely more than a hundred thousand of them, and by the curious ease with which he thought they could squash the Prussians between the two armies of Châlons and Metz. But he too was in such dire need of a few illusions! Why not keep hoping, when the glorious past was still ringing out so loud in his memory? The old tavern was so joyful, with its lattice arch hung with the pale grapes of France, all golden with sunshine! Once again, he experienced a moment of confidence, rising above the enormous sense of gnawing sadness which had gradually built up inside him.

For a moment, Maurice's gaze had followed an officer from the African Chasseurs,* accompanied by his orderly, who had just disappeared at a brisk trot round the corner of the silent house occupied by the Emperor. Then, as the orderly reappeared by himself, and drew his two horses to a halt at the tavern door, he gave a cry of surprise.

'Prosper! And there was I imagining you were in Metz!'

Prosper was from Remilly, a lowly farmhand whom he'd known as a child, when he went to spend the holidays at Uncle Fouchard's. He'd drawn the short straw, and spent three years in Africa, when war broke out; and he looked smart in his sky-blue jacket, wide red trousers with blue stripes, and red woollen belt, and with his long, bony face and strong, supple limbs, he cut an extraordinarily fine figure.

'Well well! Fancy meeting you here, Monsieur Maurice!'

But he took his time, leading the steaming horses into the stable, tending to his own in an especially paternal way. It was his love of horses, no doubt fostered in childhood, when he guided the animals along the furrow, which had made him choose the cavalry.

'We've just arrived from Monthois, you see—we've covered over ten leagues at one go,' he said when he came back, 'and Zephyr will be more than happy to get something to eat.'

Zephyr was his horse. He himself refused to eat anything, and simply accepted a coffee. He was waiting for his commanding officer, who in turn was waiting for the Emperor. It might take five minutes, it might take two hours. So he'd been told to put the horses in the shade. And when Maurice, his curiosity aroused, tried to find out what was going on, the other man gave a vague shrug.

'Don't know... Some commission, no doubt... Papers to deliver.'

Rochas, a nostalgic look in his eye, was watching the Chasseur, whose uniform brought back memories of Africa.

'Hey, lad, where were you based, back there?'

'Médéah,* sir.'

Médéah! They began to chat, feeling closer, in spite of their difference in rank. Prosper had grown used to life in a state of continual alert, always on horseback, leaving for battle as one would go to hounds, off to some great Arab-hunt. They only had one mess-tin between six of them, in each tribe; and each tribe formed a family, one man doing the cooking, another the washing, the rest pitching the tent, tending to the animals, and cleaning the weapons. Morning and afternoon would be spent on horseback, loaded down with huge saddlebags, with the sun beating straight down. In the evening, to keep away the mosquitoes, they would light huge bonfires, which they would sit around singing French songs. Often, beneath the clear, star-spangled night, they would have to get up and calm the horses, who were so lashed by the warm desert wind that they would suddenly bite each other and pull out their tethering pegs, neighing furiously. And then there was the coffee, the delicious coffee, what an important business, pounded in the bottom of a mess-tin and then filtered through a regulation-issue red belt. But there were black days too, spent far from human habitation, alone with the enemy. There were no bonfires then, no singing and feasting. Sometimes they suffered horribly from lack of sleep—and lack of food and water. But no matter! They loved this unpredictable, adventurous existence, this war of ambushes which was so suited to the glamorous pursuit of personal bravery, as entertaining as going out to conquer an island of savages, spiced up with ransacking—theft on a grand scale—and marauding, those petty thefts committed by the pilferers, whose legendary antics even had the generals laughing.

'Ah,' said Prosper, serious all of a sudden, 'it's not like that here, the fighting's different.'

And in answer to another question from Maurice, he told how they'd landed at Toulon* and made the long, laborious journey to Lunéville. It was there that they'd learned of Wissembourg and Frœschwiller. After that, he wasn't sure, and got the towns mixed up: Nancy to Saint-Mihiel, Saint-Mihiel to Metz. There must have been a large battle there on the 14th,* for the horizon had been ablaze; but he himself had seen only four Uhlans,* hiding behind a hedge. On the 16th, they had fought again,* the cannons roaring from six in the morning; and someone had told him that the dance began again on the 18th,* even more terrible than before. But the Chasseurs were no longer there, because at Gravelotte, on the 16th, the Emperor had come through fleeing in a carriage, as they lined up along one of the roads waiting to move into the line, and he'd taken them with him to escort him to Verdun. A fair old ride that had been, forty-two kilometres at a gallop, fearing every second that they'd be cut off by the Prussians.

'And Bazaine?' asked Rochas.

'Bazaine? They say he was mighty glad to have the Emperor leave him in peace.'

However, what the lieutenant had wanted to know was whether Bazaine was on his way. Prosper shrugged: who could say? Ever since the 16th, they'd spent their days marching and counter-marching in the rain, as reconnaissance, as mainguard, but with never a sign of the enemy. Now they were part of the Châlons army.

His regiment, two others from the French Chasseurs and one from the Hussars, made up the first division of reserve cavalry, under the command of General Margueritte,* of whom he spoke in glowing and affectionate terms.

'Ah, the old bugger, now there's a fellow! But what's the use, if all we can do is squelch around in the mud!'

There was a pause. Then Maurice spoke for a moment of Remilly and old Uncle Fouchard, and Prosper said he was sorry he couldn't go and shake the hand of Honoré, the staff sergeant; he must have been based more than a league away, on the other side of the Laon road. But the sound of a horse snorting made him prick up his ears, and he got up and disappeared, to make sure Zephyr didn't need anything. Little by little, soldiers of all ranks and all arms were invading the tavern, at the hour when a small coffee and something stronger to follow were the custom. There wasn't an empty table left, the air was filled with the bright, joyful colours of uniforms against green vines, splashed with sunlight. Major Bouroche had just sat down near Rochas, when Jean reported to the lieutenant with an order.

'Sir, the Captain is expecting you at three o'clock, on official business.'

With a nod of his head, Rochas confirmed that he would be on time; and Jean didn't leave straight away, but smiled at Maurice, who was lighting a cigarette. Ever since the episode in the train, there had been a tacit truce between the two men, as if each were studying the other in an increasingly good-natured way.

Prosper returned, growing impatient.

'I'm going to get myself a bite to eat if the guvnor doesn't come out of that place soon. It's no good, the Emperor might not be back before evening.'

'Tell me,' said Maurice, whose curiosity was reawakening, 'could it be news of Bazaine that you've brought?'

'Could be! They were talking about him back in Monthois.'

But there was a sudden stir. And Jean, who had remained at one of the lattice gates, turned round and said,

'The Emperor!'

At once, they all got to their feet. Between the poplar trees, a platoon of household guards could be seen approaching along the white high road, attired in luxurious uniforms that were still immaculate, with the great golden sun of their breastplates shining brightly. Immediately behind them came the Emperor, on horseback, in his own, broad space, accompanied by his staff, followed by a second platoon of household guards.

All heads were bared, and a few cheers went up. And as he passed, the Emperor, looking extremely pale, raised his head, his features drawn, and his watery gaze unsteady and almost clouded. He seemed to wake from a state of slumber, smiled weakly at the sight of the sun-filled tavern, and saluted.

Behind Jean and Maurice, Bouroche examined the Emperor thoroughly with his practised doctor's eye, and they distinctly heard him growl,

'Definitely a bad stone in there somewhere.'

Then he abruptly concluded his diagnosis.

'Done for!'

With his basic common sense, Jean nodded: bad bloody luck for an army, being landed with a commander like that! Ten minutes later, when Maurice, contented by his fine meal, had shaken hands with Prosper and left to take a stroll and smoke a few more cigarettes, it was this image that he took away with him: the Emperor, so vague and wan, passing by on his horse at a gentle trot. It was the image of the conspirator and dreamer, whose energy fails him at the vital moment. He was a very good person by all accounts, eminently capable of showing imagination and generosity, a man, moreover, of few words and stubborn determination; and extremely brave with it, scorning danger like a fatalist always ready to submit to his destiny. But when it came to moments of great crisis, he seemed to be struck with some torpor, as if paralysed when confronted with the need for action, and thereafter powerless to react against Fate, should she turn against him. And Maurice wondered if there might not be some peculiar physiological condition here, made worse by physical suffering, and if the illness which so visibly afflicted the Emperor wasn't in fact the cause of the increasing indecision and incompetence which he'd displayed since the beginning of the campaign. That would have explained everything. A single stone in a man's innards, and empires crumble.

That evening, at camp, after roll-call, there was a sudden stir of excitement. Officers ran about, passing on orders, making arrangements for departure at five o'clock the next morning. And Maurice gave a surprised start of disquiet when he realized that, yet again, everything had changed: they were no longer drawing back towards Paris, they were to march on Verdun, to meet up with Bazaine. A rumour was going round that a dispatch from Bazaine himself had arrived during the day, announcing that he was putting his plans for retreat into action; and the young man remembered Prosper and the officer from the Chasseurs, who had come from Monthois, perhaps bringing a copy of that very message. So—the Empress Regent and the Council of Ministers had triumphed, thanks to Marshal Mac-Mahon's endless indecision, they had won through their fear of seeing the Emperor return to Paris, through their stubborn desire to push the army on regardless, to make a supreme attempt to rescue the dynasty. And this wretched Emperor, this poor man who no longer had a place in his own Empire, was going to be carted off like a useless, burdensome package, along with the baggage of his troops, condemned to trail behind him the irony of his imperial entourage, his household guards, his carriages, his horses, his cooks, his wagons full of silver saucepans and champagne, all the pomp of his court mantle, embroidered with bees,* sweeping through the blood and the dirt on the high roads to defeat.

At midnight, Maurice was still awake. A feverish insomnia, fraught with nightmares, had him tossing and turning beneath the canvas. In the end, he got up and went outside, relieved to be standing up, breathing in the cool air whipped up by the wind. Huge clouds had covered the sky, and the night was growing very dark, a mournful infinity of shadow, lit up by the rare twinkle of the last, dying fires, along the edge of the camp. And surrounded by this peaceful blackness, as if crushed by the silence, the slow breathing of the hundred thousand sleeping men could be felt. Now Maurice's worries were soothed, and a feeling of kinship came over him, full of indulgent tenderness for all these sleeping beings, thousands of whom would soon be sleeping the slumber of the dead. They were fine souls, all the same! They hardly knew the meaning of discipline, they stole, and they drank. But how they'd suffered already, and what excuses they had, as the whole nation collapsed! By now, the glorious veterans of Sebastopol and Solférino made up only a tiny number, amongst all these troops who were far too young, and incapable of prolonged resistance. These four hastily gathered army corps, with nothing solid to unite them—it was an army of despair, a sacrificial herd being sent in expiation, in an attempt to assuage the ire of Fate. Up it would climb, right to the summit of its calvary, the red streams of its own blood paying in collective atonement for the sins of a nation, achieving greatness through the horror of the disaster itself.

And at that moment, as he lay deep in the trembling shadows, Maurice was suddenly conscious of an immense duty to be done. He no longer gave in to the boastful hope of carrying off legendary victories. This march on Verdun was a march to the death, and he accepted it with strong, cheerful resignation, since die he must.

CHAPTER FOUR

On 23 August, a Tuesday, at six o'clock in the morning, camp was struck, and the hundred thousand men of the Châlons army moved off, soon flowing in an immense stream, like a river of men spreading out momentarily into a lake, then resuming its course; and in spite of all the rumours which had gone round the day before, many were greatly surprised to see that instead of continuing the retreat, they were turning their backs on Paris, and heading towards the east, into the unknown.

At five in the morning, the 7th Corps was still without cartridges. For the last two days, the artillery had been wearing themselves out, trying to unload all the horses and equipment at the railway station, blocked by piles of provisions which came flooding back from Metz. And it was only at the very last minute that the wagons containing the cartridges were discovered, among the inextricable jumble of trains, and that a fatigue party, of which Jean was part, was able to bring back two hundred and forty thousand of them, loaded onto hastily requisitioned carts. Jean handed out the regulation hundred cartridges to each man in his squad, just as Gaude, the company's bugler, was giving the signal to depart. The 106th was not supposed to pass through Rheims—its marching orders were to go round the city, and rejoin the main road to Châlons. But yet again, no one had thought to stagger the departure, and so the four army corps all set off at once, causing extraordinary confusion as they came onto the first stretches of road where their paths met. Every minute, artillery and cavalry cut across infantry lines, holding them up. Entire brigades had to stop for an hour, standing to attention. And worst of all, barely ten minutes after they had set off, a terrifying storm broke out, a truly diluvian downpour which soaked the men to the skin, weighing down the capes and bags on their backs. However, the 106th had been able to take up the march again, just as the rain eased off; while Zouaves* in a neighbouring field, still forced to wait, discovered a little game to pass the time, which consisted of pelting each other with clods of earth, parcels of mud which spattered their uniforms and sent them all into gales of laughter.

Almost immediately, the sun reappeared, triumphal on that hot

August morning. And their spirits lifted, the men began steaming like a huge line of washing, strung out in the fresh air: they dried out rapidly, like filthy dogs pulled out of a bog, joking about the way the gunge had dried into large drips on their red breeches. They had to stop yet again, at every crossroads. Right on the outskirts of Rheims there was one last halt, at a bar selling drinks, with a stream of men outside.

This gave Maurice the idea of treating his squad to a drink, as a way of wishing everyone good luck.

'Corporal, with your permission...'

After a brief hesitation, Jean accepted a small glass. So did Loubet and Chouteau, the latter respectful in a shifty kind of way, ever since the corporal had exercised his authority; and Pache and Lapoulle were there too, a fine pair of lads, just as long as no one went giving them the wrong ideas.

'Your health, sir!' said Chouteau, sweet as pie.

'And yours—and may each man do his best to get back in one piece!' replied Jean, to an approving chuckle from his men.

But the line was moving again, and Captain Beaudoin had come over, looking shocked, while Lieutenant Rochas pretended to look the other way, indulgent towards his thirsty men. Already, troops were pouring onto the Châlons road, an endless ribbon lined with trees, running in a straight line across the vast plain, the stubble-fields stretching to infinity, with humps here and there caused by tall haystacks and wooden windmills with sails spinning. Further north, strings of telegraph poles sketched more roads, where dark lines indicated other regiments on the march. Many even cut across the fields, black swarms of men. Out in front, on the left, a cavalry brigade trotted along, in a dazzle of sunshine. And all that deserted horizon, sadly, boundlessly empty, began coming to life, peopled by streams of men flowing in from every direction, like an inexhaustible outpouring from some giant anthill.

Towards nine o'clock, the 106th left the Châlons road to turn left, onto the Suippes road, another dead-straight ribbon into infinity. They marched in two well-spaced columns, leaving the middle way clear for the officers to proceed freely on their own; and Maurice noticed that they seemed anxious, in contrast with the good humour and buoyant satisfaction of the soldiers, happy as sandboys to be on the move at long last. He even caught sight of Monsieur de Vineuil, the colonel, in the distance, since his squad was near the front, and he was struck by his sombre appearance, his broad frame held stiff, jogged about by his trotting horse. The music section had been relegated to the back, along with the regimental canteens. Then, accompanying the division, came the ambulances and the equipment train, followed by the convoy of the entire army corps—an enormous train of fodder wagons, covered carts full of supplies, and baggage carts, a procession of vehicles of every kind, stretching back for more than five kilometres, its endless trail glimpsed at the rare turnings in the road. Lastly, right at the back, herds of cattle rounded off the line, a scattering of huge oxen trampling in a cloud of dust; beef supplies still on the hoof, whipped along by this warring tribe on the move.

Meanwhile, from time to time, Lapoulle shifted the straps of his rucksack back onto his shoulders. On the pretext that he was the strongest, the squad's communal utensils—the large cooking-pot and the can for collecting water—were given to him to carry. This time, they'd even entrusted the company shovel to him, persuading him that it was a great honour. And he didn't complain, he walked along laughing at a song that Loubet, the squad's tenor, was charming the line of men with. Loubet's rucksack was a famous one—you could find absolutely everything in it: linen, spare sandals, a needle and thread, brushes, chocolate, a metal cup and a knife and fork, not counting the regulation rations of biscuits and coffee; and even though his cartridges were in there too, and, in addition, on top of the bag was his rolled-up blanket, the shelter-tent, and pegs, it all seemed weightless, so skilful was he at packing his bags, as he put it.

'Blasted country this is, too!' complained Chouteau every now and then, casting a look of disdain over the gloomy plains of this squalid part of Champagne.

The vast stretches of chalky land went on, unrolling endlessly, one after the other. Not a farm, not a soul to be seen, nothing but crows flying against the grey expanse, smudging it with black. Far away to their left, sombre green pinewoods crowned the gentle undulations which bordered the sky; while on the right, the course of the river Vesle could be traced by the continuous line of trees. And there, beyond the slopes, for the past league or so they'd been able to see a huge pall of smoke rising, its mass billowing out into a terrifying fire cloud which blocked the horizon.

'What's that burning over there?' came the voices from all sides.

But the explanation ran up and down the column. It was the Châlons camp, which had been burning for two days, set alight on orders from the Emperor, to save the piles of riches from the clutches of the Prussians. The rearguard cavalry had, it was said, been instructed to set fire to a large barracks, known as the yellow house, full of tents, pegs, and matting, as well as to the new warehouse, an immense, enclosed hangar, packed with heaps of mess-tins, sandals, and blankets—enough to kit out another hundred thousand men. Stacks of fodder, also set alight, were sending up smoke like gigantic torches. And at the sight of this, before the livid whirlwinds pouring from the distant hills, filling the sky with irreparable mourning, the army fell into a heavy silence as it marched across the doleful plain. Nothing could be heard now but the rhythm of their feet in the sun, while their heads kept turning, in spite of themselves, towards the swelling smoke, whose cloud of disaster seemed to follow the column for a full league.

Their cheerful mood returned when there was a general halt in a stubble-field, where the soldiers were able to sit down on their bags and have a bite to eat. The big square biscuits were fine for dunking in the soup; but the small round ones, which were light and crunchy, were a real delicacy, their only drawback being that they caused a dreadful thirst. On request, Pache took his turn to sing a hymn, and the rest of the squad joined in after him. Jean, good-naturedly, smiled on them, and left them to carry on, while Maurice began to take heart again, seeing everyone's enthusiasm, the discipline and the good mood among the men on this first day on the march. And the rest of the stretch was covered at the same cheerful pace. The last eight kilometres seemed tough, though. They had just left the village of Prosnes to their right, and had come off the main road to cut across unploughed land, sandy terrain planted with small pine-woods; and the whole division, followed by its endless convoy, entered the woods, the men sinking up to their ankles in the sand. The desert had spread yet wider, and all they encountered was a scrawny flock of sheep, guarded by a big black dog.

Finally, at about four o'clock, the 106th halted at Dontrien, a village built on the banks of the Suippe. The little river flowed between clumps of trees, and the ancient church stood in the middle of the graveyard, enveloped in the shadow of an enormous chestnut tree. And it was on the left bank, in a sloping meadow, that the regiment put up the tents. That evening, the officers told them, all four army corps would be camping alongside the Suippe, from Auberive to Heutrégiville, passing through Dontrien, Bétheniville, and Pont-Faverger, forming a camp boundary almost five leagues long.

Immediately, Gaude gave the call for supplies to be distributed, and Jean had to run off, for the corporal was their great provider, always on the lookout. He took Lapoulle with him, and half an hour later they came back, loaded down with a bloody side of beef and a bundle of wood. Beneath an oak tree, three animals from the herd following them had already been slaughtered and jointed. Lapoulle had to go back for the bread, which had been baking in the village ovens in Dontrien since noon. And that first day, everything was available in plenty, except wine and tobacco, which had never been supposed to be part of their rations anyway.

Coming back, Jean found Chouteau in the middle of putting up the tent, aided by Pache. He watched them for a moment, with the eye of an experienced old soldier who wouldn't have given tuppence for their handiwork.

'It's a good job it's going to stay fine tonight,' he said eventually. 'Otherwise, if it began to blow, we'd be taking a trip downriver... I'll have to show you how it's done.'

And he turned to Maurice, to send him with the can to fetch water. But Maurice, sitting on the grass, had taken off his shoe, to examine his right foot.

'Hello! What's up with you then?'

'It's the back of my shoe—it's rubbed my heel raw... My other sandals were falling to pieces, and I was stupid enough to buy these in Rheims, because they were a good fit. I should have chosen sailing shoes instead.'

Jean knelt down and took the foot in his hands, turning it to look with great care, as if Maurice were a child, and he nodded.

'It's no joke, this, you know... You'll have to be careful. A soldier who loses the use of his feet is good for nothing but the scrap heap. My captain, back in Italy, always said it's your legs you win battles with.'

So he ordered Pache to go and fetch the water instead. Anyway, the river was only fifty metres away. Meanwhile Loubet lit the fire at the bottom of the hole he'd just dug in the ground, and was immediately able to set the cooking-pot over it, a huge saucepan full of water, into which he plunged the artistically trussed meat. From then on, it was pure bliss, watching the soup bubble. The whole squad, now liberated from their duties, had stretched out on the grass around the fire, like a big family, full of tender concern for the meat cooking in front of them; while Loubet, a serious expression on his face, skimmed the pot with his spoon. They were like children and savages, with no other instincts than eating and sleeping, as they raced towards the unknown, with no tomorrow.

Maurice, however, had just come across a newspaper in his bag which he'd bought at Rheims, and Chouteau asked,

'Any news of the Prussians? Read it out!'

They were all getting on well together, under Jean's growing authority. Obligingly, Maurice read out the interesting bits of news, while Pache, the squad's seamstress, mended his cape for him and Lapoulle cleaned his gun. First came a great victory for Bazaine, who'd sent an entire Prussian corps flying into the Jaumont quarries; and this fiction was accompanied by dramatic details, men and horses crushed among the rocks, complete annihilation, not even a single corpse left intact for burial. Then came meticulous accounts of the pitiful state the German armies had got into since they had been in France: ill-fed, ill-equipped, reduced to utter destitution, the soldiers were dying in huge numbers, all along the roads, struck down by horrifying diseases. Another article said that the King of Prussia had diarrhoea and that Bismarck had broken his leg jumping out a window in a tavern, where some Zouaves had all but captured him. Good stuff! Lapoulle nearly split his sides laughing, while Chouteau and the rest, expressing not even the shadow of a doubt, swanked about at the thought that they would soon be scooping up those Prussians like sparrows in a field after a hailstorm. Ah, they were a brave lot, those Zouaves and Turks!* All sorts of fairy tales circulated, about Germany beginning to quake and get angry, declaring that it was dishonourable for a civilized nation to use such barbarians to defend itself. Even though they had already been decimated at Frœschwiller, they still seemed intact and invincible.

Six o'clock struck in Dontrien's little bell-tower, and Loubet shouted,

'Soup's ready!'

The squad reverently formed a circle. At the last minute, Loubet had discovered some vegetables, at the house of a peasant nearby. A perfect feast, a fragrant soup with leeks and carrots, soft as velvet on the stomach. The spoons began rattling fiercely in the small mess-tins. Then Jean, who always gave out the portions, had to share the beef out with the strictest fairness that particular day, because the men's eyes had lit up, and there would have been complaints if one piece had looked bigger than another. They licked everything clean, and stuffed themselves full to bursting.

'Whew! Lord above!' declared Chouteau, stretching out on his back when he'd finished. 'That's certainly better than a kick up the arse!'

And Maurice felt very full and very happy too, his mind taken off his foot, where the throbbing had eased. He'd come to accept this brutal companionship now, which had reverted to a state of good-natured equality, faced with the physical necessities of communal living. That night too, he slept the same, deep sleep as his other five comrades in the tent, all in a heap, happy to be in the warm, beneath the plentiful dew falling outside. It must be said that Lapoulle, egged on by Loubet, had gone to a nearby haystack to gather great armfuls of straw, in which the six fellows snored away as if in feather beds. And beneath the clear night, from Auberive to Heutrégiville, all along the pleasant banks of the Suippe, flowing gently between the willow trees, the fires of a hundred thousand men lit up the plain for five leagues, like a trail of stars.

At sunrise, they made the coffee, crushing the beans in a mess-tin with a rifle butt, and throwing them into boiling water, before sending the grounds to the bottom by adding a drop of cold water. That morning, the sun rose in regal magnificence, cloaked in great clouds of purple and gold; but even Maurice no longer noticed such spectacles in the sky and on the horizon, and only Jean, the thoughtful peasant, cast an anxious glance at the red dawn which augured rain. So before they left, since bread baked the previous day had just been handed out, and the squad had received three long loaves, he severely reprimanded Loubet and Pache for tying them to the top of their bags. The tents were already put away, the bags tied up, and nobody paid any attention. Six o'clock was ringing from all the village bell-towers when the entire army set off, cheerfully taking up the march again, bathed in the early morning hope of the new day.

In order to rejoin the Rheims to Vouziers road, the 106th almost immediately cut through cross-country paths and clambered over stubble-fields for more than an hour. Below them, towards the north, surrounded by trees, they could glimpse Bétheniville, where it was said that the Emperor had slept. And as they got back onto the Vouziers road, yesterday's plains began rolling past again, and squalid Champagne finished unfurling her poor, despairingly monotonous fields. Now it was the Arne which flowed to their left, a thin little stream, while to their right, the stark land stretched out to infinity, the horizon elongated by its flat lines. The villages passed by: Saint-Clément, whose one and only road wound along on either side of the main road; and Saint-Pierre, a large market town full of rich moneybags, who'd barricaded up their doors and windows. The main halt took place at around ten o'clock, close to another village, Saint-Étienne, where to their joy the soldiers found more tobacco. The 7th Corps had split up into several columns, and the 106th marched on alone, with only a battalion of Chasseurs* and the reserve artillery behind it; and at the bends in the road, Maurice kept turning in vain to catch another glimpse of the enormous convoy which had so fascinated him the day before: the herds of cattle had gone, now there were only cannon rolling along, magnified by the flat plains, like dark, long-legged grasshoppers.

But after Saint-Étienne, the road became atrocious, climbing with slow undulations, amid the vast, barren fields where only the never-ending pinewoods grew, with their green-black foliage so mournful among the expanses of chalky earth. This was the most desolate landscape yet. The poorly-surfaced road, waterlogged from the recent rain, was a veritable quagmire of watery clay, where their feet stuck like tar. They were extremely weary, incapable of going any further, utterly exhausted. Then, as if to put the finishing touch to it, sudden downpours started pelting down, with terrifying violence. Bogged down, the artillery almost got left behind.

Chouteau, who was carrying the squad's rice rations, was out of breath, furious at the burden weighing him down, and he threw the bundle aside, thinking that no one would see him. Loubet did.

'You shouldn't do that, it's wrong—the comrades'll go without later.'

'Ah, go on!' replied Chouteau. 'There's plenty of everything, they'll give us another one at the end of the march.'

And Loubet, carrying the bacon, persuaded by this argument, got rid of his own load too.

As for Maurice, his foot was giving him more and more trouble, his heel must have swollen up again. He limped along so painfully that Jean gave in to a growing sense of concern.

'Eh? No better then? Started up again, has it?'

Then, as they were making a short halt to let the men get their wind back, he gave him a piece of good advice.

'Take off your shoes and march barefoot, the cool mud will soothe the smarting.'

And indeed, that way Maurice was able to keep up, without too much pain; and a profound feeling of gratitude swept over him. Any squad should count itself lucky to have such a corporal, who'd already done service and knew the ins-and-outs of the profession: he was obviously an unrefined peasant, but even so, he was a good man.

It wasn't until late that evening that, after crossing the road from Châlons to Vouziers and descending a steep slope into the Semide Ravine, they reached Contreuve, where they were to camp. The countryside was changing, they were already in the Ardennes. And in the distance, from the vast, barren hillside overlooking the village, where it had been decided that the 7th Corps would set up camp, they could see the Aisne Valley, lost in the pale mist of the rain.

At six o'clock, Gaude still hadn't given the call for rations to be distributed. So, in an effort to keep himself busy, as well as being worried by the high wind which was blowing up, Jean decided to put up the tent himself. He showed his men how they should choose a piece of land on a gentle slope, hammer the pegs in at an angle, and dig a channel around the canvas, for the water to drain away. Because of his foot, Maurice found himself excused from duties; and he sat watching, surprised by the intelligent skill shown by this huge lad, who looked so clumsy. He himself was completely exhausted, yet he was sustained by the sense of hope filling every heart. They'd marched at a fair old pace from Rheims, covering sixty kilometres in two days. If they continued at the same rate, and kept going straight, there was no doubt that they would knock the German Second Army flying, and join up with Bazaine, before the Third Army, under the command of the Crown Prince of Prussia, said to be at Vitry-le-François, had had the time to move back to Verdun.

'Huh! Are they going to leave us to starve?' demanded Chouteau, noting, at seven o'clock, that still no rations had been handed out.

Sensibly, Jean had nonetheless ordered Loubet to light the fire, and then place the pot of water on it; and since there was no firewood, he had had to turn a blind eye when, to get hold of some, Loubet had made do with pulling up trellises from a neighbouring garden. But when he suggested cooking rice and bacon, they were forced to admit that both had been left behind in the mud on the Saint-Étienne road. Chouteau lied quite shamelessly, swearing that the bundle must have come loose from his bag without his having noticed.

'You're a bunch of swine!' yelled Jean, furiously. 'Throwing away good food, when there's so many poor sods with empty bellies!'

It was the same story with the three loaves of bread, which had been fastened to the tops of their bags; no one had listened to him, the rain had soaked them through, until they had disintegrated into a real soggy mess, impossible to get your teeth into.

'A proper state we're in!' he repeated. 'We had everything, and now look at us, we haven't got a crust...! Oh aye, you're a bunch of swine, all right!'

Just then, the sergeants were summoned to receive their orders, and Sergeant Sapin, with his melancholy air, came to warn the men in his section that it would be impossible to distribute any rations, and that they would have to make do with their field supplies. Apparently, the convoy had been held up en route, due to the bad weather. As for the herd of cattle, it must have lost its way, because of conflicting orders. Later, they found out that as the 5th and 12th Corps had advanced that day towards Rethel, where headquarters were to be set up, all supplies from the surrounding villages had gone in that direction, as had the local population, in their feverish desire to glimpse the Emperor; as a result, the countryside had emptied before the approach of the 7th Corps: no meat, no bread, not even any inhabitants left. And, as the final straw, a misunderstanding had resulted in the quartermasters' supplies being sent to Le Chesne-Populeux. Throughout the entire campaign, this was the constant despair of the wretched quartermasters, with all the soldiers railing against them, when their only fault was often simply that of arriving punctually at given rendezvous, which the troops did not reach.

'You filthy swine!' repeated Jean, beside himself with rage. 'Serves you right! And you just don't deserve the trouble I'm going to put myself to, digging up something for you, because it's my duty not to let you drop dead on the way, after all !'

He went off to explore, like all good corporals should, taking Pache with him, whom he liked for his gentle nature, even though he thought him too taken up with the clergy.

However, a few moments before, Loubet had spotted a little farm some two or three hundred metres away, one of the last dwellings in Contreuve, where he thought he'd caught sight of something important going on. He called to Chouteau and Lapoulle, saying,

'Come on, let's go off on our own. I've an idea that there's something to be had over there.'

And Maurice was left to watch over the pot of boiling water, with orders to keep the fire stoked up. He'd sat down on his blanket and taken off his shoe, so that the blister on his foot could dry out.

The sight of the camp fascinated him, with its squads scattered all over the place since they'd given up waiting for their rations. He became aware of a certain truth: some squads were always short of everything, while others lived in a state of continual plenty, depending on the skill and foresight of their corporal and men. In the midst of the intense excitement all around him, looking past the tents and the stacks of arms, he noticed that some squads didn't even have anything to light the fire with, others were already resigned to the fact, and lying down for the night, while others, on the contrary, were in the process of eating something or other—good, by the looks of it—with great relish. On the other hand, he was struck by the fine discipline of the reserve artillery, camped above him on the hillside. As the sun was sinking, it shone out from between two clouds and set the cannon alight, the mud from the roads already washed off by the artillery.

Meanwhile, at the little farm that Loubet and his comrades had their eye on, their brigade-chief, General Bourgain-Desfeuilles, had just settled himself in comfortably. He'd found a possible bed for the night, and was sitting at the table in front of an omelette and a roast chicken, something which put him in charming good humour; and, as Colonel de Vineuil happened to be there to take some order or other, he invited him to dinner. So they both sat eating, attended by a huge blond fellow, who'd only started work at the farm three days earlier, and who said he was from Alsace, a refugee swept along by the Frœschwiller débâcle. The general spoke freely in this man's presence, commenting on the army's march, then asking him about the road and the distance, quite forgetting that he wasn't in fact from the Ardennes. The absolute ignorance his questions betrayed ended up disturbing the colonel. He himself had lived in Mézières. He gave him a few precise directions, at which the general let out a cry.

'But it's all so stupid! How on earth are we meant to fight in country we're not familiar with!'

The colonel gave a vague, despairing shrug. He knew that, when war had been declared, all officers had been provided with maps of Germany, while he was sure not one of them possessed a map of France. What he had seen and heard over the past month was destroying him. With his slightly feeble and limited powers of command, his courage was all he had left now, which made him liked, rather than feared, by his regiment.

'Can't we eat in peace!' exclaimed the general suddenly. 'What are they bawling like that for...? Hey! You, from Alsace—go and take a look.'

But the farmer appeared, exasperated, sobbing and waving his arms about. He was being robbed, Chasseurs and Zouaves were looting his house. At first, he'd had the weakness to open up, being the only man in the village with eggs, potatoes, and rabbits to sell. He sold them without taking too much profit, pocketing the money, delivering the goods; with such success that his customers, in ever greater numbers, overwhelming and deafening him, had ended up knocking him over and taking everything, without paying. If, in the course of the campaign, many peasants hid everything away and refused the troops even a glass of water, it was precisely because of this fear of being slowly and surely overpowered by the tide of men, throwing them out of their own homes and taking the lot with them.

'Eh? my good man, leave me in peace!' replied the general, annoyed. 'We'd have to shoot a dozen of the rascals a day, and can we do that?'

And he had the door shut, so that he wouldn't have to apply harsh measures, while the colonel explained that the men hadn't received their rations, and were hungry.

Outside, Loubet had just caught sight of a field of potatoes, and he rushed into it with Lapoulle, digging with both hands, uprooting potatoes and stuffing his pockets. But Chouteau, taking a look over a low wall, suddenly whistled to them, making them run over and cry out: it was a flock of geese, ten or more magnificent birds, majestically striding about a narrow yard. Immediately, they held council, and Lapoulle was pushed forward and persuaded to climb over the wall. The combat was terrible, the goose he seized hold of nearly cut off his nose with the sharp shears of her beak. Then he grabbed her by the neck, and tried to strangle her, while she set about his arms and stomach with her strong feet. He was forced to crush her head with his fist, and still she struggled, and he hastened to make his escape, pursued by the rest of the flock, pecking at his legs.

When the three men returned, concealing the bird in a bag along with the potatoes, they found Jean and Pache also on their way back, equally pleased with their own expedition, carrying four fresh loaves and a cheese, bought from some sterling old woman.

'The water's boiling, we'll make some coffee,' said the corporal. 'We've got bread and cheese, it'll be a proper feast!'

All of a sudden, however, he noticed the goose stretched out at his feet, and he couldn't help laughing. He felt its flesh, like a real connoisseur, full of admiration.

'Oh, Lord above, what a fine beast! It must weigh twenty pounds or more!'

'It's a bird we bumped into,' explained Loubet in his rascally voice, 'who wished to make our acquaintance.'

With a wave of his hand, Jean declared that he didn't want to know any more about it. They had to live, after all. And my God, why shouldn't the poor sods have a treat, after all, when they'd forgotten what poultry even tasted like?

Loubet was already lighting a fire. Pache and Lapoulle set about violently plucking the goose. Chouteau, who'd gone running off to the artillery to find a bit of string, came back and strung it up between two bayonets, in front of the hearty blaze, and Maurice was given the task of turning it with a flick of the hand from time to time. Underneath, the fat dripped into the squad's mess-tin. The whole regiment, drawn by the delicious smell, came over and gathered round. And what a feast it was! Roast goose, boiled potatoes, and bread and cheese! When Jean had finished carving the bird, the squad stuffed themselves full to bursting. No portions this time— each man just shovelled in as much as he could hold. They even took a piece over to the artillerymen who'd provided the string.

Meanwhile, that evening, the regiment's officers went hungry. Due to mistaken directions, the canteen wagon had got lost—somewhere on the trail of the big convoy, no doubt. If the soldiers suffered when there was no distribution, they managed to find food more often than not, helping each other out, each squad's men pooling their resources; while the officer, isolated and left to his own devices, starved, unable to fight back, as soon as the canteen failed to provide.

So Chouteau, who'd heard Captain Beaudoin ranting about the disappearance of the supply wagon, sniggered as he delved into the goose's carcass, and saw him passing by with his proud, stiff demeanour. And he glanced sidelong at him, pointing him out.

'Just look at him! His nose is twitching... He'd give a hundred sous for the parson's nose.'

They all laughed at the hungry captain, who'd been incapable of winning the affection of his men, too young and too harsh with them—a martinet, they called him. For a moment, he seemed to be on the point of questioning the squad about the scandal it was creating with its goose. But no doubt the fear of letting his hunger show made him draw away, head held high, as if he hadn't seen a thing.

As for Lieutenant Rochas, also suffering from dreadful hunger, he walked around the lucky squad with a brave smile on his face. Now, he was adored by his men, first because he loathed the captain, that whippersnapper fresh out of Saint-Cyr,* and secondly because he'd carried the soldier's bag, like the rest of them. However, he wasn't always easygoing, showing a coarseness at times that made them want to slap him.

Jean, consulting the comrades with a quick glance, got up, and nodded to Rochas to follow him behind the tent.

'Listen, sir, no offence meant, but if you'd like to...'

And he handed him a quarter of a loaf and a mess-tin, in which a leg of goose was lying on a bed of six large potatoes.

That night, once again, there was no need to rock them to sleep. The six men lay digesting the bird, fists curled tight. And they had reason to thank the corporal for the sturdy way he'd put up the tent, for they didn't even notice the fierce gust of wind which blew over at about two o'clock, accompanied by a squall of rain: tents were blown away, men awoke with a start, soaked through, and had to dash around among the shadows; while their own tent stood up to it, and they were safe and dry, not a single drop of rain touched them, thanks to the channels into which the downpour flowed.

At daybreak, Maurice woke up, and seeing as they weren't to set off until eight o'clock, it occurred to him to climb up the hill to the reserve artillery encampment, to shake cousin Honoré by the hand. His foot, rested after a good night's sleep, was less painful. He still found it an object of wonder to see the artillery park so beautifully set out, with its six battery pieces all properly lined up, followed by the caissons, gun carriages, fodder wagons, and forges. Further off, the tethered horses whinnied, nostrils flaring at the rising sun. And he found Honoré's tent straight away, thanks to the perfect order which assigned a row of tents to each man attending a particular piece, so that a camp's outward appearance was enough to indicate the number of cannon it comprised.

When Maurice arrived, the artillery soldiers, already up and about, were drinking their coffee; and a quarrel broke out between Adolphe, the forward driver, and Louis the gun-layer, his companion. During the three years that they'd been 'married'— according to the custom which teamed up a driver and a server— they'd got on well, except when it came to food. Louis, who was better educated and extremely intelligent, accepted the state of dependency in which the man on horseback keeps the footsoldier, and so he would put up the tent, go on fatigues, and look after the soup, while Adolphe busied himself with his two horses, with an air of absolute superiority. But Louis, dark and wiry, victim of an excessively large appetite, rebelled when the other man, who was very tall, with profuse, blond whiskers, decided to serve himself the lion's share. That morning, the quarrel had started because Louis, who'd made the coffee, accused Adolphe of drinking the lot. They had to be reconciled.

Each morning, as soon as reveille sounded, Honoré went to see his cannon, and had the night dew wiped from its surface as he stood and watched, just as if he were cosseting a beloved animal, fearful that it might catch cold. And there he was, looking on with a paternal eye as it gleamed in the cool dawn air, when he recognized Maurice.

'Well, well! I knew the 106th was nearby, I received a letter from Remilly yesterday, and I was going to come down... Come and join me for some white wine.'

So that they could be alone, he led him towards the little farm looted by the soldiers the night before, where the incorrigible peasant, grasping as ever, had just set up a sort of drinks stall by putting a barrel of white wine on tap. On a plank outside his door, he handed out his wares at four sous the glass, assisted by the lad whom he'd taken on three days earlier, the blond colossus from Alsace.

Honoré was just clinking glasses with Maurice when his gaze fell upon this man. He looked hard at him for a moment, stupefied. Then a dreadful oath escaped him.

'Hell and damnation! It's Goliath!'

And he sprang forward to grab him by the throat. But the peasant, thinking that his house was about to be ransacked a second time, jumped back, and barricaded his door. For a moment, confusion reigned, and all the soldiers standing around surged forward, while the artillery sergeant shouted furiously, choking with rage,

'Open up! Open up, you damned idiot!... He's a spy, I tell you, he's a spy!'

By now, Maurice was no longer in any doubt. He'd recognized the man perfectly as the same one who'd been released from the camp at Mulhouse for want of proof; and it was indeed Goliath, old Fouchard's former farmhand at Remilly. When, finally, the peasant consented to open his door, they searched the house in vain—the man from Alsace had vanished, that blond colossus with the pleasant features, whom General Bourgain-Desfeuilles had interrogated so fruitlessly the day before, and in whose presence, as he dined, he had confessed himself with such complete lack of concern. No doubt the fellow had hopped out of a window at the back, which they found open; but they scoured the surrounding area quite in vain, for the man, tall as he was, had evaporated into thin air, like the morning mist.

Maurice had to take Honoré aside, because his despair would have given too much away to his comrades, and there was no need for them to become involved in this sad family affair.

'Hell and damnation! I could quite happily have strangled him...! It's just that this letter I've had made me so furious with him.'

And as the two men sat down, leaning against a haystack a few paces away from the farmhouse, he gave the letter to his cousin.

It was the age-old story, this thwarted love between Honoré Fouchard and Silvine Morange. Brown-haired, with beautiful, submissive eyes, she had lost her mother—a seduced factory-girl at

Raucourt—when she was very little; and it was Doctor Dalichamp, her unofficial godfather, a decent man who was always ready to adopt the children of the poor wretches he delivered, who'd had the idea of placing her as a young servant at old Fouchard's. It was true that the peasant, whose desire for wealth had drawn him to the butcher's trade, taking his meat-cart around twenty neighbouring villages, was a deeply avaricious and mercilessly harsh man; but he would look to the little girl, and if she could work she would have some sort of future. In any case, she would be saved from the debauchery of the factory. And, naturally, it came to pass that, at old Fouchard's, the son of the house and the little servant fell in love. Honoré had been sixteen when Silvine was twelve, and when she was sixteen, he was twenty; he was forced go into the military lottery, delighted to draw a lucky number, and determined to marry her. Because of a rare sense of honour, which stemmed from the boy's calm, reflective nature, nothing had passed between them but long embraces in the barn. But when he spoke of the marriage to his father, the old man, exasperated and stubborn, declared that it would be over his dead body; and he quietly kept the girl on, hoping that they would satisfy each other, and that it would pass. For more than eighteen months afterwards, the youngsters worshipped each other, wanting each other, yet never touching. Then, after an atrocious scene between the two men, the son, unable to stay any longer, joined up, and was sent to Africa, while the old man stubbornly hung on to his servant, with whom he was quite happy. And then the terrible thing happened: Silvine, who had sworn she would wait for him, found herself one evening, two weeks later, in the arms of a farmhand who'd been taken on a few months before—Goliath Steinberg, the Prussian as he was called, a tall, good-natured lad with fine, blond hair and a broad, pink face that was always smiling, and who was Honoré's comrade and confidant. Had old Fouchard surreptitiously encouraged this affair? She didn't even know herself; she was struck as if by lightning, pregnant, and now accepted the necessity of marrying Goliath. Nor did he refuse, but simply put off the formalities until the baby was born. Then, quite suddenly, the day before she gave birth, he disappeared. They recounted later how he'd gone to work on another farm, over Beaumont way. All that had been three years ago, and at this precise moment, no one was in any doubt that this Goliath, such a pleasant man, who so casually got young girls pregnant, was one of those spies with which Germany was populating our eastern provinces. When Honoré, in Africa, learned of all this, he spent three months in hospital, as if the land's mighty sun had smote him on the back of the neck with a burning brand; and he'd never wanted to take advantage of any leave to go back to the country, for fear of seeing Silvine again, and the child.

While Maurice read the letter, the artilleryman's hands trembled. It was a letter from Silvine, the first, the only one she'd ever written to him. What emotion had prompted her to do it—this submissive, silent girl, whose beautiful dark eyes sometimes took on a look of extraordinary resolve and determination, in her continual state of servility? She said simply that she knew he'd been sent to war, and that it hurt her so much to think that he might die, believing she no longer loved him. She loved him still, she'd never loved anyone but him; and she said this over and over again, for four pages, in phrases which repeated each other, without trying to make excuses, not even trying to explain what had happened. Not a word about the child, either, and nothing but an infinitely tender word of farewell.

Maurice, in whom his cousin had confided in the old days, was deeply affected by the letter. Looking up, he saw that he was in tears, and embraced him like a brother.

'My poor Honoré!'

But the artillery sergeant was already hiding away his emotion. Carefully, he replaced the letter against his breast, and buttoned his jacket back up.

'Yes, things like that really shake you up... Oh, if only I could have strangled the bastard!... Well, we shall see.'

The bugles were sounding for camp to be struck, and both had to run to reach their tents in time. In the event, preparations for departure dragged on, the troops stood waiting, bags on backs, until nearly nine o'clock. Their commanders seemed to be in the grip of uncertainty, and the fine resolve of the first two days, and those sixty kilometres that the 7th Corps had covered, had disappeared. And a peculiarly worrying piece of news had been going round since morning: it concerned the northward march of the other three army corps, the 1st at Juniville, the 5th and 12th at Rethel, a completely illogical route, which was being explained away by the need to stock up on supplies. Weren't they heading for Verdun any more? Why had a day been wasted? The worst of it was that the Prussians couldn't be far off by now, because the officers had just warned the men not to tarry, and that anyone trailing behind might be seized by advance enemy cavalry.

It was now 25 August, and Maurice, recalling afterwards Goliath's abrupt disappearance, remained convinced that this man was one of those who passed on information to the German staff about the precise itinerary of the Châlons army, and who made them decide to change the forward position of the Third Army. The next day, the Crown Prince of Prussia was leaving Revigny, it was the beginning of the manœuvre, the attack on their flank, the gigantic envelopment achieved by forced marches, proceeding in an admirably well-ordered manner across Champagne and the Ardennes. While the French would hesitate and waver on the spot, struck down as if by some sudden paralysis, the Prussians were covering up to forty kilometres a day, to form a massive circle of beaters, forcing the herd of men they were tracking onward, towards the forests and the frontier.

At last they set off, and that day the army effectively swung round to its left; the 7th Corps simply covered the two short leagues which separated Contreuve from Vouziers, while the 5th and 12th Corps stayed put at Rethel, and the 1st halted at Altigny. From Contreuve to the Aisne Valley, the naked plains began to unroll before them once again; as they neared Vouziers, the road weaved through the grey land, with its desolate hills, and not a single tree in sight; and the march, short as it was, was covered at such a troubled, weary pace that it seemed terribly drawn-out. From midday onwards, they halted on the left bank of the Aisne, camping among the barren landscape whose final escarpments overlooked the valley, and from here they kept watch over the riverside Monthois road, which they expected the enemy to use for its approach.

And it was with genuine disbelief that Maurice saw the Margueritte division—all the reserve cavalry which had been ordered to back up the 7th Corps and carry out reconnaissance for the army's left flank—coming towards them, making its way along this very Monthois road. The rumour went round that it was retreating to Le Chesne-Populeux. Why were troops being withdrawn from the only flank which was under threat? Why were these two thousand cavalrymen being made to move to the centre, where they could only be entirely useless, instead of sending them way on ahead as reconnaissance? The worst of it was that, landing as they did slap bang in the middle of the 7th Corps's manœuvres, they almost cut through its columns, causing an inextricable tangle of men, cannon, and horses. Some African Chasseurs had to wait for almost two hours before they could enter Vouziers.

It was by chance at this point that Maurice recognized Prosper, who had urged his horse over to the edge of a pond; and they were able to talk for a moment. The Chasseur appeared stunned and baffled, didn't know a thing, hadn't seen a thing since Rheims: except that he'd seen two more Uhlans, blasted fellows, who kept appearing and disappearing, and no one ever knew where they'd come from or where they were going. Stories were already being told about four Uhlans galloping into a town, waving their revolvers, passing through, and taking it, twenty kilometres from their army corps. They were everywhere, they preceded the columns, buzzing like bees, a moving curtain behind which the infantry concealed its manœuvres, marching in complete safety, as if in peacetime. And Maurice felt his heart contract sharply within him, as he looked down on the road obstructed by Chasseurs and Hussars, being put to such bad use.

'Well then, goodbye,' he said, shaking Prosper by the hand. 'Maybe they've need of you up there after all.'

But the Chasseur seemed exasperated at being forced to exercise such a profession. He stroked Zephyr with a distraught hand, and replied,

'Oh Lord! They kill the animals, and do nothing with the men... It's sickening!'

That evening, when Maurice went to take off his sandal and inspect his heel, which was throbbing and swollen, he tore away the skin. Blood spurted and he cried out in pain. And Jean, who happened to be nearby, seemed to feel a powerful wave of concern and pity surge through him.

'Hey, that's getting serious, you'll be left on the flank... You must get that seen to. Here, let me do it.'

Kneeling down, he bathed the wound himself, and dressed it with some clean linen which he took from his bag. And his gestures were maternal, exercised with all the gentleness of a skilled man, whose large fingers knew how to move delicately when they needed to.

An overwhelming feeling of tenderness came over Maurice, his eyes filled with tears, and words of friendship rose from his heart to his lips, as if he'd discovered his own brother in the form of this once loathed peasant, whom he'd held in such disdain only the day before.

'You know, you're a good soul, you are... Thanks, old chap.'

And Jean, looking very happy, answered him in the same affectionate tone,* smiling that serene smile of his.

'Now then, my lad, I've still some tobacco left. How about a cigarette?'

CHAPTER FIVE

The next day, 26 August, Maurice woke up aching all over, his shoulders stiff from the night spent in the tent. He still wasn't used to the hard ground; and as they'd been forbidden to take off their footwear the previous evening, and the sergeants had gone round in the darkness, feeling to make sure that each man had his shoes properly laced up, his foot was hardly any better, hot, swollen, and more painful than before; added to which his legs must have caught a chill, because he'd been foolish enough to sleep with them sticking out of the tent.

Jean said at once,

'Listen, lad, if we have to march today, you'd better go and see the Major, and get them to put you in one of the carts.'

But no one knew what was going on, and all sorts of conflicting rumours went round. At one point, they thought they were about to set off again and struck camp, and the entire army corps got going and marched through Vouziers, leaving only a brigade from the 2nd Division on the left bank of the Aisne, to keep watch over the Monthois road. Then they stopped abruptly on the right bank, on the other side of town, and the rifle stacks were set up in the fields and meadows lining either side of the Grand-Pré road. At this point, the sight of the 4th Hussars trotting briskly off down it sparked off all sorts of speculation.

'If we're going to hang on here, then I'm staying put,' declared Maurice, who hated the idea of the major and the ambulance.

And in fact, they soon discovered that they would be camping there until General Douay could find out for certain which route the enemy was taking. Ever since the day before, when he'd seen the Margueritte division heading back up towards Le Chesne, he'd had a growing sense of unease, knowing that his position was no longer covered, that not a single soldier was left to guard the Argonne Passes, and that he might well be attacked at any moment. So he'd decided to send the 4th Hussars on ahead as reconnaissance, as far as the Grand-Pré and Croix-aux-Bois Passes, with orders to bring him back news at all costs.

The previous day, thanks to the efforts of the mayor of Vouziers, bread and meat had been distributed, as well as fodder for the animals, and that morning, at about ten o'clock, the men had just been granted permission to prepare themselves some soup, in case they might not have time to do so later on, when a second lot of troops, the Bordas brigade, set out along the route the Hussars had taken, and started everyone wondering again. What was all this, then? Were they leaving? Weren't they going to be allowed to eat in peace, now the pot was on the go? But the officers explained that the Bordas brigade had orders to occupy Buzancy, a few kilometres away. It was true that there'd been talk of the Hussars stumbling across large numbers of enemy squadrons and the brigade being sent to get them out.

For Maurice, those few hours were ones of delicious repose. He stretched himself out halfway down the hill in the field where the regiment was camped; and, limbs leaden with exhaustion, he looked down onto the green valley of the Aisne and the meadows planted with clumps of trees, the river winding lazily between them. Ahead of him, shutting off the valley, Vouziers rose up like an amphitheatre, showing off its rows of rooftops, dominated by the slender church spire and its dome-topped tower. Down by the bridge, smoke billowed from the tanneries' tall chimneys; and on the far side, he could see the walls of a large mill, covered in flour, set on the leafy, green riverbanks. And this small-town skyline, lost among the grass, seemed full of gentle charm, as if he'd got back those sensitive, dreamer's eyes of his. It was his youth returning to him, all those journeys he'd made to Vouziers back then, when he lived in Le Chesne, his home town. For an hour, he forgot about everything.

The soup had long been finished up and the waiting went on until, at about half past two, a dull but mounting restlessness began to take over the whole camp. Orders travelled up and down the ranks, the meadows were emptied of soldiers, the troops climbed to the top of the hill and lined up along the ridge between the villages of Chestres and Falaise, which lay about four or five kilometres apart. The sappers were already digging trenches and building epaulements; while to the left, the reserve artillery took up position on a low hill. And word spread that General Bordas had just sent a messenger to say that, having encountered superior forces at Grand-Pré, he'd been obliged to withdraw to Buzancy, raising fears that his line of retreat to Vouziers would soon be cut off. Moreover, the commander of the

7th Corps, thinking an attack imminent, had made his men take up battle positions, so as to withstand the first assault until the rest of the army arrived to back them up; one of his aides-de-camp had set off with a letter for the Marshal, alerting him to the situation and requesting help. Finally, afraid that the endless supply convoy might hinder their progress, having caught up with the army overnight and now bringing up the rear yet again, he ordered it to move on at once, and off it went, haphazardly, towards Chagny. This was battle.

'So, sir, it's serious this time, is it?' Maurice ventured to ask Rochas.

'Yes, it bloody well is!' replied the lieutenant, waving his long arms around. 'You just wait and see, things'll hot up soon!'

The soldiers were all delighted to hear this. Ever since the battle line had formed from Chestres to Falaise, the level of excitement in camp had risen higher and higher, and the men were full of feverish impatience. At last, they'd be getting a look at the bloody Prussians who, according to the papers, were so shattered from marching, so exhausted by illness, and all of them starving and in rags! The prospect of sending them arse over elbow at the first encounter boosted everyone's courage.

'It's not at all a bad thing that we're about to meet up,' declared Jean. 'We've been playing hide-and-seek long enough since we lost each other back there at the border, after that battle of theirs... But are these the same ones who beat MacMahon?'

Maurice hesitated, unable to answer. After what he'd read at Rheims he found it difficult to believe that the Third Army, led by the Crown Prince of Prussia, could be at Vouziers when, yesterday, it could only just have been camped near Vitry-le-François. True, there had been talk of a Fourth Army, under the orders of the Prince of Saxony,* which would advance along the Meuse: this was probably it, even though, considering the distance involved, he was astonished at how promptly it had occupied Grand-Pré. But what left him well and truly stunned and quite bewildered was hearing General Bourgain-Desfeuilles question a peasant from Falaise, asking if the Meuse passed through Buzancy, and if there were any sturdy bridges there. What was more, in his blissful ignorance the general proclaimed that they were going to be attacked by a column of a hundred thousand men coming from Grand-Pré, while another sixty thousand were on their way from Sainte-Menehould.

'How's your foot?' Jean asked Maurice.

'I can't feel it anymore,' he laughed. 'It'll be fine, even if we do fight.'

It was true—he was so buoyed up by nerves and excitement that he felt as if he were floating. To think that he hadn't fired a single cartridge all campaign! He'd been to the frontier, he'd passed south of Mulhouse on that night of dread and fear, without seeing a single Prussian, without firing a single shot; and he'd had to beat a retreat right back to Belfort, and to Rheims, and now, yet again, he'd been marching towards the enemy for five days, his rifle still intact and useless. He was overwhelmed by a growing need, a slow, angry urge to shoulder his weapon and at least let off a shot, just to ease the tension. In nigh on six weeks since he'd joined up in a fit of enthusiasm, dreaming of fighting for the morrow, all he'd done was weary his poor, delicate, gentlemanly feet with fleeing and tramping, far from the battlefields. And as they all waited anxiously, he was among the most impatient of all, his searching gaze on the Grand-Pré road stretching straight ahead into infinity, between the fine, tall trees. Beneath him the rolling valley unfurled, and the Aisne flowed like a silver ribbon between the willows and the poplar trees; and his gaze came back, unerringly, to the road ahead.

At about four o'clock, the alarm went up. The 4th Hussars were on their way back, after a long detour; and stories started going round, more and more exaggerated the nearer they came, of battle with the Uhlans, which served to confirm the general conviction that an attack was imminent. Two hours later another messenger arrived, scared and explaining that General Bordas no longer dared leave Grand-Pré, convinced that the road to Vouziers was blocked. This wasn't yet the case, since the messenger had just got through unhindered. But that might change at any moment, and General Dumont, the division commander, set off at once, together with the one brigade he still had, to extricate the one which had been left behind in distress. The sun was sinking behind Vouziers, where the rooftops stood silhouetted against a great, red cloud. For a long time, they could still see the brigade, moving away between the double line of trees, until eventually it was lost among the deepening shadows.

Colonel de Vineuil came over to make sure that his regiment was well settled in for the night. He was astonished not to find Captain Beaudoin at his post; and when the captain returned from Vouziers, excusing his absence by saying that he had dined with Baroness Ladicourt, he received a harsh reprimand, which he nonetheless heard out in silence, with all the correctness befitting a fine officer.

'Well, lads,' repeated the colonel, passing among his men, 'we'll be attacked tonight, no doubt, or certainly at daybreak tomorrow morning... Make sure you're ready, and remember—the 106th has never run away.'

They cheered him, for since setting out the exhaustion and despondency had become so overwhelming that they'd all rather just have a 'scrap' and get it over with. Rifles were checked and firing-pins changed. As the soup had been eaten that morning, they made do now with coffee and army biscuits. Orders had been issued not to go to sleep. Advance guards were posted fifteen hundred metres away, and sentries were dispatched as far as the banks of the river. The officers all kept watch around the camp fires. And every now and then, in the flickering light of one of the fires, the brocaded uniforms of the general-in-chief and his staff could be seen shadowed against a low wall, moving about excitedly, running towards the road, listening for the sound of hooves, mortal dread about the fate of the 3rd Division dominating the camp.

At about one o'clock in the morning Maurice was put on lookout duty at the edge of a field of plum trees, between the river and the road. The night was black as ink. As soon as he found himself alone, enveloped in the crushing silence of the sleeping countryside, he felt fear creep over him, a dreadful fear that he'd never experienced before, that he would never be able to conquer, and he was seized with trembling shame and anger. He turned to reassure himself by looking at the campfires; but they must have been hidden by a coppice, for behind him lay nothing but a sea of darkness; alone, far, far away, a few lights still burned in Vouziers, where the inhabitants, probably on the alert and quaking with fear at the thought of battle, were still awake. What finally chilled him was the realization, when he shouldered his rifle, that he couldn't even see the sights clearly. Then began the cruellest wait of all, as he funnelled all his strength into his sense of hearing, straining his ears for imperceptible sounds, until eventually all he could hear was a roaring sound, like thunder. The distant trickle of water, the slight rustle of leaves, an insect scrabbling around—every noise was huge and echoing. Wasn't that horses galloping, an endless rumble of artillery over there, making straight for him? And over to his left, hadn't he heard hushed whispers and muffled voices, scouts crawling through the shadows, preparing a surprise attack? Three times he nearly let off a warning shot. Fear of being mistaken and making himself a laughing stock only put him more on edge. He knelt down and leaned his left shoulder against a tree; it felt as if he'd been there for hours, that they'd forgotten him, and the army must have left without him. Then all of a sudden, he was no longer afraid; for there on the road, which he knew was two hundred metres away, he could distinctly make out the rhythmic steps of soldiers on the march. All at once, he knew that these were the troops in distress, this was General Dumont bringing back the Bordas brigade, whose return they'd been waiting for so impatiently. At that moment, a guard came to relieve him; his watch had barely lasted the regulation hour.

It was indeed the 3rd Division returning to camp. The relief was enormous. But security was doubled, for the news they brought with them confirmed all the suspicions about the enemy approach. The few prisoners who'd been brought back—several gloomy Uhlans draped in their greatcoats—refused to talk. And first light appeared, with a livid dawn that augured a rainy morning, as still they waited and waited, impatient and irritable. It was now nearly fourteen hours since the men had dared sleep. At about seven o'clock, Lieutenant Rochas told them that MacMahon was on his way with the entire army. The truth was that, in response to the dispatch he'd sent the day before, declaring that there was bound to be fighting near Vouziers, General Douay had received a letter from the Marshal telling him to stand his ground until he could bring help: the advance had been halted, the 1st Corps was heading for Terron, the 5th for Buzancy, while the 12th would stay at Le Chesne, as a second line of defence. So the anticipation became keener, it was no simple skirmish they were about to engage in, but a great battle, which would bring the whole army into the Aisne Valley, diverted away from the Meuse and marching south from now on. Yet they still didn't dare cook the soup and had to make do once again with coffee and army biscuits, because the 'scrap' was set for midday—everyone said so, although nobody knew why. An aide-de-camp had just been sent off to the Marshal to hurry up the emergency troops, as the approach of the two enemy armies became increasingly certain. Three hours later, a second officer galloped off for Le Chesne, where the general headquarters had been set up, with instructions to bring back orders immediately, for the feeling of anxiety had risen to fever pitch in the wake of further information supplied by a local mayor, who claimed to have seen a hundred thousand men at Grand-Pré, with another hundred thousand approaching near Buzancy.

Midday, and still no sign of any Prussians. One o'clock, two o'clock—still nothing. And their weariness began to grow, and with it, their doubt. Mocking voices began making fun of the generals. Maybe it was their own shadows on the wall they'd seen. Glasses, that's what they needed. Proper bunch of clowns they'd look, if nothing came along after they'd mucked everyone around like that! One fellow yelled,

'So it's Mulhouse all over again, is it?'

Maurice heard, and his heart lurched at this painful memory. He recalled the senseless flight, the panic which had carried the 7th Corps away with it, and never a German showing his face for ten leagues around. And he had the distinct sensation, he just knew, that the episode was beginning all over again. For there to have been no enemy attack, twenty-four hours after the skirmish at Grand-Pré, meant that the 4th Hussars must simply have bumped into a few reconnaissance scouts from the cavalry. The main columns must still be a long way off, perhaps two days' march away. Suddenly he grew terrified at the thought, realizing how much time they'd just wasted. In the space of three days, they hadn't even covered two leagues, between Contreuve and Vouziers. On the 25th and 26th, the other army corps had moved to the north, supposedly to stock up on supplies; while today, the 27th, here they were, heading south into a battle that no one was offering them. On the trail of the 4th Hussars, near the abandoned Argonne Passes, the Bordas brigade had thought it was done for and dragged the entire division to its rescue behind it, then the 7th Corps, and now the entire army—all in vain. And Maurice reflected on how priceless each hour was, in this crazy plan to join up with Bazaine, a plan which only a general of true genius would have been capable of carrying through, with solid troops, and only by bulldozing his way ahead, straight through any obstacles.

'We're done for!' he said to Jean, seized by despair, in a sudden burst of lucidity.

Then, as Jean looked at him, wide-eyed and unable to comprehend, he continued softly, for his ears only, speaking of their commanders.

'It's not that they're bad, so much as stupid, that's the thing—and unlucky, too! They haven't a clue, they've got no foresight, no plans, no ideas, no lucky breaks!... Come on, everything's against us, we're done for!'

And this feeling of discouragement, which Maurice reasoned through like the well-educated, intelligent man he was, increased and gradually weighed heavier and heavier over the troops, immobilized for no reason, getting wound up with all this waiting around. Furtively, doubt and a presentiment of the real situation began to wreak their work upon these slow wits; and there wasn't one, however blinkered he might be, who didn't have the uneasy feeling that they'd been poorly led, wrongly delayed, and pushed haphazardly into the most disastrous venture. What the hell were they doing there, for God's sake, if the Prussians weren't coming? Either they fought, right there and then, or they went off somewhere to sleep in peace. They'd had enough. Ever since the last aide-de-camp had left to bring back orders, concern had been mounting steadily by the minute; groups had formed, arguing and talking loudly. The officers, themselves frantic with worry, had no idea how to answer those soldiers who dared ask them questions. And so when, at five o'clock, the rumour spread that the aides-de-camp had returned, and that the army was about to retreat, a burden was lifted from everyone's shoulders, and there was a heartfelt sigh of joy and relief.

At last, common sense had got the better of them! The Emperor and the Marshal, who'd never been for this march onto Verdun and were worried to learn that, once again, they'd been too slow and would find themselves up against the army of the Crown Prince of Prussia, had abandoned the improbable idea of joining up with Bazaine, in favour of beating a retreat back through the northern strongholds and so withdrawing to Paris. The 7th Corps received the order to move back towards Chagny, via Le Chesne, while the 5th Corps was to march on to Poix, and the 1st and 12th to Vendresse. Well, in that case, seeing as they were retreating, why advance as far as the Aisne, why so many days and so much fatigue, when from Rheims it was so easy and so logical to take up positions in the Marne Valley which would be strong from the very start? Was there no direction at all, no military talent, no straightforward common

sense? But there were no more questions asked, just forgiveness, in
sheer relief at the decision, which was so reasonable, and the only
sensible one if they were to get themselves out of the trap they'd
fallen into. From the generals right down to the simple soldiers,
everyone felt that they would be strong again, invincible outside
Paris, and that this was, inevitably, where they would defeat the
Prussians. However, they had to move out of Vouziers at first light,
to be on the march towards Le Chesne before they were attacked;
and at once the camp grew extraordinarily animated, with bugles
sounding and orders being passed down; meanwhile the baggage and
supply convoy had already been sent on ahead, so it wouldn't ham-
per the rearguard.

Maurice was overjoyed. Then, as he attempted to explain to Jean
the retreating manœuvre they were about to execute, a cry of pain
escaped him: his excitement was gone; there was his foot again, like
some lead weight, stuck on the end of his leg.

'What's up? Starting again, is it?' asked the corporal in despair. It
was he who came up with an idea, full of practical common sense.

'Listen here, lad, you told me yesterday that you knew folk up
there, in town. You should get permission from the Major to have
yourself driven over to Le Chesne in a cart, you could get a good
night's sleep there, in a warm bed. Tomorrow, if you can walk better,
we'll pick you up when we pass through... Hey? That suit you?'

Right there in Falaise, the village close to where they were
camped, Maurice had bumped into an old friend of his father's, the
owner of a small farm; he was just about to drive his daughter over to
Le Chesne, near one of his aunts, and the horse stood waiting, harnessed to a small cart.

Things with Major Bouroche, though, nearly turned sour from
the very start.

'It's my foot, it's blistered, doctor, sir...'

At once Bouroche, shaking his powerful head with its lion's mane,
roared,

'I'm not the "doctor, sir"... What sort of a bloody soldier are you?'

And as Maurice, frightened, stammered his excuses, he went on,

'I'm the Major, you lout, you hear me?'

Then, noticing who he was dealing with, he must have felt somewhat ashamed, and became even angrier.

'Your foot—a fine story!... Yes, yes, you can have permission. Go in a cart, go in a balloon if you like! We've had enough of you hobbledehoys and schemers!'

As Jean helped Maurice hoist himself up into the cart, the latter turned to thank him; and the two men fell into each other's arms, as if they'd never see each other again. Who could tell, in all the upheaval of the retreat, with the Prussians there? Maurice was surprised by the deep affection which already drew him to this man. He turned around twice more to wave him goodbye; and he left the camp, where they were preparing to light great fires to fool the enemy, while they themselves slipped off in absolute silence, before first light.

En route, the farmer went on and on about what terrible times they were living in. He hadn't had the courage to stay in Falaise; and he was already regretting having left, saying over and over again that he'd be ruined if the enemy set fire to his house. His daughter, a tall, pale creature, just sat and cried. But Maurice, almost drunk with fatigue, didn't hear a word of it and fell asleep sitting up, rocked by the brisk trot of the little horse, which managed to cover the four leagues from Vouziers to Le Chesne in under an hour and a half. It wasn't yet seven o'clock, and dusk was only just beginning to gather, when the young man, shivering and astonished, alighted at the bridge over the canal in the square, opposite the narrow house where he'd been born, and where he'd spent twenty years of his existence. That was where he headed for, automatically, even though the house had been sold to a veterinary surgeon eighteen months previously. And, when the farmer asked him, he replied that he knew exactly where he was going, and thanked him profusely for being so obliging.

However, when he found himself in the middle of the little triangle, near the well, he just stood there, dizzy, his mind a blank. Where was he going? Abruptly, he remembered that he was heading for the notary's, whose house was next door to the one he'd grown up in, and whose mother—lovely old Madame Desroches—used to spoil him when he was little and they were neighbours. But he barely recognized Le Chesne, for the tiny town, normally so lifeless, was caught up in the extraordinary hustle and bustle which an army corps, camped at the gates, had brought with it, filling the streets with officers, messengers, and servants, wanderers and laggards of every kind. He had no trouble finding the canal which marked a line from one end of the town to the other, cutting diagonally across the main square, where the narrow, stone bridge linked the two triangles; on the far bank, there was the market still, all right, with its mossy roofs, the Rue Berond disappearing off to the left, and the road to Sedan running to the right. There was so much buzzing in the Rue de Vouziers opposite, though, packed with swarming crowds as far as the town hall, that it wasn't until he looked up from where he was standing and recognized the slate-covered steeple above the notary's house that he could be sure that this was indeed the same street corner where he'd played hopscotch. In the square, it looked as if a space was being cleared, and men were keeping curious onlookers at bay. And there, beyond the well, he was amazed to catch sight of a sort of depot, taking up large amounts of room, full of carriages, wagons, and carts, a whole encampment of luggage that he'd surely seen somewhere before.

The sun had just vanished into the smooth, blood-red water of the canal, and Maurice was just deciding what to do, when a woman nearby, who'd been staring closely at him for a moment or two, exclaimed,

'Lord above! It can't be! You're the Levasseur boy, aren't you?'

Then it was his turn to recognize her—Madame Combette, the wife of the pharmacist, whose shop stood on the square. As he began to explain that he was going to ask nice old Madame Desroches to put him up for the night, she pulled him aside excitedly.

'No, no, come to our house, I'll tell you all about it...'

Inside the pharmacy, having carefully shut the door behind them, she said,

'Don't you know, then, my dear boy? The Emperor's staying with the Desroches... Their house has been commandeered for him, and they're not at all pleased with the great honour being bestowed on them, I can tell you. When you think that they forced that poor old grandmother—gone seventy, she is—to give up her room, and climb up to the attic to sleep in the maidservant's quarters!... Look, every-thing you see over there, in the square, belongs to the Emperor, that's his trunks, you see?'

And then Maurice did remember them, all those carriages and wagons, the whole, splendid train of the imperial household, that he'd seen at Rheims.

'Oh! My dear boy, if you only knew what they pulled out of there, silver plate, bottles of wine, baskets of provisions, fine linen and all!

Went on for two whole hours, non-stop. I wonder where they've managed to cram it all, because the house isn't big... Look, look! What a fire they've made up in that kitchen!'

He looked at the little white, two-storey house on the corner of the square and the Rue de Vouziers, calm and genteel-looking from the outside, and he could see the interior in his mind's eye, with its central downstairs hallway, and four rooms on each floor, as if he'd been there only the day before. Above, near the corner, the first-floor window which opened onto the square was already lit up, and the pharmacist's wife explained that this was the Emperor's room. However, as she'd said, it was the kitchen that blazed brightest of all, with its ground-floor window overlooking the Rue de Vouziers. Never had the inhabitants of Le Chesne been treated to such a spectacle. A stream of curious bystanders, constantly coming and going, blocked the road, gawping at this furnace where the Emperor's dinner roasted and bubbled. To let in more air, the cooks had flung the windows wide open. There were three of them, dressed in dazzling chef's whites, busy before a row of spit-roasting chickens, stirring sauces at the bottom of enormous copper saucepans which shone like gold. The old folk couldn't remember ever having seen so much fire burning and food cooking all at once, not even at the Hôtel du Lion d'Argent for the grandest feasts.

Combette, the pharmacist, a lean, lively little man, came home very excited by everything he'd just seen and heard. As deputy mayor, he seemed to be in the know. It had been about half-past three when MacMahon had telegraphed Bazaine to say that the arrival of the Crown Prince of Prussia was forcing him to withdraw to the northern strongholds: and another dispatch was to be sent to the Minister of War, similarly warning him of the retreat and explaining the terrible danger that the army was in of being cut off and crushed. Well, they could whistle for the dispatch to Bazaine, for all communication with Metz appeared to have been suspended for the past several days. The other one, though, was more serious; and lowering his voice, the pharmacist told them how he'd heard a superior officer saying: 'If they get word of this in Paris, we're done for!' No one could ignore how harshly the Empress Regent and the Council of Ministers were pushing the march forward. Meanwhile, the confusion grew worse by the hour, and the most extraordinary news flooded in about the approach of the German armies. Was it possible that the Crown Prince of Prussia was in Châlons? And, in that case, just whose troops had the 7th Corps bumped into in the Argonne Passes?

'They haven't got a clue back at headquarters,' continued the pharmacist, arms flailing in despair. 'Oh, what a mess! Mind you, it'll all be fine if the army's on the retreat by tomorrow.'

Then, a fine fellow at heart, he said,

'Well then, my young friend, I'll put a dressing on that foot of yours, you shall dine with us, and then you can sleep upstairs in the little room belonging to my apprentice, who's run off.'

But Maurice was tormented by the need to see, to find out, and before he would do anything else, he was determined to pursue his original idea, and visit the house opposite to see old Madame Desroches.

He was surprised when no one stopped him at the door, which in all the tumult going on in the square had been left open, and wasn't even guarded. Officers, staff, and others were coming in and out all the time; and the bustle in the blaze-filled kitchen seemed to have set the whole house astir. On the stairs, however, not a single lamp was lit, and he had to feel his way up. On the first-floor landing, he stopped for a few seconds, heart thumping, in front of the door of the room where he knew the Emperor was staying; but nothing, not a sound came from inside, just a deathly hush. Upstairs, Madame Desroches was afraid of him at first, as he stood on the threshold of the maidservant's roomwhere she'd been obliged to seek refuge. Then she recognized him.

'Ah! My child, what dreadful times to meet again in!... I'd quite willingly have given the Emperor my house, I would; but those people of his, with him, they're just too rude! If you'd seen the way they grabbed everything, and they'll set light to the place with all that fire!... As for him, the poor man looks like death warmed up, and he's so very sad...'

When the young man took his leave, reassuring her as he left, she accompanied him, and leaned over the banisters.

'Look!' she murmured. 'You can see him from here... Oh, yes! We're all lost, now. Farewell, my child!'

And Maurice stood there on the stair, in the darkness. He craned his neck, and, through the glass of a transom window, glimpsed a sight which would stamp itself indelibly on his memory.

There at the back of the cold, genteel room was the Emperor, sitting at a little table laid with a single setting and lit at either end by a candlestick. In the background, two aides-de-camp stood by in silence. A maître d'hôtel waited near the table. The glass was untouched, the bread uneaten, and in the middle of the plate lay a chicken breast, going cold. The Emperor sat motionless, looking at the tablecloth, his eyes failing and watery, just as they'd been before, at Rheims. But he seemed wearier, and when he finally made up his mind and had lifted two mouthfuls to his lips, with what seemed to be an immense effort, he pushed the rest away. He had eaten. An expression of secretly endured suffering made his pale face look more wan than ever.

Downstairs, as Maurice was passing the dining room, the door was suddenly flung open and inside, in the flickering glow of the candles and the steam rising off the food, he saw a table full of equerries, aides-de-camp, and chamberlains, busy emptying the bottles from the wagons, gobbling down the game, and mopping up the sauces, accompanied by much shouting. Ever since the Marshal's dispatch had been sent off, the knowledge that they were definitely about to retreat had sent them into raptures. In eight days they would be in Paris, and sleeping in clean sheets at long last.

Then Maurice was suddenly conscious of the terrible weariness that had been overwhelming him: it was absolutely certain, the whole army was drawing back, and all he had to do was sleep and wait for the 7th Corps to pass through. He walked back across the square and once again found himself at the house of Combette, the pharmacist, where he ate his food as if in a trance. Then he felt someone bandaging his foot and showing him up to a bedroom. And next, black night, obliteration. He slept flat out, without a murmur. However, after an indeterminate length of time—hours, centuries perhaps—a shudder shook his sleep, and made him sit bolt upright, among the shadows. Where was he? What was the continuous rumble of thunder that had woken him? At once he remembered, and ran to the window to have a look. Down below, in the darkness, in the square where the nights were usually so calm, the artillery was marching past, an endless, trotting procession of men, horses, and cannon that caused the little, dead houses to shake. At the sight of this sudden departure, he was seized by an irrational fear. What time could it be? The town hall clock struck four. And he forced himself to calm down, telling himself that they were simply carrying out the order to withdraw, issued the day before; until turning his head, he saw something which well and truly frightened him: at the notary's, a light still burned in the corner window; and at regular intervals, the shadow of the Emperor could be seen quite clearly, casting a sombre profile.

Maurice swiftly pulled on his breeches, to go downstairs. However, Combette appeared, holding a candlestick and waving his hand.

'I saw you from down in the street as I was coming back from the town hall, and I came to let you know... Just imagine, they haven't let me get to bed, we've just spent two hours, the mayor and I, on new requisitions... Oh, yes, it's all change again... He was bloody well right, that officer, not wanting us to send off that dispatch to Paris!'

On and on he went, in unfinished, jumbled sentences, and eventually, with a pang of anguish, the young man understood, dumbfounded. Towards midnight, a dispatch had arrived for the Emperor from the Minister of War, in answer to the one from the Marshal. No one knew the exact wording; but at the town hall, an aide-de-camp had said out loud that the Empress and the Council of Ministers feared a revolution in Paris if the Emperor were to return, abandoning Bazaine. The dispatch was ill-informed about the true positions of the Germans, and seemed to believe in a head start which the Châlons army no longer possessed; it demanded that they march onward, in spite of everything, and did so with extraordinary urgency and passion.

'The Emperor sent for the Marshal,' added the apothecary, 'and they've been holed up together for nearly an hour. Naturally, I don't know what they may have said to each other, but what all the officers have told me is that we're not beating a retreat anymore, and the march on the Meuse is to be resumed... We've just requisitioned all the ovens in town for the 1st Corps, which will replace the 12th here tomorrow morning—as you see, their artillery's leaving for Besace as we speak... This is it, this time—you're off to battle!'

He stopped. He too was looking towards the lighted window, at the notary's. Then, with an air of pensive curiosity, he said in a low voice:

'Well, well... What could they have said to each other?... It's odd, all the same, to withdraw at six in the evening, faced by the threat of danger, only to go headlong into that danger at midnight, when the situation hasn't changed!'

Maurice was still listening to the rumbling of the cannon, down there in the dark little town, listening to the ceaselessly trotting hooves, to the tide of men flowing towards the Meuse, towards the terrible unknown of the morrow. And, cast upon the flimsy, genteel curtains across the window, he saw the shadow of the Emperor passing regularly to and fro, this sick man pacing back and forth, kept from his bed by insomnia, trapped by his need to move around, despite all his suffering, his ears ringing with the noise of all these horses and men that he was allowing to be sent to their deaths. So, a few hours had been enough, and now disaster was decided on and accepted. What, indeed, could they have said to each other, the Emperor and the Marshal? Both had been warned of the misfortune they were marching towards, had been convinced, that evening, of defeat, seeing the awful conditions the army was going to find itself in, and they couldn't see things any differently in the morning, when the peril was growing with every hour. General Palikao's plan—the lightning march on Montmédy—had been foolhardy even on the 23rd and perhaps just about possible on the 25th, providing the troops had been solid and led by a genius; but now, on the 27th, it was becoming an act of sheer folly, as the commanders continued to prevaricate and the troops became increasingly demoralized. If they both knew this, then why were they giving in to the pitiless voices whipping up their indecision? The Marshal was perhaps no more than a narrow-minded, obedient soldier at heart, noble in his self-denial. And the Emperor, no longer giving orders, merely awaited his fate. They were being asked for their lives, and the life of the army: and they were giving them. This was the night the crime was committed, the abominable night when a nation was assassinated; from then on, the army was in dire straits, a hundred thousand men were sent to the slaughter.

Thinking of this, despairing and shivering, Maurice followed the shadow upon old Madame Desroches's flimsy muslin curtains, that feverish, pacing shadow, which moved as if hounded by the pitiless voices from Paris. Hadn't the Empress prayed that night for the death of the father, to make way for the son to reign? Forward march! Forward march! No looking back, onwards in the rain, through the mud, towards extermination, so that the Empire in its death-throes can play its final hand down to the very last card. Forward march! Forward march! Die like a hero upon piles of your people's corpses, strike the whole world with tender admiration if you want your descendants to be forgiven! And without a doubt the Emperor was marching to his death. Downstairs, the kitchen no longer glowed, the equerries and aides-de-camp and chamberlains were all asleep, and the whole house stood in darkness; while the shadow, all alone, paced ceaselessly back and forth, resigned to the inevitable sacrifice, amid the deafening row made by the 12th Corps, still marching past in the darkness.

Suddenly, it occurred to Maurice that if the advance march had been resumed, the 7th Corps would not be coming back through Le Chesne; and he imagined himself getting left behind, separated from his regiment, having deserted his post. His foot wasn't aching anymore: a skilful dressing and several hours of total rest had soothed the inflammation. After Combette had given him a pair of his own boots, which were wide-fitting and comfortable, he wanted to be up and off without delay, hoping to meet up with the 106th still on the road from Le Chesne to Vouziers. The pharmacist tried in vain to hold him back, and had all but decided to drive him back himself, in his carriage, when Fernand, his apprentice, reappeared, explaining that he'd been to say hello to a cousin of his. It was this tall, pale, cowardly-looking lad who harnessed up the horses and drove Maurice back. It wasn't yet four o'clock and a deluge was tumbling from the inky sky, while the lanterns on the carriage grew dim, barely lighting the road, amid the vast, drowned landscape, full of loud noises which made them halt every kilometre, thinking they could hear an army on the march.

Down near Vouziers, however, Jean hadn't slept at all. Ever since Maurice had explained to him how this withdrawal would save the day, he'd been watching, making sure his men stayed close, waiting for the order to depart, which the officers might give at any minute. At about two o'clock, deep in the shadows, starred red by the camp-fires, a loud noise of horses' hooves carried across the camp: it was the cavalry, leaving for the vanguard near Ballay and Quatre-Champs, to keep watch over the Boult-aux-Bois and Croix-aux-Bois roads. An hour later, the infantry and artillery began setting off in turn, finally leaving Falaise and Chestres and the positions they'd so stubbornly defended for two long days against an enemy who wasn't coming. The sky had clouded over, the night was still dark, and each regiment moved off in absolute silence, a row of shadows slipping away, deep into the darkness. But their hearts all pounded with elation, as though they'd escaped from an ambush. Already, they saw themselves approaching the walls of Paris, on the eve of revenge.

In the dense night, Jean kept his eyes well open. The road was lined with trees, and it seemed to him that they were crossing vast prairies. Then there were slopes, climbing uphill and down. They were just coming to a village, which must have been Ballay, when the heavy layer of cloud covering the sky burst, releasing a violent downpour. The men had already taken such a soaking that it didn't even anger them now, and they just hunched their shoulders. But they had passed Ballay; and the nearer they got to Quatre-Champs, the stronger the great, furious gusts of wind began to blow. Further on, when they'd climbed up onto the great plateau, with its bare terrain stretching all the way to Noirval, the hurricane began to rage, and they were battered by a terrifying deluge. And it was in the middle of these vast expanses of countryside that the order to halt brought all the regiments to a standstill, one by one. The whole of the 7th Corps, some thirty thousand men or more, found itself standing there as day was breaking, a muddy day, streaming with grey water.

What was going on? Why had they halted? Disquiet was already snaking through the ranks; some claimed that the marching orders had just been changed. They were made to stand to attention, and forbidden to relax and sit down. At times, the wind swept so violently over the high plateau that they had to huddle close together, so as not to be blown away. The rain blinded them, hacking at their skin, icy cold, trickling beneath their clothes. And two hours went by, an interminable wait, and no one knew why, their hearts tight with anguish yet again.

As it grew lighter, Jean tried to work out where they were. Over to the north-west, on the other side of Quatre-Champs, someone had pointed out the road to Le Chesne running along the hillside. So why had they turned right instead of left? Then his attention was drawn to the staff headquarters, based at the Converserie, a farm which stood on the edge of the plateau. There, everyone seemed very scared, officers were running round and arguing, gesturing wildly. Nothing was coming, so what were they waiting for? The plateau lay like a sort of amphitheatre, with stubble-fields reaching into infinity, dominated to the north and east by tree-lined heights: thick woodland stretched to the south, while, through a gap to the west, the Aisne Valley could be glimpsed, and the little white houses in Vouziers. Beneath the Converserie, the slate-covered steeple of Quatre-Champs rose up, washed out by the raging downpour, and the few poor, mossy village roofs appeared to melt beneath the onslaught. And as Jean's gaze traced the road's ascent, he quite clearly saw a carriage approaching at a brisk trot, coming along the stony road which had been turned into a torrent.

It was Maurice, who had at last caught sight of the 7th Corps from the hillside opposite, as they rounded a bend. He'd been scouring the countryside for two hours, misled by directions given him by a peasant, and led astray in particular by the unwillingness of his driver, whose fear of the Prussians was making him ill. As soon as he reached the farm, he leapt out of the carriage and made straight for his regiment.

Stupefied, Jean shouted,

'What on earth are you doing here? Why? We were coming to pick you up!'

Maurice shrugged, and told him of his anger and sorrow.

'Ah! Yes... We're not going that way anymore, we're heading over there, to die, all of us!'

'Right,' said the other after a pause, turning pale. 'At least we'll be together when we get our brains smashed in.'

And so the two men greeted each other as they had parted, with an embrace. With the rain still beating down, the simple soldier rejoined the ranks, while the corporal set a good example, soaking wet and uncomplaining.

But now the news was going round, and it was official. They were no longer withdrawing to Paris, but marching once again on the Meuse. One of the Marshal's aides-de-camp had just brought the 7th Corps the order to go to Nouart and set up camp; while the 5th Corps, which was making for Beauclair, was to take the army's right flank, and the 1st would replace the 12th at Le Chesne, marching on Besace, on the left flank. And if thirty-odd thousand soldiers had been kept waiting there for nearly three hours, standing to attention, buffeted by furious gales, it was because, in all the deplorable confusion caused by this fresh change of battle fronts, General Douay was desperately worried about the fate of the supply convoy, which had been sent on ahead somewhere near Chagny the day before. They would have to wait for it to catch up with the army corps. Some said it had been intercepted by the convoy of the 12th Corps, at Le Chesne. What was more, part of their equipment—all the artillery's mobile forges—had gone the wrong way, and was now coming back from Terron along the Vouziers road, where it was sure to fall into the hands of the Germans. Never had there been greater disorder, and never had their anxiety been more acute.

Real despair now reigned among the soldiers. Many wanted to sit on their rucksacks in the mud, on this waterlogged plateau, and wait for death in the rain. They scorned and sneered at the commanders: oh! fine lot they were, no brains, undoing in the evening what they'd done in the morning, dawdling when the enemy wasn't there and disappearing as soon as it came into view! This final demoralization was the last straw, transforming the army into a herd stripped of all faith and discipline, being led to the slaughter wherever the winding road happened to take it. Back near Vouziers there was a burst of gunfire, as the 7th Corps's rearguard exchanged shots with the German vanguard; and a moment ago, all eyes had turned to the Aisne Valley, where they could see thick, black swirls of smoke rising into a clear patch of sky: they knew that this was the village of Falaise burning, set on fire by the Uhlans. Rage took hold of the men. What? So the Prussians were there now! Two days they'd waited for them, to give them just enough time to get there. And then they'd decamped. Deep down, furtively, in the hearts of even the most blinkered men, anger was mounting at the irreparable mistake which had been made, anger at the idiotic waiting and the trap they'd fallen into: the Fourth Army's scouts keeping the Bordas brigade amused, halting and immobilizing the army corps at Châlons, one after the other, just so that the Crown Prince of Prussia could come galloping along with the Third Army. And now, thanks to the Marshal's ignorance, still unsure which troops he had in front of him, they were beginning to meet up, and the 7th and 5th Corps were going to be harried, under constant threat of disaster.

Maurice watched Falaise burning on the horizon. There was one consolation, however: the convoy, which they'd believed lost, emerged from the Le Chesne road. While the 1st Division waited at Quatre-Champs, guarding the endless line of baggage as it filed past, the 2nd set off again at once, and reached Boult-aux-Bois through the forest, while 3rd was posted up on the Belleville heights, to keep the lines of communication open. And as the 106th finally left the plateau, just as the rain started to fall twice as heavily as before, and resumed the treacherous march towards the Meuse, into the unknown, Maurice again saw the shadow of the Emperor against old Madame Desroches's flimsy curtains. Oh! This army, full of hopelessness, this army in distress, being sent to certain destruction—all for the sake of a dynasty! Forward march! Foward march! No looking back, onwards in the rain, through the mud, on towards extermination!

CHAPTER SIX

'Jesus Christ!' said Chouteau the next morning, waking up frozen and exhausted inside the tent. 'What I wouldn't give for a nice drop of broth with some meat in it!'

At Boult-aux-Bois, where they had camped, the only food they'd had the previous evening had been a measly distribution of potatoes, as the constant marches and counter-marches made the supply corps increasingly bewildered and chaotic, never managing to meet the troops at the pre-arranged rendezvous. In all the confusion on the roads, they no longer knew where to find the migrating herds, and shortages weren't far off.

Loubet stretched and gave a hopeless sneer.

'Too bloody right! No more spit-roast goose for us.'

The squad was sullen and gloomy. It was bad news, having no food. That, and this never-ending rain and the mud they'd just slept in.

Seeing Pache making the sign of the cross, having quietly said his prayers to himself, Chouteau started up furiously again,

'Go on, ask that God of yours to send us a couple of sausages and a bottle each.'

'Oh! If only we had a loaf, as much bread as we could eat!' sighed Lapoulle, who suffered more keenly from hunger than the others, tortured by his huge appetite.

But Lieutenant Rochas told them to be quiet. They should be ashamed of themselves, always thinking of their bellies! Now, he simply tightened his belt a notch, he did. Ever since things had taken a decisive turn for the worse, and they'd been hearing the odd burst of gunfire in the distance, his stubborn confidence had been completely restored. Since the Prussians were there now, it couldn't be simpler: they'd fight them! And he shrugged, standing behind Captain Beaudoin—this youngster, as he called him—who was devastated because he'd lost all his luggage for good, this time, and was going around pale and tight-lipped, unable to calm down. No food—that was bearable! What infuriated him was having no clean shirt to change into!

Maurice had just woken up, shivering and exhausted. Thanks to the wide shoes, though, his foot hadn't become any more inflamed. But yesterday's downpour, from which his greatcoat was still heavily damp, had left him aching all over. And, as he went on an errand to fetch water for the coffee, he looked over to the plain, on the edge of which lay Boult-aux-Bois: forests stretched west and north, a hillside climbed up to the village of Belleville; while, near Buzancy in the east, great, flat terrain unrolled, and hamlets hid among the gently undulating folds. Was that where they were expecting the enemy to show? As he returned from the stream, carrying the bottle full of water, a family of peasants called tearfully to him from the door of their little farm, and asked him if the soldiers were going to stay at long last, to defend them. The 5th Corps had already passed through the region three times, sent back and forth by conflicting orders. Yesterday, thay'd heard the sound of cannons coming from the direction of Bar.

There was no doubt that the Prussians were no more than two leagues away. And when Maurice told these poor folk that the 7th Corps, too, was probably going to be on its way again, they bemoaned their fate. So they were abandoning them; these soldiers couldn't possibly be here to fight, not if they kept reappearing only to disappear again, always on the run.

'Anyone who wants sugar', said Loubet as he served the coffee, 'can dip their thumb in and wait for it to melt.'

No one laughed. Well, it was a nuisance, having to drink coffee without sugar; especially when there weren't any biscuits left, either! The day before, to take their minds off the long wait on the Quatre-Champs Plateau, nearly all the men had finished off the provisions from their bags, right down to the last crumbs. Happily, though, the squad discovered a dozen potatoes, which they shared amongst themselves.

Maurice's stomach was in a sorry state, and he lamented,

'If I'd known, I'd have bought some bread in Le Chesne!'

Jean listened, but said nothing. He'd had a quarrel with Chouteau when he got up, after the latter insolently refused to go and look for firewood, saying that it wasn't his turn. Since things had been going downhill, discipline had been getting worse, and eventually the commanders no longer dared hand out any reprimands. And Jean, in his fine, calm way, had realized that if he wanted to avoid open rebellion, he'd have to play down his authority as corporal. He'd

become an easygoing chap, and appeared to his men as just an ordinary comrade, one whose experience continued to bring them huge
advantages. Even if his squad was no longer so well nourished,
at least they weren't yet starving, unlike so many others. It was
Maurice's suffering, though, that touched him most of all. He sensed
that he was growing weak, and looked at him anxiously, wondering
how this frail young man would manage to hold out.

When Jean heard Maurice complaining about having no bread,
he got up, disappeared for a moment, then came back, after rummaging in his bag. Then, slipping a biscuit into Maurice's hand, he
said,

'Here! Hide this, I haven't enough for everyone.'

'But what about you?' asked the young man, deeply touched.

'Oh! Don't you worry about me... I've still got two left.'

It was true, he'd carefully saved three biscuits in case they went
into battle—he knew how hungry you got on the battlefield. Anyway,
he'd just eaten a potato. That was enough for him. He'd see, later on.

At about ten o'clock, the 7th Corps set off yet again. The Marshal's first intention must have been to send it through Buzancy, to
Stenay, where it would have crossed the Meuse. But the Prussians,
who were gaining on the Châlons army, must have been at Stenay
already, and some even said they were at Buzancy, and so the 7th
Corps, driven back north, had just received the order to make for
Besace, some twenty kilometres or so from Boult-aux-Bois, in order
to cross the Meuse from there at Mouzon the following day. Their
departure was cheerless and the men grumbled, stomachs half-
empty, limbs only half-rested, exhausted by the delays and fatigue of
the past few days; and the gloom-laden officers, succumbing to the
feeling of unease about the catastrophe towards which they were
marching, complained about the lack of action and grew annoyed
that they hadn't gone to back up the 5th Corps near Buzancy when
they'd heard the cannon. That corps must be beating a retreat, too,
moving back up towards Nouart; while the 12th Corps was leaving
Besace for Mouzon and the 1st headed for Raucourt. It was like the
stampede of a herd, harried by dogs, rushing desperately, after endless delays and dawdling, towards the longed-for Meuse.

When the 106th left Boult-aux-Bois in the wake of the cavalry and
artillery, and joined the three divisions, moving in a mighty stream
across the plain, lining it with men on the march, the sky clouded

over once again, filling up with slow-moving white clouds whose mournful appearance accentuated the sad mood of the soldiers. The 106th followed the main Buzancy road, which was lined with magnificent poplars. In the village of Germond, where steam was rising from the piles of manure lying outside houses all along the roadside, women sobbed and clutched their children, holding them out towards the passing troops, as if begging them to take them with them. There wasn't a single morsel of bread left, not even a potato. Then, instead of carrying on towards Buzancy, the 106th turned left and went back in the direction of Authe; and when they saw Belleville again, on the other side of the plain, on the hillside, the town they had been through the day before, it dawned quite clearly on the men that they were retracing their steps.

'Bloody hell!' growled Chouteau. 'Do they think we're completely stupid?'

Loubet added,

'They're just two-bit generals, they're all over the bloody place! Easy to see our legwork doesn't cost them much!'

Everyone was getting angry. It wasn't right, tiring men out like this, sending them walkabout just for the hell of it. And on they marched, across the barren plain, between great folds of land, in a column formed of two rows, one on either side, while the officers rode down the middle; but it wasn't the jaunty, jokey, song-filled march of the day after Rheims, in Champagne, when they'd cheerfully carried their bags, when the hope of getting there ahead of the Prussians, and beating them, had lightened the load: now they dragged their feet, silent, irritated, full of hatred for their rifles, digging into their shoulders, and their bags, weighing them down, all faith in their commanders now vanished, and victims to such hopelessness that they just trudged along like a herd of beasts, cowering before the inexorable crack of the whip. The wretched army had started its climb to calvary.

For the past few minutes, however, something had caught Maurice's interest. To his left, the land rose in undulating terraces, and he'd just spotted a trooper riding out of a small wood, far away. Almost immediately, another appeared, and then another. All three stood motionless, no bigger than a fist, their lines fine and precise, like toys. He thought that this must be some sort of Hussar detachment, some reconnaissance scouts coming back, when he was startled by something glinting on their shoulders, reflections, no doubt, from copper epaulettes.

'Look, over there!' he said, nudging Jean next to him. 'Uhlans!'

The corporal stared, wide-eyed.

'Well, well!'

They were, indeed, Uhlans, the first Prussians the 106th had set eyes on. In almost six weeks of the campaign, not only had they failed to fire a single cartridge, but they'd still to see an actual enemy. Word went round, and all eyes turned to look, with mounting curiosity. They seemed in fine fettle, these Uhlans.

'One of them looks nice and plump,' remarked Loubet.

But on a plateau, to the left of a small wood, an entire squadron of them came into view. Faced with such a threatening apparition, the column came to a halt. Orders came down the line, and the 106th went to take up position behind some trees on the banks of a stream. Some of the artillery were already turning round and galloping back, setting up on a hillock. Then, for nearly two hours, they stayed there, ready for battle, and they lingered, but nothing further happened. On the horizon the amassed enemy cavalry stood immobile. Finally, realising that they were wasting precious time, they set off again.

'Oh, well,' murmured Jean regretfully, 'it's not going to be this time, either.'

Maurice's hands, too, were itching at least to let off a shot. And his thoughts returned to the mistake they'd made yesterday, by not going to back up the 5th Corps. If the Prussians weren't mounting any attacks, then it could only be because they didn't have enough infantry at their disposal; which meant that their cavalry displays in the distance could have only one purpose—to delay the army corps on the march. They'd just fallen into the trap, yet again. Indeed, from that moment on, the 106th was forever catching sight of the Uhlans, on their left, at every hill and turn: they would follow, keep watch, and disappear behind a farm, only to reappear round the edge of a wood.

Little by little, the soldiers grew angry, seeing themselves surrounded like this from a distance, like being caught in the meshes of an invisible net.

'They're really beginning to get on our nerves!' even Pache and Lapoulle kept saying. 'It'd help if we could send a few bullets their way!'

But on they marched, marching, marching, painfully, their steps already heavy and quick to tire. This part of the journey was an uneasy one, they could feel the enemy approaching from every side, just as one can sense a storm gathering, before it appears over the horizon. Strict orders were issued to keep the rearguard well in line, and there were no more stragglers, for they were sure that behind the army corps were the Prussians, sweeping up. While the enemy infantry approached at a thundering pace, the French regiments tramped around on the spot, harried and paralysed.

At Authe, the sky brightened, and Maurice, who was using the sun as his guide, noticed that instead of heading back more in the direction of Le Chesne, which was a good three leagues away, they were turning to march due east. It was two o'clock and now, after shivering for two days in the rain, they suffered in the baking heat. The road climbed across the deserted plains, winding in long twists and turns. There wasn't a house nor a soul to be seen, barely a wretched little wood here and there, in the middle of the naked, melancholy lands; and the dismal silence of the solitude overtook the soldiers, who hung their heads, dripping with sweat and dragging their feet. At last, they came to Saint-Pierremont, a few empty houses sitting on a hillock. They didn't march through the village, and Maurice noticed that they immediately turned left and began heading north again, towards Besace. This time he understood which route they were taking, trying to reach Mouzon before the Prussians. But could they succeed, with such weary and demoralized troops? At Saint-Pierremont, the three Uhlans reappeared in the distance at a turning on one of the roads from Buzancy; and as the rearguard was leaving the village, a battery was unmasked, and a few shells came down, though no damage was caused. No answering shots were fired, and the march continued, growing more and more tortuous.

Three long leagues lay between Saint-Pierremont and Besace, and when Maurice told Jean this, he spread his hands in despair: the men would never manage twelve kilometres, he could tell, the signs were unmistakable—shortness of breath and a distracted look on their faces. The road climbed up and up between the two hillsides, which gradually closed in on each other. They had to make a halt. But resting made their limbs go completely numb; and by the time they set off again, it was worse than before: the regiments got nowhere, and men began falling down. Seeing Maurice turn pale, eyes rolling with exhaustion, Jean began talking, contrary to habit, trying to keep him awake by bombarding him with a barrage of words, as they automatically followed the mechanical marching motion.

'So, your sister lives in Sedan, maybe we'll be passing through.'

'Through Sedan? Not a chance. We're not going there, we'd be mad to.'

'She young, your sister?'

'She's the same age as me—I told you before, we're twins.'

'Does she look like you?'

'Yes, she's blonde too, oh! such soft curls!... And she's tiny, with such a slender face, and never loud with it, oh no!... Not my Henriette!'

'Are you very close?'

'Yes, yes...'

There was a pause, and looking at Maurice, Jean noticed that his eyelids were drooping, and he was about to fall over.

'Hey! My poor lad... Stand up, God help me!... Give me your rifle a moment, it'll give you a break... We're going to leave half the men behind at this rate, God knows we can't go any further today!'

He'd just spotted Oches opposite, with its tumbledown houses few and far between ranged upon a hillside. The village was dominated by the yellow church, perched high up among the trees.

'That's where we'll be sleeping, I'll be bound.'

He'd guessed right. Seeing how very weary his troops were, General Douay had given up hope of ever reaching Besace that day. What decided him above all, though, was the arrival of the convoy, that troublesome supply train he'd been dragging behind him since Rheims, which had hampered the march so badly with its three leagues of wagons and livestock. In Quatre-Champs he'd given the order for it to head straight for Saint-Pierremont; and only at Oches did the teams of horses join up with the army corps, in such a state of exhaustion that the animals refused to go any further. It was already five o'clock. Apprehensive about entering Stonne Gorge, the general thought it best to abandon the plan to complete the march as the Marshal had instructed. They halted and set up camp, with the convoy standing in the meadows below, guarded by a division, while the artillery established itself on the hillsides behind, and the brigade which was to act as the rearguard the next day kept to the high ground, facing Saint-Pierremont. Another division, which included the Bourgain-Desfeuilles brigade, bivouacked on a wide plateau bordered by an oak wood, behind the church.

Such was the confusion over choosing places to camp that by the time the 106th was finally able to install itself on the edge of the wood, night was already falling .

'Damn this!' said Chouteau furiously. 'I'm not eating, I'm going to sleep!'

The others echoed his complaint. Many hadn't even the strength to put up their tents, and fell asleep where they dropped, like dead weights. In any case, for them to eat, there would have to have been a distribution from supplies; and with the supply corps waiting for the 7th on ahead at Besace, it certainly wasn't at Oches. Things had become so slack, and discipline so poor, that no one even bothered sounding the bugle to summon the corporals. It was every man for himself. From then on, no more rations were distributed, and the soldiers had to live off the provisions they were meant to have in their bags; but their bags were empty, few even found a crust, the crumbs left over from the plenty that they'd ended up with in Vouziers. There was coffee; and the least tired among them again drank it without sugar.

When Jean turned round to share one of his biscuits with Maurice, while he ate the other, he found him fast asleep. For a moment he thought of waking him: then he stoically put the biscuits back at the bottom of his bag, taking the utmost care, as if he were hiding gold: and so he made do with coffee, like his comrades. He'd ordered the tent to be put up, and they were all lying in it when Loubet returned from an expedition, with some carrots he'd found in a nearby field. As it was impossible to cook them, the men crunched them raw; but they aggravated their hunger, and made Pache ill.

'No, no, let him sleep,' Jean told Chouteau, who was shaking Maurice to give him his share.

'Ah!' said Lapoulle. 'Tomorrow, when we're in Angoulême,* we'll have bread... I had a cousin who was a soldier in Angoulême. Good garrison.'

They were stunned. Chouteau cried,

'What do you mean, Angoulême?... What a prize idiot, he thinks he's in Angoulême!'

And it was impossible to get any explanation from Lapoulle. He thought they were going to Angoulême. That morning, when they'd seen the Uhlans, it had been he who'd insisted that they were Bazaine's soldiers.

So the camp sank into inky darkness and a deathly silence. In spite of the cool night air, they'd been forbidden to light fires. They knew that the Prussians were only a few kilometres away, and even noises were hushed, for fear of raising the alarm. The officers had already warned their men that they would be leaving at about four in the morning, to make up for lost time; and everyone made haste and slept gluttonously, thoroughly worn out. The heavy breathing of these masses of men rose up into the shadows above the scattered encampments, like the breathing of the earth itself.

Suddenly, a shot woke the squad. The darkness was still dense, it must have been about three o'clock. Everyone got to their feet, the alarm grew closer, and they all thought it was an enemy attack. But it was only Loubet, who'd woken up and decided to go foraging in the oak wood, where there were bound to be a few rabbits: what a feast, if he could bring back a pair for his comrades at first light! However, as he was searching for a good place to hide, he heard men approaching, talking and stepping on branches, and he took fright and let off a shot, thinking it was Prussians he was dealing with.

Maurice, Jean, and the others were already drawing near when a hoarse voice cried out,

'For God's sake, don't shoot!'

There, at the edge of the wood, stood a tall, skinny man with a thick, bushy beard that all but obscured his face. He was wearing a grey smock, with a red belt round his waist and a rifle slung over his shoulder. Immediately, he explained that he was French, a sergeant in the guerrillas, and that he'd come from Dieulet Wood with two of his men to give some information to the general.

'Oy! Cabasse! Ducat!' he shouted, turning round. 'Oy! Come on, then, you lazy bastards!'

The other two were probably scared, but they approached all the same. Ducat was short, fat and pale with wispy hair, and Cabasse was a tall, brusque man, with a tanned face and a long nose shaped like a knife-blade.

Meanwhile, Maurice had been looking closely at the sergeant in surprise. Finally he asked,

'Tell me, aren't you Guillaume Sambuc, from Remilly?'

And when the man looked worried, and after some hesitation said that yes, he was, Maurice took a small step back, for this man Sambuc was a notorious villain. He was the legitimate son of a family of woodcutters which had gone to the dogs, with a drunkard for a father, who'd been found one evening in a corner of the wood with his throat cut, while mother and daughter turned to begging and stealing for a living, before disappearing and ending up in some brothel. As for Guillaume, he'd turned poacher and smuggler; only one of this wolf's litter had grown up an honest man, and that was Prosper, the African Chasseur, who had taken work as a farmhand, because he hated the forest, before getting the chance to become a soldier.

'I saw your brother at Rheims and Vouziers,' said Maurice. 'He's well.'

Sambuc made no reply. Then to cut the conversation short, he said,

'Take me to the General. Tell him that some guerrillas from Dieulet Wood are here with some important information for him.'

As they returned to camp, Maurice thought about these guerrilla companies, in whom so much hope had been placed and who were already the cause of complaints from all over the region. They were meant to be waging ambush warfare, waiting in the hedgerows for the enemy, harassing it, killing its lookouts and holding the woods so that not a single Prussian could get out. The truth of it was that they were beginning to terrorize the peasants, affording them poor defence and ransacking their fields. Out of loathing for the regular army service, all the deranked soldiers hastened to join up, glad to have escaped from the discipline and to be roaming the bushes like marauding bandits, sleeping and wandering wherever the road led them. Some of these companies' recruits were truly deplorable.

'Oy, Cabasse! Oy, Ducat!' repeated Sambuc, turning round to call out at every step. 'Move it, you pair of gits!'

Maurice sensed that the other two were also dangerous men. Cabasse, the tall, harsh-featured man, had been born in Toulon, and worked as a waiter in a café in Marseilles, then ended up in Sedan as a travelling salesman, selling goods from the south, and he'd had a close brush with the police over a theft which had never been cleared up. Ducat, the short, fat one, was a former bailiff from Bainville, who'd been forced to sell off his practice after a series of unsavoury incidents involving little girls; he'd just risked the court of assizes again, for the same filth, at Raucourt, where he kept the books in a factory. He could quote Latin, while the other could barely read; but the two made a pair, all right, an unsettling pair of shady characters.

Camp was already stirring. Jean and Maurice took the guerrillas to Captain Beaudoin, who led them to Colonel de Vineuil. He questioned them; but Sambuc was very conscious of his rank and insisted on talking to the general; and when General Bourgain-Desfeuilles, who'd slept at the house of the Oches curate, appeared in the presbytery doorway, morose because he'd had to get up in the middle of the night to spend yet another day of famine and fatigue, he gave a furious welcome to the men who had been brought to him.

'Where have they come from? What do they want?... Oh! It's you lot, from the guerrillas! More hobblers, eh?'

'Sir,' explained Sambuc, unperturbed, 'we and our comrades are occupying Dieulet Wood...'

'Dieulet Wood? Where's that, then?'

'Between Stenay and Mouzon, sir.'

'Stenay, Mouzon, never heard of 'em! How am I supposed to get my bearings, with all these new names?'

Embarrassed, Colonel de Vineuil discreetly intervened, to remind him that Stenay and Mouzon were on the Meuse, and that, as the Germans had cut off the first of these towns, they were going to cross the river using the bridge at Mouzon, further north.

'Anyway, sir,' continued Sambuc, 'we came to warn you that Dieulet Wood is full of Prussians right now... When the 5th Corps was leaving Bois-les-Dames yesterday, there was a bit of a scuffle over near Nouart.'

'What! Fighting, yesterday?'

'Oh yes, sir, the 5th Corps withdrew fighting, and it must be in Beaumont by now... So, while a few comrades have gone to let them know what the enemy's up to, us lot thought we'd come and tell you how things stand, so you can come and help, because the 5th's going to find itself with sixty thousand men on its hands tomorrow, and that's a sure bet.'

General Bourgain-Desfeuilles shrugged at the figure.

'Sixty thousand men, go on! Why not make it a hundred thousand?... You're dreaming, lad. Fear's making you see double. There can't be sixty thousand men so near us, we'd know it if there were.'

And he stood firm. In vain, Sambuc called upon Ducat and Cabasse to back him up.

'We've seen the cannons,' confirmed the Provençal. 'Those sods must be raving mad, risking them on these forest roads, the mud's almost knee-deep after all this rain the past few days.'

'Someone's guiding them, no doubt about it,' declared the former bailiff.

But since Vouziers, the general had lost faith in this story of the two converging German armies that they'd been harping on to him about, as he put it. And he didn't even judge it relevant to have the guerrillas taken to the commander of the 7th Corps, although the men were convinced they'd just spoken to the man himself. Well, if they'd listened to every peasant and prowler claiming to bring them information, they couldn't have set foot outside their tents without getting caught up in God knows what. However, since they knew the area, he ordered the three men to stay and accompany the column.

'All the same,' said Jean to Maurice, as they went back to fold up the tent, 'they're good blokes, coming four leagues cross-country to warn us.'

The young man agreed, and thought they were right to do so; he too knew the area, and was tormented by mortal dread when he thought about the Prussians being in Dieulet Wood, moving towards Sommauthe and Beaumont. He sat down, exhausted already, before they'd even begun to march, his stomach empty, his chest tight with anxiety, as morning dawned on the day that he knew was going to be a terrible one.

Despairing to see him so pale, the corporal asked him with fatherly concern,

'Still no good, eh? Is it your foot again?'

Maurice shook his head. His foot was much better, in his wide boots.

'Are you hungry, then?'

And seeing that he couldn't answer, Jean secretly took one of his two biscuits from his bag; and telling a simple lie, he said,

'Here, I saved yours for you... I ate the other one just now.'

It was growing light when the 7th Corps left Oches and began the march to Mouzon through Besace, where it should have stopped for the night. The troublesome convoy had already left, accompanied by the 1st Division; and if the wagons which were firmly harnessed up proceeded at a brisk pace, the others, requisition wagons, empty and useless for the most part, made particularly slow progress up the slopes of Stonne Gorge. The road was uphill, especially once they'd passed the hamlet of Berlière, nestling between the wooded hills which rose above it. At about eight o'clock, the moment when the other two divisions finally set off, Marshal MacMahon appeared, and was exasperated to find that troops he'd presumed to have left Besace that morning were in fact still there, when they'd only have had a few kilometres to go to reach Mouzon. So he had a heated argument with General Douay. It was decided that the 1st Division and the convoy would be allowed to continue their march to Mouzon, but that, to avoid the cumbersome, slow-moving vanguard causing any more delay for the other two divisions, they'd take the Raucourt and Autrecourt road, in order to cross the Meuse at Villers. Yet again they were heading northwards, as the Marshal hastened to put the river between his army and the enemy. They must be on the right bank by evening, at all costs. And the rearguard was still at Oches when, from a distant hilltop, near Saint-Pierremont, a Prussian battery fired, playing the same game they'd started the day before. At first they made the mistake of firing back, but then the last troops withdrew.

Until almost eleven o'clock, the 106th slowly followed the winding road along the floor of Stonne Gorge, between the high knolls. To the left rose high summits, bare and craggy, while gentler slopes to the right were covered with woodland. The sun had reappeared and it was very hot in the narrow valley, where the solitude hung heavily over them. Beyond Berlière, which was dominated by a tall, mournful cross, there wasn't a single farm, not a soul, not a single animal grazing in the pastures. And the men, who were already so tired, and had been starving since the day before, who'd hardly slept and had nothing to eat, were already beginning to drag their feet, their courage gone, and anger brimming up inside them.

Then, abruptly, as they halted at the roadside, the cannon boomed out over to the right. The retort sounded so loud and clear that the fighting couldn't be more than two leagues away. The effect it had upon these men, tired of withdrawing, edgy from all the waiting, was extraordinary. All stood trembling, their fatigue forgotten: why weren't they marching? They wanted to get in there, anything rather than carry on running away as the army dissolved, never knowing where to or why.

General Bourgain-Desfeuilles had in fact just climbed up onto a hillock on the right, taking Colonel de Vineuil with him to look at the lie of the land. They could see them, in between two small woods, field glasses trained on the countryside; and they at once dispatched an aide-de-camp who was with them, to say that the guerrillas were to be sent to them, if they were still there. A few men, Jean, Maurice, and some others, accompanied them, in case they needed help.

As soon as the general caught sight of Sambuc, he shouted,

'Damn country, all these endless bloody hills and woods... Listen, where is it, where's the fighting?'

Sambuc, with Ducat and Cabasse close on his heels, looked at the vast horizon for a moment, without answering. And nearby, Maurice stared too, transfixed by the woods and valleys which unfurled for leagues around. It was an infinite ocean, full of huge, slow waves. The forests formed dark green splashes on the yellow countryside, while beneath the burning sun, the distant hills lay submerged beneath a russet haze. And although they could see nothing, not even a trace of smoke in the clear sky, still the cannon boomed, like the distant, gathering roar of a storm.

'That's Sommauthe, on the right,' said Sambuc eventually, pointing to a high hilltop, crowned with greenery. 'There's Voncq, on the left... It's Beaumont where they're fighting, sir.'

'Yes, Varniforêt or Beaumont,' confirmed Ducat.

The general mumbled under his breath.

'Beaumont, Beaumont, you never know in this blasted place.'

Then, aloud, he said,

'And how far away's this Beaumont then?'

'About ten kilometres, if you take the Le Chesne to Stenay road which goes past over there.'

The cannonfire went on, and seemed to be approaching from west to east, like a relentless rumbling of thunder. Sambuc added,

'Blast me! It's hotting up... I thought this would happen, I warned you this morning, sir: it's those batteries we saw in Dieulet Woods, mark my words. The 5th Corps must have the whole army that's come from Buzancy and Beauclair on its hands right this very minute.'

There was a pause, and far away the battle rumbled louder than ever. Maurice felt a furious urge to cry out, and gritted his teeth. Why weren't they marching towards the cannon right now, instead of doing all this talking? He'd never felt so exhilarated. Each shot echoed through his breast, lifting him up, making him want to be there at once, be part of it, get it over with. Were they going to pass this battle by yet again, brush past it, and not fire a shot? What a swindle, dragging them around like this, always running away, ever since war had been declared! At Vouziers, all they'd heard was gunfire from the rearguard. At Oches, the enemy had simply fired cannon at them from behind for a bit. And they were going to run, they wouldn't be racing off to help their comrades this time, either! Maurice looked at Jean, who like him was very pale, with feverish, glittering eyes. At the violent boom of the cannon, hearts leapt in every breast.

But there was further delay as one of the general staff came climbing the narrow path up the hillock. It was General Douay, rushing up, looking worried. And, when he'd personally interrogated the guerrillas, he let out a cry of despair. Even if he had been warned that morning, what could he have done? The Marshal's wishes were quite explicit: the Meuse must be crossed before evening, come what may. And then, now that they were all spread out and marching towards Raucourt, how could he reassemble the troops and direct them swiftly towards Beaumont? Surely they'd get there too late? The 5th Corps must already be in retreat near Mouzon; and the cannon showed this quite clearly, progressing further and further eastwards, like a hurricane full of hail and disaster, moving on and away. General Douay raised his arms in frustration above the line of the vast horizon, with its hills and valleys, fields and forests, furious at his own impotence; and the order was given to continue marching to Raucourt.

Oh! What a march that was, through Stonne Gorge, between the high ridges, while to the right, beyond the woods, the cannon went on booming! At the head of the 106th, Colonel de Vineuil sat bolt upright upon his horse, his face stiff and pale and his eyelids fluttering, as if blinking back tears. Captain Beaudoin chewed silently on his moustache, while Lieutenant Rochas swore under his breath, muttering curses at himself and everyone else. And the soldiers, even those who had no desire to fight, even the least courageous, felt a need to yell and strike out welling up inside them, and with it anger at their continual defeat, and rage that yet again they were making off with heavy, unsteady steps, while down below those damn Prussians were slitting their comrades' throats.

Just below Stonne, where the winding path descends between small knolls, the road widened and the troops began crossing vast expanses, broken up by clumps of trees. Since leaving Oches, the 106th, now in the rearguard, had been expecting to be attacked at any minute; for the enemy was following the columns step by step, keeping a close eye on it, no doubt watching for the right moment to grab it by the tail. Cavalry units, taking advantage of the slightest fold in the terrain, tried to sneak up on its flanks. Several squadrons of the Prussian Guard were seen emerging from behind a wood; but when they saw the display put on by a Hussar regiment, clearing the road as it advanced, they stopped. And thanks to this respite, the retreat continued in quite an orderly fashion until they were nearing Raucourt, when they saw a spectacle which unsettled them more than ever, and demoralized the soldiers once and for all. Suddenly, coming along a road which cut across their route, they caught sight of a crowd rushing headlong, with officers wounded, soldiers scattering and unarmed, convoy wagons galloping along, men and beasts fleeing, the wind of disaster behind them. It was the debris from a brigade of the 1st Division, which was escorting the convoy and had left that morning for Mouzon, through Besace. After a wrong turning and a terrible stroke of bad luck, they and part of the convoy had fallen straight into the path of the routed 5th Corps, at Varniforêt, near Beaumont. Surprised and outnumbered, with their flank coming under attack, they'd fled, and their panic brought them back, bloodied, haggard, and half-mad, their terror making their comrades distraught. The tales they told sowed panic among the men, it was as if they'd been brought by the thunderous rumbling of the cannon, which had been heard, unceasingly, since midday.

And so the mood was fraught as they passed through Raucourt, in dread and disarray. Should they turn right towards Autrecourt, so they could cross the Meuse at Villers, as planned? General Douay, troubled and hesitant, was afraid of finding the bridge blocked, perhaps already in Prussian hands. He preferred to carry straight on, along Haraucourt Pass, in order to reach Remilly before nightfall. After Mouzon, Villers, and after Villers, Remilly: still they retreated,

with the Uhlans galloping after them. There were only six kilometres still to go, but it was already five o'clock, and they could
barely stand! They had been on their feet since daybreak, it had
taken twelve hours to cover barely three leagues, shuffling along,
exhausted by the endless hanging around, filled with acute dread and
fear. The men had hardly slept for the past two nights, and they
hadn't eaten their fill since Vouziers. They were fainting from hunger. In Raucourt, they made a pitiful sight.

It was a rich little town, with numerous factories, a broad street
with fine buildings on either side, and a charming little church and
town hall. However, the night which the Emperor and Marshal
MacMahon had spent there* had completely drained its resources,
with all the clutter of the staff and the imperial household, and then
the whole of the 1st Corps passing through, flowing down the road
all morning like some river, emptying the bakeries and the grocers',
even sweeping the crumbs from the houses of the well-to-do. They
found no bread, no wine, no sugar, nothing either to eat or drink.
There had been ladies standing at their front doors, handing out
glasses of wine and mugs of soup, draining barrels and saucepans
right down to the very last drop. But all that was over, and when the
first regiments of the 7th Corps began filing through at about three
o'clock, there was utter despair. What? Still more of them? Was it
starting all over again? Once more, the broad street ferried past
exhausted men, covered in dust, dying of hunger, and there wasn't a
mouthful of food left to give them. Many stopped and knocked on
doors, arms stretched out towards the windows, begging someone to
throw them a crust of bread. And women began sobbing, gesturing
that they couldn't, they had nothing left to give.

On the corner of the Rue des Dix-Potiers, Maurice grew dizzy,
and reeled. When Jean began to fuss, he said,

'No, leave me, I'm finished... I'd rather die here.'

He collapsed onto a milestone. The corporal pretended to be
harsh, like an angry boss.

'Bloody hell! How pathetic can you get? Do you want to get picked
up by the Prussians? Come on, get up!'

Then, seeing that the young man could no longer answer and had
turned ashen, his eyes shut, only semi-conscious, Jean swore again,
but this time in a voice of infinite pity.

'Bloody hell! Bloody hell!'

Running to a nearby fountain he filled his mess-tin with water, and came back to bathe Maurice's face. Then, making no attempt this time to conceal what he was doing, he took from his bag his last biscuit, saved with such care, and began to break it into little pieces and push them between Maurice's teeth. The starving man opened his eyes, and devoured them.

'But what about you?' he asked suddenly, remembering. 'Didn't you eat it after all?'

'Oh!' said Jean, 'I'm a tough old bird, me, I can wait... All I need is a good dose of pond nectar, and I'll be right as rain!'

He went to fill up his mess-tin again, and drained it at one go, smacking his lips. And he too had a pale, hollow look about him, so consumed by hunger that his hands trembled.

'Off we go! Come on, lad, we've got to catch up with the others.'

Maurice leaned against Jean's arm, and let himself be led like a child. No woman's arm had ever given him such a warm glow. With everything collapsing around him, in the midst of utter misery, with death staring him in the face, it brought him a delicious sense of comfort to feel someone loving him and looking after him; and per-haps the idea that the heart which was all his own belonged to a simple man, a peasant who'd kept close to the earth—someone who'd at first repulsed him—now added unutterable sweetness to his sense of gratitude. Wasn't this the brotherly love that existed in those first days of the world, the friendship which rose above all culture, all class, the friendship of two men, united as a single soul by their mutual need for help, confronted by hostile Nature? He could hear his humanity beating in Jean's breast, and he was proud for himself, feeling it beat more strongly, giving him succour and devo-tion; while Jean, without analysing what he felt, was full of joy, protecting his friend's grace and intelligence—qualities which in him had remained rudimentary. Ever since the violent death of his wife, snatched from him by a terrible tragedy, he'd thought he'd a heart of stone, and had sworn never again to look upon the creatures who bring so much suffering, even when they aren't bad in them-selves. And for both men, this friendship grew into a sort of expan-sion of the soul: they didn't embrace, yet they touched deep inside, they were one and the same, however different they might be, upon that terrible road to Remilly, one supporting the other, merged now into a single being, full of suffering and pity.

As the rearguard was leaving Raucourt, the Germans began entering the town at the other end; and two of their batteries were immediately put into position on the high ground, to the left, and opened fire. At that moment the 106th, coming down the road which ran alongside the river Emmane, found itself in the line of fire. One shell sliced through a poplar tree on the river's edge; another buried itself in the meadow next to Captain Beaudoin, failing to explode. But the gorge closed in as it neared Haraucourt, and they were squashed into the narrow corridor, dominated on either side by tree-covered ridges; if a mere handful of Prussians had prepared an ambush up there, there was bound to be a disaster. With shells falling on their tail and the threat of a possible attack to the right and left of them, the troops now advanced, overcome by a sinking sense of dread, in a hurry to get out of this dangerous gorge. It rekindled a final burst of energy in even the weariest of them. Soldiers who only a while before had been trudging from one door to the next through Raucourt, began to push on, cheerful, lively again, urged on by danger's stinging spurs. Even the horses seemed to realize that a single minute wasted might cost them dear. And the head of the column must have been in Remilly when the march was suddenly brought to a halt.

'Bloody hell!' said Chouteau. 'They're not going to leave us here, are they?'

The 106th hadn't yet reached Haraucourt, and still the shells kept raining down.

As the regiment marked time, waiting to set off again, a shell exploded to the right; luckily, no one was injured. Five endless, excruciating minutes trickled by. Still they didn't budge, some obstacle was blocking the road ahead, some wall which had suddenly sprung up. And the colonel watched, standing up in the stirrups, and trembled, sensing rising panic among the men behind him.

'Everyone knows we've been betrayed,' burst out Chouteau angrily.

And then muttering broke out, a continuous, growing, exasperated growl as fear cracked the whip. Yes! Yes! They'd been brought here to be betrayed and handed over to the Prussians. In the face of such relentless misfortune, with mistakes made on such an excessive scale, to their blinkered minds treason was the only possible explanation left for such a string of disasters.

'We've been betrayed!' repeated panic-stricken voices.

Loubet got carried away.

'It's the Emperor, that's who it is up there, the swine, come to stop us, blocking up the road with all his baggage!'

Immediately, the word spread. It was confirmed—the obstruction was due to the imperial household passing by, moving through the column. And it brought on a wave of loathing and abominable remarks, all the hatred which the Emperor's servants inspired, taking over the towns where they slept, unpacking all their provisions, their basketloads of wine, their silver plate, in front of soldiers who had nothing left, stoking up fires in the kitchens while these poor devils were tightening their belts! Oh! This wretched Emperor, stripped now of his throne and his command, like a child lost in his own Empire, carted off like a useless package, in among the baggage of his troops, condemned to drag with him the irony of his ceremonial entourage, his household guards, his carriages, his horses, his cooks, his wagons, all the pomp of his court mantle, embroidered with bees, sweeping through the blood and the mud on the high roads to defeat!

Two more shells fell, one after the other. Lieutenant Rochas's képi was blown off in the blast. The ranks closed in and there was a surge, a sudden wave which sent out wide ripples. There were strangled cries and Lapoulle shouted angrily for them to advance. One minute more, perhaps, and there would be an appalling catastrophe, a stampede which would trample the men at the end of this corridor, in a furious crush.

The colonel turned round, his face very pale.

'Lads, lads, let's be patient. I've sent someone on to have a look... We're about to march on...'

But they weren't marching on, and the seconds seemed like centuries. Jean had already taken hold of Maurice's hand again, full of a fine, brave feeling of calm, whispering to him that if the comrades surged forward, the two of them would leap to the left, and climb up into the woods on the other side of the river. He glanced around to see if he could spot the guerrillas, thinking that they must know the roads round here; but someone told him they'd disappeared as they were marching through Raucourt. And all of a sudden they began moving again, rounding a bend in the road, and were safe from the German batteries. Later they learned that, in the chaos of that awful day, it had been the Bonnemain division—four cavalry regiments—which had cut across the path of the 7th Corps and brought it to a standstill.

Night was falling when the 106th marched through Angecourt. There were still hills on the right; but to the left the gorge began to widen, and a bluish valley appeared in the distance. At last, from the heights at Remilly, through the evening mists, they saw a pale, silver ribbon lying among the massive, rolling country of fields and meadows. It was the Meuse, the longed-for Meuse, where victory seemed sure to dwell.

And stretching his arm towards the tiny, far-off lights, springing up gaily among the greenery down in the fertile valley, which had such sweet charm in the soft twilight, Maurice said to Jean, with the joyous relief of a man returning to a beloved country,

'Look! Down there... That's Sedan!'

CHAPTER SEVEN

In Remilly, a terrifying jumble of men, horses, and carts stood blocking the road which wound down to the Meuse. Halfway down, outside the church, some of the cannon wheels had become entangled, and no amount of cursing and bumping could get them to budge. Below, near the mill, where a waterfall rumbled from the Emmane, a whole line of upturned carts lay in the way; and an endless flow of soldiers built up, hammering at the door of the Hôtel de la Croix de Malte, in the vain search for a glass of wine.

The furious surge of men made its way to join the crush further on, at the village's southernmost point, separated from the river by a clump of trees, where that morning the sappers had constructed a pontoon bridge. To the right was a ferry, and set in the long grass was the ferryhouse, solitary, with fading paintwork. Large fires had been lit on either bank and the flames, stoked up from time to time, would set the night on fire, illuminating the water and riverbanks with a glow as bright as day. Then the enormous bottleneck of soldiers could be seen waiting, but the footbridge would only let two men over at a time, and on the pontoon itself, which at its widest was only three metres across, cavalry, artillery and pack-horses filed across, at an infernally slow pace. They said that there was still a brigade there from the 1st Corps, a munitions convoy, not counting the four cavalry regiments of the Bonnemain division. And behind them came the whole of the 7th Corps, thirty-odd thousand men, believing the enemy on their heels, hurrying fearfully to reach the safety of the far bank.

For a moment, they were filled with despair. What? On the march since morning, nothing to eat, only just managed to get themselves out of that terrible place, Haraucourt Gorge, by running hell for leather—all that, just to come up against an insurmountable wall, into all this panic, all this disarray! The last to arrive might not see their turn come for hours; and every man was well aware that even if the Prussians dared not continue their pursuit by night, they'd still be there at daybreak. However, they were ordered to stack arms, and set up camp on the vast, bare hillsides, whose slopes, bordered by the Mouzon road, ran down to the meadows of the Meuse. At the rear, high on a plateau, the reserve artillery prepared for battle and trained its guns on the gorge, so that if need be, it could fire onto the exit. And the waiting began again, full of rebellion and fear.

Meanwhile, the 106th had installed itself above the road in a stubble-field overlooking the vast plain. The men had abandoned their rifles with some regret, glancing back over their shoulders, haunted by the fear of attack. All were silent, their expressions set and impassive, merely grumbling a few angry words under their breath every now and then. It was not far off nine o'clock, they'd been there for two hours; and even though they were exhausted, many were unable to sleep and lay shivering on the ground, listening out for the faintest noise in the distance. They no longer fought against the hunger which gnawed at them: they would eat over there, on the other side of the water, and if there wasn't anything else, they'd eat grass. But the congestion just seemed to get worse, the officers that General Douay had posted near the pontoon came back every twenty minutes with the same infuriating news—that it would take hours yet. In the end, the general decided to force a path down to the pontoon himself. They could see him in the crowd, battling his way through, speeding up the march.

Maurice, sitting leaning against an embankment with Jean, again pointed north.

'Sedan's right at the bottom... And look, there's Bazeilles... And then Douzy, and then Carignan on the right... No doubt that's where we'll be joining forces, at Carignan... Oh! if only it were light, you'd see just how big it all is.'

And the sweep of his hand took in the immense valley, full of darkness. The sky was not so black that they couldn't trace the river's pale course through the dark, unfurling meadows. Groups of trees formed more substantial masses, especially a row of poplars to the left, like some fantastical dyke obscuring the horizon. Then in the background, behind Sedan, which was studded with small, bright lights, the shadows lay heaped up, as if all the Ardennes forests had flung their curtain of hundred-year oak trees across it.

Jean's gaze returned to the pontoon bridge below them.

'Just look at that!... The whole lot's going to bugger over. We'll never get across.'

On either side of the river the fires were burning brighter, and their light was now so strong that the scene appeared before his panic-stricken eyes with all the vividness of a hallucination. The ferries supporting the timbers had gradually sunk beneath the weight of the cavalry and artillery which had been filing across since the morning, and so the roadway was now several inches below water. The cavalrymen were crossing now, two by two, in an unbroken line, emerging from the shadows on one bank to disappear into the shadows of the other; the bridge was no longer visible, they seemed to be walking on water, this violently lit water, with fire dancing on its surface. The horses advanced, neighing, manes bristling and legs stiff in terror at the ground shifting beneath them, as they felt it slipping away. Standing in the stirrups, pulling the reins in tight, over went the cavalry, over they went, draped in their long, white greatcoats, only their helmets showing, blazing red from the reflections. They might have been phantom horsemen, off to a war of shadows, with hair made of flames.

A low groan rose from Jean's tear-choked throat.

'Oh! I'm so hungry!'

Meanwhile, around them, the men had fallen asleep in spite of the gnawing at their bellies. Their weariness was too much, it overwhelmed their fear, laying them flat on their backs, mouths open, obliterated beneath the moonless sky. From one end of the bare slopes to the other, a deathly silence had fallen over the waiting men.

'Oh! I'm so hungry I could eat dirt!'

That was the cry that Jean, so hardened to misfortune and so silent, could hold back no longer, the cry he blurted out in spite of himself, delirious with hunger, after eating nothing for nearly thirty-six hours. Then, seeing that it would be another two or even three hours before their regiment would cross the Meuse, Maurice made a decision.

'Listen, I've got an uncle round here, you know, Uncle Fouchard, the one I told you about... He lives up there, about five or six hundred metres away, and I wasn't too sure; but if you're hungry... Damn it, old Fouchard will surely give us some bread !'

And he led his companion away, unprotesting. Old Fouchard's little farm stood at the exit from Haraucourt Gorge, near the plateau where the reserve artillery had taken up position. It was a low-slung house, with fairly large buildings, a barn, cowshed, and stables; and on the other side of the road, in a sort of shed, the peasant had installed his travelling butcher's trade, the abattoir where he himself killed the animals and then took them round the villages in his cart.

As they drew near, Maurice was surprised to see that not a single light was lit.

'Ah! The old miser, he'll have barricaded himself in, he won't open up.'

But then he saw something which stopped him dead. Outside the farm were a dozen soldiers, marauders, starving men, no doubt, out to see what they could find. At first they'd called out, then knocked; and now, seeing the house lying silent and in darkness, they began banging on the door with sticks, trying to force the lock. Loud voices shouted angry orders.

'Christ alive! C'mon, smash the bloody door in for me if there's no one home!'

Suddenly a shutter flew open in an attic skylight, and a tall old man in a smock appeared, bare-headed, with a candle in one hand and a rifle in the other. Beneath the shock of white hair was a square face, scored by long creases, and he had a strong nose, large, pale eyes, and a determined chin.

'So, you're thieves, are you, smashing everything up?' he shouted in a harsh voice. 'What do you want?'

The soldiers, a little nonplussed, began to back off.

'We're starving, we want something to eat.'

'I've nothing, not a crust... Do you think I keep enough to feed a hundred thousand men, just like that?... There were more of you this morning, oh yes! General Ducrot's bunch, up they came and took everything I had.'

One by one, the soldiers drew near.

'Open up anyway, we'll have a rest, you're sure to find something or other...'

And they were starting to hammer on the door again when the old man put his candle down on the ledge and shouldered his gun.

'As sure as there's a candle sitting there, I'll blow the head off the first man as lays a finger on my door!'

At that point it almost turned into a battle. Curses began to fly, a voice shouted that the peasant ought to get what was coming to him, he was just like all the rest, he'd rather chuck his bread down the well than give a single mouthful to a soldier. And the rifle barrels were turning on him, they were about to shoot him at almost point blank range; he didn't take a single step back, but stood there, stubborn and angry in the candlelight.

'Nothing at all! Not even a crust! They took everything I had!'

Frightened, Maurice threw himself forward, followed by Jean.

'Comrades, comrades...'

He turned the soldier's rifles aside; and looking up, pleaded,

'Look, see reason... Don't you recognize me? It's me.'

'Who's me?'

'Maurice Levasseur, your nephew.'

Old Fouchard picked up the candle. He probably did recognize him. But he persisted, intent on not even having to give up a glass of water.

'Nephew or no, how can I tell in this stinking darkness?... Piss off, the lot of you, or I'll shoot!'

'Even at me, Father?' came a loud voice all of a sudden, rising above the din.

The others stepped aside, and a sergeant apeared in the flickering candlelight. It was Honoré; his battery was less than two hundred metres away, and he'd been fighting the irresistible urge to come and knock at the door for two whole hours. He'd sworn never again to cross that threshold, and in all the four years he'd been in the service, he hadn't exchanged so much as a letter with the father he now called up to in such a curt manner. The marauding soldiers were already beginning to chatter excitedly, deciding what to do. The old man's son, and an officer, too! Nothing for it, it wasn't looking good, they'd better go look further afield! And off they ran, vanishing into the thick, black night.

When Fouchard realized that he'd been saved from pillage, he said simply, with no trace of emotion in his voice, as if he'd seen his son only the day before,

'Oh, it's you... Right! I'm on my way down.'

He took a long time about it. Inside, they could hear him locking and unlocking doors, going through the routine of a man making sure nothing's left lying around. Then, at last, the door opened, but only a crack, and sturdy fist kept it barely ajar.

'You—come in! And no one else!'

However, despite his obvious repugnance, he couldn't refuse his nephew shelter.

'Go on then, you as well!'

He tried ruthlessly to shut the door on Jean, and Maurice had to plead with him. But he wouldn't give way: no, no! He didn't need thieves and strangers in his shouse, wrecking his furniture! Finally Honoré rammed the door with his shoulder and got Jean inside, and the old man had to give in, muttering threats under his breath. He hadn't let go of his rifle. Then, when he'd led them into the main room and propped the rifle against the sideboard, placing the candle on the table, he lapsed into a stubborn silence.

'Come on, Father, we're starving hungry. Surely you can give us lot some bread and cheese, can't you?'

There was no reply, and he appeared not to have heard, repeatedly turning back to the window, listening to make sure that no other gangs had come to lay siege to his house.

'Look, Uncle, Jean's been a brother to me. He took the last crumbs from his own mouth for me. And we've been through so much together!'

He turned round, made sure nothing was missing, and didn't even look at them. Then he finally made up his mind, though still without saying a word. Suddenly he picked up the candle and left them in the dark, carefully locking the door behind him so that no one could follow. They heard him going down the stairs into the cellar. Again, he took a long time. And when he returned, barricading everything up again on his way, he placed a large loaf of bread and a cheese in the middle of the table, still silent; not that his anger had passed, mind you, this silence of his was no more than politic, for you never did know where talking might lead you. In any case, the three men threw themselves on the food and devoured it. All that could be heard was the furious sound of chewing.

Honoré got up and went to the sideboard to fetch a pitcher of water.

'Father, you could have let us have some wine.'

Calm now, and sure of himself, Fouchard found his tongue.

'Wine? None left, not a drop!... Those others, Ducrot's lot, drank me dry and ate me out of house and home!'

He was lying and despite his efforts, the way he kept blinking his large, pale eyes betrayed him. For the last two days he'd been making his livestock disappear, both the few beasts he used on the farm and those he kept for his butcher's trade; he led them away by night, and hid them God knows where, deep in some wood, or down an

abandoned quarry. And he'd just spent hours hiding away everything in his house—bread, wine, the least provisions, right down to
the flour and salt, so effectively, in fact, that it would have been
pointless to rifle through the cupboards. The house was quite empty.
He'd even refused to sell anything to the first soldiers who'd come
along. You never knew, a better occasion might come his way; and
hazy business schemes began sketching themselves out inside the
patient, wily old miser's head.

Maurice, who'd nearly eaten his fill, was the first to speak.

'And what about my sister, Henriette? Is it long since you've seen
her?'

The old man kept pacing up and down, glancing at Jean, who was
wolfing down great mouthfuls of bread; then, not bothering to hurry
himself, he said, as if after lengthy reflection,

'Henriette? Yes, I saw her in Sedan the other month... But I
caught sight of her husband Weiss this morning. He was with Monsieur Delaherche, who'd taken him in his carriage to see the army
crossing at Mouzon, for a spot of fun...'

A look of profound irony flickered over the peasant's impassive
features.

'Mind you, they may have seen too much of the army for their
liking, and maybe it wasn't so much fun after all; because the road's
been impassable since three o'clock, there's been so many soldiers
turning tail and blocking the way.'

In the same quiet, almost indifferent tone, he recounted some of
the details of the defeat of the 5th Corps, which had been taken by
surprise in Beaumont* just as the men were preparing their soup, and
been forced to retreat, sent packing by the Bavarians all the way back
to Mouzon. Some of the scattered soldiers passing through Remilly,
wild with panic, had shouted over to him that de Failly had sold
them out to Bismarck yet again. And Maurice thought back to the
panic-stricken marches they'd made over the last two days on Marshal MacMahon's orders, hastening the retreat, wanting to cross the
Meuse at all costs, after so many precious days had been lost because
of a hesitancy which was quite incomprehensible. It was too late. No
doubt the Marshal, who'd been so angry when he found the 7th
Corps at Oches instead of Besace where he'd imagined them to be,
must have been convinced that the 5th Corps was already camped at
Mouzon, when in fact it had been delayed, and been crushed at

Beaumont. But what could you demand of troops who'd been poorly led, who were so demoralized by all the waiting and running away, and who were dying of hunger and exhaustion?

Eventually, Fouchard went to stand behind Jean, astonished at the rate at which the mouthfuls were vanishing. In a cold, mocking voice he said,

'That better, then?'

The corporal looked up, and replied in the same no-nonsense, country manner,

'Getting there, thank you!'

Since they arrived, Honoré had stopped eating now and then, despite being so hungry, and turned his head, thinking he heard a noise. If he had, after a long struggle, broken his solemn oath never to set foot in this house again, it had been because of his irresistible desire to see Silvine. He kept the letter he'd received from her at Rheims beneath his shirt, tucked right against the skin—that tender letter, where she'd told him that she loved him, that she would never love anyone but him, in spite of the cruel past, in spite of Goliath and the little Charlot she'd borne him. He thought of nothing but her any more, and was worried not to have seen her yet, while steeling himself, so that he wouldn't betray his anxiety to his father. But his passion got the better of him, and in a voice which he forced to sound neutral, he asked,

'And Silvine—isn't she here any more?'

Fouchard glanced sidelong at his son, and glowed with secret mirth.

'Yes, she's here.'

Then he fell quiet, and spat at length; after a pause, the artillery-man was obliged to try again.

'Has she gone to bed, then?'

'Oh no, no.'

Finally, the old man deigned to explain that he'd been to Raucourt market that morning, in spite of it all, with his cart and his servant. Well, no reason for folks to stop eating meat, or for not going about your business, just because there's soldiers passing through. So, just like any other Tuesday, he'd taken a sheep and a quarter of beef that way; and he was just packing up when the 7th Corps arrived and landed him right in the middle of a dreadful fight. People were running and jostling. Afraid of having his horse and cart stolen, he'd gone, leaving Silvine behind, who'd just then been off doing the shopping in town.

'Oh, she'll be back all right!' he concluded in his quiet voice. 'She must have gone for shelter at Dr Dalichamp's, her godfather... She's a brave girl, all the same, even though she looks as if all she knows what to do is what you tell her... Oh yes, she's got some good qualities, that girl.'

Was he making fun of him? Did he want to explain why he'd kept this girl on, after she'd caused a rift between him and his son, and in spite of the Prussian's child, from whom she refused to be separated? Once again he gave that sidelong glance, and that silent laugh.

'Charlot's here, asleep in his room, so she won't be long.'

Honoré looked at his father, lips trembling, and he stared so hard that the old man started pacing up and down again. And then silence again, endless silence, while he mechanically cut himself more bread and went on eating. Jean, too, carried on, not feeling any need to speak. Maurice had eaten his fill and sat with his elbows on the table, looking at the furniture, the old sideboard, the old grandfather clock, dreaming of days gone by spent in Remilly with his sister Henriette, during the holidays. The minutes ticked past, the clock struck eleven.

'Hell!' he murmured. 'We mustn't let them leave without us!'

He went to open the window, and old Fouchard made no objection. Below him lay the whole valley, dark and hollow, a sea of shadows. When his eyes grew accustomed to the darkness, however, the pontoon bridge was clearly visible, lit up by the fires on either bank. Cavalrymen were still crossing, clad in their huge, white greatcoats, like phantom riders, whose horses walked on water, lashed by a wind of terror. And it was endless, interminable, forever at the same slow, dreamlike pace. To the right, the naked hillsides, where the army lay sleeping, still stood unstirring, amid a deathly hush.

'Oh well!' shrugged Maurice in despair. 'It'll be tomorrow morning, then.'

He left the window open, and old Fouchard seized his rifle and leapt over the window-sill, as agile as a young man. They heard him marching up and down for a moment, with a regular step, like a sentry; then, not a sound but the distant, heavy rumble from the overburdened pontoon bridge: no doubt he'd sat down by the roadside, his mind more at rest out there, where he could see danger coming, and be ready to bound back inside and defend his house.

Every minute, Honoré looked at the clock. He was growing more and more worried. It was only six kilometres from Raucourt to Remilly: barely more than an hour's walk for a sturdy young girl like Silvine. Why wasn't she back? It was hours since the old man had lost her, in the confusion caused by an entire army corps swamping the countryside and blocking the roads. There must surely have been some catastrophe; and he imagined her having a dreadful accident, lying lost out in a field somewhere, trampled by horses.

Suddenly, though, all three got up. They could hear someone running down the road, and they had just heard the old man cocking his gun.

'Who goes there?' shouted the latter roughly. 'Is that you, Silvine?'

There was no reply. He threatened to shoot, and repeated the question. Then a breathless, panting voice managed,

'Yes, yes, it's me, Fouchard.'

Then, without pausing, she asked,

'What about Charlot?'

'He's in bed, asleep.'

'Oh! Good, thank you.'

At once she stopped hurrying and heaved a great sigh, releasing all her worry and fatigue.

'Come in through the window,' Fouchard instructed. 'We've got company.'

And jumping into the room, she stood transfixed before the three men. In the flickering candlelight she stood there in front of them, with her deep, tanned skin, thick, black hair, lovely, big eyes, which were enough to give her beauty, and her oval face, full of strong, submissive calm. But at the same moment, the sudden sight of Honoré brought all the blood from her heart rushing to her cheeks; and yet, she wasn't surprised to find him there, because she'd thought about him, galloping back from Raucourt.

Choked and faint, he pretended to be perfectly unaffected.

'Good evening, Silvine.'

'Good evening, Honoré.'

Then, to stop herself bursting into tears, she looked away and smiled at Maurice, whom she'd only just recognized. Jean's presence made her uncomfortable. She was stifling, and took off the scarf from around her neck.

Honoré spoke again, but not in the familiar way he once had.

'We were worried about you, Silvine, what with all those Prussians coming.'

She suddenly grew pale again, devastation all over her face; and involuntarily glancing towards the room where Charlot was asleep, she waved her hand, as if she were trying to brush away the abominable vision, and murmured,

'Oh yes! The Prussians. Yes, I saw them.'

She collapsed, exhausted, on to a chair, and recounted how she'd sought refuge with her godfather, Dr Dalichamp, when the 7th Corps invaded Remilly, hoping that Fouchard would think of coming to pick her up there before he went home. The Grand-Rue was blocked by such a jostling crowd that not even a dog could have ventured out. And she'd waited more or less patiently until nearly four o'clock, shredding linen with some ladies; for the doctor, thinking that some of the wounded from Metz and Verdun would be sent to them if any fighting took place in the area, had been busy for the past two weeks, setting up a field hospital in the main room of the town hall. People arrived, saying they might need to make use of it immediately; and indeed, they'd heard the cannons booming since midday, over by Beaumont. But it was still a long way off, and they hadn't been afraid, when all at once, just as the last French soldiers were leaving Raucourt, a shell had landed with a terrifying crash, falling straight through the roof of a nearby house. Two more followed, launched by a German battery bombarding the rearguard of the 7th Corps. The wounded from Beaumont were already in the town hall, waiting for the doctor to come and operate on them, and they were scared that a shell might finish them off where they lay, on the straw mattresses. The injured began getting up, mad with terror, trying to go down into the cellars, in spite of the broken bones which made them shriek with pain.

'And then,' Silvine went on, 'don't ask me how, but suddenly it all went quiet... I climbed up at the window to look out onto the road and the area round about. I couldn't see a soul any more, not a single pair of red breeches, and then I heard these great, heavy footsteps; and a voice shouted something, and all the gun barrels hit the ground at the same time... There, at the end of the road, were little, dark men, all dirty they looked, with horrible big heads and helmets on, like our fire brigade. Someone told me they were Bavarians... Then, looking up, I saw, oh! thousands and thousands of them, streaming in from the roads and fields and woods, endless columns of them, packed tight together. All at once the countryside turned black with them. It was a black invasion,* they were like black grasshoppers, more and more of them, and before you could even blink, you couldn't even see the ground.'

She shuddered, and waved her hand again, brushing off the dreadful memory.

'And after that, we didn't have a clue what happened... Apparently, these men had been marching for three days, and they'd just fought like madmen at Beaumont. So they were starving hungry, their eyes were popping out of their heads, they looked half-crazy... The officers didn't even attempt to hold them back—they all went barging into houses and shops, breaking down doors and windows, smashing furniture, looking for food and drink and eating anything they could get their hands on. At Simmonot, the grocer's, I spotted one of them dipping his helmet into the bottom of a molasses barrel. Others were biting into sides of raw bacon. Others chewed flour. The place was already cleaned out, they told them, because soldiers had been coming through for the past forty-eight hours; but even so, they came across supplies which had no doubt been hidden; which made them determined to tear the lot apart, thinking that food was being kept from them. In less than an hour, they'd shattered the windows, plundered the cupboards and raided the cellars at the grocer's, the butcher's and baker's, and even in people's houses... At the doctor's, you can't imagine the like, I caught one big soldier eating all the soap. It was in the cellar that they caused the most damage, though. You could hear them from upstairs, howling like dogs, smashing all the bottles, opening the taps on all the barrels, and all the wine came pouring out like a fountain. They came up with their hands all red from squelching around in the wine they'd spilt all over the place. . . And I tell you, this'll show you what they're like when they start behaving like savages, Monsieur Dalichamp tried in vain to stop a soldier drinking a litre of opium syrup he'd found. The poor man'll be dead now, for sure, for he was in such pain when I left!'

A violent tremor ran through her, and she put her hands over her eyes, to block out the picture in her mind's eye.

'No! Oh no! I've seen too much, it's choking me!'

Old Fouchard, who had stayed on the road, came closer and stood outside the window to listen; the tales of all this pillage troubled him: he'd been told that the Prussians paid good money for everything—surely they weren't about to turn into thieves now, were they? Maurice and Jean also grew excited, hearing such details about an enemy this girl had actually seen, whereas they hadn't managed to come face to face with it in a whole month of fighting; Honoré, meanwhile, sat pensively, mouth twisted in distress, eyes for her alone, thinking only of the old unhappiness which had parted them.

But at that moment, the door to the next room opened and little Charlot appeared. He must have heard his mother's voice, and ran up to her in his nightshirt for a kiss. Pink and blond and very sturdy, he had a shock of pale, curly hair and big, blue eyes.

Silvine shivered, seeing him there so suddenly, as if surprised by the image he called up in her. Didn't she know this beloved child of hers any more, to look on him with such terror, as if he were the very embodiment of her nightmare? Then she burst into tears.

'My poor little one!'

And she hugged him passionately to her, clutching him to her neck, while a pale Honoré noted the extraordinary resemblance between Charlot and Goliath: he could see that same square, blond head, all the features of the Germanic race in a fine, healthy infant frame, all fresh-faced and smiling. The Prussian's son, 'the Prussian' as the wags in Remilly called him! And there was his French mother, hugging him to her breast, still shaking and torn from the sight of the invasion!

'My poor little one, come on, be good, back to bed!... Time for bye-byes, my poor little one!'

She carried him out of the room. Afterwards, when she came back, she'd stopped crying and recovered her calm expression, docile and full of courage.

It was Honoré who spoke first, a tremor in his voice.

'So, what about the Prussians...?'

'—Oh, yes! The Prussians... Well, they'd broken, pillaged, eaten, and drunk everything. And they were stealing linen, napkins, sheets, even curtains, ripping them into long strips to bandage their feet with. I saw some whose feet were just one big open wound, they'd walked so far. Outside the doctor's house, by the edge of a stream, there was a group of them who'd taken off their boots, and they were binding their heels with ladies' frilly blouses, probably stolen from that pretty Madame Lefèvre, the factory owner's wife... They plundered and plundered right until it was dark. The houses had no doors left, they just lay wide open to the street, all the doorways and windows on the ground floor gaping wide, and you could see bits of broken furniture inside, such a massacre, even the mildest person would have gone wild with rage... And I was like a mad woman, I couldn't stay a moment longer. It was no use them trying to hold me back, telling me all the roads were blocked and I'd get killed for sure, I left, and when I got out of Raucourt I ran straight for the fields on the right. There were loads of carts full of French and Prussians coming from Beaumont. Two of them passed quite close by me, in the darkness, and they were crying and groaning, and I just ran, oh! I ran and ran, through fields and woods, and I don't know where I went, I took a long way round, near Villers... Three times I hid, thinking I could hear soldiers. But the only person I met was another woman, she was running too, running away from Beaumont she was, and the things she told me made my hair stand on end... Anyway, I'm here now, and I'm so miserable, oh! I'm just so miserable!'

Once again, she was choked by tears. She was haunted, she couldn't stop thinking about it, repeating what the woman from Beaumont had told her. This lady, who lived on the main village street, had been watching the German artillery march down it since nightfall. A line of soldiers stood on each side bearing resin torches, lighting up the road with a red, fiery glow. And down the middle flowed the river of horses, cannons, and caissons, urged on at a hellish pace, at a furious gallop. This was the wild rush for victory, a diabolical pursuit of the French troops, hurrying to finish them off, hastening to crush them, down there in some dank ditch. They respected nothing, breaking everything, barging through regardless. Any horse which fell was immediately cut free of the harness, trampled and crushed, flung aside like bleeding wreckage. Men who wanted to cross over were knocked down too, and hacked to pieces beneath the wheels. In this hurricane, the starving drivers didn't even bother to stop, but just caught the loaves of bread chucked their way; while the torch-bearers held out sides of meat to them on the tips of their bayonets. Then, with the same blade, they pricked their horses' flanks, causing them to kick, terror-stricken, and gallop on faster. And the night drew in, and still the artillery drove past, to a violent, stormy crescendo and a frenzy of cheers.

Despite paying close attention to her story, Maurice was quite overcome by exhaustion, after this gluttony, and his head drooped forward on to the table, between his arms. Jean struggled to stay awake for a moment longer, and then he too gave up, and fell asleep at the other end of the table. Old Fouchard had gone back down to the road, and Honoré found himself alone with Silvine, now sitting motionless before the still wide-open window.

Then the sergeant rose and went over to the window. Outside, the night still lay vast and black, swollen by the laboured breathing of the troops. But more resonant sounds, of banging and squeaking, drifted up to him. Now the artillery was marching across the half-submerged pontoon below. Some of the horses reared up in fright, feeling the shift of the water. Some of the caissons half-slipped, and had to be thrown into the river. And seeing this retreat on to the far bank, so slow-moving and laborious, which had been going on since the day before and certainly wouldn't be complete by daybreak, the young man thought of that other artillery, whose savage torrent was sweeping full tilt through Beaumont, knocking over everything in its path, trampling over man and beast in order to go faster.

Honoré moved closer to Silvine, with these shadows, quivering, wild with fear, before him, and said softly,

'Are you unhappy?'

'Oh! Yes, I am!'

She sensed that he was about to talk about It, that abominable thing, and she lowered her head.

'Tell me, how did it happen?... I'd like to know...'

But she couldn't reply.

'Did he force you?... Did you consent?'

Then she stammered, in a strangled voice,

'God! I don't know, I swear I don't even know myself... But don't you see, it would be wrong of me to lie! And I can't excuse myself, oh no! I can't say he beat me... You'd gone, I was beside myself, and it just happened, I don't know how, I just don't know!'

She broke off in sobs, and he waited for a moment, pale, with a lump in his throat. But the idea that she didn't want to lie calmed him. He continued to ask questions, his head swimming with so many things he still couldn't comprehend.

'My father kept you on here, then?'

She didn't look up, growing calmer, recovering her brave air of resignation.

'I do my work, I never did cost much to feed, and now I've an extra mouth with me, he took advantage of it to lower my wages... Now he can be sure that I have to do whatever he orders me to.'

'But why did you stay?'

At once, she was so surprised that she looked up at him.

'Stay? Where could I go? At least here my little one and I have food, and no one bothers us.'

There was a renewed silence. Now they were looking into each other's eyes; and far away, across the dark valley, the whispering of the crowd drifted up to them louder than ever, while the cannons rumbled on and on across the pontoon. Through the shadows came a cry, a loud, lost human or animal cry, of boundless pity.

'Listen, Silvine,' began Honoré slowly, 'you sent me a letter which brought me great joy... I'd never have come back otherwise. But I read that letter again this evening, and there are things in it that no one could say better than you did...'

At first she paled, hearing him talk of this. Perhaps he was angry that she'd dared write to him, like some shameless woman. Then, as he explained, she went red all over.

'I know well enough that you don't want to lie, and that's why I believe what you put down on paper... Yes, I believe it utterly now... You were right to think that if I'd died in this war, without ever seeing you again, it would have caused me great pain, going like that, telling myself you didn't love me... And so, seeing as you still love me, seeing as you only ever loved me...'

He grew tongue-tied and lost for words, shaken by an extraordinary emotion.

'Listen, Silvine, if those filthy Prussians don't kill me, I still want you. Yes! we'll get married, as soon as I'm out of the army.'

She stood up, and fell into the young man's arms with a cry. She couldn't speak, all the blood in her veins went coursing to her cheeks. He sat down on the chair and took her onto his lap.

'I've thought long and hard about it, and this is what I came back here to tell you... If my father refuses to give us his blessing, we'll go away, the world's a big enough place... And as for your little one, well, we can't strangle him, can we, for God's sake? There'll be others, and I'll end up not knowing the difference, among all the rest.'

She was forgiven. She struggled to come to terms with such enormous happiness, and finally murmured,

'No, it can't be possible, it's too much. You might regret it one day. But how good you are, Honoré, and how I do love you!'

He silenced her with a kiss on the lips. And already she lacked the strength to refuse the joy coming to her, and all the happy life she had thought dead forever. With an involuntary, irresistible movement, she flung her arms around him, held him tight, and kissed him back, with all her strength as a woman, as if he were a regained possession, hers alone, and no one could ever take him away from her again. The man she had lost was hers once more, and she'd rather die than ever let him be taken from her again.

But just then a sound reached them, as the great tumult of the reveille filled the thick, black night. Orders were shouted, bugles rang out, and there was a great stirring from the naked lands, a moving, hazy sea, whose swell was already rushing down to the road. Below, the fires on either bank were almost out, and it was now impossible to see anything but a confused, shuffling mass; he couldn't even tell whether they were still crossing the river or not. And never had such dread, such terror, such panic come through the shadows.

Old Fouchard came to the window, shouting that they were leaving. Waking, shivering and numb, Maurice and Jean stood up. Honoré swiftly squeezed Silvine's hands in his own.

'I promise you... Wait for me.'

She was lost for words, and gazed at him with all her soul, in one long, last look, as he leapt out of the window at top speed to rejoin his regiment.

'Farewell, Father!'

'Farewell, son!'

And that was it, peasant and soldier took leave of each other just as they'd said their greeting, no embraces, a father and son who had no need to see each other to live their lives.

Once they, too, had left the farm, Maurice and Jean galloped back down the steep slopes. Below, the 106th wasn't where they'd left it; all the regiments were already on the move; and they had to run even further, and were sent all over the place looking for it. At last, with no idea where they were, surrounded by terrible confusion, they stumbled across their company, which was being led by Lieutenant Rochas; as for Captain Beaudoin and the regiment itself, no doubt they were elsewhere. And then Maurice was dumbstruck; he realized that the muddle of men, beasts, and cannon was leaving Remilly and retreating towards Sedan, along the road which followed the left bank. Now what? What was going on? They were no longer crossing the Meuse, but beating a retreat towards the north!

An officer from the Chasseurs, who was there for some reason which no one could explain, said aloud,

'Bloody hell! We should have buggered off on the 28th when we were at Le Chesne!'

Other voices explained what was happening, news was coming in. At about two o'clock that morning, one of Marshal MacMahon's aides-de-camp had come to tell General Douay that the entire army was under orders to withdraw to Sedan, and there wasn't a minute to lose. The 5th Corps, crushed at Beaumont, had taken three more corps with it into the jaws of disaster. At that moment the general, who was keeping watch near the pontoon, despaired to see that only his third division had crossed the river. Day would dawn, and they might be attacked at any moment. So he sent warning to all his commanders that they must each reach Sedan under their own steam, by the swiftest route. He himself, after abandoning the bridge and giving orders for it to be destroyed, made his way along the left bank with his second division and the reserve artillery; the third division, meanwhile, followed the right bank; and the first, broken up at Beaumont, in disarray, fled no one knew where. All that was left of the 7th Corps, which hadn't yet been into battle, was scattered sections, lost on the roads, galloping into the shadows.

It wasn't yet three, and the night was still dark. Even though he knew the countryside, Maurice didn't know where he was heading, unable to stop, caught up in the overflowing torrent, the terror-stricken crowd coursing down the road. Many of them, soldiers from every kind of unit, ragged, covered in blood and dust, had escaped from the crushing defeat at Beaumont, mingling with the regiments and sowing fear among the men. The same noises were carried up to them from the whole valley, across the river, the trampling of other herds, other flights, the 1st Corps, which had just left Carignan and Douzy, the 12th, which had left Mouzon along with the debris of the

5th; all of them shattered, swept along by the same logical, invincible force which had been pursuing the army north since the 28th, forcing it back down into the impasse where it was to perish.

However, as Beaudoin's company marched through Pont-Maugis, the first light of dawn appeared; and Maurice could see where he was now, with the Liry Hills on his left and the Meuse on his right, running alongside the road. But the grey dawn shed an infinitely sad light over Bazeilles and Balan, mere blurs across the plain; while a livid Sedan, Sedan, city of nightmares and mourning, rose up on the horizon, above the huge, dark curtain of the forest. And after Wadelincourt, when they'd at last reached the Porte de Tourcy, they had to negotiate, plead, grow angry, and practically lay siege to the city walls, before the governor would lower the drawbridge for them. It was five o'clock. The 7th Corps entered Sedan, reeling from cold, hunger, and exhaustion.

CHAPTER EIGHT

What with all the turmoil at the end of the Wadelincourt Road, on the Place de Tourcy, Jean got separated from Maurice; he ran about, getting lost among the trampling crush, but couldn't find him. It was really unfortunate, because he'd accepted the young man's offer to take him to his sister's house: there they'd rest, and even sleep in a proper bed. Everything was in such a mess, all the regiments were so mixed up, with no more marching orders and no commanders either, that the men were more or less free to do as they pleased. Once they'd had a few hours' sleep, there'd be time enough to get their bearings and rejoin their comrades.

Panicking, Jean found himself on the Tourcy viaduct overlooking the vast plains, which the governor had deliberately had flooded by the river. Then, making his way through another entrance to the city, he crossed the bridge over the Meuse, and it seemed to him that in spite of the dawn spreading across the sky, night was coming down again over this cramped town, squeezed between the ramparts, with its damp roads lined with tall houses. He couldn't even remember the name of Maurice's brother-in-law, all he knew was that his sister was called Henriette. Where should he go? Who could he ask? A mechanical movement was the only thing that kept his feet propelling him forward, and he knew that if he stopped, he'd fall over. Like a drowning man, all he could hear was a dull, droning sound, all he could distinguish was the continuous, babbling flood of men and beasts sweeping him along. Having eaten at Remilly, lack of sleep was what bothered him the most; and around him, yet again, tiredness was triumphing over hunger, as the herd of shadows stumbled through the unfamiliar streets. At each step, a man would collapse onto the pavement and roll into a doorway, where he would fall asleep, sprawled out like the dead.

Looking up, Jean read a street sign on the wall: Avenue de la Sous-Préfecture. At the end of it was a monument, standing in a garden. And on the corner of the avenue, he caught sight of a trooper, a Chasseur, whom he thought he recognized. Wasn't that Prosper, the lad from Remilly he'd seen at Vouziers with Maurice? He'd dismounted and his horse was haggard, wobbly on its feet, suffering from such hunger that it was reaching out to eat the planks of a wagon parked by the side of the road. For two days now, the stores had issued no feed for the horses, and they were dying of exhaustion. His large teeth made a rasping noise against the wood, while the Chasseur just stood and cried.

Jean started to walk away, then turned back, thinking that the lad must know where Maurice's relations lived, but he could no longer see him. Despair swept over him, he wandered from one street to another, found himself outside the Sous-Préfecture and pushed on as far as the Place Turenne. There, for a moment, he thought he'd been saved when he spotted Lieutenant Rochas standing outside the town hall, right at the foot of the statue, together with some of the men from his company. If he couldn't find his friend, he'd go back to the regiment, and then at least he could sleep in the tent. Since Captain Beaudoin hadn't reappeared, also carried off somewhere, the lieutenant was trying to reassemble his men, gathering informa-tion, asking in vain where the division's encampment had been set up. But as they moved further into town, instead of growing, the company shrank. One soldier went into an inn, gesturing wildly, and never came back out again. Three more stopped outside a grocer's, waylaid by some Zouaves who'd cracked open a small barrel of brandy. Several were already lying in the gutter, while others wanted to leave but kept falling down again, in a dazed stupor. Chouteau and Loubet had just disappeared down a dark alley after a fat woman carrying a loaf of bread, nudging each other. And the lieutenant had been left with no one but Pache and Lapoulle and ten or so comrades.

Standing beneath the bronze statue of Turenne,* Rochas was mak-ing a considerable effort to stay on his feet and keep his eyes open. When he recognized Jean, he murmured,

'Oh! It's you, Corporal! Where are your men?'

Jean shrugged, indicating that he didn't know. But Pache, point-ing to Lapoulle and dissolving into tears, answered,

'We're here, there's just us two... May the good Lord have pity on us, this misery is too much to bear!'

The other man, the hearty eater, was looking greedily at Jean's hands, outraged to see them always empty these days. Perhaps, in his half-waking state, he'd dreamt that the corporal had been to collect the rations.

'Damn and blast it!' he growled. 'We'll have to pull our belts in again, then!'

Gaude the bugler, who'd leaned against the railings to await the order for the rallying cry, had fallen asleep, sliding straight to the ground, flat on his back. One by one, each of them succumbed and started snoring, hands curled into tight fists. Only Sergeant Sapin still had his eyes open, with his pinched nose and small, pale face, as if he could read his misfortune writ upon the horizon of this strange town.

Lieutenant Rochas, though, had surrendered to the irresistible urge to sit down. He tried to give an order.

'Corporal, you must... you must...'

And the words evaded him, his mouth was thick with fatigue; and all of a sudden he collapsed as well, floored just like the others.

Afraid that he'd be next to fall down in the street, Jean walked on. He was absolutely determined to find a bed. On the other side of the square he'd spotted General Bourgain-Desfeuilles up at one of the windows in the Hôtel da la Croix d'Or, already in his shirt sleeves, about to snuggle down between fine, white sheets. Why overdo it, why suffer any more? And he felt a sudden surge of joy as a name sprung from his memory, the name of the mill owner who employed Maurice's brother-in-law: Monsieur Delaherche! Yes, that was it. He stopped an old man who was walking past.

'Where does Monsieur Delaherche live?'

'Rue Maqua, almost on the corner of the Rue au Beurre, the fine, big house with all the carvings outside.'

Then the old man ran after him.

'Say, you're from the 106th, aren't you... If it's your regiment you're after, it's left town again, past the Château there... I just met your colonel, Monsieur de Vineuil—I used to know him well, when he was at Mézières.'

But Jean was off, with a furious, impatient wave of the hand. No! No! Now he was sure of finding Maurice again, he wasn't going to sleep on hard ground. But deep down he felt a twinge of remorse, for he could still picture the tall figure of the colonel, a man so hardened to fatigue, despite his age, sleeping beneath the tent, like his men. He turned straight into the Grande-Rue, and got lost again in the growing tumult inside the town, eventually going up to a little boy, who led him to the Rue Maqua.

This was where a great-uncle of the present Delaherche had in the previous century built the monumental factory which had been in the family for a hundred and sixty years. In Sedan, there are textile mills like this, dating from the first years of Louis XV's reign,* which are as big as the Louvre, with façades of majestic proportions. The one on the Rue Maqua had three floors of tall windows, framed by classical carvings; inside was a palatial courtyard, still planted with gigantic elms, ancient trees dating back to its foundation. Here, three generations of Delaherches had made considerable fortunes. The father of Jules, the present owner, had inherited the factory from a cousin who had died without an heir, so that now a younger branch of the family reigned. This father had increased the prosperity of the house, but he was a man of roguish morals, and had made his wife very unhappy. So when she was widowed, she trembled at the thought of her son getting up to the same old tricks, and forced herself to keep him tied to her apron strings like some good-natured, overgrown child until he was over fifty, by marrying him to a very simple-hearted and devoted woman. The worst of it was that life has terrible ways of exacting revenge. It so happened that Delaherche's wife died, and he, now weaned of his youthful dependence, became infatuated with a young widow from Charleville, pretty Madame Maginot, about whom there were all sorts of gossip, and eventually, the previous autumn, he had married her, in spite of his mother's remonstrances. Sedan was a very puritanical town and had always judged Charleville extremely harshly for being a place of festivities and frivolity. In any case, the marriage would never have been concluded if Gilberte hadn't been the niece of Colonel de Vineuil, who was next in line to be promoted to general. This kinship, and the idea that he was marrying into a military family, greatly flattered the mill owner.

That morning, on learning that the army would be passing through Mouzon, Delaherche had taken his bookkeeper Weiss with him on the carriage ride that old Fouchard had told Maurice about. Tall and fat, with a ruddy complexion, large nose, and thick lips, he had an expansive nature, and demonstrated that cheerful curiosity typical of French gentry, who love to watch the fine displays of troops go marching past. Having discovered from the pharmacist in Mouzon that the Emperor was staying at the Baybel farm,* he'd gone up there, seen him, and almost even talked with him, quite a wonderful story which he hadn't tired of telling ever since he'd got back. But what an awful return journey it had been, through all the panic in Beaumont, with the roads blocked by fleeing men! The carriage had almost gone into the ditch at least twenty times. It wasn't until nightfall that the two men returned, encountering one obstacle after another. And this pleasure-trip on which Delaherche had set out, this army he'd gone to see marching past, two leagues away, and which was now bringing him back, caught up in its galloping retreat, the whole unforeseen, tragic adventure caused him to say ten times over on the way home,

'And there was me, thinking it was marching towards Verdun, and not wanting to miss the chance to see it!... Well, I've seen it now, and I think we'll be seeing it in Sedan, a bit more than we'd like, too!'

That morning, woken at five o'clock by the loud rumble of the 7th Corps marching through the town, like the noise of sluice-gates being opened, he'd dressed in haste; and he recognized the first person he came across in the Place Turenne as being Captain Beaudoin. The year before, in Charleville, the captain had been part of the pretty Madame Maginot's circle of friends; in fact, before the marriage, Gilberte had introduced them to each other. The story which had been whispered about them in those days was that the captain, having nothing left to desire, had withdrawn out of a sense of delicacy to leave the way clear for the mill owner, not wishing to deprive his lady-friend of the very substantial fortune which was coming her way.

'It's you! How come?' cried Delaherche. 'Good Lord, and what a state you're in, too!'

Beaudoin, normally so correctly and finely turned out, was in a pitiful condition, his uniform covered in mud and his hands and face black with grime. In exasperation, he'd just made his way there with some Turks, at a loss to understand how on earth he'd managed to lose his company. Just like everyone else, he was dropping from hunger and fatigue; but that wasn't the worst of his despair: what caused him acute discomfort was that he'd been unable to change his shirt since Rheims.

'Just imagine,' he groaned, 'they lost my bags at Vouziers. Good-for-nothing halfwits! I'd wring their necks if I ever got my hands on them!... I've nothing left, not a handkerchief, not even a pair of socks! I tell you, it's enough to send a fellow mad!'

Delaherche immediately insisted on taking him home with him. But he protested: no! no! He didn't look human any more, and he didn't want to frighten anybody. The mill owner had to swear that neither his mother nor his wife was up yet. And in any case, he would provide him with soap, water, linen, everything he needed, in fact.

The clock was just striking seven when Captain Beaudoin— washed, brushed, and wearing one of the husband's shirts beneath his uniform—appeared in the high-ceilinged, grey-panelled dining room. Madame Delaherche, the mother, was already there, always up at first light in spite of her seventy-eight years. White-haired, her nose had shrunk and her mouth no longer laughed in her long, thin face. She rose and was extremely polite, inviting the captain to sit down and take one of the cups of coffee which had been served.

'Perhaps, sir, you would prefer some meat and wine after all your labours?'

But he exclaimed,

'A thousand thanks, ma'am, but a little milk and some bread and butter will do me most good.'

At that moment a door was joyfully pushed open and in came Gilberte, hand outstretched. Delaherche must have let her know, for she never usually rose before ten o'clock. She was tall, and looked strong and supple, with beautiful dark hair and eyes, and yet her complexion was very pink and her expression merry and a little wild, without a trace of malice. Her beige dressing gown, embroidered in red silk, had come from Paris.

'Ah! Captain,' she said brightly, shaking the young man by the hand, 'how very kind of you to stop by our poor little country backwater!'

But then she was the first to laugh at her own thoughtlessness.

'Why, how silly of me! You'd be more than happy not to be in Sedan, under such circumstances... But I'm so happy to see you again!'

Indeed, her lovely eyes shone with pleasure. And Madame Delaherche, who must surely have known what the wagging tongues of Charleville used to say, stared hard at them both with her unwavering gaze. For his part, the captain was most discreet, like a man who merely had happy memories of the hospitable house where he'd been received in the past.

They breakfasted, and Delaherche came straight back to the

excursion he'd made the day before, unable to resist the temptation
to tell the tale anew.

'You know, I saw the Emperor at Baybel.'

And he was off, nothing could stop him after that. First, he gave a
description of the farm, a large, square building with a central courtyard, enclosed by railings, which sat upon a small rise overlooking
Mouzon, to the left of the Carignan road. Then he came back to the
subject of the 12th Corps, camped among the hillside vineyards,
with whom he had crossed paths—superb troops they were, sparkling in the sun, and the sight of them had filled him with immense,
patriotic joy.

'So you see, there I was when all of a sudden the Emperor comes
down from the farm, where he'd stopped to rest and eat. He had an
overcoat flung over his general's uniform, even though the sun was
very hot. Behind him there was a servant, carrying a camp stool... He
didn't look well, if you ask me, oh no, he stooped, he had great
difficulty walking, his face was all yellow—in short, he was a sick
man... Not that it surprised me, though, because the pharmacist in
Mouzon who'd advised me to push on to Baybel had just told me
that an aide-de-camp had come dashing into his shop to buy remedies... oh, you know what I mean, remedies for...'

The presence of his mother and wife prevented him from being
any more explicit about the dysentery the Emperor had been suffering from since Le Chesne, and which was forcing him to make stops
at farmhouses along the way.

'In a word, there was the servant, unfolding the camp stool at the
edge of a cornfield, near a coppice, and the Emperor goes and sits
down... He sat there stock still, all in a heap, like a little old man
warming his aches and pains in the sun. His dull gaze scanned the
vast horizon, the Meuse down below, flowing through the valley, and
the wooded hillsides opposite, with the peaks disappearing into the
distance, the treetops of Dieulet Woods to the left, leafy green Sommauthe hillock on the right...* He was surrounded by aides-de-camp
and senior officers; and a colonel of dragoons, who'd already asked
me about the lie of the land, had just waved at me to move off, when
all of a sudden...'

Delaherche got up, for now he was reaching the thrilling climax of
his story and wanted to act out his words.

'All of a sudden, there's the sound of explosions and just ahead, in front of Dieulet Woods, we can see shells tracing arcs in the sky... To me, it was like a firework being let off in broad daylight, upon my word, so it was!... Of course, round the Emperor, they were all exclaiming and getting worried. My dragoon colonel comes running back to me, and asks if I can tell exactly where the fighting's going on. Straight away, I tell him: "That's Beaumont, not the slightest doubt about it." He goes back to where the Emperor's sitting, where an aide-de-camp's spreading out a map before him. The Emperor didn't want to believe that that's where the fighting was. Well, what could I do but stand my ground? Especially with the shells flying through the air, getting nearer, following the Mouzon road... And then, as clear as I can see you now, sir, I saw the Emperor turn his pale features in my direction. Yes, for one moment he looked at me with his watery eyes, full of sadness and defiance. And then his head bowed back over the map, and he never moved another muscle.'

Delaherche, who'd been an ardent Bonapartist at the time of the referendum, had, since the first defeats, begun to admit that the Empire had made some mistakes. But he still defended the dynasty itself, and pitied Napoleon III, whom everyone was letting down. To hear him, the true authors of our misfortunes were none other than the Republican opposition deputies, who'd prevented the necessary numbers of men and credits being voted through.

'And did the Emperor return to the farm?' asked Captain Beaudoin.

'Goodness me, sir, I haven't a clue, I left him sitting on his camp stool... It was midday, the battle was getting closer, and I was starting to think about getting back... All I can add is that one general, to whom I pointed out Carignan in the distance, on the plain behind us, seemed stupefied to learn that the Belgian frontier was there, only a few kilometres away... Ah! That poor Emperor, a fine lot they are!'

Gilberte, smiling and utterly at ease, just like in the old days when she was still a widow and received him in her drawing room, attended to the captain, passing him toast and butter. She insisted that he accept a room and a bed; but he declined, and it was agreed that he would simply rest for a couple of hours on the sofa in Delaherche's study, before rejoining his regiment. As he took the sugar bowl from the young woman's hands, Madame Delaherche, who hadn't once taken her eyes off them, quite clearly saw them squeeze each other's fingers; and she no longer had any doubts.

But a maid had just appeared.

'Monsieur, there's a soldier downstairs, asking for the address of Monsieur Weiss.'

Delaherche was not proud, as they say, and liked talking to the lowly of this world, always eager for a friendly chat.

'Weiss's address! Well, well, how odd... Show the soldier in.'

Jean entered, so exhausted that he swayed on his feet. Noticing his captain seated at table with two ladies, he gave a slight start, and pulled back the hand which he'd automatically put out to lean against a chair. Then he replied briefly to the questions asked by the mill owner, who'd taken on the role of fine fellow and soldier's friend. In a few words, he explained his friendship with Maurice and why he was looking for him.

'He's a corporal in my company,' said the captain eventually, to cut the tale short.

He questioned him in turn, wishing to know what had become of the regiment. And as Jean told him how the colonel had just been seen making his way across town, at the head of what was left of his men, to camp further north, Gilberte again spoke too hastily, with the impulsiveness typical of a pretty woman who rarely thinks before she opens her mouth.

'My uncle—oh! why didn't he come and breakfast here? We would have prepared a room for him... Why don't we send someone to fetch him?'

But Madame Delaherche made a gesture full of sovereign authority. The ancient blood of the border-town gentry ran through her veins, rich with the manly virtues of unswerving patriotism. She broke her severe silence only to say,

'Leave Monsieur de Vineuil be; he has his duty to do.'

This resulted in an awkward atmosphere. Delaherche led the captain to his study, and insisted on preparing the sofa for him with his own hands; and Gilberte went off, despite the reprimand, like a bird shaking out its wings, carefree even in a storm; while the maid to whom Jean had been entrusted led him through the factory court-yards, through a maze of corridors and staircases.

The Weisses lived on the Rue des Voyards; but their house, which belonged to Delaherche, was connected to the monumental edifice on the Rue Maqua. At that time, this Rue des Voyards was one of the narrowest in Sedan, a tiny crack of a street, overshadowed by the proximity of the rampart which ran alongside it. The roofs of the tall buildings almost met in the middle, and the dark alleys looked like the mouths of cellars, especially at the end where the high school wall rose up. However, Weiss had his house and heating provided for him, the whole of the third floor to himself, and he was comfortable here, close to his office, able to pop down to it in his slippers without having to step outside. He had been a happy man since marrying Henriette; he'd long yearned after her, when he knew her at Le Chesne, at the house of her father, the tax collector; at six years old, she'd become the housewife, taking her dead mother's place. Whereas he, after entering the General Refinery almost in a labouring capacity, had got himself an education and risen to bookkeeper, by dint of sheer hard work. Still, for his dream to come true, it had taken first the death of her father and then the deplorable conduct in Paris of her brother, this Maurice, to whom his twin sister was something of a maidservant, and for whom she had sacrificed everything in order to make a gentleman of him. Brought up at home like Cinderella, with reading and writing the sum total of her education, she'd just sold the house and furniture and still not managed to fill the gulf made by the young man's follies, when good, kind Weiss had rushed forward to offer her all he possessed, with his strong arms and all his heart; and she'd agreed to marry him, moved to tears by his affection, accepting him in a very wise, considered way, full of tender esteem if not passionate love. Now, fortune was beginning to smile on them, for Delaherche had talked about making Weiss a partner in the business. When children came along, they would be truly happy.

'Careful!' said the servant to Jean. 'The stairs are steep.'

Indeed they were, and just as he was stumbling around in pitch darkness, a door was briskly opened, casting a shaft of light down the stairwell. And he heard a soft voice saying,

'It's him.'

'Madame Weiss,' called the servant, 'this is a soldier who asked to see you.'

There was a gentle, satisfied laugh, and the soft voice replied,

'Good! Good! I know who it is.'

Then, as the corporal stood on the doorstep, awkward and at a loss for words, she said,

'Come in, Monsieur Jean... Maurice arrived two hours ago, and we've been waiting for you, oh! so impatiently!'

Then, in the room's pale light, he saw her, strikingly like Maurice, displaying that extraordinary resemblance of twins that makes their faces almost copies of each other. She was smaller, though, and even more slight and frail to look at, with her rather wide mouth and delicate features beneath wonderful blonde hair, bright blonde, the colour of ripe oats. And what set her apart from her brother above all were her grey eyes, calm and courageous, where the heroic soul of their grandfather, the hero of the Grande Armée, lived on. She spoke little and moved noiselessly, with such deft activity and such laughing sweetness that wherever she walked, it felt like a caress brushing through the air.

'Come through here, Monsieur Jean,' she repeated. 'Everything will soon be ready.'

He stammered, unable even to find the words to thank her, overcome by emotion at being received in such a brotherly fashion. What was more, his eyelids were drooping, and he could only make her out through the invincible sleep which had hold of him, like a sort of mist in which she floated, hazily, above the ground. Was this merely a charming apparition, then, this helpful young woman, smiling at him with such simplicity? It seemed to him that she was touching his hand, and that he could feel hers, small and firm, loyal, like an old friend.

After that, Jean wasn't quite conscious of what was happening. They were in the dining room, and there was bread and meat on the table; but he wouldn't have had the strength to put the morsels in his mouth. There was a man, sitting in a chair. Then he recognized him as Weiss, the man he'd seen at Mulhouse. But what he was saying, with slow gestures and an air of despondency, he couldn't understand. On a trestle bed which had been set up in front of the stove, Maurice was already asleep, his face immobile, for all the world as if he were dead. And Henriette began bustling around a sofa with a mattress thrown onto it; she fetched a bolster, pillow, and blankets; and with swift, deft hands, she made it up with white sheets, wonderful white sheets, white as snow.

Oh! All Jean could see were those white sheets, the sheets he'd longed for so fervently! For six whole weeks he hadn't got undressed, hadn't slept in a real bed. He was greedy and impatient as a child, feeling an irresistible passion urging him to slip into the whiteness, the freshness, and lose himself inside it. No sooner was he left by himself than he was barefoot, in his shirt-tails, and he got into bed and burrowed down, grunting like a contented animal. The pale morning light came in through the high window, and when he half-opened his eyes, already keeling over into sleep, he saw once again an apparition of Henriette, hazier now, insubstantial, tiptoeing in with a carafe and a glass which she'd forgotten, and placing them on the table beside him. She seemed to stay there for a few seconds, looking down at them both, him and her brother, with her peaceful smile, full of infinite kindness. Then she melted away. And between the white sheets he slept, oblivious.

Hours, years went by. Jean and Maurice were no more— dreamless, unconscious even of the faint pulsing in their veins. Ten years or ten minutes—time had ceased to count; and it was as if their overworked bodies were taking revenge, satisfying themselves by the death of their whole being. Abruptly they both gave a start, waking at the same moment. What was the matter? What was going on, how long had they been asleep? The same, pale light fell from the high window. They were worn out, their joints had stiffened, their limbs were even more weary, and their mouths tasted even more bitter, than when they had gone to bed. Luckily, they couldn't have been asleep for more than an hour. And they weren't surprised to see Weiss sitting on the same chair as before, in the same bowed position, apparently waiting for them to wake up.

'Bloody hell!' stammered Jean. 'We've got to be up and back with the regiment before noon!'

He leapt out of bed onto the tiled floor with a small cry of pain, and got dressed.

'Before noon!' echoed Weiss. 'You do know that it's seven in the evening, and you've been asleep for about twelve hours?'

Seven o'clock! Good God! They were filled with alarm. Jean was already fully dressed and ready to rush off, while Maurice, still in bed, began groaning that his legs were like lead weights. How were they going to find their comrades? Hadn't the army already gone? And both grew angry—they shouldn't have been left to sleep for so long. But Weiss gave a shrug of despair.

'Good Lord, for all that they've done, you did just as well to stay in bed.'

Since morning, he'd been wandering up and down Sedan. He'd only just returned home, distraught by the inaction of the troops on this day, 31 August, time which was so precious, and now lost to inexplicable delay. There was only one possible excuse—that the men were too exhausted, and absolutely had to have some rest; and yet he couldn't understand why the retreat shouldn't have resumed once they'd slept for the necessary few hours.

'I don't pretend,' he went on, 'to know anything about it myself, but I just know—oh yes!—I just know that the army's in a very bad position in Sedan... the 12th Corps is in Bazeilles, and there was some fighting there this morning; the 1st is spread along the Givonne river, from the village of La Moncelle to Garenne Wood; while the 7th is camped out on the Floing Plateau, and the 5th is half in ruins, and piling up right under the ramparts, over by the Château... And that's what frightens me, knowing that they're all lined up round the town, just waiting for the Prussians. I'd have been off straight away, if it'd been me, oh yes! I'd have made for Mézières. I know the lie of the land, and there's no other line of retreat, otherwise we'll get tripped up in Belgium... And then, just look! Come and see this...'

He took Jean by the hand, and drew him over to the window.

'Look over there, on the hilltops.'

Above the ramparts, and above the neighbouring buildings, the window opened out onto the Meuse Valley, to the south of Sedan. There was the river, rolling through the vast plains, with Remilly to the left, Pont-Maugis and Wadelincourt opposite, and Frénois to the right; and the hillsides spread out their green slopes, first Le Liry, then La Marfée and La Croix-Piau, with their large tracts of woods. In the fading light, a profound softness lay over the vast horizon, limpid as crystal.

'Can't you see those black lines, marching all along the hilltops there, like columns of black ants?'

Jean stared hard, while Maurice, kneeling on his bed, craned his neck to see.

'Oh! Yes!' they cried together. 'There's one line, and there's another, and another, and another! They're everywhere!'

'Well,' continued Weiss, 'those are the Prussians... I've been watching them since this morning, and still they keep on coming and coming! Oh! I promise you, our soldiers might be waiting for them, but they're certainly in a hurry to get here!... And everyone who lives here has seen them, just like me, there's really only the generals who can't see what's staring them in the face. I was talking to a general just now and he shrugged, and told me that Marshal MacMahon was absolutely convinced that he was looking at barely seventy thousand men out there. I hope to God he's got his facts right! The ground's crawling with them, and still those black ants just keep on coming!'

At that moment, Maurice threw himself back on the bed, and burst into loud sobs. Henriette came in, smiling as she had that morning. Hastily, she approached in alarm.

'What is it?'

But he pushed her away.

'No, no! Leave me alone, abandon me, I've never been anything but a sorrow to you. When I think that you went without new clothes, and there was me at school! Oh, yes! I made fine use of that education, didn't I!... And then I nearly brought dishonour on our name, I don't know where I'd be right now, if you hadn't bled yourself dry to make amends for all my foolishness!'

She began smiling again.

'My poor dear, you haven't woken up very cheerful, have you?... But come now, all that's over and done with, all forgotten! Aren't you doing your duty as a Frenchman now? I've been so proud of you, since you joined up, I really have.'

And as if appealing to him for help, she turned towards Jean. He was looking at her, a little surprised to find her less beautiful than before, thinner and paler now that he wasn't looking at her through the half-hallucinating eyes of his exhausted state. What was still striking was her likeness to her brother; and yet at that moment, the profound differences in their nature were quite clear: he, with a woman's nervous disposition, shaken by the sickness of the age, going through the social and historical crisis of his race, capable of the loftiest enthusiasm and the most acute discouragement from one moment to the next; and she, so shy, as submissive as a Cinderella, looking like a resigned little housewife, with her firm brow and brave eyes, carved from the blessed wood of which martyrs are made.

'Proud of me!' cried Maurice. 'But there's nothing to be proud of, nothing at all! For a whole month now, we've been running away like the cowards we are.'

'Lord!' said Jean, down-to-earth as ever. 'We aren't the only ones, we're only doing what we're told.'

But the young man broke down again, even more violently than before.

'Exactly, and I've had enough of it!... It's enough to make you weep tears of blood to see the endless defeats, gormless commanders, soldiers being led dumbly to the slaughterhouse like a herd of cattle... Now look, we're caught in a dead end. You can all see that the Prussians are coming from every direction; and we're going to be crushed flat, the army's lost... No, no! I'm staying here, I'd rather they shot me for desertion... Jean, you go without me. No! I'm not going back there, I'm staying right here.'

He flung himself onto his pillow, in a fresh fit of sobbing. He was completely carried away by this irresistible, nervous release, one of those sudden, steep descents into despair—despising the whole world, despising himself—which affected him so often. His sister knew him well, and stayed calm.

'It would be very bad of you, my dear Maurice, to desert your post in time of danger.'

In an instant, he was sitting up.

'All right, then! Give me my rifle, I'll blow my brains out, it'll be quicker that way.'

Then, stretching out his arm and pointing to Weiss, who stood silent and motionless, he said,

'Look! He's the only one with any sense around here! Yes, he's the only one who saw things clearly... Do you remember, Jean, what he was telling me, outside Mulhouse, a month ago?'

'It's true,' nodded the corporal, 'the gentleman did say we'd be beaten.'

And it all came back to them, that night of dread, the waiting, full of fear, as the full-blown disaster of Frœschwiller could already be felt passing over the dreary sky, while Weiss voiced his fears, Germany ready for war, with better commanders, better arms, swept up on a great wave of patriotism, and France scared, left in disarray, delayed and waylaid, with neither the commanders nor the weapons she needed. Now his awful prediction was coming true.

Weiss raised trembling hands. There was a look of deep pain on his kindly face.

'Oh! It's no triumph to be proved right,' he murmured. 'I'm no genius, but it was so plain to see, when you knew how things stood!... But if we're beaten, we can still kill a few of those accursed Prussians. That's my consolation, I think we're going to be left on the field, and I'd like a few Prussians to be left lying there, too, a whole heap of them, enough to cover the ground!'

He stood up, and pointed to the Meuse Valley. His large, short-sighted eyes, which had made him unfit for military service, burned with a bright flame.

'Jesus Christ! Oh, yes! I'd fight, if they'd let me... I don't know if it's because they're the masters now, in my country, my Alsace, where the Cossacks already did such harm years ago, but I can't think of them, I can't imagine them here, in our houses, without feeling this furious desire to bleed a dozen of them to death... Oh! If only they hadn't declared me unfit, if only I were a soldier!'

Then, after a brief pause,

'And anyway, who knows?'

It was hope—the need, even amongst the most disillusioned, to believe victory still possible. And Maurice, ashamed now of his tears, listened to him, clinging to this dream. For hadn't the rumour gone round the day before that Bazaine was at Verdun? Fortune certainly owed France a miracle, this France she'd made glorious for so long. Henriette had disappeared without a word; and when she returned, she wasn't surprised to find her brother up and dressed, ready to depart. She insisted that they eat, he and Jean. They were obliged to sit down at the table, but the mouthfuls of food choked them, and waves of nausea had them retching, still sluggish from their heavy sleep. Cautious man that he was, Jean cut a loaf in two and put one half in Maurice's bag and the other in his own. Daylight was fading, they had to go. And Henriette, standing at the window, watching the Prussian troops far away on La Marfée, those black ants filing endlessly past, little by little lost in the thickening shadow, couldn't help letting out a cry.

'Oh! this war, this dreadful war!'

At once Maurice teased her, taking his revenge.

'What's this, little sister? You're the one who wants us to fight, and now you're cursing the war!'

She turned round and flung back at him, feisty as ever,

'It's true, I abhor it, I think it's unfair and abominable... Perhaps it's just because I'm a woman. All this killing revolts me. Why not talk things over and come to an understanding?'

Jean, good fellow that he was, nodded his approval. Nothing seemed simpler to him, an uneducated man, than for everyone to agree, if good enough reasons were given. But Maurice, back in the thrall of his learning, was thinking about the necessity of war, war which is life itself, war which is the law of the world. After all, wasn't it man, full of pity, who had introduced the idea of peace and justice, while impassive nature is nothing but an endless massacre?

'Come to an understanding?' he cried. 'Yes—hundreds of years from now. If all people became a single nation, then you could, possibly, conceive of the coming of that golden age; and yet, wouldn't the end of war be the end of humanity itself?... I was being stupid, just now; we have to fight, because that's the way of the world.'

Now it was his turn to smile, and he repeated Weiss's words.

'Anyway, who knows?'

Once more, he was held fast by indestructible illusion, by a deep need to be blind to the truth, his nervous sensitivity exaggerating and distorting everything.

'By the way,' he went on, 'what about cousin Gunther?'

'Cousin Gunther?' said Henriette. 'But he's part of the Prussian Guard... Is the Guard near here?'

Weiss shrugged to say he didn't know, as did the two soldiers, unable to reply since even the generals didn't know which enemies they had before them.

'Let's go, I'll drive you,' he declared. 'I found out where the 106th was camping just now.'

Then he told his wife that he wouldn't be coming back but would stay overnight in Bazeilles. He'd recently bought a little house there, which he'd only just finished working on, to make it inhabitable even in cold weather. It was next to a dye-works belonging to Monsieur Delaherche. And he was obviously worried about the supplies he'd already placed in the cellar—a cask of wine and two sacks of potatoes; he declared that he was sure marauders would loot the house if it were left empty, whereas he'd no doubt keep it safe by staying there that night. His wife stared at him as he spoke.

'Don't worry,' he added with a smile, 'I haven't anything else in mind other than looking after our few sticks of furniture. And I promise, if the village is attacked, if there's any danger at all, I'll come straight back.'

'Go on, then,' she said. 'But be sure to come back, or I'll be over to fetch you.'

At the door, Henriette embraced Maurice tenderly. Then she held out her hand to Jean, and kept his in hers for a few seconds, in a friendly way.

'I'm placing my brother back in your charge... Oh yes, he's told me how kind you've been to him, and I love you for it.'

He was so overcome that all he could do was hold her small, frail, but firm hand tightly in his, in his turn. And once again, he saw her as he had when he arrived, the Henriette with hair like ripe oats, so light, so full of laughter with her self-effacing manner that she filled the air around her like a caress.

Down in the street they discovered Sedan in darkness again, as it had been that morning. Twilight was already flooding through the narrow streets, and confused activity was choking up the roads. Most of the shops had shut, the houses seemed lifeless, while outside, people were squashed together. However, just as they reached the Place de l'Hôtel-de-Ville, without too much difficulty, they came across Delaherche, hanging around out of curiosity. Immediately he gave a cry and seemed delighted to recognize Maurice, and told them that he himself had just driven Captain Beaudoin back to near Floing, where the regiment was situated; and his customary satisfaction grew still further on learning that Weiss was to stay overnight in Bazeilles; for, as he'd only just been telling the captain, he too had resolved to spend the night there at the dye-works, just in case.

'We can set off together, Weiss... But meanwhile, let's go as far as the Sous-Préfecture, we might catch a glimpse of the Emperor.'

Ever since he'd almost spoken to him at Baybel's farm, he could think of nothing but Napoleon III; and he ended up dragging the two soldiers along with him. There were only a few groups standing around, whispering, on the Place de la Sous-Préfecture; while from time to time officers rushed past in panic. A melancholy shadow was already staining the trees, and to their right they could hear the Meuse flowing noisily past, below the houses. In the crowd, people were already talking about how the Emperor, having made the painful decision to leave Carignan only the day before, at eleven o'clock at night, had absolutely refused to carry on as far as Mézières, in order to stay close to the danger and avoid demoralizing the troops. Others said that he was no longer there but had fled, leaving one of his lieutenants as a decoy, clothed in his uniform, so like him that it had the army fooled. Others gave their word of honour that they'd seen carriages entering the Sous-Préfet's garden, loaded with imperial treasures, a hundred million francs in gold, in new twenty-franc coins. In fact, it was only the imperial household's equipment, the charabanc, the two carriages, the twelve vans, whose passage had caused such a stir as they passed through the villages of Courcelles, Le Chesne, and Raucourt, swelling in the popular imagination until it became an enormous procession hampering the army's advance, which had finally ended up there, in shame and loathing, hidden from view behind the Sous-Préfet's lilacs.

Near Delaherche, who was standing on tiptoe to peer in at the ground-floor windows, was an old woman, a poor local day-labourer, her back twisted and hands gnarled, worn away by work, and she was mumbling between her teeth,

'An emperor... I'd really like to see one, I would... just to have a look...'

Suddenly, grabbing hold of Maurice's arm, Delaherche exclaimed,

'Look! It's him... There, look, in the window on the left... Oh! No mistake, I saw him right up close yesterday, I recognize him... He's lifted the curtain, see, that pale face against the glass.'

The old woman, who'd overheard him, stood open-mouthed. There was indeed a cadaverous face at the window, like an apparition, eyes dull, features in decay, moustache turning white in the final hour of agony. And the old woman, stupefied, immediately turned her back and left, throwing up her hands in utter disdain.

'An emperor, that thing! Of all the stupid ideas...!'

There was a Zouave nearby, one of the disbanded soldiers who were in no hurry to get back to their army corps. He waved his rifle in the air, spitting out threats; and he said to a comrade,

'Hang on while I put a bullet through his skull!'

Delaherche intervened, full of indignation. But the Emperor had already vanished. The loud roar of the Meuse rumbled on, and an infinitely sad cry seemed to have been uttered in the thickening shadows. Here and there, other noises grumbled in the distance. Was it the terrible order, 'Forward march! Forward march!', issued from

Paris, which had pushed this man from one stage to the next, trailing the irony of his imperial escort along the highroads of defeat, driven now to the brink of the appalling disaster he foresaw, and which he had come to meet? How many fine people were going to die because of him, and how this sick man's world, his whole being had come to grief, this sentimental dreamer, silently enduring the mournful wait for destiny!

Weiss and Delaherche accompanied the two soldiers as far as Floing Plateau.

'Farewell!' said Maurice, kissing his brother-in-law.

'Good God no, not farewell, just goodbye for now!' cried the mill owner jovially.

Jean, with his nose for such things, found the 106th straight away, its tents lined up on the slope of the plateau, behind the graveyard. Night had almost fallen; but large masses still showed clearly the dark layers of the town's rooftops, then, beyond that, Balan and Bazeilles, lying in the meadows which unrolled as far as the chain of hills from Remilly to Frénois; while on the left, the black blotch of Garenne Wood stretched away from them, and on the right, down below, the wide, pale ribbon of the Meuse flowed gleaming past. Maurice watched this vast horizon for a moment, as it faded to nothing in the darkness.

'Ah! Here comes the Corporal!' said Chouteau. 'Has he been to collect supplies?'

A buzz rose from the men. All day long the soldiers, some singly, some in little groups, had been reassembling to form such a jostling crowd that the commanders had even given up asking for explanations. They shut their eyes, happy simply to accept those willing to come back.

Captain Beaudoin, in any case, had only just arrived, and Lieutenant Rochas hadn't brought back the scattered company until about two o'clock, down to a third of its numbers. Now, it was getting back to about full strength. Some of the soldiers were drunk, others sober, having failed to find even a morsel of bread; and yet again, rations hadn't been issued. Loubet, however, had managed to cook up some cabbages, which he'd unrooted from a garden nearby; but he had neither salt nor fat, and the men's stomachs went on complaining of starvation.

'Come on, Corporal, seeing as you're always so crafty!' said

Chouteau mockingly. 'Oh! It's not for me, I've already had a hearty meal with Loubet, at a lady's house.'

Anxious faces turned towards Jean, the squad had waited for him, especially Pache and Lapoulle, who hadn't had any luck and had been counting on him, for he could get flour out of a stone, as they put it. And Jean, full of pity for them, his conscience racked with guilt at having abandoned his men, shared the half-loaf of bread with them from his rucksack.

'Jesus! Jesus!' repeated Lapoulle, devouring the food, grunting with satisfaction and unable to find anything else to say, while Pache said a quiet *Pater* and *Ave* under his breath, to make sure that the next day, Heaven would again send him food.

Gaude the bugler had just sounded the call, with a huge fanfare. There was no retreat, though, and the camp sank straight into utter silence. And when he'd checked that everyone in his half-section was present, Sergeant Sapin, with his thin, poorly face and pinched nose, said softly,

'There'll be a few missing, tomorrow evening.'

Then, as Jean looked at him, he added in a calm, sure manner, eyes staring far into the shadows,

'Oh! I'll be killed tomorrow, I will.'

It was nine o'clock, and the night was beginning to grow icy, for mists had drifted up from the Meuse, shutting out the stars. And Maurice, lying near Jean beneath a hedge, gave a shiver, saying that they'd do better to go and lie down in the tent. But they were shattered, and stiffer than ever after the rest they'd had, and neither could sleep. They envied Lieutenant Rochas next to them who, dismissing any idea of shelter, had simply wrapped himself in a blanket and was now snoring like a hero on the damp earth. Long after that, their interest was held by the little flame of a candle burning in a large tent, where the colonel and several officers were still awake. Monsieur de Vineuil had seemed very worried all evening because he didn't have any orders for the following morning. He sensed that his regiment was exposed, placed too far forward, even though it had already moved back, abandoning the advanced position which it had occupied that morning. General Bourgain-Desfeuilles hadn't put in an appearance, and was said to be sick in bed at the Hôtel de la Croix d'Or; and the colonel had to decide to send an officer to him, to warn him that the 7th Corps's new position seemed dangerous, spread out as they were, obliged to defend too long a front, from the loop of the Meuse to Garenne Woods. Battle was sure to commence at first light. They had no more than seven or eight hours of this still, black calm ahead of them. As the little light went out in the colonel's tent, Maurice was utterly astonished to see Captain Beaudoin pass close by him, walking furtively along the hedge, and disappear in the direction of Sedan.

The night was growing streadily thicker, and the billowing mists rising from the river cloaked all in a mournful fog.

'Are you asleep, Jean?'

He was, and Maurice was all alone. The idea of going to join Lapoulle and the others in the tent made him weary. He listened to their snores answering those of Rochas, and he envied them. Maybe, if great captains slept soundly on the eve of battle, it was simply because they were tired. From the whole of the enormous camp, submerged in the darkness, he could hear only this deep breath of slumber, one huge, soft sigh. Nothing else existed, all he knew was that the 5th Corps must be camping somewhere nearby, beneath the ramparts, that the 1st was stretched out from Garenne Woods to the village of La Moncelle, while the 12th, on the other side of the city, was occupying Bazeilles; and all were asleep, the slow rhythm sounded from the nearest tents to those furthest away, deep down in the vague shadows, over a league away. Then, beyond that, was more of the unknown, from where noises also reached him every now and then, so far away, so faint, that he might have thought it was just a buzzing in his ears: the distant gallop of the cavalry, the muffled rumbling of cannon, and above all the heavy tread of men marching, the black swarm of human ants filing across the high ground, a surrounding movement that even night itself had been unable to halt. And down below, weren't those more fires suddenly going out, voices calling now and then, a feeling of growing dread, filling this last night, as they waited fearfully for the day?

Maurice fumbled for Jean's hand and took it in his. Only then, reassured, did he fall asleep. In the distance, the only remaining sound came from a bell in Sedan, tolling the hours one by one.

PART TWO

CHAPTER ONE

In the small, dark bedroom in Bazeilles, a sudden disturbance made Weiss jump out of bed. He listened: it was the cannon. Fumbling, he had to light a candle to see what time his watch said: four o'clock, the day was only barely beginning.* Briskly, he put on his pince-nez and glanced up and down the main road, the road to Douzy which went through the village; but it was filled by a sort of thick dust, and he couldn't make out a thing. So he went through to the other bedroom overlooking the meadows, towards the Meuse; and there, he realized that the morning mists were rising from the river, and engulfing the horizon. The cannon boomed louder there, behind the veil, across the water. All of a sudden a French battery answered, so close and with such a crash that the walls of the little house shook.

Weiss's house was situated near the centre of Bazeilles, on the right, before the Place de l'Église. The front of the house, set back a little, overlooked the road, a single upper storey with three windows and a loft at the top; but at the back there was quite an enormous garden, which sloped down towards the meadows, offering an immense panorama of the hillside, from Remilly to Frénois. And in the fervour of his new-found ownership it wasn't until about two o'clock that Weiss had finally got to bed, after hiding all his provisions down in the cellar and contriving to protect the furniture from bullets as much as possible, by standing mattresses up against the windows. Anger boiled up inside him at the thought of the Prussians coming to sack this house, which he'd so longed for and acquired with such difficulty, and which he'd as yet had so little time to enjoy.

But a voice called to him from the road outside,

'I say, Weiss, can you hear that?'

Below, he discovered Delaherche, who'd also wanted to stay overnight at the dye-works, a large, brick building which adjoined Weiss's house. All the workers, moreover, had fled through the woods into Belgium; and only the concierge was left to guard it: a stonemason's widow called Françoise Quittard. Trembling and distraught, even she would have run off with the others if it hadn't been for her son, little Auguste, a small boy of ten who was so sick with typhoid that he couldn't be moved.

'I say,' repeated Delaherche, 'd'you hear that, it's well and truly begun... We'd be well advised to go straight back to Sedan.'

Weiss had made a solemn promise to his wife to leave Bazeilles at the first sign of any serious danger, and he was still firmly resolved to keep that promise. But this was only artillery combat for the moment, at long range and somewhat at random, through the early morning mists.

'Let's wait, damn it!' he replied. 'There's no hurry.'

In any case, Delaherche's curiosity was so keen and agitated that it lent him courage. He hadn't slept a wink himself, so fascinated was he by the preparations being made for the defence. Warned that he would be attacked at daybreak, General Lebrun,* the 12th Corps commander, had spent all night entrenching his men in Bazeilles, which he had orders not to allow to be occupied at any cost. Barricades blocked the main road and side-streets; garrisons of a few men occupied every house; every lane, every garden was transformed into a fortress. And from three o'clock, in the ink-black night, the troops were woken noiselessly and took up their battle positions, rifles freshly greased, ammunition belts filled with the regulation ninety cartridges. And so the first boom of the enemy cannon hadn't taken anyone by surprise, and the French batteries set up at the rear between Balan and Bazeilles had immediately set about replying, just to show they were there, for they were simply firing blind, through the fog.

'You know that the dye-works will be vigorously defended,' began Delaherche. 'I've an entire section to myself. Come and see.'

Indeed, forty or so marines had been posted there, headed by a lieutenant, a tall, blond, and very young chap who seemed strong-willed and full of energy. His men had already taken possession of the building, some making loopholes in the shutters on the first floor, looking onto the road, while others made slits in the low courtyard wall, overlooking the meadows at the back.

In the middle of the yard, Delaherche and Weiss found the lieutenant, watching, straining his eyes to see into the distance through the morning mists.

'Bloody fog!' he murmured. 'We're not going to be able to fight blindfold.'

Then, after a pause, and apparently at random, he said,

'What day is it today?'

'Thursday,' answered Weiss.

'Thursday, that's right... Damn it all! We don't even know where we are, you'd think the world had ceased to be!'

But just then, above the incessant rumbling of the cannon came a fierce burst of gunfire, right on the edge of the fields, five or six hundred metres away. And it was like a sudden, dramatic change of scene: the sun began to come up, the mists of the Meuse evaporated into fine shreds of muslin, and blue sky appeared, clear and limpid. It was an exquisite prelude to a sublime summer's day.

'Ah!' exclaimed Delaherche. 'They're crossing the railway bridge. Can you see them, trying to gain ground, all along the line... But how stupid not to have blown up the bridge!'

The lieutenant gave a silent, angry shrug. The charges had been laid, he said; but the day before, after battling for four hours to recapture the bridge, they had forgotten to light the fuse.

'Just our luck,' he said curtly.

Weiss watched, trying to take this in. In Bazeilles, the French occupied a very strong position. Built on either side of the Douzy road, the village overlooked the plain; and it could only be reached by this route, which turned to the left and passed in front of the castle, and one other, to the right, which led to the railway bridge and cut across the Place de l'Église. Thus the Germans had to cross the meadows and the ploughed fields, whose vast, open spaces lined the Meuse and the railway track. Knowing them to be generally cautious, it seemed most unlikely that the real attack would come from that side. Nevertheless, huge masses continued coming across the bridge, in spite of the massacre being inflicted on the ranks by the machine guns stationed at the entrance to Bazeilles; and as soon as they were across, the men would take up positions as skirmishers, flinging themselves behind the few willows, and columns would then regroup and advance. That was where the rising rattle of gunfire was coming from.

'Well, well!' remarked Weiss. 'Those are Bavarians. I can see their tufted helmets quite clearly.'

But he thought he could see other columns, half-hidden behind the railway line, making their way towards the road they themselves were in, trying to reach the distant trees in order to close in on Bazeilles from an angle. If they managed to find the same kind of shelter in Montivilliers Park, the village could be taken. He had a vague, fleeting sense of this. Then, as the frontal assault grew worse, the feeling passed.

Abruptly, he turned towards Floing Heights, which could be seen to the north, above the town of Sedan. A battery up there had just opened fire, and palls of smoke rose into the bright sunshine, while the sound of the explosions reached them very clearly. It must have been about five o'clock.

'Come on!' he murmured. 'The dance is almost done.'

The marine lieutenant, who was also watching, nodded with utter certainty, and said,

'Oh! Bazeilles is the most important spot. This is where the fate of the battle will be decided.'

'You think so?' cried Weiss.

'No doubt about it. You can be sure that that's what the Marshal had in mind when he came to tell us last night to fight to the very last man, rather than let the village be taken.'

Weiss nodded, and glanced along the horizon; then, hesitantly, as if he were talking to himself, he said,

'No, no, that's not it, that's just not it!... I'm afraid of something else, I am, but I daren't say exactly what.'

And he fell silent. He simply spread his arms very wide, like a vice; and facing north, he brought his hands together, as if the jaws of the vice had suddenly snapped shut.

This was what he had feared, ever since the day before, knowing the countryside and realizing where the two armies were heading. Even now, as the vast plain broadened beneath the radiant light, his gaze kept returning to the hills on the left bank, where, all day and all night, a black line of ant-like German troops had scurried across. Above Remilly a battery fired. Another, whose shells were just starting to land near them, had taken position at Pont-Maugis, by the edge of the river. He folded his pince-nez, placing one lens on top of the other to scrutinize the wooded slopes; but all he could see were the little palls of white smoke from the cannon, rising every minute over the brows of the hills: so where was it gathered now, the flood of men which had streamed past? It was only when he looked beyond

Noyers and Frénois, on La Marfée, that he finally made out a cluster of uniforms and horses at the edge of a pinewood—officers, no doubt, a general staff of sorts. Further off was the loop of the Meuse, blocking the west, and on this side there was no other line of retreat onto Mézières than a narrow road which ran alongside the Saint-Albert gap, between the river and the Ardennes Forest. Only yesterday, he'd ventured to mention this unique line of retreat to a general whom he'd met quite by chance down a lane in the Givonne Valley, and whom he later discovered to be General Ducrot, the 1st Corps commander. If the army didn't retreat at once via this route, if it waited for the Prussians to come and cut it off after crossing the Meuse at Donchery, it would surely be immobilized, cornered at the frontier. And by evening of that same day it was already too late, as confirmation came that Uhlans had taken the bridge, yet another one which hadn't been blown up—this time because no one had thought to bring any gunpowder with them. And in despair, Weiss told himself that the flood of men, the stream of black ants, must now be on Donchery Plain, marching towards the Saint-Albert gap, pushing their vanguard on towards Saint-Menges and Floing, to where he'd driven Jean and Maurice the day before. In the dazzling sun, the church tower in Floing could be seen from very far away, like a fine, white needle.

Then, to the east, was the other arm of the vice. Although he could just see the battle line of the 7th Corps to the north, from Illy Plateau to Floing Plateau, feebly supported by the 5th, placed as reserves beneath the ramparts, it was impossible to know what was happening to the east, the length of the Givonne Valley, where the 1st Corps was lined up from Givonne Wood to the village of Daigny. But the cannon boomed out from this side, too, so there must be fighting in Chevalier Wood, this side of the village. And what worried him was that since the day before, peasants had been warning that the Prussians had reached Francheval; meaning that the movement taking place to the west, via Donchery, was also occurring to the east, via Francheval, and that the jaws of the vice would succeed in meeting up, there to the north, on Illy Calvary, if the pincer movement were not stopped. He knew nothing of military tactics, he had only his common sense to draw on, and he trembled to see this immense triangle, the Meuse forming one side, with the other two represented by the 7th Corps to the north and the 1st to the east, while the 12th, south in Bazeilles, made up the furthest angle, all three standing with backs turned, waiting who knew why or how for an enemy which was approaching from every direction. In the middle, lying as if in the depths of a dungeon, was the town of Sedan, armed with broken-down cannons and with no munitions or supplies.

'Just listen,' said Weiss, repeating the gesture, holding out his arms and then bringing them together, 'that's what will happen, if your generals don't watch out... They're just keeping you distracted, in Bazeilles...'*

But he explained it badly and got it all mixed up, and the lieutenant, unfamiliar with the area, couldn't understand what he meant. So he shrugged impatiently, full of disdain for this gentleman in his overcoat and spectacles, who thought he knew better than the Marshal. Irritated to hear him repeat that the attack on Bazeilles might have no purpose other than to create a diversion and conceal their true plan, he finally cried,

'Give it a rest!... We're going to chuck your precious Bavarians in the Meuse, I'll have you know, and then they'll see how distracted we are!'*

For the past few moments, the enemy marksmen seemed to have been drawing closer, and bullets began hitting the bricks of the dyeworks with dull thuds; and sheltered behind the low wall of the yard, the soldiers were now answering back. Not a second went by without the sharp crack of a rifle.

'Yes, chuck them into the Meuse!' murmured Weiss. 'And walk over their bodies to regain the Carignan road, yes, that would certainly be a very good thing!'

Then, turning to Delaherche, who'd dodged behind the pump to avoid the bullets, he said,

'No matter, the real plan would have been to get out last night, and head for Mézières; if I were in their shoes, I'd rather be back there... But never mind, we'll have to fight, because it's impossible to retreat now.'

'Are you coming?' asked Delaherche, who in spite of his burning curiosity was beginning to grow pale. 'If we delay any longer, we won't be able to get back to Sedan.'

'Yes, just a minute, and I'll be with you.'

Despite the danger he stayed on his feet, determined to find out what was happening. On the right, the plains, which had been flooded at the governor's behest, protected the town, forming a vast lake which stretched from Torcy to Balan: a motionless expanse of delicate blue in the morning sun. But the water stopped at the entrance to Bazeilles, and Bavarians had in fact advanced across the field, taking advantage of the shallowest ditch, the smallest tree. They must have been within five hundred metres of them; and what struck Weiss was the deliberate pace at which they moved, the patience with which they gained ground, breaking cover as seldom as possible. What was more, they were backed up by powerful artillery, and the cool, pure air was full of shells whistling past. He looked up and saw that the Pont-Maugis battery wasn't the only one firing onto Bazeilles: two more, positioned halfway up Le Liry, had also opened fire, battering the village and even sweeping beyond the bare terrains of La Moncelle, where the 12th Corps reserves were placed, even as far as the wooded slopes of Daigny, which was occupied by a division of the 1st Corps. Every hilltop on the left bank was going up in flames. The cannon seemed to spring from the earth, like an ever-lengthening belt: one battery at Noyers, firing down onto Balan, one at Wadelincourt, firing onto Sedan, one at Frénois, below the woods of La Marfée— a formidable battery this, its shells sailing over the town and exploding among the troops of the 7th Corps on Floing Plateau. These hillsides he so loved, this string of ridges he'd always believed existed solely to please the eye, sealing off the valley in the distance with such a cheerful stretch of green, Weiss now viewed with nothing but terrified concern; suddenly they'd become a frightening, gigantic fortress which was crushing Sedan's useless fortifications.

A light fall of plaster made him look up. A bullet had just chipped the corner of his house, he could see the façade from over the neighbouring wall. Very upset, he muttered,

'Are they about to knock it down, the bastards?'

But behind him another small, soft noise took him by surprise. And as he turned, he saw a soldier, struck right in the heart, toppling backwards. His legs convulsed for a moment, and his face remained young and peaceful, struck down in an instant. He was the first of the dead, and Weiss was particularly disturbed by the crash of his rifle as it bounced over the flagstones in the yard.

'Oh! No, no, that's it, I'm off,' stammered Delaherche. 'If you aren't coming, I'll go by myself.'

The lieutenant, who was beginning to find them a pain, broke in,

'Certainly, gentlemen, you'd do well to go... We could be attacked any minute now.'

Then, after glancing towards the meadows, where the Bavarians were gaining ground, Weiss made up his mind to follow Delaherche. But in the road, on the other side, he decided to double-lock his door; and he was just joining his companion at last when a fresh sight stopped them both in their tracks.

At the end of the road, about three hundred metres away, the Place de l'Église was coming under attack from a strong Bavarian column which was pouring in from the Douzy road. The marine infantry regiment charged with defending the square appeared to hold their fire for a moment, as if to let the column advance. Then, all at once, when it was neatly assembled opposite, an extraordinary and quite unexpected manœuvre took place: the soldiers flung themselves to either side of the road, many lying flat; and into the space suddenly created, the machine guns, which had been drawn up at the other end, spewed out a hail of bullets. It was as if the enemy column had been swept aside. The soldiers leapt up, charging at the scattered Bavarians with fixed bayonets, managing to knock them down and push them right back. Twice the manœuvre was repeated, with the same success. On the corner of a small street, inside a little house, three women had stayed behind; and they stood there calmly at one of the windows, laughing and applauding, apparently entertained by the performance.

'Oh blast it!' said Weiss suddenly. 'I've forgotten to lock the cellar door and remove the key... Wait for me, I'll only be a minute.'

The first attack appeared to have been repulsed, and Delaherche, eager to stay and carry on watching, was now in less of a hurry to be off. He stood outside the dye-works, talking to the concierge, who'd come out for a moment into the doorway of the ground-floor room where she lived.

'My poor Françoise, you should come with us. It's a terrible thing, a woman all on her own in the middle of all this dreadful business!'

She threw up trembling hands.

'Oh sir! Of course I'd have fled, if it hadn't been for poor little Auguste here being ill... Come in, sir, and you'll see him.'

He didn't enter, but poked his head round the corner and nodded, catching sight of the lad lying in snow-white sheets, his face all purple and hot, staring at his mother with fever-bright eyes.

'Yes, I see what you mean,' he began again, 'but why don't you bring him with you? I'll put you up in Sedan... Wrap him up in a warm blanket, and come with us.'

'Oh no, sir! That's impossible. The doctor said it would surely kill him... If only his poor father were still alive! But there's only the two of us now, and we must make sure we're there for each other... And anyway, these Prussians wouldn't hurt a woman on her own with a sick child, now, would they?'

At that moment, Weiss returned, happy that he'd safely barricaded up his house.

'They'll have to smash the lot to get in there now... Now, let's get going! It's not going to be a smooth ride, we'll have to take cover from these houses if we don't want to get hit.'

Indeed, the enemy must have been preparing for a fresh attack, for the gunfire grew twice as loud and the shells never once stopped whistling through the air. Two had already fallen on to the road, about a hundred metres away; another had just implanted itself in the soft earth of the next-door garden, failing to explode.

'Ah! Well then, Françoise,' he said, 'I'd like to embrace your little Auguste... But he's not as poorly as all that, just give him another couple of days, and he'll be out of danger... Keep your spirits up, and above all get back inside quick, and keep yourself out of sight.'

Finally, the two men left.

'Goodbye, Françoise.'

'Goodbye, gentlemen.'

And at that very moment, there was a terrifying crash. It was a shell, which destroyed the chimney on Weiss's house, then fell onto the pavement, where it exploded with such a bang that all the windows nearby were shattered. Thick dust and heavy smoke at first obscured their vision. Then the front of the building reappeared, gutted; and there lay Françoise, sprawled across the threshold, dead, her body broken and her head all mangled, a human rag, all red and horrible.

Weiss hurled himself over to her. All he could do was swear, stammering,

'Bloody hell! Bloody hell!'

Oh yes, she was dead all right. He bent down, felt her hands; and straightening up again, he found himself looking at the purple face of little Auguste, who had raised his head to look at his mother. He didn't speak, he didn't cry, he just opened his great big, feverish eyes unnaturally wide, before the dreadful body that he no longer recognized.

'Bloody hell!' Weiss managed to cry at last. 'Look, now they've started killing women!'

He got back up, and shook his fist at the Bavarians, whose helmets were just reappearing over by the church. And the sight of the roof of his house, half-demolished by the fall of the chimney, was the final straw, sending him flying into a fury.

'You dirty bastards! You're killing women and you're destroying my home!... No, no! It's just not possible, I can't just leave like this, I'm staying put!'

He sprang forward and in a single bound came back with the rifle and cartridges belonging to the dead soldier. For special occasions, when he wanted to see things really clearly, he always kept about him a pair of glasses, which generally he didn't wear, embarrassed, in a touching and coquettish way, about wearing them in front of his young wife. With a swift hand, he tore off his pince-nez and replaced it with the glasses; and this large gentleman in his overcoat, with his round, good-natured face transfigured by anger, almost comical and proud with heroism, began shooting, firing into the mass of Bavarians at the bottom of the road. It was in his blood, he said, he'd been itching to bring a few of them down ever since the stories of 1814, which had been his childhood lullabies, back there in Alsace.

'Oh! The dirty bastards, the dirty bastards!'

And he carried on, firing so rapidly that the muzzle of his rifle began to burn his fingers.

The attack was going to be dreadful. Over by the meadows, the shooting had ceased. Having taken control of a small stream, over-hung by poplars and willows, the Bavarians were preparing to storm the houses which defended the Place de l'Église; their marksmen had wisely drawn back, and only the sun now slumbered in a blanket of gold above the rolling grasses, discoloured here and there by patches of black, the bodies of dead soldiers. So the lieutenant had simply abandoned the factory yard, leaving a guard behind, realizing that from now on the danger would come from the direction of the road.

Briskly, he lined his men up along the pavement, with orders to barricade themselves in upstairs should the enemy take control of the square, and to defend themselves down to the very last cartridge. Lying flat on the ground, sheltered behind milestones, making use of anything which stuck out, the men fired at will; and along the broad roadway, sunny and deserted, a hurricane of lead raged, streaked with smoke, like a shower of hail being chased by high winds. A young girl was seen rushing panic-stricken across the road, without getting hit. Then an old man, a peasant dressed in a smock, stubbornly determined to lead his horse back into the stable, was struck right between the eyes, with such force that it sent him flying into the middle of the road. The church roof had just been blown in by a falling shell. Two more shells had set houses on fire, and now they blazed in the bright light, with a crackling of timbers. And the inhabitants who'd preferred to die where they stood rather than flee to Belgium, were finally driven mad by the sight of the wretched Françoise, lying mangled near her sick child, the peasant with a bullet in his skull, and all this fire and destruction. Gentlemen, workers, people in overcoats or overalls fired furiously from the windows.

'Oh! The swine!' shouted Weiss. 'They've come round the back... I saw them, sneaking along by the railway line... Listen! Can you hear them, there, on the left?'

He was right, a burst of gunfire had just exploded behind Montivilliers Park, where the trees bordered the road. If the enemy gained possession of the park, Bazeilles was lost. But the violence of the gunfire was itself proof that the commander of the 12th Corps had foreseen the move, and that the park was defended.

'Watch out, then, you fool!' cried the lieutenant, forcing Weiss to cling to the wall. 'You'll get cut in half!'

This large, bespectacled man who was so brave had finally caught his interest, as well as making him smile; and, hearing a shell coming, he'd acted in a brotherly manner and got him out of the way. The projectile fell some ten paces off and burst, showering them both with shrapnel. The gentleman was left standing, not a scratch on him, while the lieutenant found himself with both legs shattered.

'Well, there we are, ' he murmured, 'it's me who's had it.'

Lying on the pavement, he moved himself into a sitting position

against the door, near the woman already sprawled across the threshold. And his young features retained their stubborn, energetic air.

'No matter, lads, listen carefully to me... Take your time firing,
don't hurry. I'll tell you when to fall on them with bayonets.'

He carried on giving orders, head held high, surveying the enemy
in the distance. Another house, opposite, had caught fire. The crackling of gunfire and the sound of exploding shells ripped through the
dusty, smoke-filled air. Soldiers fell at the corner of every tiny street,
and the dead—some isolated, others piled up together—formed
dark heaps, splattered with red. And over the village rose a terrifying
clamour, the threat of thousands of men rushing upon a few hundred
brave souls resolved to die.

Then Delaherche, who was still calling Weiss, asked one last time,
'Aren't you coming?... Too bad, I'm going without you, farewell!'

It was about seven o'clock, and he'd hung on too long. As long as
he could walk alongside houses, he made use of doors and bits of
walls, edging into the smallest corners at every volley. He would
never have thought himself so young and agile, sneaking along with
the suppleness of a grass-snake. At the edge of Bazeilles, however,
when he had to cover nearly three hundred metres of deserted,
naked road, raked by the batteries from Le Liry, he felt himself
shivering, even though he was soaked with sweat. For a moment
longer he walked on, bent double, in a ditch. Then he set off wildly,
galloping straight ahead, explosions booming in his ears like thun-
derclaps. His eyes burned, he felt as though he were moving through
fire. It lasted an eternity. Suddenly he caught sight of a little house to
his left; and he hurried towards it and sought shelter, a huge weight
taken off his chest. There were people around him, men and horses.
At first, he couldn't make out anyone at all. Then what he saw
astonished him.

Wasn't that the Emperor, with all his military staff? He hesitated,
even though he'd boasted of knowing him by sight since the moment
he'd almost spoken to him in Baybel; then he stood, open-mouthed.
It was indeed Napoleon III, looking taller on horseback, and his
moustache was so stiffly waxed and his cheeks so strongly rouged
that Delaherche immediately thought how much younger he
seemed, all powdered up like an actor. He'd surely got them to make
him up, so that his army wouldn't have to face the spectacle of his
pale, ghastly mask, ravaged by suffering, with its gaunt features and

clouded eyes. Alerted at five in the morning that there was fighting in Bazeilles, he had made his way there, silent and mournful as a ghost, the life painted back into his cheeks with vermilion.*

There was a brickyard nearby, which offered some shelter. Opposite, a hail of bullets riddled the walls, and every second shells came crashing down onto the road. The entire escort had come to a halt.

'Sire,' murmured a voice, 'it really is dangerous...'

But the Emperor turned, and with a single wave of his hand ordered his staff to line up in the narrow lane which ran alongside the brickyard. There, men and beasts would be completely hidden.

'Truly, Sire, it's sheer folly... Sire, we beseech you...'

But he simply repeated the gesture, as if to say that the appearance of a group of uniforms on this deserted road would surely attract the attention of the batteries on the left bank. And all alone, he moved forward, amidst the shells and bullets, without haste, at his normal, mournful, indifferent pace, to meet his fate. Doubtless behind him he could hear that implacable voice, propelling him to the front, that voice from Paris, calling 'Forward march! Forward march! Die like a hero, on the heaped-up corpses of your subjects, let the whole world be struck with awe and admiration, so that your son may reign!' And on he marched, urging his horse on step by step. He kept on marching for another hundred metres. The he stopped, waiting for the end he'd come in search of. Around him, the bullets whistled like desert winds and a shell exploded, showering him with earth. His horse bridled, trembling all over, instinctively recoiling in the face of death, which passed by every moment, not differentiating between man or beast. Then, after this endless pause, realizing with fatalistic resignation that it wasn't here that his destiny lay, the Emperor came calmly back, for all the world as if his only purpose had been to establish exactly where the German batteries were placed.

'Sire, what courage!... For the grace of God, please don't risk yourself further...'

But, with yet another wave of his hand, he motioned to his staff to follow him, not sparing them this time any more than he spared himself; and he climbed up through the fields towards La Moncelle, over the barren country of La Rapaille. One captain was killed and two horses brought down. The regiments of the 12th Corps watched him pass before them and disappear like a phantom, no salute, no cheering.

Delaherche had seen all this. And it left him shaking, especially at the thought that as soon as he left the brickyard, he too would find himself fully exposed to the firing. He hung back, listening now to some officers who'd come off their horses and remained behind.

'I tell you, he was killed outright, cut in two by a shell.'

'No, no, I saw him being carried off... It was just a wound, a splinter in his thigh...'

'What time was this?'

'About half-past six, an hour ago... Up there, it was, near La Moncelle, on a track...'

'So he's gone back to Sedan, then?'

'Yes, of course.'

Who were they talking about? Suddenly Delaherche realised that it was Marshal MacMahon, who'd been wounded on his way to the outposts. The Marshal—wounded!* Just our luck, like the marine lieutenant had said. And he was just pondering the implications of this accident when a messenger came past at full gallop, and, recognizing a comrade, yelled out,

'General Ducrot's Commander-in-Chief!... The whole army's to concentrate at Illy, and then beat a retreat to Mézières!'

The messenger was already galloping off into the distance and entering Bazeilles, under a fresh hail of bullets; while Delaherche, alarmed at these extraordinary items of news, coming one after the other, made up his mind and began heading for home, running all the way to Balan, from where he finally reached Sedan without too much trouble.

In Bazeilles, the messenger was still galloping on, looking for the commanding officers, to give them their orders. And on galloped the news, too, Marshal MacMahon wounded, General Ducrot appointed Commander-in-Chief, and the whole army withdrawing to Illy.

'What? What are they saying?' cried Weiss, already black with gunpowder. 'Retreat to Mézières—now! But that's sheer madness, we'll never get through!'

He began to despair, full of remorse that this was precisely the advice he'd given the day before to General Ducrot of all people, who was now in supreme command. Yes, certainly, the day before that had been the only plan to follow: retreat, immediate retreat, through the Saint-Albert gap. But that route must be blocked by now, for that was where the entire black swarm of Prussians had gone, down below on Donchery Plain. And weighing up folly for folly, there was only one left, a brave and desperate measure, which meant chucking the Bavarians into the Meuse and marching over them to pick up the Carignan road.

Hitching his glasses sharply back into place every second or so, Weiss explained the situation to the lieutenant, who was still sitting propped up against the door, both his legs blown off, extremely pale, bleeding to death.

'Lieutenant, I can assure you I'm right... Tell your men not to give up. You can see that we've won. Just one more try, and we'll tip them into the river!'

He was right, the second Bavarian attack had just been fought off. Once again, the machine guns had swept the Place de l'Église quite clean, and piles of bodies lay covering the paving stones in the bright sunlight; and from every lane, the enemy were being chased into the meadows with bayonets at their backs, causing a scattered flight towards the river which would undoubtedly have turned into a rout had there only been fresh troops to back up the marines, who were already exhausted and decimated. What was more, in Montivilliers Park the gunfire was hardly getting any nearer, which suggested that here, too, reinforcements would have cleared the wood.

'Tell your men, Lieutenant... Fix bayonets! Fix bayonets!'

Waxen pale, his voice failing, the lieutenant still had just enough strength to murmur,

'You heard him, lads—fix bayonets!'

And that was his last breath, he died, head stubbornly held erect, eyes open, still watching the battle. Flies were already buzzing around Françoise, landing on her shattered skull; while poor little Auguste lying in bed, now delirious with fever, called out to her, asking for a drink in low, pleading tones.

'Mother, wake up, get up... I'm thirsty, really thirsty...'

But their instructions were quite strict, and the officers had to order the retreat, devastated that they couldn't pursue the advantage they'd just won. Obviously General Ducrot, haunted by the fear of the enemy's pincer movement, had decided to sacrifice everything in a vain attempt to escape from its embrace. The Place de l'Église was evacuated, the troops withdrew lane by lane, and soon the road was empty. Women could be heard sobbing and crying, men cursed, shaking their fists in anger to see themselves abandoned in this way.

Many locked themselves in, resolved to defend their homes to the death.

'Well, I'm not buggering off, oh no I'm not!' shouted Weiss, beside himself. 'No! I'd rather die like a dog!... Just let them come and smash my furniture and drink my wine, just let them try!'

He had nothing left but his anger, that inextinguishable, fighting fury at the thought that a complete stranger was going to enter his house, sit on his chair, and drink from his glass. It was something that made his whole being revolt, sweeping aside his everyday life with his wife, his possessions, his rational, petty bourgeois cautiousness. And he locked himself inside his house, barricading himself in, pacing up and down like some caged animal, going from one room to the next, making sure that every opening was securely blocked. He counted up his cartridges; he still had about forty left. Then, just as he was about to take one last look in the direction of the Meuse, to make sure that there was no sign of an attack threatened from across the meadows, the sight of the slopes on the left bank made him pause yet again. Flurries of smoke quite clearly showed the positions of the Prussian batteries. And overlooking the formidable Frénois battery, at the corner of one of the little woods on La Marfée, there was that cluster of uniforms again, more numerous now than before, standing in such a bright burst of sunlight that, if he put his pince-nez over his glasses, he could make out the gold on their helmets and epaulettes.

'Dirty bastards! Dirty bastards!' he said, over and over again, shaking his fist.

It was the King of Prussia and his staff, up there on La Marfée. At seven o'clock he had left Vendresse, where he'd spent the night, and now there he was, up there, out of harm's way, with the entire Meuse Valley before him—the battlefield, a rolling, boundless expanse. The huge relief map extended from one edge of the sky to the other; while he, standing on the hill, looked on, as if from his own private throne in this gigantic royal box.

In the centre, outlined against the dark backdrop of the Ardennes Forest, which hung from the horizon like a curtain of ancient green, was Sedan, its geometrically designed fortifications submerged to the south and west by the flooded riverside meadows. In Bazeilles, homes were already on fire, and a fog of battle-dust swirled through the village. Then, to the east, from La Moncelle to Givonne, all that

could be seen were a few regiments of the 12th and 1st Corps, like
lines of insects crossing the stubble-fields, disappearing every now
and then into the narrow hollow where the hamlets lay hidden; and
opposite was the reverse of the picture, with pale fields stained by the
green expanse of Chevalier Wood. But above all, to the north, the 7th
Corps was plainly visible, its black dots advancing and filling Floing
Plateau, a broad swathe of reddish land which stretched from tiny
Garenne Wood down to the grass meadows at the water's edge.
Beyond lay Floing, Saint-Menges, Fleigneux, and Illy, villages lost
amid the swelling terrain, an entire region twisted and fragmented
by steep slopes. And on the left there was also the Meuse, slow-
sliding waters of bright silver in the brilliant sunshine, meandering
round the Iges peninsula in a huge, lazy embrace, blocking any way
through to Mézières, leaving only the one entry point between the
far bank and the impenetrable forests—the Saint-Albert gap.

The hundred thousand men* and five hundred cannon of the
French army were all here, piled up and hounded into this triangle;
and when the King of Prussia turned to the west, he could see
another plain, Donchery, where empty fields broadened towards Bri-
ancourt, Marancourt, and Vrigne-aux-Bois, a grey landscape stretching out of sight, with clouds of dust rising up under the blue sky; and
when he turned to the east, there too, opposite the French lines, so
tightly packed together, was an immense space, with a swarm of
villages, first Douzy and Carignan, then climbing up to Rubécourt,
Pouru-aux-Bois, Francheval, Villers-Cernay, as far as La Chapelle,
close to the border. All around him, the land belonged to him, he
could move his armies' two hundred and fifty thousand men and
eight hundred cannons at will, and take in the whole of their invading march with one sweeping glance. On one side, the XIth Corps
was already advancing on Saint-Menges, while the Vth Corps was at
Vrigne-aux-Bois, and the Württemberg Division stood waiting near
Donchery; and although the trees and hills blocked his view on the
other side, he could still guess at the movements of the XIIth Corps,
for he'd just seen it enter Chevalier Wood, and knew that the scouts
must have reached Villers-Cernay. These were the arms of the vice,
the Crown Prince of Prussia's army on the left, the Crown Prince of
Saxony's on the right, branching out and climbing up in an inexorable movement, while the two Bavarian corps hurled themselves at
Bazeilles.

At King William's feet, from Remilly to Frénois, the batteries thundered on relentlessly almost without interruption, covering La Moncelle and Daigny with shells which flew over the town of Sedan and swept across the northern plains. It was barely gone eight o'clock, and already he awaited the battle's inevitable outcome, eyes fixed on the giant chessboard, busy leading these human specks of dust, the furious charge of these few black dots, lost amidst eternal, smiling nature.

CHAPTER TWO

In the small hours on Floing Plateau, in the thick fog, Gaude the bugler sounded the reveille with all his might. The air was so drenched, though, that the joyous call was muffled. The company's men, who'd been unable to summon up the courage even to pitch their tents and had simply rolled up in the canvas, lying down in the mud, didn't wake, already corpselike, their pale faces set hard by sleep and fatigue. They had to be shaken one by one to drag them from the void; and they rose like men brought back from the dead, their features livid and their eyes filled with the terror of living.

Jean had woken Maurice.

'What is it? Where are we?'

Full of alarm, he tried to look, but saw only the sea of grey in which the shadows of his comrades appeared to be floating. You could hardly see twenty metres. His sense of direction had gone completely and he had no idea where Sedan was. Just then, however, somewhere far, far away, the sound of cannonfire reached his ears.

'Oh, yes! Today's the day we're going to fight... So much the better! We'll get all this over and done with!'

Other voices around him were saying the same thing; and there was a grim sense of satisfaction, they felt they must escape from this nightmare and at long last set eyes on those Prussians they'd come looking for and been running away from for so many, fatal hours! So, now they were going to send a bullet or two their way, and get rid of some of these cartridges they'd lugged so far, without firing a single one! This time everyone could feel it, it was the inevitable battle.

But the cannon in Bazeilles boomed louder, and Jean stood and listened.

'Where are they firing from?'

'Well,' replied Maurice, 'it sounds to me as if it's somewhere near the Meuse... Only thing is, I'm damned if I know where I am.'

'Listen, lad,' the corporal then said, 'you're not to leave my side, because you've got to know what's what, you see, if you don't want to get hit by anything nasty... I've seen it all already, I have, and I'll keep my eyes peeled for the both of us.'

Meanwhile the squad was beginning to grumble, angry because

they had nothing to put in their bellies. Impossible to light a fire
without any dry wood, especially in such foul weather! At the very
moment that battle was being joined, the subject of food came back
to the fore, urgent, critical. Heroes, maybe, but stomachs first and
foremost. Eating was all that concerned them; how lovingly they'd
lick out the pot on days when there was a good drop of soup to be
had! And what childish, savage tantrums there were when there
wasn't enough bread!

'No food, no fighting,' declared Chouteau. 'I'm buggered if I'm
going to put my neck on the line today!'

He was recovering his revolutionary spirit, this tall fellow, the
house-painter, fancy Montmartre talker and workers' club theorist,
spoiling the few sound ideas he'd grasped here and there in the most
terrible tangle of lies and rubbish.

'What's more,' he went on, 'they must have been taking the piss,
telling us the Prussians were sick and dying of starvation, that
they didn't have so much as their shirts left, and that people were
finding them in the street all filthy and dressed in rags, like
paupers.'

Loubet began to laugh, like a streetwise Parisian who'd drifted his
way through every odd job going in Les Halles.

'Oh, right! We're the ones starving and dropping like flies, we're
the ones you'd throw a penny to when we go by in our knackered
boots and our beggars' rags... And what about their great victories!
What a bunch of jokers, telling us we'd just taken Bismarck prisoner
and pushed a whole army into a quarry... No, I ask you, they've just
been taking the piss!'

Pache and Lapoulle, listening to this, clenched their fists and nodded vigorously. Others began getting angry, too, for the countless lies
in the papers had ended up having a disastrous effect. All their
confidence was dead and gone, they didn't believe in anything anymore. The imagination of these overgrown children, which at the
start had been so fertile with extraordinary hope, was now sinking to
the level of a crazed nightmare.

'Of course they are!' took up Chouteau again. 'There's nothing
clever about it, we've been sold out, that's all... You all know that.'

Lapoulle, with his rustic simplicity, grew exasperated every time
that word was mentioned.

'Oh! Sold out! There must be some low sorts around!'

'Sold out! Just like Judas sold out his master,' murmured Pache, forever haunted by memories of biblical stories.

Chouteau grew excited.

'I mean, good grief, it's simple enough! We all know the sums involved... MacMahon got three million and the other generals got a million each, to bring us here... It was all set up in Paris, last spring; and last night they let off a rocket—you know, to tell them everything's ready and they could come and get us.'

Maurice was disgusted at the stupidity of this invention. Before, Chouteau had amused him, and he'd almost been won over by his working-class eloquence and wit. Now, though, he couldn't stand the corrupting influence of this idle workman, who bad-mouthed every task, just to put the others off.

'Why do you say such absurd things?' he cried. 'You know it's not true.'

'What d'you mean, not true?... So it's not true, now, that we've been betrayed?... Aha! Well, well, aristo, are you one of them, too? One of the gang of traitors, one of those dirty bastards?'

He approached threateningly.

'You know, you should say so, Mr High-and-Mighty, because we wouldn't wait for Bismarck, we'd settle up with you right here and now.'

The others were starting to mutter, too, and Jean thought he should step in.

'Quiet there! The first one to move will go on report!'

But Chouteau, sniggered, jeering at him. He couldn't give a toss about going on fucking report! He'd fight or not, just as he pleased; and they'd better not get him riled, because it wasn't just the Prussians his cartridges would do for. Now that the battle had begun, the little discipline that fear had kept in place was falling apart: what could they do to him? He'd bugger off, just as soon as he'd had enough. And he spoke coarsely, stirring the men up against the corporal who was letting them starve to death. Oh, yes, it was all his fault that the squad hadn't eaten for three days, while the rest of the comrades had had soup and meat. But Mr Fancy here had gone off on a binge with the aristo, to see some tarts. They'd seen them, they had, in Sedan.

'You pigged out on the squad's money—go on, I dare you to deny it, you greedy bastard!'

Suddenly, things turned nasty. Lapoulle was clenching his fists, while Pache, despite his gentle nature, was wild with hunger and wanted an explanation. The most reasonable of them still was Loubet, who began laughing in his wise way, saying how stupid it was for them to be fighting each other when the Prussians were just round the corner. He wasn't one for quarrelling, not with fists or with guns; and alluding to the few hundred francs he'd received as a military replacement, he added,

'Honestly! If that's all they think I'm worth!... I'll give 'em exactly what they paid for.'

Maurice and Jean, however, irritated by all this stupid aggressiveness, began responding violently, denying that they were to blame, when, all of a sudden, a loud voice boomed out of the fog.

'What's all this, then? What's all this? Which of you bloody conscripts are quarrelling?'

And Lieutenant Rochas appeared, képi yellowed by the rain, buttons missing from his greatcoat, his entire skinny, lanky person in a pitifully neglected, wretched state. And yet he was full of victorious bravado, with sparkling eyes and bristling moustache.

'Sir,' replied Jean, beside himself with rage, 'it's these men, they're shouting about us being sold out... Yes, the generals are supposed to have sold us out...'

Inside Rochas' tiny mind, the idea of treason didn't seem so wide of the mark, since it would explain the defeats he couldn't bring himself to accept.

'Well, now! And what the hell has it got to do with them if they have?... Is it any of their business?... It doesn't alter the fact that the Prussians are here now, and we're going to give them a thrashing to remember.'

Far away, behind the thick curtain of the fog, the cannon in Bazeilles boomed on and on. He flung his arms wide open.

'Hey! This is it, this time... We're going to send them packing, and let them feel the end of our rifle butts!'

For him, the sound of the cannonfire had erased everything else: the slow pace and uncertainties of the march, the demoralized state of the troops, the Beaumont disaster, the recent agony of their forced retreat back to Sedan. Now that they were fighting, victory was assured, wasn't it? He hadn't learned or forgotten anything at all, retaining his boastful disdain for the enemy, his complete ignorance of the modern conditions of warfare, with his stubborn certitude that a veteran of Africa, the Crimea, and Italy simply couldn't be beaten. It really would be too ridiculous to start now, at his age!

Suddenly, he laughed from ear to ear. A surge of tenderness came over the good fellow, one of those which made his soldiers adore him, in spite of the thumpings he sometimes handed out.

'Listen, lads, instead of arguing, you'd be better off having a drop to drink... Yes, I'm going to stand you a drink, you can toast my good health.'

And he pulled out a bottle of brandy from a deep pocket in his greatcoat, adding with his triumphant air that it had been a gift from a lady. The day before, it was true, they'd seen him sitting back in some bar in Floing, being very forward with the barmaid, whom he was holding on his knee. Laughing good-naturedly now, the soldiers held out their mess-tins, and he cheerfully poured their drinks himself.

'Lads, if you have any, you must drink to your sweethearts, and to the glory of France... They're the only things I know about—so here's to happiness!'

'Quite true, sir, here's to you, and to us all!'

They all drank up, reconciled, spirits rekindled. It was kind of him, this drop of something in the cold wee hours, just as they were about to march to meet the enemy. Maurice felt the liquid spreading through his veins, restoring the warmth and half-tipsy feeling of the illusion. Why shouldn't they beat the Prussians? Didn't battles produce surprises sometimes, unexpected reversals of fortune which still caused astonishment long after they'd passed into history? The fellow added that Bazaine was on the march and was expected here before evening: oh! this was reliable information that an aide-de-camp to one of the generals had given him; and even though he pointed towards Belgium as being the direction that Bazaine would be coming from, Maurice abandoned himself to one of those surges of hope without which he simply couldn't exist. Perhaps this was revenge, at last.

'What are we waiting for, sir?' he ventured. 'Aren't we marching, then?'

Rochas shrugged, as if to say he hadn't any such orders. Then, after a pause, he said,

'Has anyone seen the Captain?'

No one answered. Jean recalled seeing him leave during the night and head for Sedan; but a wise soldier never sees a commanding officer when off duty. He was keeping quiet when, turning round, he caught sight of a shadow making its way back along the hedge.

'Here he is now,' he said.

It was indeed Captain Beaudoin. They were all amazed to see how impeccably turned out he was, uniform brushed and shoes polished, striking quite a drastic contrast to the lieutenant's own pitiful state. What was more, there was a coquettishness to him, as if he'd dressed for the ladies, with his white gloves and curled moustache, and a faint perfume of Persian lilac, the scent of a pretty woman's plush dressing room.

'Well, well!' sniggered Loubet. 'So the Captain's found his bags!'

No one smiled, though, for they knew he wouldn't be amused. He was detested by his men, and kept them at arm's length. A nasty piece of work, Rochas called him. Since the first defeats, he'd seemed to be in a state of utter shock; and the disaster everyone predicted seemed to him improper, rather than anything else. Bonapartist by conviction, destined for the brightest of futures, enjoying the influence of several social circles, he could feel his fortune floundering in the mud. People said he had a very fine tenor voice, to which he owed a great deal. He wasn't unintelligent, either, although he knew nothing about his profession, his only desire being to please, and he showed great bravery when necessary, without overdoing it.

'Look at this fog!' he merely said, relieved to find his company, which he'd been looking for for over half an hour, afraid that he'd got lost.

The battalion immediately set off, for an order had come at last. More fog must have begun billowing up from the Meuse, because they were practically groping their way along through a whitish sort of dew which fell as fine drizzle. And then Maurice saw a striking vision suddenly looming out of the fog—Colonel de Vineuil* at the corner of two roads, sitting quite still on his horse, very tall and pale, like a marble statue of despair, his mount shivering in the cold morning air, nostrils flared in the direction of the cannon. But above all this, ten paces further back, floated the regiment's standard, borne by the second lieutenant on duty, its cover already off; in the soft, shifting whiteness of the mists, it appeared to be high up in a dreamy sky, an apparition of glory, trembling and about to vanish. The gold-plated eagle was covered in water, and the silk tricolour, embroidered with the place names of victories, was faded, discoloured by smoke, and full of holes from ancient wounds; and all that really lent some bright sparkle to this image of obliteration were the enamelled branches of the Légion d'Honneur, pinned to the colonel's sash.

Flag and colonel disappeared, swallowed up by a fresh wave of fog, and the battalion advanced further, not knowing where they were going, as if moving through wet cotton wool. They had marched downhill, and were now climbing back up a narrow track. Then the cry to halt rang out. And there they stayed, standing to attention, shoulders weighed down by their rucksacks, forbidden to make a move. They must have been on a plateau; but even so, it was still impossible to see further than twenty paces ahead, they couldn't make out a thing. It was seven o'clock, the cannon seemed to have got nearer, more batteries were firing from the other side of Sedan, and they were coming closer and closer.

'Oh!' said Sergeant Sapin suddenly to Jean and Maurice. 'I'm going to be killed today.'

He hadn't opened his mouth since reveille and seemed to be lost in a dream, with his haggard features, big, beautiful eyes, and small, pinched nose.

'What an idea!' protested Jean. 'How can we say what'll happen to us!... You know it could be any one of us, or even no one at all.'

But the sergeant nodded, completely sure of himself.

'Oh! It might just as well have happened already... I'm going to be killed today.'

Heads turned in his direction, and someone asked if he'd seen it in a dream. No, he hadn't dreamt it; he could just sense it, there it was.

'It's annoying, too, because I was going to get married when I got back home.'

His eyes wavered once again, and his whole life passed before him. Born to parents with a small grocer's shop in Lyons, his mother had spoiled him but died young; unable to get on with his father, he'd stayed with the regiment out of total disgust at it all, unwilling to get himself bought out of service; and then, one time on leave, he'd come to an understanding with one of his cousins, and they'd discovered a new taste for life, happily planning to set up in business together, thanks to the few francs she would bring to the marriage.

He was educated, able to read and write, spell and add up. For a year, now, the joy of this shared future was all he'd been living for.

He shuddered, shaking himself free from his thoughts, calmly repeating,

'Yes, how annoying, I'm going to be killed today.'

No one spoke again, and the waiting went on. They didn't even know whether they were facing the enemy or had their backs to them. Vague noises emerged from the fog every now and then: the creaking of wheels, the tramping of crowds, and horses trotting in the distance. It was the troops on the move, their manœuvres hidden by the fog, as the whole of the 7th Corps took up battle positions. For a moment now, though, the mists appeared to have been thinning out. They floated away like fine shreds of muslin, revealing corners of the horizon, still hazy, the dull, blue colour of deep water. It was during one of these clear spells that they saw the regiments of the African Chasseurs, part of the Margueritte division, filing past like ghostly horsemen. Bolt upright in the saddle, wearing their regulation coats with the broad, red belts, they urged on their horses, slender beasts half-obscured beneath their complicated saddlebag arrangement. Squadron followed squadron; and every one of them, emerging from the haze, would then vanish back into it, seeming to melt as it touched the fine drizzle. They were probably a nuisance, being led away because no one knew what to do with them, as had been the case ever since the outset of the campaign. They had hardly even used them as scouts, and now, with battle about to commence, they were being led from one valley to another, precious and utterly useless.

Maurice watched, thinking of Prosper.

'Look!' he murmured. 'Maybe that's him, there!'

'Who?' asked Jean.

'That lad from Remilly—you know, the one whose brother we met at Oches.'

But the Chasseurs had already gone past, and they heard another sudden sound of galloping, as a staff officer came hurtling down the track. This time, it was Jean who recognized their brigadier, Bourgain-Desfeuilles, furiously waving his arms. So, he'd finally deigned to leave the Hôtel de la Croix d'Or; and his bad mood plainly illustrated his anger at having to rise so early, in conditions of food and lodging which were quite deplorable.

His thunderous voice carried distinctly over to them.

'What? Moselle, Meuse—whatever! That water over there, for God's sake!'

The fog, however, was lifting. Just as in Bazeilles it was sudden, like scenery being unveiled behind the floating stage curtain, slowly rising up to the awning. Bright sunshine streamed down from the blue sky. And Maurice immediately recognized where it was they'd been waiting.

'Ah!' he said to Jean. 'We're on the Plateau d'Algérie... See, across the valley, opposite, that village—that's Floing; and over there's Saint-Menges; and behind that, Fleigneux... Then right back there, in the Ardennes Forest, you see those spindly trees on the horizon— that's the frontier...'

He carried on, arm outstretched. The Plateau d'Algérie, a reddish strip of land three kilometres long, sloped gently down from Garenne Wood to the Meuse, separated from it by grassland. This was where General Douay had positioned the 7th Corps, despairing that he lacked the men to defend such a drawn-out line and forge a solid link to the 1st Corps, set at right-angles to the 7th, occupying the Givonne Valley from Garenne Wood to Daigny.

'See? It's huge, isn't it, huge!'

Maurice turned, tracing the curve of the horizon with his hand. South and west from the Plateau d'Algérie the whole, enormous battlefield stretched out: first Sedan, with its citadel rising above the rooftops; then Balan and Bazeilles, in a persistent, murky shroud of smoke; then, in the background, the heights of the left bank, Le Liry, La Marfée, and La Croix-Piau. It was to the west, though, towards Donchery, that the real view lay. The loop of the Meuse encircled the Iges peninsula with a pale ribbon; and there, the narrow Saint-Albert road was clearly visible, running between the riverbank and a steep hillside, crowned further off by Seugnon, a little wood, the tail-end of Falizette Woods. At the top of the slope, at the Maison-Rouge crossroads, emerged the Vrigne-aux-Bois and Donchery road.

'You see, that way we could withdraw to Mézières.'

At that very moment, however, the first of the cannon boomed out from Saint-Menges. Shreds of fog still lingered down in the valley, and they could see nothing but a confused mass moving through the Saint-Albert gap.

'Ah! Here they come,' said Maurice, without naming the Prussians, instinctively lowering his voice. 'They've cut us off, we're done for!'

It was not yet eight o'clock. The cannonfire, which was growing more intense near Bazeilles, could also be heard now to the east, in the Givonne Valley, which they couldn't see: that was the moment that the Crown Prince of Saxony's army, emerging from Chevalier Wood, began approaching the 1st Corps, just outside Daigny. And now that the XIth Prussian Corps, marching towards Floing, was opening fire on General Douay's troops, battle was joined on every side, from north to south, all across this huge expanse which spread over several leagues.

Maurice had just begun to realize what an irreparable fault they'd committed by not withdrawing to Mézières during the night. But the consequences were as yet unclear to him. Only a gnawing, instinctive sense of danger made him cast a worried glance at the neighbouring hills, overlooking the Plateau d'Algérie. If they hadn't had time to beat a retreat, then why hadn't they decided to occupy this high ground, backed up against the border, ready to cross into Belgium if they should find themselves outnumbered? Two points seemed particularly menacing: Hattoy Hill on the left, above Floing, and Illy Calvary to their right, a stone cross set between two linden trees. The previous day, General Douay had assigned a regiment to occupy Hattoy Hill; at daybreak, it had withdrawn, too much out on a limb. As for Illy Calvary, it was to be defended by the 1st Corps's left flank. The countryside stretched out from Sedan to the Ardennes Forest, vast and bare, scored by deep valleys; and this was clearly where the key to the battle lay, at the foot of this cross and these two linden trees, from where the gunfire could sweep over all the surrounding land.

Three more cannon blasts boomed out. Then, a whole salvo. This time, they saw a wisp of smoke rising from a low hillside, to the left of Saint-Menges.

'Right,' said Jean, 'our turn.'

But nothing happened. The men, still standing motionless, to attention, had nothing to do but watch the fine way that the 2nd Division was laid out, drawn up outside Floing, its left flank forming an L-shape opposite the Meuse, to stave off an attack from that side. The 3rd Division was placed on the left, as far as Garenne Wood, below Illy, while the 1st, solidly dug in at Beaumont, was in the second line. Overnight, the sappers had worked on building defences. Even now, as they began coming under fire from the Prussians, they were still digging out shelter trenches and raising epaulements.

However, gunshots rang out down in Floing, although they ceased immediately, and Captain Beaudoin's company received the order to move back three hundred metres. They were just entering a huge, square cabbagefield when the captain cried sharply,

'Everyone lie flat!'

They had to lie down. The cabbages were soaked with heavy dew, their thick, green-gold leaves trapping drops as pure and brilliant as enormous diamonds.

'Sights at four hundred metres!' cried the captain again.

Maurice propped up the barrel of his rifle on a cabbage in front of him. But now they couldn't see a thing, down at ground level like this; the land stretched out, confused, lined with green. He nudged Jean's elbow to his right, asking him what the hell they were doing here. Jean, experienced in battle, showed him a battery they were setting up on a small hill nearby. Obviously, they'd been put here to give it support. Curiosity getting the better of him, Maurice stood up again, eager to see whether Honoré and his field-gun were part of it; but the reserve artillery were at the back, behind a clump of trees.

'For God's sake!' yelled Rochas. 'Will you please lie down!'

And Maurice was barely back on the ground when a shell came whistling past. After that, they didn't stop. The Prussians' aim was adjusted, but only slowly, and the first shells landed well beyond the battery, which began returning fire. What was more, many of the shells failed to explode, their fall cushioned by the soft earth; and at first there were endless jokes about how cack-handed these bloody Krauts were.

'Well, there we are!' said Loubet. 'Their fireworks are just damp squibs!'

'Bet you they pissed on them!' added Chouteau, sniggering.

Even Lieutenant Rochas joined in.

'Didn't I tell you these good-for-nothings couldn't even aim a cannon straight?'

But a shell exploded ten metres away, showering the company with earth. Although Loubet shouted jokingly to his comrades to get their clothes brushes out of their rucksacks, Chouteau turned pale and fell silent. He'd never seen battle before; nor had Pache or Lapoulle, for that matter, no one in the squad had, except Jean. Eyes blinked and misted over a little, voices grew squeaky, as if sticking in throats. Quite in control of himself, Maurice forced himself to examine his own reactions: he wasn't frightened yet, because he didn't believe he was in any danger; all he could feel was an uneasy sensation in his stomach, while his mind went blank and he couldn't string two ideas together. But ever since he'd marvelled at the fine order of the troops, he'd felt hope, like dizziness, welling up inside him. He'd now reached the point where, if only they could get at the enemy with their bayonets, he no longer had any doubts about victory.

'Listen!' he murmured. 'There's flies everywhere.'

It was the third time he'd heard what sounded like a swarm of bees.

'No, there aren't,' laughed Jean. 'They're bullets.'

More faint noises of buzzing wings went past. The whole squad turned to look, drawn by the sound. The men craned their necks, it was irresistible, they just couldn't keep still.

'Listen,' Loubet advised Lapoulle, making fun of his simple nature, 'when you see a bullet coming, all you have to do is hold one finger up in front of your nose, like this: it cuts the air, and the bullet goes either left or right.'

'But I can't see them,' said Lapoulle.

A huge laugh erupted around him.

'Oh! The clever boy can't see them!... Open those baby blues of yours, you idiot!... Look! There's one, and look! There's another... Didn't you see that one? It was green.'

And Lapoulle opened his eyes wide, and put a finger up in front of his nose, while Pache, feeling for the scapular he was wearing, wished he could have stretched it so that it covered his whole chest like a breastplate.

Rochas, who'd stayed on his feet, cried out in his mocking voice,

'Lads, there's no law against waving at the shells, you know. But it's no good trying it with the bullets, there's just too many of 'em!'

At that moment, an exploding shell shattered the skull of a soldier in the first row. There wasn't even a cry: a spurt of blood and brains, and that was it.

'Poor sod,' said Sergeant Sapin simply, very calm and pale. 'Who's next?'

But it was impossible to hear one another by now, and it was this terrible din that caused Maurice the most discomfort. The battery beside them fired ceaselessly, rumbling on and on, making the ground shudder; and the machine guns ripped through the air faster and faster, it was unbearable. Were they going to lie in this cabbagefield for ever? They still couldn't see anything, still didn't know what was going on. It was impossible to get any sort of idea of the battle: was it a big battle, or even a real one? Above the flat line of the fields, Maurice could recognize only the round, wooded crest of Hattoy Hill, far, far away and still deserted. On the horizon, in any case, there wasn't a single Prussian to be seen. Only wisps of smoke rose up, floating for a moment in the sunlight. And when he turned his head, he was astonished to catch sight of a peasant, down in a secluded valley, protected by steep slopes, unhurriedly tilling his field, taking his time, pushing the plough behind a large, white horse. Why waste a day? The wheat wasn't going to stop growing just because there was a battle going on, nor would the world stop living.

Overcome by impatience, Maurice stood up. In a single glance, he saw the batteries at Saint-Menges which were bombarding them, overhung by tawny smoke, and above all, he saw once again the black path of the Prussians, coming from Saint-Albert, a swarming, blurred, invading horde. Already Jean was grabbing him by the legs and dragging him violently back down.

'Are you mad? You'll get yourself killed!'

Rochas, too, began swearing at him.

'Will you please lie down! What sort of comedians are you, getting yourselves killed before you've even been ordered to!'

'But sir,' said Maurice, 'you're not lying down!'

'Me? That's different, I have to know what's going on.'

Captain Beaudoin, too, had bravely stayed standing up. He never once opened his mouth to speak, though, nothing linked him with his men, and he seemed unable to stay put, trudging from one end of the field to the other.

More waiting, and still nothing happened. Maurice was suffocating beneath the weight of his rucksack, bearing down on his back and chest in this prone position, which grew so painful after a while. The men had been strongly advised not to discard their rucksacks except in the direst circumstances.

'Say, are we going to spend all day like this?' he eventually asked Jean.

'Possibly... At Solférino, it was a field of carrots. We spent five hours there, noses to the ground.'

Then, being a practical fellow, he added,

'What are you complaining about? It's not that bad here. There'll be plenty of time to get closer to the action later on. Come on, everyone's got to have a turn. If we all got killed right away, there'd be no one left for the end.'

'Oh!' Maurice suddenly cut in. 'Just look at that smoke up on Hattoy Hill... They've taken it, now there'll be merry hell to pay!'

For a moment, as the first tremblings of fear started creeping in, his dread and curiosity had something to feed on. Not for a minute did he take his eyes off the rounded top of the hill, which was the only bump of land he could see above the receding line of huge fields down at eye level. Hattoy Hill was much too far away for him to be able to make out the gunners in the battery the Prussians had just set up on the top; in fact all he could see, above a coppice which must have been concealing the cannon, were the clouds of smoke which followed each salvo. Just as he'd suspected, it was indeed grave that the enemy had taken control of the position General Douay had been forced to abandon. It commanded the surrounding plateaux. The batteries immediately opened fire on the 7th Corps's 2nd Division, decimating it. Their aim was improving and the French battery, with Beaudoin's company lying nearby, had two of its gunners killed one after the other. A piece of shrapnel even managed to wound one of the company's men, a quartermaster. His left heel was wrenched off and he began screaming in agony, as if he'd suddenly gone mad.

'Shut up, you animal!' said Rochas. 'What on earth are you blubbering about a little scratch like that for?'

Suddenly calm, the man fell quiet and lapsed into a stupefied, motionless state, clutching his foot in his hand.

And the terrible artillery duel continued over the heads of the prone regiments, getting worse and worse, in that mournful, scorching countryside, with not a soul to be seen beneath the burning sun. There was only the thunder, that hurricane of destruction, rumbling across the solitude. The hours would trickle past, and never once would it stop. But the superior nature of the German artillery was becoming evident, almost all the shells from their percussion guns exploding, covering enormous distances; whereas the French shells, all on time-fuses, which didn't carry nearly so far, usually burst into flames in mid-air before reaching their target. And there was nothing the men could do but make themselves as small as possible, huddling down in the furrows. They couldn't even let off some steam and experience the heady sensation of firing a few shots; who could they shoot at? There wasn't a soul to be seen on the empty horizon!

'Will we ever start firing?' Maurice kept on asking, beside himself. 'I'd give five whole francs just to hit one of them. It's maddening, being fired at like this without being able to answer back.'

'Hang on, it may still happen,' replied Jean calmly.

But the sound of galloping to their left made them turn and look. They recognized General Douay, followed by his staff, who'd come over to check on how his troops were standing up to the dreadful onslaught from Hattoy Hill. He seemed satisfied, and was just giving out a few orders when General Bourgain-Desfeuilles also appeared, emerging from a narrow track. In spite of the fact that his duties were normally purely ceremonial, he trotted along quite unconcerned through the shower of missiles, stubbornly sticking to the routine he'd picked up in Africa, having failed to learn a single lesson. He was shouting and waving, just like Rochas.

'They'll be here any minute now, they'll be here for hand-to-hand fighting!'

Then, spotting General Douay, he drew near.

'Sir, is it true about the Marshal being wounded?'

'Yes, I'm afraid so... I just received a note from General Ducrot, telling me that the Marshal had appointed him to take over command of the army.'

'Ah! So it's General Ducrot!... And what are our orders?'

The general shrugged in despair. Since the day before, he'd sensed that the army was lost and had insisted in vain that they take control of the positions on Saint-Menges and Illy, to ensure the retreat to Mézières.

'Ducrot's reverted to our plan—all the troops are to gather on Illy Plateau.'

And he shrugged again, as if to say that it was too late now.

The booming of the cannon swept aside his words, but their meaning had reached Maurice's ears only too clearly, leaving him petrified. What! Marshal MacMahon wounded, General Ducrot in command in his place, the whole army retreating north of Sedan! And here were these poor bloody soldiers, completely ignorant of such grave news, getting themselves killed! Here they were, being drawn into this appalling fight by some accident, by some chance, at the whim of a new commander-in-chief! He felt the army sinking into confusion and terminal disarray, with no chief, no plan, tugged every which way; and meanwhile the Germans were going straight for their goal with their customary rectitude, and with machine-like precision.

General Bourgain-Desfeuilles was already heading off when General Douay received a new message, brought to him by a Hussar covered in dust; he called the other man back sharply.

'General! General!'

His voice was so loud and so full of thunderous emotion and surprise that it could be heard above the noise of the artillery.

'General! It's not Ducrot any more, it's Wimpffen!... Yes, he arrived yesterday, right in the middle of the Beaumont rout, to replace de Failly as the 5th Corps commander... And he's written to me to say that he's had an official letter from the War Minister, placing him at the head of the army in the event of the command falling vacant... And we're not withdrawing any more, either, our orders are to retake and defend our original positions.'

General Bourgain-Desfeuilles listened to him, wide-eyed.

'Good Lord!' he finally got out. 'So now they tell us... Mind you, I couldn't care less.'

And off he galloped, genuinely unconcerned at heart, for he'd regarded war as merely a means of getting promoted to major-general, and was anxious only to see an end to this blasted campaign as soon as possible, since it was bringing so little joy to them all.

At this, jeers went up from the soldiers in Beaudoin's company. Maurice said nothing, but he shared Chouteau and Loubet's views as they joked with irrepressible disdain. This way, that way, any way I tell you! Well, now, here were commanders who could all agree and weren't trying to take all the credit—my arse! With chiefs like that, surely the best thing to do was just lie down and give up? Three commanders in two hours—three jokers who couldn't even grasp what had to be done, and all giving out different orders! No, but really, it was enough to demoralize and try the patience of the Good Lord himself! And again, those fatal accusations of treason popped up—now Ducrot and Wimpffen were after Bismarck's three million, just like MacMahon.

General Douay was still there, alone, out in front of his staff, gazing into the distance at the Prussian positions, lost in a reverie of infinite sadness. He looked long and hard at Hattoy Hill, from where the shells were landing at his feet. Then, having turned towards Illy Plateau, he called over an officer to take an order there to the brigade of the 5th Corps, which he'd requested from General de Wimpffen the day before and which linked him to General Ducrot's left flank. And they could hear him saying, quite distinctly,

'If the Prussians get hold of the Calvary, we couldn't hold out an hour here, we'd be beaten back to Sedan.'

He left, disappearing with his escort around the bend in the track, and the gunfire grew fiercer. No doubt they'd spotted him. The shells, which up until then had only come from in front of them, began raining down right across them, from the left. It was the Frénois battery and one other, up on the Iges peninsula, crossing fire with the one on Hattoy Hill. They swept across the entire Plateau d'Algérie. From then on, the company's position became appalling. The men, busy keeping an eye on what was happening opposite, now had this other worry to the rear, and were at a loss to know which danger they should flee from first. One after the other, three soldiers were killed, and two wounded men screamed.

And that was how Sergeant Sapin met the death he'd been expecting. He'd turned and seen the shell approaching too late to get out of its way.

'Oh! Here it comes!' he said simply.

His little face with its lovely, big eyes showed only profound sadness, but no terror. His stomach was ripped open. And he began to moan.

'Oh! Don't leave me here, take me to the ambulance, I beg you... Take me to the ambulance.'

Rochas wanted to shut him up. He was about to tell him brutally that there was no point bothering two comrades for a wound like that. Then, taking pity on him, he said,

'My poor boy, just hang on for the stretcher-bearers to come and get you.'

But the wretched man went on, sobbing now, distraught to see the happiness he'd dreamed of ebbing away with his blood.

'Take me away, take me away...'

Captain Beaudoin, his frayed nerves no doubt exasperated by the

moaning, asked for two volunteers to carry the man to a small wood
nearby, where there should be a field ambulance. Bounding forward
and signalling to the others to stay where they were, Chouteau and
Loubet stood up and seized hold of the sergeant, one taking his
shoulders, the other his feet; and they trotted briskly off with him.
On the way, however, they felt him grow stiff and die, with a final
shudder.

'Hey, he's dead,' declared Loubet. 'Put him down.'

Chouteau pushed on furiously.

'Will you move it, lazybones! I'm hardly going to leave him here,
so that they can call us back!'

They ran on with the body as far as the little wood, chucked him
down by a tree and ran off. They weren't seen again until that
evening.

The firing redoubled, the nearby battery had just been strengthened by two more guns; and in the growing din, fear, mad fear
gripped Maurice. At first he hadn't had these cold sweats and that
churning, painful feeling in the pit of the stomach, that irresistible
need to get up and run off at a gallop, yelling. No doubt this was
because it was only just sinking in, as often happens with nervous,
sensitive temperaments. But Jean, who was keeping an eye on him,
caught him in his strong grip, pulling him roughly to him, reading
this fit of cowardice in the wavering look which had come into his
eyes. He swore at him in a low voice, like a father, trying to shame
him with violent words, for he knew that only kicks could put the
courage back into men. Others, too, were shivering, Pache had tears
in his eyes, giving a soft whimper, in spite of himself, like a child's
cry, which he couldn't hold back. And Lapoulle had an accident, his
insides so churned up that he had to pull his trousers down before he
could reach the hedge nearby. They jeered at him, throwing handfuls
of earth at his naked backside, exposed to the shells and bullets.
Many were similarly affected, relieving themselves amid much joking, which helped boost everyone's courage.

'You bloody coward,' Jean kept on at Maurice, 'you're not going to
be ill like them... You'll feel the back of my hand across your face,
you will, if you don't behave yourself!'

He was still egging him on with these taunts when, abruptly, four
hundred metres ahead of them, they caught sight of about ten men,
wearing dark uniforms, emerging from a small wood. At last, here

were the Prussians, whom they recognized from their pointed helmets, the first Prussians they'd seen within range of their rifles since
the beginning of the campaign. Other squadrons followed the first;
and in front of them, they could see the small clouds of dust which
the shells threw up from the ground. It was all nice and precise, the
Prussians were delicately defined, like little lead soldiers, all standing
in neat rows. Then, as the shells began raining down more heavily,
they drew back, and disappeared again behind the trees.

But Beaudoin's company had seen them, and they could still see
them there. The rifles had gone off all by themselves. Maurice was
the first to let off his. Jean, Pache, Lapoulle, and the others all
followed suit. There had been no order to do so, and the captain
wanted to stop the firing; only a sharp gesture from Rochas, indicating that this release was necessary, made him give in. So at last they
were shooting, at last they were making use of these cartridges they'd
been lugging around for over a month, without ever firing a single
one! Of them all, Maurice was the most cheered by it, putting aside
his fear and forgetting everything in the noise of the bullets. The
edge of the wood remained mournful, not a leaf stirred, and not a
single Prussian reappeared; and still they went on shooting at the
motionless trees.

Then, looking up, Maurice was surprised to spot Colonel de
Vineuil a few steps away on his horse, both man and beast impassive,
as if made of stone. Facing the enemy, the colonel waited in the line
of fire. The whole of the 106th must have drawn back here, other
companies were lying flat in neighbouring fields, and the gunfire was
getting closer and closer. And the young man saw the standard, too,
in the solid grasp of the subaltern. But this time, it wasn't that ghost
of a flag, drowned in the morning mists. Beneath the burning sun the
gold-plated eagle gleamed, the silk tricolour was vibrant with bright
hues, despite being gloriously battle-worn. High up against the blue
sky, in the middle of the cannonade, it floated like a victory flag.

Why shouldn't they win, now that they were actually fighting?
Maurice and the rest fired furiously, burning up their gunpowder,
firing into the distant woods, and a slow, silent shower of tiny
branches pattered to the ground.

CHAPTER THREE

Henriette couldn't sleep all night. Knowing that her husband was in Bazeilles, so close to the German lines, was torture. In vain, she repeated to herself his promise to come home at the first hint of danger; and every other minute, she strained her ears, thinking she could hear him. At about ten o'clock, as she was about to go to bed, she opened the window and leaned on the sill, lost in thought.

The night was very dark, and she could hardly make out the pavement of the Rue des Voyards down below, a narrow, obscure corridor squeezed between the ancient houses. In the distance, near the school, all that could be seen was the smoky star of a street lamp. The sulphurous smell of cellars and saltpetre rose on the air, the yowling of an angry cat, the heavy footsteps of a soldier who had lost his way. And behind her, throughout Sedan, came unusual noises, the sudden sound of galloping, continuous rumblings, passing like deathly shivers. She listened, heart pounding, and still she couldn't recognize her husband's footsteps coming round the corner of the street.

Hours passed, and now she was worried about the distant lights she could see in the countryside, beyond the ramparts. It was so dark that she had to try mentally to piece the land together. The huge, pale tablecloth down below had to be the flooded meadows. So what was that fire she'd seen burning and then going out, up there, probably on La Marfée? Others were glowing all around, in Pont-Maugis, Noyers, Frénois, mysterious fires which flickered as if above a numerous crowd seething in the shadows. More sinister, though, were the extraordinary noises which gave her the shivers, the tramping sound of people on the march, animals huffing, weapons clanking, an entire cavalcade passing deep in these infernal shadows. Suddenly a cannon boomed out, a single, formidable blast, terrifying by the utter silence which followed. It made her blood run cold. What on earth was it? Probably a signal, some manœuvre successfully accomplished, a signal to say that they were ready, down there, and that the sun could come up.

At about two o'clock, Henriette flung herself fully dressed onto the bed, neglecting even to close the window. Fatigue and fear were weighing her down. What was it that made her shiver feverishly like this, when she was usually so calm, her step so light that one didn't even notice she was there? She slept badly, numb, with a nagging awareness of the disaster which lurked in the black sky. All of a sudden, in the middle of her fitful sleep, the cannon began again, muffled explosions, far away; and on and on it went, regular and stubborn. Shivering, she sat up in bed. Where was she? She couldn't make out her surroundings, no longer able to see her room, which seemed to be filled by thick smoke. Then she realized what it was: fog rising from the river near by must have crept into the room. Outside, the cannonfire redoubled. She leapt out of bed and ran to the window to listen.

One of Sedan's clocks was striking four. First light was beginning to break through, murky and dirty through the brownish fog. It was impossible to see anything, she couldn't even make out the school buildings any more, a few metres away. My God, where was the firing coming from? Her first thought was for her brother Maurice, for the shots were so muted that they seemed to be coming from the north, above the town. Then, she no longer had any doubts, the firing was there, right in front of her, and she trembled, thinking of her husband. It was definitely in Bazeilles. However, for some moments she was reassured, for every now and then it seemed that the explosions were coming from the right. Maybe they were fighting in Donchery, where she knew they'd been unable to blow up the bridge. Then she succumbed to a moment of cruel indecision: was it Donchery, or Bazeilles? It was becoming impossible to work it out, what with the buzzing which filled her head. Before long, she was in such torment that she knew she couldn't stay there a moment longer, just waiting. Quivering to know this instant, she threw a shawl over her shoulders and went out, searching for news.

Down below in the Rue des Voyards, Henriette hesitated briefly, seeing the town still so dark beneath the blind fog which submerged it. Dawn hadn't reached down as far as the damp cobbles, between the old, smoke-smudged buildings. At the back of a shady club in the Rue au Beurre, all she saw were two drunken Turks with a girl. She had to turn into the Rue Maqua before she found any life: soldiers whose shadows flitted furtively along the pavements, cowards, perhaps, seeking somewhere to hide; a tall Cuirassier who'd got lost and was busy looking for his captain, knocking furiously on every door; a whole collection of townsfolk, sweating with fear at having left it so late, now making up their minds to pile into a carriage and see whether there was still time to get to Bouillon, in Belgium, to where half Sedan had been emigrating for the past two days. Instinctively, she headed for the Sous-Préfecture, where she was sure she'd get some information; and it occurred to her to cut through the back-streets, eager to avoid meeting anyone. On the Rue du Four and the Rue des Laboureurs, however, she couldn't get past: they were full of cannons, a whole line of guns, ammunition chests, and gun carriages, which must have been tucked away here the day before and appeared to have since been forgotten. There wasn't even anyone guarding them. It made a chill run through her, to see all this useless, mournful artillery sleeping here abandoned at the back of these deserted streets. So she had to go back, through the Place du Collège, towards the Grande-Rue where, outside the Hôtel de l'Europe,* messengers were holding the horses, awaiting their superior officers, who could be heard raising loud voices in the glaringly lit dining room. On the Place du Rivage and the Place Turenne there were even more people, worried groups of townsfolk, women, and children, all mixed up with the scattered, panicking troops; and it was here that she saw a general come swearing out of the Hôtel de la Croix d'Or and set off at a raging gallop, nearly bowling everyone over. For a moment, she thought of going to the town hall; then in the end she took the Rue du Pont-de-Meuse, pushing on towards the Sous-Préfecture.

Never before had Sedan struck her as the tragic city it now seemed, seen in the light of the murky, fog-muffled dawn. The houses looked dead; many had been empty and abandoned for the past two days; the rest were hermetically sealed up, victims of the terror-stricken insomnia which could be felt in the air. It was a cold, shivery morning, the streets were still half-deserted, peopled only by frightened shadows, marked by abrupt departures, among the collection of dubious characters which had already started hanging around the day before. Daylight would grow brighter and the town more crowded, submerged beneath the disaster. It was half-past five, and the noise of the cannon could hardly be heard here, muffled by the tall, black buildings.

At the Sous-Préfecture, Henriette knew the concierge's daughter, Rose, a small blonde girl, pretty and delicate-looking, who worked at

Delaherche's factory. She went straight into the lodge. Her mother wasn't there, but Rose greeted her with her usual warmth.

'Oh! My dear ma'am, we just can't keep on our feet a moment longer. Mother's gone to rest a little. Can you imagine it, we've had to be up all night, with all these endless comings and goings!'

And without waiting to be asked, she went on and on about it, thoroughly excited by all the extraordinary things she'd seen since the day before.

'The Marshal slept well, he did. But it's that poor Emperor I worry about! No, you just can't imagine how he suffers!... Just imagine, yesterday evening I went to help take up the laundry. And there I was going into the room next to the dressing room, when I heard groans, oh! such groans they were, just like someone was dying. And there I stood, trembling, my blood running cold, as I realized that it was the Emperor... Apparently, he's got some terrible illness makes him cry out like that. When there are people around, he holds it in; but as soon as he's on his own, he just can't help it, he cries out and moans, it's enough to make your hair stand up on end.'

'Where have they been fighting since this morning, do you know?' asked Henriette, trying to interrupt.

Rose waved the question aside; and she went on,

'Well, you know, I wanted to find out more, so I went back up there four or five times in the night, and put my ear to the partition... He was still moaning away, he never stopped, I'm sure he can't have got a wink of sleep... Awful, isn't it, to suffer like that, with all those worries he must have going round inside his head! I mean, it's such a mess, it's bedlam up there! They all seem to be quite mad, I swear! And there's always someone else arriving, and doors slamming, and people shouting at each other and others crying, and the house is in chaos, it's sheer pillage, there's officers drinking out of bottles and sleeping in the beds with their boots still on!... Mind you, the Emperor's the nicest of them all, and the one as takes up least room, hiding away in that corner of his to groan.'

Then, when Henriette repeated her question,

'Where are they fighting? In Bazeilles, since this morning!... A soldier came on horseback to tell the Marshal, and he went straight in to the Emperor, to warn him... The Marshal's already been gone ten minutes, and I think the Emperor's going to meet him there, because they're getting him dressed, upstairs... I just this minute saw them combing his hair and sprucing him up, putting all sorts of bits and bobs on his face.'

But Henriette, having found out what she'd wanted at last, was off.

'Thank you, Rose. I'm in a hurry.'

And the young girl obligingly accompanied her out into the road, calling after her,

'At your service, Madame Weiss. I know I can tell you everything.'

Henriette went swiftly back home to the Rue des Voyards. She was sure she'd find her husband already back; and it even occurred to her that he must be very worried, not to find her at home, and so she pressed on even faster. As she was approaching the house she looked up, expecting to spot him leaning out of the window, watching out for her. But the window, still wide open, was empty. When she'd climbed the stairs and glanced in at all three rooms, she stood frozen, her heart gripped with fear at finding only this icy fog, with the cannon still pounding and pounding away. They were still firing, down there. She stood at the window again for a moment. Now that she'd been told, even though the wall of morning mist was just as impenetrable as ever, she could see perfectly well that there was fighting in Bazeilles, with the crack of machine-gun fire and the deafening salvos from the French batteries answering the distant German ones. The explosions seemed to be coming closer together, and the battle was growing fiercer every minute.

Why didn't Weiss come back? He'd promised so faithfully to return home at the first sign of attack! Henriette became more and more worried, imagining obstacles in his way, the road being cut off, shelling already making it dangerous to retreat. Maybe even something awful had happened to him. She pushed the thought aside, her hope urging her firmly to take action. For a moment, she thought about going there herself and setting off to meet her husband. Doubts, though, held her back: perhaps they'd pass each other; and what would become of her if she missed him? And think how anxious he'd be if he came back to find her not there! Other than that, the folly of going to Bazeilles at this time seemed to her quite natural, with no trace of misplaced heroism, something which was just part of being a busy wife, silently doing what had to be done for the good of her family. Wherever her husband was, that, quite simply, was where she must be.

Suddenly an idea struck her, and leaving the window she said out loud,

'What about Monsieur Delaherche... I'll go and see...'

She'd just remembered that the mill owner, too, had spent the night in Bazeilles, and that if he was back home, he could give her news. She promptly went back downstairs. Instead of going out onto the Rue des Voyards, she crossed the narrow courtyard and took the passage leading to the vast factory buildings, whose monumental façade overlooked the Rue Maqua. Emerging into what had once been the inner garden, now paved over, leaving only a lawn bordered by superb trees, giant elms dating from the previous century, she was astonished at first to catch sight of a sentry guarding a locked shed door; then she remembered why—she'd been told the day before that the coffers of the 7th Corps had been put in there; and it had a peculiar effect on her, knowing that all that gold was there, millions, apparently, hidden in this shed, while people were already getting killed nearby. But just as she was mounting the back stairs up to Gilberte's room, another surprise pulled her up short, a meeting so unexpected that she went back down the three steps she'd already climbed, unsure whether she dared knock at the door or not. A soldier had just passed her by, a captain, as airy as an apparition, vanishing as swiftly as he had appeared; she had, however, had time to recognize him, for she'd seen him at Charleville, at Gilberte's house, Madame Maginot as she then was. She took a few steps into the courtyard and looked up at the two bedroom windows high up, where the shutters were still closed. Then she decided to go up anyway.

On the first floor, she had intended to knock at the dressing-room door, as a childhood friend, someone intimate who sometimes came like this to talk in the mornings. But in the haste of departure the door hadn't been shut properly, and was standing ajar. All she had to do was give it a push, and she was in the dressing room, and then in the bedroom itself. The room had a very high ceiling, from which hung full drapes of red velvet which entirely enveloped the large bed. Not a sound could be heard in the humid silence which follows a night of pleasure, just steady, barely audible breathing, floating on a faint, evaporated scent of lilac.

'Gilberte!' called Henriette softly.

The young woman had gone straight back to sleep; and lying in the pale light coming in between the red curtains at the windows, her pretty, rounded head had rolled off the pillow and was leaning on one of her bare arms, surrounded by her remarkable, loose black hair.

'Gilberte!'

She stirred, then stretched, without opening her eyes.

'Yes, farewell... Oh! Please...'

Then, lifting her head, she recognized Henriette.

'Oh! It's you... What time is it?'

When she was told that it was striking six, she seemed embarrassed, and to hide her unease said jokingly that this was no time to be waking people up. Then, as soon as she was asked about her husband, she said,

'But he isn't home yet, he won't be until about nine o'clock, I think... Why did you think he'd be back so soon?'

Seeing her smiling and still lazy from her contented sleep, Henriette had to insist.

'I'm telling you, they've been fighting in Bazeilles since first light, and since I'm very worried about my husband...'

'Oh! My dear,' exclaimed Gilberte, 'how wrong you are... Mine is such a cautious man that he'd have been here long ago if there were the slightest sign of danger... As long as you don't see him, you needn't worry...'

Henriette was quite struck by this remark. It was true, Delaherche wasn't the sort of man to put himself needlessly at risk. She was entirely reassured, and went over to open the curtains and fold back the shutters; and the bright, orange light from the sky flooded the room as the sun began to break through the fog, lending it a golden hue. One of the windows stayed open a little, and now they could hear the cannon, inside the large, warm room, which only a moment ago had been so stuffy and tightly shut.

Gilberte, half sitting up, with one elbow resting on the pillow, was looking at the sky with her pretty, sparkling eyes.

'So, they're fighting,' she murmured.

Her nightshirt had slipped down, and one of her shoulders was bare, the flesh delicate and pink beneath the scattered black tresses; and a pervasive smell, the smell of love, rose from her as she awoke.

'My God, they're fighting this morning! How ridiculous it is, to fight!'

However, Henriette's gaze had strayed to a pair of army issue gloves, a man's gloves left behind on a pedestal table; and she couldn't help giving a start. Gilberte blushed deeply, beckoning her to her bedside with a confused, affectionate gesture. Then, burying her face against her shoulder, she said,

'Yes, I could tell that you knew, that you'd seen him... Darling, don't be too harsh on me. He's an old friend, I did confess my weakness to you in Charleville before, you remember...'

She lowered her voice even further, and went on with fondness and a hint of laughter,

'Yesterday, he begged and begged me to, when I saw him again... Just think, this morning he's fighting, maybe they'll kill him... How could I refuse?'

It was so charming and heroic, to see her all tender and full of joy, giving this final gift of pleasure, a night of happiness donated on the eve of battle. That was why she was smiling, in spite of her embarrassment, dizzy as a sparrow. She would never have had the heart to shut her door on him, not when circumstances made it so easy for them to meet.

'Do you blame me?'

Henriette had listened to her very gravely. These things surprised her, because she couldn't comprehend them. Perhaps she was different. Since that morning, her heart had been with her husband and her brother, out there under fire. How could someone sleep so peacefully and be so full of amorous delight when there were loved ones in danger?

'But darling, what about your husband and that boy, too—doesn't it make you sick at heart, not to be with them?... Hasn't it occurred to you that they might be brought back at any minute, with their heads cracked open?'

Gilberte sharply swept the horrible image aside, with her adorably bare arm.

'Oh! My God! What sort of a thing to say is that? How mean of you to spoil my morning!... No, no, I don't even want to think about it, it's all too sad!'

And in spite of herself Henriette smiled, too. She recalled their childhood days, when Gilberte's father, Commander de Vineuil, appointed Chief of Customs for Charleville after being wounded, had sent his daughter to stay on a farm near Le Chesne-Populeux, worried to hear her coughing, for he was haunted by the memory of his wife, who had just been carried off by consumption while still very young. The little girl had only been nine years old, but she was already disturbingly coquettish; she would put on performances and always insisted on playing the queen, draping herself in all the scarves she could find, saving the silver paper from chocolates to make herself bracelets and crowns. Later on, she stayed just the same, and at twenty had married Forestry Inspector Maginot. Mézières, squeezed between its ramparts, didn't agree with her, and she went on living in Charleville, where she liked the less constrained lifestyle, brightened up by parties. Her father had since died, and she enjoyed complete freedom, with a convenient husband who was such a nonentity that she felt no remorse. Provincial spitefulness had credited her at the time with many lovers, but in reality, she'd only forgotten herself with Captain Beaudoin, among the crowd of uniforms in which she lived, thanks to old contacts of her father's and her relationship to Colonel de Vineuil. There was no trace of wilful malice in her, she merely adored pleasure; and it seemed certain that, in taking a lover, she'd given in to her irresistible need to be happy and beautiful.

'It's very wrong to have taken up with him again,' Henriette said eventually, in her serious way.

Gilberte had already hushed her, with one of her pretty, caressing gestures.

'Oh! But darling, when I couldn't do otherwise and it was just this once... You do know, I'd rather die now than deceive my new husband.'

Neither of them said anything more, holding each other in an affectionate embrace, even though they were so profoundly different. They could hear their hearts beating, they would have been able to understand the different language each was talking, one living only for pleasure, giving of herself, sharing herself, the other one deeply, uniquely devoted, with that great, silent heroism which is the mark of a strong soul.

'It's true, they're fighting!' Gilberte finally exclaimed. 'I must hurry up and get dressed.'

Since they'd fallen silent, the noise of the explosions had in fact appeared to grow louder. And she leapt out of bed and made Henriette help her, not wishing to call the chambermaid, putting on her shoes and immediately getting into a dress, so that she'd be ready to receive visitors and go downstairs, if needed. As she was quickly finishing her hair, there was a knock at the door, and, recognizing the voice of old Madame Delaherche, she ran to open it.

'Of course you may come in, Mother dear.'

With her habitual carelessness she let her in, not noticing that the officer's gloves were still lying there on the table. Henriette vainly rushed to grab them and throw them behind an armchair. Madame Delaherche must have seen them, for she remained speechless for a few moments, as if unable to draw breath. Involuntarily, she glanced around the room, and stopped at the red-draped bed, curtains still wide open to reveal its crumpled sheets.

'So, it was Madame Weiss who came to wake you... You've managed to sleep, my dear...'

Obviously, this wasn't what she had come up to say. Oh! This marriage, which her son had insisted on against her will, in the crisis of middle age, after twenty passionless years with a morose, skinny wife; he'd been so reasonable up until then, but now his head had been quite turned by youthful yearning for this pretty widow, who was so flighty and carefree. She'd promised herself that she would look to the present, and now here was the past repeating itself! But should she say anything? Her role in the house had been reduced now to one of mute reproach, always keeping herself shut away in her room, practising a rigid, devout existence. This time, however, the misdemeanour was such a serious one that she resolved to warn her son.

Reddening, Gilberte replied,

'Yes, I slept well for a few hours, anyway... You do know that Jules hasn't come home...'

Madame Delaherche cut her off with a gesture. Since the cannon had begun to boom, she'd been worried, watching for her son to return. She was a heroic mother, though. And she remembered what it was she had come up here to do.

'Your uncle, the Colonel, has sent us a pencilled note along with Major Bouroche, to ask whether we would let them set up a hospital here... He knows that we have room for it in the factory, and I've already placed the courtyard and drying room at these gentlemen's disposal... The only thing is, you should come down.'

'Oh! Right away, right away!' said Henriette, stepping forward. 'We'll help.'

Gilberte herself seemed very moved and full of passion for this
new role of nurse. She barely took the time to knot a lace shawl over
her hair; and the three women went downstairs. There, as they came
into the huge porch, through the open double doors, they saw a
gathering outside in the road. A low-slung carriage was slowly pulling up, a sort of cart with a single horse hitched to it, which a Zouave
lieutenant was leading by the bridle. And they thought this was the
first of the wounded being brought in.

'Yes, yes, this way, come in!'

But they were mistaken. The wounded man lying on the floor of
the cart was Marshal MacMahon, his left buttock half blown away,
being taken back to the Sous-Préfecture after being given a preliminary dressing in a little gardener's house. His head was bare and he
was half-undressed, the gold braid on his uniform soiled with blood
and dust. Without speaking, he lifted his head and looked around
him vaguely. Then, noticing the three women standing there frozen,
hands clasped at the sight of the grave misfortune which was passing
by—this wounding of the army's commander which was like a
wound to the entire army, from one of the very first shells—he
bowed his head slightly with a faint, fatherly smile. Around him, a
few curious people had taken off their hats. Others were already
busily talking about how General Ducrot had just been named
Commander-in-Chief. It was half-past seven.

'And what about the Emperor?' Henriette asked a bookseller,
standing outside his door.

'He went by nearly an hour ago,' replied her neighbour. 'I went
with him, I saw him leave by the Porte de Balan... There's a rumour
going round that a cannonball took his head off.'

But the grocer opposite grew angry.

'Give it a rest! What lies! The only people who'll leave their hides
behind are the good ones!'

Near the Place du Collège, the cart carrying the Marshal got lost
among the swollen crowds, where the most extraordinary pieces of
news from the battlefield were already going round. The fog was
clearing and the streets were filling with sunlight.

But a rough voice called out from the courtyard,

'Ladies! It's here you're needed, not out there!'

All three went back inside, where they found themselves confronted with Major Bouroche, who'd already flung his uniform into

a corner and donned a large, white apron. His huge head and wiry, bushy hair, his lion's mane, was aflame with haste and energy, above this as yet spotless expanse of white. They found the sight of him so terrifying that at once they were in his thrall, obeying at the merest sign, falling over each other to please him.

'We've nothing here... Get me linen, try to find some more mattresses, show my men where to find the pump...'

They ran here and there, everywhere at once, his utterly dedicated servants.

The factory was an excellent choice for a hospital. Above all, it had the drying room, an immense, glassed-in room where easily a hundred beds could be set up; and next door was a warehouse, where they would be wonderfully placed for carrying out operations; a long table had just been carried in, the pump was only a few steps away, and those with minor injuries could wait on the neighbouring lawn. Not only that, but it was really very pleasant, with the ancient elm trees providing delicious shade.

Bouroche preferred to set everything up straight away in Sedan, foreseeing the massacre, the dreadful onslaught which would fling the troops onto the town. He'd had to make do with leaving two first-aid field ambulances near the 7th Corps, behind Floing, from where they were to send the wounded on to him, after applying basic dressings. All the squads of stretcher-bearers were out there, given the task of going under fire to gather up the fallen men, equipped with supplies from the carriages and wagons. And apart from two of his aides who'd stayed behind on the battlefield, Bouroche had brought his entire staff with him, two majors, second class, and three under-assistants, who would probably be sufficient for the operations. Besides these, there were three pharmacists and a dozen nurses.

However, he was constantly in a temper, for he was unable to do anything without passion.

'What the hell are you doing? Move those mattresses closer together!... We'll put straw down in that corner, if need be.'

The cannon were rumbling, and he was well aware that any minute now, the work was going to start coming in, carriages full of bleeding flesh; and roughly he began setting up the large, still empty room. Next, more preparations got under way in the warehouse: boxes of dressings and medicines were lined up and opened on a shelf, bundles of shredded linen, bandages, compresses, sheets, equipment for fractures; while on another shelf, next to a big pot of thick cerate ointment and a bottle of chloroform, the surgical kits were rolled out, the bright steel of the instruments, probes, tweezers, knives, scissors, saws, an entire arsenal of them, every possible shape of sharp, cutting things for delving, incising, slicing, and chopping. However, there weren't enough bowls.

'You must have bowls and buckets and saucepans, whatever you like... We can't get up to our necks in blood, can we!... And sponges, try to find me some sponges!'

Madame Delaherche rushed off, returning with three maids in tow, arms piled up with every single bowl she could find. Standing before the surgical kits, Gilberte had beckoned Henriette over, pointing them out to her with a slight shudder. They took each other's hand, standing there in silence, their contact imbued with the mute terror and anxious pity which overwhelmed them.

'Oh! Darling, and to think they could cut off a bit of you!'

'Those poor people!'

Bouroche had just had a mattress placed on the big table, and he was covering it with an oilcloth, when the clatter of hooves was heard in the porch. It was one of the first ambulances coming into the courtyard. Inside, though, were ten men with only minor injuries, sitting face to face, most of them with an arm in a sling, some with head wounds, their foreheads bandaged up. They just needed to be helped down; and the doctor began his rounds.

As Henriette was gently helping a very young soldier, whose shoulder had been pierced by a bullet, to take off his greatcoat, a process which drew cries of pain from him, she noticed the number of his regiment.

'But you're from the 106th! Do you belong to Beaudoin's company?'

No, he was from Ravaud's. But he did know Jean Macquart, and thought he was right in saying that his squad hadn't yet gone into battle. And this information, vague as it was, was enough to make the young woman rejoice: her brother was alive, and once she'd kissed her husband, whom she was still expecting any minute now, her relief would be quite complete.

Just then, looking up, Henriette was startled to see Delaherche a few steps away, in the middle of a group of people, recounting the terrible dangers he'd just run, coming back from Bazeilles to Sedan. How had he got there? She hadn't seen him come in.

'Isn't my husband with you?'

Delaherche, however, whose wife and mother were indulgently asking him questions, was in no hurry.

'Hang on, in a minute.'

Then, picking up his tale again,

'Between Bazeilles and Balan, I nearly got killed dozens of times. The shells and bullets were hailing down, it was like a hurricane!... And I met the Emperor, oh! a jolly good chap he is... Then, I went on my way again, from Balan to here...'

Henriette tugged at his sleeve.

'What about my husband?'

'Weiss? He's there, Weiss is!'

'What do you mean, there?'

'Well, he picked up this dead soldier's rifle, and he's fighting.'

'Fighting? What for?'

'Oh! He's gone mad! He wouldn't follow me back, and so, naturally, I left him there.'

Wide-eyed and staring, Henriette just looked at him. There was a pause. Then, quite calmly, she made up her mind.

'Right, I'm going there.'

What did she mean, going there? But it was impossible, it was mad! Delaherche mentioned the bullets again, and the shells sweeping across the road. Gilberte had taken both hands into hers again, to hold her back, while Madame Delaherche, too, exhausted herself trying to show her the blind folly of her plan. In her gentle, simple way, she just repeated,

'No, it's no use, I'm going.'

And she was insistent, agreeing only to take the black lace which Gilberte was wearing on her head. Still hoping to dissuade her, Delaherche ended up declaring that he would go with her, at least as far as the Porte de Balan. However, he'd just caught sight of the sentry who, in all the turmoil caused by the setting up of the hospital, hadn't stopped pacing up and down outside the shed where the coffers of the 7th Corps were locked up; and he suddenly remembered them and panicked, and went over to have a quick look to make sure the millions were still there. Henriette was already making for the door.

'Wait for me, will you! You're as mad as that husband of yours, I swear!'

As it happened, another ambulance was coming in and they had to let it pass. This one, smaller than the last, just a two-wheeler, contained two seriously injured men lying on straw mattresses. The first one to be taken off, with the utmost care, was just a mass of bloody flesh, with one broken hand and a gash in his side from a piece of shrapnel. The second man's right leg had been crushed. Bouroche had him put straight onto the oilcloth-covered mattress and began the first operation, surrounded by the constant comings and goings of the nurses and his assistants. Madame Delaherche and Gilberte, sitting near the lawn, rolled up bandages.

Outside, Delaherche had caught up with Henriette.

'My dear Madame Weiss, come on, you surely aren't going to go ahead with this foolish plan... How are you going to find Weiss back there? He probably isn't even there any more, he's probably making his way back across the fields by now... I assure you, Bazeilles is quite inaccessible.'

But she wasn't listening to him, and began walking faster, turning down the Rue du Ménil to the Porte de Balan. It was nearly nine o'clock, and in Sedan the dark shiver of the morning had gone, with that lonely, fumbling awakening in the thick fog. Strong sunlight cut sharply through the shadows cast by the houses, and a nervous crowd filled the pavements, where messengers were continually galloping back and forth. The largest groups were those that formed around the few unarmed soldiers who'd already returned, some with minor wounds, others in an extraordinarily nervous and excited state, waving and shouting. And yet the town would have looked more or less as it did on any normal day, if it hadn't been for the closed-up shop fronts, the lifeless façades, where there wasn't a single open shutter to be seen. And then there were the cannon, the unrelenting cannon, causing every stone, the ground, the walls, even the slates on the roofs to tremble.

Delaherche was going through a particularly unpleasant tussle with himself, torn between his duty to be courageous, which told him to stay with Henriette, and his terror of making the journey back to Bazeilles through the shelling. All of a sudden, as they reached the Porte de Balan, a crowd of mounted officers arrived and separated them. People swarmed round the gates, waiting for news.

In vain, he ran here and there, looking for the young woman: she must have been outside the walls, hurrying on her way down the road. And refusing to go to unnecessary lengths, he surprised himself by saying aloud,

'Oh, never mind! Anyway, what's the point!'

Then Delaherche wandered around Sedan, just a curious gentleman who didn't want to miss any of the spectacle, although he was steadily growing more and more anxious. What was going to become of all this? And if the army were defeated, wouldn't the town suffer badly? The answers to these questions remained obscure, too dependent on the turn events might take. However, this didn't stop him trembling in fear for his factory and his property on the Rue Maqua, to where he'd moved all his valuables, tucked away in a safe place. He went to the town hall, found the town council in permanent session, and hung around for quite a while, without learning anything new at all, except that the battle was going extremely badly. The army no longer knew whom to obey, forced to withdraw by General Ducrot during the two hours of his command, then made to advance again by General de Wimpffen as he took over; and these incomprehensible vacillations, these positions they'd abandoned, only to be forced to retake them, the complete lack of any sort of plan or dynamic leadership, were simply speeding the disaster on.

After this, Delaherche pushed on as far as the Sous-Préfecture to find out whether the Emperor had reappeared. All they could manage was news of Marshal MacMahon; his wound, which posed little real danger, had been dressed by a surgeon, and he was now safely in bed. Towards eleven o'clock, however, as he was once again pounding the pavement, Delaherche was delayed for a moment in the Grand-Rue, outside the Hôtel de l'Europe, by a slow-moving procession, its riders covered in dust and the gloomy horses proceeding at walking pace. And at their head he recognized the Emperor, returning from four hours spent on the battlefield. Death had obviously not claimed him, after all. The sweat of fear as he marched through their defeat had made the powder wear off his cheeks, his waxed moustache had grown soft and limp, and his sallow features had taken on the pained stupor of a dying man. One officer, dismounting outside the hotel, began explaining to a group the way they'd come, from La Moncelle to Givonne, all along the little valley, among the soldiers of the 1st Corps, driven back onto the right bank of the stream by the Saxon Corps; and they had come back along the track which ran through Givonne Valley, amid such congestion that, even had the Emperor wished to return to the front where his troops were positioned, he wouldn't have been able to do so without great difficulty. And in any case, what was the use?

As Delaherche was listening to this, a violent explosion shook the area. It was a shell which had demolished a chimney on the Rue Saint-Barbe, near the Prison. People rushed for cover and women could be heard screaming. He was clinging to a wall when a fresh blast shattered the windows of a neighbouring house. Things were clearly in a dreadful state if they were now bombarding Sedan; and he ran back home to the Rue Maqua, so desperate to know what was happening that he didn't even stop when he got there, climbing swiftly up onto the roof where he had a terrace overlooking the town and the surrounding countryside.

At once, he was somewhat reassured. The fighting was taking place to the north of the town, and the German batteries on La Marfée and at Frénois were sending their fire right over the houses to sweep across the Plateau d'Algérie; and he even watched the flight of the shells with interest, and the immense curves of light-coloured smoke which they left above Sedan, like invisible birds leaving fine trails of grey feathers. At first, it seemed obvious to him that the shells which had crashed through the roofs around him had been missiles which had strayed off course. They were not yet bombarding the town. Then, looking more closely, he thought he could see that they must be responding to the occasional shots being fired from the cannon on the square. He turned round and examined the citadel to the north, with all its impressive, complicated mass of fortifications, the blackish stretches of wall, the green panels of glacis, a geometric proliferation of bastions and the three giant, dominating corners—the Scots, the Grand Jardin, and La Rochette—with their menacing edges; and next, like some cyclopean extension on the west side, was the Nassau Fort, followed by the Palatinate one above the Le Ménil district. It gave him the melancholy impression of enormity and yet, at the same time, childishness. What good was it now, confronted by these cannon, whose missiles flew so effortlessly from one edge of the sky to the other? Besides, the square was undefended, with neither the guns, nor the ammunition, nor the men necessary. It had been scarcely three weeks ago that the town governor had organized a National Guard, made up of local volunteers, who were to man the few guns in working order. That was how there came to be three cannon firing from the Palatinate Fort, while there must have been about half a dozen of them at the Porte de Paris. The only trouble was that there were only seven or eight charges to lay per gun, so the shots were being let off sparingly, exploding only once every half-hour, and then merely to satisfy honour, for the shells didn't carry far and landed in the meadows opposite. The enemy batteries showed their disdain by replying less and less often, almost out of charity.

It was precisely these batteries which interested Delaherche up on the roof. His sharp eyes were raking over the slopes of La Marfée when he suddenly thought of the telescope he used to amuse himself with, training it on the surrounding area from high up on the terrace. He went down to find it, came back again, and set it in position; and as he was getting his bearings, edging it over the fields, trees, and houses, he chanced on the group of uniforms which Weiss had distinguished from Bazeilles, on the edge of a pine wood, just above the large battery at Frénois. Thanks to the magnifying lens, however, he could see them so clearly that he could have actually counted the number of officers in the staff. Several were half-reclining on the grass, others were standing in groups; and to the fore was a single man, who looked thin and wiry, wearing an undecorated uniform, but whose masterly presence was unmistakable. It was indeed the King of Prussia, hardly taller than half his finger, like one of those minuscule lead toy soldiers. He was nonetheless adamant, subsequently, that he'd never taken his eyes off him, forever coming back to this infinitely small figure, whose face, no bigger than a lentil, was just a pale dot beneath the vast, blue sky.

It wasn't yet midday, and the King had been surveying the mathematical, inexorable march of his armies since nine. On and on they progressed, following the designated routes, completing the circle, step by step closing in their wall of men and artillery around Sedan. The one on the left, which had come across the flat terrain of Donchery Plain, continued to file out of the Saint-Albert gap, moving beyond Saint-Menges and starting to reach Fleigneux; and behind the XIth Corps, which was violently entangled with General Douay's troops, he could quite distinctly see the Vth Corps slipping through, taking advantage of the woods to head for Illy Plateau;

meanwhile, more and more batteries were adding to the numbers, forming a line of thundering guns, growing longer and longer, little by little setting the whole horizon on fire. From that point on, the army on the right was to occupy the whole of the Givonne Valley, the XIIth Corps having seized La Moncelle, while the Guard had just come through Daigny, and was already following the stream back up, also marching towards the Calvary, having forced General Ducrot to withdraw behind Garenne Wood. It just needed one more effort, and the Crown Prince of Prussia would join up with the Crown Prince of Saxony, in the middle of these naked fields, right on the edge of the Ardennes Forest. South of the town, Bazeilles was no longer visible, it had disappeared in the smoke of the fires, in the savage dust of a raging struggle.

And the King had been calmly watching and waiting since morning. An hour, two hours to go, maybe three: it was only a matter of time, one cog was turning another, the grinding machine was moving and would complete its course. Beneath the infinite, sunny skies the battlefield was shrinking, the entire, furious crush of black dots was tumbling and piling up higher and higher around Sedan. Windows in the town were shining, one house appeared to be on fire, to the left, on the edge of the suburb of La Cassine. Then, beyond that, in the newly deserted fields near Donchery and near Carignan, there reigned a warm, luminous peace, with the clear waters of the Meuse, trees full of the joys of life, huge, fertile lands, and expanses of green meadows lying in the powerful midday heat.

With a single word, the King asked a question. He wanted to know every particle of this human dust under his command on the giant chessboard, he wanted to hold it in the palm of his hand. To his right, a flight of swallows, taking fright at the noise of the cannon, wheeled and went climbing high into the sky, vanishing south.

CHAPTER FOUR

On the Balan road, Henriette had been able to walk quickly at first. It was barely after nine o'clock and the wide road, lined with houses and gardens, was still clear, although it grew steadily more obstructed the nearer it got to the village, filled with fleeing locals and troops on the move. With each fresh surge of people, Henriette clung close to the walls, slipping through in spite of them. Slender and inconspicuous in her dark dress, her fine blond hair and tiny, pale face half-covered by the black lace shawl, she escaped their notice, and nothing slowed her light-footed, silent steps.

In Balan, however, there was a regiment of marine infantry blocking the road. It was a compact mass of men awaiting orders, in the shelter of the tall trees which concealed them. She stood on tiptoe, and still couldn't see to the end. But she tried to make herself smaller than ever and thread her way through. She was elbowed back, and felt rifle butts digging into her sides. She'd hardly gone twenty paces when cries of protest started up. A captain turned to look and lost his temper.

'Hey! Are you mad, woman?... Where are you going?'

'To Bazeilles.'

'Bazeilles! Oh, you are, are you!'

Laughter broke out all around. They pointed at her, joking. The captain, also amused, spoke again.

'Bazeilles—well, my girl, you ought to take us with you!... We were there just now, and hopefully we're going back; but I warn you, it's no picnic back there.'

'I'm going to Bazeilles to be with my husband,' Henriette replied in her soft voice, while her light blue eyes retained their air of calm resolution.

'My poor child, you can see for yourself that it's impossible to get through... It's no place for a woman just now... You'll find your husband later on. Come on, show some sense!'

She had to give in and she stopped, standing and stretching up on tiptoe every two minutes to look into the distance, stubbornly determined to continue on her way. She gleaned information from what she could hear being said around her. Some of the officers were complaining bitterly about the order to retreat which had forced them to abandon Bazeilles at a quarter past eight, when General Ducrot, assuming command from the Marshal, had taken it into his head to concentrate all the troops on Illy Plateau. The worst of it was that, because the 1st Corps had withdrawn too early, leaving Givonne Valley open to the Germans, the 12th Corps, already under fierce frontal attack, had been outflanked on its left. Now that General de Wimpffen was taking over from General Ducrot, they were reverting to the original plan, and the order had suddenly arrived to reoccupy Bazeilles at any cost, so as to push the Bavarians into the Meuse. Wasn't it ridiculous, making them abandon a position which they now had to reconquer? They were willing to get killed, but not just for the hell of it!

There was a strong surge among the men and horses, and General de Wimpffen appeared, standing up in the stirrups, his face aflame and his voice full of excitement, shouting,

'My friends, we cannot withdraw, for then truly all would be lost... If we must beat a retreat, we'll do so via Carignan, not Mézières... But the victory will be ours, you beat them this morning, and you can beat them again!'

He made off, galloping away along a lane which climbed up towards La Moncelle. Rumour had it that he'd just had a violent argument with General Ducrot, each man defending his own plan and attacking the other, one declaring that it had been impossible to retreat via Mézières since first thing that morning, the other prophesying that if they didn't retreat onto Illy Plateau before evening, the army would be surrounded. And each accused the other of knowing neither the terrain nor the real positions of the troops. The worst of it was that they were both right.

For some moments, however, Henriette's mind had been taken off her need to press on. She'd just recognized an entire family from Bazeilles who'd collapsed by the wayside, a poor weaver with his wife and three daughters, the oldest of whom was no more than nine years old. They were in such a daze from fatigue and despair that they'd been unable to go any further, and had slumped down by a wall.

'Oh! Dear lady,' said the woman to Henriette, 'we've nothing left... Our house was on the Place de l'Église, as you know. And now a shell's gone and set fire to it. I don't know how we and the children managed to get out of there alive...'

Recalling it, the three little girls began sobbing again, crying out, while their mother recounted the disaster in detail, accompanied by wild gestures.

'I saw the loom go up in smoke like a piece of dry kindling... The bed and the furniture all went up faster than handfuls of straw... Even the clock, oh, yes! I didn't have time to carry it out with me.'

'Oh God Almighty!' swore the man, eyes brimming full of tears. 'What's to become of us?'

To calm them, Henriette merely said, her voice trembling slightly,

'You're together, both of you safe and sound, and you still have your little girls: what are you complaining for?'

Then she questioned them, trying to find out what was happening in Bazeilles, whether they'd seen her husband and what her own house had looked like when they last saw it. But shivering with fear, they gave conflicting answers. No, they hadn't seen Monsieur Weiss. But one of the little girls cried that yes, she'd seen him, he'd been lying on the pavement with a big black hole in the middle of his head, and her father gave her a clout to shut her up, because, he said, she was lying for sure. As for the house, it must still have been standing when they fled; they even remembered, as they were passing, having noticed that the doors and windows had been carefully closed up, as if there hadn't been a soul at home. In any case, at that point the Bavarians were only occupying the Place de l'Église, and they were having to take the village street by street and house by house. The only thing was, they must have made some progress by now, and no doubt the whole of Bazeilles was on fire. And the wretched people went on talking about it with fumbling, fearful hands, calling up the atrocious vision, the roofs in flames, the streams of blood, the bodies littering the ground.

'So what about my husband?' repeated Henriette.

They couldn't answer any more, they were sobbing between clasped hands. And she was left in a state of terrible anxiety, not losing her resolve, just a slight tremor on her lips. What should she believe? It was all very well telling herself that the child had been mistaken—she could see her husband lying across the road with a bullet hole in his head. Then there was the report of the closed-up house which worried her: why? Wasn't he there any more? The conviction that he'd been killed suddenly froze her heart to ice. Perhaps he'd just been injured, though; and the need to go there, be there, seized her with such force that she would have tried to shove her way through the mass yet again, if the bugles hadn't at that very minute sounded for them to advance.

Many of these young soldiers had come from Toulon, Rochefort or Brest,* with scarcely any training, never having fired a gun; and since that morning they'd been fighting with bravery and solidarity worthy of veterans. Faced with the enemy, these troops who'd marched so poorly from Rheims to Mouzon, burdened by their inexperience, were now proving to be the most disciplined of men, bound by the most brotherly ties of duty and self-denial. The bugles had only had to sound, and back they went into the fire, taking up the attack in spite of their hearts being heavy with anger. Three times they'd been promised a division to support them, but it hadn't come. They felt abandoned, sacrificed. Leading them back like this into Bazeilles, after they'd been forced to evacuate the village, was asking each man to lay down his life. And they knew it, they gave their lives without protest, closing ranks, leaving the shelter of the trees, to step back into the fire of shells and bullets.

Henriette breathed a huge sigh of relief. At last they were march-ing! She followed them, hoping to arrive with them, ready to run if they began to. But they'd already halted again. Now the missiles were raining down, and if they were to reconquer Bazeilles, they'd have to fight for every single metre of road, taking over lanes and houses and gardens to both right and left. The first rows had opened fire, and now they were advancing in fits and starts, the slightest obstacles causing long minutes to be wasted. She'd never get there if she carried on queuing up like this, waiting for victory. She made up her mind and dived to her right, between two hedges, onto a little lane which ran down into the meadows.

Henriette's plan at this point was to reach Bazeilles by crossing the vast meadows on the banks of the Meuse. But she didn't really have any clear idea as to how. Suddenly she stopped short, at the edge of a small, motionless sea which was blocking her way on this side. It was the floodwaters, where the low-lying lands had been transformed into a defensive lake, and which hadn't even occurred to her. For a moment she thought of going back; then, at the risk of leaving her shoes behind, she went on, following the edge of the field, through the sodden grass, sinking in right up to her ankles. This was practicable for about a hundred metres. Then she came up against a garden wall: the ground dipped, and two metres of water were lapping against the other side. It was impossible to get through. Her little fists clenched, and she had to strain every muscle to stop herself dissolving into tears. When she'd got over the worst, she edged along the wall and discovered a little lane which ran between the scattered houses. This time she thought she was safe, for she knew this maze, this labyrinth of tangled lanes, whose web ended up nonetheless in the village.

Only then did the shells start falling. Henriette stood frozen, very pale, deafened by a dreadful blast which left her wrapped in its draught. A shell had just exploded in front of her, only a few metres away. She turned her head and examined the high ground above the left bank, where smoke was rising from the German batteries; and she understood, and set off again, eyes staring at the horizon, watching for the shells so she could avoid them. The rash temerity of her journey wasn't without great sang-froid, all the calm courage of which her little soul, her good, housewifely soul, was capable. She wanted not to be killed, she wanted to find her husband, take him back with her, live together, happy again. The shells now fell continuously, she dodged along beneath walls, threw herself behind milestones, taking advantage of the slightest cover. However, she came upon an open space, the rutted end of a road, already littered with shrapnel; and she was waiting round the corner of a barn when, before her, poking out of a sort of hole, she noticed the curious face of a child, watching. It was a little boy of ten, barefoot, dressed only in a ragged shirt and trousers, some sort of vagabond, who was most amused by the battle. His small black eyes sparkled, and with each explosion he gave an exhilarated exclamation,

'Oh! Aren't they funny!... Don't budge, here comes another one!... Boom! What a racket that one made!... Don't budge, don't budge!'

And as each missile came over, he dived down into the hole then resurfaced, like some twittering bird, only to plunge back down again.

Then Henriette noticed that the shells were coming from Le Liry, and that the batteries at Pont-Maugis and Noyers were now firing only on Balan. She could see the smoke quite distinctly, after every volley; then she would hear the whistling almost immediately, followed by the explosion. There must have been a brief respite, the wisps of smoke slowly dispersed.

'They must be having a drink!' cried the little boy. 'Quick! Come on, give me your hand, we're going to clear off out of here!'

He took her hand and forced her to follow him; and off they both galloped, side by side, bent double, and crossed the open space. At the other end, as they flung themselves behind a haystack and turned to look, they saw another shell approach, falling right on the barn and exactly where they'd been only moments before. The blast was appalling and the barn collapsed.

At this, the boy danced about, wild with joy, finding it all a wonderful lark.

'Bravo! Now that's what I call damage!... Huh? 'Bout time, too, don't you think?'

For the second time, however, Henriette bumped into an insurmountable obstacle, garden walls, with no way round. Her little companion carried on laughing, saying that there was always a way through if you wanted it badly enough. He climbed up onto the top of a wall, then helped her to get over it. In a single bound, they found themselves standing in a vegetable garden, between rows of peas and runner beans. Fences everywhere. To get out of the garden, they had to walk through a gardener's house. Whistling, arms swinging by his sides, he went in first, quite unabashed. He pushed open a door, found himself in a bedroom, walked through into another, where there was an old woman, probably the only soul left. She stood by a table, seemingly in a daze. She watched these two strangers stroll through her house; and not a word did she say, nor they, either. Already on the other side, they came out into a lane, which they were able to follow for some way. Then they came up against more problems, and so it went on for nearly another kilometre, leaping over walls, climbing over hedges, cutting through via the shortest route, through shed doors, windows in houses, wherever the route they managed to create happened to take them. Dogs howled and they were almost trampled by a cow galloping past at a furious rate. Meanwhile they must have been getting closer, for they could smell the burning, and huge, reddish clouds of smoke, like airy, flying pancakes, were constantly veiling the sun.

All of a sudden the boy stopped, and stood before Henriette.

'Tell me, Madame, where is it you're going in fact?'

'But you can see for yourself, I'm going to Bazeilles.'

He whistled, and gave one of his high-pitched laughs like a real good-for-nothing lad playing truant, and having a whale of a time.

'Bazeilles... Oh! No way, that's not for me... I'm off elsewhere, I am. Good evening to you!'

And he spun on his heel and was off just as he'd come, without her being able to tell where he'd come from nor where he'd gone. She'd found him in a hole, and she lost sight of him round the end of a wall; and she would never set eyes on him again.

Once she was alone, Henriette felt a peculiar sense of fear. It had hardly been any protection, having this wild child for company; but he'd distracted her with his chatter. Now she began to tremble, in spite of her usual courage. The shells were no longer falling, the Germans had stopped firing onto Bazeilles, probably afraid of killing their own men, who were now in control of the village. However, for the past few minutes she'd been hearing the whistle of bullets, that noise like the loud buzzing of large flies they'd told her about, and which she now recognized. In the distance there was such a raging cacophany that she couldn't even make out the sound of the gunfire through the violent din. As she rounded the edge of a house she heard a dull thud next to her ear, and a fall of plaster, stopping her dead in her tracks: a bullet had just grazed the front of the house, leaving her quite pale. Then, before she could ask herself whether she was brave enough to go on, she received what felt like a hammer-blow to her forehead and fell to her knees, stunned. A second bullet, ricocheting, had brushed her just above her left eyebrow, leaving only a deep graze behind. Touching her forehead, she found her hands red with blood. But she could feel that her skull was still solid and intact beneath her fingers; and she repeated out loud, to give herself courage,

'It's nothing, it's nothing... Look, I'm not scared, no! I'm not scared...'

It was true, she picked herself up and from then on walked through the gunfire with the carelessness of someone removed from their body, beyond reason, laying down their life. She no longer even tried to protect herself, walking straight on, head held high, lengthening her stride only because she wanted to get there quicker. The missiles crashed down around her, and dozens of times she was almost killed, without appearing even to notice. Her light-footed haste, her habit of just getting quietly on with everything, seemed to help her, making her pass by so lithe and slender that she slipped through danger's net. At last she was in Bazeilles, and cut across a field of lucerne to get back onto the road, the main road which passed through the village. Coming out onto the road, she saw that her house, two hundred paces to her right, was burning, the flames invisible in the bright sunlight, the roof already half caved in, the windows spewing out great whirling clouds of black smoke. She broke into a gallop, and ran until she was gasping for breath.

Weiss had been holed up there since eight o'clock that morning, cut off from the withdrawing troops. It had immediately become impossible to return to Sedan, for the Bavarians had broken through at Montivilliers Park and blocked the line of retreat. He was all alone, armed with his rifle and remaining cartridges, when he spotted a group of about ten soldiers outside his front door, who, like him, had stayed behind. Now, finding themselves isolated from their comrades, they were searching high and low for somewhere to take cover, so that at least the enemy would have to pay dearly for their hides. Swiftly, he ran downstairs to open the door and the house gained an instant garrison—captain, corporal, and eight men, all outraged, furious, and determined not to give themselves up.

'Laurent! Fancy seeing you here!' exclaimed Weiss, surprised to spot among their number a tall, skinny lad, holding a rifle which he'd found on the ground near some corpse.

Laurent, in working blue shirt and trousers, had a job as a gardener's assistant in the neighbourhood. He was about thirty, and had recently lost his mother and his wife: both had been struck down by the same virulent bout of fever.

'Why not?' he replied. 'I've nothing left but this carcass of mine, and I might as well give that... Anyway, you know what, I'm actually looking forward to it, because I'm not a bad shot. I'm going to have a fine time, killing off one of those bastards out there every time I pull the trigger.'

The captain and corporal had already set about inspecting the house. Nothing much could be done on the ground floor, so they just pushed the furniture up against the door and windows, to barricade them as sturdily as possible. Then they got down to organizing the defence proper in the three small first-floor rooms and the loft, nodding approvingly at the preparations that Weiss had already made by placing mattresses against the shutters, leaving narrow slits at intervals between the slats for firing through. As the captain ventured to lean forward to take a look at the surrounding positions, he heard whimpering, the sound of a child in tears.

'What's that noise?' he asked.

Once again, Weiss had a vision of little Auguste lying sick in the dye-works next door, his burning, fevered cheeks crimson against the white sheets, begging for water and calling out for his mother; while she lay on the tiled floor, incapable of answering him now, her skull blown to bits. At the thought of this, Weiss motioned sorrowfully towards the dye-works.

'It's a poor little mite crying next door,' he replied. 'His mother's been killed by a shell.'

'Christ Almighty!' murmured Laurent. 'We're really going to have to make them pay for this.'

As yet, the only objects reaching anywhere near the front of the house were a few stray bullets. Weiss and the captain, followed by the gardener and two soldiers, climbed up into the loft, from where they had a better view of the road. They could see diagonally across it as far as the Place de l'Église. Although they were now in control of the square, the Bavarians didn't lower their guard, but advanced as cautiously and painstakingly as before. At the corner of a narrow lane, a handful of infantry managed to hold them off for almost another quarter of an hour, their bullets flying so thick and fast that the bodies started to pile up. Then, before the Bavarians could get any further, they had to lay siege to a house on the corner opposite. Every now and then, the figure of a woman could be glimpsed through the smoke, shouldering a rifle and shooting out of one of the windows. The house belonged to a baker, and inside were a number of soldiers who'd been left behind among the villagers. When the house was eventually captured, screams rang out, and a terrible flailing tangle of people went tumbling all the way over to the opposite wall, revealing a flash of the woman's skirt, a man's jacket, and a shock of white hair. They heard the crack of the firing squad, and blood spurted right up the wall. The Germans were implacable: anyone caught carrying weapons and who wasn't part of either warring army was shot on the spot, guilty of overstepping their rights as mere civilians. In the face of such furious resistance from this village, German anger grew uncontrollably, and the appalling losses which they had been suffering now for nigh on five hours goaded them into exacting a terrible revenge. The gutters ran red with blood, dead bodies lay blocking the streets, and the haunting groans of dying men rose from the crossroads, which had turned into mere charnel pits. Now, each time the Bavarians took a house by storm, they could be seen tossing lighted straw inside: some came running up with blazing torches, others splashed paraffin over the walls. Before long, whole streets were on fire. Bazeilles was ablaze.*

Meanwhile, at the heart of the village, Weiss's tightly shuttered house stood alone, still looking like some menacing citadel, grimly determined not to surrender.

'Watch out! Here they come!' yelled the captain.

A salvo burst from the loft and the first floor, bringing down three Bavarians who were advancing, sticking close to the walls. The rest withdrew to take cover at each bend in the road. And so the siege of the house began, with such a shower of bullets raking the walls that it sounded like a storm of hailstones. The shooting continued unabated for nearly ten minutes, tearing holes in the plaster, although real damage was slight. However, one of the men up in the loft with the captain was careless enough to show himself at a sky-light, and a bullet caught him right in the middle of his forehead, killing him stone dead.

'Christ! One down already!' muttered the captain. 'Come on, watch yourselves—we can't afford to go letting ourselves get shot just for the hell of it!'

He too had picked up a rifle, and was firing out of the window from behind a shutter. But it was Laurent, the gardener, who really won his admiration. Kneeling down with his gun-barrel wedged into one of the narrow slits in the shutters, he was like a hunter lying in wait. He would never let off a shot until he was completely sure of his aim: and he would even tell them the result in advance.

'This one's for that short officer in blue over there: through the heart... This is for the other one, that tall, thin one, further off: right between the eyes... And this one's for him with the ginger beard, that fat one who's been getting on my nerves: in the belly...'

Every single time, the man he had picked out would drop to the ground, struck as if by lightning, and hit exactly where he had indicated. And on went Laurent, quite peaceably, never rushing his shot: as he said, he had plenty of work to keep him going—killing them all off one by one this way would take some time.

'If only my eyes weren't so bad!' Weiss kept saying, beside himself with fury.

He had smashed his glasses, and was distraught. He still had his pince-nez, but there was so much sweat streaming down his face that it was impossible to get it to keep it in place. Often he just fired at random, in a frenzy, hands shaking. His usual calm had vanished, swept away on a rising tide of violent emotion.

'Don't rush it, you'll never get anywhere like that,' Laurent kept telling him. 'Look, take your aim carefully—see, that one over there, the one who's lost his helmet, over by the corner of the grocer's... Well done. You see? You've got him in the foot, and now he's hopping around in his own blood.'

Weiss's face had grown somewhat pale as he watched.

'Finish him off,' he murmured.

'What? And waste a good bullet? You must be joking. Far better to blast another of 'em with it.'

By now, their attackers must have noticed this formidable aim coming from the skylights up in the loft. Not one of their men could move forward without being brought down. So they brought in a new line of troops, with orders to concentrate all their fire-power on the roof. From then on, the position in the loft became untenable: the tiles were perforated as easily as if they'd been no more than paper-thin, as the bullets came crashing through from all sides, buzzing like swarms of angry bees. Death might strike at any minute.

'Let's move down to the first floor,' said the captain. 'We can still hold out down there.'

However, as he made for the ladder, a bullet struck him in the groin, throwing him to the floor.

'Christ! Too late!'

Aided by the one remaining soldier, Weiss and Laurent were determined to get him down the stairs, in spite of his protests not to waste their time: he was done for, and it made no difference to him whether he died upstairs or down. Once he had been laid on a bed in one of the first-floor bedrooms, however, he tried to continue coordinating the defence.

'Fire straight into the thick of them, don't bother about the rest. As long as your fire doesn't slack off, they're far too careful to take any risks.'

And indeed, the siege of the little house went on and on and on.

Time and time again, it looked as if it would topple and collapse
beneath the storm of metal raining down on it: and yet, battered by
volleys of gunfire, surrounded by haze and smoke, still it stood firm,
holed and mutilated perhaps, but spitting bullets from every fissure
nonetheless. Utterly exasperated at losing so much time and so many
lives for a mere pile of bricks, its attackers yelled and fired wildly at it
from a distance, not bold enough as yet to make a dash forward to
kick in the door and downstairs windows.

'Watch out!' shouted the corporal. 'There goes one of the
shutters!'

The bullets were coming with such force that they'd just torn a
shutter off its hinges. But Weiss sprang forward and pushed a wardrobe up against the window: and sheltering behind it, Laurent was
safe to carry on firing. At his feet lay one of the soldiers: his jaw had
been shot to pieces and he was losing a lot of blood. Another was hit
in the throat, and rolled over to the wall, where he began groaning
endlessly, his whole body wracked by convulsive shudders. Now
there were only eight of them left, not counting the captain. He lay
propped up against the wall, too weak to talk, but still using his
hands to give orders. The three first-floor bedrooms were now
almost as intolerable as the loft, because the mattresses, ripped to
shreds, were no longer able to keep out the bullets: shards of plaster
flew from the walls and ceiling, corners were chipped off the furniture, and the sides of the wardrobe were splintering as if an axe were
being taken to them. The worst of it was that their ammunition was
about to run out.

'Pity!' grumbled Laurent. 'We were doing so well, too!'

Suddenly, Weiss had an idea.

'Hang on!'

He'd just remembered the dead soldier lying up in the loft. He
climbed the stairs and searched the body, looking for the cartridges
that the man would have had left over. An entire section of the roof
had caved in, and he was astonished to catch sight of the blue sky, a
broad expanse of cheerful light. He kept low to avoid the bullets,
crawling forward on his hands and knees. Then, as soon as he
grasped the extra cartridges—some thirty or so—he turned tail, and
galloped hurriedly back downstairs.

However, just as he was sharing out this fresh supply with the
gardener, safely back on the floor below, a soldier let out a cry and

toppled forward. Now there were only seven left, and seconds later they were down to six: a bullet caught the corporal in the left eye, and blew his brains out.

From that moment on, Weiss was completely oblivious to all else. He and the five who were left continued to fire like men demented, exhausting their supply of ammunition; and the thought of surrendering never even entered their heads. Throughout the three small rooms, the floor was strewn with broken furniture. Dead bodies lay blocking doorways, and over in a corner a wounded man kept up a ghastly, interminable moaning. Everywhere they trod, blood squelched underfoot. A trickle of red liquid had crept down the stairs. The air was unbreathable, scorched with powder, filled with smoke and thick with acrid, nauseating dust. Flames from gun-barrels streaked through the darkness, now almost as black as night.

'Jesus Christ!' exclaimed Weiss. 'They're bringing up the cannon!'

It was true. In their despair at ever getting rid of this enraged bunch of men holding them up, the Bavarians were wheeling a cannon into position on the corner of the Place de l'Église. Maybe, once their cannonballs had reduced the house to rubble, they would get through at long last. At the sight of the immense military honour being conferred on them by the enemy, who judged them worthy of their heavy artillery, the jubilant, ferocious mood of the besieged men knew no bounds, and set them sneering in scorn. What cowardly bastards, bringing on the big guns! Laurent, still kneeling, aimed carefully at the gunners, getting his man each time: and he was so effective that at first the Germans were unable to prime the cannon for firing. Five or even six minutes passed before the first shot boomed out, and even then, it was aimed too high, and merely tore a chunk out of the roof.

The end, though, was nigh. They searched the bodies, but to no avail: there wasn't a single cartridge to be found. Wild-eyed and exhausted, the six men fumbled around, looking desperately for anything they might hurl from the window to stop the enemy. One man showed himself at the window, shouting angrily and waving his fists, and was mown down in a volley of lead. And then there were five. What could they do? Go downstairs and try to make their escape through the garden and across the meadows? At that very moment, chaos erupted in the rooms below, and a furious, seething mass of men came rushing up the stairs: the Bavarians had finally managed

to make their way round to the other side of the house, break down
the back door and force their way inside. A horrific scuffle broke out
in the small rooms, amid the dead bodies and the wrecked, scattered
furniture. One of the soldiers was pierced through the heart by a
bayonet, and the remaining two were taken prisoner. The captain,
who had just breathed his last, was still sitting there, his mouth open,
arm raised as if giving an order.

Meanwhile, a large, fair-haired officer armed with a revolver, his
bloodshot eyes apparently about to pop out of their sockets, caught
sight of Weiss and Laurent, one in an overcoat, the other in his blue
shirt.

'Who are you?' he barked violently at them in French. 'What the
hell do you think you're doing here?'

Then he noticed that they were covered in black gunpowder; the
truth suddenly dawned on him, and he showered them with a storm
of German insults, his voice trembling with rage. He was already
taking aim to blow their heads off himself, when the soldiers under
his command swooped forward and seized them, forcing them down
the stairs. The two men were swept away and tossed along by the
raging sea of human bodies, and then flung into the road. As they
went hurtling over to the far wall, the jeering and cursing from the
soldiers outside reached such a pitch that the commanding officers
could no longer make themselves heard. Some two or three minutes
went by while the large, fair-haired officer tried to extract them from
the crush, in order to proceed to their execution, and they had time
to stand up and take a look around them.

Other houses were catching fire—soon there would be nothing
left of Bazeilles but a blazing inferno. Sheets of flame were beginning
to flicker at the upper windows of the church. A group of soldiers
chased an old lady from her home, and then forced her to provide
them with matches, so they could set fire to her curtains and bedding. Firebrands of burning straw were tossed through doors and
windows, torrents of paraffin were sluiced here, there, and everywhere, and so the flames spread, leaping from house to house. The
German troops had been reduced to a rampaging horde of barbarians, driven wild by the long struggle, intent on avenging their dead,
lying there in great heaps beneath their feet as they advanced.
Groups of men waded screaming through the smoke and sparks,
adding to the terrifying din—the agonized groans of the dying, the

gunshots, the buildings crashing down around them. They lost sight of each other through the swirling flurries of livid dust, which blocked out the sun and filled the air with an unbearable stench of soot and blood, as if all the atrocities of this massacre were hanging suspended in it. And the killing didn't cease, the work of destruction went on, in every corner of the village: the beast had been let loose, the senseless anger, the mad rage of man eating man.

And then finally Weiss caught sight of his own house in flames before him. Soldiers armed with firebrands had come running, while others fed the blaze by chucking on the splintered remains of furniture. Flames spread rapidly through the ground floor, and smoke billowed out from every gaping wound in the roof and walls. But next door, the dye-works had already caught alight: and, horror of all horrors, the voice of little Auguste could still be heard as he lay in bed, delirious with fever, crying out for his mother: while the pitiful woman's skirts, as she lay sprawled across the threshold with her skull blown to bits, were starting to catch fire.

'Mummy, I'm thirsty... Mummy, bring me some water...'

The flames roared, the voice fell silent, and all that could be heard were the deafening cheers of the conquerors.

But above the noise and shouting a terrible cry suddenly rang out. Henriette had finally managed to get through and had just seen her husband, standing with his back against the wall, facing the firing squad. The soldiers were taking aim.

She flung herself at him.

'Oh my God! What's happening? Surely they aren't going to kill you?'

Weiss looked at her, dumbfounded. Her! His wife! The woman he'd yearned for so, the woman he loved with such tenderness and adoration! He came to with a shudder, bewildered. What had he done? What on earth had made him stay and fight, instead of returning home to her, as he had sworn he would? In a sudden burst of lucidity, he saw their violent separation to come, and his precious happiness lost now for ever. Then he started at the sight of the blood on her forehead, and in a mechanical, faltering voice he said,

'Are you hurt? You must be mad, coming here.'

She cut him short, angrily waving his words aside.

'What, me? Oh, it's nothing, just a scratch... But you! What about you? Why are they holding you like this? I don't want them to kill you!'

In the middle of the crowded road, the officer was still struggling to give some room to the firing squad. At the sight of this woman clinging to one of the prisoners, he began again in his harsh, guttural French:

'Oh no, come on, none of this nonsense. Where did you spring from? What do you want?'

'I want my husband.'

'This man here, your husband?... He's been found guilty. Justice must be done.'

'I want my husband.'

'Come along now, be sensible... Move aside, we don't want to hurt you.'

'I want my husband.'

Abandoning all hope of persuading her, the officer was about to give the order for her to be forcibly removed from the prisoner's arms when Laurent, who until then had stood by, passive and silent, ventured to intervene.

'Listen captain, I'm the one who massacred so many of your men, and it's only right and proper that you should shoot me. Especially when I've no one left in this world, no mother, no wife, no children... But this gentleman here's married... Come on, let him go. Then you can give me what I've got coming.'

'Did you ever hear such nonsense!' thundered the captain, beside himself with rage. 'What kind of fool do you take me for? Someone kindly remove this woman!'

He had to repeat the order in German. A soldier stepped forward. He was a squat Bavarian with a huge head, bristling with red hair and a bushy beard, beneath which only a square, broad nose and large blue eyes could be seen. He was a terrifying sight, all covered in blood, like some bear emerging from its cavernous lair, a hairy beast smeared with the blood of the prey it has just crushed to death. With heart-rending cries, Henriette screamed,

'I want my husband! Kill me with my husband!'

But the officer proudly thumped his chest, proclaiming that he was no murderer, and that while there might be some who killed innocent people, he certainly wasn't one of them. It wasn't her they'd found guilty, and he'd sooner cut off his own hand than harm a single hair of her head.

As the Bavarian drew near, Henriette clung desperately to Weiss, pressing against him with every inch of her body.

'Oh my love! Please, I beg you, keep me with you, let me die with you...!'

Tears streamed down Weiss's cheeks. Without answering, he forced himself to prise her grip away from his shoulders and waist, as the desolate woman clutched convulsively at him.

'Oh, you don't love me anymore! You want to die without me!... Keep me with you, they'll tire of it in the end, they'll kill us both together.'

He managed to prise away one of her poor little hands, and pressing it to his lips, kissed it, while he set about making the other one let go.

'No! No! Keep me with you! I want to die...'

Finally, after much effort, he held both her hands in his. Until then he had been silent, avoiding saying anything. Now he simply said,

'Farewell, beloved wife.'

Without waiting to be prompted, he flung her into the arms of the Bavarian, who carried her off. She struggled and cried out, while the soldier spoke to her, no doubt trying to calm her with his coarse stream of words. Making a violent effort, she freed her head, and saw everything.

It was all over in a couple of seconds. Weiss's pince-nez had slipped down as he bid her farewell, and he thrust it sharply back onto his nose, as if he wanted to be able to look death in the face. Stepping back, he leaned against the wall, and folded his arms. His face wore an exalted look, and the courage in the heart of this great, peaceable fellow in his torn, ragged jacket suddenly lent him an extraordinary beauty. Laurent, standing at his side, had merely thrust his hands in his pockets. He seemed outraged by the cruelty of the scene before him, by the abominable deeds of these savages, who slaughtered men in front of their wives. Drawing himself up, he stared at them long and hard, then spat out, his voice full of contempt,

'Filthy swine!'

But the officer had already raised his sword, and the two men slumped to the floor like sacks of flour. The gardener fell face down in the mud, while the other, the bookkeeper, collapsed on his side, at the foot of the wall. Before he died, his body gave one final spasm, his eyelids twitched, and his mouth twisted. The officer walked up to him and prodded him with his foot, to make sure he was really dead.

Henriette had seen everything, seen his dying eyes seeking hers, seen his death agony, with its sickening shudder, seen that great boot poking at the body. She didn't utter a single cry, just bit into whatever she could, silently and furiously. Her teeth sank into a hand. The Bavarian let out an almighty yelp of pain, knocked her off her feet, and came close to striking her. Their faces touched: never would she forget that beard and that red hair, spattered with blood, nor those wide blue eyes, bursting with fury.

Afterwards, Henriette was unable to recall the details of what happened next. She had one wish, and one wish only—to go back to her husband's body, take him away, and watch over him. But it was like walking through a nightmare, and every step she took, obstacles loomed up to block her path. The crackle of gunfire had broken out again, and a great wave surged through the German troops holding Bazeilles: the marine infantry had finally arrived, and the fighting began again with such ferocity that the young woman was flung to the left, into a narrow side-road, where a group of petrified villagers stood huddling together. Whatever happened now, though, the battle's outcome could be in no doubt, for it was far too late for them to regain the positions they had previously abandoned. The infantry hung on for almost half an hour, laying down their lives with a dedication that was magnificent to behold. But enemy reinforcements kept on pouring in, flowing from all directions, from the meadows, from the roads, from Montivilliers Park. From that moment on, nothing on earth could have dislodged them from the village which they had paid for so dearly, where several thousands of their own men lay dead and dying among the blood and flames. The work of destruction was almost complete now, and there was nothing left but a charred mess of scattered limbs and smoking debris. Bazeilles lay prostrate, with its throat slit and its lifeblood drained, reduced to a pile of smouldering ashes.

One last time, Henriette caught sight of her little house standing in the distance, its floors collapsing in a whirlwind of flying sparks. Opposite, she could still see the inert form of her husband, lying dead at the foot of the wall. However, a fresh tide of people caught her up as the bugles started sounding the retreat, and she was swept away somehow among the withdrawing troops. She became a mere object, a tumbling, spinning piece of flotsam, tossed and trampled in the crushing tide of the crowd streaming down the road. And she no longer had any idea where she was, eventually finding herself sitting in someone's kitchen in Balan, surrounded by total strangers, sobbing away with her head slumped on the table.

CHAPTER FIVE

At ten o'clock on the Plateau d'Algérie, Beaudoin's company was still lying in the field of cabbages where it had been all morning. The crossfire from the batteries up on Hattoy Hill and on the Iges peninsula, which had grown fiercer than ever, had just killed another two of its men; and still no order came to march on: were they to spend the whole day there, letting themselves get shot at without putting up a fight?

The men weren't even allowed to release the tension by firing their rifles any more. Captain Beaudoin had managed to make them hold fire, halting the furious but useless fusillade of the little wood opposite, where there didn't appear to be a single Prussian left. The sun was starting to beat down on them and they were getting burned, lying there on the ground beneath the flaming sky.

Jean, turning round, was worried to see that Maurice's head had slumped forward, his cheek resting on the ground, eyes shut. He was very pale and showed no sign of life.

'Hey! What's up?'

But Maurice had quite simply fallen asleep. All the waiting and exhaustion had got the better of him, in spite of death flying all around. He woke with a start and his eyes opened, wide and calm, only to be filled again by the cloudy panic of battle. He never did work out how long he'd been asleep. He felt as if he were emerging from an infinite, delicious nothingness.

'Well! How odd!' he murmured. 'I've been asleep!... Oh! It's done me good.'

It was true, he was less conscious now of the painful, tight feeling at his temples and about his ribs, that constricting, bone-crunching fear. He teased Lapoulle, who'd been worrying about Chouteau and Loubet ever since they'd disappeared and was talking about going to look for them. That was rich! Just so he could go and shelter behind a tree and smoke a pipe! Pache was convinced that they'd been kept back at the field hospital, where they were short of stretcher-bearers. And another bloody awful profession that was, going to gather up the wounded under fire! Then, haunted by his rustic superstitions, he added that it was unlucky to touch the dead—you died of it.

'God Almighty, will you shut up!' yelled Lieutenant Rochas. 'As if you could!'

High up on his horse, Colonel de Vineuil had turned to look. And he gave a smile, the only one that morning. Then he sank back into his motionless state, impassive as ever beneath the falling shells, awaiting orders.

Maurice, showing interest now in the stretcher-bearers, watched them as they searched among the dips and hollows. There must have been a first-aid post somewhere up the track, behind a hillock, and its crew had set about exploring the plateau. Swiftly they put up a tent, while the necessary equipment was unpacked from the waggon, consisting of a few tools, instruments, and dressings, enough for making hasty bandages before taking the injured to Sedan, as and when they could get hold of vehicles to transport them, for these would soon be in short supply. The post was manned only by assistants. It was the stretcher-bearers, more than anyone else, who acted like heroes, stubbornly and without glory. They could see them, dressed in grey with a red cross on their helmets and armbands, slowly and calmly venturing out under fire, going right up to where soldiers had fallen. They crawled along on their hands and knees, trying to use the cover of ditches and hedges, of any little dips in the land, without ever needlessly exposing themselves to danger for the sake of it. Then, as soon as they found men lying on the ground, the tough job began, for many had fainted, and they had to distinguish the wounded from the dead. Some had ended up face down, mouths lying in a pool of blood, choking; others had mouths full of mud as if they'd bitten into the ground; others were lying flung all over the place, in heaps, arms and legs twisted, ribcages half crushed. The stretcher-bearers carefully untangled them, gathering up any who were still breathing, straightening out their limbs, raising their heads, and trying to clean them up as best they could. Each man carried a bottle of fresh water, which he used only sparingly. And they could often be seen kneeling down for minutes at a time, trying desperately to resuscitate an injured man, waiting for him to open his eyes.

About fifty metres away to his left, Maurice watched one who was trying to locate the injury of a young soldier who had a thin trail of blood dripping from his sleeve. There was a haemorrhage there somewhere, and the Red Cross man eventually found it and staunched the bleeding by compressing the artery. In urgent cases they would give first aid like this, binding and splinting limbs to avoid jolting fractures, so that patients could be moved without danger. And it was transporting them that became their main task: they supported those able to walk and carried the rest, either in their arms, like infants, or piggyback, the men's arms about their necks; and sometimes two or three of them, or four, depending on how awkward it was, would make a chair by grasping each others' fists, or carry the wounded off lying down, holding them by the arms or legs. Apart from the regulation stretchers they also invented all sorts of ingenious contraptions, improvising stretchers with rifles bound together by rucksack straps. And they could be seen all over the barren plain where the shells rained down, working alone or in groups, dashing across with their burdens, heads down, feeling their way forward, showing admirable, cautious heroism.

As Maurice was watching one on his right, a skinny, feeble lad who was carrying a heavy sergeant around his neck, his legs buckling like a worker-ant carrying a grain of wheat far too big for him, he saw them get sent up in the air by a shell and disappear in the explosion. When the smoke had cleared, the sergeant came back into view, on his back, with no fresh injuries, while the stretcher-bearer lay with his sides ripped open. Another man took his place, yet another industrious worker-ant who, having gone over to his comrade and sensed that he was dead, picked up the wounded man in his turn, and carried him off.

Maurice teased Lapoulle.

'Tell you what, if you like that job more, why don't you go and give them a hand!'

For a while now, the batteries at Saint-Menges had been raging away, and the hail of missiles had grown thicker; and Captain Beaudoin, still nervously pacing up and down in front of his company, eventually went up to the colonel. It was a shame to wear down the men's morale like this for hours on end, without making use of them.

'I've no orders,' replied the colonel stoically.

Once again they saw General Douay passing at a gallop, followed by his staff. He'd just encountered General de Wimpffen, who'd come rushing up to beg him to hold fast, something he'd felt able to promise, but only on the strict condition that Illy Calvary, to his right, should be defended. If they lost their position on Illy he could no longer answer for anything, retreat would be unavoidable. General de Wimpffen declared that the troops of the 1st Corps would take possession of the Calvary; and indeed, almost immediately they saw a regiment of Zouaves take up position; reassured by the sight, General Douay agreed to send the Dumont division to the rescue of the 12th Corps, which was in grave danger. A quarter of an hour later, however, as he came back to verify that the left flank was solid, he exclaimed as he looked up and saw that the Calvary was empty: there were no Zouaves left, the plateau had been abandoned, and the hellish fire from the Fleigneux batteries was making it impossible to hold in any case. And in despair, seeing disaster ahead, he was rapidly moving his men over to the right when he landed right in the middle of the routed Dumont division, falling back in chaos and panic, mixed up with the debris of the 1st Corps. The latter, having made a move to retreat, had been unable to retake the positions it had held that morning, abandoning Daigny to the XIIth Saxon Corps and Givonne to the Prussian Guard, and had been forced to move northwards, through Garenne Wood, under cannonfire from batteries which the enemy was placing on every hilltop, from one end of the valley to the other. The terrible ring of iron and flames was closing in, part of the Guard continued its march upon Illy, from east to west, circling the hills; while from west to east behind the XIth Corps, which had control of Saint-Menges, the Vth Corps was still on the move, passing Fleigneux, bringing its cannons constantly further forward with bold impudence, so convinced of the ignorance and impotence of the French troops that it didn't even wait for the infantry to come and lend its support. It was midday, and the whole of the horizon was ablaze and booming, sending crossfire down on the 7th and 1st Corps.

At that moment, while the enemy artillery were preparing for the final attack on the Calvary, General Douay resolved to make a last effort to retake it. He issued orders and personally threw himself into the midst of the fleeing men from Dumont division, and succeeded in regrouping a column, which he launched onto the Calvary. It held out there for a few minutes; but the bullets were whistling past so thick and fast, and such a deluge of shells swept across the empty fields, with not a tree in sight, that panic immediately broke out among the men, sending them rushing down the slopes, rolling them headlong like wisps of straw surprised by a storm. The general persisted, bringing up other regiments.

A messenger galloping past cried out an order to Colonel de Vineuil through the awful din. The colonel was already standing up in the stirrups, his face aflame; and with a sweeping gesture from his sword, pointing at the Calvary, he shouted,

'At last, it's our turn, lads!... Forward, to the top!'

The 106th, stirred by this, began to move. Beaudoin's company was one of the first to get up, the men joking that they'd grown rusty and had earth in their joints. But as soon as they set off, the firing became so intense that they had to jump into the shelter trenches. And on they ran, bent double.

'Look out, lad!' Jean said again and again to Maurice. 'This is it... Don't even poke your nose out, or they'll shoot it off for sure... And make sure you keep those bones of yours close to you, unless you want to leave a few behind. Anyone who gets out of this the other end's a good 'un.'

Maurice hardly heard him, with all the buzzing and the clamour of the crowd which was filling his head. He no longer knew whether he was afraid or not, but just ran, carried along by the galloping of the others, with no will of his own, his only desire being to get it all over with there and then. Such was the extent to which he'd been reduced to a mere drop in this surging torrent, that when there was a sudden recoiling movement at the far end of the trench, before the bare terrain still left to climb, he at once felt panic overwhelm him and was ready to take flight. It was unbridled instinct taking over in him, his muscles rebelling, following every change in the tide.

Some men were already turning back when the colonel rushed forward.

'Come on, lads, you're not going to do this to me, are you? You're not going to act like cowards... Remember! The 106th has never run away, you'd be the first to disgrace the flag...'

He urged his horse on, blocking the path of the fleeing men, finding the right words for each of them, speaking of France in a voice that shook with tears.

Lieutenant Rochas was so moved that he flew into a terrible rage, raising his sword and using it like a stick to beat the men with.

'You bastards! I'll get you up that hill with a good kick up the arse,

I will! You bloody well obey, or the first man to turn tail will get his face smashed in!'

But the colonel was revolted by such violence and talk of soldiers being pushed into battle with kicks up the behind.

'No, no, Lieutenant, they'll all follow me... Right, lads? You wouldn't let your poor old colonel have it out with the Prussians all by himself, would you?... Forward march, to the top!'

He set off, and indeed they did all follow him, for he'd spoken in such a brave, fatherly way that they couldn't abandon him, or else they wouldn't be worth much at all. In any case, he was the only one to cross the bare fields on his great horse quite calmly, while the men spread out, scattering into sniping positions, making use of any cover they could find. The ground was getting steeper, and there were at least five hundred metres of stubble and beetroot fields to cover before they would reach the top. Instead of carrying out a classic textbook assault, as in manœuvres, in straight lines, soon there were only stooped backs to be seen running close to the ground, with soldiers on their own or in small groups, climbing and then suddenly leaping like insects, reaching the summit through cunning and agility. The enemy batteries must have seen them, for shells pounded the soil with such frequency that there were no gaps between the explosions any more. Five men were killed, and one lieutenant was blown clean in two.

Maurice and Jean had been lucky enough to come upon a hedge, behind which they could gallop along without being seen. Even so, a bullet still managed to pierce a hole in the side of one of their comrades' heads, and he fell down, getting tangled up in their legs. They had to kick him aside. But the dead no longer counted, there were too many of them. A glimpse of a wounded man, screaming and using both hands to stop his entrails from falling out, a horse which was still hanging on, its hindquarters blown apart, all this horrifying agony, all the horror of the battlefield, ended up no longer having any effect on them. The only thing that bothered them was the midday sun beating down, boring into their shoulders.

'God, I'm thirsty!' stammered Maurice.'It feels like my throat's full of soot. Can you smell that scorched smell, like singed wool?'

Jean nodded.

'It was like that at Solférino, too. Maybe that's what war smells like... Hang on, I've still got some brandy left, we can have a drink.'

Calmly, they stopped behind the hedge for a minute. But instead of quenching their thirst, the brandy burned their stomachs. It was infuriating, having that scorched taste in their mouths. And then they began to feel starving hungry, and would happily have tucked into the half loaf of bread that Maurice had in his knapsack; except how could they? Behind them, all along the hedge, more and more men were coming up in their wake, pushing them on. Finally they leapt up the final slope in a single bound. They were on top of the plateau, right at the foot of the Calvary, the ancient cross, worn away by the winds and the rain, standing between two spindly linden trees.

'Ah! By God, here we are!' cried Jean. 'The important thing now is to stay here!'

He was right, the place was hardly pleasant, as Lapoulle remarked dolefully, making the rest of the company laugh. Once again they all lay down in a stubble-field; but even so, three more men were killed. Up there, it was as if a roaring hurricane had been unleashed, shells came sailing over in such huge numbers from Saint-Menges, Fleigneux, and Givonne that it was like a violent rainstorm, the onslaught seeming to make steam rise from the ground. Obviously they couldn't hold on to the position for very long unless some artillery came double quick to back up these troops which had been so rashly committed to the fight. It was said that General Douay had given the order to send up two batteries from the reserve artillery; and every other moment the men looked around anxiously, waiting for the cannons that never came.

'This is ridiculous, quite ridiculous!' Captain Beaudoin said over and over again, pacing jerkily up and down again. 'You don't just send a regiment in like this without making sure it gets back-up straight away.'

Then, spotting a dip in the ground, on the left, he shouted to Rochas,

'I say, Lieutenant, the company could dig in over there.'

Rochas, standing motionless, shrugged his shoulders.

'Oh, sir, whether it's here or over there, makes no difference, it's the same old game. It's best not to move at all.'

At this Captain Beaudoin, who never swore, lost his temper.

'But Jesus Christ! None of us will make it! We can't just let ourselves be massacred like this!'

And he insisted, wanting to go and see personally whether the position he'd pointed out was better. But he hadn't gone ten paces before he vanished in a sudden explosion, his right leg shattered by a shell. He fell over backwards, emitting a shriek like a woman caught unawares.

'It was bound to happen,' murmured Rochas. 'It's no use moving around so much—whatever you've got coming to you, you'll get it anyway.'

Seeing their captain fall, some of the company's men got up; and as he began to call for help, begging for someone to carry him off, Jean ended up running over to him with Maurice right behind.

'My friends, oh, heavens! don't leave me here, take me to the ambulance!'

'Lord! it's not going to be easy, sir... But we can still try...'

They were already trying to work out which end to pick him up by when they spotted two stretcher-bearers sheltering behind the hedge which they themselves had come along, apparently looking for some work to do. They waved madly at them and persuaded them to come over. They'd be saved, as long as they could get back to the ambulance without any nasty accidents. But it was a long way away, and the iron hailstorm was growing fiercer again.

As the stretcher-bearers, having bound the leg tightly to hold it in place, were carrying the captain away sitting on their clasped fists, one of his arms around each of them, Colonel de Vineuil, who'd been informed, came up to them, urging on his horse. He'd known the young man ever since his graduation from the military academy at Saint-Cyr; he was very fond of him and seemed very upset.

'My poor child, be brave... It'll be nothing, they'll save you, you'll see...'

The captain gave a sigh of relief, as if he'd suddenly found large reserves of courage at long last.

'No, no, it's over, I prefer it that way. What's exasperating is having to wait for the unavoidable.'

They took him away, the stretcher-bearers being lucky enough to reach the hedge without any trouble, and they ran swiftly along behind it, carrying their load. When the colonel saw them disappear behind the clump of trees where the ambulance was situated, he breathed a sigh of relief.

'But, sir!' Maurice suddenly cried. 'You're wounded, too!'

He'd just noticed that his commander's left boot was covered in blood. The heel must have been torn off, and part of the leather had dug right into the flesh of his foot.

Monsieur de Vineuil calmy leaned over in the saddle and looked at his foot for a moment, which must have been stinging and feeling very heavy, hanging there.

'Yes, indeed,' he murmured, 'I got that just now... It's nothing, doesn't stop me sitting on a horse...'

And returning to take his place at the head of his regiment, he added,

'When one's on horseback and one can stay there, everything's all right still.'

At last, the two batteries from the reserve artillery were arriving. For the worried men this came as a huge relief, as if these cannons were their ramparts, salvation, the thunder which would silence the enemy guns opposite. In any case, it was a superb sight, as the batteries arrived in faultless battle order, each gun followed by its ammunition wagon, the drivers riding on the near-horses, holding the bridle of the off-horses, the gunners sitting on the weapons chests, corporals and artillery sergeants cantering along in their proper places. They might have been on parade, careful to maintain the distance between them while advancing at a furious pace across the stubble, with a dull rumbling like a storm.

Maurice, who'd lain down again in a furrow, got up, all excited, to say to Jean,

'Hey, look! That one getting into position on the left, that's Honoré's battery. I recognize his men.'

Jean slapped him back down to the ground.

'Lie flat! And play dead!'

Neither of them, though, lost sight of the battery, cheeks pressed against the soil, fascinated by its manœuvres, hearts beating violently at the sight of such calm, industrious courage from these men, whom they still expected to bring them victory.

Suddenly, to their left, on top of a treeless hilltop, the battery had come to a halt; and it took them only a minute, the gunners leapt down from the weapons-chests, unhitched the limber, the drivers left the guns in position, and made their horses execute a half-circle to take them fifteen metres back, facing the enemy, stock still. The six guns were already set up, widely spaced apart, paired into three

sections under the command of the lieutenants, all six coming under
the orders of a very tall, skinny captain, who angrily marked out the
plateau. And after he'd made his calculations, they heard him cry
out,

'Sights at sixteen hundred metres!'

Their target was to be the Prussian battery left of Fleigneux,
behind the undergrowth, whose deadly fire was making Illy Calvary
untenable.

'You see,' began Maurice again, unable to keep quiet, 'Honoré's
gun is in the middle section. There he is, leaning over next to the
gun-layer... That's wee Louis: we drank a glass with him in Vouziers, remember?... And the off-side driver, there, the one sitting up
so straight on his horse, the magnificent arab beast, that's
Adolphe...'

The field gun, with its six gunners and the sergeant, then beyond
that the limber and four horses mounted by the two drivers, followed
by the ammunition wagon, which was drawn by six horses and three
drivers, and then the supply wagons, forage carts, and the mobile
smithy, all made up an entire train of men, beasts, and equipment,
stretching back in a straight line for about a hundred metres; not
counting the spare horses, the extra ammunition wagon, the men
and animals intended to plug any gaps, waiting over to the right, so
as not to put themselves needlessly at risk in the line of fire.

Honoré, though, was busy loading his gun. The two middle gunners had already gone to fetch the cartridge and shell from the
ammunition chest, where the corporal and engineer were keeping
watch; and suddenly, having inserted the cartridge—a powder
charge wrapped in serge—and carefully pushed it in with the ramrod, the forward gunners slid the shell likewise into place, studs
grating along the grooves of the barrel. Swiftly, the second gun-layer
used the pin to pierce the cartridge and plunged the linstock into the
vent. Honoré wanted to lay this first charge himself, and was half-
crouched over the mounting, turning the screw to adjust the range,
and making slight hand signals to indicate in which direction the
gunner behind the cannon should aim, operating a lever to move the
gun imperceptibly over to the right or to the left.

'That should do it!' he said, straightening up.

The captain, his tall frame bent double, came over to check the
range. Next to each cannon, the second gunner stood holding the

cord, ready to pull on the striker, the saw-toothed blade which lit the cap. And slowly, the orders were called out by number.

'Gun number one—fire!... Gun number two—fire!...'

All six guns went off, the cannons recoiled and were wheeled back into place, while the artillery sergeants noted that the aim had fallen far too short. They corrected it, and the manœuvre started again, always the same; it was the slow deliberateness with which they performed their mechanical task, this calm precision, which sustained morale among the men. The weapon, that beloved beast, drew a little family around itself, brought closer together because they all took a share in the task. The gun was the tie that bound them, their sole concern, everything existed for the gun alone—vans, wagons, horses, men, the lot. It was this which gave the battery its strong cohesion, working together calmly and solidly like a well-ordered household.

Among the men in the 106th, cheers had greeted the first salvo. At last—they were going to shut up those Prussian cannon! However, they were immediately disappointed when they saw the shells falling short only halfway there, most of them exploding in mid-air, before they'd even got as far as the bushes near where the enemy artillery lay hidden.

'Honoré says,' began Maurice yet again, 'that compared to his, all the other guns aren't worth tuppence... His, though—oh! He'd sleep next to it, you'd never find its like! Just see how fondly he looks at it, just watch how he makes them wipe it down to stop it overheating!'

He and Jean joked about this, cheered to see the artillery putting on such a brave show. After three rounds, though, the Prussians had adjusted their aim: first it had been too long, but now it was so precise that shells were dropping right on top of the French guns; and in spite of their best efforts to lengthen their range, the latter still couldn't manage it. One of Honoré's gunners was killed—the one at the front, on the left. They shoved the body aside and the drill carried on as before, careful and steady. Missiles exploded, raining down from all directions; and around each gun, the same methodical activity went on, cartridge and shells put in place, sights set, shot fired, gun wheeled back into place, and it was as if the men were so thoroughly absorbed in the task that they could neither see nor hear anything else.

What struck Maurice most strongly of all, however, was the attitude of the drivers, positioned fifteen metres back but sitting bolt upright in the saddle, facing the enemy. There was Adolphe, broad across the chest, with his thick blond moustache and red face; it required real pride and courage to sit there without even blinking, watching the shells coming straight for you, not even able to gnaw at your knuckles to distract yourself. The gunners working at least had something to keep them occupied; but the drivers just sat there, still as stones, seeing only death before them, with all the time in the world to reflect on it and wait for it to come. They were forced to sit facing the enemy—if they turned their backs, the urge to flee would prove too much for both the men and their mounts. Facing danger forces one to brave it out. No heroism is greater, yet none more humble.

Another soldier had had his head blown off, and two wagon horses were in their death throes, their bellies ripped open; the enemy fire continued, so deadly that the entire battery was going to be put out of action if they insisted on staying where they were. They had to sidestep this terrible aim, even though it would be awkward to change position. The captain hesitated no longer, yelling out the order,

'Limber up!'

The perilous manœuvre was carried out at frightening speed: the drivers executed another semicircle, drawing up the limber into place, and the gunners hitched it back to the guns. In doing this, however, they presented an extended front to the enemy, who took the opportunity to intensify their fire. The battery filed off at a brisk trot, tracing an arc among the furrows, and moved about fifty metres further to the right, setting up on a small plateau on the far side of the 106th. The guns were unhitched and the drivers once again found themselves face to face with the enemy; the firing began again, without pause, making such a commotion that the ground wouldn't stop shaking.

This time Maurice cried out. Yet again, after three rounds, the Prussian batteries had readjusted their aim and the third shell had landed right on top of Honoré's gun. They could see him rush forward and feel the fresh wound with a trembling hand—an entire chunk of the bronze muzzle had been torn away. But it could still be loaded, and once they'd removed the body of another gunner from between the wheels, the manœuvre began again. The gunner's blood had splashed onto the gun carriage.

'No, it's not Louis,' Maurice continued thinking aloud. 'There he is, laying the charge. He must be wounded, though, because he's only using his left arm... Oh! poor old Louis. He and Adolphe got on so well as long as he, the gunner, the foot soldier, was happy to be the humble servant of the driver, the man on horseback—despite the fact that he's actually the more skilled of the two...'

Jean, who'd been quiet up until now, interrupted him with a cry of anguish.

'They'll never hold out, it's no good!'

It was true—in less than five minutes this second position had become as untenable as the first. Missiles came hammering down with the same accuracy as before. A shell blew up one of the guns, killing a lieutenant and two men. Not a single shot went to waste, with such devastating effect that if they insisted on staying there much longer, there'd be neither cannon nor artillery personnel left. The destruction was crushing and complete.

Then the captain cried out for the second time,

'Limber up!'

The manœuvre began again, the drivers galloped round once more in a semicircle, allowing the gunners to hitch the cannons back up. This time, though, in the middle of the process, an explosion shot a hole in Louis's throat, tearing off his jaw, and he slumped over the mounting which he'd been lifting. And as Adolphe was coming round, just as their lines stood side-on to the enemy, they took a furious broadside: he keeled over, chest ripped open, arms flung wide. In a final spasm, he took the other man in his arms and they lay locked in an embrace, grotesquely twisted, married even unto death.

In spite of the dead horses, and in spite of the chaos into which the ranks had been thrown by the broadside, the entire battery was already climbing back up the slope and had taken up a position further forward, a few metres away from where Maurice and Jean were lying. For the third time, the guns were unhitched and the men on horseback found themselves once again facing the enemy, while the cannons reopened fire without delay, showing stubborn, invincible heroism.

'It's all over!' said Maurice, his voice faltering.

For the sky and the land seemed to have merged into one. Stones were splitting open and sometimes the sun was hidden by thick smoke. In the midst of the terrifying din, horses could be seen cowering, deafened by the noise. The captain was visible everywhere he went, far too tall. He was brought down, sliced in two, and fell like a toppled flagpole.

They kept on at their task, however, especially around Honoré's cannon, steadily and stubbornly. Honoré, despite his sergeant's stripes, had to get down and do the drill himself, for there were only three gunners left. He laid the charge and pulled the striker, while the other three went to the ammunition chest, loaded the gun, and employed the brush and the ramrod. Extra men and horses had been sent for to fill the gaps carved out by death; they were slow to come, and in the meantime they just had to make do and wait. What really got to them was that they still couldn't get their aim right, and almost all the missiles exploded in mid-air, without causing any real damage to the batteries opposite and their horribly effective bombardment. Suddenly, Honoré swore so loudly that they could hear him even above the sound of the thunder: of all the bloody luck! The right-hand wheel of his gun had been blown off! Jesus Christ! One leg gone, the poor old girl fallen over on her side, nose to the ground, all askew and no good for anything now! Huge tears rolled down his cheeks, and he took her neck between frantic hands, as if the warmth and tenderness of his embrace would be enough to put her right again. The best gun of all, the only one to have got a few shells over to the other side! And he was seized by a mad resolve—he would replace the wheel there and then, under fire. When he'd been to the trail-chest to fetch the spare wheel himself, assisted by another gunner, the emergency operation began—the most dangerous one possible to perform on the battlefield. Luckily, the extra men and horses had finally arrived, and two more gunners came to help.

Yet again, though, the battery was in a state of confusion. There was a limit even to these mad heroics. The order was going to be given to withdraw once and for all.

'Hurry, comrades!' Honoré kept on. 'We can at least wheel her off, and then they won't get hold of her!'

His overriding concern was to save his cannon, as if he were saving the flag. And he was still talking when he was struck down, his right arm torn off, his left side ripped open. He fell on his cannon and remained there, as if lying in state, his eyes to the front, features intact, handsome and angry, looking towards the enemy. A letter had slipped out from under his torn uniform; his clenched hands had grasped hold of it, and drop by drop it became stained with his blood.

The only lieutenant left alive flung out the command,

'Limber up!'

One of the wagons had blown up, with a sound of fireworks fusing and exploding. They had to make the decision to take horses from another wagon, in order to salvage a cannon whose team had been left on the field. And this last time, when the drivers had turned and the four remaining guns had been hitched back up, they set off at a gallop, not stopping until they'd gone about a thousand metres, behind the first trees of Garenne Wood.

Maurice had seen it all. With a small shudder of horror, he repeated mechanically,

'Poor lad! Oh, the poor lad!'

His distress seemed to make the gnawing pain in his stomach even worse. The animal within him was beginning to revolt: all his force was spent, and he was dying of hunger. His vision was becoming blurred, and he was no longer even conscious of the danger the regiment was in, now that the battery had been forced to retreat. Substantial numbers of men could attack the plateau at any moment.

'Listen,' he said to Jean, 'I must have something to eat... I'd rather eat and then be killed straight away!'

He opened his rucksack, took out the bread in two trembling hands and ravenously bit into it. Bullets whistled past, two shells burst only metres away. But for him nothing else existed, nothing but the need to quell his hunger.

'Jean, do you want some?'

Jean was staring at him, dazed and wide-eyed, his stomach tortured by the same desire.

'All right then, I will, I can't bear it.'

They shared the bread, greedily finishing it off, worrying about nothing else so long as there was still a mouthful left. And it was only afterwards that they saw their colonel again, high up on his horse, with blood coming from his boot. The 106th was overrun from every side. Other companies had already been put to flight. Then, forced to give way to the torrent, raising his sword, eyes full of tears, Monsieur de Vineuil cried,

'Lads! God have mercy on the souls he's abandoned today!'

He was surrounded by groups of fleeing soldiers, and a dip in the landscape hid him from view.

Then, somehow, Jean and Maurice found themselves behind the hedge, along with the remains of their company. There were forty men left at most, with Lieutenant Rochas at their head; they had the standard with them, and the subaltern bearing it had wound the silk around the pole to try to protect it. They scurried to the end of the hedge and threw themselves into a small clump of trees growing on a slope, where Rochas ordered them to start firing again. Scattered and concealed like snipers, the men could hold out; and they were helped by the fact that there was a major cavalry manœuvre going on to their right, and the regiments were being brought back into line to give it support.

It was then that Maurice understood the slow, invincible grip which was now closing in on them for good. That morning, he'd seen the Prussians break through via the Saint-Albert gap and reach Saint-Menges, then Fleigneux; and now, behind Garenne Wood, he heard the booming of the cannon of the Prussian Guard, and began to glimpse other German uniforms coming down from the Givonne Hills. A few minutes more and the circle would be complete, the Guard would join up with the Vth Corps, surrounding the French artillery with a living wall, a thundering cordon of artillery. It must have been with the desperate notion of making one last attempt, of finding some way to break through this marching wall, that one of the reserve cavalry divisions, led by General Margueritte, began gathering behind a fold in the land, ready to charge. This would be a charge to the death, with no hope of accomplishing anything, merely a gesture to uphold French honour. And Maurice, thinking of Prosper, witnessed the awesome spectacle.

Ever since the small hours, Prosper had done nothing but make his horse trudge from one end of Illy Plateau to the other, constantly marching and counter-marching. They'd been woken at dawn, one by one, without the reveille being sounded; and to make the coffee, they'd cleverly shielded each fire with an overcoat, so as not to alert the Prussians. After that, they'd been left in total ignorance, they could hear the cannon and see the smoke and the infantry moving around far away, but they knew nothing of the battle, its importance, what the outcome was, or why their generals had left them so utterly inactive. As for Prosper, he was thoroughly exhausted. What made them suffer were these sleepless nights, as their fatigue mounted up and the trotting of their horses induced irresistible drowsiness. He hallucinated, seeing himself on the ground, snoring away on a pebble mattress, he dreamed he was in a proper bed with clean, white sheets. For minutes at a time he was actually asleep in the saddle, just some object on the move, carried wherever his horse chose to trot. Sometimes comrades had toppled off their mounts that way. They were all so tired that the sound of the reveille no longer woke them up, and they had to be pulled to their feet, tugged and kicked out of the void.

'What the hell are they doing? What the bloody hell are they doing to us?' said Prosper over and over again, trying to shake off the inexorable torpor.

The cannon had been booming since six o'clock. As they climbed up a hillside, two of his comrades were killed by a shell, right there beside him; and further on, three more were left lying on the ground, bullet-holes piercing their skin before they even knew what was coming, or where it was coming from. This military parade was infuriating; it was futile and dangerous, across a battlefield. Finally, at about one o'clock, he realized that they were deciding to kill them cleanly at least. The entire Margueritte division, three regiments of the African Chasseurs, one of the French Chasseurs, and one of Hussars, had been assembled in a dip in the landscape, a little below the Calvary, to the left of the road. The trumpets had sounded to dismount. And the order from the officers rang out,

'Saddle up the horses and secure the saddlebags!'

Dismounting, Prosper stretched and patted Zephyr down. Poor old horse, he was about as dead on his feet as his master, completely shattered by the rotten job he was being forced to do. On top of all that, he was heavily laden: there was clothing in the saddlebags and an overcoat rolled up over the top, shirt, trousers, shoulderbag for grooming behind the saddle, and then across it the bag of provisions, not counting the goatskin, waterbottle, and mess-tin. The cavalry officer felt his heart overflow with tender pity as he tightened the girth and made sure that everything was secure.

It was a nasty moment. Prosper, who was no more of a coward than the next man, lit up a cigarette, his mouth was so dry. Just before a charge, every man can tell himself, 'This time, it's your turn!' It lasted a good five or six minutes, as General Margueritte reportedly went on ahead to get the lie of the land. They waited. The five regiments had formed three columns, each one seven squadrons deep, to give the cannons something to chew on.

Suddenly, the trumpets sounded: to your mounts! Almost simultaneously, another call rang out: draw swords!

Each regiment's colonel had already galloped on twenty-five metres ahead of the front line to his battle position. The captains were at their posts, out in front of their men. And the waiting began again, amid a deathly hush. Not a sound, not a whisper could be heard beneath the blazing sun. Only the beating of their hearts. One order to go, the very last, and then this motionless mass would stir and rush forward like a hurricane.

Just then, however, an officer appeared over the crest of the hill, riding on horseback and wounded, with two men supporting him. At first they didn't recognize him. Then a rumbling came up from the men, rising to a wild clamour. It was General Margueritte, who'd been shot through both cheeks, and who'd no doubt die from his wounds. Unable to speak, he waved his arms in the enemy's direction.

Still the clamour grew.

'Our General!... Revenge, revenge!'

Then raising his sword aloft, the colonel of the 1st Regiment boomed out,

'Charge!'

The trumpets sounded and the mass began to stir, at a trot at first. Prosper was in the first row of men, but almost at the far end of the right flank. The centre is where the danger is greatest, for this is where the enemy instinctively concentrates its fire. As they came over the crest of the hill and began descending the other side, towards the vast plain, he could make out quite distinctly the Prussian squares they were being flung at, a thousand metres away. Apart from that, he trotted along as if in a dream, feeling floaty and light-headed because he'd been asleep, and with an extraordinarily empty sensation in his head, which left him completely devoid of thought. It was the machine taking over, propelled onwards by an irresistible impulse. Again and again, they were told to feel their boots touching the next man's, to make the ranks as serried as possible and rock solid. Then, as the trot began to accelerate and turned into a raging gallop, the African Chasseurs began emitting wild shrieks like Arabs, terrifying their horses. Before long they were rushing headlong, hell for leather, at an infernal gallop, letting out ferocious yells which the crackling bullets accompanied like a hailstorm, rattling down upon everything metal, mess-tins, water bottles, the copper trim on their uniforms and on the harnesses. Through the hail came the hurricane blast of wind and thunder that set the ground trembling, leaving a smell of scorched wool and sweating beasts rising up into the sunlight.

At five hundred metres, Prosper slipped beneath the impact of a terrifying surge forward which swept everything away with it. He grabbed at Zephyr's mane and managed to get back into the saddle. The battered centre ranks, demolished by the gunfire, swung to the side, while the two flanks began to spin round, doubling back to gather momentum. It was the final, predicted annihilation of the 1st Squadron. Dead horses cluttered the ground, some killed outright, others struggling in violent agony; unseated horsemen could be seen running as fast as their little legs could carry them, trying to find a horse. The dead were already strewn across the plain, and many riderless horses kept on cantering, coming back into position of their own accord to return to the fire at a mad pace, as if drawn by the smell of gunpowder. The charge began once more, the 2nd Squadron advanced with mounting fury, men clinging low to their horses' necks, swords held by their knees, ready to strike. They covered another two hundred metres, amid the deafening clamour of the storm. But yet again the centre ranks crumbled beneath the gunfire, men and beasts began to fall, as inextricably tangled bodies halted the charge. And so the 2nd Squadron was broken in its turn, wiped out, giving up its place to those that followed.

By the time the third charge took place, in this stubborn display of heroics, Prosper found himself mixed up among Hussars and French Chasseurs. The regiments were becoming confused, and now they were just one enormous wave, perpetually breaking and gathering, sweeping everything up in its path. He was no longer conscious of anything at all, but abandoned himself to his horse, brave old Zephyr whom he loved so dearly, and who appeared to have been panicked by an injury to his ear. Now he was among the centre ranks, and other horses were rearing up and toppling over around him, some men being thrown to the ground as if blown off by a gust of wind, while others, killed outright, stayed in the saddle, continuing the charge, their eyes suddenly lifeless. And this time, in the wake of the two hundred metres they gained once more, the stubble-field reappeared, covered in the dead and the dying. There were some with their heads buried in the ground. Others, who'd fallen face up, gazed at the sun with terror-stricken eyes coming out of their sockets. Then there was the large, black horse of an officer, its stomach blown open, which was trying in vain to get back up, forelegs all tangled up in its guts. As the gunfire intensified again, the outer flanks swung round one more time, and doubled back to concentrate their numbers.

In the end, it wasn't until they got as far as the 4th Squadron and the fourth attempt that they managed to reach the Prussian lines. Sword held high, Prosper swung down on their helmets and dark-coloured uniforms, seeing them through a fog. There was blood coming from somewhere, he saw that Zephyr's mouth was bleeding, and he imagined that it must have come from biting into the enemy ranks. The clamour around him had reached such a pitch that he could no longer hear himself shouting, even though the cry that must have been coming from his mouth was tearing his throat out. Behind the first of the Prussian lines, however, was another, and another, and yet another. Heroism was futile, these deeply massed men were like long grass, engulfing horses and riders alike. It was no use hacking away at them, for there were always more left. The gunfire raged with such intensity, and at point-blank range, that uniforms began catching fire. Everything went dark, swallowed up in the bayonets among the crushed chests and cracked skulls. The regiments would leave two-thirds of their numbers behind, and all that remained of the charge was the glorious folly of having tried it at all. Suddenly Zephyr was struck right in the chest and collapsed to the ground, crushing Prosper's right hip beneath him; the pain was so intense that he lost consciousness.

Maurice and Jean, who'd been following the heroic gallop of the squadrons, exclaimed angrily,

'Jesus Christ! What bloody good's bravery?'

And they kept firing, crouched behind the bushes on their low hill where they found themselves deployed as snipers. Rochas himself had picked up a rifle and was firing. But Illy Plateau was well and truly lost this time, the Prussian troops were invading it from every side. It was probably about two o'clock, and the junction was now complete—the Vth Corps and the Prussian Guard had at last met up, closing the loop.

All of a sudden, Jean fell to the ground.

'That's it,' he stammered, 'I've had it.'

It was as if he'd been struck a violent blow to the top of his head with a hammer—his képi had been torn off and was now lying behind him. At first, he thought his skull had been cracked open and that his brains were showing through. For some moments he didn't dare touch the spot, sure there'd be a hole. Then he risked it, and examined his fingers, which were covered in sticky, red blood. The pain was so overpowering that he passed out.

Just at that moment, Rochas was issuing orders to withdraw. There was a Prussian company only two or three hundred metres away. They were going to be caught.

'Don't hurry, just turn around and keep firing... We'll regroup back there, behind that low wall.'

But Maurice was in despair.

'Sir, we're not going to leave the corporal here, are we?'

'If he's had it, what do you want me to do?'

'No! No, he's still breathing... We can carry him off!'

Rochas shrugged, as if to say that you couldn't burden yourself with every man that fell. On the battlefield, the wounded no longer count. Then Maurice pleaded with Pache and Lapoulle.

'Come on, give me a hand, I'm not strong enough to manage all by myself.'

They didn't hear him, they weren't listening, they were thinking only of themselves, survival instincts working overtime. They were already sliding to their knees and disappearing off at high speed behind the little wall. The Prussians were a mere hundred metres away.

Crying with rage, left alone with an unconscious Jean, Maurice put his arms around him and tried to carry him. But it was true, he was too weak and feeble, worn out by fatigue and anxiety. He stumbled at the first attempt, and fell over with his load. If only he could spot a stretcher-bearer somewhere! He looked frantically about him, thought he recognized one among the fleeing men, and waved desperately at him. No one turned back to help. He gathered his last ounce of strength, took hold of Jean again, and managed about thirty paces; and when a shell exploded nearby, he thought it was all over and that he, too, was going to die, on top of the body of his friend.

Slowly, Maurice picked himself up. He felt for wounds and found none, not even a scratch. So why didn't he just make a run for it then? There was still time, it would only take him a couple of bounds to reach the little wall, and he'd be safe. Fear welled up inside him again, making him panic. He took one leap and was running away, when a bond stronger than the fear of death held him back. No! He couldn't do it, he couldn't possibly abandon Jean like that. It would have tortured every cell in his body, for the brotherly affection which had grown up between him and this peasant went to the very depths of his soul, right to the roots of life itself. Perhaps it even went back as far as those first days on earth: now, as then, it was as if only two humans existed, and neither could have abandoned the other without abandoning part of himself.

If Maurice hadn't eaten that crust of bread an hour before, while the shells were falling all around him, he'd never have found the strength to do what he did next. As it was, he couldn't remember any of it afterwards. He must have heaved Jean up onto his shoulders and then dragged him off with him, stopping and starting dozens of times among the stubble and the undergrowth, stumbling over every stone, yet struggling back to his feet every time. What kept him going was an invincible will-power, a refusal to give up which would have made him carry a whole mountain if he'd had to. Behind the wall he found Rochas and the few remaining men from their squad, still firing, defending the flag, which the subaltern was carrying under his arm.

No line of retreat had been signalled to the army corps in the event of failure. This lack of foresight and state of confusion left each general to do as he saw fit, and by now they'd all found themselves being forced back to Sedan by the fearsome embrace of the victorious German armies. The 7th Corps's 2nd Division was withdrawing in a fairly orderly manner, but what was left of the other divisions, together with those from the 1st Corps, were already heading for the city in an appalling mess, like a torrent of anger and sheer panic sweeping men and beasts along with it.

Just then, however, Maurice saw with joy that Jean was opening his eyes; and as he ran to a nearby stream to fetch water to wash his face, he was astounded: on his right, on the floor of the sheltered valley, protected by steep slopes, he saw the very same peasant he'd noticed that morning, still plodding steadily on, pushing the plough behind a large, grey horse. Why waste a day? It wasn't because there was a battle going on that the wheat would stop growing, nor the world cease to live.

CHAPTER SIX

High up on the roof terrace, where he'd gone to get an overview of the situation, Delaherche eventually began to grow restless and impatient, anxious to know what was going on. He could see for himself that the shells were passing over the town, and that the three or four which had destroyed the roofs of the surrounding houses could only be the occasional replies to the firing from the Palatinate Fort, which was so slow and ineffectual. Of the battle itself, though, he could see nothing, and the urge to find out what was happening, and find out now, was fuelling his fear of losing both his life and fortune to the catastrophe. He went back down, leaving his field glasses trained towards the German batteries.

Downstairs, however, he paused for a moment on seeing the garden which lay in the middle of the factory. It was nearly one o'clock, and the hospital was overflowing with wounded men. There was an endless stream of ambulances drawing up now beneath the porch. They were already short of the standard two- and four-wheel vehicles. Now there were trail-frames, forage and supply wagons, anything that could be requisitioned on the battlefield; even carts and farm-wagons began appearing, taken from farmyards and harnessed up to stray horses. Into these were piled all the men who'd been gathered up and hastily bandaged by the first-aid field ambulances. What they unloaded was a gruesome collection of poor wretches, some a greenish hue, others purple from asphyxia; many had passed out and others emitted sharp cries of pain; some were so numb with shock that they abandoned themselves to the nurses' care with terror in their eyes, while a few shook so violently on being touched that they died on the spot. The influx became so huge that there weren't going to be enough mattresses in the vast, low-ceilinged room, and Major Bouroche gave orders to start using the large bed of straw he'd had spread out at one end. However, he and his assistants were still able to handle all the operations between them. He'd simply asked for a second table to be set up in the warehouse where he was working, equipped with a mattress and oilcloth. One of his assistants swiftly stuffed a chloroform-soaked towel under the patient's nose. The thin, steel blade gleamed, the saws made only the slightest rasping sound, blood would spurt out, and the flow was instantly staunched. Patients were brought rapidly to and from the operating table, leaving barely enough time to sponge down the oilcloth in between. And at the other end of the garden, behind the laburnum trees, where they'd had to start a charnel heap to get rid of the bodies, they also flung the amputated arms and legs and all the bits of flesh and bone left behind on the tables.

Sitting beneath one of the tall trees, Madame Delaherche and Gilberte couldn't roll bandages fast enough. Bouroche, passing by with his face red and hot and his apron already bloodstained, threw a bundle of linen at Delaherche, yelling,

'Here, take this! Do something, make yourself useful for God's sake!'

But the mill owner protested.

'Sorry! I must get back to see what's happening. We don't even know whether we're still alive...'

Then, his lips brushing his wife's hair, he said,

'My poor Gilberte! To think that a shell could send all this up in smoke! It's terrifying.'

She raised her head, her face very pale, and glanced around with a shudder. Then that involuntary, irrepressible smile reappeared on her lips.

'Oh, yes! It is terrifying, what with all these men being cut up... How odd that I can stay where I am and not faint.'

Madame Delaherche had watched her son kiss the young woman's hair. She made a move as if to push the image away, thinking of that other man who also must have kissed her hair last night. But her elderly hands trembled, and she murmured,

'Lord, such suffering! It makes you forget your own.'

Delaherche left, explaining that he would be straight back with something definite to report. As soon as he reached the Rue Maqua, he was astonished to see how many soldiers were coming back unarmed, uniforms in tatters and covered in dust. The men he actually tried to question were unable to give him any detailed information: some replied in a daze that they didn't know; others said so much, waving their arms around so wildly and talking in such exaggerated terms that they appeared quite mad. So he instinctively headed back to the Sous-Préfecture, assuming that this was where any news would be arriving. As he was crossing the Place du Collège,

two cannons, no doubt the only two guns left of a battery, drew up at
a gallop and came to a halt against the kerbstone. In the Grande-Rue,
it was hard not to notice that the city was starting to become cluttered with the first of the men fleeing the battle: three Hussars
without horses were sitting in a doorway, sharing a loaf of bread;
another two were hesitantly leading their mounts, unsure where to
stable them; officers ran around in desperation, apparently without a
clue as to where they were going. On the Place Turenne, a second
lieutenant advised him not to hang around too long, because shells
were landing frequently on the square, and only a few moments
earlier a blast had mangled the iron railings surrounding the statue
of the famous captain who had conquered the Palatinate. Just as he
was making his way hurriedly down the Rue de la Sous-Préfecture,
he actually saw two projectiles explode with a dreadful racket on the
Pont de Meuse.

He was standing awkwardly outside the concierge's door, trying
to find some pretext for summoning one of the aides-de-camp and
questioning him, when a young voice called out to him from
within.

'Monsieur Delaherche! Quick, come in, it isn't nice out there.'

It was Rose, a girl who worked for him, and whom he hadn't
thought of before. Thanks to her, every door would be open to him.
He entered the lodge and accepted her invitation to sit down.

'Just imagine, all this has made Mama quite unwell, and she's
gone to bed. There's only me here now, you see, because Papa's part
of the National Guard up at the Citadel... A little while ago, the
Emperor decided to show how brave he was again, and he went back
out and got right to the end of the road, as far as the bridge. A shell
even landed right in front of him, and one of his equerries' horses
was killed. And then he came back... Well, what else could he do?'

'So, you know what the situation is, then... What have these
gentlemen been saying?'

She looked at him in amazement. She still seemed fresh-faced and
happy, with her fine hair and bright, childlike eyes, busying herself
among all these dreadful goings on, without really understanding
what was happening.

'No, I don't know anything... At about midday, I took a letter up
for Marshal MacMahon. The Emperor was with him... They shut
themselves away in there for an hour, the Marshal lying in his bed

and the Emperor sitting on a chair at his side... I do know that,
because I saw them when the door was opened.'

'So, what were they saying?'

Again, she looked at him, and she couldn't help laughing.

'But I don't know—how could I? No one on this earth knows
what they said to each other.'

It was true, and he made as if to apologize for having asked such a
stupid question. However, he was obsessed by the thought of that
vital conversation: how fascinating it must have been! What solution
had they come up with?

'Now,' went on Rose, 'the Emperor's gone back into his own
room, and he's in conference with two generals who've just arrived
from the battlefield.'

She broke off, and glanced up the steps.

'Look! Here comes one of them now... And look! There's the
other one!'

He hurried out and recognized them as Generals Ducrot and
Douay, whose horses were waiting for them. He watched them
climb into the saddle and then gallop off. Following the surrender
of Illy Plateau, both men had come running to warn the Emperor
that the battle was lost. They gave him precise details of the situation, telling him that both the army and Sedan were now surrounded on all sides, and that the disaster would be truly
appalling.

In his room, the Emperor wandered up and down in silence for a
few minutes, his gait unsteady and ailing. The only man left with
him now was a single aide-de-camp, standing mutely by one of the
doors. And the Emperor went on pacing up and down, from the
fireplace to the window, his face drained of colour and now distorted
by a nervous twitch. His back seemed to have grown more stooped,
as if an entire world had collapsed on it; and his lifeless gaze, eyes
veiled by heavy lids, displayed the resignation of the fatalist who'd
gambled and lost his final hand against Fate. But each time he
reached the half-open window, a shudder made him pause for a
second.

During one of these momentary pauses, he raised a shaky hand
and murmured,

'Oh! The cannon, the cannon! It's been going on and on all day!'

Indeed, from where he was standing, the boom of the batteries on

La Marfée and Frénois was extraordinarily violent. It was like a rumble of thunder which made the windows and even the walls tremble, a stubborn, incessant, exasperating din. He must have been thinking that any further struggle was futile, and that it was little short of criminal to keep up the resistance. What good would any more bloodshed do, any more crushed limbs and heads blown off, yet more dead, to add to those already scattered about the countryside? If they really were beaten, and it was all over, why carry on with the massacre? There was enough abomination and pain crying out beneath the sun already.

Returning from the window, the Emperor began to tremble again and he lifted up his hands.

'Oh! The cannon! The cannon! It just won't stop!'

Perhaps the horrible realization of his own responsibilities was dawning on him, as he imagined the bleeding corpses lying back there in their thousands due to his misdeeds; or perhaps it was simply that his dreamer's heart was moved to pity, that he was just a good man haunted by humanitarian concerns. Even as Fate was dealing him this dreadful blow, breaking and destroying his destiny like some wisp of straw, he managed to find tears for others, overwhelmed by the senseless butchery which was still going on, powerless to bear it any longer. Now this diabolical cannonade was causing his heart to pound in his chest as if it would burst, making his pain even worse.

'Oh! The cannon! Make it stop, make it stop right now!'

And this Emperor, who'd lost his throne and given up his powers to the Empress Regent, this army leader who'd lost his authority, since handing over supreme command to Marshal Bazaine, was suddenly conscious once more of his own powers, and he felt an overwhelming need to prove himself master one last time. Ever since Châlons, he'd kept to the shadows without giving a single order, had resigned himself to being no more than some useless, nameless burden, getting in the way, being bundled along with his troops' baggage. And it was only in defeat that the Emperor in him reawoke; the first and only order he still had to give, out of the terror and pity in his heart, was to hoist the white flag over the Citadel, to ask for an armistice.

'Oh! The cannon! The cannon!... Take a sheet, a tablecloth, take anything! Quick, run and tell them that they're to shut up!'

The aide-de-camp hurried out of the room, and the Emperor went on pacing unsteadily back and forth, from the chimney-place to the window, while the batteries still thundered away, shaking the entire house.

Downstairs, Delaherche was still chatting to Rose when a duty sergeant came running up to them.

'Mademoiselle, we can't find anything, and I can't even seem to find a maid anywhere... I don't suppose you've got any material, a piece of white material?'

'How about a towel?'

'No, no, not big enough... Something like a sheet torn in half.'

Obligingly, Rose had already dashed over to the linen cupboard.

'The only thing is, I don't have any sheets cut up... A large piece of white material... No! I can't see anything that would do the trick... Aha! Here we are—how about a tablecloth?'

'Perfect! Exactly what I need.'

As he was leaving, he added,

'We're going to use it as a white flag to hoist above the citadel and ask for peace... Thank you, Mademoiselle.'

Delaherche gave an involuntary leap of joy. At last, they were going to be left alone! Then, sensing that it wasn't really very patriotic to be so glad, he contained himself. But his heart pounded with relief nonetheless, and he watched a colonel and a captain, with the sergeant in their wake, coming hurriedly out of the Sous-Préfecture. The colonel was carrying the rolled-up tablecloth under his arm. It occurred to Delaherche that he might follow them, and he took leave of Rose, who was extremely proud to have furnished the piece of material. Just then, the clock struck two.

Outside the town hall, Delaherche was jostled by floods of haggard-looking soldiers coming down from the Cassine district. He lost sight of the colonel and abandoned the idea of going to see the white flag being put up. They certainly wouldn't let him into the Keep; and for another thing, hearing talk of shells landing on the school, a new fear came over him: what if his factory had caught fire since he'd left it? Agitated and restless again, he headed back home, hurrying to mask his own anxiety. But groups of people blocked the streets and obstacles were already springing up again at every cross-roads. Not until he reached the Rue Maqua did he breathe a sigh of relief on seeing the monumental façade of his house undamaged, with not even a wisp of smoke or a spark to be seen. He went inside and called out to his mother and wife.

'Everything's all right, they're hoisting the white flag, there's going to be an armistice!'

Then he stopped short, for the sight of the hospital was truly appalling.

In the huge drying room, whose main door had been left open, not only were all the mattresses occupied, but there was no longer any room left even on the bed of straw spread out at the far end. They were starting to lay straw down in between the beds, squashing the injured up close together. Already they'd counted nearly two hundred, and still they kept coming in. The wide windows shed a white light across this heaped-up human suffering. Sometimes, someone made too brusque a movement, and an involuntary cry rang out. Dying breaths gasped out onto the damp air. In the background was a soft, incessant moaning, which sounded almost like singing. And the silence deepened into a sort of resigned stupor, taking on the doleful, despondent air of a room for the dead, broken only by the whispers and footsteps of the nurses. The soldiers' wounds, hastily bandaged on the battlefield, some still exposed to the air, displayed their distress for all to see, between the tatters of their greatcoats and torn trousers. Feet with shoes still on stretched out mangled and bleeding. Limbs hung inert from knees and elbows, as if a hammer had been taken to them. There were broken hands and fingers about to fall off, dangling by no more than a thread of skin. Fractured arms and legs appeared to be most common, held stiff with pain, like lead weights. The most worrying injuries of all, though, were those to the stomach, trunk, and skull. Blood poured from horrific gashes to the ribcage, intestines had wound into knots and pushed up the skin, and kidneys which had been damaged, sliced into, made bodies twist into frenzied, contorted attitudes. Some men's lungs had been pierced right through, some with so tiny a puncture that there wasn't any bleeding, others by such a yawning gash that life gushed out in a flood of red; and haemorrhages, the injuries no one could see, would suddenly strike men down, making them delirious, turning their faces black. But the head injuries were by far the worst; shattered jawbones with teeth and tongues reduced to a bloody pulp; smashed sockets with an eyeball half hanging out; skulls split open and brains showing through. Wherever the bullets had entered the spinal cord or brain tissue the men lay like corpses, lifeless and comatose; while others, suffering from fractures and fever, tossed and turned, asking for water in low, pleading voices.

Then, next door, in the warehouse where they were operating, there was yet more horror. In this first rush, they were performing emergency operations only, where the desperate condition of the patient made it vital. If there was any risk of haemorrhage, Bouroche would decide on an immediate amputation. Likewise, if shrapnel was lodged anywhere dangerous, such as the base of the neck, under the arms, in the groin, inside elbow, or the back of the thigh, he went straight in and dug it out from deep down inside the wound. Other injuries, which he preferred to leave for observation, were simply dressed by the nurses on his instructions. He himself had already carried out four amputations, staggering them with a few bullet extractions to give himself a rest in between major operations; and he was starting to get tired. There were only two operating tables, his and one other, where one of his assistants was at work. They'd simply hung a sheet down the middle, so that the patients couldn't see each other. And even though they sponged down the tables, they were still red; and the buckets of water, which needed only a glassful of blood to turn them from clear to crimson, and which they swilled out a few steps away over a tub of daisies, looked as if they were full of pure blood being flung over the lawn, drenching the flowers. Even though the air flowed in freely from outside, the stale smell of chloroform rose up in nauseous waves from the tables, bandages, and surgical equipment.

A compassionate man deep down, Delaherche was still shaking in sympathy when his attention was caught by a landau drawing up beneath the porch. No doubt this gentleman's carriage had been the only thing they could find, and they'd piled in the wounded. There were eight of them, crowded in one on top of the other. The mill owner gave a cry of shock and terror on recognizing the last one to be brought down as Captain Beaudoin.

'Oh! My poor friend!... Wait here! I'll get my mother and my wife to come out to you.'

They came running, leaving two servant girls to carry on rolling up bandages. The nurses who'd taken hold of the captain carried him into the room; and they were about to set him on a pile of straw when Delaherche noticed a soldier lying on a mattress, motionless, face sallow, eyes wide open.

'Hold on, this one's dead!'

'Hey, he's right, ' murmured one of the nurses. 'No point him taking up space.'

He and a colleague picked up the corpse and carried it out to the improvised charnel heap behind the laburnums. A dozen bodies already lay lined up, grown stiff as their dying breath left them, some with their feet pointed, as if their suffering had stretched them, others lying crooked, twisted into atrocious positions. Some were grimacing, eyes rolled up to show the whites, teeth bared by snarling lips; while many of them, drawn and terribly sad, still had great big tears on their cheeks. A very young soldier, who'd been small and skinny, had had his head half blown away, and he was clutching a woman's photograph to his breast with convulsed hands; it was one of those pale, cheap-quality photographs, and it was spattered with blood. And lying at the feet of the dead, flung on any old how, were piles of amputated arms and legs and everything that could be carved out or chopped off on the operating table, like sweepings from a butcher's shop, flesh and blood offcuts shoved into a corner.

Standing in front of Captain Beaudoin, Gilberte gave a shudder. My God! How pale he was, lying there on the mattress, his face white beneath all that horrid dirt! And the thought that, only a few hours before, he had held her in his arms, full of life and smelling so sweet, left her frozen with fear. She fell to her knees.

'My dear, how terrible! But it's nothing serious, is it?'

Automatically, she took out her handkerchief and wiped his face, unable to bear to see him like this, all dirty and sweaty with soil and gunpowder. She felt as if she was easing his suffering by cleaning him up a little.

'That's right, isn't it? It's nothing, just your leg.'

The captain opened his eyes with some difficulty, half-submerged in sleep. He recognized his friends, and tried to smile.

'Yes, it's only my leg... I didn't even feel it happen, I just thought I'd tripped and fallen...'

But his speech was laboured.

'Oh! I'm thirsty, I'm so thirsty!'

Madame Delaherche, who was leaning over him on the other side of the mattress, hurried off. She ran to fetch a glass and a carafe of water, with a drop of cognac added. And when the captain had greedily drained his glass she was obliged to share the rest between the other patients lying next to him: hands reached out and voices pleaded fervently with her. A Zouave began sobbing because there wasn't any left for him.

Meanwhile, Delaherche tried to have a word with the major, to see if he would treat the captain out of turn. Bouroche had just walked into the room in his blood-soaked apron, his broad face covered in sweat and seemingly set on fire by his leonine mane of hair: and as he passed, men tried to sit up and stop him, all desperate to be seen to straight away, to be saved, to know what their fate was to be: 'Me next, sir, me next!' Faltering prayers followed him across the room and fumbling fingers clutched at his clothes. But he was completely absorbed in what he was doing, huffing and puffing away wearily, getting his work organized and taking no notice of anyone else. He talked out loud to himself, counting the patients off on his fingers, assigning numbers to them and sorting them into categories: this one, then this one, then another; one, two, three; jaw, arm, thigh; while the assistant accompanying him listened carefully, trying to remember it all.

'Major,' said Delaherche, 'there's a captain here, Captain Beaudoin...'

Bouroche cut him short.

'What? Beaudoin, here?... Oh, poor sod!'

He went over and stood before the wounded man. However, he must have seen at a glance how serious his condition was, for immediately, without even stooping to examine the injured leg, he said,

'Right! He's to be brought to me straight away, as soon as I've finished the operation they're preparing at the moment.'

And he went back into the warehouse, followed by Delaherche, who was unwilling to let him out of his sight in case he forgot his promise.

This time, the operation was to amputate an arm at the socket by the Lisfranc method, something surgeons referred to as a nice little job, an elegant, swift piece of work, which took forty seconds from start to finish, if that. Chloroform was already being administered, while an assistant grasped the shoulder in both hands, four fingers of each under the armpit, thumbs on top. Then, armed with a long, slim knife, Bouroche called out 'Sit him up!', grabbed the deltoid, pierced the arm and cut through the muscle; then, slicing back upwards, he severed the joint in one go; and off came the arm, lopped off in three swift strokes. The assistant had slid his thumbs over the humeral artery to act as a tourniquet and stop the flow of blood. 'Lie him back down!' Bouroche couldn't help chuckling as he began stitching up the wound, for it had taken him a mere thirty-five seconds. All that was left now was to tack the flap of flesh back over the wound, like a flat epaulette. It was a pretty sight, because this was a dangerous operation—a man could lose all his blood in three minutes from the humeral artery, not to mention the fact that every time a patient was knocked out with chloroform, there was a risk that he might die.

Frozen to the spot, Delaherche would gladly have fled. But he didn't have time to, for the arm was already lying on the table. The soldier who'd been operated on, a recruit, a sturdy peasant, caught sight of the arm as it was being carried away to behind the laburnums, just as he was coming round. He looked down sharply at his shoulder, saw it sliced through and bleeding. He was furiously angry.

'Oh! Jesus Christ! What a stupid thing to do!'

Bouroche, drained, made no reply. Then he said heartily,

'I acted for the best, son, I didn't want you kicking the bucket... And anyway, I asked you, and you said yes.'

'I said yes! I said yes! D'you think I knew what I was saying?'

His anger dissolved, and he began crying bitterly.

'What the fuck am I meant to do now?'

They carried him back to the straw, and gave the table and oilcloth a rough wipe down; and once again the buckets of red water were sent sloshing across the lawn, drenching the white tub of daisies with blood.

But Delaherche was astonished that he could still hear the cannon. Why on earth didn't they stop? Surely Rose's tablecloth must be flying over the citadel by now. Yet it was quite the opposite, the Prussian batteries seemed to have started to intensify their fire. It made such a racket that no one could hear themselves speak, the ground shuddered so violently that even the least nervous of them shook from head to toe, filled with mounting dread. Jolts that brought hearts leaping into throats could hardly be good for those either at or on the operating tables. The entire hospital was being turned upside down, panic-stricken, driving everyone to exasperation.

'It was all over, so why are they still firing?' exclaimed Delaherche, ears straining anxiously, all the time imagining that what he was hearing would be the final shot.

Then, turning back to Bouroche to remind him about the captain, he was astounded to discover him lying on the ground, face down on a bale of hay, both arms stripped to the shoulders and plunged into two buckets of icy water. His strength and morale completely drained, the major had collapsed in utter exhaustion, brought down by an overwhelming sense of sadness and desolation, going through one of those agonizing moments when the doctor feels completely powerless. He was a solid man, though, with a tough hide and a steady heart. But he'd just been struck by that feeling of 'What's the point?' The sense that he'd never manage it all, that he couldn't do everything, had suddenly paralysed him. What was the point? Whatever he did, death would always be the strongest.

Two nurses brought Captain Beaudoin over on a stretcher.

'Major,' ventured Delaherche, 'here's the captain.'

Bouroche opened his eyes, drew his arms out of the buckets, shook them off and dried them on the straw. Then, getting to his knees, he said,

'Bloody hell, yes! Another one... Come on, then, the day's not over yet!'

And he was back on his feet, refreshed, shaking his leonine head with its wild mane of hair, the compelling call of discipline and the need for action setting him back on track.

Gilberte and Madame Delaherche had followed the stretcher through; and when the captain had been laid on the oilcloth covering the mattress, they stood a few paces back.

'Right! It's just above the right ankle,' Bouroche was saying, talking a lot to distract the patient. 'Not serious if it's there. Get better in no time... Now, let's have a look at it.'

He was visibly concerned, however, by Beaudoin's torpid state. He looked at the first-aid dressing, a single band which had been pulled tight and kept in place on the trouser-leg by the sheath of a bayonet. He grumbled beneath his breath, wondering what sort of idiot could have done that. Then all of a sudden, he shut up. He'd just worked it out: it must have happened on the way there, in the landau full of wounded men; the bandage must have come loose and slipped down, so that it no longer exerted any pressure on the wound, and this had led to extensive haemorrhaging.

Bouroche flew into a violent rage, shouting at one of the nurses who was helping him.

'You useless bugger! Start cutting, quick!'

The nurse cut open the trouser-leg and pants, as well as the shoe and sock. First the leg, then the foot appeared, bare and deathly pale, all stained with blood. There, above the ankle, was a dreadful hole, where the blast of the shell had caused a ragged shred of red material to embed itself. A jagged lump of flesh, where the muscle stuck out, was poking messily out of the wound.

Gilberte had to lean against one of the posts for support. Oh! That flesh, that flesh! Once so white, and now so bloody and mangled! Despite her horror, she just couldn't take her eyes off it.

'Christ!' Bouroche declared. 'They've made a fine old mess of you!'

He touched the foot, found that it was cold, and was unable to detect a pulse. His face had grown extremely grave, and he was grimacing in a way peculiar to him when presented with worrying cases.

'Christ!' he repeated. 'This foot's gone bad!'

The captain, whose fear was preventing him from sliding into unconsciousness, was watching him and waiting; finally, he said,

'Do you think so, sir?'

Bouroche's tactics, though, were never to ask a patient directly for permission to operate when an amputation was necessary. He preferred to let them resign themselves to the idea.

'Foot's gone bad,' he murmured, as if thinking out loud. 'We shan't be able to save it.'

Nervously, Beaudoin spoke again.

'Look here, sir, we ought to get it over with, don't you think?'

'I think you're a brave man, Captain, and that you'll let me do what has to be done.'

Captain Beaudoin's eyes paled and misted over with a brownish sort of mist. He had understood. However, in spite of the unbearable fear which was choking him, he answered simply and bravely,

'Do it, sir.'

It didn't take long to get him ready. The assistant was already holding the chloroform-soaked towel, and it was placed directly under the patient's nose. Then, as he underwent that brief struggle that precedes anaesthesia, two nurses slid the captain round on the mattress, so that his legs swung free; one of them kept hold of his left leg, while an assistant, seizing hold of his right, squeezed it roughly between his hands, right at the root of the thigh, to compress the arteries.

When Gilberte saw Bouroche approaching with the narrow blade, she was able to stand it no longer.

'No, no! This is awful!'

She started to faint and leant against Madame Delaherche, who had to put out a hand to stop her from falling.

'Why don't you leave the room, then?'

But they both stayed where they were. They turned away, not wanting to see, standing still, trembling, pressed against each other in spite of the lack of tenderness between them.

It must have been at this point that the cannon boomed loudest of all. It was three o'clock, and a frustrated and disappointed Delaherche declared that it was all quite beyond him. For now there could be no doubt that, far from falling silent, the Prussian batteries were firing more fiercely than ever. Why? What was going on? The bombardment was infernal, the ground shook, the air was on fire. All around Sedan the eight hundred cannon of the German armies, the bronze cordon, were firing simultaneously, thundering down ceaselessly on the neighbouring fields; and the converging fire, with blows raining down on the centre from all the surrounding heights, would burn down the town and reduce it to pulp within two hours. The worst of it was that shells were starting to hit houses again. The explosions blasted out more and more frequently. One shell fell on the Rue des Voyards. Another grazed one of the tall chimneys on the factory, and debris came down outside the warehouse.

Bouroche looked up, grumbling.

'Are they trying to finish our wounded off for us?... This din's unbearable!'

Meanwhile, the nurse was keeping the captain's leg straight; and with a rapid, circular incision, the major cut right through the skin, below the knee, five centimetres down from where he wanted to saw through the bone. Then, moving swiftly, using the same slim blade to save time, he cut aside the skin and lifted it away all around the leg, just like orange peel. However, just as he was about to slice into the muscle, a nurse came up and spoke into his ear.

'Number two's just gone.'

The major couldn't hear him above the dreadful noise.

'Speak up, man, for God's sake! My eardrums are fit to burst, what with their bloody cannon!'

'Number two's just gone.'

'Which one was that, number two?'

'The arm.'

'Oh, right! Well, bring me number three, then, the jaw!'

And with extraordinary deftness, without interrupting his movement, he sliced into the muscle with a single incision, cutting right to the bone. He exposed the tibia and fibula and put a three-tailed compress between them to keep them in place. Then, with one stroke of the saw, he chopped them both off. The foot was left behind in the hands of the nurse who'd been holding it.

There was little blood, thanks to the pressure the assistant was exerting on the thigh, higher up. The three arteries were rapidly sewn up. But the major shook his head; and when the assistant took his fingers away, he examined the wound, murmuring, certain that the patient couldn't yet hear him.

'Blast. The arterioles aren't bleeding.'

Then, with a wave of his hand, he concluded his diagnosis: another poor sod for the scrap heap! Immense fatigue and sadness reappeared on his sweat-covered face, that despair, that 'What's the point?', when not even four out of ten can be saved. He wiped his brow and set about folding the skin over, to make the three closing stitches.

Gilberte had just turned back round. Delaherche had told her it was over and she could look again. However, she caught sight of the captain's foot, which the nurse was taking out to behind the laburnums. The charnel heap was still growing, two more bodies were laid out, one with a black, wide-open mouth, who looked as if he was still yelling, the other curled up in some awful agony, shrunk down to the size of a puny, deformed child. The worst of it was that the pile of remains was starting to spill over into the neighbouring alley. The nurse hesitated, unsure as to where to put the captain's foot. In the end, he decided to chuck it onto the pile.

'There we are! All done!' said the major to Beaudoin, who was being brought round. 'You're out of danger.'

The captain, though, felt none of that joyful awakening that comes with successful operations. He sat up a little, then fell back, stammering in a feeble voice,

'Thank you, sir. I'd rather it was over and done with.'

However, he could feel the alcohol dressing stinging the wound. And as they brought up the stretcher to carry him back, a terrible explosion shook through the building: a shell had landed behind the warehouse, in the little yard where the pump stood. Windows shattered and glass went flying, and thick smoke filled the hospital. In the main room, the wounded sat up in panic on their straw bedding, crying out in terror, trying to run away.

Delaherche dashed forward in alarm to assess the damage. Were they going to set fire to his house now, and destroy it? What on earth was going on? If the Emperor wanted them to stop, why had they started all over again?

'Jesus Christ! Get a move on!' yelled Bouroche to the terror-stricken nurses. 'Wash the table down and bring me number three!'

They washed the table and flung the buckets of red water out over the lawn again. The tub of daisies was nothing but a bloody mess by now, greenery and flowers all torn and battered by the blood. When they'd brought him number three the major, by way of a rest, began looking for a bullet which must have lodged itself beneath the tongue, after smashing through the lower jaw. There was a lot of blood, and it made his fingers stick together.

In the main room, Captain Beaudoin was back on his mattress. Gilberte and Madame Delaherche had followed the stretcher back through. Even Delaherche himself came to talk for a moment, in spite of his agitated state.

'You must rest, Captain. We'll prepare a room for you, you can come and stay with us.'

Lying there prostrate, however, the injured man suddenly woke, and in a moment of lucidity, said,

'No, I think I'm going to die.'

He looked at all three of them, eyes wide, full of the fear of death.

'Oh! Captain, what are you saying?' murmured Gilberte, trying to smile, chilled through. 'You'll be up and about in a month.'

He shook his head, now looking only at her, huge regret for life written all over his face, sensing the cowardice of going like this, too young, without having exhausted the joys of living.

'I'm going to die, I'm going to die... Oh! How horrible...'

Then, all at once, he caught sight of his torn, dirty uniform and grimy hands, and it seemed to pain him to find himself in such a state in front of ladies. He was overcome by shame for having let himself go in such a way, and the thought that he wasn't correctly turned out was what finally restored his courage. He managed to speak in a cheerful tone of voice.

'Only, if I do die, I'd like to go with clean hands... Madame, would you be so kind as to bring me a wet towel?'

Gilberte ran off to return with the towel, and she insisted on rubbing his hands for him herself. After that he showed enormous courage, anxious to end his life like a true gentleman. Delaherche offered words of encouragement and helped his wife to make him comfortable. Looking at this dying man, when old Madame Delaherche saw how the household was rallying round to help him, she felt her rancour subside. Yet again she would keep quiet, although she knew what was going on and had sworn to tell her son everything. What was the point of upsetting everyone, now that death was taking away the sin?

It was over almost immediately. Captain Beaudoin, growing weaker and weaker, relapsed into his exhausted state. An icy sweat broke out on his brow and neck. He opened his eyes for an instant longer, and fumbled around as if he were feeling for the bedcovers, which he began pulling up under his chin, his twisted hands making gentle, persistent movements.

'Oh! I'm cold, I'm so cold!'

And he passed away, went out, without so much as a hiccup, and on his face, calm and thinner of late, there remained an expression of infinite sadness.

Delaherche saw to it that instead of being taken to the charnel heap, the body was placed in a shed next door. He tried to make Gilberte go up to her room, for she was sobbing and distraught. But she declared that she'd be too scared up there now, on her own, and that she'd rather stay with her mother-in-law, among the hustle and bustle of the hospital, which would take her mind off it. She was already running off to give water to an African Chasseur who was delirious with fever, and helping a nurse to bandage the hand of a young soldier, a recruit only twenty years old, who'd walked all the way from the battlefield with his thumb torn off; and because he was kind and funny, making light of his injury in a carefree way, like some Parisian wit, in the end it cheered her up, too.

While the captain had been in his final agony, the bombardment seemed to have grown even fiercer, and a second shell had landed in the garden, splitting one of the hundred-year-old trees. People began crying in terror that the whole of Sedan was burning, because a sizeable fire had started in the district of La Cassine. If the shelling carried on for much longer and with such violence, it would all be over.

'This is impossible, I'm going back!' said Delaherche, beside himself with rage.

'Where to?' asked Bouroche.

'The Sous-Préfecture, of course, to find out whether the Emperor was having us on when he talked about hoisting the white flag.'

For a moment the major just stood there, stunned by the idea of the white flag, of defeat, of capitulation, coming as it did on top of his feeling of powerlessness to save all these poor sods they kept bringing him, all shot to pieces. He shrugged in fury and despair.

'Oh, go to hell! We're buggered anyway!'

Outside, Delaherche found it more difficult than ever to fight his way through the swelling numbers of people. The streets were getting busier by the minute, flooded with scattered soldiers. He questioned a few of the officers he came across: none had seen the white flag flying over the citadel. Finally he found a colonel who declared that he'd glimpsed it momentarily, just enough time for it to be hoisted and then lowered again. That would explain everything, for either the Germans hadn't seen it at all, or, having seen it appear and then disappear, they'd redoubled their fire, realizing that the end was in sight. There was even a rumour going round already about a general who, seeing the white flag appear, had flown into a rage, leapt forward and torn it out of the soldier's hands, snapping the flagpole in two and stamping on the material. And still the Prussian batteries went on firing, shells were raining down on roofs and streets, houses were ablaze, and on the corner of the Place Turenne a woman lay with her skull blasted open.

At the Sous-Préfecture, Rose wasn't in the concierge's lodge when

Delaherche got there. All the doors were standing wide open—the rout had begun. So he went upstairs; the only people he bumped into were in a blind panic, and no one asked him any questions at all. On the first floor, as he was wondering which way to go, he came across the young woman.

'Oh, Monsieur Delaherche, it's all going wrong! Quick! Look through here if you want to see the Emperor.'

She was right, for a door to their left hadn't been closed properly, and was standing ajar; through the crack, they could see the Emperor, who had begun walking unsteadily back and forth again, from the fireplace to the window. He plodded on relentlessly, despite being in intolerable pain.

An aide-de-camp had just entered, and it was he who had left the door ajar. They could hear the Emperor asking him, in a tense, despondent voice,

'For Heaven's sake, sir, tell me why they're still firing, when I've already given the order to raise the white flag?'

It had become an unbearable torment for him to hear this relentless cannonfire, getting more and more violent as each minute passed. He couldn't approach the window without it striking at his very heart. More blood, more human lives wasted due to his mistakes! Every minute, more needless deaths piled up. Revolted by it all, this compassionate dreamer had already asked the same, despairing question ten times over of those who entered his room.

'For Heaven's sake, tell me why they're still firing, when I've already given the order to raise the white flag?'

The aide-de-camp murmured a reply, which Delaherche couldn't catch. The Emperor, meanwhile, hadn't stopped pacing, but he gave in to the desire to turn away from the window, where he faltered before the cannon's ceaseless thunder. He'd grown paler than ever and his long face, all mournful and drawn, the morning's powder only partly removed, told of his agony.

Just then a small, sprightly man in a dusty uniform, whom Delaherche recognized as being General Lebrun, crossed the landing and pushed open the door, without being announced. At once, the Emperor's anguished voice could be heard asking, yet again,

'For Heaven's sake, General, tell me why they're still firing, when I've already given the order to raise the white flag?'

The aide-de-camp left the room, the door was shut behind him, and Delaherche was unable even to hear the general's reply. There was nothing to be seen or heard.

'Ah!' repeated Rose. 'It's all going wrong, I can tell by those gentlemen's faces. It's just like my tablecloth, I won't be seeing that again, someone told me they'd ripped it up... But the Emperor's the one I feel sorry for in all this, because he's more poorly than the Marshal, he'd be better off in bed than in there, driving himself mad with all that pacing up and down.'

She was very upset, and her pretty, blonde head displayed genuine pity. Delaherche, whose Bonapartist fervour had grown singularly cooler over the last few days, thought her a little silly. Downstairs, though, he stayed with her a moment longer, watching for General Lebrun to leave. And when the latter reappeared, he followed him.

General Lebrun had explained to the Emperor that if they wanted to ask for an armistice, then a letter would have to be signed by the French Commander-in-Chief and handed over to the Commander-in-Chief of the German armies. Then he'd volunteered to write the letter himself and set about finding General de Wimpffen, who would sign it. He left with the letter, his only fear being that he wouldn't be able to locate de Wimpffen, since he didn't know whereabouts on the battlefield he might be. Moreover, the chaos in Sedan was becoming such that he couldn't let his horse go any faster than walking pace; which meant that Delaherche was able to accompany him as far as the Porte du Ménil.

Once on the main road, however, Lebrun urged his horse into a gallop, and as luck would have it, just as he was entering Balan he spotted General de Wimpffen. A few minutes earlier, the latter had written the following to the Emperor: 'Sire, come and take your place at the head of your troops. It will be an honour for them to forge a passage for you through the enemy lines.' As a result, he flew into a furious temper at the merest mention of an armistice. Absolutely not! He wouldn't sign anything of the kind, he wanted to fight! It was half-past three. And it was shortly after this that the heroic, desperate attempt took place, the last push, to try to make a break through the Bavarian lines, by marching one last time on Bazeilles. In the streets of Sedan and the neighbouring fields, they lied to the troops to give them heart, crying 'Bazaine's coming! Bazaine's coming!' Since that morning, this was what many had been dreaming of, and with each new battery that the Germans unveiled, they thought they were hearing the cannon of the Metz army. About twelve hundred men were assembled, scattered soldiers from all the army corps, armed with a whole mixture of weapons; and the little column launched itself gloriously into the road raked by machine-gun fire, taking it at a run. At first the effort was superb, the men who fell didn't slow the momentum of the rest, and they covered nearly five hundred metres of ground, displaying truly ferocious courage. But soon gaps began to appear in the ranks, and even the bravest of them pulled back. What could they do when they were so devastatingly outnumbered? It was nothing but the rash folly of an army chief who didn't want to be beaten. General de Wimpffen ended up on his own with General Lebrun, on the road to Balan and Bazeilles, which they now had to abandon once and for all. The only thing left to do was to beat a retreat back to the walls of Sedan.

As soon as he'd lost sight of the general, Delaherche hurried back to the factory, with one thing on his mind—to set up his observation post again and follow events from a distance. However, as he reached home he bumped into Colonel de Vineuil coming in, and he paused for a moment as the officer was carried through on a sort of barrow, lying half-unconscious on a bed of hay, his boot covered in blood. The colonel had stubbornly insisted on rallying what was left of his regiment until he had fallen from his horse. He was immediately taken to a first-floor bedroom, and Bouroche, rushing up and finding that it was only a cracked ankle, simply dressed the wound for the time being, after removing the bits of boot leather. He was swamped by work and thoroughly worn out, and he went back downstairs yelling that he'd rather cut off one of his own legs than carry on doing his job in such unhygienic conditions, without the right equipment or the necessary support staff. In fact, downstairs they were at a loss as to where to put the wounded, and had decided to lay them on the lawn, in the grass. There were two of them waiting already, lamenting in the open air beneath the shells which continued to rain down. The number of men brought into the hospital since midday now stood at over four hundred, and the major had asked for surgeons to be sent for, but no one had come as yet except for a young doctor from the town. He couldn't be everywhere at once, he probed and sawed and sewed back up, quite beside himself, despairing to see them keep on bringing him more work than he could possibly manage. Gilberte, drunk with horror and nauseous from so much blood and tears, had stayed close by her uncle, the colonel, leaving Madame Delaherche downstairs to give water to the feverish and wipe the damp faces of the dying.

Up on the roof terrace, Delaherche was rapidly trying to take stock of the situation. The town had suffered less than one would have thought, for there was just a single fire belching out thick, black smoke in the district of La Cassine. The firing from the Palatinate Fort had ceased, probably due to lack of ammunition. The guns at the Porte de Paris were the only ones still letting off the occasional round. What immediately caught his attention was the fact that a white flag had once again been hoisted above the Keep; but they couldn't have seen it from the battlefield, because the firing went on with the same ferocity. The nearby roofs hid the Balan road from view, and he was unable to follow the movements of the troops. Meanwhile, looking through the telescope which he'd left trained on the distance, his gaze fell upon the German staff, which he'd already seen in that very same place at midday. The master figure, the min-uscule toy soldier, no taller than half his little finger, whom he thought he recognized as the King of Prussia, was still standing there in his dark uniform, slightly in front of the other officers, most of them lying on the grass, shining in their gold braid. There were foreign officers present too, aides-de-camp, generals, court officials, and princes, all holding field glasses; all had been following the death throes of the French army since morning, as if watching a show at the theatre. And the fearsome drama was now reaching its conclusion.

From the wooded heights of La Marfée, the King had just wit-nessed the convergence of his troops. It was done, the Third Army was taking possession of Illy Plateau, under the orders of his son, the Crown Prince of Prussia, who had come round via Saint-Menges and Fleigneux; while the Fourth Army, commanded by the Crown Prince of Saxony, had approached the rendezvous from the side via Daigny and Givonne, skirting around Garenne Wood. Thus the XIth and Vth Corps joined up with the XIIth and the Prussian Guard. And the supreme effort to smash the circle just as it was closing in, that futile and glorious charge by the Margueritte divison, had wrung a cry of admiration from the King. 'Oh, how brave!'* Now the mathematical, relentless surrounding manœuvre was coming to a close, the jaws of the vice had met up, and with a single glance he could take in the whole of this enormous wall of men and cannon, enveloping the vanquished army. To the north, the embrace was becoming tighter and tighter, forcing men to flee to Sedan, under redoubled fire from the batteries which formed an unbroken line around the horizon. To the south the conquered village of Bazeilles, mournful and deserted, had almost stopped burning, throwing up great swirling clouds of smoke and sparks; while the Bavarians, now in control of Balan, were lining up the cannon three hundred metres from the city gates. From their positions on the left bank at Pont-Maugis, Noyers, Frénois, and Wadelincourt, from where they'd been firing non-stop for nearly twelve hours, the other batteries were thundering out louder than ever, completing the unbreachable cordon of flames, right up to where the King was standing.

The King, however, was tired, and let his field glasses drop for a moment; he went on watching without them. The slanting sun sank towards the woods, ready to set in a pure, flawless sky. Its golden rays drenched the vast landscape, bathing it in such a limpid light that the slightest details were picked out with peculiar clarity. He could distinguish the houses in Sedan, with the little black bars at the windows, the ramparts, and the fortress, making up the complicated defences whose edges cut sharp lines against the sky. Then, around the town, scattered here and there among the fields, were brightly painted villages, like farms in toy-boxes, Donchery to the left on the edge of the flat plain, Douzy and Carignan to the right, in the meadows. He felt as if he could have counted each and every tree in the Ardennes Forest, an ocean of greenery vanishing into the frontier. The Meuse, with its lazy curves, was no more than a river of fine-spun gold beneath the slanting light. And the horrific, bloody battle was transformed into a delicate tableau viewed from such a height, as the sun bid its farewell: dead horsemen and disembowelled horses strewed gaily coloured patches across Floing Plateau; to the right, towards Givonne, the eye was drawn to the last throes of the retreat, where little black dots were running and stumbling, caught up in a whirlwind; meanwhile, on the Iges pensinsula to the left, a Bavarian battery with match-stick sized cannons looked like some well-oiled machine, so easy was it to follow its movements, regular as clockwork. This was an unhoped for, crushing victory, and the King felt no remorse at the sight of the tiny corpses, all these thousands of men who took up less room than the dust on the roads, in the immense valley where the fires in Bazeilles, the massacres up on Illy, and the fear and dread in Sedan could not prevent impassive nature from being beautiful, at the serene end of a lovely day.

All at once, however, Delaherche caught sight of a French general climbing up the slopes of La Marfée, dressed in a blue tunic and riding a black horse, a Hussar before him bearing a white flag. It was General Reille, to whom the Emperor had entrusted the following letter to be delivered to the King of Prussia:*

'Sire and brother, having failed to die among my men, it remains only for me to surrender my sword unto the hands of Your Majesty. I remain, Your Majesty, your Brother, Napoleon.'

In his haste to bring an end to the killing, since he was no longer in control, the Emperor was giving himself up, hoping to mollify the conqueror. And Delaherche watched as General Reille stopped ten paces from the King, dismounted, and then walked forward to hand him the letter, unarmed and holding only a riding crop. The sun sank in a vast, pink pool of light, the King sat down on a chair, leaned against the back of another chair, held for him by a secretary, and replied that he accepted the sword, pending the arrival of an officer to negotiate the terms of surrender.

CHAPTER SEVEN

At that hour, all around Sedan, a terrified mass of men, horses, and cannon was surging back towards the city, flooding in from all the positions which had been lost, from Floing, Illy Plateau, Garenne Wood, Givonne Valley, and the Bazeilles road. The fortified city, upon which they'd made the disastrous decision to converge, was becoming a deadly temptation, offering shelter to those fleeing and a safe haven to which even the bravest of men allowed themselves to be led, as morale plummeted and panic set in. There, behind the ramparts, they imagined that they'd finally escape from the terrible artillery, which had been rumbling on now for nearly twelve hours; and they had neither conscience nor reason left, the animal in them had taken over the human, wild instinct sent them galloping to find a bolt-hole, somewhere to go to ground, somewhere to sleep.

At the foot of the low wall, Maurice was bathing Jean's face with cool water, and when he saw him open his eyes he gave a cry of joy.

'Oh! You poor sod, I thought you'd had it!... By the way, not that I'm blaming you or anything, but boy, are you heavy!'

Still dazed, Jean seemed to wake as if from a dream. Then he must have realized, remembered, for two big, fat tears rolled down his cheeks. Maurice, this boy who was so frail, whom he loved so dearly and whom he'd tended to like a child, had been so moved by friendship that he'd managed to find the strength to carry him all this way!

'Hold on while I have a squint at that head of yours.'

The wound was hardly anything, just a graze to the scalp which had bled profusely. His hair, now matted with blood, had formed a sort of plug across the gash. So Maurice took care not to get it wet and risk the wound reopening.

'There, you're clean and looking human again... Hang on, let me put this on you.'

And picking up the nearby képi of a dead soldier, he placed it carefully on Jean's head.

'Just the right size... Now, if you can walk, we'll be a fine pair of fellows.'

Jean got up and shook his head to make sure it was in one piece. His skull felt a bit heavy, but that was all. It'd be absolutely fine. His simple soul was flooded with tenderness, he grabbed Maurice and hugged him tightly to his breast, and all he could say was,

'Oh! You dear, dear lad!'

But the Prussians were coming, and it was no time to be hanging around behind walls. Lieutenant Rochas was already beating a retreat, together with the few men he had left, protecting the flag which the subaltern was still carrying under his arm, rolled up around the flagpole. Being very tall, Lapoulle was able to see over the coping and let off a few extra rounds; Pache, meanwhile, had slung his rifle back over his shoulder, probably considering that enough was enough, and that by rights they should be due a bit of food and some sleep by now. Jean and Maurice, bent double, hurried to join them. Rifles and ammunition weren't in short supply—you just had to bend down and pick them up. Once again they armed themselves, for everything, knapsack and all, had been left back on the battle-field, when one had had to carry the other over his shoulder. The wall ran right to the edge of Garenne Wood, and thinking they were home and dry, the little group flung itself eagerly behind a farm and from there made its way into the trees.

'Aha!' said Rochas, as blithely and unshakeably confident as ever. 'We'll stop here a moment to catch our breath before we get back to the attack.'

From the very first steps, each man sensed that they were entering some kind of hell; but they couldn't turn back, they had to cut through the wood come what may, for it was their only line of retreat. Right now it was a terrifying place, where death and despair lurked. Realizing that this was where the troops were withdrawing to, the Prussians were peppering it with bullets and bombarding it with shells. It was as if a storm were whipping through the wood, whirling and raging, turning the branches to shreds. Shells sliced through trees, bullets brought down showers of leaves, plaintive cries seemed to come from the cleft trunks, and the fallen boughs seemed to sob with sap. It was like the distress of a crowd in chains, the cries and terror of thousands of people, nailed to the ground, unable to flee from the hail of bullets. Never had the taste of fear been so strong as here in the beleaguered forest.

As soon as they rejoined their comrades, Maurice and Jean grew scared. At that point they were passing through a group of tall trees, and were able to run. But the bullets came whistling past so thick and fast, and from all directions, that it was impossible to tell where they were coming from and so take cover when dashing from one tree to the next. Two men were killed, shot in the face and back. In front of Maurice an ancient oak keeled over, its trunk smashed by a shell, falling with tragic and heroic majesty, crushing everything around it. And just as the young man leapt back out of its way, a colossal beech tree to his left, which had just had its crown blasted off by another shell, began to break up and topple over, like a pillar in some cathedral. Where could he run to? Which way should he turn? On every single side branches came crashing down, like in some enormous building on the verge of collapse, where one room with crumbling ceilings succeeds another. Then, having flung themselves into a thicket to avoid being crushed by the huge trees, it was Jean who was nearly cut in two by a missile which, luckily, failed to explode. Now they could go no further through the inextricable tangle of bushes. The fine stalks clung to their shoulders; the long grass twined itself around their ankles; sudden walls of undergrowth stopped them in their tracks, while foliage flew about them as the giant scythe sliced through the wood. Beside them another man, killed outright by a bullet in the forehead, remained upright, wedged between two young birch trees. Prisoners of the thicket, they felt death brush past them dozens of times.

'Jesus bloody Christ!' said Maurice. 'We'll never get out of here!'

He was a livid white, and had begun to shiver again; even Jean, brave as he was, who only that morning had offered him succour, grew pale, feeling an icy chill creep over him. It was fear, horrendous fear, contagious and irresistible. They were thirsty again, burning dry, their mouths so parched they couldn't stand it, throats contracting so tightly that it was as violent and painful as strangulation. With the thirst came sickness and nausea in the pit of the stomach; and pins and needles pricked at their legs. As they endured the all-too physical symptoms of fear, feeling as if their heads were in a vice, they could see thousands of black dots flying past, as if they were seeing right into the flying cloud of bullets.

'Bloody hell!' stammered Jean. 'Drives me mad having to stand here risking our necks for other people, while they're off somewhere else, happily smoking their pipes!'

Distraught and frantic, Maurice added,

'Too right, why does it have to be me and not someone else?'

Here was the ego in revolt, the selfish fury of the individual unwilling to sacrifice himself, end it all, for the sake of the species.

'It'd be nice,' began Jean again, 'if we just knew why, or even if it was going to do any good!'

Then he lifted his eyes to the sky.

'And to cap it all, the bloody sun can't get the hint and bugger off! When it's set and gone dark, maybe we won't have to fight anymore!'

For a long while now, with no other way of knowing what time it was, not even conscious of time, he'd been keeping an eye on the sun's slow descent, and it seemed to him to have come to a halt and stopped where it was, above the wood on the left bank. It wasn't even a question of cowardice on his part, simply an urgent, pressing need not to have to hear either bullets or shells, a need to go elsewhere, to burrow into the ground and lose himself in it. If it weren't for human respect and the glory of doing your duty in front of your comrades, you'd lose your head and make a run for it in spite of yourself.

Once again, Maurice and Jean were getting used to it: their extreme panic had left them with a sort of unconsciousness, a light-headed feeling, which was a bit like courage. In the end, they didn't even bother hurrying through the accursed wood. The feeling of horror had built up again among the population of bombarded trees, killed at their posts, keeling over on every side like huge, motionless soldiers. Beneath the foliage, in the delicious, greenish half-light deep down in mysterious, moss-carpeted sanctuaries, blew the brutal wind of death. Isolated streams were violated, dying men went through their death throes in even the remotest corners, where only lovers had strayed before. One man, who'd been shot through the chest, had time to cry out 'I've been hit!' before falling flat on his face, stone dead. Another, both legs blown off by a shell, just carried on laughing, unaware of his injury, thinking he'd simply bumped into a tree-root. Others, with fatal wounds to arms and legs, kept on talking and running for several metres, before suddenly seizing up and falling over. In the first few seconds the deepest wounds couldn't be felt, and it was only later on that the dreadful suffering began, spurting out in cries and sobs.

Oh! Treacherous wood, slaughtered forest, where little by little the distressed screams of the dying added to the sobbing of the mortally wounded trees! At the foot of an oak tree Maurice and Jean spotted a Zouave who was letting out a continuous cry like an animal with its throat ripped open, his innards hanging out. Further on, another man was on fire: his blue belt was burning and the flames were licking upwards, scorching his beard; but his back was probably broken, for he couldn't move, and he was weeping bitterly. Then there was a captain whose left arm had been torn off and his right side slashed all the way down to his thigh, and he was lying sprawled on his stomach, dragging himself along by his elbows, begging and pleading for someone to finish him off in a shrill, terrifying voice. And then there others, yet more, enduring atrocious suffering, strewn over the grassy paths in such huge numbers that they had to be careful not to tread on them as they passed. The dead and wounded, though, no longer counted. A comrade who fell was abandoned and forgotten. Without even a backward glance. It was Fate. Someone else's turn next—maybe yours!

All at once, as they reached the edge of the wood, a cry rang out.

'Over here!'

It was the subaltern carrying the flag, who'd just caught a bullet in his left lung. He'd gone down spitting mouthfuls of blood. And when he saw that no one was stopping, he found the strength to pick himself up and cry,

'The flag!'

With a single bound, Rochas doubled back and seized the flag; the pole had snapped; meanwhile the subaltern was murmuring something, his words thick with bloody foam.

'I've had it, I don't care about me!... But save the flag!'

And there he stayed, alone, twisting on the moss in this delicious, woody glen, his clenched hands tearing out the grass, chest arched in death throes which went on for hours.

At last they emerged from the terrifying wood. Along with Maurice and Jean, only Lieutenant Rochas, Pache, and Lapoulle were left of the little band. Gaude, whom they'd lost track of, also emerged from a thicket and galloped to catch up with his comrades, bugle slung over his shoulder. It was such a relief to find themselves back on clear ground, breathing easily. The bullets had stopped whistling past, and no shells were landing on this side of the valley.

Just then, outside a farm gate, they heard someone swearing, and caught sight of an angry general on a horse steaming with sweat. It was General Bourgain-Desfeuilles, their brigade commander, also covered in dust and apparently exhausted. His fat, ruddy face, the mark of someone who lives life to the full, expressed his sheer exasperation at the disaster, which he regarded as some kind of personal misfortune. His soldiers had seen nothing of him since that morning. He'd probably got lost on the battlefield, running after the debris of his brigade, quite capable of getting himself killed in his anger at these Prussian batteries which were sweeping away the Empire, and with it his fortune as a favoured officer at the Tuileries.*

'God Almighty!' he bellowed. 'There's nobody left, you can't even find out what's going on in this bloody place!'

The people who lived on the farm must have gone to hide down in the woods. Eventually, a very old woman appeared in the doorway, probably some servant they'd left behind, stuck there because of her bad legs.

'Hey! Grandma! Over here!... Where's Belgium?'

She stared at him, dazed, not appearing to understand. At that point he went completely overboard, forgetting that this was a peasant woman he was talking to, yelling that he'd no desire whatsoever to get himself trapped like some rabbit by returning to Sedan, and that he was going to bugger off across the frontier, and bloody quick, too! A few soldiers had drawn near and were listening to him.

'But sir,' said a sergeant, 'you can't get through anymore, there's Prussians all over the place... It was this morning we should have buggered off.'

In fact, stories were already going round about companies which had been separated from their regiments and who, without meaning to, had crossed the frontier; and others, later on, who'd even managed to make a courageous breakthrough across enemy lines, before the circle closed up completely.

The general shrugged, beside himself.

'Come on, with solid chaps like you lot we can go wherever we want, right?... Surely I can find fifty chaps still willing to stick their necks out!'

Then, turning back to the old peasant woman, he cried,

'Hey! God Almighty, Grandma! Answer me!... Where's bloody Belgium?'

This time, she understood. She pointed her bony hand towards the great woods.

'Over there! Over there!'

'Eh? What's that?... Those houses there?'

'No, further than that, much further!... Over there, right over there!'

At this, the general began to choke with rage.

'This is absolutely disgraceful! What sort of country is it, for God's sake? You never know what bloody shape it is!... First Belgium was there, and we were afraid we'd fall over the border by accident; and now we actually want to go there, it's disappeared!... No, I ask you, this really is too much! Let them capture me, let them do what they will with me, I'm off to bed!'

There was a bend in the road and they descended into Fond de Givonne, a suburb enclosed by hillsides, where the road climbing up to the woods was bordered by little houses and gardens. Just at this moment it was overrun by such a mass of fugitives that Lieutenant Rochas, together with Pache, Lapoulle, and Gaude, found themselves sort of stuck outside an inn, at the corner of a crossroads. Jean and Maurice had to struggle to reach them. All were surprised to hear a thick, drunken voice calling them over.

'Hey! Fancy meeting you here! Oy! You lot! Well I never, fancy meeting you here!'

They recognized Chouteau in the inn, leaning at one of the ground-floor windows. He was very drunk and managed to say, between a couple of hiccups,

'C'mon, don't be shy if you're thirsty... Still some left for comrades...'

He gave a vague wave over his shoulder and called out to someone at the back of the room.

'Shift it, slowcoach! Get these gentlemen something to eat...'

Then it was Loubet's turn to heave into view, a full bottle in either hand, waving them around and giggling. He was less drunk than his friend and shouted in his joking, Parisian way, with the nasal twang of the coconut sellers on public holidays,

'Roll up, roll up! Cold drinks this way!'

They hadn't set eyes on them since they'd sloped off on the pretext of carrying Sergeant Sapin to the field ambulance. No doubt they'd gone walkabout after that, wandering around, avoiding anywhere shells were falling. And this was where they'd eventually ended up, in an inn which was being looted.

Lieutenant Rochas was indignant.

'Just you wait, you thieves, I'll teach you to sit there and drink while we're all out here killing ourselves!'

Chouteau, however, wouldn't accept the reprimand.

'Bah! Listen, you old loony, there's no lieutenants around here, just free men... Haven't you been screwed enough by the Prussians already, or do you fancy a few more?'

Rochas had to be held back from going over to smash his face in. Meanwhile Loubet, with his arms full of bottles, tried to restore peace.

'Leave it alone! We shouldn't get at each other—we're all brothers here!'

And noticing Lapoulle and Pache, his two comrades from the squad, he said,

'Don't just stand there like a couple of lemons, come on in and get some drink down you!'

For a second Lapoulle hesitated, dimly aware that it wouldn't really be right to whoop it up while so many poor sods were dying of thirst out there. But he was so shattered, so worn out by hunger and thirst! All of a sudden, he made up his mind and bounded into the inn without a word, pushing Pache ahead of him; Pache didn't protest, equally as silent and tempted as the other man. And they didn't come out again.

'Bunch of no-goods!' yelled Rochas. 'Should be shot, the lot of them!'

Now he only had Jean, Maurice, and Gaude with him, and in spite of their best efforts they all found themselves gradually drifting away, carried off by the torrent of fleeing men as it coursed down the middle of the road. They were already a long way from the inn. This was what a rout looked like, a muddy river of men rolling down towards the ditches of Sedan, like the mass of soil and stones that a storm buffeting the high ground sends tumbling down into the valley. And from all the neighbouring plains, in a panic, at a gallop, down every slope, along every fold of land, down the Floing road, through Pierremont, through the graveyard, over the Champ de Mars, and through Fond de Givonne came the same crowd, swelling with every minute, streaming down. How could you reproach these wretched men for acting as they did, when they'd been waiting motionless for twelve whole hours, enduring the artillery onslaught of an invisible enemy against whom they were powerless? Now the batteries were aiming at them head on, from the side, to their rear, the lines of fire were moving closer and closer together as the army beat its retreat to the city, and they were being crushed wholesale, squashed to a human pulp at the bottom of the treacherous hole into which they'd been swept. Some regiments from the 7th Corps were withdrawing in fairly good order, especially around Floing. In Fond de Givonne, however, ranks and officers had ceased to exist, the troops jostled frantically, a mixture of all the debris, Zouaves, Turks, Chasseurs, Fantassins,* most of them unarmed, uniforms torn and dirty, hands and faces black with grime and bloodshot eyes popping out of sockets, mouths swollen and puffy from so much swearing. Now and then a riderless horse dashed forward at a gallop, sending soldiers flying and leaving a long wake of panic through the crowd. Then cannon came tearing past, the remnants of batteries, with artillerymen who seemed to be drunk and carried away, not bothering to cry out a warning and crushing everything in their path. The trampling of the herd continued, a compact file of men serried side by side, headlong flight where any gaps were immediately filled as they obeyed instinct and hastened to get to Sedan and take cover, behind a wall.

Once again, Jean looked up and turned towards the setting sun. Through the thick dust kicked up by the pounding feet, the sun's rays still burned the sweat-covered faces. It was a beautiful day, and the sky was a wondrous blue.

'It isn't half knackering,' he said, 'what with this bloody sun which won't take the hint and bugger off!'

Suddenly Maurice, looking at a young woman clinging to the wall of a house, in danger of being crushed by the crowd, was dumbstruck to see that it was his sister Henriette. For almost a minute he stared at her, standing open-mouthed. It was she who spoke first, apparently unsurprised to see him.

'They shot him in Bazeilles... Yes, I was there... And I've got this idea, because I want to get his body back...'

She named neither the Prussians nor Weiss. People should understand. And Maurice did. He adored her, and he burst out sobbing.

'My poor darling!'

At about ten o'clock, when she had come to, Henriette had found herself in Balan, in a kitchen belonging to complete strangers, her head slumped on the table, crying. But her tears had ceased. Inside this silent woman, so frail, the heroine was already coming to life. She feared nothing, her soul was firm and invincible. In the midst of her pain she thought only of retrieving her husband's body, so that she could bury him. Her first plan was simply to go back to Bazeilles. Everyone was against it, telling her how utterly impossible an idea it was. So in the end, she began looking for someone, a man, to accompany her, or to agree to take the necessary measures. Her choice fell on one of her cousins, who'd once been the assistant manager of the General Refinery at Le Chesne, at the time when Weiss was employed there. He'd been very fond of her husband, and he wouldn't refuse to help. Two years ago, after his wife came into an inheritance, he'd retired to a fine property called the Hermitage, whose grounds lay near Sedan, on the other side from Fond de Givonne. So it was to the Hermitage she was going, meeting obstacles at every step, in constant danger of being trampled and killed.

Maurice, listening to a brief outline of her plan, nodded his approval.

'Cousin Dubreuil's always been good to us... He'll help you.'

Then he had an idea of his own. Lieutenant Rochas wanted to save the flag. They'd already suggested cutting it up and each putting a piece of it beneath his shirt, or even burying it at the foot of a tree and making a note of where it was, so that they could dig it up later on. But it was too painful to think of their flag being shredded up or buried like some dead body. They'd rather find another way.

So when Maurice suggested giving the flag to someone they could trust, who would hide and if need be defend it, until the day he could hand it back to them, unharmed, everyone agreed.

'Well!' the young man said to his sister. 'We'll come with you to see whether Dubreuil's at the Hermitage... In any case, I don't like leaving you on your own.'

It wasn't easy to extricate themselves from the crowd but they managed it, and chose a track that climbed to their left. They found themselves in a veritable maze of paths and lanes, a whole village full of market gardens and small holdings all jumbled up together, running alongside walls, turning sharply, coming to dead-ends: it was a wonderfully entrenched spot for guerrilla warfare, with corners where ten men could have held out for hours against an entire regiment. Already gunshots were starting to crackle in the air, for the area overlooked Sedan and the Prussian Guard was on its way over from the other side of the valley.

When Maurice and Henriette, leading the rest, had taken first a left then a right turn between two never-ending walls, they suddenly emerged to find themselves standing before the wide-open gate into the Hermitage. The property, along with its modest grounds, was spread across three levels of terraced land; and it was on one of these terraces that the main building stood, a large, square house approached by an avenue of ancient elm trees. Opposite, separated by the narrow, deeply banking valley, were other properties on the edge of a wood.

Henriette was worried to see the gate standing so brutally open like that.

'They're not here, they must have left.'

Indeed, the day before Dubreuil had resigned himself to taking his wife and family to Bouillon, predicting the oncoming disaster. But the house wasn't empty, for they could see something moving through the trees, from a distance. Just as the young woman ventured out onto the main avenue, she recoiled before the corpse of a Prussian soldier.

'Blimey!' exclaimed Rochas. 'There's already been some action here, then!'

Eager to find out what had happened, everyone pushed on towards the house. What they saw there told all: the ground-floor doors and windows must have been battered in with rifle-butts and were now yawning wide to reveal ransacked rooms within, while the furniture had been chucked outside and was lying on the gravelled terrace at the bottom of the steps. An entire sky-blue suite from the drawing room stood out from the rest, a sofa and twelve chairs arranged any old how, higgledy-piggledy, around a large, pedestal table in white marble which had been cleft open. Zouaves, Chasseurs, infantry soldiers, and others from the marine infantry were running behind the buildings and down the avenue firing into the copse opposite, across the valley.

'Sir, it's those Prussian bastards,' a Zouave explained to Rochas. 'We discovered them in the middle of wrecking the place. As you can see, we've given them what they deserved... Trouble is, the sods keep coming back ten to one, and it's not going to be an easy job.'

The bodies of three more Prussian soldiers were lying on the terrace. This time Henriette looked at them, her thoughts no doubt on her husband, who was also sleeping, back there, disfigured by blood and dust; and as she did so, a bullet whizzed past her ear and hit a tree behind her. Jean leapt forward.

'Don't stay out here!... Quick, quick, go and hide in the house!'

Since seeing her again so changed, so overwrought with distress, Jean had been heartbroken with pity whenever he looked at her, recalling how she'd appeared to him the day before, with her happy, homely smile. At first he couldn't think of what to say, unsure whether she even recognized him or not. He would gladly have devoted himself to her, and given her back some joy and peace of mind.

'Wait for us inside... If there's any hint of danger, we'll be right in there to come and get you out.'

But she shrugged indifferently.

'What's the point?'

However, her brother also urged her to do so, and she was forced to climb up the steps, pausing for a moment in the hall to glance back at the avenue, thus allowing her full view of the fighting.

Behind one of the first elm trees were Maurice and Jean. The trunks, a hundred years old and of gigantic proportions, could easily shelter two men. Further down Gaude, the bugler, had joined Lieutenant Rochas, who was stubbornly keeping the flag, there being no one else he could entrust it to; he'd placed it nearby, against a tree, while he fired. Every single tree hid someone. From one end of the avenue to the other, Zouaves, Chasseurs, and marine infantry kept themselves concealed, only showing their faces when they needed to fire.

In the little wood opposite, the number of Prussians must have been rising steadily, for the gunfire was growing more intense. They couldn't see anyone, only barely catching a fleeting glimpse of a soldier's profile now and then, as he bounded from one tree to the next. A country cottage with green shutters was also occupied by snipers firing through the half-open windows on the ground floor. It was about four o'clock, and the noise of the cannon was slowing down and gradually growing quieter; yet here they were, still getting killed, as if it were something personal, stuck down here in the back of beyond where they couldn't even see the white flag flying above the citadel. Right up until nightfall, in spite of the armistice, there were places like this where the battle stubbornly raged on, and in Fond de Givonne and the gardens of Petit-Pont they could also hear persistent gunfire.

They carried on for ages, peppering each other with bullets across the valley. From time to time, whenever a man was foolish enough to break cover, he would fall, shot through the chest. Three more dead bodies now lay in the avenue. An injured man, lying face down, was groaning horribly, but no one thought of turning him over to ease his agony.

Suddenly looking up, Jean saw Henriette, who had quietly slipped back from the house, turn the poor man over onto his back and slide a knapsack under his head. He ran forward and dragged her roughly back behind the tree where he and Maurice had taken cover.

'Are you trying to get yourself killed or something?'

She seemed unaware of how rashly she'd acted.

'Of course not... Only, I was scared, all by myself in the hall... I'd rather be out here.'

So she stayed with them. They sat her down at their feet, against the trunk, while they went on using up the last of their cartridges, firing right and left with such fury that their fear and exhaustion vanished. They became completely oblivious to everything, their movements entirely automatic, heads devoid of thought; even the instinct of self-preservation had deserted them.

'Look, Maurice,' said Henriette suddenly, 'that dead man in front of us, isn't that a soldier from the Prussian Guard?'

For the past few moments she'd been carefully studying one of the corpses left behind by the enemy, a squat boy with a thick moustache lying on his side in the gravel. His pointed helmet had rolled a few steps away, and his jugular was severed. The corpse was indeed wearing the uniform of the Guard: dark grey trousers, blue tunic, and white braids, with his overcoat rolled up and slung over his shoulder.

'I promise you, it's the Guard... I've got a picture at home... And there's that photograph Cousin Gunther sent us...'

She broke off and, as calm as ever, walked right up to the dead man, before they could even try to stop her. She bent over the body.

'Red epaulettes!' she cried. 'See? I'd have bet you anything.'

And back she came, while bullets flew past her ears like hailstones.

'Yes, red epaulettes, it was bound to happen... It's Cousin Gunther's regiment.'

After that, neither Jean nor Maurice could make her keep cover or stay still. She kept moving, peeping out, constantly preoccupied with trying to see across into the little wood. The other two went on firing, pushing her back with their knees when she leaned out too far. No doubt the Prussians were starting to feel that there were now enough of them to launch an attack, for they were beginning to break cover, like a rolling mass overflowing between the trees; and they suffered appalling losses, every French bullet hit its target, bringing their men down.

'Look!' said Jean. 'Maybe that's your cousin, there... That officer who's just come out of the house with the green shutters opposite.'

It was in fact a captain, indentifiable by the gold collar on his tunic and the golden eagle on his helmet, which the slanting rays of the sun had set ablaze. He wasn't wearing epaulettes, and had a sword in his hand as he shouted out an order in a curt voice; he was such a short distance away, barely two hundred metres, that they could see him quite clearly, slight in stature, with a harsh pink face and a fine blond moustache.

Henriette looked him up and down with her keen gaze.

'It certainly is him,' she replied, registering no surprise. 'I recognize him perfectly.'

Maurice reacted wildly, and was already getting him in his sights.

'Our own cousin! Good God Almighty, he's going to pay us back for Weiss!'

But she leapt up, trembling, and turned the rifle aside, so that the shot veered off somewhere over their heads.

'No, no, not between family, not between people who know each other... It's monstrous!'

Suddenly she was just a woman again, and she collapsed behind the tree, racked with sobs. The horror was getting too much for her, and she was a mass of fear and pain.

Rochas, however, was triumphant. The firing all around him, coming from a handful of soldiers whom he was urging on in his thundering tones, had grown so fierce when they caught sight of the Prussians that the latter had edged off, retreating into the wood.

'Stand firm, lads! Don't lose your grip! Look! They're chicken! They're running away! We'll give them what for!'

He was cheerful and seemed to have gained a huge boost of confidence. There had been no defeats. This handful of men opposite him was the entire German army, and he was about to send them all flying in one fell swoop, no trouble at all. His tall, lanky frame and long, bony face with its hooked nose curving to a rough, good-natured mouth, was wreathed in a boastful smile, the picture of the jovial trooper slotting the conquest of the globe in between his girl and a good bottle of wine.

'Hell's bells, lads, the only reason we're here is to give them a good hiding... Can't turn out any other way. Eh? Be too much of a change for us, to be beaten. Beaten? Is that possible? One more try, lads, and they'll turn tail like frightened rabbits!'

He yelled and waved his arms, his deluded ignorance making him so brave that the soldiers took heart too. Abruptly, he cried,

'Kick 'em up the arse! Kick 'em up the arse, all the way to the frontier! Victory's ours! Victory's ours!'

But just then, as the enemy across the valley did indeed appear to be withdrawing, a dreadful volley of gunfire exploded to their left. It was the same old encircling movement, from an entire detachment of the Prussian Guard which had come round via Fond de Givonne. After that, it became impossible to defend the Hermitage any longer, the dozen soldiers still holding out on the terraces found themselves caught between two lines of fire and in danger of being cut off from Sedan. Men fell, and for a moment confusion reigned. Prussians were already coming over the walls and running up the paths in such huge numbers that they began fighting them with bayonets. A bare-headed Zouave, a handsome, black-bearded man with a torn jacket, was making an especially gruesome effort, piercing chests until the ribs cracked, turning stomachs into jelly, wiping off the bright red blood from one in the torso of the next; and when his blade broke, he carried on, smashing their skulls with his rifle butt; and when he stumbled and lost his weapon altogether, he leapt at the throat of a big, fat Prussian, using such force that both men rolled onto the ground and over to the broken-down kitchen door, locked in a mortal embrace. In between the trees, in every corner of the lawns, more slaughter piled up yet more dead bodies. It was on the steps, though, that the fighting was fiercest, around the sky-blue sofa and chairs, as a raging tangle of men blew each other's heads off at point-blank range, tearing out teeth and nails for want of knives to slash through to the heart.

And then Gaude, wearing that long-suffering look of his, like a man who's had troubles but never talks about them, was seized by some heroic madness. As they faced this final defeat, even though he knew that his company had been devastated and not a single man could answer his call, he grabbed hold of his bugle, put it to his lips and gave the rallying cry, blowing with such a hurricane force that he seemed to be trying to raise the dead. The Prussians were coming and he wouldn't budge, but merely blew harder, trumpeting for all he was worth. A volley of bullets cut him down, and his final breath left his body as a ringing brass note that made a shudder fill the sky.

Rochas, standing there, uncomprehending, had made no attempt to run away. He waited, stammering,

'Well? What is it? What is it?'

It didn't even enter his head that this was defeat again. Everything was changing, even the way they fought one another. Shouldn't these people have stayed on the other side of the valley and waited for us to go and conquer them? But however many you killed, they just kept on coming. What sort of a damned war was this, anyway, where the enemy ganged up on you ten to one, and only showed its face in the evening, after a whole day of putting you to rout with careful cannonfire? Stunned and distraught, having understood nothing about the campaign up until now, he felt himself being surrounded and swept off by some superior force which he could no longer resist, even though he repeated mechanically, over and over again, stubborn as ever,

'Take courage, lads, victory awaits!'

Meanwhile, he swiftly seized the flag. His last thought was to hide it, to keep it from the Prussians. But even though the pole had snapped it still got tangled up in his legs and he nearly fell over. Bullets whistled past, he sensed the presence of death, he ripped and tore at the flag, trying to destroy it. And just then, he was hit in the neck and chest and collapsed among the tricolour shreds, enveloping him like garments. He lived for a moment longer, eyes open wide, maybe seeing a vision rising up on the horizon of what war was really about, that abominable struggle between life and death which should be accepted by a heart full of gravity and resignation, as if it were law. Then he gave a slight hiccup and expired, as bewildered as a child, like some poor creature of limited intelligence, some carefree insect crushed by huge, impassive Nature. And with him vanished a legend.

As soon as the Prussians had started arriving, Jean and Maurice had beaten a retreat from one tree to the next, keeping Henriette protected behind them as best they could. They didn't stop firing, and would let off a round before taking cover again. Maurice knew that there was a little gate up at the top of the grounds, and luckily they found it open. Swiftly, all three slipped through. They found themselves on a narrow path winding between two high walls. However, as they neared the end of it they heard the sound of gunfire and dived to their left into another lane. As luck would have it, it was a dead end. They were forced to come galloping back and turn right, under a hail of bullets. Afterwards, none of them could remember which way they'd gone. At every bend in the wall in this inextricable maze, shots were being fired. There were drawn-out gun-battles in gateways, and the slightest obstacles were defended and taken by storm, with fearful relentlessness. Then, all of a sudden, they came out onto the Fond de Givonne road, near Sedan.

Jean looked up one last time and gazed towards the west, where an immense, pink light was creeping across the sky; and at last he gave a huge sigh of relief.

'Ah! Look, the bloody sun's going down now!'

Meanwhile, all three ran on and on, without stopping to pause for breath. All around them the tail-end of the crowd of fugitives was still pouring down the middle of the road, gathering speed like an overflowing torrent. When they reached the Porte de Balan, they had to wait, caught up in a savage crush. The chains on the drawbridge had broken, and the only feasible way left to get over was via the footbridge, which meant that horses and cannon were unable to cross. At the Castle postern, by the Porte de la Cassine, they heard that the congestion was even more appalling. It was a frantic rush, as all the debris of the army came tumbling down from the slopes, hurling itself at the town, landing with a noise like a canal lock being sprung, like water going down a sewer. The baneful attraction of these city walls had ended up breaking the will of even the bravest of them.

Maurice took Henriette into his arms; and shivering with impatience, he said,

'Surely they're not going to close the gates before everyone's in?'

That was exactly what the crowd was afraid of. Meanwhile, soldiers were already camping out on the embankment to the left and right of them; and batteries, plus a whole hotch-potch of guns, cannon, and horses, had come to grief in the ditches.

However, repeated bugle-calls rang out, soon followed by the clear signal to retreat. The stragglers were being summoned. Some were still arriving at a breakneck pace, and occasional gunshots rang out in the surrounding villages, becoming more and more isolated. Detachments of troops were left along the inner ledge of the parapet to defend the approaches to the city; and finally the gates were closed. The Prussians were now only a hundred metres behind. They could see them coming and going on the Balan road, steadily taking possession of houses and gardens.

Maurice and Jean, pushing Henriette ahead of them to protect her from being jostled by the crowd, were among the last to enter Sedan. The clock was striking six. It was nearly an hour since the cannon had ceased. Little by little, the isolated gunfire fell silent, too. And then nothing was left of the deafening noise, the atrocious thunder which had been rumbling on since morning, only a dead nothingness. Night was approaching, cloaking everything in a terrifying, lugubrious silence.

CHAPTER EIGHT

At about half-past five, before the gates were shut, Delaherche had gone back again to the Sous-Préfecture, worried about what the consequences would be now that he knew the battle was lost. He stayed there for nearly three hours, plodding up and down the court-yard on the lookout, stopping every officer who passed; and that was how he came to learn of the rapid developments. A letter of sur-render had been sent and then withdrawn by General de Wimpffen, the Emperor having accorded him plenary powers so he could go to Prussian headquarters and plead for the least humiliating conditions possible for the defeated army. Lastly, he learned that there was a Council of War in progress, its purpose to decide whether they should attempt to keep up the fight and defend the fortress. This council consisted of about twenty top-ranking officers, and seemed to Delaherche to go on for ever; while it was in session, the mill owner climbed up and down the steps twenty times if he climbed them once. Then suddenly, at a quarter past eight, he saw General de Wimpffen coming down them, bright red in the face, his eyes all puffy, with a colonel and two more generals in his wake. They leapt into the saddle and trotted off over the Pont de Meuse. It meant that surrender had been accepted, and was now inevitable.

Reassured, Delaherche discovered that he was starving hungry, and resolved to return home. However, no sooner was he out in the open than he hesitated, seeing the appalling congestion that was now clogging the streets. Roads and squares were full to bursting, stuffed with so many men, horses and guns that the compacted mass looked as if it had been forced in with some giant pestle. While the regi-ments which had made an orderly retreat were bivouacking up on the ramparts, the city had been submerged beneath a sort of peat, teeming with the scattered debris of the army, with runaways from every corps and all disciplines, flowing thicker and slower until it was impossible to move even a muscle. The wheels of countless cannon, wagons, and carts had all got tangled up. The horses, whipped and jostled from all sides, had no room to move either forward or back. And the men, deaf to all threats, began charging into houses, devour-ing anything they came across, sleeping wherever they could, in bedrooms, cellars, anywhere. Many collapsed in doorways, blocking the entrance. Others, lacking the strength to go any further, lay sprawled on the pavement, sleeping like the dead, not even moving out of the way of the feet which trampled over their limbs, preferring to get crushed rather than have to change position.

It was then that Delaherche realized how absolutely crucial it was for them to surrender. At certain crossroads, ammunition chests were lying side by side, touching, and it would take only a single Prussian shell to fall on one of them for the rest to blow up too; and the whole of Sedan would have gone up like a torch. Anyway, what were you supposed to do with such a wretched collection of men, beaten by hunger and fatigue, with no ammunition or provisions left? It would have taken all day merely to clear the streets. The fortress itself was unarmed, and the city had no supplies. At the Council of War, these were precisely the reasons cited by the sensible ones among them, keeping the situation in perspective in spite of their deep patriotic grief; and even the most foolhardy officers, the ones who shuddered and cried that the army couldn't just surrender like that, had to hang their heads in shame, unable to find any practicable way to start fighting again the next day.

On the Place de Turenne and the Place du Rivage, Delaherche painstakingly managed to force his way through the crush. Passing the Hôtel de la Croix d'Or, he caught a sorry glimpse of the dining room, where generals were sitting dumbly around the empty table. There was nothing left, not even any bread. But General Bourgain-Desfeuilles, ranting and raving away in the kitchen, must have unearthed something, for he suddenly went very quiet and dashed upstairs, awkwardly clutching a piece of greasepaper between his hands. Such a crowd had gathered on the square to gawp through the windows at this gloomy dining table, swept bare by the dearth of food, that the mill owner had to elbow his way through, like walking through treacle, sometimes getting pushed and losing ground he'd already covered. In the Grande-Rue, however, the wall became insurmountable, and for a moment he lost hope. An entire battery of guns appeared to have been flung down one on top of the other. He decided to climb up on the gun carriages, and clambered over the guns, jumping from wheel to wheel, almost breaking his legs in the process. Then he found his path blocked by horses; he ducked down, reduced to having to weave his way through their legs and beneath the bellies of the poor, half-starved beasts. After another quarter of an hour spent trying to get through, as he was reaching the Rue Saint-Michel, he took fright at the obstacles mounting up in his path and decided to turn down this road and then make his way round via the Rue des Laboureurs, in the hope that the back streets would be clearer. As bad luck would have it, though, a band of drunken soldiers had laid siege to a house of ill repute along the way; and he retraced his steps, afraid of getting caught up in the scuffle. From then on, he pushed on stubbornly right to the end of the Grande-Rue, sometimes balancing on carriage shafts, sometimes clambering over wagons. On the Place du Collège he was carried along for about thirty paces on the shoulders of the crowd. He fell to the ground again and almost got his sides kicked in, only managing to save himself by clinging to some railings. When he finally reached the Rue Maqua, sweating, his clothes in shreds, the journey from the Sous-Préfecture back home, which normally lasted less than five minutes, had taken him over an hour of exhausting effort.

To prevent people from barging into the hospital and garden, Major Bouroche had taken the precaution of posting two guards at the gate. Delaherche was relieved to see it, because it had just occurred to him that his house might have become a target for looters. When he saw the hospital from the garden, poorly lit by a few lanterns, giving off a feverish, foul stench, the sight sent a fresh chill through him. He stumbled against a soldier who'd fallen asleep on the pavings, and he remembered that the man had been guarding the coffers of the 7th Corps since that morning; his officers had probably forgotten all about him, and he'd been so worn out that he'd simply lain down and gone to sleep where he was. As for the rest of the house, it looked empty, the ground floor stood in darkness and the doors were open. The servants must still be at the hospital, for there was no one in the kitchen, just a little lamp smoking away sadly all by itself. He lit a candle and climbed softly up the main staircase, so as not to wake his mother and his wife, whom he'd begged to go up to bed after such a hard and traumatic day.

On entering his study, however, he gave a start. There on the sofa, where Captain Beaudoin had slept for a few hours the day before, a soldier lay stretched out; and it was only when he recognized him as Maurice, Henriette's brother, that he understood. On turning round, moreover, he saw yet another soldier, this one lying on a rug and wrapped in a blanket; it was Jean, the man he'd seen briefly prior to the battle. Both were sleeping like the dead, crushed by fatigue. He didn't stop, but went straight into his wife's room next door. There was a lamp burning on the the corner of a table, and silence quivered all around. Gilberte had flung herself onto the bed fully clothed, probably afraid of some new catastrophe. She slept as calm as could be, while next to her on a chair, only her head drooping forward to touch the edge of the mattress, Henriette too was asleep, nightmares disturbing her slumber and huge tears welling up beneath her eyelids. He watched them for a moment, tempted to wake the young woman up and find out what had happened. Had she gone to Bazeilles? Maybe if he questioned her she could give him news of his dye-works? But pity got the better of him and he drew back, while his mother appeared silently in the doorway and motioned to him to follow her.

As they walked through the dining room, he said in astonishment, 'What's all this? Haven't you gone to bed yet?'

At first she simply shook her head; then, in a half-whisper, she said,

'I can't sleep, I've been sitting in an armchair next to the Colonel... He's just got up a very high temperature, and he keeps waking up and asking me questions... I just don't know what to say to him. Please, go in and see him.'

Monsieur de Vineuil had already gone back to sleep. His long, ruddy face was barely visible against the pillow, covered by the great snow-drift of his moustache. Madame Delaherche had propped a newspaper in front of the lamp, and his corner of the room was in semi-darkness; the bright light fell sharply on her, sitting bolt upright against the back of the chair, her hands lying loosely on her lap, her eyes gazing into the distance, lost in a tragic reverie.

'Wait,' she murmured, 'I think he heard you—look, he's waking up again.'

The colonel was indeed opening his eyes, and looked at Delaherche without turning his head. He recognized him and immediately asked, in a voice trembling with fever,

'It's over, isn't it? We've surrendered.'

The mill owner, catching a look from his mother, was about to lie to him. But what was the use? He shrugged hopelessly.

'What could they do? If you could just see the streets in town!...

General de Wimpffen's just left for the Prussian headquarters to thrash out the terms of surrender.'

Monsieur de Vineuil shut his eyes again, a long shudder ran through him and a muted cry of despair escaped his lips.

'Oh, God! Oh, God!'

In a jumpy voice, his eyes still closed, he went on,

'Oh! What I wanted should have been done yesterday... Oh yes, I knew the area all right, and I told the General what it was I was afraid of; but they wouldn't listen, not even to him... Up there, above Saint-Menges, all the way to Fleigneux, all the high ground had been taken, the army was above Sedan and had control of the Saint-Albert gap... If we'd waited there our positions would have been unassailable, the Mézières road would have stayed open...'

His speech became slurred and he muttered a few more unintelligible words, while the vision of the battle evoked by his fever grew gradually blurred, swept away by slumber. He slept, still dreaming of victory, perhaps.

'Does the Major think he'll pull through?' Delaherche asked in a low voice.

Madame Delaherche nodded.

'Dreadful, though, those injuries he's got on his feet,' he said. 'He'll have to stay in bed for a long time, won't he?'

This time she remained silent, as if she were herself lost in all the deep pain of defeat. She belonged to another generation, she was part of the old, tough bourgeoisie of the border country which once upon a time had defended its cities so fiercely. In the bright glow of the lamp her severe features, with the pinched nose and compressed lips, told of her anger and suffering, revolt brewing up in her and preventing her from sleeping.

Seeing this, Delaherche felt isolated and overcome by a truly terrible feeling of distress. He found that once again he was unbearably hungry, and he thought it must simply be weakness which was stripping him of his courage like this. He tiptoed out of the room and went downstairs into the kitchen, carrying his candle. Here, though, he discovered even more melancholy, for the stove had gone out, the sideboard was bare, and the teacloths had been scattered any old how. It was as if the winds of disaster had even swept through here, taking with them all the pleasures of eating and drinking. At first he despaired of even finding a crust to eat, for any remaining bread had been taken to the hospital to accompany the soup. Then, at the back of a cupboard, he discovered some beans left over from the day before, which had been forgotten. And he ate them without butter, without bread, standing where he was, not daring to go upstairs with such a meal, eating hurriedly in the middle of the gloomy kitchen, which the spluttering little lamp filled with paraffin fumes.

It was only just gone ten o'clock and Delaherche had nothing to do while he waited to find out whether the surrender had finally been signed. He felt a nagging worry, he was afraid that the fighting would start afresh, and the thought of what would happen then, although he didn't say as much, filled him with terror and preyed heavily on his mind. Having gone back up to his study, where Maurice and Jean hadn't stirred, he tried in vain to stretch out in an armchair: but sleep evaded him, the noise of shells kept making him sit up with a start, just as he was slipping off into unconsciousness. The horrific bombardment which had thundered all day was still pounding in his ears; he listened for a moment, terrified, and found himself trembling at the profound silence which now enveloped him. Unable to sleep, he decided he would rather get up again, and he wandered through the darkened rooms, keeping away from the bedroom where his mother was sitting with the colonel: the way she stared at him as he walked around ended up annoying him. Twice he went back to see whether Henriette had woken up, and then was transfixed by the sight of his wife's face, which was so peaceful. At a loss as to what to do, he roamed around, going up and down the stairs, until two o'clock in the morning.

This couldn't go on. Delaherche decided to return once more to the Sous-Préfecture, well aware that rest would be impossible until he found out what was happening. But down in the street, confronted by the chaos, he was seized by despair: he'd never have the strength to get there and back again through all the obstacles along the way, the mere memory of which was enough to make his limbs start aching. As he stood hesitating, he saw the major arriving, out of breath and cursing.

'God Almighty! Nearly wore me bloody feet off!'

He'd had to go to the town hall to beg the mayor to requisition chloroform and send it to him at daybreak, for his supplies were exhausted, there were urgent operations to perform, and he was afraid he'd have to carve up the poor buggers, as he put it, without sending them to sleep.

'Well?' asked Delaherche.

'Well, the thing is, they don't know whether the pharmacies have got any left!'

But the mill owner couldn't care less about the chloroform. He tried again.

'No, not that... Is it all over, back there? Have they signed with the Prussians?'

The major waved violently.

'Nothing's been done at all!' he cried. 'Wimpffen's just got back... Those scoundrels deserve a good hiding by all accounts, the things they're demanding... Oh! Why don't we just start fighting again and die, the lot of us! It'd be better that way!'

Delaherche listened, turning pale.

'But are you sure what you're saying is true?'

'I got it from those gentry on the local council which is in permanent session... An officer came from the Sous-Préfecture and told them everything.'

He went into more detail. The meeting between General de Wimpffen, General Moltke, and Bismarck had taken place at the Château de Bellevue, near Donchery. He was a fearsome character, General Moltke—a harsh, pinched man, clean-shaven like some mathematician, winning battles from inside his office, wielding algebra! He'd made it clear from the very start that he was fully aware of the desperate situation the French army found itself in:* no supplies, no ammunition, disorder in the ranks and low morale, the absolute impossibilty of breaking free of the iron circle squeezed tight around it; while the German armies had occupied the strongest positions and could burn the city to the ground in two hours flat. He coldly set out what he wanted: the entire French army to be taken prisoner, along with weapons and equipment.* Bismarck simply lent him his support, like some good-natured mastiff. After this, General de Wimpffen had exhausted himself trying to resist such terms—the most severe ever imposed on a defeated army. He explained how unlucky he'd been, and how heroic his soldiers had proved themselves, and how dangerous it would be to push such a proud nation right to the brink. For three whole hours he threatened, begged, and talked by turns with superb, desperate eloquence, asking that they satisfy themselves with interning the defeated men down in deepest France, or even in Algeria; and the sole concession that they eventually obtained was that any officer who promised,* in writing and upon his honour, never to serve again, would be free to go home. Finally, they agreed to extend the armistice until ten o'clock the next morning. If by then these terms hadn't been accepted, the Prussian batteries would reopen fire, and the city would be burned down.

'That's ridiculous!' cried Delaherche. 'You don't just burn a city down like that, when it's done nothing to deserve it!'

Then the major made him quite beside himself, as he added that the officers he'd just seen at the Hôtel de l'Europe had been talking of a mass exodus before first light. Ever since the German demands had become known, the men had been noticeably over-excited and the most outrageous projects were being mooted. The thought that it wouldn't be honourable to take advantage of the darkness like that and break the truce, without giving any warning, wasn't about to stop anyone; and they were making far-fetched plans for picking up the march to Carignan, right through Bavarian lines, under cover of night, taking back Illy Plateau by surprise, unblocking the Mézières road, or making some unstoppable push to get them directly over the border into Belgium. Others, it was true, were saying nothing, aware that disaster was now fated, and they would have accepted anything, signed anything at all, just to put an end to it, with a happy cry of relief.

'Good night!' concluded Bouroche. 'I'm going to try and get a couple of hours' sleep. God knows I need it.'

Left to himself, Delaherche spluttered with rage. What! Was it true that they were going to start fighting all over again, that they were going to set fire to Sedan? It was becoming an inevitability, a terrifying certainty, as soon as the sun came up high enough over the hills to shed light on the full horror of the massacre. And mechanically he climbed the steep stairs to the attic yet again, and found himself among the chimney stacks, on the edge of the narrow terrace overlooking the town. But now, at this hour, he was up there in pitch darkness, in the middle of an endless, rolling sea of tall, dark waves, and at first he couldn't make anything out. Then, below him, he recognized the confused bulk of the factory buildings, first to loom out of the night: there was the engine-room, there were the workshops, the drying rooms, the warehouses; and seeing this huge block of buildings which constituted his pride and his fortune, he felt a wave of self-pity surge over him, as he dwelt on the fact that in only a few hours there would be nothing left of it but ashes. His gaze wandered back to the horizon and swept across the vast blackness, where tomorrow's threat lay sleeping. South, near Bazeilles, sparks were flying up into the air above the collapsing embers of the houses; meanwhile to the north the farm at Garenne Wood, which had been set alight that evening, was still burning, bathing the trees in a huge pool of blood-red light. There were no other fires to be seen, just these two, separated by an unfathomable gulf, across which only occasional, terrifying sounds travelled. Somewhere over there, maybe very far away, maybe on the ramparts, someone was crying. In vain, he tried to see through the veil of night to make out Le Liry, La Marfée, the batteries at Frénois and Wadelincourt, the cordon of bronze beasts he could sense standing there, necks outstretched, maws gaping open. And as his gaze came back to the city itself, he could hear it sigh with dread all around him. It wasn't just the uneasy sleep of the soldiers who'd collapsed in the streets, nor merely the muffled creaking caused by men, animals, and guns. What he thought he could sense in the air was the restless insomnia of the entire gentry, his neighbours, who like him were unable to sleep, shaking with fear, waiting for the dawn. They must all know that the surrender hadn't been signed, and were now counting the hours, quaking at the thought that if nothing was signed, all that would be left for them to do would be to hide in the cellars and die there, crushed and walled in under the rubble. He thought he could hear a frantic voice coming up from the Rue des Voyards, screaming murder, amid a sudden clash of arms. He leaned forward and stood there in the dense night, lost in a fog-filled, utterly starless sky, enveloped in such a shudder that his hair stood up on end all over his body.

Downstairs on the sofa, Maurice woke up at daybreak. His limbs were stiff and he lay still, eyes fixed on the windows, which little by little grew white with a livid dawn. Atrocious memories came back to him of the battle they'd lost, the flight, the disaster, all in this clear, cruel waking light. He saw it all again, down to the smallest detail, and he suffered horribly at the thought of their defeat, which he could still feel ringing in the very roots of his being, as if he felt he was the one to blame. He reasoned with the pain, analysing his emotions, finding his skill for self-destruction even more sharply

honed than before. Wasn't it true that he was just a nobody, a mere
passer-by as far as the era was concerned—admittedly, one with a
brilliant education, yet crassly ignorant of everything he ought to
have known about, and conceited to the point of blindness, cor-
rupted by the pursuit of pleasure and the delusory prosperity of the
Emperor's reign? Then something else came to mind: his grandfather, born in 1780, had been one of the heroes of Napoleon's
Grande Armée, one of the conquerors at Austerlitz, Wagram, and
Friedland; his father, born in 1811, had been reduced to the level of a
bureaucrat, a petty, mediocre employee, a tax collector in Le Chesne-
Populeux, where he'd worked himself into the ground; and now
there was him, born in 1841, raised to be a gentleman, a qualified
lawyer, capable of the most sublime enthusiasm and the basest stupidity, defeated at Sedan, part of a disaster whose magnitude he
sensed only too keenly, bringing an end to an era; such degeneracy in
the race would explain how the grandsons of France had come to
lose where their grandfathers had been victorious, and it weighed
heavily upon his heart, like some hereditary disease, slowly deterior-
ating, eventually leading to the fated destruction, once the hour had
come. Had this been victory, how brave and triumphant he would
have felt! But in defeat, with his feminine, nervous disposition, he
fell prey to one of those overwhelming attacks of despair which
brings the whole world crashing down with it. There was nothing
left, France was dead. Tears choked him, he wept and wrung his
hands, reverting to the faltering prayers of his childhood.

'Oh, God! Please take me... Oh, God! Please take all the poor
wretches who are suffering!'

Jean, lying on the floor wrapped in the blanket, began to stir. After
a while, he sat up in astonishment.

'What is it, lad? You feeling ill?'

Then, realizing that this was another case of silly ideas that should
be kicked right out, as he put it, he adopted a fatherly approach.

'Come on, what's the matter? You shouldn't go upsetting yourself
about a load of nonsense.'

'Oh!' wailed Maurice. 'We've well and truly had it this time! We
might as well get ready to become Prussians!'

And when his comrade, hard-headed illiterate that he was, registered his amazement at such talk, he tried to make him understand
how their race had exhausted itself, and how it was necessary now for

it to disappear beneath a wave of new blood. But the peasant gave a stubborn shake of the head, rejecting the explanation.

'What? D'you mean my land won't be mine any more? D'you think I'd let the Prussians come and take it away from me so long as I'm not six feet under, so long as I've got two arms to fight with? Give over!'

Then he, too, explained how he saw things, but with difficulty, as and when the words came to him. Yes, they'd taken a hell of a beating! But he didn't think they were all dead just yet, there were still a few left, and they'd certainly be enough to rebuild their houses, as long as they were sturdy fellows and worked hard, and didn't drink away their earnings. When a family pulled together and scrimped and saved, you could always manage to get out of a hole, even with the worst of luck on your side. And it's not always a bad thing to get a bit of a slap in the face sometimes: it makes you stop and think. And God! Even if it was true that there was a bit of rot about and a few unhealthy limbs, well! Far better see them lopped off and on the ground rather than let them kill you off like some cholera.

'Had it? No, oh, no,' he repeated again and again. 'Me, I've not had it, that's not the way I see it!'

And wounded though he was, with his hair still sticky with the blood from his graze, he stood right up, suddenly feeling an indestructible urge to live, to take up his tools or pick up the plough, to rebuild his house, just as he'd said he would. He came from old, wise, stubborn soil, from the land of reason, toil, and thrift.

'Mind you,' he went on, 'I do feel sorry for the Emperor... Things seemed to be going well, we were getting a good price for corn... But he was just too stupid, when it comes down to it—you just don't get mixed up in dreadful business like that.'

Maurice, still overcome, gave another dejected shrug.

'The Emperor! Oh, him... I used to really like that man, in spite of all my beliefs in freedom and the republic... Oh, I did! It was in my blood, probably from my grandfather... And now look! That's all gone rotten, too, and what's to become of us?'

His eyes took on a wild look and he let out such a cry of pain that Jean, suddenly worried, was about to get up again when he saw Henriette coming in. She'd just woken up, hearing the sound of their voices from next door. A pallid light now filled the room.

'You've come just in time to give him a scolding,' he said, pretending to laugh. 'He's not behaving himself at all.'

But the sight of his sister, looking so pale and distressed, had touched Maurice, causing him to pull himself together. He opened his arms to draw her to his breast; and when she flung her arms about his neck, an intense feeling of warmth flooded over him. She too was weeping, and their tears mingled on their cheeks.

'Oh, my poor, poor darling, I'm so sorry I haven't the courage you need to comfort you!... Such a good man, he was, your husband Weiss, and he loved you so very much! Whatever's to become of you? You've always been the one to suffer, and you never, ever complain... I know I've already been the source of much grief for you, and who knows whether I may yet cause you even more!'

She made him hush, placing her hand over his mouth, and just then Delaherche came into the room quite beside himself, in a dreadful state. He'd eventually come down from the roof terrace, suddenly starving again, prey to one of those nervous appetites which tiredness only makes worse; and on re-entering the kitchen to get himself a hot drink, he'd discovered the cook sitting there with one of her relatives, a joiner from Bazeilles, whom she was just serving with some mulled wine. It was then that this man, one of the last inhabitants to have left the village, amid the fires, had told him that his dye-works had been completely destroyed and was now no more than a heap of rubble.

'Eh? The scoundrels! Can you believe it?' he stuttered to Jean and Maurice. 'Everything's lost now for sure, they'll set fire to Sedan in the morning, just like they set fire to Bazeilles yesterday... I'm ruined, completely ruined!'

He was suddenly struck by the sight of the bruise on Henriette's forehead, and he recalled that he hadn't yet had the chance to talk to her.

'So it is true, you did go there, you got that bruise... Oh! Poor Weiss!'

Realizing abruptly from the sight of the young woman's red-rimmed eyes that she knew her husband was dead, he let slip a horrible detail which the joiner had told him only a minute ago.

'Poor Weiss! It seems they burned him... Yes, they gathered up all the bodies of the inhabitants who took up arms, and chucked them into the blaze of one of the houses which were on fire, and then poured oil over them.'

Henriette listened, frozen with horror. Oh God! Not even to have the consolation of finding and burying the body of her poor, dead husband, now that the wind was to scatter his ashes! Once again Maurice clasped her to his breast, calling her his poor little Cinderella in a soothing voice, and begging not to upset herself so, she was such a brave girl.

After a pause, Delaherche, standing at the window watching the daylight getting brighter, turned round sharply and said to the two soldiers,

'Oh, by the way, I'd forgotten... I came up to warn you that down there in the shed where they put the coffers, there's an officer handing out the money to the men, so that the Prussians won't get hold of it... You ought to go down and see, the money could come in useful if we're not all dead by this evening.'

It was good advice, and Maurice and Jean went downstairs after Henriette had agreed to take her brother's place on the sofa. As for Delaherche, he walked through to the next room where Gilberte, with her peaceful face, was still sleeping like a baby; the noise of talking and sobbing hadn't even caused her to stir in her sleep. From there, he looked round the door into the room where his mother was looking after Monsieur de Vineuil; but she'd dozed off in her chair, and the colonel, eyes shut, hadn't moved, drained by the fever.

He opened his eyes wide, and asked,

'Well? It's over, isn't it?'

Annoyed by the question, which detained him just as he was hoping to get away, Delaherche angrily clenched his fists, stifling the irritation in his voice.

'Oh, yes! It's over all right. Until it starts again, that is!... Nothing's been signed.'

The colonel, in a very low voice, continued, on the verge of delirium,

'Oh, God! Let me die before it's over!... I can't hear the cannon. Why aren't they still firing?... Up there, at Saint-Menges and Fleigneux, we've got control of all the roads, we'll tip the Prussians into the Meuse if they try to come back to Sedan and attack us! The city's at our feet, it's like an obstacle, it makes our positions even stronger... Forward march! The 7th Corps to take the lead, and the 12th to safeguard the retreat...'

And his hands fumbled with the edge of the sheet, moving as if to the trot of the horse which was carrying him in his dream. Gradually, they moved more slowly, as his words grew heavy and he fell asleep. They stopped, and he lay there, not breathing, completely knocked out.

'Get some rest,' whispered Delaherche. 'I'll be back when I've got some news.'

Then, making sure not to wake his mother, he slipped out, and vanished.

Down in the shed, Jean and Maurice did discover an officer handing out money, sitting on one of the kitchen chairs, protected only by one small, white, wooden table, with no pen or receipt, or any sort of papers at all for that matter, handing over fortunes. He simply plunged his hand into moneybags bulging with gold pieces; and without even bothering to count the sum, he swiftly filled the képis of every sergeant in the 7th Corps with handfuls of gold as they filed past. It was agreed that the sergeants would then share out the money between the soldiers in their half of the section. Each received the gold awkwardly, uneasily, emptying the képi into his pockets, so as not to be caught outside on the streets with all this gold on show. Not a word was exchanged, just the tinkling of the coins, amid the stupefaction of these poor devils, seeing themselves showered with such riches when there wasn't even a loaf of bread or a bottle of wine left to buy in the entire town.

When Jean and Maurice stepped forward, the officer at first withdrew the fistful of gold he was holding.

'Neither of you's a sergeant... Only sergeants are allowed...'

Then, tired of it all already and impatient to get it over and done with, he said,

'Oh, here, you take it anyway, corporal... Let's get a move on—next, please!'

And he dropped the gold coins into the képi that Jean was holding out. The latter, moved at the size of the sum, which came to nearly six hundred francs, immediately asked Maurice to take half. You never knew, they might suddenly get separated.

They shared it out in the garden, outside the hospital; and then they went back in, having recognized the company's drummer, Bastian, lying on the straw, almost in the doorway itself. He was a large, cheerful lad who'd been unlucky enough to catch a stray bullet in the groin at about five o'clock, when the battle had already finished. He had been dying since yesterday.

In the pale morning light, as the men were beginning to wake up, the sight of the hospital sent a chill through them. Three more men had died during the night, without anyone noticing; and the nurses were hurrying to make room for others, carrying away the bodies. Those who'd been operated on the day before, and were still groggy, began opening their eyes wide and looking around them in terror at the huge dormitory full of suffering, where this herd of men was lying on the straw, half-slaughtered. Even though they'd swept the floor the previous evening and done a bit of cleaning up in the aftermath of the bloody butchery of the operations, the badly mopped floor still showed traces of blood, and a huge, blood stained sponge, like a brain, was floating in a bucket; someone's hand had been forgotten and was lying at the door of the warehouse, with all its fingers broken. These were the scraps left over from the slaughter, the horrible morning-after remains of a massacre, seen in the dismal dawning of the day. The restlessness, the turbulent need to live of the first few hours, had given way now to a feeling of oppression beneath fever's weight. The damp silence was disturbed only by the occasional, stammered moan, muffled by sleep. Glassy eyes were afraid to face the daylight, furred-up mouths exhaled stale breath, and the whole room began to sink into that rhythm of days without end, livid and foul-smelling, broken up by suffering, which the poor, lame wretches were going to live through. After two or three months they might eventually make it, but minus a limb.

Bouroche, who was about to go back on duty after a few hours' rest, stopped in front of the drummer, Bastian, then moved on, with an imperceptible shrug of his shoulders. Nothing to be done there. The drummer, though, had opened his eyes; and as if he'd suddenly been brought back to life, his keen gaze followed a sergeant who'd had the idea of coming in, gold-filled képi in his hand, to see whether there were any of his own men among these poor devils. In fact he found two, and gave each one twenty francs. More sergeants came in, and gold began showering down on the straw. And Bastian, managing to sit up, held out his hands, trembling in his death throes.

'Me too! Me too!'

The sergeant wanted to pass him by, like Bouroche had done. What was the use? Then, giving in to a kind-hearted impulse, he threw the coins into the already cold hands, without even bothering to count them.

'Me too! Me too!'

Bastian slumped back onto the straw. He tried to pick up the gold, but it kept slipping through his hands, and for a while his stiff fingers fumbled in vain. Then he died.

'Good night! Our friend's blown out his candle!' said the man next to him, a small, dark, pinch-faced Zouave. 'How irritating, just when you've got the money for a drop of something!'

His left foot was held fast in some sort of contraption. He managed to raise himself, though, and crawl along on his knees and elbows; and when he reached the dead man he gathered up the lot, searching between his fingers and rummaging through the folds of his greatcoat. When he got back to his place, noticing that people were looking at him, he merely said,

'No point it going to waste, is there?'

Maurice, feeling a pang of anguish at the sight of all this human distress, hastily pulled Jean away. As they crossed the floor of the operating room, they saw Bouroche, exasperated because he hadn't been able to get hold of any chloroform; he'd decided to go ahead anyway and cut off the leg of a poor little soldier who was about twenty years old. They fled, so that they wouldn't have to hear it.

Just then, Delaherche came back in from the street. He waved at them, shouting,

'Quick, quick! Come upstairs! We're about to have breakfast. Cook's managed to get hold of some milk. It's no bad thing, too, we certainly need to get something hot inside us!'

And in spite of his best efforts, he couldn't suppress his joy. He lowered his voice, adding in a tone that radiated happiness,

'It's the real thing, this time! General de Wimpffen's set off to sign the surrender!'

Oh! What a huge relief it was—his factory saved, the awful nightmare dispelled, life would begin again, tough, yes, but life all the same, life! The clock had been striking nine when young Rose, who'd come running through the partly cleared streets to this side of town to get bread from an aunt who had a bakery, had recounted to him the morning's events at the Sous-Préfecture. At eight o'clock, General de Wimpffen had called another Council of War, comprised of over thirty generals, to whom he'd explained what had come of his approach, how futile his attempts had been, and how harsh were the demands of their victorious enemy. His hands had been trembling and violent emotion brought tears to his eyes. He was still talking when a colonel from the Prussian staff presented himself as a negotiator, on behalf of General Moltke, to remind him that if no decision had been taken by ten o'clock, they would reopen fire on Sedan. At this, faced by the harsh reality of the situation, the Council had no choice but to authorize the general to return to the Château de Bellevue, and agree to all the Prussians' conditions. He should be there by now, and the entire French army was prisoner, arms, equipment, and all.

Next, Rose went into elaborate detail about the extraordinary stir the news was causing in town. At the Sous-Préfecture she'd seen officers ripping off their epaulettes, breaking down in tears like children. On the bridge, armoured cavalry were tossing their sabres into the Meuse; and a whole regiment had filed past, each man throwing his weapon into the river, watching the water splash up and close over it. On the street, soldiers seized their rifles by the barrels and smashed the butts against the walls: and the artillerymen, who'd removed the firing mechanisms from the machine guns, got rid of them by dropping them down drains. Some burned and some buried regimental flags. On the Place Turenne an old sergeant got up on a milestone and began insulting the army commanders, calling them cowards, as if seized by a sudden fit of madness. Others seemed dazed, and cried huge, silent tears. But it had to be said, by far the majority of the men had eyes sparkling with delight, their whole bearing suddenly lighter, relieved. At last their misery was at an end, they were prisoners, and there'd be no more fighting! They'd been suffering for so many days now, with too much marching and not enough to eat! Anyway, what good was fighting when they weren't the strongest side? Good job too that the commanders had betrayed them, if it got it over and done with right away! It was such a delicious feeling to be able to tell yourself you were going to have white bread to eat, and sleep in proper beds again!

Upstairs, as Delaherche was going back into the dining room with Maurice and Jean, his mother called out to him.

'Could you come here, I'm worried about the Colonel.'

Monsieur de Vineuil, his eyes wide open, had started to talk out loud again, recounting the breathless dream brought on by the fever.

'What does it matter? If the Prussians cut us off from Mézières...
There they are, they'll end up coming round Falizette Wood, while
the others climb up along the Givonne stream... The frontier's
behind us, and we can just jump across, as soon as we've killed as
many of them as possible... Yesterday, that's what I wanted...'

But his burning gaze had just alighted on Delaherche. He recog-
nised him and seemed to come back down to earth and emerge from
his half-sleeping hallucination; and landing with a bump in the cruel
world of reality, he asked for a third time,

'It's over, isn't it?'

Suddenly, the mill owner was unable to stop himself blurting out
how happy he was.

'Oh, yes! Thank God! Over and done with... The surrender must
have been signed by now.'

Violently the colonel got to his feet, in spite of his bandaged foot;
and taking up his sword which was lying on a chair nearby, he tried
to snap it in half. But his hands trembled too much, and the steel
blade slipped.

'Watch out! He'll cut himself!' cried Delaherche. 'That thing's
dangerous, somebody take it away from him!'

It was Madame Delaherche who took hold of the sword. Then,
seeing the look of despair on Monsieur de Vineuil's face, instead of
hiding it as her son told her to, she deftly broke it in two, over her
knee, with a remarkable strength of which even she wouldn't have
thought her poor old hands capable. The colonel had lain back on the
pillows, and he began weeping, watching his old friend with an air of
infinite tenderness.

In the dining room, meanwhile, cook had served up bowls of hot,
milky coffee for them all. Henriette and Gilberte had woken up, the
latter rested from a good night's sleep, fresh-faced and bright-eyed;
and she tenderly embraced her friend, telling her that she pitied her
from the very depths of her soul. Maurice sat near his sister while
Jean, feeling slightly awkward at having also been obliged to accept
the invitation, found himself opposite Delaherche. Madame Delaherche would not on any account agree to come to the table, and a
bowl was taken to her, from which she drank, saying nothing. Next
door, however, the five ate breakfast in silence at first, but they soon
struck up a lively conversation. They were in a sorry state, ravenously hungry, and how could they help but rejoice to find themselves

sitting here, unharmed and in good health, while thousands of poor devils were still lying in the surrounding fields? In the large, cool dining room the clean, white tablecloth was a joy to behold, and the steaming hot bowls of milky coffee seemed quite exquisite.

They talked. Delaherche, who'd already regained his confident, rich industrialist's bearing, all good heart, a boss who enjoys being popular and is harsh only when faced with failure, came back to the subject of Napoleon III, whose face had been haunting him and exciting his idle curiosity for the past two days. He addressed his words to Jean, having only this simple soul to talk to.

'Oh yes, sir! I can tell you, the Emperor had me well and truly fooled... I mean, it's all very well for those sycophants of his to plead extenuating circumstances—he's obviously the main cause, the unique cause of the disasters which have befallen us.'

He was already forgetting that, only months before, as an ardent Bonapartist, he had worked to make the referendum a triumph. And he'd reached the stage where he no longer even pitied the one they would later call the man of Sedan, accusing him of every possible iniquity.

'The man's incompetent, that's something we have to acknowledge here and now; but that's not the point... He's a dreamer, he's got something missing, it just looked as if he was doing well while luck was on his side... No, you see, we mustn't try to pity him by saying that he's been deceived himself, or that the opposition refused to let him have the men and the funds necessary. He's the one who's deceived us, it's his mistakes and vices which have landed us in the dreadful mess we're in now.'

Maurice, who didn't want to say anything, was unable to hold back a smile; while Jean, ill at ease with all this talk of politics and scared of saying something stupid, merely replied,

'Mind you, they do say he's a decent sort of man.'

But these few words, so modestly spoken, caused Delaherche to leap to his feet. All the fear he'd lived through, all his anguish burst out in a cry of outraged passion turned to hatred.

'A decent sort of man! Well, that's easily said!... Do you know, sir, that my factory's been hit three times, and it's no thanks to the Emperor that it hasn't been burned to the ground!... Do you know that I—yes, I alone—am set to lose about a hundred thousand francs because of all this silly business! Oh, no! No! Look at us, France has been invaded, set alight, wiped out, our industry's been brought to a halt, trade's been destroyed, it's all just too much! We've had just about enough of decent men like him, God preserve us from them!... He's landed face down in the muck and gore, and let him stay there, I say!'

He clenched his fist and gave an energetic impression of shoving some poor, struggling wretch under water and holding him there. Then he finished off his coffee with a smack of his lips. Gilberte had involuntarily smiled at the absent-minded look of suffering on Henriette's face, as she fed her like a child. When the bowls were empty they lingered on, in the happy tranquillity of the cool dining room.

And at that very moment, Napoleon III was in the humble dwelling of the weaver on the Donchery road. At five o'clock that morning he'd insisted on leaving the Sous-Préfecture, uneasy at the thought of Sedan all around him, menacing and remorseful, while the need to appease his tender-hearted nature by obtaining better terms of surrender for his unfortunate army was still tormenting him. He wanted to see the King of Prussia.* He had climbed into a hired carriage and followed the broad highway lined with tall poplar trees, making this, his first foray into exile in the chill, dawn air, sensing the scale of the fall from greatness which he left behind in his flight; and it was on this road that he had just encountered Bismarck, who'd come hurrying to meet him, wearing an old helmet and large, well-polished boots, wishing only to keep him distracted and stop him from seeing the King until the surrender was signed. The King was still in Vendresse, some fourteen kilometres away. Where could he go? Where could he stop and wait? Out there, lost beneath the storm clouds, the Tuileries Palace had disappeared. Sedan seemed to have suddenly faded into the distance, far away, as if cut off from him by a river of blood. There were no longer any imperial châteaux left in France, nor any official residences, not even a corner in the house of the humblest civil servant, where he dared sit down. And so the weaver's house was where he ended up, a miserable-looking place he'd seen by the roadside, with its narrow vegetable garden surrounded by a hedge and a single upstairs room with mournful little windows. Upstairs, the plainly whitewashed bedroom with its tiled floor boasted no furniture other than a white, wooden table and two wicker chairs. There he waited patiently for hours, at first with Bismarck for company, who smiled to hear him talk of generosity, and then alone, as wretched as could be, his sallow face pressed against the window, taking another look at French soil and the Meuse which flowed so prettily through the vast, fertile fields.

Then the next day, and during the days which followed, came the other abominable stages: at the Château de Bellevue, that pleasant, bourgeois mansion where he slept and where he wept, after his meeting with the King; then the cruel departure, avoiding Sedan for fear of what the angry, famished, vanquished men might do, crossing the pontoon bridge which the Prussians had put up at Iges, making the long detour to the north of the town, taking shortcuts and back roads through Floing, Fleigneux, and Illy, the entire, sorry flight undertaken in an open carriage; and there, on tragic Illy Plateau, all covered with corpses, the legendary encounter took place. The wretched Emperor, unable now even to tolerate the trotting of his horse, had been overcome by yet another violent bout of illness, perhaps automatically smoking his ever-present cigarette, and a herd of prisoners, haggard, covered in blood and dust, being brought back from Fleigneux to Sedan, had lined up at the side of the road to let the carriage past; the first few men stayed silent, the next began muttering, and little by little they grew more and more exasperated, bursting out into catcalls, fists clenched in an insulting gesture of malediction. After that, he still had to make the interminable journey across the battlefield, covering another league of rutted track, among the debris and the dead bodies, their eyes wide open and full of menace, and then there was the barren countryside with its vast, silent woodland, the frontier over the crest of a hill, and then the end of it all, descending into the land beyond, the road lined with fir trees on the floor of the narrow valley.

And what a night was his first spent in exile, at an inn, the Hôtel de la Poste in Bouillon,* surrounded by such a crowd of French refugees, as well as the merely curious, that the Emperor felt he should show his face, amid murmurs and whistling! His room, with three windows overlooking the square and the Semoy river, was an ordinary one with chairs upholstered in red damask, a mahogany wardrobe with a mirror, and a metal clock standing on the mantelpiece, flanked by seashells and vases of artificial flowers in glass cases. On either side of the door were little twin beds. An aide-de-camp slept in one, so tired that he went to sleep at nine o'clock, hands tightly clenched. In the other, the Emperor tossed and turned for a long time without being able to sleep; and he got up and tried to relieve his pain by pacing the room, with only the pictures on either side of the fireplace to take his mind off it; one depicted Rouget de l'Isle* singing the 'Marseillaise', and the other the Last Judgement, with archangels calling up all the dead from the earth with a furious trumpet call, resurrecting those fallen on the killing fields of war, and sending them up to bear witness before God.

In Sedan, the long train of the imperial household with all its burdensome, benighted baggage had been abandoned behind the Sous-Préfet's lilacs. No one knew how to make it disappear, how to remove it from the sight of the poor folks dying in misery, for the aggressive, insolent air it had taken on and the horrible irony bestowed on it by defeat were becoming quite intolerable. They had to wait for a very dark night. Horses, carriages, wagons, with their silver saucepans, spits for roasting, and their baskets of vintage wines, all left Sedan in great secrecy, and they too made for Belgium, along the darkened roads, with little noise, stealing nervously away.

PART THREE

CHAPTER ONE

Throughout the endless day of the battle, back at Remilly, where old Fouchard's little farm sat perched on the hillside, Silvine hadn't taken her eyes off Sedan, watching it through the thunder and smoke of the cannons, trembling all over, thinking of Honoré. The next day she grew more and more concerned, for accurate news proved impossible to come by, what with the Prussians guarding the roads, refusing to answer questions and in any case not knowing anything themselves. Yesterday's bright sunshine was gone and showers had fallen, casting a sad, dreary light across the valley.

Towards evening, old Fouchard—equally tormented behind his deliberate silence, with barely a thought for his son but anxious to find out how others' misfortunes were going to work to his advantage—was standing out on his doorstep so that he would see anything coming, when he noticed a tall lad dressed in a smock, who'd been wandering up and down the road for the past few moments, looking rather awkward. He was so astonished when he realized who it was that he called out loud to him, in spite of the fact that three Prussians were passing.

'Prosper? Is that really you?'

The African Chasseur signalled frantically to him to keep his mouth shut. Then, drawing near, he said in a low voice,

'Yes, it's me. I've had about enough of fighting for no reason, so I sneaked off... You wouldn't be needing a farmhand by any chance, would you, Fouchard?'

At once, the old man recovered his natural caution. A farmhand was exactly what he was looking for. But it wouldn't do to say so.

'A farmhand? Good Lord, no, not just now... But come in anyway, and have a drink. You don't think I'd leave you languishing out here in the road, do you?'

Inside, Silvine was putting the soup on, while little Charlot clung to her skirts, laughing and playing. At first, she didn't recognize Prosper, even though he'd worked with her in the past; and it was only when she brought through the two glasses and a bottle of wine that she looked at him properly. She cried out, thinking only of Honoré.

'Ah! You've been there, haven't you?... Is Honoré all right?'

Prosper was about to reply, then hesitated. For two days he'd been living in a daydream, while a whole series of violent, vague events passed him by, none of which he could quite remember. He was in no doubt that he thought he'd seen Honoré lying dead, draped over a cannon; but he couldn't swear to it anymore; and what point was there upsetting people when you weren't quite sure?

'Honoré,' he murmured, 'I don't know... I couldn't say...'

She stared at him, insistent.

'So you haven't seen him?'

He slowly drew his hands apart, shaking his head.

'Who can tell! So much has happened, so very much! I mean, of all this blasted war, I couldn't even begin to tell you the half of what's gone on!... Hell, no! I couldn't even tell you where I've been to... Honestly, we're like a lot of halfwits!'

And gulping down a glass of wine, he sat there gloomily, eyes lost in the shadows of his memory.

'All I remember is that it was already getting dark by the time I came to... When I came off my horse in the middle of the charge, the sun was high in the sky. I must have been lying there for hours, and my right leg was trapped beneath my old pal Zephyr, who'd been shot right through the heart... I can assure you, it wasn't a pleasant position to be in, what with a pile of dead comrades around me and not another living soul in sight, knowing that I'd snuff it, too, unless someone came and picked me up... I tried gently to free my hip; but it was impossible, Zephyr weighed a bloody ton. He was still warm. I stroked him and called to him, talking kindly all the time. And I'll never forget what happened next, you know: he opened his eyes, he tried so hard, and lifted up his poor, old head, which was lying on the ground, next to mine. And we talked. 'Poor old thing,' I said to him, 'I don't mean to reproach you, but are you trying to take me with you, holding me so tight?' Of course, he didn't say yes. But I could see by the troubled look in his eyes how terrible it was for him to leave me. And I don't know how it came about, whether he did it on purpose or whether it was just a spasm, but his body suddenly shook, throwing him over to one side. I managed to get up—oh, I was in a dreadful state, my leg was like a lead weight... But it didn't matter, I took Zephyr's head in my arms, and carried on talking to him, saying all the things that came straight from the heart, telling him he was a good horse and I loved him, and that I'd always remember him. He listened to me, and he seemed so happy! Then his body shook again and he died, and those big, empty eyes of his were still on me, right to the end... It's funny, you know, and no one will believe me: but the simple truth of it is that there were great big tears in his eyes... My poor Zephyr was crying, just like a man.'

Choking with grief, Prosper had to break off, in tears again himself. He gulped down another glass of wine and went on with his story in broken, unfinished sentences. It had been growing darker now, and there'd been just a red rag of light still glowing in the sky, on the edge of the battlefield, lengthening the gigantic shadows of the dead horses. He'd probably stayed behind a long time next to his own, with his dead leg making it impossible for him to move away. Then he started walking anyway, spurred on by a sudden feeling of panic, the need not to be alone, to be with his comrades again, so that he wouldn't be so afraid. Likewise, other forgotten wounded lagged behind, appearing from all around, from ditches and brambles and every hidden nook and cranny, trying to join up with others, forming small groups of four or five, little communities where together it wasn't so hard to suffer and die. That was how he came across two soldiers from the 43rd in Garenne Wood, who didn't have a scratch on them but were lying low there like a couple of hares gone to ground, waiting for night to fall. When they found out that he knew the area, they told him about their idea for escaping into Belgium, reaching the border through the woods, before daylight. At first he refused to lead them, preferring to make straight for Remilly, where he was sure of finding shelter; the only thing was, how to get hold of a smock and trousers? Not to mention that from Garenne Wood to Remilly, at opposite ends of the valley, he hadn't a hope of crossing the countless Prussian lines. So in the end, he agreed to act as guide for his two comrades. His leg had warmed up, and they were lucky enough to be given a loaf of bread at a farm. The clock in the distance was striking nine o'clock as they set off again. The only serious danger they got themselves into was at La Chapelle, where they landed smack bang in the middle of an enemy guardpost, which proceeded to take aim and fire into the shadows, while they slid along on their bellies and galloped back on all fours, making for the woods, ears straining, hands fumbling to feel the way. Rounding a bend in the road, they crept up on a guard who'd lost his way, leaping onto his shoulders and slitting his throat with the slash of a knife. After that the roads were clear, and they went on their way laughing and whistling. And towards three o'clock in the morning, they reached a small Belgian village and stopped at a farmer's house, a good man who, upon being woken, immediately opened his barn for them, where they slept soundly on bales of hay.

The sun was already high in the sky when Prosper awoke. His comrades were still snoring as he opened his eyes, and he spotted their host busy harnessing up a horse to a large cart, piled high with bread, rice, coffee, sugar and all sorts of provisions, hidden under sacks of charcoal; and he learned that the man had two married daughters living in France, in Raucourt, and that he was going to take the food to them, knowing they'd nothing left since the Bavarians had been through the town. He'd got hold of the necessary safe-conduct papers only that morning. Prosper suddenly had the crazy notion of getting up there with him on the bench, and going back to that little corner of the world for which he was already feeling homesick. Nothing could be simpler, he'd hop off in Remilly, which the farmer had to pass through. The matter was settled in a couple of minutes; the farmer lent him the precious smock and trousers and told everyone that he was his farmhand; and so, towards six o'clock, he was climbing down from the cart outside the church, having been stopped only two or three times at German checkpoints.

'No, I'd had enough!' Prosper said again, after a pause. 'I mean, if only they'd at least made some use of us, like back there in Africa! But just going in one direction only to retrace your steps, feeling completely useless, well, that's no kind of existence... And now poor old Zephyr's dead, I'd be all on my own, so the only thing left for me to do is get back to the land. True, isn't it? Better than being a prisoner of the Prussians... You've got horses, Fouchard, just you see if I don't love them and take care of them!'

There was a glint in the old man's eye. He clinked glasses again, and concluded without haste,

'Hell! If it does you a favour, I'm happy enough to take you on anyway... But as for wages—well, we'll have to leave that until after the war's over, because I really don't need anyone, and times are just too hard at the moment.'

Silvine, still sitting there with Charlot on her lap, hadn't taken her eyes off Prosper. When she saw him rise to go straight to the stable and get to know the animals, she asked him yet again,

'So you haven't seen Honoré?'

Hearing the question again so abruptly he started, as if it had suddenly lit a bright light in a dark corner of his memory. Still he hesitated, then made up his mind to tell her anyway.

'Listen, I didn't want to upset you just now, but I think Honoré got left behind back there.'

'What do you mean, left behind?'

'Well, I think the Prussians did for him... I saw him half lying across a cannon, staring straight ahead, with a hole beneath his heart.'

There was a silence. Silvine had turned horribly pale, while old Fouchard, transfixed, put his glass back on the table, having just emptied out the last of the bottle.

'Are you really sure?' she asked, her voice choked.

'Lord! As sure as you can be about something you've seen... It was up on a small hill, next to three trees, and I feel as if I could find it again even with my eyes closed.'

Something inside her crumbled. The boy who'd forgiven her, who'd made a solemn promise to her, the boy she was to marry as soon as he was back from the war and the campaign was over! They'd gone and killed him, he was lying out there with a bullet beneath his heart! Never had she felt her love for him so strongly, she needed to see him again so badly, to get him back all the same, even if it was just to bury him, that it roused her, taking her out of her normal, passive self.

She put Charlot down roughly and cried,

'Right! I won't believe that until I've seen it with my own eyes... Seeing as you know where it is, you can drive me there. And then, if it is true, if we do find him, we'll bring him back home.'

Tears choked her and she collapsed over the table, shaken by long, drawn-out sobs, while the little boy, dumbstruck at the way his mother had jostled him, also burst into tears. She picked him up again and squeezed him to her, stammering in a distraught voice,

'My poor child! My poor child!'

Old Fouchard sat there in dismay. In his own way, he did love his son, all the same. Old memories must have come flooding back to him from long ago, when his wife was still alive and Honoré was still at school; and two fat tears welled up in his red-rimmed eyes and trickled down the tanned, leathery skin of his cheeks. It was more than ten years since he'd cried. He began to curse, getting angry with this son who was his, but whom he would never see again.

'God Almighty! It's a dreadful thing when they take away the only son you have!'

However, when a little calm had been restored, Fouchard was extremely troubled to hear Silvine still talking about going back to find Honoré's body. She was adamant, no longer crying but maintaining a desperate, unassailable silence; he no longer recognized the girl who was usually so docile and carried out her chores so dutifully: her large, submissive eyes, which were enough to make her beautiful, had taken on a fierce determination, while her brow remained pale beneath the thick fall of brown hair. She'd torn off a red scarf she'd been wearing about her shoulders and was all in black, like a widow. In vain, he tried to tell her how difficult it would be to find out where he was, and the dangers she could face, and how little hope there was of finding the body. She stopped bothering even to answer, and he could see that she would go by herself and do something stupid, unless he took care of things; and that bothered him, because it could complicate things for him with the Prussian authorities. In the end, though, he decided to go and see Remilly's mayor, who was a distant cousin of his, and between them they concocted a story: Silvine was put down as Honoré's rightful widow, and Prosper became her brother; this way, the Bavarian colonel who'd been installed down in the village, at the Hôtel de la Croix de Malte, was quite willing to issue brother and sister with a pass, authorizing them to bring back her husband's body if they found it. Night had fallen, and it was as much as they could do to persuade the young woman to wait for daybreak before setting off.

The next day, Fouchard refused point blank to let them harness up one of his horses, afraid he'd never see it again. Who was to say the Prussians wouldn't confiscate both cart and horse? Eventually he agreed, with bad grace, to lend them his donkey, a small, grey beast, along with a narrow cart just big enough to hold a body. He gave lengthy instructions to Prosper, who had slept well, but was anxious at the prospect of the expedition, now that he'd rested and was trying to remember the way there. At the last minute Silvine went to take the cover off her own bed, folding it up and placing it at the bottom of the cart. As she was about to leave, she came running back to kiss Charlot.

'Fouchard, I'm entrusting him to you, make sure he doesn't go playing with matches.'

'Yes, yes! Don't you worry!'

They had taken a long while getting ready, and it was nearly seven o'clock by the time Silvine and Prosper were finally descending the steep slopes of Remilly, walking behind the little grey donkey as it plodded along before the cart, head bowed. It had rained heavily during the night, and the lanes had been turned into rivers of mud; and big, white clouds sailed sad and gloomy across the sky.

Prosper, wishing to take the shortest route, had decided to cut through Sedan. But just before Pont-Maugis a Prussian guard post stopped the cart and held them up for over an hour; and once the pass had been handed back and forth between four or five officers, they were free to continue their journey with the donkey, on condition that they take the long way round, via Bazeilles, turning off left onto a path which ran across the fields. They were given no reason for this, but the Prussians were probably afraid of congesting the city even more. When Silvine passed the railway bridge over the Meuse, the fateful bridge that they hadn't blown up, but which had cost the Bavarians so dear, she spotted the body of an artilleryman floating aimlessly downstream. It got caught up in a clump of grass and was momentarily stopped in its course, then swung round on itself and set off once again.

As they traversed Bazeilles, with the donkey slowing to a walk, they encountered destruction from one end of the village to the other, all the abominable ruination war can wreak in passing, as devastating as a raging hurricane. The dead had already been collected up from the streets, and there was only one corpse left lying on the village cobbles; the rain was washing away the blood, leaving red puddles with murky debris, shreds which still seemed to bear something resembling hair. But the fear that clutched at the hearts of those who saw it came from the rubble that only three days before had been the cheerful village of Bazeilles, with its pretty houses and gardens, now lying in a state of collapse and destruction with only charred bits of wall to show. The church in the middle of the square was still burning, a huge pyre of smoking timbers sending up an endless pall of thick, black smoke, spreading out in the sky like the plume on a hearse. Entire streets had disappeared, with nothing left on either side, just blackened heaps of rubble lining the gutter, a sooty, ashen mess, an inky slurry which covered everything. At every crossroads, the corner houses had been razed to the ground, as if the wind of fire that had passed through had carried them away with it. Others had suffered less, one was still standing, all alone, while those on either side of it appeared to have been hacked down by machine-gun fire, their carcasses like stripped skeletons. And there was an unbearable smell in the air, the nauseating stench that followed the fire, particularly the acrid odour of paraffin, which had been poured all over the floors. Then there was the mute desolation of what they had tried to salvage, pitiful sticks of furniture thrown out of windows, lying smashed on the pavement, broken-legged, wobbly tables, cupboards rent open, split down the middle, linen lying around torn and soiled, sad leftovers from the pillage, disintegrating in the rain. Behind a gaping façade, through ceilings which had caved in, a clock could be seen, intact, hanging high up a wall on a chimney breast.

'Oh! The bastards!' groaned Prosper. Only two days ago he'd still been a soldier, and he felt his blood beginning to boil at the sight of such abomination.

He clenched his fists, and a very pale Silvine had to stare hard at him to calm him each time they passed a sentry along the road. The Bavarians had, in fact, posted sentries near houses which were still burning; and it was as if these men, standing with loaded rifles and fixed bayonets, were guarding the fires, to make sure that the flames finished their work. Curious onlookers and interested parties wandering past were sent on their way with a threatening wave and a guttural shout if they tried to linger. Groups of villagers stood at a distance, silent, quivering with suppressed rage. One very young woman, with dishevelled hair and a mud-spattered dress, was stubbornly hanging on outside the smoking ruins of a little house, trying to get in and sort through the burning embers, in spite of the sentry barring her way. They said that her child had been burned inside. And all of a sudden, as the Bavarian shoved her brutally aside, she turned and spat at him, venting all her hopeless fury right in his face, using vile insults and dreadful words, which at last brought her some small relief. He couldn't have understood, but looked at her anxiously, backing off. Three of his comrades came running up and took the woman off his hands, leading her away screaming. Before the rubble of another house a man and two little girls were lying collapsed on the ground, wretched and exhausted, sobbing and at a loss as to where to go, having seen everything they possessed go up in smoke. However, a patrol of soldiers came by and dispersed the curious, and the road grew deserted once again, with only the gloomy, dour-faced sentries left, keeping an eye out to make sure that their heartless orders were respected.

'Bastards! The bastards!' repeated Prosper under his breath. 'What I wouldn't give to strangle a couple of them.'

Yet again Silvine made him hush. She shivered. Inside a shed which had been spared by the fire was a dog which had been forgotten and left there for two days, and he was howling and howling so pitifully that terror crept over the low sky, from which a fine drizzle had begun to fall. That was when they came upon the carts, outside Montivilliers Park. There were three of them, standing in line, piled high with dead bodies; they were those large excrement carts which are filled by the shovel-load each morning as they go up and down the roads, clearing up from the day before; and in similar fashion they'd been filled with corpses, stopping for each body to be thrown in, moving off again with wheels creaking loudly, stopping again further on, covering the whole of Bazeilles until the pile overflowed. There they stood on the road, waiting motionless to be taken away to the public tip, the nearby charnel pit. Feet were poking out, sticking up into the air. A head lolled back, half torn-off. When the three carts set off once more, jolting through the puddles, a long, pale hand which had been hanging out began trailing against a wheel; and bit by bit the hand was worn away, scraped right down to the bone.

In the village of Balan, the rain stopped. Prosper persuaded Silvine to eat some bread which he'd had the foresight to bring with him. It was already eleven o'clock. But as they neared Sedan, they were stopped by yet another Prussian checkpoint; and this time it was awful, the officer lost his temper and refused even to give them back their pass, which he maintained was a forgery, and all this in impeccable French. On his orders some soldiers pushed the donkey and cart into a warehouse. What were they to do? How could they carry on their journey? Silvine, beside herself with despair, had an idea, remembering her cousin Dubreuil, one of old Fouchard's relatives whom she knew and whose property, the Hermitage, was only a few hundred metres away, at the top of the narrow streets which overlooked the faubourg. She took Prosper with her, since as long as they left the cart behind they were free to go. They ran off to find the gate to the Hermitage lying wide open. And from a distance, as they started down the avenue lined with ancient elms, they were greeted by a sight which quite astonished them.

'Blimey!' said Prosper. 'Easy time they're having of it!'

There, at the foot of the steps, on the gravelled terrace, a joyous party was in full swing. Set around a marble pedestal table was a ring of armchairs and a sofa in sky-blue satin, forming a bizarre open-air drawing room which must have been drenched with rain since the day before. Lolling at either end of the table were two Zouaves, apparently in fits of laughter. A little Fantassin, leaning forward in an armchair, seemed to be clutching his belly. All three were nonchalantly leaning on the arms of their chairs, and a Chasseur was reaching out a hand, as if to pick up a glass off the table. Obviously they'd cleaned out the cellar and were making merry.

'How come they're still here?' murmured Prosper, growing more incredulous the nearer they got. 'Don't the idiots give a damn about the Prussians?'

But Silvine, eyes widening, suddenly cried out and clapped her hand to her mouth in horror. The soldiers weren't moving, they were dead. The two Zouaves were stiff, their hands all twisted, and they hadn't any faces left, their noses had been ripped off and their eyes had popped out of their sockets. The laughter on the face of the one holding his belly had been caused by a bullet which had split his lips open and smashed his teeth. It was a truly appalling sight, these poor wretches chatting away, with glassy stares and open mouths, all frozen and forever still. Had they dragged themselves here while they were still alive, so that they could die together? Or was it rather the Prussians playing a prank, rounding them up and then sitting them down in a circle, in mockery of the gay old French spirit?

'Funny sort of joke, anyway!' said Prosper, turning pale.

And looking at the other bodies, strewn down the avenue, at the foot of trees, on the lawns, these thirty-odd brave souls whose bodies included that of Lieutenant Rochas, riddled with bullets and wrapped in the flag, he added, with a solemn, deeply respectful air,

'Quite a massacre there was here! I'd be surprised if we found the gentleman you're looking for.'

Silvine was already entering the house, with its windows and doors smashed in and yawning open in the damp air. He was right, there obviously wasn't anyone home, the masters of the house must have left before the battle. Then, as she persisted and made her way into the kitchen, she again let out a frightened cry. Two bodies had rolled under the sink, one a Zouave, a handsome, black-bearded man, and the other a huge, red-haired Prussian, both locked in a furious embrace. The teeth of one man had sunk into the cheek of the other, their stiff arms hadn't loosened their grip and were still making their snapped spines crack, tying the two bodies into such a knot of eternal rage that they would have to be buried together.

Prosper hurried to lead Silvine away, since there was nothing to keep them in this open house which only death now inhabited. And when they returned in despair to the checkpoint where the donkey and cart had been detained, they were lucky enough to find that, as well as the officer who had been so harsh with them, there was now a general who was making a tour of the battlefield. He asked to have a look at the pass and then handed it back to Silvine, with a gesture of pity for the poor woman, indicating that she be allowed to continue her search for her husband, with her donkey. Without waiting any longer, the narrow cart in tow, she and her companion climbed back up towards the Fond de Givonne, obeying their new orders not to pass through Sedan.

Next, they turned left to reach Illy Plateau, along the road through Garenne Wood. But there again they were held up, and there were so many obstacles that a dozen times they thought they wouldn't be able to get through the woods. At each step, they found trees cut down by shells like felled giants, blocking their path. This was the bombarded forest, where the cannonade had sliced through age-old existences, as if scything through a section of the old guard, standing firm and motionless as veterans. Trunks were lying all over the place, denuded, full of holes and split open, like torsos; and this field of destruction, this massacre of branches weeping with sap, had the frightened, distressed aspect of a human battlefield. And then there were the bodies, too, soldiers fallen like comrades-in-arms alongside the trees. One lieutenant, with a bleeding mouth, still had both hands digging into the earth, pulling out handfuls of grass.

Futher on, a captain had died lying on his belly, face raised up, shouting out in agony. Others seemed to be sleeping in the under-growth, while a Zouave whose blue belt had caught fire had had his beard and hair completely burned off. And several times, as they made their way along this narrow, forest path, they had to move a body to one side so that the donkey and cart could get through.

All of a sudden, in a shallow valley, the horror ceased. No doubt the battle had passed by without touching this delicious little corner of nature. Not a tree had been touched, not a single wound had bled onto the moss. A stream trickled through the duckweed, and the path alongside was overshadowed by tall beech trees. There was an intense charm and adorable peacefulness about the coolness of the bubbling water and the quiet rustling of the greenery.

Prosper pulled the donkey to a halt to water him at the stream.

'Oh! How lovely it is here!' he said, unable to suppress a cry of relief.

Silvine looked around in astonishment, concerned to find that she, too, felt relaxed and happy here. Why should there be such calm and happiness in this remote spot, when all around there was nothing but grief and suffering? She indicated hopelessly that they should hurry.

'Quick, quick, let's go!... Where is it? Where are you sure you saw Honoré?'

And fifty paces on, as they emerged at long last from the woods onto Illy Plateau, the barren plain suddenly unfurled before them. This time it was a genuine battlefield, bare landscape stretching to the horizon beneath the great, pale sky, washed down by continual showers of rain. Here the dead were not heaped up, the Prussians must have all been buried already, for there wasn't a single one left to be seen among the scattered French corpses sown all along the roads and in the stubble, at the bottom of hollows, at random, as the battle had left them... The first one they came across, lying against a hedge, was a sergeant, a superb-looking man, young and strong, who seemed to be smiling through his half-open lips, his face calm. A hundred metres further on, however, they saw another, lying across the road, horribly mutilated, his head half blown away, shoulders splattered with bits of brain. Then after the isolated bodies lying here and there, they found small groups, they saw seven in a row, kneeling down, shouldering their rifles, struck as they were firing; and nearby, an NCO had fallen too, as he was giving a command.

The road then ran along the bottom of a narrow ravine, and it was there that they were again seized by horror, opposite a sort of ditch where a whole company appeared to have gone down under machine-gun fire: it was filled with dead bodies, like a landslide of men, tumbling down, all broken and tangled up together, their twisted hands clawing at the yellow earth, unable to hold them back. And a black flock of crows flew croaking overhead; and swarms of flies were already buzzing over the corpses, obstinately coming back again and again in their thousands to drink the fresh blood from the wounds.

'So where is it?' repeated Silvine.

They were walking along a ploughed field which was completely covered in rucksacks. Some regiment or other must have got rid of them here in a moment of panic, the enemy too close behind. The debris strewn across the ground bore witness to the episodes of the battle. In a field of beetroot, scattered képis like broad-petalled poppies, shreds of uniforms, epaulettes, and belts told of a fierce skirmish, one of the rare hand-to-hand combats in the formidable artillery duel which had lasted for twelve hours. But what they most frequently stumbled across at every step were the remains of weapons, sabres, bayonets, and rifles, so many of them that they were like some sort of vegetation, a harvest which had grown naturally, in one abominable day. Mess-tins and water bottles were also strewn along the roads, with all that had fallen out of torn-open rucksacks—rice, brushes, cartridges. The fields gave way to more fields, amidst massive destruction, fences ripped up, trees burnt as if by fire, even the ground itself cratered by shells, trampled and hardened by the gallop of the crowd, so ravaged that it seemed it must remain forever infertile. The rain engulfed everything in its pale dampness, and a persistent smell rose from the ground, that battlefield smell which reeks of rotten straw and burnt cloth, a mixture of gunpowder and decay.

Silvine, weary of these fields of death, which she seemed to have been walking through for miles and miles, looked around in growing dread.

'Where is it, then? Where is it?'

Prosper, however, didn't reply, and was starting to get worried. What upset him, even more than the bodies of his comrades-in-arms, were the numerous dead horses they passed, the poor animals lying on their sides. Some of them were truly lamentable, lying in horrendous positions, heads torn off, flanks open, leaving their entrails to spill out. Many were lying on their backs, their bellies huge, legs sticking up in the air like warning posts. The boundless plain was bumpy with them. Some weren't yet dead after two days of agony; and the slightest sound made them raise their suffering heads, moving right and left, then letting them drop back on the ground; while others, lying motionless, gave a loud cry every now and then, that cry dying horses make, so peculiar to them, and so full of pain that it made the very air quiver. And Prosper, with aching heart, thought of Zephyr, wondering whether he might see him again.

All of a sudden he felt the ground shudder beneath the raging charge of galloping hooves. He turned round and just had time to shout to his companion,

'The horses, the horses!... Quick, behind that wall!'

From high up on a neighbouring slope a hundred or so loose, riderless horses, some still carrying full kit, were coming hurtling down the hill towards them at a hellish pace. They were abandoned animals, left behind on the battlefield, instinctively gathering into herds. Having had neither hay nor oats for two days, they'd grazed the patchy grass bare, started eating hedges and chewing the bark off the trees. And when they felt hunger clutching too tight at their bellies, pricking at them like spurs, they all set off together at a mad gallop, charging across the mute, deserted countryside, crushing the dead and finishing off the wounded.

The whirlwind was getting nearer, and Silvine only just had time to pull the donkey and cart into the shelter of the little wall.

'My God! They're going to destroy everything!'

But the horses had cleared the obstacle, there was just a rumbling sound of thunder, and already they were galloping off on the other side, tearing down a little track to the corner of a wood, disappearing behind it.

When Silvine had led the donkey back onto the road, she demanded that Prosper answer her question.

'So, where is it?'

He stood and looked to all four corners of the horizon.

'There were three trees, I have to find those three trees... Oh! Lord, you don't really see straight when you're fighting, and afterwards it's not that easy to know which way you went!'

Then, seeing two men and a woman to their left, he thought he'd ask them. As he approached, however, the woman fled and the men waved threateningly at him to keep away; and he saw others like them, all of whom avoided him, slipping into the bushes like shifty, prowling animals, squalidly clothed, unspeakably dirty and suspicious-looking, like thieves. Then, noticing that wherever these unpleasant people had passed the dead no longer had their shoes on, leaving their feet bare and white, he finally realized that they were the vultures who went around after the German armies, plundering the corpses, an organized band of mean predators* roving in the wake of the invasion. A tall, skinny man galloped off in front of them, shoulders weighed down under a rucksack, pockets jangling with watches and silver coins stolen from inside clothing.

However, one boy of about thirteen or fourteen allowed Prosper to approach him, and when the latter, recognizing him as French, began hurling insults at him, he protested. What was this? Weren't you allowed to earn your living now? He was picking up rifles, he got five sous for each one he found. That morning, fleeing his village after having had nothing to fill his belly with since the day before, he'd been taken on by a Luxembourg businessman who'd made an agreement with the Prussians to collect up all the rifles lying on the battlefield. The fact was, the Prussians were afraid that if these weapons were picked up by peasants living on the border, they'd be taken over into Belgium to be smuggled back into France. And so a whole swarm of poor beggars was hunting for rifles, looking for their five sous, rummaging through the grass, just like women bending over in the fields, picking dandelions.

'Foul job!' growled Prosper.

'Hell! Got to eat,' replied the boy. 'I'm not robbing anyone.'

Then, seeing as he wasn't from round there and couldn't give him any information, he simply pointed out a little farm nearby, where he'd seen some life.

Prosper thanked him and was walking off to join Silvine when he spotted a rifle half buried in a furrow. At first, he was careful not to point it out. Then he suddenly turned back, shouting almost in spite of himself,

'Here! There's another one, that'll be five more sous for you!'

As they approached the farm, Silvine noticed other peasants busy digging long trenches with pickaxes. These, however, were under direct orders from Prussian officers who, armed merely with switches, surveyed the labour, standing by stiff and silent. The villagers had been conscripted into burying the dead for fear that the rainy weather would speed up the process of decay. Two carts of corpses stood there, and a team of men was unloading them and laying them swiftly side by side, without even stopping to search them or look at their faces; while three men with large shovels followed behind, covering the row in such a thin layer of earth that the rain was already starting to make cracks appear in the ground. So hasty was the work that before a fortnight was out, plague would be wafting up through these crevices. Silvine couldn't help stopping at the edge of the ditch and examining the faces of each of these wretched bodies as they were brought down. She shuddered in horror, dreadfully afraid that she recognized Honoré's features in every bloody face. Wasn't he that poor man whose left eye was missing? Or maybe that one, whose jaw had been cracked open? If she didn't hurry up and find him somewhere on this hazy, endless plain, they were sure to take him and throw him onto the pile along with the others.

So she ran to catch up with Prosper, who'd walked up to the farm gate with the donkey.

'Oh God! Where is it, then?... Ask them, find out!'

Inside the farm there were only Prussians, accompanied by a servant and her child who had come out of the woods where they'd almost died of hunger and thirst. It was a corner of homely comfort and honest rest after the strains of the last few days. Soldiers were carefully brushing down their uniforms, pegged out on washing lines. Another was finishing a deft repair to his trousers, while the party's cook had lit a large fire in the middle of the farmyard, where a large pot of soup was on the boil, giving off a delicious smell of cabbage and bacon. Victory was already being organized in a perfectly peaceful, disciplined way. They looked like bourgeois folk who had come home and were sitting down to smoke their long pipes. By the door, sitting on a bench, a big, red-headed man had taken the servant's son into his arms, a toddler of about five or six; and he was bouncing him on his knee, saying words of endearment to him in German, highly amused to see the child laughing at this foreign language with its harsh syllables that he didn't understand.

Prosper immediately turned his back, fearful of some fresh mis-hap. But these Prussians were undoubtedly good people. They smiled at the little donkey, and didn't even bother to come over and ask to see their pass.

After that, their search became frantic. The sun appeared for a moment between two clouds, already low on the horizon. Was night going to fall and take them by surprise, on this endless graveyard? A fresh shower drowned out the sunshine, and around them there was only the pale rain stretching into infinity, water like clouds of dust, blocking out everything, roads, fields and trees. Prosper no longer knew where he was, he was lost and admitted as much. Behind them, the donkey trotted along at the same pace, head down, pulling the little cart, plodding along like the docile, resigned beast that it was. They headed north, then came back towards Sedan. They had lost all sense of direction, twice they retraced their steps, realizing that they were covering the same ground. No doubt they were going round in circles, and finally, despairing and exhausted, they stopped where three roads met, lashed by the rain, with no strength left to search further.

However, they were surprised to hear the sound of moaning, and pushed on as far as an isolated little house on their left, where they discovered two wounded men lying at the back of one of the rooms. The doors were wide open; and for two days they'd been shivering with fever, without so much as a dressing, and had seen no one, not a soul. Above all, they were consumed with thirst, while the rain beat-ing against the window panes trickled down outside. They were unable to move, and immediately cried out 'Water! Water!', that painful, greedy cry with which the wounded pursue passers-by at the slightest sound of footsteps to rouse them from their drowsy state.

When Silvine had taken them water, Prosper, who'd recognized the worse off of the two as a comrade from his regiment in the African Chasseurs, realized that they couldn't be all that far from the fields where the Margueritte division had charged. The wounded man eventually managed a vague wave: yes, it was over there, you turned left after you passed a large field of lucerne. Without waiting for more information, Silvine wanted to set off again. She'd just found help for the two injured men, hailing a passing team of men who were gathering up the dead. She took the donkey's halter once more and led it over the slippery ground, impatient to be there, beyond the field of lucerne.

Suddenly Prosper stopped.

'It must be round here. Look! There are the three trees, on the right... You see the wheel tracks? And there's a broken ammunition wagon, over there... At last, we've found it!'

Silvine shuddered and rushed forward, looking at the faces of two dead men, two artillery men who had fallen by the side of the road.

'But he's not here, he's not here!... You must have been mistaken... Yes! It must have been some sort of fancy, something you just imagined you saw!'

Little by little she was overcome by wild hope, delirous with joy.

'What if you were mistaken, what if he was alive! Of course he's alive, since he isn't here!'

All at once, she gave a muffled cry. She had just turned round, and found herself standing right on the site of the battery. It was a dreadful sight, the ground looked like an earthquake had hit it, debris lay all over the place, dead men sprawling everywhere, in gruesome positions, with twisted arms, legs bent under, heads crooked, screaming through their wide open, white-toothed mouths. One brigadier had died in a terrified spasm, both hands clamped over his eyes, as if he hadn't wanted to look. A few gold pieces which a lieutenant had been carrying in his belt had flowed out along with his blood, and were lying scattered among his entrails. Adolphe, the driver and Louis, the gunner, the couple, lying one on top of the other, eyes hanging out of their sockets, were still locked in a fierce embrace, married even unto death. And last of all there was Honoré, lying on his crooked gun, as if he were lying in state, struck in the side and shoulder, his face intact and handsome with rage, still looking towards the Prussian batteries.

'Oh! My darling,' sobbed Silvine, 'my darling...'

She fell to her knees on the waterlogged earth, hands clasped together in a mad surge of grief. This word, the only one which came to her, told of the tenderness she had just lost in this man, who was such a good man, who'd forgiven her and agreed to make her his wife, in spite of everything. Now all her hope was gone, she couldn't go on. She'd never loved another, and she would love him forever. The rain ceased and a croaking flock of crows, circling above the three trees, were like a threat to her. Were they going to snatch him from her, the cherished dead she had taken such pains to find? Crawling on her knees, with a trembling hand she brushed away the greedy flies which were buzzing around the wide-open eyes, where she was still seeking Honoré's gaze.

Clutched between his fingers, however, she glimpsed a blood-stained piece of paper. She grew worried and tried to prise it out, tugging gently at it. The dead man didn't want to give it up, and kept hold of it so tightly that it would only have come free in pieces. It was the letter she had written to him, the letter he'd kept under his shirt, against his skin, clutched as if to say farewell, in his final convulsion. And when she saw what it was she felt a deep, penetrating joy in the midst of her grief, quite overcome to see that he was thinking of her when he died. Oh! Of course she'd let him keep it, the precious letter! She wouldn't take it back, since he was so stubbornly intent on taking it with him into the ground. A fresh fit of weeping came as a release, with tears that were now warm and soft. She stood up, and kissed his hands, his brow, saying just that one, infinitely caressing word.

'My darling... My darling...'

Meanwhile the sun was sinking, and Prosper had gone to fetch the bedspread. Slowly and devotedly, they picked up Honoré's body and laid him on the cover, spread out on the ground; then, after wrapping it around him, they lifted him onto the cart. The rain was threatening to start again, and they were setting off with the donkey, a mournful little procession across the treacherous plain, when a distant rumbling of thunder was heard.

Again Prosper cried out,

'The horses! The horses!'

It was another charge of stray horses, on the loose and starving hungry. This time they were coming over a huge, flat stubble-field, a tightly packed mass, manes flying in the wind, nostrils covered in foam; and an oblique ray of red sun cast the shadow of their frenetic course right to the far end of the plain. Silvine immediately flung herself in front of the cart, both arms raised, as if to try and stop them, with a furious, frightened gesture. Luckily, they veered off to the left, led away by a piece of sloping ground. They would have trampled everything to bits. The ground shook beneath them, their hooves sending up a shower of stones, a hail of grapeshot which injured the donkey's head. And they disappeared down into a ravine.

'It's the hunger driving them mad,' said Prosper. 'Poor beasts!'

After bandaging the donkey's ear with her handkerchief, Silvine again took the bridle. And the lugubrious little procession crossed back over the plain, in the opposite direction, to cover once again the two leagues which separated them from Remilly. Prosper stopped at every step to look at the dead horses, his heart heavy at having to leave like this without seeing Zephyr again.

A little below Garenne Wood, as they were turning left to pick up the route they'd taken that morning, a German outpost demanded to see their pass. And instead of directing them away from Sedan, this time they were ordered to go through the city, or risk arrest. There was no point arguing, these were new orders. In any case, it would shorten their journey home by a couple of kilometres and exhausted as they were, they were more than happy.

Once in Sedan, however, they came up against a most unusual obstruction. As soon as they'd passed the fortifications, a stench enveloped them, from a knee-high layer of dung. The city had become squalid, a cesspool where for three days the refuse and excrement of a hundred thousand men had been accumulating. There were all sorts of rubbish filling out this human litter, straw and hay, causing the animals' manure to rot. Worst of all were the carcasses of horses, slaughtered and cut up right there in the street, fouling the air. The entrails were rotting in the sun, heads and bones were lying on the cobbles, crawling with flies. Plague would start blowing this way for sure, if they didn't hurry up and sweep this disgusting layer of muck into the sewers; on the Rue du Ménil, Rue Maqua, and even on the Place Turenne it was up to twenty centimetres deep. What was more, the Prussian authorities had put up white notices conscripting the inhabitants into service for the next day, ordering everyone, be they labourers, merchants, bourgeois, or magistrates, to set to work armed with brooms and buckets, under threat of the harshest punitive measures if the city wasn't clean by evening; and they could already see the chief magistrate outside his front door, scraping the cobbles clean and piling the filth into a wheelbarrow with a coal-shovel.

Silvine and Prosper, who had turned down the Grande-Rue, were able to take only a few paces at a time through this fetid mud. On top of this the streets were full of unrest, which halted their progress at every step. It was the moment the Prussians began searching houses to flush out the soldiers who were hiding and stubbornly refusing to give themselves up. The previous day at about two o'clock, when General de Wimpffen had returned from the Château de Belleville after signing the surrender, the rumour had immediately gone round that the captured army was to be imprisoned on the Iges peninsula while they waited for convoys to be organized to take them back to Germany. Very few officers were minded to take advantage of the clause which set them free, on condition that they promised in writing not to fight again. Only one general, Bourgain-Desfeuilles, was said to have made this undertaking, using his rheumatism as a pretext; and only that morning jeers had greeted his departure as he climbed into a carriage outside the Hôtel de la Croix d'Or. Since the small hours the process of decommissioning had been under way, the soldiers had to parade onto the Place Turenne, each throwing down his weapons, rifles, bayonets, onto the growing pile in the corner of the square, like some heap of old scrap. There was a Prussian detachment on duty, under the command of a young officer, a tall, pale lad in a sky-blue tunic, wearing a fur hat crowned by a cockerel feather, watching over the disarming with a haughtily correct stance and white-gloved hands. When a Zouave had defiantly refused to give up his rifle, the officer had had him taken away, saying, without a trace of an accent, 'Shoot that man!' The rest went on gloomily filing past, mechanically throwing away their weapons, anxious to get it over with. But how many of them were already unarmed, their rifles lying back there around the countryside! And how many of them, since the day before, had been hiding, dreaming of disappearing amid the indescribable confusion! Houses had been invaded and were still full of these stubborn souls who wouldn't respond to the calls to surrender, who stayed holed up in corners. Searching the city, the German patrols even found men cowering under pieces of furniture. And when large numbers refused to come out of the cellars, even after being discovered, the patrols decided to fire down on them through the basement windows. It was a man-hunt, a truly appalling running to ground.

At the Pont de Meuse, the donkey was stopped by a crowd blocking its way. The officer in charge of the checkpoint, thinking they were selling bread or meat or something, wanted to verify the contents of the cart; and when he pulled back the cover, he gave one startled look at the body; then he waved them through. But they still couldn't move forward, for the congestion grew worse as one of the first convoys of prisoners passed, being led to the Iges peninsula by a Prussian detachment. The herd was endless, men jostled each other, treading on one another' heels, dressed in their tattered uniforms, heads bowed, eyes averted, with the stoop and dangling arms of the vanquished who no longer even have a knife to slit their own throats with. The harsh voice of their guard was like a whip urging them on, cutting across the silent exodus, with only the noise of the slapping of their large boots in the thick mud. There had just been another shower, and nothing was more pitiful to see than this herd of dispossessed soldiers, like vagabonds or highway beggars, trudging on beneath the rain.

Suddenly Prosper, whose former Chasseur's heart was pounding fit to burst with suppressed rage, nudged Silvine with his elbow, pointing to two passing soldiers. He'd recognized Maurice and Jean being led away with their comrades, marching side by side like brothers; and when the cart had at last set off again behind the convoy, he was able to trace their progress as far as Torcy, on that flat road leading to Iges through the allotments and market gardens.

'Ah!' murmured Silvine, looking towards Honoré's body, overcome by the sight before her. 'Perhaps the dead are the lucky ones, after all!'

Night, which caught up with them at Wadelincourt, had long fallen by the time they got back to Remilly in the pitch black. Old Fouchard stood dumbfounded before the body of his son, for he'd been convinced that they wouldn't find it. He had spent his day tying up a nice bit of business. Officers' horses, stolen off the battlefield, were at present selling for twenty francs apiece; and he had bought three for forty-five.

CHAPTER TWO

As the column of prisoners was leaving Torcy there was such a scramble that Maurice was separated from Jean. No matter how fast he ran to catch up, he just got more lost. And when he finally arrived at the bridge over the canal which cuts across the base of the Iges peninsula, he found himself mixed up with African Chasseurs and unable to rejoin his regiment.

Two cannons, pointing towards the interior of the peninsula, defended the bridge. Immediately beyond the canal, in a country house, the Prussian staff had set up headquarters under the orders of a commandant, responsible for receiving and guarding the prisoners. Formalities were brief—they simply counted the men in like sheep as they arrived in the crush, without worrying too much about uniforms or serial numbers; and the herds of men rushed in, setting themselves down wherever the roads happened to lead them.

Maurice thought he could ask for help from a Bavarian officer, who was happily smoking away, sitting astride a chair.

'Where should I go, sir, for the 106th infantry regiment?'

Was it that, exceptionally, this officer didn't understand French? Or did he find it amusing to send some poor sod of a soldier off course? He smiled, raised a hand, and signalled to him to carry straight on.

Even though Maurice was from the area, he'd never been to the peninsula, and for him this was a voyage of discovery, as if a gust of wind had sent him off to a distant isle. First he walked past the Tour à Glaire to his left, a fine property with small but very charming grounds, situated on the banks of the Meuse. The road then followed the course of the river, which flowed round to the right, beneath steep-sided banks. Little by little it circled slowly upwards to flow around the hillock in the middle of the peninsula, where there were old quarries and excavations with narrow, winding paths. Further downstream was a mill. Then the road turned off, descending back down to the village of Iges, built on the slope and connected to the far bank by a ferry, in front of Saint-Albert Mill. Finally, ploughed fields and meadows opened out into a vast, flat stretch of treeless landscape, hemmed in by the rounded curve of the river. Maurice looked in vain across the bumpy slopes of the hillside; all he could see were cavalry and artillery getting settled in. Again he asked for help, addressing a brigadier in the African Chasseurs, who could tell him nothing. Night was beginning to fall, and he sat down for a moment on a milestone, his legs aching.

Then, as despair suddenly flooded over him, he saw opposite, across the Meuse, the accursed fields where he had fought two days before. In the fading light of this rainy day it was a dreary vision, the horizon stretching out mournfully, soaked in mud. The Saint-Albert gap, that narrow passage along which the Prussians had come, ran all the way around the bend, as far as a whitish mass of fallen rocks from the quarry. Beyond Seugnon Hill were the leafy treetops of Falizette Wood. But right in front of him, slightly to the left, was Saint-Menges, where the road sloped down to meet the ferry; at the centre was the summit of Hattoy Hill, with Illy far away, in the distance, Fleigneux hidden behind a fold in the land, and Floing lying nearer, on the right. He recognized the field where he'd lain for hours among the cabbages, the plateau that the reserve artillery had tried to defend, and the brow of the hill where he'd seen Honoré die on top of his devastated cannon. And the appalling extent of the disaster rose up again, overwhelming him with suffering and disgust until it actually made him sick.

However, the fear that nightfall might take him by surprise made him take up his search once more. Perhaps the 106th was camping somewhere lower down, beyond the village. All he found there were those roving for loot, and he decided to walk around the peninsula, following the curve of the river. As he walked through a field of potatoes he took the precaution of digging up a few tubers and filling his pockets with them: they weren't yet ready to eat, but he had nothing else, for to add to his woes, Jean had taken it upon himself to carry the two loaves of bread that Delaherche had given them when they left. What struck him now was the considerable number of horses he came across on the barren lands whose gentle slopes rolled down from the central hillock to the Meuse, towards Donchery. Why on earth had they brought all these animals with them? How were they going to feed them? It was already pitch black by the time he got to a little wood at the water's edge, where he was surprised to find the Emperor's Household Cavalry escort already settled in, drying themselves by large fires. These gentlemen, camping away from the

rest, had good-quality tents, saucepans on the boil, and a cow tethered to a tree. He was immediately conscious that they were looking
at him askance, his sadly neglected infantry uniform all tattered and
caked in mud. However, they did allow him to bake his potatoes in
the ashes, and he retired to the foot of a tree about a hundred metres
away to eat them. It had stopped raining, the sky had cleared, stars
were shining very brightly deep in the blue shadows. He realized that
this was where he was going to spend the night, ready to continue his
search the following morning. He was dog tired, and if it started to
rain again the tree would give him some shelter.

He couldn't get to sleep, though, haunted by the thought of this
vast prison, open to the night air, where he felt shut in. The Prussians had had an extraordinarily intelligent idea in herding the eighty
thousand remaining men of the Châlons army onto the peninsula. It
must have measured three and a half kilometres long by about one
and a half wide, easily enough to accommodate the huge, routed herd
of conquered men. And he was all too well aware of the unbroken
ring of water which surrounded them, the loop of the Meuse on
three sides and the bypass canal at the base, uniting the two close-
lying riverbeds. That was where the only access lay—the bridge,
which was defended by the two cannons. So nothing could have been
easier than to guard this camp, in spite of its size. He'd already
noticed the cordon of German sentinels on the other side, one every
fifty paces, placed near the water's edge, under orders to fire at any
man who tried to swim to freedom. Uhlans galloped behind them,
moving between the different outposts; while further off, scattered
across the vast countryside, you could have counted the black lines of
the Prussian regiments, a triple cordon, alive and on the move, wall-
ing in the imprisoned army.

Now, in any case, his eyes open wide and sleepless, Maurice saw
nothing but shadows, illuminated here and there by the campfires.
But beyond the pale ribbon of the Meuse he could still clearly make
out the motionless outlines of the sentinels. Beneath the bright star-
light they stood black and straight; and at regular intervals he could
hear their guttural call, a menacing watch-cry fading away into the
loud gurgling of the river. At the sound of these harsh, foreign
syllables coming through this beautiful, starlit French night, the
whole nightmare of the day before yesterday began to reawaken in
him, in those places he'd seen again only an hour ago, on an Illy

Plateau still cluttered with bodies, and in the treacherous outskirts of Sedan where a world had turned to dust. Leaning his head against the root of a tree in the damp air of the woods, he again sank down into despair like the day before, on Delaherche's sofa; and what tormented him now, making his wounded pride prick him more than ever, was the question of what would happen tomorrow, and the need to measure their failure, to find out exactly into what sort of ruins yesterday's world had collapsed. Since the Emperor had surrendered his sword to the King, wasn't this abominable war now over? But he recalled what two Bavarian soldiers had said to him, as they were leading the prisoners to Iges. 'We all in France, we all to Paris!' Half-asleep, he had a sudden vision of what was happening, the Empire swept away, carried off in a climate of universal loathing, a Republic proclaimed amid an explosion of patriotic fervour, while the legend of 1792 summoned up old ghosts, the soldiers from the call-up, armies of volunteers purging the foreigners from the soil of the fatherland. And inside his poor, sick head everything grew muddled, the demands of the victors, the harsh nature of the conquest, the obstinacy of the conquered to fight until their very last drop of blood, and these eighty thousand men held captive, first here on the peninsula, then in German fortresses, for weeks, months, maybe years. Everything was crumbling and disintegrating for ever, in boundless misery.

The cry of the sentinels, which had gradually been getting louder, rang out in front of him, then faded into the distance. He had woken up and was turning over on the hard ground when a shot ripped through the profound silence. At once the sound of a death rattle came through the black night; there was a splash of water and the brief struggle of a body sinking down to the bottom. It was probably some poor soul who'd got a bullet right through the heart as he tried to escape by swimming across the Meuse.

The next day, Maurice was up at daybreak. The sky was still clear and he was in a hurry to rejoin Jean and his comrades in the company. For a moment he thought about taking another look around inland; then he decided to complete his tour round the outside. As he came to the edge of the canal, he noticed the remains of the 106th, a thousand men camping along the bank, which was sheltered only by a thin line of poplar trees. The previous day, if he'd turned left instead of walking straight ahead, he'd have caught up with his regiment. Nearly all the infantry regiments were crammed in here, all along the bank running from the Tour à Glaire to the Château de Villette, another country residence surrounded by a few tumbledown houses towards Donchery; they were all camped near the bridge, close to the only way out, obeying that instinct to head for freedom which makes huge flocks trample each other against the gate on the threshold of the sheepfold.

Jean cried out with joy.

'Ah! There you are, at last! I thought you'd fallen in the river!'

There he was, with what was left of the squad—Pache, Lapoulle, Loubet, and Chouteau. The latter, having slept beneath a doorway in Sedan, had found themselves reunited again in the great shake-down. What was more, there was no longer a commander in the company save the corporal, death having reaped Sergeant Sapin, Lieutenant Rochas, and Captain Beaudoin. And even though the conquerors had got rid of ranks, deciding that the prisoners should obey only German officers, all four were nonetheless keeping close to Jean, knowing him to be wise and experienced, a good man to follow in difficult situations. And so that morning harmony and goodwill reigned, despite the fact that some were stupid and others headstrong. First of all he'd found them somewhere just about dry to spend the night, between two irrigation channels, where they had lain down with only a single canvas between them. Then he'd managed to get hold of firewood and a saucepan, which Loubet had used to make the coffee, whose delicious warmth had raised their spirits. It had stopped raining, it promised to be a wonderful day, and they still had a few biscuits and some bacon left; and then again, as Chouteau said, it was really nice not to have obey anyone anymore and just while away the time as you pleased. Even if they were shut in, there was plenty of room. In any case, they'd be gone in two or three days. Such was the atmosphere that this first day, Sunday, 4 September, went by cheerfully.

As for Maurice, feeling stronger now that he'd rejoined his comrades, practically the only thing that bothered him was the Prussian music, which went on nearly all afternoon on the other side of the canal. Towards evening there were choirs, too. Beyond the cordon of sentinels, they could see soldiers walking in small groups, singing in slow, high-pitched voices, celebrating Sunday.

'Oh! That music!' an exasperated Maurice cried at last. 'It's really getting to me!'

Jean shrugged, less on edge.

'Lord! They've good reason to be pleased. And anyway, maybe they think it's keeping us entertained... It hasn't been a bad day, let's not complain.'

As evening fell, however, the rain began again. It was a disaster. A number of soldiers had forced their way into the few abandoned houses on the peninsula. Several had managed to put up tents. But the majority, with no sort of shelter whatsoever, not even a blanket, had to spend the night out of doors, in the pouring rain.

At about one in the morning Maurice, who'd dozed off from sheer weariness, woke to find himself in a veritable lake of water. The channels had overflown, swollen by the downpour, submerging the piece of ground he was lying on. Chouteau and Loubet cursed angrily, while Pache began to shake Lapoulle, who was still fast asleep with fists curled tight, in spite of the soaking. Then Jean remembered the poplar trees planted along the canal and ran for shelter with his men, who spent the rest of the dreadful night sitting half doubled-up, backs against the tree-trunks, legs pulled up under them, to escape the worst of the drips.

And the next day and the day after that were truly awful, with continuous showers, coming down so hard and so often that their clothes didn't have time to dry out in between. Famine set in, they had neither biscuits, bacon, nor coffee left. During those two days, the Monday and Tuesday, they lived on potatoes stolen from neighbouring fields; but by the end of the second day even these were becoming so scarce that soldiers with any money were buying them for up to five sous apiece. The bugles sounded the call for rations to be distributed, and the corporal had even hurried off to a large barn at Tour à Glaire, where rumour had it that bread rations were being given out. The first time, though, he'd waited there for almost three hours in vain; then, a second time, he'd got into a fight with a Bavarian. If the French officers could do nothing, being powerless to act, had the German staff simply dumped the conquered army out in the rain with the intention of letting it starve to death? They appeared to have taken no precautions whatever, and no effort at all had been made to feed the eighty thousand men who were starting to die in this terrifying hell that the soldiers would later call the Camp of Misery, a name so full of suffering that even the bravest would forever shudder on hearing it.

On his return from the long and useless waits outside the barn Jean, despite his usual calm, would fly into a rage.

'Are they taking the piss, sounding the call when there's nothing? I'll be damned if I'm going to bother going again!'

But at the slightest call, off he'd hurry yet again. These regulation calls were quite inhuman; and they had another effect, which made Maurice's heart bleed. Each time the bugles sounded, the French horses, abandoned and on the loose over on the other side of the canal, came running up and dashed into the water to rejoin their regiments, driven wild by these familiar fanfares reaching them like a spur in their sides. But they were exhausted and got swept away by the current, and very few reached the far bank. They struggled pitifully, drowning in such huge numbers that the canal was already cluttered with their floating, bloated bodies. As for those who did reach the other side, they were seized by a sort of madness, galloping away, off into the penisula's empty fields.

'More meat for the crows!' said Maurice sadly, recalling the disturbing numbers of horses he had come across. 'If we stay here a few more days, we'll all end up eating each other! Oh! The poor things!'

The night of Tuesday to Wednesday was particularly terrible. Jean, who was beginning to have serious fears about Maurice's feverish state, forced him to wrap up in a tattered blanket which they'd bought off a Zouave for ten francs; while he himself, his greatcoat like a sodden sponge, took the full force of the ceaseless deluge that night. Their position beneath the poplar trees was becoming intolerable: the mud flowed like a river and the waterlogged ground formed deep puddles. The worst of it was that their stomachs were empty, the evening meal having consisted of two beetroots between the six of them, and they hadn't even been able to eat them cooked, because they didn't have any dry wood, and the root's cool sweetness had soon turned to an unbearable burning sensation. Not to mention that dysentery was breaking out, caused by fatigue, poor food, and the persistent damp. A dozen times Jean, leaning against the same tree as before, his legs under water, had felt to check that Maurice hadn't thrown off the blanket in his restless sleep. Ever since his companion had saved him from the Prussians by taking him into his arms up on Illy Plateau, he had repaid his debt a hundredfold.

Without making a conscious effort to do so, he had devoted himself
entirely to Maurice, completely forgetting himself for love of the
other man; and it was an obscure and steadfast thing coming from
this peasant, who'd stayed close to the land, and who couldn't find
the words to express his feelings. He'd already given him food from
his own mouth, as the others in the squad said; and now he would
have given his own skin to clothe the other, to protect his shoulders
and warm his feet. And amid the savage selfishness all around them,
in this corner of suffering humanity where hunger was enraging
their appetites, it was perhaps to this total self-abnegation that he
owed the unexpected reward of maintaining his calm bearing and his
good health; for he alone was still strong and still more or less in his
right mind.

So, after this awful night, Jean set in motion a plan which had
been nagging at him.

'Listen, lad, seeing as they're not giving us anything to eat and
leaving us here in this blasted hole, we ought to stir ourselves, if we
don't want to die like dogs... Your legs still good?'

Fortunately the sun had come back out, and had quite warmed
Maurice through.

'Of course my legs are still good!'

'Right, then, we're off to explore... We've got some money, and I'll
be damned if we can't find something to buy. And don't let's bother
with the others, they aren't worth it, let them sort themselves out!'

It was true, Loubet and Chouteau had disgusted them with their
sly selfishness, looting anything they could and never sharing with
their comrades; likewise there wasn't much good could be said of
Lapoulle, who was just a fathead, nor Pache, the sneak.

So the two of them set off down the path that Maurice had already
followed along the Meuse. The grounds of the Tour à Glaire and the
house itself had been devastated, pillaged, lawns furrowed as if a
storm had hit them, trees felled, buildings overrun. A ragged crowd
of mud-covered soldiers, hollow-cheeked and eyes fever-bright, were
squatting there like gypsies, living like wolves in the filthy rooms, not
daring to go out for fear of losing their place for the night. Further
on, up the hillsides, they walked through the cavalry and artillery
encampments, which until then had been so correctly turned out,
but now they too had fallen, this torture by starvation reducing them
to chaos, terrorizing the horses and sending the men roaming across

the fields in groups bent on destruction. To the right, in front of the mill, they saw an endless queue of artillerymen and African Chasseurs slowly filing past: the miller was selling them flour, two handfuls in their handkerchief for a franc. But afraid of having to wait too long, they passed on, hoping to find something better in the village of Iges; and they were filled with dismay when they got there, for it was bare and mournful, like some Algerian village after a swarm of locusts: not a crumb of food was left, no bread, no vegetables, no meat; it was as if the wretched houses had been scraped clean with fingernails. They were told that General Lebrun was staying at the mayor's house. He had done his best to try to set up a voucher system, to be paid back after the war, so as to make it easier to feed the troops, but in vain. There was nothing left, money was becoming useless. Only the day before, a biscuit had cost two francs, a bottle of wine seven, a small glass of brandy twenty sous, and a pipe of tobacco ten. And now there had to be officers guarding the general's house and the shacks nearby, swords drawn, for there were bands of scroungers constantly battering down doors, stealing everything, even drinking the oil from lamps.

Three Zouaves called to Maurice and Jean. Between the five of them, they could get something done.

'Come on... There's horses snuffing it, and if we just had a bit of dry wood...'

They rushed into a peasant's house, breaking down cupboard doors, ripping the thatch from the roof. A few officers came racing up, threatening them with their revolvers, and made them run off.

When Jean saw that the few inhabitants who'd remained on Iges were as wretched and starving as the soldiers, he regretted having shunned the flour at the mill.

'We should go back, maybe there's still some left.'

But Maurice was growing so weary and so weak with hunger that Jean left him in a nook in the quarry, sitting on a rock facing the broad Sedan horizon. After queuing for three-quarters of an hour, he finally returned with a cloth full of flour. And they could think of nothing else to do than eat it just as it was, in handfuls. It wasn't bad, it didn't smell of anything, it just had a stale, pastry taste. They were even lucky enough to come across a natural pool of fresh rainwater in the rock, which was pure enough, and they quenched their thirst with relish.

Then, when Jean suggested that they stay there for the afternoon, Maurice reacted violently.

'No, no, not here!... It'd make me ill if I had to look at that for too long...'

With a trembling hand he pointed to the immense horizon, to Hattoy Hill, Illy and Floing Plateaux, Garenne Wood, all those hateful fields of massacre and defeat.

'Just now, when I was waiting for you, I had to turn my back on it, otherwise I'd have ended up howling with rage—yes, howling! Just like a tormented dog... You can't imagine the pain it causes me, it's driving me mad!'

Jean looked at him, astonished to see such bleeding pride, and again he was disturbed to catch that wandering look of madness in his eyes which he'd already noticed. He pretended to make a joke of it.

'Right! That's easy enough, we'll give ourselves a change of scenery.'

So they wandered around until the end of the day, wherever the paths led them. They visited the flat part of the peninsula, hoping to find some potatoes still left; but the artillerymen had taken up the ploughs and turned the fields over, gleaning and gathering up everything. They retraced their steps, once again making their way through idle, dying crowds, soldiers trailing their hunger around with them, strewing the ground with their numbed bodies, hundreds of them collapsing beneath the bright sun. Every hour they too succumbed, and had to sit down. Then a gnawing sense of frustration would make them get back up and start prowling round again, as if goaded by that instinct which makes an animal look for food. It seemed to have gone on for months, and yet the minutes went by in a flash. Inland, towards Donchery, they were frightened by the horses and had to shelter behind a wall, where they stayed for a long time, utterly exhausted, their hazy eyes watching these mad beasts go galloping across the red sky of the sunset.

Just as Maurice had predicted, the thousands of horses which had been imprisoned along with the army, and which they were unable to feed, presented a danger that was increasing day by day. First they had chewed the bark off the trees, then they had begun attacking trellises and fences and any planks they came across, and now they were starting on each other. They could be seen flinging themselves at one another, trying to tear out bits of tail, which they then chewed on furiously, foaming at the mouth. It was at night, though, that they became most terrible of all, as if the darkness haunted them with nightmares. They flocked together, charging on the few tents still standing, attracted by the smell of the straw. The men tried in vain to keep them off, lighting huge fires, which seemed to make them even more excited. Their whinnying was so pitiful and so frightening that it was like the howling of wild beasts. The men would chase them off, and they would come back fiercer and in greater numbers. And every moment, through the darkness, came the long, agonizing cry of some lost soldier, who'd just been crushed under their raging hooves.

The sun was still on the horizon when Jean and Maurice, on their way back to the camp, were surprised to meet the other four men from their squad, crouching in a ditch, apparently plotting some dirty deed. At once Loubet called them over and Chouteau said,

'It's about dinner tonight... We're going to starve to death, it's thirty-six hours now since we last had anything to put in our bellies... So, seeing as there're horses around, and horsemeat isn't at all bad...'

'Don't you think, Corporal? Are you with us?' went on Loubet. 'Because the more there are of us, the better it'll be, with such a huge animal... Look! There's one over there we've been watching for the past hour, that big roan who doesn't look too well. It'll be easier to finish it off that way.'

He pointed to a horse which had just collapsed from hunger at the edge of a devastated field of beetroot. Fallen and lying on his side, he would raise his head every now and then, looking around with his mournful eyes, sighing a big, sad sigh.

'Oh! It's taking ages!' groaned Lapoulle, tormented by his enormous appetite. 'What d'you think, shall I hit it on the head?'

Loubet, though, stopped him. Thanks a lot! And get themselves into trouble with the Prussians, who'd forbidden them, on pain of death, to kill a single horse, for fear that the abandoned carcasses would encourage plague? They'd have to wait for the cover of night. And that was why all four were huddled in the ditch, keeping watch, glinting eyes never straying from the animal.

'Corporal,' asked Pache in a slightly faltering voice, 'you're the one with the ideas round here, couldn't you kill it without hurting it?'

Jean held his hands up in disgust, refusing the cruel task. Kill that poor, dying beast? Oh, no, not him! His first instinct had been to flee, taking Maurice with him, so that neither of them should have to take part in this appalling butchery. But when he saw how pale his companion was, he chided himself for being so sensitive. My God, animals were created as food for humans, after all! They couldn't let themselves starve to death when there was meat available. And he was happy to see Maurice perking up a bit at the thought that they were going to eat, and so he said, in his good-natured way,

'Good grief, no, I haven't any bright ideas, and if we have to kill it without hurting it...'

'Well I don't give a toss,' interrupted Lapoulle. 'Just you wait and see!'

When the two newcomers had sat down in the ditch, the waiting began again. From time to time one of the men would get up and make sure that the horse was still there, neck stretching out towards the cool breezes coming off the Meuse, towards the setting sun, trying to soak up all the life from it. Then at last, when dusk had slowly gathered in, the six got to their feet, looking all around with frightened, worried faces to make sure nobody could see them.

'Oh, hell!' cried Chouteau. 'It's time!'

The countryside was still light, with a shady, twilight glow. And Lapoulle was the first to run up to the horse, followed by the other five. He had picked up a large, round stone from the ditch, and he rushed at the horse and began smashing its skull, both arms held out straight, as if he were wielding a hammer. At the second blow, however, the animal tried to get back up. Chouteau and Loubet flung themselves across its legs, trying to hold it down, shouting to the others to help them. The horse neighed in a voice that was almost human, frantic and in pain, he struggled, and if he hadn't been half-dead with hunger, he'd have broken them like pieces of glass. However, his head was moving about too much, the blows no longer hit home, and Loubet couldn't finish him off.

'Jesus! His bones are tough!... Hold him down, then, so I can kill him!'

Jean and Maurice, chilled, didn't hear Chouteau's calls for help, just stood there with arms hanging limply by their sides, unable to decide whether to intervene.

And suddenly Pache, in a fit of instinctive religious compassion, fell to his knees on the ground, clasping his hands together and beginning to stammer out prayers, as if he were at the bedside of a dying man.

'Lord, have mercy on his soul...'

Once again Lapoulle missed, managing only to tear off one of the wretched horse's ears, and the animal fell back with a loud cry.

'Hang on, hang on!' scolded Chouteau. 'We've got to finish this, he'll get us caught... Loubet, don't you let go of him!'

He had taken his knife out of his pocket, a small knife with a blade no longer than his finger. And sprawled on the beast's belly with one arm round its neck, he stuck the blade in, digging into this living flesh, carving out chunks until he found and cut through the artery. With a single bound he leapt to one side and the blood spurted out, gushing forth like water from a fountain, while the horse's feet twitched and violent shudders ran across his skin. It took the beast nearly five minutes to die. His huge eyes opened wide, full of sadness and terror, and stared at the haggard men waiting for him to die. They clouded over and then the light in them died.

'Dear God,' stuttered Pache, still on his knees, 'give him succour, take him into thy keeping.'

Then, when the horse had stopped moving, they had enormous difficulty getting a good piece of meat off the body. Loubet, who'd practised every trade, knew very well how they should go about getting a fillet. However, being a clumsy butcher and having only the little knife to work with, he got lost in all that hot flesh, still pulsating with life. And when Lapoulle, growing impatient, started to help by opening up the belly, completely unnecessarily, the carnage became quite appalling. They delved into the blood and guts with ferocious haste, like wolves sinking their teeth into the carcass of their prey.

'I'm not really sure which part this could be,' said Loubet, standing up with his arms full of an enormous chunk of meat. 'But it's enough to stuff our faces with, anyway.'

Jean and Maurice, seized with horror, had turned away. However, hunger urged them on and they followed the group of men as they galloped off to avoid getting caught near the carved-up horse. Chouteau had just made a real find, three huge beetroots which had been overlooked, and he carried them off. Loubet, to lighten his burden, had unloaded the meat onto Lapoulle's shoulders; while Pache carried the squad's cooking-pot, which they'd been dragging around with them in case they made a good catch. And the six of them galloped off, without stopping to catch their breath, as if they were being pursued.

All of a sudden, Loubet stopped the others.

'This is stupid, we don't even know where we're going to cook the thing.'

Jean, who was calming down, suggested the quarries. They were no more than three hundred metres away, and there were hidey-holes where they could light a fire without being seen. When they got there, however, all sorts of problems arose. First, there was the question of firewood; fortunately they discovered a roadmender's barrow which Lapoulle broke up by stamping on the planks. Next, there was absolutely no drinking water to be found. During the day, the strong sun had dried up all the natural little pools of rainwater. There was a pump on the peninsula, but it was too far away, at the château of the Tour à Glaire, and you could queue up there 'til midnight, and even then you were lucky if one of your comrades didn't knock over your mess-tin with his elbow. As for the few wells in the neighbourhood, they had been dry for two days now, and all you drew up was mud. All there was left was the water from the Meuse, whose bank lay on the other side of the road.

'I'll go with the cooking-pot,' suggested Jean.

They all cried out in protest.

'Oh, no! We don't want to be poisoned—it's full of corpses!'

The Meuse was indeed full of the bodies of men and horses. Every minute they could see them floating past, stomachs ballooning, already turning green and decomposing. Many of them had come to a standstill in the grasses on the riverbanks, fouling the air, constantly bobbing and swaying with the current. Almost all the soldiers who'd drunk from this abominable water had found themselves taken ill with appalling stomach cramps, followed by sickness and dysentery.

However, they would have to resign themselves to it. Maurice explained that once the water had been boiled, it wouldn't be dangerous any more.

'Right, I'll go then,' repeated Jean, taking Lapoulle with him.

When the cooking-pot was finally full of water and the meat had been put in, black night was upon them. Loubet had peeled the beetroots to cook them in the broth, a real out-of-this-world treat, as he put it; and they all stood fanning the flames, feeding the remains of the wheelbarrow under the pot. Their long shadows danced about bizarrely at the bottom of this hole in the rocks. Then they couldn't wait any longer, and pounced on the revolting stew, sharing out the meat with fumbling, trembling hands, not even bothering to take the time to use the knife. But they retched, in spite of themselves. What they noticed most of all was the lack of salt, their stomachs refusing to keep down the tasteless beetroot broth and the half-cooked pieces of meat, all slimy and tasting of clay. They began to vomit almost immediately. Pache couldn't go on, Chouteau and Loubet cursed the lousy blasted nag they'd had so much trouble getting into the pot in the first place, and was now giving them gutache. Only Lapoulle dined copiously; but it nearly killed him later on that night, when he and the other three returned to the spot beneath the poplar trees by the canal to sleep.

On the way Maurice wordlessly took hold of Jean's arm and led him onto a track leading off across country. His comrades produced a sort of furious disgust in him, and he had half an idea to go and sleep in the little wood where he'd spent the first night. It was a good idea of which Jean heartily approved once he was lying on the sloping ground, dry as a bone, sheltered by thick foliage. They stayed there until it was well and truly light, and even managed to sleep deeply, which restored some of their strength.

The next day was a Thursday. But they didn't really know where they were any more, they were simply happy that fine weather seemed to be setting in again. In spite of his reluctance, Jean persuaded Maurice to return to the banks of the canal to see whether their regiment was meant to be leaving that day. Prisoners were departing daily now, with columns of anything from a thousand to twelve hundred men being led off to the German fortresses. Two days earlier, in front of the Prussian guard post, they'd seen a convoy of officers and generals heading for the railway at Pont-à-Mousson. Everyone was burning with the need, the furious desire to leave this terrible place, the Camp of Misery. Oh! If only their turn could have come! And when they found the 106th still camped out on the bank, in the growing chaos caused by all their suffering, they plunged into deep despair.

However, at one point that day Maurice and Jean thought they were going to eat. Since morning, a sort of trade had developed between the prisoners and the Bavarians above the canal; the prisoners threw money wrapped in a handkerchief, and the Bavarians sent it back with brown bread or coarse, barely cured tobacco. Even soldiers who hadn't any money managed to strike deals by throwing them white army-issue gloves, to which they seemed to be partial. For two hours, along the edge of the canal, this primitive form of bargaining had bundles flying through the air. However, when Maurice threw a hundred sous coin in his necktie, the Bavarian who threw him back a loaf of bread flung it in such a fashion that, either through clumsiness or out of spite, it fell into the water. At this, the Germans burst out laughing. Twice Maurice tried again, and twice the bread took a soaking. Then, drawn by the laughter, officers came running up, forbidding their men to sell anything at all to the prisoners, at the risk of being severely punished. The trade ceased, and Jean had to calm Maurice, who was shaking his fists at the brigands, yelling at them to send him back his hundred sous pieces.

In spite of the bright sun, it was another dreadful day. There were two alerts, two bugle-calls, causing Jean to dash to the barn where the distributions were supposed to take place. But on both occasions, all he got was elbows in his ribs in all the jostling. The Prussians, in spite of their remarkable talent for organization, continued to treat the conquered army with brutal negligence. Following complaints from Generals Douay and Lebrun, they'd sent in a few sheep and carts of bread; but they took such poor precautions that by the time they reached the bridge, the sheep had all been grabbed and the carts stripped bare, so that the troops camped more than a hundred metres away still didn't get anything. The scroungers and convoy thieves were practically the only ones who got to eat. So Jean, realizing what the trick was, as he put it, finally led Maurice to a place near the bridge so that they, too, could keep a look out for the food.

It was already four o'clock and they still hadn't eaten anything on this fine, sunny Thursday, when all of a sudden they were delighted to spot Delaherche. A few of Sedan's well-to-do had managed, with great difficulty, to obtain permission to go and see the prisoners and take them provisions; and Maurice had already mentioned several times how surprised he was not to have any news from Henriette. As soon as they recognized Delaherche from a distance, carrying a basket and bearing a baguette under each arm, they rushed forward; but yet again they got there too late, for there was such a surge that the basket and one of the loaves had disappeared, whipped away, vanished, without even the mill owner himself noticing how they came to be taken.

'Oh! My poor friends!' he faltered, dumbstruck and totally overcome, he who'd arrived all smiles, jovial and not too proud, ever eager to make himself popular.

Jean had got hold of the remaining loaf and was defending it; and while he and Maurice, sitting by the side of the road, devoured it in huge bites, Delaherche gave them all the news. His wife, thank God! was very well. But he was worried about the colonel, who had fallen into a deep depression, even though his mother continued to keep him company from morning to night.

'And what about my sister?' asked Maurice.

'Of course, your sister!... She was with me, it was she who brought the two loaves of bread. But she had to stay over there, on the other side of the canal. The guard wouldn't dream of giving her a pass... You know that the Prussians have strictly forbidden women from entering the peninsula.'

Then he spoke of Henriette and her vain attempts to come and see her brother and help him. In Sedan, chance had brought her face to face with Cousin Gunther, the captain in the Prussian Guard. He'd been walking past in his tough, cold manner, affecting not to recognize her. She herself, feeling ill, as if confronted with one of her husband's assassins, had at first quickened her pace. Then, suddenly changing her mind, which she couldn't explain at all, she'd turned back and told him everything, Weiss's death, the lot, in a harsh, reproachful voice. And all he'd done was give a vague sort of wave as he learned of his relative's appalling death: it was a hazard of war, he could very well have been killed himself. Hardly a shiver had run across his soldier's face. Then, when she'd spoken to him of her brother being held prisoner, begging him to intervene to let her visit him, he had refused to get involved. His orders were quite categorical, he spoke of the German wishes as if he were discussing religion. As she left him, she had the distinct impression that he saw himself in France as a kind of upholder of justice, full of intolerance and haughtiness towards the hereditary enemy, brought up to hate the race he was now punishing.

'Anyway,' concluded Delaherche, 'at least you'll have eaten this evening; but what upsets me is that I'm afraid I won't be able to get permission to come again.'

He asked if they had any messages they'd like him to take, and he obligingly took letters written in pencil which other soldiers entrusted to him, for they'd seen Bavarians laughing and lighting their pipes with those they had promised to pass on themselves.

Then, as Maurice and Jean accompanied him as far as the bridge, Delaherche cried out,

'But look! There's Henriette, over there!... You can see her waving her handkerchief.'

And there she was, behind the line of sentinels, a slim little figure among the crowd, a white dot fluttering in the sun. And they were both deeply moved, tears sprang to their eyes, and they raised their arms and replied by waving furiously at her.

It was the next day, a Friday, that for Maurice was the most abominable of all. However, after another peaceful night in the little wood, he'd been lucky enough to eat more bread, for Jean had discovered a woman at the Château de Villette selling it for ten francs per pound. But that day they witnessed a terrifying scene, the nightmare of which haunted them long afterwards.

The day before, Chouteau had noticed that Pache was no longer complaining and had a dizzy, contented air, like a man who has eaten his fill. It immediately occurred to him that the deceitful bugger must have a hiding place somewhere, especially since that morning he'd seen him slip away for almost an hour, then reappear, hiding a smile, with his mouth full. He must surely have had some sort of windfall, picked up provisions from some fight or other. And Chouteau began winding up Loubet and Lapoulle, especially the latter. Hey? What a rotten bloke for having food and not sharing it with his comrades!

'You never know, we'll follow him this evening... We'll see if he dares stuff his face all by himself, when there're poor sods standing next to him starving to death!'

'Yes, yes! That's it, we'll follow him!' Lapoulle echoed violently. 'We'll see about that!'

He clenched his fists, for the mere hope of eating at last was driving him mad. His huge appetite tormented him more than the others, and it had become such torture that he'd even tried chewing grass. Since the day before yesterday, since that night when the horsemeat and beetroot had given him such terrible dysentery, he'd had nothing to eat, his enormous body so clumsy, despite its strength, that he never managed to catch anything in the scramble to pillage the provisions. He would have paid in blood for a pound of bread.

As night was falling, Pache slipped away between the trees in Tour à Glaire, and the other three carefully hurried after him.

'He mustn't suspect anything,' repeated Chouteau. 'Watch out, in case he turns round.'

A hundred paces further on, however, Pache evidently believed he was alone, for he began walking swiftly without even glancing behind him. They were able to follow him with ease right up into the nearby quarries, and they crept up on him just as he was uncovering two large stones to take out half a loaf of bread from underneath. It was the last of his provisions, he had enough left for one more meal.

'Jesus, you little sneak!' yelled Lapoulle. 'So that's why you've been hiding from us!... Just you give me that, that's my share!'

Why should he give away his bread? Though naturally timid, anger made him get to his feet, while he clutched the morsel to his heart with all his strength. He was hungry, too.

'Leave me alone, d'you hear? It's mine!'

Then seeing Lapoulle's raised fist he took flight, galloping off, tearing down the quarries into the barren terrain towards Donchery. The other three gave chase, panting, running as fast as their legs could carry them. But he was gaining ground, lighter than them, in such a panic, so determined to hold on to what was his that he seemed to be carried along on the wind. He'd covered nearly a kilometre and was approaching the little wood, at the water's edge, when he encountered Jean and Maurice, returning for the night to their shelter. As he passed, he cried out to them for help, while they, astonished to see this man-hunt rushing past them at a raging gallop, just stood there on the edge of a field. And that was how they came to see it all happen.

As bad luck would have it, Pache stumbled against a stone and fell over. The other three were already upon him, swearing and shouting, whipped up by the chase, like wolves unleashed upon their prey.

'Jesus, will you give me that!' cried Lapoulle. 'Or I'll give you what for!'

And he was raising his fist again when Chouteau passed the

slim-bladed knife to him, fully open, the one he'd used to slit the horse's throat.

'Here! Take the knife!'

But Jean leapt forward to prevent some tragedy from happening, also losing his head, talking about throwing them all in prison; this made Loubet call him a Prussian, laughing nastily because there were no commanders any more, and only the Prussians gave orders.

'Jesus Christ!' repeated Lapoulle. 'Will you give me that!'

In spite of the terror which had made him turn quite pale, Pache clutched the bread even tighter to his chest, an obstinate, starving peasant who never gives up what belongs to him.

'No!'

And then it was over, the brute planted the knife in his throat with such violence that the wretched man didn't even cry out. His arms went limp and the piece of bread rolled to the ground into the blood which had spurted out.

Faced with this stupid, insane murder, Maurice, who up until then had stood quite still, also seemed suddenly to be seized by madness. He waved threateningly at the three men, calling them murderers with such vehemence that he shook all over. But Lapoulle didn't even seem to hear him. Still on the ground, crouching near the body, he was devouring the bread, which was splattered with drops of red; the look on his face was one of animal stupidity, as if dazed by the loud noise his jaws were making; while Chouteau and Loubet, seeing him satisfy his hunger in such a terrifying fashion, didn't even dare to claim their share.

It was now completely dark, the night was clear with a fine, starry sky; and soon Maurice and Jean, having reached their little wood, could only see Lapoulle, lurking down by the Meuse. The other two had vanished, no doubt returning to the edge of the canal, worried about the body they had left behind. He, on the contrary, seemed to be scared of going back to join his comrades. After the dazed feeling the murder had left him with, his stomach heavy with the large, hastily swallowed piece of bread, he had obviously been gripped by dread, which made him keep on the move, not daring to return along the road now blocked by the body, instead trudging ceaselessly along the riverbank, his steps wobbly with indecision. Was it remorse waking within him, deep down in his dark soul? Or was it just fear of being found out? Back and forth he went, like some animal before the bars of his cage, feeling a sudden, growing need to flee, a need which was almost like physical pain, which made him feel as if he'd die if he didn't satisfy it. He had to run and run and run, get out of this prison where he'd just killed a man, and right now. Instead he collapsed, and for a long time remained sprawled on his belly in the long grass on the riverbank.

Maurice, revolted by it all, was having similar thoughts.

'Listen, I can't stay here any longer. I swear I'll go mad... I'm amazed that my body's held out, I'm not in too bad a shape. But mentally I'm going round the bend, quite round the bend... If you make me stay one more day in this hell, I'm lost... Please, I beg you, let's go, let's go, now!'

And he began explaining his far-fetched plans for escaping. They would swim across the Meuse and leap on the sentinels, strangling them with a bit of rope he had in his pocket; or they would hit them over the head with rocks; or else they would buy their silence and clothe themselves in their uniforms, so as to cross the Prussian lines.

'Hush, lad!' Jean kept saying in despair. 'It scares me to hear you saying such foolish things. Is it reasonable, all that? Or even possible?... We'll see, tomorrow. Hush, now!'

Even though his own heart was overflowing with anger and disgust, he hadn't lost his common sense as hunger weakened him, among the nightmares of this life which plumbed the very depths of human wretchedness. And as his companion's panic grew, and he spoke of throwing himself into the Meuse, he had to hold him back, even using violence, his eyes full of tears, pleading and scolding. Then, suddenly, he said,

'Hey! Look!'

He had heard a splash in the water. They saw Lapoulle, who'd removed his greatcoat to stop it hindering him and decided to let himself slip into the river; his shirt formed a conspicuous patch of white, moving downstream against the sliding black water. He swam, taking it gently, no doubt looking for a place to land; while over on the opposite bank the slender, immobile outlines of the sentinels were clearly visible. Suddenly a flash ripped through the night, and a shot went rattling right over to the rocks of Montimont. The water simply boiled up, as if a pair of wildly thrashing oars had slapped down hard on it. And that was all, the body of Lapoulle, the patch of white, began drifting downstream, limp and abandoned to the current.

The next day, which was a Saturday, Jean took Maurice back to the camp of the 106th at first light, hoping anew that they would leave today. No orders had been given, though, and it seemed as if the regiment had been forgotten. Many had already gone, the peninsula was emptying, and those left behind were sinking into a seriously ill state. For eight long days now insanity had been breeding and gathering inside this hell. When the rain had stopped and the sun come beating down, it had served only to exchange one torment for another. The extreme hot weather was finishing the men off and making the cases of dysentery look worryingly like an epidemic. The refuse and excrement of this entire, sick army fouled the air with a revolting stink. It was no longer possible to walk along the Meuse or the canal, such was the stench of the drowned horses and soldiers rotting among the grasses. And in the fields, the horses which had starved to death were starting to decompose, sending up such a violent whiff of plague that the Prussians, who were beginning to fear for their own men, had brought spades and pickaxes across and were forcing the prisoners to bury the bodies.

But at least that Saturday the food shortages came to an end. As there were now fewer of them and provisions were arriving from all over the place, the situation turned from one of utter destitution to one of over-abundance. They had as much bread, meat, and even wine as they could consume, and they ate from dawn till dusk, fit to burst. Night fell and they were still eating, and went on doing so until the next morning. Many died as a result.

During the daytime, Jean's sole concern was to keep an eye on Maurice, for he suspected him capable of the wildest excesses. He'd been drinking, and was talking of slapping a German officer in the face so that they'd take him away. That evening, since Jean had discovered an empty corner in a cellar in one of the Tour à Glaire's outbuildings, he thought it would be wise to bring his companion here to sleep, and that a good, peaceful night might calm him down a bit. But it was the worst night of their stay, a night filled with terror, and they didn't get a wink of sleep. The cellar was full of other soldiers, with two lying in the same corner as them, in the process of dying, washed out by dysentery; and as soon as it was fully dark they just wouldn't stop emitting low groans and inarticulate cries, a death agony which grew steadily louder and louder. Deep in the shadows it became so abominable that the others lying nearby, trying to sleep, lost their tempers, shouting to the dying men to shut up. But they couldn't hear them, the groaning went on, getting louder, drowning out everything else; while outside, the drunken shouts of their comrades carried over to them, still eating, unable to get their fill.

It was then that Maurice started to grow distressed. He'd tried to get away from the horrible groans of pain which were bringing him out in a clammy, anxious sweat; but as he was getting up, feeling his way along, he'd trodden on someone's limbs and he fell back down again, walled in with these dying men. He stopped even trying to get away. In his head he saw the whole terrifying disaster, from their departure from Rheims right up until the crushing defeat of Sedan. It seemed to him that the passion of the Châlons army finally came to an end that night, in the inky dark of this cellar, where two soldiers were groaning and stopping their comrades from sleeping. The army of despair, the sacrificial herd, sent into a holocaust, had paid for the sins of them all, each time it had stopped, paid with the red streams of its own blood. And now, its throat slit without glory, spat upon, it was being put through torture, suffering a punishment far crueller than any it deserved. It was too much to take, it made him seethe with anger, starved of justice, leaving him with a burning need to avenge himself on destiny.

When dawn broke, one of the soldiers was dead and the other still groaning.

'Come on, lad, quick,' said Jean, gently. 'It's best if we go out for some air.'

Outside, though, where it was already a fine, hot morning, once they'd followed the riverbank round and found themselves near the village of Iges Maurice got even more excited, shaking his fist over towards the vast, sunlit horizon of the battlefield, with Illy Plateau opposite, Saint-Menges to the left, and Garenne Wood on the right.

'No, no! I can't bear seeing that anymore, I can't bear it! That's what's breaking my heart, always seeing that in front of me, it's doing my head in... Take me away, take me away from here, right now!'

That day was Sunday again, and peals of bells came ringing over to them from Sedan, while in the distance they could already hear the sound of German music. But the 106th still had no orders to leave, and Jean, scared by Maurice's worsening delirium, decided to try out something he'd been mulling over since the day before. On the road, in front of the Prussian guardpost, preparations were being made for the departure of another regiment, the 5th infantry. Confusion reigned within the column, where an officer who spoke bad French was having trouble counting up the men. And so both of them, after ripping the collar and buttons off their uniforms so that their regiment number wouldn't give them away, made off amid the crush, crossed the bridge, and found themselves on the far side. No doubt Chouteau and Loubet had had the same idea, for they spotted them behind them, looking around nervously like murderers.

Oh! What a relief that first, happy minute was! Outside it was like being resurrected, seeing living light, a boundless sky, like a flowering renaissance of all their hopes. Whatever their misfortune might be at present, they no longer feared it, but laughed about it as they walked out of the terrifying nightmare of the Camp of Misery.

CHAPTER THREE

That morning, Jean and Maurice had heard the joyful calls of the bugles for the last time; and now they were on the march, heading for Germany among the herd of prisoners, preceded and brought up at the rear by platoons of Prussian soldiers, while others watched over them to left and right with fixed bayonets. At each guard post they passed, all they heard now were the German trumpets, with their shrill, sad tone.

Maurice was happy to see that the column was turning left and would pass through Sedan. Perhaps he'd be lucky enough to see his sister Henriette again. But the five kilometres which separated the Iges peninsula from the city sufficed to take the edge off his happiness at being out of the cesspit he'd been suffering in for the past nine days. This was a different sort of torture, this pathetic convoy of prisoners, unarmed soldiers, hands hanging loosely by their sides, being led like sheep, shuffling forward with hurried, frightened steps. Dressed in rags, soiled from being left in their own filth, emaciated from over a week of fasting, they looked no better than tramps, shady scroungers whom the police would have descended on and rounded up off the streets. From Torcy and beyond, as men began to stop and women started coming out into doorways to watch with an air of sombre commiseration, Maurice was overwhelmed by a rush of shame and bowed his head, a bitter taste in his mouth.

Jean, with his practical outlook and a thicker skin than Maurice, could only think about how stupid it had been of them to leave without bringing a loaf of bread each. In the panic of departure, they had even left without eating; and once again, hunger was weakening their stride. Other prisoners must have been in the same situation, for several held out money, begging people to sell them something. One, a very tall man who looked very ill, was waving a gold coin in the air, his long arm holding it out over the heads of the soldiers in the escort, in despair at finding nothing to buy. And it was then that Jean, who was keeping a lookout, noticed a bakery in the distance and a pile of about a dozen loaves. Immediately, before anyone else, he threw over a hundred sous and tried to get two of the loaves. Then as the Prussian walking near him shoved him brutally back, he was determined at least to get his money back. But the captain in charge of the column, a short bald man with an insolent face, was already running up. He raised the butt of his revolver above Jean's head and swore that the first one to move would get his skull split open. They all bowed their shoulders and lowered their eyes, while the march went on to the dull tramp of feet, like a quivering, submissive herd of animals.

'Oh! What I wouldn't give to slap him!' muttered a seething Maurice. 'Smash his teeth in with the back of my hand!'

After that he just couldn't bear the sight of this captain and his haughty face that deserved to be slapped. Moreover, they were entering Sedan and crossing the Pont de Meuse; and the scenes of brutality started again, getting more and more frequent. One woman who tried to kiss a very young sergeant, probably his mother, was shoved aside so roughly with a rifle butt that she fell down. On the Place Turenne it was the townsfolk who were jostled because they were throwing provisions to the prisoners. In the Grande-Rue one prisoner slipped over trying to take a bottle that a lady was holding out to him, and he was kicked back onto his feet. After watching these wretched, defeated cattle tramping through for the past week, being driven along with sticks, Sedan still wasn't used to it, and with each fresh convoy that passed it grew restless, stirred by a silent fever of pity and revolt.

Meanwhile Jean was also wondering about Henriette; and suddenly he thought of Delaherche. He nudged his friend.

'Hey? Keep an eye out in a moment, in case we go down their street!'

And in fact, as they entered the Rue Maqua, they noticed several people in the distance leaning out of one of the monumental factory windows. Then they recognized them as Delaherche and his wife Gilberte, leaning on their elbows, with the tall, severe face of Madame Delaherche behind them. They had loaves of bread and the mill owner was tossing them to the starving men holding out their trembling, imploring hands.

Maurice had immediately noticed that his sister wasn't there; while Jean, worried to see the loaves flying through the air, was afraid that there wouldn't be any left for them. He waved his hand, shouting,

'Over here! Over here!'

It was a moment of almost joyous surprise for the Delaherche family. Their faces, all pale with pity, lit up, and they were so happy at the encounter that they couldn't help waving madly. And Gilberte insisted on throwing the last loaf into Jean's arms herself, which she did with such adorable clumsiness that she burst out into pretty laughter.

Unable to stop, Maurice turned round and shouted in a worried, questioning voice,

'Henriette? What about Henriette?'

Delaherche gave a lengthy reply. But his voice was drowned beneath the tramp of feet. He must have realized that the young man hadn't heard him, for he used more signs, repeating one in particular, pointing south. The column was already turning into the Rue du Ménil and the factory façade disappeared from view, along with the three heads leaning out, while one hand still waved a handkerchief.

'What did he say?' asked Jean.

Maurice, in torment, was looking back in vain.

'I don't know, I didn't understand... Now I'll be all worried until I get news of her.'

And on they trudged, the Prussians hurried the march on with their brutal, conquerors' spirit, and the herd left Sedan by the Porte du Ménil, stretched out into a long line which hastened along, like sheep afraid of the dogs.

When they passed through Bazeilles Jean and Maurice thought about Weiss, looking for the ashes of the little house which he had so valiantly defended. Back in the Camp of Misery they'd been told stories of how the village had been destroyed, with the fires and the massacres; and what they saw went way beyond the abominations they had imagined. Twelve days on, the piles of rubble were still smoking. Crumbling walls had given way, and only ten houses remained intact. What comforted them a little, though, was when they came upon carts full of Bavarian helmets and rifles, gathered up after the fight. The proof that they had killed a lot of these throat-cutters and arsonists came as some relief.

It was in Douzy that the main halt was to take place, to allow the men to eat. Not that they got there without suffering. The prisoners tired very rapidly, exhausted by the days without food. The ones who'd stuffed themselves the day before were now feeling faint and heavy, their legs giving way under them; for their greed, far from restoring their lost strength, had only made them weaker. Consequently when they stopped in a meadow, on the left of the village, the wretched men just collapsed onto the grass, lacking the courage to eat. There wasn't any wine, and charitably minded women who tried to bring them some bottles were chased off by the guards. One of them, taking fright, fell over and dislocated her ankle; and there were cries and tears and utterly appalling scenes while the Prussians, who had confiscated the bottles, drank them. The peasants' tender pity for the poor soldiers being led away into captivity showed itself with every step they took, although they were said to be harsh and hostile towards the generals. Right there in Douzy a few days before, the locals had booed a passing convoy of generals who were giving themselves up, as promised, at Pont-à-Mousson. The roads weren't safe for officers: men in smocks, escaped soldiers, deserters maybe, leapt on them with pitchforks, trying to slaughter them, calling them cowards and traitors, the myth of treachery that, even twenty years on, would mean that any officers who had worn the epaulette were still condemned to loathing in this part of the country.

Maurice and Jean ate half their bread, which they were lucky enough to wash down with a few drops of brandy, thanks to a kindly farmer who had managed to fill up their flask. What was awful, though, was setting off again afterwards. They were supposed to be sleeping in Mouzon, and even though it was a short march away, the effort required seemed too much for them. The men couldn't get up without crying out, for even the shortest rest made their tired limbs stiffen up. Many had bleeding feet and took off their boots so that they could carry on. They were still ravaged by dysentery; one man fell in the first kilometre and had to be sat up against a mound of earth. Further on two more collapsed at the foot of a hedge, where it wasn't until evening that an old woman discovered them. All were swaying on their feet, leaning on sticks which the Prussians, perhaps mockingly, had allowed them to cut on the edge of a small wood. They were just a rabble of beggars, covered in wounds, haggard and out of breath. And the violence began again as anyone who strayed out of line, even to answer a call of nature, was beaten back into the herd with sticks. At the tail-end the escort platoon was under orders to prod on any stragglers with bayonets in their backs. When one sergeant refused to go any further, the captain ordered two of his men to take him

under the arms and drag him along, until the wretched man consented to walk again. The captain was the worst torment of all,
that face that deserved to be slapped, that little bald officer who
abused the fact that he spoke very good French to insult the
prisoners in their own language, using short, stinging phrases like
cracks of a whip.

'Oh!' Maurice repeated angrily. 'If only I could hold him down
and draw out all his blood, drop by drop!'

He had no strength left at all, even sicker from repressed anger
than physical exhaustion. Everything infuriated him, even the shrill
calls of the Prussian trumpets, which so made his flesh crawl that he
could have howled like an animal. He'd never get to the end of this
cruel journey without getting his head smashed in. Even now, when
they passed through the tiniest hamlets, he already suffered horribly
when he saw the women looking at him with deep pity. What would
it be like when they entered Germany, and entire populations of
towns jostled to greet him with an insulting leer as he went past?
And he conjured up visions of the cattle trucks they were going to be
piled into, the revolting conditions and torments of the journey, their
sad existence inside the fortresses, beneath the snow-laden winter
skies. No! Not that! He'd rather die right now, he'd rather risk
leaving his carcass at some turning in the road, on French soil, than
rot away over there, down in some dark blockhouse, maybe for
months on end!

'Listen,' he said to Jean in a low voice as he marched beside him,
'we'll wait until we're going past the edge of a wood, and then leap
into the trees and run for it... The Belgian border's not far off, we're
sure to find someone who'll lead us there.'

Jean shuddered, of clearer and cooler mind, despite the feeling of
revolt which was beginning to make him dream of escaping too.

'Are you completely mad? They'll shoot, and then we'll both be
dead.'

But Maurice waved him off and said that they might well miss,
and anyway, even if they did die, so what!

'Fine!' continued Jean. 'But what are we to do afterwards, in these
uniforms? You know very well the place is full of Prussian checkpoints. We'd need different clothes at least... It's too dangerous, lad,
I'd never dream of letting you do anything so daft.'

And he had to hold him back, seizing him by the arm, pulling him towards him, as if they were holding each other up, while he continued to calm him down, in his gruff, tender way.

Just then the sound of whispering behind their backs made them turn their heads. It was Chouteau and Loubet, who'd left the Iges peninsula that morning at the same time as them, and whom they'd avoided up until now. Now the two rogues were marching on their heels. Chouteau must have overheard Maurice and his plan to escape through a copse, for he was making it his own. He murmured to the back of their necks,

'Tell you what, we're in on it with you. Buggering off's a great idea. Some of the comrades have gone already—surely we're not going to let ourselves get dragged like dogs all the way to their country, the pigs... Hey? How about it, the four of us, giving it a go?'

Maurice got all fired up again, and Jean had to turn and say to the tempter,

'If you're in such a hurry, why don't you go on ahead... What do you expect to happen, anyway?'

Faced with the corporal's direct gaze, Chouteau was somewhat put off. He let slip the real reason for his insistence.

'Lord! If there's four of us, it'll be easier... One or two of us are sure to make it.'

Then, shaking his head vigorously, Jean refused outright. He didn't trust the kind gentleman, as he put it, he was afraid some sort of treachery might be afoot. He had to exercise all his authority over Maurice to prevent him giving in, for just then an opportunity presented itself as they walked past a very dense little wood, separated from the road only by a field strewn with undergrowth. Wouldn't they be saved if they just went galloping across that field and disappeared into the bushes?

Up until then, Loubet had said nothing. His worried nose sniffed the wind, the shrewd lad's keen eyes watching out for the right moment, quite determined that he wasn't going to rot away in Germany. He must have trusted his legs and his cunning, which had always got him out of trouble in the past. And all at once he made up his mind.

'Oh, hell! I've had enough, I'm off!'

He'd already taken a bound into the neighbouring field when Chouteau copied him, galloping off beside him. Immediately two Prussians from the escort set off in pursuit, without it occurring to either of them to stop them with a bullet. And the scene was so brief that at first they didn't realize it was happening. Loubet, swerving through the undergrowth, was sure to get away while Chouteau, not so agile, was already on the point of being caught. But with a supreme effort the latter closed the distance between them and threw himself between his comrade's legs, pulling him to the ground; and while the two Prussians flung themselves on the man on the ground to hold him down, the other jumped into the woods and vanished. A few shots rang out as they remembered their weapons. There was even an attempt to hunt him down through the trees, but it was futile.

Meanwhile, on the ground, the two soldiers were laying into Loubet. The captain was outraged and rushed forward, talking about making an example of him; and with this encouragement, they carried on kicking and striking him with their rifle butts with such force that, by the time the unlucky man was picked up off the ground, he had a broken arm and a fractured skull. He died before they reached Mouzon, in a a little cart belonging to a peasant who'd been kind enough to take him.

'You see?' was all Jean would murmur in Maurice's ear.

With a single glance back at the impenetrable wood both men let show their anger at the bastard who was now running free; while they ended up feeling full of pity for his victim, the poor devil; sure, he'd been a bit of a worthless good-for-nothing, but he'd been a happy fellow all the same, one who could look after himself and wasn't stupid. It just went to prove that no matter how clever you were, you could still be had one day!

In Mouzon, in spite of this dreadful lesson, the idea of running away began to haunt Maurice yet again. They'd arrived so exhausted that the Prussians had been obliged to help the prisoners to put up the few tents at their disposal. The encampment was near the town, on low, marshy ground; and the worst of it was that another convoy had camped there the night before and the ground was invisible beneath a layer of waste; it was an absolute cesspit, revoltingly filthy. In order to protect themselves they had to lay down large, flat stones which they luckily found nearby. The evening, in any case, wasn't so rough, the Prussians had eased off somewhat since the captain had disappeared, probably staying at an inn somewhere. At first the soldiers tolerated it when children threw fruit to the prisoners, tossing apples and pears over their heads. Then they allowed locals to swarm into the camp, and soon there was a crowd of improvised traders, men and women dealing in bread, wine, even cigars. All those with money ate, drank, and smoked. In the pale twilight, it was like a corner of some travelling fair, bustling with noise.

Behind their tent, however, Maurice was getting het up, telling Jean over and over again,

'I can't take any more, I'm off as soon as it's dark... Tomorrow we'll be moving away from the border and it'll be too late.'

'Fine, then, let's go!' said Jean eventually, his own resistance worn down, giving in to the haunting idea of fleeing. 'We'll see whether we get to pay with our hides.'

But from then on he began looking closely at the traders around them. Some of his comrades had got hold of smocks and trousers, and the rumour was going round that kind-hearted locals had set up veritable clothes shops to make it easier for prisoners to escape. And almost at once his attention was drawn to a pretty girl, a tall, blonde sixteen-year-old with magnificent eyes, who was carrying three loaves of bread in a basket. She wasn't shouting out her wares like all the others, and had an engaging, nervous smile on her face, her steps halting. He stared at her and their eyes met, fixed for a moment on one another. Then she drew near, with the embarrassed smile of a beautiful girl putting herself forward.

'Would you like some bread?'

He didn't reply, but made a slight, questioning gesture. Then as she nodded her head he ventured, in a very low voice,

'Are there clothes in there?'

'Yes, under the loaves.'

And she began to shout out her wares very loudly: 'Bread! Bread! Who wants to buy some bread?' When Maurice tried to slip her twenty francs, however, she sharply drew back her hand and ran off, leaving them the basket. They saw her turn round once more, though, her beautiful eyes sending them a look full of laughing, tender emotion.

Once they had hold of the basket Jean and Maurice became extremely anxious. They'd moved away from their tent, and were in such a panic that they were quite unable to find their way back to it. Where could they go? How could they change their clothes? It seemed to them that everyone was staring at the basket, which Jean was carrying awkwardly, and that they could all see clear as day what it contained. Finally they made up their minds, and entered the first empty tent they could find, where each frantically put on a pair of trousers and a smock, hiding their uniforms beneath the loaves of bread. And they left the whole lot behind. However, they'd only been able to find one woollen hat, which Jean had made Maurice put on. He himself was left bare-headed, which made it even more dangerous, and he thought he'd never get away. So he hung on, searching for something to put on his head, when it occurred to him to buy the hat of a very grubby old man selling cigars.

'Three sous apiece, five sous the pair, Brussels cigars!'

Since the battle of Sedan there had been no customs controls on the border and floods of Belgians had been coming through quite freely; the raggedy old man had managed to make a very handsome profit; not that this stopped him from making wild demands once he realized why they wanted to buy his hat off him, a greasy felt object full of holes. He would only part with it for two five-franc pieces, groaning that he was sure to catch cold.

In the meantime Jean had had another idea, to buy up his stock as well, the three dozen cigars he still had left. And without pausing, the hat pulled down over his eyes, he shouted,

'Three sous the pair, three sous the pair, Brussels cigars!'

This time, they were on their way. He signalled to Maurice to walk on ahead. The latter chanced upon an umbrella lying on the ground; and since it was spitting slightly, he casually opened it as they approached the line of sentinels.

'Three sous the pair, three sous the pair, Brussels cigars!'

In a few minutes, Jean had been relieved of his wares. People pushed forward, laughing: now here was a reasonable man, who wasn't out to rob poor folk! Drawn by the bargain, Prussians came over, too, and he had to do business with them. He had manœuvred so as to be able to cross the guarded fence, and he sold his last two cigars to a fat, bearded sergeant who didn't speak a word of French.

'Don't walk so fast, for God's sake!' Jean kept saying to Maurice's back. 'You'll get us caught.'

In spite of themselves, their legs were running away with them. It cost them a huge effort to stop for a moment at the corner of two roads, where groups of people were standing outside an inn. There were townsfolk chatting away peacefully with German soldiers; and they pretended to listen to them, even risked saying a few words themselves about the rain which could well set in for the whole night. One man, a fattish gentleman, kept staring at them, making them shake. Then, as he smiled so kindly at them, they ventured to say, very softly,

'Sir, is the road into Belgium guarded?'

'Yes, but first go through these woods, then turn left, across the fields.'

In the woods, in the great, dark silence of the motionless trees, when they could no longer hear a single sound and nothing stirred and they thought they were safe, an extraordinary rush of emotion flung them into each other's arms. Maurice cried, sobbing heavily, while tears ran slowly down Jean's cheeks. It was the sense of release after their long ordeal, the joy of telling themselves that the pain might be about to show them some mercy. And they clung to each other in an endless embrace, brothers bonded by all they had suffered together; and the kiss they exchanged then seemed to be the sweetest and the strongest of their entire lives, a kiss unlike any they had ever received from a woman, a kiss of immortal friendship and absolute certitude that their two hearts would from now on be one, for ever and ever.

'My boy,' said Jean in a trembling voice, when they had pulled apart, 'it's good to have got this far, but we're not there yet... We should try and get our bearings.'

Even though Maurice wasn't familiar with this part of the frontier, he swore that all they had to do was carry straight on. So the two of them, one behind the other, slipped through, walking carefully, right to the edge of the copse. There, recalling the directions given by the obliging gentleman, they tried to turn left to cut through the stubble-fields. But just as they came to a road lined with poplar trees they spotted the fire of a Prussian checkpoint blocking the way. A sentry's bayonet was gleaming, soldiers were chatting and finishing off their soup. They doubled back, diving deep into the woods, terrified of being pursued. They thought they could hear voices and footsteps, they beat their way through the thicket for nearly an hour, becoming completely disorientated, going round in circles, sometimes heading off at a gallop like animals fleeing through the bushes, and sometimes standing motionless, sweating with fear, before motionless oak trees which they had mistaken for Prussians. At last they came out onto to the poplar-lined road once more, ten paces away from the guard post, near the soldiers, who were happily warming themselves by the fire.

'Rotten luck!' groaned Maurice. 'This wood's got a spell on it.'

This time, though, someone heard them. Branches had snapped and stones been turned. And when they began to run off when challenged by the sentry, the guards picked up their weapons and rounds were fired, riddling the copse with bullets.

'Jesus Christ!' swore Jean in a muffled voice, suppressing a cry of pain.

A bullet had whipped across his left calf, and the force of the blow had flung him against a tree.

'You hit?' asked Maurice anxiously.

'Yes, in the leg, I'm done for!'

They were still listening, panting, dreading the noise of someone crashing along in pursuit on their heels. But the shots had ceased, and everything was still again, amid a dead, quivering silence which was settling back over the woods. Obviously, the guards couldn't be bothered to venture into the trees.

Jean, forcing himself to get back up, stifled a moan. Maurice gave him support.

'Can't you walk?'

'I don't think so!'

He was overcome by anger, despite his usual calm. He clenched his fists and could have hit himself.

'Oh! Jesus bloody Christ! How unlucky can you get! Getting shot in the foot just when you need to make a run for it! It stinks, I tell you!... Carry on without me, go on!'

Maurice merely replied brightly,

'Don't be stupid!'

He took his arm and helped him along, both of them hurrying to get away. After a few painful paces, which cost them a truly heroic effort, they stopped, nervous again, noticing a house ahead of them, like a small farm on the edge of the woods. There were no lights shining in the windows and the gate into the courtyard was wide open, leading to the dark, empty building. And when they'd plucked up the courage to walk into the courtyard, they were astonished to find that it contained a horse, all saddled up, without any clue as to why he was standing there. Perhaps his master was coming back, maybe he was lying behind some bush with a hole in his head. They never did find out.

However, Maurice had suddenly thought of a plan, and it seemed to cheer him up considerably.

'Listen, the border's too far off and anyway, we'd definitely need a guide... Whereas if we went to Remilly, to Uncle Fouchard's place, I know I could get you there with my eyes shut, I know all the lanes and byways by heart... Hey? It's an idea—I'll help you up on this horse, and Uncle Fouchard will take us in for sure.'

First he wanted to examine the leg. There were two holes—the bullet must have exited after breaking the tibia. The bleeding was slight, and he made do with bandaging the calf up tightly with his handkerchief.

'Carry on without me!' repeated Jean.

'Shut up, don't be stupid!'

Once Jean was firmly ensconced in the saddle, Maurice took the horse's bridle and they set off. It must have been nearly eleven o'clock, and he was fairly sure of making the journey in three hours, even if they proceeded only at walking pace. But an unforeseen problem caused him a moment of despair: how were they to cross the Meuse and get onto the left bank? The Pont du Mouzon was certainly under guard. Eventually he remembered that there was a ferry downstream in Villers; and trusting to luck they made for the village, across the meadows and ploughed fields on the right bank, hoping to find fortune on their side at last. At first everything went quite well, they only had to avoid a single cavalry patrol, staying motionless for a quarter of an hour in the shadow of a wall. It had started raining again, and the problem was that for Maurice, it was becoming very difficult to walk, forced to squelch around in the waterlogged ground alongside the horse; luckily the animal was an extremely docile, good-natured creature. In Villers, luck did indeed turn out to be on their side: the ferry, which had only just taken a Bavarian officer across at this late hour, was able to take them on board straight away and set them down on the far bank without further ado. The danger and exhaustion didn't start until they got to the village, where they almost fell into the hands of the sentries placed at intervals all along the Remilly road. Once again they dived through fields and down random tracks and narrow, overgrown paths. The slightest obstacles forced them to make enormous detours. They clambered over hedges and ditches, beat a path through impenetrable thickets. Jean, who was becoming feverish beneath the drizzle, had slumped across the saddle, half-fainting, both hands clutching at the horse's mane; while Maurice, who was now holding the bridle in his right hand, had to hold him by the legs to stop him sliding off. For over a league and more than two hours, the endless journey went on and on, with sudden jolts and bumps and losses of balance, when every minute beast and men risked falling flat on their faces. The convoy was a picture of utter misery, covered in mud, the horse trembling on its feet, the man it was carrying lying inert, as if a final hiccup had carried him off, while the other, distraught and frantic, kept on going, sustained only by his sense of brotherly charity. The day began to dawn and it might have been about five o'clock when they finally got to Remilly.

In the yard on his little farm overlooking the village, at the point where the Haraucourt Pass emerged, old Fouchard was loading two sheep into his cart which had been killed the day before. The sight of his nephew with such a pitiful entourage sent him into such a state that after the preliminary explanations he cried out brutally,

'What! Keep you and your friend here?... And get into all sorts of trouble with the Prussians? Oh no, I don't think so! I'd rather drop dead!'

However, he didn't dare stop Maurice and Prosper from getting Jean down off the horse and laying him on the large kitchen table. Silvine ran off to fetch her own bolster, which she slipped under the head of the wounded, still unconscious man. But the old man began moaning, infuriated at the sight of this man on his table, saying that it wasn't a good place for him, and asking why they didn't take him to the hospital straight away, seeing as they were fortunate enough to have one in Remilly, near the church, in the old schoolhouse, housed in the remains of a former convent, and where the hall was spacious and just right.

'To hospital!' cried Maurice in his turn. 'So that the Prussians can send him to Germany once he's better, since all the wounded belong to them!... Are you making fun of me, Uncle? I didn't bring him all the way here just to give him up to them!'

Things started to get nasty and the uncle was talking about kicking them out, when Henriette's name came into it.

'Henriette? What do you mean?' asked the young man.

And he eventually found out that his sister had been in Remilly for two days now, so mortally stricken with grief that to remain in Sedan, where she'd lived so happily, had become quite unbearable for her. A meeting with Doctor Dalichamp from Raucourt, with whom she was acquainted, had made her decide to come and live with old Fouchard, in a little room, so that she could devote herself entirely to tending to the injured at the hospital nearby. It was the only thing, she said, which could take her mind off things. She paid for her food and lodging, and on the farm she was the source of a thousand little comforts which made the old man look upon her with indulgence. Things were always sweet, when he was making money.

'Oh! So my sister's here!' repeated Maurice. 'That's what Monsieur Delaherche was trying to tell me when he waved at me like that, and I didn't understand!... Well, then! If she's here, that settles it, we're staying.'

In spite of his tiredness he was determined to go and get her there and then from the hospital, where she had spent the night; and his uncle was getting angry now because he couldn't set off with his cart and two dead sheep and ply his travelling butcher's trade, so long as this blasted business of the wounded man who'd suddenly been foisted on him wasn't settled.

When Maurice brought Henriette back they came upon old Fouchard, carefully examining the horse which Prosper had led into the stable. The animal was tired, but strong as an ox, and Fouchard liked what he saw! Laughing, the young man told him he could have it as a present. Henriette, for her part, took him aside and explained to him that Jean would pay his way, that she would look after him herself and tend to him in the little room behind the stable, where they could be sure no Prussians would come looking for him. And the old boy, sullen and still unconvinced that he'd make any real profit out of it in the end, nonetheless ended up climbing into his cart and setting off, leaving her free to act as she saw fit.

So in a few minutes, helped by Silvine and Prosper, Henriette arranged the room, had Jean brought in and put him to bed in fresh sheets, while he gave no sign of life other than vague mumblings. He opened his eyes and looked around, without appearing to see anyone. Maurice was finishing off a glass of wine and some leftover meat, suddenly shattered, exhausted now that he had relaxed, when Doctor Dalichamp arrived, as he did every morning on his way to the hospital; and the young man found the strength to follow him and his sister to the sick man's bedside, anxious to find out how bad it was.

The doctor was a short man with a big, round head and greying hair and side-whiskers. His red face had grown tough, like a peasant's, from spending all his time out in the open, always on his way to relieve suffering somewhere; while his lively eyes, stubborn nose and kindly mouth told of a whole life spent helping others, a bit barmy sometimes, and no medical genius, but someone whom long experience had made into an excellent healer.

When he'd examined Jean, who was still dozing, he murmured,

'I'm afraid it might become necessary to amputate.'

This was a blow for Maurice and Henriette. However, he added,

'It may just be possible to save his leg, but it would need a lot of care, and it would take a very long time... At the moment, he's so physically and morally depressed that the only thing to do is to let him sleep... We'll see tomorrow.'

Then, after applying a dressing, he turned his attention to Maurice, whom he'd known as a child.

'And you, my fine fellow, would be better off in bed than on that chair.'

The young man stared straight ahead of him, eyes lost in the distance, as if he hadn't heard him. In the dizziness of his fatigue a fever was rising again, an extraordinarily over-excited nervousness, all the suffering and all the revolt which had built up since the beginning of the campaign. The sight of his friend lying there, dying, and the sense of his own defeat, naked, unarmed, good for nothing, the thought that so many heroic efforts had come to such distress, threw him into a frenetic need to rebel against destiny. Finally he spoke.

'No, no! It isn't over. No! I have to go... No! Now that he's going to be here for weeks, maybe months, I can't just stay here, I want to go right away... Don't you think so, Doctor? You'll help me, you'll give me the means to escape and get back to Paris, won't you?'

Trembling, Henriette took him into her arms.

'What are you saying? Weak as you are, and after all that suffering! I'll keep you here, I'll never, ever let you leave!... Haven't you paid your debt? Think of me, too, you'd be leaving me on my own, and now you're all I have.'

Their tears mingled. They kissed each other, distraught, with that adoration and tenderness which twins have for one another, with a closer bond, as if created in the womb. But he just got more worked up.

'Honestly, I have to go... They're waiting for me, I'd die of worry if I didn't go... You can't imagine how it churns me up inside when I think of having to sit and do nothing. I tell you, it can't end like this, we have to avenge ourselves, against whom or what, I don't know, but we must avenge ourselves for such tragedy, if we're to have the courage to carry on!'

Doctor Dalichamp, who'd been watching the scene with keen interest, made a sign to Henriette not to reply. Once Maurice had slept no doubt he'd be calmer; and he slept all day and all the following night, for over twenty hours, without moving so much as a toe. But when he awoke the next morning, his determination to leave reappeared, unshakeable. He wasn't feverish any more, but his mood was gloomy and worried, impatient to escape from all the temptations to live peacefully which he could feel around him. In tears, his sister realized that she shouldn't insist. And when Doctor Dalichamp called, he promised to help him to escape, thanks to the papers of a hospital aide who'd just died in Raucourt. Maurice would don the grey smock and red cross armband and pass via Belgium, from where he could get back into Paris, which was still open.

That day he didn't leave the farm, hiding, waiting for night. He hardly opened his mouth, except to try to persuade Prosper to come with him.

'Come on, aren't you tempted to go back and see the Prussians?'

The former African Chasseur, finishing off some bread and cheese, raised his knife in the air.

'Oh! From what we've seen of them, it's hardly worth it!... If cavalry's no good for anything, now, except getting killed once it's all over, why should I want to go back?... Goodness, no! They've already done more than enough to annoy me, by not giving me anything decent to do!'

There was a pause, and then he spoke again, no doubt to stifle the uneasiness he felt in his soldier's heart.

'And anyway, there's too much work to be done here, now. There's all the ploughing about to start, and then it'll be time for sowing. Got to think of the land, too, haven't we? Because it's all very well to go off fighting, but what would become of us, if we stopped ploughing the fields?... I can't just abandon the work, you see. It's not that I think old Fouchard'll be reasonable, because I doubt I'll ever see the colour of his money; but the animals have started to get fond of me; and this morning, by God! while I was up there in the Vieux-Clos field, I was looking at Sedan in the distance, damn the place, and I didn't half feel reassured, being up here all alone, out in the sun, with my animals, pushing the plough!'

As soon as night fell, Doctor Dalichamp was there with his carriage. He insisted on driving Maurice all the way to the border himself. Old Fouchard, happy to see at least one of them pushing off, went down to the road to keep a look out, and make sure that there weren't any patrols on the prowl; while Silvine finished mending the old hospital smock, with the armband bearing the red cross sewn on its sleeve. Before they left the doctor, taking another look at Jean's leg, couldn't promise that it could be saved. The wounded man was still lying dead to the world, not recognizing anyone, not speaking. And Maurice was about to go without having said goodbye to him when, bending over to kiss him, he saw his eyes open very wide, his lips moved, and he said in a weak voice,

'Are you leaving?'

Then, as everyone stood astonished,

'Yes, I heard you, while I couldn't move... In that case, take all the money. Feel in my trouser pocket.'

They had about two hundred francs each left from the regiment's money, which they'd shared between them.

'The money!' exclaimed Maurice. 'But you need it more than I do, I've got both my legs! With two hundred francs, I've enough to get back to Paris, and it'll cost me nothing at all to get done in after that... Goodbye, anyway, old chap, and thank you for all the good, wise things you've done, because without you I'd be lying on the edge of some field by now, for sure, like a dead dog.'

Jean signalled him to hush.

'You don't owe me a thing, we're quits... I'm the one the Prussians would have picked up back there, if you hadn't carried me off on your back. And yesterday you rescued me from their clutches again... You've paid twice over, it should be my turn now, to give up my life... Oh! I'll be in a bad way, not being with you any more!'

His voice was quivering and tears came to his eyes.

'Kiss me, lad.'

They kissed, and it was like back in the woods the day before; at the heart of his embrace lay the brotherly love born of the dangers they had faced together, those few weeks of heroic life they had shared, uniting them more closely than years of ordinary friendship could have done. The days without bread, the nights without sleep, the excessive tiredness, death ever present, were all part of their emotion. Can two hearts ever start beating separately again, once they've been so fused together by the giving of each to the other? But while the kiss exchanged in the shadows of the trees had been full of the new hope which escape was opening up to them, this one, now, shuddered with the fears that parting brings. Would they see each other again, one day? And how? In what circumstances—joy or sorrow? Doctor Dalichamp had already got back into his carriage and was calling to Maurice. At last he embraced his sister Henriette, with all his soul, as she gazed at him through silent tears, pale beneath her widow's black mourning.

'It's my brother I'm entrusting to you... Look after him, love him like I love him!'

CHAPTER FOUR

It was a large, tiled room with plain whitewashed walls, which had formerly been used to store fruit. The sweet smell of apples and pears still lingered; and the only pieces of furniture were an iron bedstead, a white wooden table, and two chairs, as well as an old, deep-sided walnut cupboard full of all sorts of things. The atmosphere, though, was one of deep, soothing calm, where only the muffled sounds from the nearby stable could be heard, the faint clicks of clogs and the lowing of the animals. Through the south-facing window the bright sunshine poured in. All that could be seen was the edge of a hillside, a cornfield bordering a little wood. And this mysterious, secluded room was so well hidden from view that no one on earth could have suspected it existed.

Henriette sorted things out straight away: it was understood that, in order to avoid arousing suspicion, only she and the doctor would go in to Jean. Silvine was never to go in, unless she herself summoned her. Very early in the morning the cleaning was done by the two women; and then the door stayed shut all day, as if walled up. At night, if the sick man needed anyone, he had only to knock on the wall, for Henriette's room was next door. And so Jean suddenly found himself cut off from the rest of the world after weeks of violent crowding, seeing only this young woman, who was so gentle and whose light footsteps made no sound. He saw her again as he'd seen her that first time, back in Sedan, like an apparition, with her slightly over-large mouth, her delicate features, and that fine hair the colour of ripe oats, tending him with an air of infinite kindness.

For the first few days the sick man's fever was so high that Henriette rarely left his side. Each morning, as he was passing, Doctor Dalichamp came in, on the pretext of collecting her and taking her to the hospital with him, and he would examine Jean and change his dressings. Since the bullet had exited after fracturing the tibia, he was astonished to see what a bad state the wound was in, and he was afraid that the presence of a splinter which the probe failed to locate might force him to have to shorten the bone. He had spoken to Jean about this, who'd been appalled by the thought of one leg being shorter than the other, and making him lame; oh no! He'd rather die than remain a cripple. And so, keeping an eye on the wound, the doctor made do with dressing it with lint soaked in olive oil and phenic acid and inserting a drain, a rubber tube, at its base to remove the pus. But he did warn him that if he didn't operate, it could take an extremely long time to heal. By the second week, though, the fever had begun to subside and his condition improved, as long as he stayed absolutely still.

So Jean and Henriette's intimacy became routine. Habits developed between them, and it seemed as if they had never lived any other way, and that they would always live like this. She spent with him all the time she didn't spend at the hospital, making sure that he ate and drank regularly, helping him to turn over, her grip stronger than one would have suspected to see her slender arms. Sometimes they would chat together, but most often they said nothing at all, especially in the beginning. But they never seemed to get bored, and it was an extremely gentle way of life, surrounded by such restfulness, with him still battle-torn and she dressed in mourning, heartbroken by her recent loss. At first he'd felt a little awkward, for he was well aware that she was above him, almost a lady, in fact, while he was nothing but a peasant and a soldier. He barely knew how to read or write. Then he was gradually reassured, seeing that she treated him without any pride, as her equal, and this made him bold enough to show her his true self, intelligent in his own way, full of calm common sense. What was more, he himself was surprised to find that he felt somehow finer and lighter, full of new ideas: perhaps the abominable life he'd been leading for the past two months had made him emerge refined by all the physical and moral suffering. However, what finally won him over was the realization that she didn't really know much more than he did. When she was still very young, after her mother's death, she'd become a sort of Cinderella, the little mother in charge of her three men, as she put it, grandfather, father, and brother, and she hadn't had time for learning. Reading, writing, a little spelling and arithmetic, yes, but much more than that was quite beyond her. And she no longer intimidated him, and the only thing that placed her so far above the rest was knowing how extraordinarily good and unusually courageous she was, beneath that exterior of the self-effacing little woman who was happy doing life's lowly chores.

They got on together straight away, talking about Maurice. If she did so much for him, it was because he was Maurice's friend, his brother, the brave, helpful man to whom she in turn was repaying a debt from her heart. As she got to know him better she was filled with gratitude and growing affection for this man who was simple and good, with a solid way of thinking; and as she tended to him like a child, he too contracted a debt of infinite gratitude, and could have kissed her hands for every cup of broth she brought him. The bond of tender sympathy between them grew closer each day in the profound solitude they inhabited, troubled by the same griefs. When they had exhausted his memories, those details she tirelessly requested of their painful march from Rheims to Sedan, they would always come back to the same question: what was Maurice doing now? Why didn't he write? Was Paris really under so tight a blockade that they should receive no more news? So far they'd only had one letter from him, postmarked Rouen, three days after his departure, in which he explained in a few lines how he'd come to stop off in the city following a long detour, in order to reach Paris. And now they had heard nothing for a week, total silence.

In the morning, once Doctor Dalichamp had dressed the wound, he liked to stay on for a few minutes. Sometimes he even came back in the evening and would stay even longer; he was their sole link with the world, that vast outside world, turned upside down by catastrophes. News came only through him, his heart was ardently patriotic, overflowing with anger and sorrow at each defeat. And so he rarely talked of anything but the invasion of floods of Prussians, who since Sedan had been gradually spreading all over France, like a black tide. Each day brought with it new grief, and he would sit on one of the two chairs by the bed, overcome, talking about how the situation was getting worse and worse, gesturing with trembling hands. Often his pockets were stuffed full of Belgian newspapers, which he would leave behind. At several weeks' remove, the echo of each disaster would thus reach this remote room, and the two poor, suffering beings who found themselves enclosed in it were brought even closer together.

So it was that Henriette, reading from old newspapers,* recounted to Jean the events of Metz, the great, heroic battles which had stopped and started again three times, a day apart. It was already five weeks since they had happened, but it was the first he'd heard of them, and he listened, his heart heavy as he recognized the same

misery and defeats that he himself had gone through. In the quivering silence of the room Henriette, in her slightly sing-song voice, like
a schoolgirl concentrating hard, clearly picked out each phrase, and
the woeful story unfolded. After Frœschwiller, after Spickeren, at
the time when a crushed 1st Corps was dragging the 5th with it into
rout, the other corps, spaced from Metz to Bitche, were hesitating,
falling back in consternation at these disasters, and finally concentrating in front of the fortified camp on the right bank of the
Moselle. But what a lot of precious time had been lost, instead of
making a hasty retreat back to Paris—a retreat which was now going
to become so difficult! The Emperor had had to cede command to
Marshal Bazaine, of whom they expected victory. So, on the 14th,
came Borny, where the army was attacked just as it was finally making up its mind to move on to the left bank, facing two German
armies, first the Steinmetz army menacing the fortified camp, standing motionless opposite, then that of Frederick Charles, which had
crossed the river upstream and was making its way along the left
bank to cut Bazaine off from the rest of France; Borny was where the
first shots hadn't rung out until three o'clock in the afternoon, Borny
was the victory with no tomorrow, leaving the French corps masters
of their positions, but immobilizing them astride the Moselle, while
the wheeling manœuvre of the German Second Army was being
completed. Then on the 16th, it was Rezonville, with all the army
corps finally on the left bank, only the 3rd and 4th lagging behind,
held back by the appalling congestion building up at the crossroads
of the Étain and Mars-la-Tour roads, following the daring attack
that morning by the Prussian cavalry and artillery, which had
blocked them both off, leading to a slow, muddled battle which, up
until two o'clock, Bazaine could have won, as he had only a handful
of men to deal with ahead of him, but which he ended up losing,
afraid for some reason of being cut off from Metz; the battle was
immense, covering miles and miles of hills and plains, where the
French, attacked at the front and on the flank, had worked wonders
not to gain any ground, leaving the enemy time to concentrate,
thereby complying with the Prussian plan to force them back on to
the other side of the river. At last, on the 18th, after returning to
positions in front of the fortified camp, came Saint-Privat, the
supreme struggle, with a battlefront thirteen kilometres long, two
hundred thousand Germans with seven hundred cannon against one

hundred and twenty thousand French, with only five hundred guns, Germans facing Germany, the French facing France, as if the invaders had become the invaded, as a result of the peculiar pivotal movement which had occurred, the most frightening crush happening from two o'clock onwards, with the Prussian Guard driven back, hacked down, Bazaine victorious for some time, his left flank strong and unshakeable right up until the moment, towards evening, that the weaker right flank had had to abandon Saint-Privat, amidst horrible carnage, taking the entire army down with it, defeated, pushed back south of Metz and from then on squeezed inside a ring of iron.

As Henriette read, Jean would constantly interrupt her, saying,

'Well, well! And there was us lot been waiting for Bazaine ever since we'd left Rheims!'

The dispatch from the Marshal dated the 19th, after Saint-Privat, in which he talked about resuming the retreat via Montmédy, and which had been the reason why the Châlons army had marched on, now seemed to be nothing more than the report of a beaten general trying to play down his defeat; and it wasn't until later, not until the 29th, when the news reached him that an army was on its way to rescue him, that he had made a final effort, on the right bank in Noiseville; but it was so half-hearted that on 1 September, the very day on which the Châlons army was crushed at Sedan, the Metz army was withdrawing, well and truly paralysed, sacrificing its life for France. The Marshal, who up until then might have been nothing worse than a mediocre commander, neglecting to get through while roads were still open and then genuinely being blocked by superior forces, would now, in the grip of his political preoccupations, become a conspirator and a traitor.

In the newspapers brought by Doctor Dalichamp, however, Bazaine was still the great man, the brave soldier to whom France still looked for her salvation. Jean made her repeat whole passages, trying to understand how the German Third Army, under the Crown Prince of Prussia, had managed to pursue them while the First and Second Armies were blocking off Metz, both with such large numbers of men and cannons that they'd been able to dip into them to detach a Fourth Army which, under the orders of the Crown Prince of Saxony, had put the finishing touches to the disaster of Sedan. Then, finally brought up to date, on the bed of pain to which his wound kept him pinned, he forced himself nevertheless to take hope.

'So that's why—we weren't the strongest!... Never mind, the figures are there: Bazaine has a hundred and fifty thousand men, three hundred thousand rifles and more than five hundred cannon; so he must be planning to deal them a hell of a blow.'*

Henriette nodded her head, going along with what he said, to avoid making him even gloomier. These vast troop movements were quite beyond her, but she could sense the inevitable calamity ahead. Her voice remained clear, she could have read like this for hours on end, simply glad to keep him amused. But sometimes, during an account of a massacre, she began to stutter, eyes filling with a sudden flood of tears. No doubt thoughts of her husband had come back to her, struck down back there, shoved against the wall by that Bavarian officer's foot.

'If it's too upsetting for you,' Jean said, surprised, 'you should stop reading out the battles to me.'

But she instantly pulled herself together, her manner very gentle and indulgent.

'No, no, please forgive me, it does me good as well, honestly.'

One evening during the first days of October, as a furious wind was raging outside, she came back from the hospital and entered the room, full of emotion, saying,

'It's a letter from Maurice! The doctor just handed it to me.'

With each morning that passed they'd both been getting more and more worried that the young man was showing no sign of life; especially as for over a week the rumour had been abroad that Paris was completely besieged, and they despaired of getting any news at all, wondering anxiously what could have become of him after leaving Rouen. Now his silence was explained, for the letter which he'd addressed to Doctor Dalichamp on the 18th, the very day that the last trains were leaving for Le Havre, had made an enormous detour, and it was a miracle that it had got there at all, having gone astray twenty times on the way.

'Oh! The dear lad!' exclaimed Jean, happy as could be. 'Read it to me, quick.'

The wind grew even more violent and rattled the window like a battering ram. And bringing the lamp to the bedside table, Henriette started to read, sitting so close to Jean that their heads almost touched. Inside the peaceful room they were warm and snug, while outside the storm raged.

It was a long letter, eight pages in all, in which Maurice first explained that as soon as he'd arrived on the 16th, he'd been lucky enough to get enrolled into one of the regiments of the line whose numbers were being brought back up to full strength. Then he went back over what had happened, recounting with extraordinary excitement what he'd learned of the events of that terrible month. After the pain and stupefaction caused by Wissembourg and Frœschwiller, Paris had grown calmer, harbouring hopes of revenge, falling back on yet more illusions—the victorious legend of the army, Bazaine's command, the levy en masse, imaginary victories, with wholesale slaughters of the Prussians being reported to parliament even by the ministers themselves. Then abruptly, he told how the second thunderbolt had struck Paris on 3 September:* hopes shattered, the ignorant, self-confident city devastated by this crushing blow from fate, and cries of 'Depose him! Depose him!' ringing out on the boulevards by evening; then the short, gloomy night session during which Jules Favre had read out the proposals for the removal from power which the people were demanding. And the following day was 4 September, when a world crumbled, and the Second Empire was swept away in the débâcle of its sins and vices, with the whole population pouring out onto the streets, a torrent of half a million men filling the Place de la Concorde in the bright sunshine of this fine Sunday, making its way as far as the railings of the Legislative Assembly, blocked by barely a handful of soldiers with their rifle butts held aloft, and then breaking down the doors, invading the assembly room from where Jules Favre, Gambetta, and other deputies from the left would go on to proclaim the Republic* at the Hôtel de Ville, while, on the Place Saint-Germain-l'Auxerrois, a little door in the Louvre opened a crack to let out the Empress Regent,* dressed all in black, accompanied by a single female companion, both of them trembling, fleeing, huddling into the back of a passing cab, which took them jolting far away from the Tuileries, which the crowds were now streaming through. That same day, Napoleon III had left the inn in Bouillon where he had just spent his first night in exile, and was heading for Wilhelmshöhe.*

Gravely, Jean interrupted Henriette.

'So we're living in a Republic now, are we?... Well, good job too, if it helps us beat the Prussians!'

But he shook his head, for he'd always been taught to fear a

Republic when he was a peasant. Added to which, it hardly seemed a good idea to be facing the enemy when you couldn't agree amongst yourselves. But something had had to change, in any case, for the Empire was definitely rotten, and no one wanted any more to do with it.

Henriette finished the letter, which ended by signalling the approach of the Germans. On the 13th, the same day that a government for National Defence was being set up in Tours,* they had seen them east of Paris,* advancing as far as Lagny. By the 14th and 15th they were at the gates, at Créteil and Joinville-le-Pont. On the 18th, however, the morning that Maurice had written, he still didn't appear to believe that it would be possible to besiege Paris completely, a ringing confidence had seized him again, he looked on the siege as some kind of insolent and risky attempt doomed to fail before three weeks were out, counting on the relief armies which would surely be sent from the provinces, not to mention the Metz army, which was already on the march, making its way there via Verdun and Rheims. And then the links on the iron belt had joined together, locking Paris in, and now the city, cut off from the world, was nothing but a gigantic prison for two million living souls, from where there arose only a deathly hush.

'Oh! My God!' murmured Henriette breathlessly. 'How long is all this going to carry on? Shall we ever see him again?'

A gust of wind bowed the trees in the distance, and caused the farm's ancient timbers to groan. If the winter was to be a harsh one, what suffering these poor soldiers would undergo, without fire or bread, fighting in the snow!

'Well!' concluded Jean. 'Very nice it is too, that letter, and it's good to have some news... We must never give up hope.'

And so day by day, the month of October went by, with sad, grey skies where the wind paused only to bring along even darker ridges of clouds. Jean's wound scarred infinitely slowly, and the draining tube still didn't show the healthy pus that would have allowed the doctor to remove it; and the patient had grown a lot weaker, stubbornly refusing any operation, too afraid of being left an invalid. The remote little room now seemed to be slumbering in an atmosphere of waiting and resignation, sometimes disturbed by sudden anxiety, for no precise reason, and news reached them only vaguely and from a distance, as if they were waking from a nightmare. The abominable war, the massacres and disasters went on back there, somewhere, without them knowing what the truth really was, without them hearing anything except the loud, muffled cry from their slaughtered country. And the wind swept away the leaves beneath the gloomy sky, and there were long, deep silences in the barren countryside, where only the croaking of the crows fell upon the air, announcing a hard winter to come.

One of their topics of conversation had become the hospital, which Henriette rarely left except to keep Jean company. In the evening, when she came home, he would question her, coming to know each of her patients, wanting to be told who was dying and who was getting better; and she, never running short of things to say about these matters which so filled her heart, would recount her days to him right down to the smallest details.

'Oh!' she was always saying. 'Those poor boys, those poor boys!'

The hospital was no longer the place, in the middle of a battle in full swing, where fresh blood flowed and amputations took place on healthy, red flesh. It had sunk to the level of a decaying hospice, smelling of death and fever, damp with long convalescence and interminable agony. Doctor Dalichamp had had immense trouble getting hold of the necessary beds, mattresses, and sheets; and every day the task of providing for his patients, finding them bread, meat, and dried vegetables, not to mention bandages, compresses, and equipment, forced him to perform yet more miracles. Having being refused any help, even chloroform, by the Prussians in the Military Hospital in Sedan, he had everything sent over from Belgium. However, he took in German as well as French wounded, in particular a dozen Bavarians who'd been picked up in Bazeilles. These soldiers and enemies, who before had rushed at each other's throats, were now lying side by side, peaceable in their shared suffering. And what a frightful, miserable place it was, those two long halls in Remilly's old school, each containing about fifty beds, in the weak light filtering in through the high windows!

Ten days after the battle, wounded men were still being brought in, found lying in corners, forgotten. Four had been left behind in a house in Balan with no medical attention whatsoever, surviving goodness only knows how, probably thanks to the charity of some neighbour; and their injuries were swarming with maggots, they were as good as dead, poisoned by their vile wounds. It was this putrefaction which nothing could stop, hovering over and emptying whole rows of beds. As soon as one stepped inside, the smell of rotting flesh would stick in the gullet. Wound drains suppurated, dripping drops of fetid pus. Often flesh had to be reopened, to extract yet more splinters which had gone unnoticed. Then abcesses developed, floods waiting to burst further down the body. Exhausted, emaciated, pale-faced, the wretches endured all sorts of torment. Some, prostrate, barely drawing breath, spent their days lying on their backs, their eyelids closed and black, like corpses already halfway to decay. The rest, unable to sleep, troubled by anxious insomnia, drenched in floods of sweat, were highly excited, as if the catastrophe had driven them insane. And whether they were violent or calm, once the shivering of contagious fever came over them, that was the end of it, the poison triumphed, flitting from one man to the next, sweeping them all away in the same torrent of victorious decay.

Worst of all, though, was the room of the condemned, those afflicted by dysentery, typhus, and smallpox. Many of them had black pox. They tossed about, calling out in constant delirium, rising to their feet and standing up on their beds like spectres. Some, whose lungs were affected, were dying of pneumonia, with hacking coughs. Others were always yelling and could only be calmed by the trickle of cold water with which their wounds were constantly being cooled. The hour they all waited for, when dressings were changed, was the only time of day when a little calm entered the room, airing the beds and relaxing the bodies which had grown stiff from always lying in the same position. It was also the hour they dreaded, for not a day went by without the doctor noticing sorrowfully, as he examined the wounds, that some poor devil had blue dots showing on the skin, patches of gangrene creeping in. The operation would take place the next day. Another bit of arm or leg cut off. Sometimes, the gangrene even climbed higher, and they had to start all over again, until the whole limb had been gnawed away. Then the man's whole body would be affected, invaded by livid typhus blotches, and he would have to be taken away, reeling and distraught, into the room of the condemned, where he would succumb, his flesh already dead and smelling like a corpse even before the final agony set in.

Every evening on her return, Henriette would answer Jean's questions in a voice shaking with the same emotion.

'Oh! The poor boys, the poor boys!'

And the details were always the same, the daily torments of this hell. A shoulder had been disarticulated, a foot chopped off, a humerus bone sectioned yet again; but would the gangrene or the rotting infection show any mercy? Or they'd just buried another one of them, usually French, sometimes German. It was rare for the day to end without some hastily constructed coffin, made from four planks of wood, being taken furtively out of the hospital at dusk accompanied by a single nurse, often the young woman herself, so that the man wouldn't have to be buried like some dog. In Remilly's little cemetery, two trenches had been dug; and they slept side by side, Germans on the left, French on the right, reconciled in the earth.

Jean, although he'd never seen them, ended up taking an interest in some of the patients. He would ask after them.

'What about "Poor Child", how's he doing today?'

He was a young trooper, a volunteer from the 5th infantry regiment, who wasn't yet twenty. The nickname 'Poor Child' had stuck because when he talked about himself, he would always use these words; and when someone asked him one day why he did so, he replied that this was what his mother always called him. And he was a poor child, too, for he was dying of pleurisy, brought on by a wound to his left side.

'Oh! The dear boy,' Henriette would say, who'd become motherly towards the soldier, 'he's not well, he was coughing all day... It breaks my heart to hear him.'

'And how about your bear, Gutmann?' said Jean, with a faint smile. 'Is the doctor more hopeful for him?'

'Yes, we may be able to save him. But he's suffering dreadfully.'

Even though they were full of pity for him, neither could mention Gutmann without a sort of tender-hearted gaiety. When the young woman had arrived at the hospital on her first day, she'd been shocked to recognize this Bavarian soldier as the man with the red hair and beard, big blue eyes, and broad, square nose who'd carried her off in his arms in Bazeilles while her husband was being shot. He recognized her, too; but he couldn't talk, for a bullet, entering through the back of the neck, had removed half his tongue. And after spending two days recoiling in horror and shuddering in spite of herself every time she went near his bed, she was won over by the way his eyes followed her about the room, desperate and full of gentleness. Was he no longer the monster with blood-spattered whiskers and eyes rolling in anger who'd been haunting her with such awful memories? She had to make an effort to find the same person there now, inside this unhappy man, who seemed so good-natured and docile as he underwent such appalling suffering. His case—this sudden handicap—was rare, and it touched everyone in the hospital. No one was quite sure he was even called Gutmann: they called him that because the only sound he could manage was a two-syllable groan which sounded something like it. As for the rest of it, all they thought they knew was that he was married and had children. He must have been able to understand a few French words, for he would sometimes answer with a violent nod or shake of the head. Married? Yes, yes! Children? Yes, yes! One day he'd seemed moved by the sight of flour, which led them to believe that he might have been a miller. And that was all. Where was the mill? Where was the distant, Bavarian village where they were weeping for him now, his wife and his children? Was he going to die a stranger, with no name, leaving his loved ones back there to wait for ever and ever?

'Today,' recounted Henriette to Jean one evening, 'Gutmann blew me kisses... I can't give him a drink, or do even the slightest thing for him any more, without him putting his fingers to his lips, in a gesture of burning gratitude... You mustn't laugh, it's just too terrible, being sort of buried like that before your time.'

Meanwhile, towards the end of October, Jean was getting much better. The doctor agreed to take out the draining tube, even though he was still concerned; and the wound seemed nonetheless to heal over fairly quickly. The convalescent was already getting out of bed and spending hours and hours walking about his room, sitting at the window, saddened to see the clouds sailing past. Then he got bored and talked about doing something to keep busy, making himself useful on the farm. One thing which secretly made him uneasy was the matter of money, for he thought that his two hundred francs must surely have been spent by now, after six long weeks. For old Fouchard to continue being on good terms with him, Henriette must be paying for him. This thought became unbearable, he didn't dare talk it over with her, and so was deeply relieved when it was agreed that he would work as a new farmhand, given the job of taking care of things indoors along with Silvine, while Prosper busied himself with the farming, outside.

In spite of the dreadful times, an extra hand certainly wasn't one too many at old Fouchard's, where business was booming. While the rest of the country was gasping for breath, bled dry, he had managed to expand his travelling butcher's trade to such an extent that he was now slaughtering three times and four times as many livestock as before. Stories were told of how, right from 31 August, he'd struck splendid deals with the Prussians. He who, on the 30th, had been defending his door against the soldiers of the 7th Corps, brandishing his rifle, refusing to sell them even a small loaf of bread, shouting that his house was quite empty, had set himself up as seller of all things at the first appearance of an enemy soldier, digging out the most extraordinary provisions from his cellars, bringing back whole herds of beasts from the secret places where he had hidden them. And since that day he'd become one of the largest suppliers of meat to the German armies, displaying an astonishing talent for getting his merchandise sold, and paid for, in between requisitions. Others had suffered because of the victors' sometimes brutal demands: but he hadn't yet supplied one bushel of flour, or one gallon of wine, or one quarter of beef, without finding good, sound money at the other end. They talked about him a lot, in Remilly, finding it wicked, coming from a man who'd only just lost his own son to the war and never even visited his grave, which Silvine was alone in tending. But even so, they respected him for getting richer when even the craftiest were going to the wall. And he would shrug mockingly and growl, with that stubborn set to him,

'Patriotic, I'm more patriotic than the lot of them!... I ask you, is it patriotic to stuff the Prussians up to here with food for free? I make them pay for everything, I do... Well, we'll see, later on!'

On only his second day up, Jean spent too much time on his feet, and what the doctor had been afraid of actually happened: the wound opened up again, grew very inflamed, and made his leg swell up, and he had to go back to bed. In the end, Dalichamp began to suspect the presence of a splinter, which the effort of two days' exercise had managed to dislodge. He felt around and was lucky enough to be able to extract it. Not that it went entirely smoothly, for it brought on a violent bout of fever which exhausted Jean yet again. Never before had he sunk to such a feeble state. And Henriette took up her post as faithful guardian again, sitting in the room where winter was spreading gloominess and chill. The first days of November had come, the east wind had already brought a flurry of snow, and it was very cold inside the four empty walls, on the bare, tiled floor. Since there was no fireplace, they decided to put in a stove, and the roaring of the fire brightened their solitude a little.

The days went by, monotonously, and for Jean and Henriette this first week of his relapse was definitely the most miserable of their long period of forced intimacy. Was there no end to the suffering? Was danger always going to reappear, weren't they allowed to hope for an end to all this misery? Their thoughts constantly flew to Maurice, from whom they'd received no further news. They were told that other people were getting letters, slim little notes brought by carrier pigeons.* No doubt some German bullet had killed the pigeon that had been delivering their own joy and affection, as it flew across the wide, free sky. Everything seemed to recede, die out, disappear, deep in this precocious winter. Echoes of the war came to them only after considerable delay, and the few newspapers which Dalichamp still brought them were sometimes a week old. Much of their sadness came from this ignorance, what they didn't know and could only guess at, from the long death cry which, in spite of everything, they could hear in the silent countryside around the farm.

One morning, Doctor Dalichamp arrived in a terrible state, his hands shaking. He took a Belgian paper from his pocket and flung it on the bed, exclaiming,

'Oh! My friends, France is dead, Bazaine has just betrayed us!'*

Jean, leaning back on two pillows, drowsing, woke up.

'What do you mean, betrayed?'

'Just that—he's handed over Metz and the army. It's Sedan all over again, but this time it's the rest of our flesh and blood!'

Then, picking up the paper again, he read out,

'One hundred and fifty thousand prisoners, a hundred and fifty-three eagles and standards, five hundred and forty-one field guns, seventy-three machine guns, eight hundred siege guns, three hundred thousand rifles, two thousand cartloads of military equipment, munitions for eighty-five batteries...'

And on he went, giving the details: Marshal Bazaine stuck inside Metz with the army, utterly powerless, making no effort to break the ring of iron which was tightening around him; his long parleys with Prince Frederick Charles, his hesitant, hazy political schemes, his ambition to play a deciding role which even he seemed unable to define properly; then all the complicated negotiations, with dubious, lying emissaries sent to Bismarck, the King, and the Empress Regent who, eventually, would refuse to treat with the enemy on anything which was based on handing over territory; and then the inescapable catastrophe, fate finishing its work, famine in Metz, forced capitulation, commanders and soldiers reduced to accepting the conquerors' harsh terms. France no longer had an army.

'Jesus Christ!' swore Jean under his breath; he didn't understand everything, but up until then he'd still seen Bazaine as the great captain, their only possible saviour. 'So what now, what are we going to do? What's become of them, up in Paris?'

The doctor was just going on to the news from Paris, which was quite disastrous. He pointed out that the newspaper was dated 5 November. The surrender of Metz had occurred on 27 October, and the news had only reached Paris on the 30th. After the defeats already endured at Chevilly, Bagneux, and Malmaison, after the fighting and defeat at Le Bourget,* this news had burst upon them like a thunderclap, striking at the despairing populace, who were irritated by the weakness and impotence of the government for National Defence. And so the next day, the 31st, a real insurrection* had sprung up, with an immense crowd pouring onto the Place de l'Hôtel de Ville, streaming into the rooms and taking prisoner members of the government whom the National Guard had finally given up to them, for fear of seeing the triumph of the revolutionaries who were clamouring for the Commune. And the Belgian paper added the most insulting comments about mighty Paris, torn asunder by civil war just as the enemy was knocking at the gates. Wasn't this the mark of final decay, the puddle of mud and blood into which an entire world was about to collapse?

'It's true,' murmured Jean, quite pale, 'you just don't start hitting each other when the Prussians are at the door!'

Henriette, who'd said nothing up until then, preferring not to open her mouth about such political matters, was unable to suppress a cry. All she could think of was her brother.

'My God! I only hope Maurice doesn't go getting mixed up in all this business, what with him being so headstrong!'

There was a pause and the doctor, an ardent patriot, spoke again.

'Whatever, even if there aren't any soldiers left, there'll be others springing up. Metz has surrendered, even Paris could surrender, and it still won't be the end of France... Oh, yes, it's like the peasants say, there's life in the old dog yet!'

They could see, though, that he was forcing his hopes up. He spoke of the new army which was being assembled on the Loire and whose debut, near Artenay, had been none too auspicious: but it would toughen up and march to Paris's rescue. Above all he was fired up by the proclamations made by Gambetta, who had left Paris by hot-air balloon on 7 October, and the next day had installed himself in Tours, calling all the citizens to arms, speaking a language that was at once so manly and so moderate that the entire country was giving way to this dictatorship for the public safety. And wasn't there meant to be another army in the north, and another in the east, wouldn't soldiers rise up out of the ground inspired by faith alone? This was the provinces rising up, with their irrepressible will to create whatever was lacking, to fight on to the last sou, to the final drop of blood.

'Hmph!' concluded the doctor, getting up to go. 'I've often given up on patients who were up and about a week later.'

Jean smiled.

'Make me better soon, Doctor, so that I can get back to my post.'

However, he and Henriette were left deeply upset by all this bad news. That very evening there was a fall of snow, and the next day, when Henriette came back all shivering from the hospital, she announced that Gutmann was dead. The sharp cold was decimating the patients and emptying the rows of beds. The wretched mute, with his amputated tongue, had taken two days to die. In his final hours she had stayed by his bedside, for he'd had such a pleading look on his face. He was trying to talk to her through his tears, perhaps he was trying to tell her his real name and the name of the distant village where a woman and her children were waiting for him. And so he had passed away unknown, his fumbling fingers sending her a last kiss, as if to thank her once again for her kindness and care. She alone accompanied him to the cemetery, where the frozen soil, this heavy, foreign soil, thudded dully onto his firwood coffin along with chunks of snow.

The following day, yet again, Henriette said on her return,

'Poor Child is dead.'

This time, she cried.

'If only you'd seen him, all delirious! He was calling me: Mummy! Mummy! And he was holding out his arms so tenderly that I had to take him onto my lap... Oh! The poor thing, his suffering had so wasted him that he weighed no more than a little boy... And I cradled him so he could die happy, yes! I cradled him, me, the woman he was calling his mother, and I'm only a few years older than him... He was crying, and I couldn't help crying too, I'm still crying...'

She had to break off, choked by tears.

'When he died, several times he stammered his nickname: Poor child, poor child... Oh! Yes, yes, they're poor children all right, all those brave boys, some of them so young, and your awful war's taking away their limbs and putting them through such suffering before it lays them in the earth!'

Every day, now, Henriette would return in the same state, overcome by someone's death, and the suffering they saw through others brought them even closer together, during the doleful hours they spent so alone, there in the large, peaceful room. They were very sweet hours, though, for a tenderness had developed between them, in these two hearts which little by little had come to know each other, and they thought it was fraternal. He, with his deeply thoughtful nature, had been elevated by their constant companionship; and she, seeing that he was such a good and sensible man, no longer even thought about the fact that he was of humble birth, and had tilled the soil before taking up the soldier's pack. They got on very well together, forming an excellent couple, as Silvine would say, with her grave smile. Moreover, there wasn't the slightest hint of awkwardness between them, as Henriette continued to tend to his leg without either of them once averting their candid gaze. Still dressed in black, in her widow's mourning, she seemed to have ceased being a woman.

Jean, though, during those long afternoons when he found himself alone, couldn't help daydreaming. What he felt for her was boundless gratitude, a kind of devout respect, which would have made him push away any thought of love as sacrilegious. But even so he told himself that, if he'd had a wife like her, so sweet and gentle, and so active, then life would have been a true paradise. His misfortune, those unhappy years he had spent in Rognes, the disaster of his marriage, and the violent death of his wife—he would see all his past come back to visit him, and miss the tenderness, with the vague, barely formulated hope of making another bid for happiness. He would close his eyes and let drowsiness creep over him, and then he would see a confused vision* of himself in Remilly, remarried, owner of a field which provided enough to feed a family of good, unambitious folk. It was such a hazy vision that it didn't really exist, and surely never would. He no longer believed himself capable of anything but friendship, he only loved Henriette like this because he was Maurice's brother. Then this vague dream of marriage eventually grew into a sort of consolation, one of those imagined things that one knows can never become reality, but which one toys with in moments of sadness.

As for Henriette, nothing of this had even touched her. After the dreadful events in Bazeilles, her heart was broken in two; and if some sense of relief, some new feeling of tenderness had entered it, it could only be unconscious: just like the hidden movement inside a germinating seed, giving no visible sign of the process secretly under way. She was unaware even of the pleasure she'd begun to experience in the hours and hours spent by Jean's bed, reading to him from the newspapers, even though it brought the two of them nothing but sorrow. If her hand happened to brush his, she never felt so much as a spark; she'd never dreamed about the future, never hoped that she might be loved again. And yet the only place she could forget, the only place that gave her any comfort, was this room. Whenever she found herself there, keeping herself busy in her sweet, gently industrious way, it seemed as if her brother were about to come back at any moment, that everything would work itself out, that they would all end up being happy and stay together for ever. And she would talk of it quite easily, for it seemed so natural that things should be so, and it never occurred to her to examine her own feelings more closely as she chastely, unconsciously, gave all her heart.

One afternoon, however, as she was setting off for the hospital, the sight of a Prussian captain and two other officers standing in the kitchen made her freeze in terror, making her realize the deep affection she held for Jean. Obviously these men had learned about the wounded man's presence at the farm and had come to claim him as their prisoner: his departure was inevitable, then captivity in Germany, deep inside some fortress. She listened trembling, her heart thumping.

The captain, a large man who spoke French, was reproaching old Fouchard violently.

'This can't go on, you're making fun of us... I came here in person to warn you that if it happens again, I'll hold you responsible, oh yes! I'll know just how to deal with you!'

The old man, quite calmly, feigned stupefaction, as if he hadn't understood, arms hanging loosely at his sides.

'What's this, sir, what's all this about?'

'Oh! Don't give me all that nonsense, you know full well that those three cows you sold us last Sunday were rotten... Just that, rotten; well, sick, they'd died of some nasty disease—because they poisoned my men, and two of them must be dead by now.'

Old Fouchard instantly recoiled with indignation.

'Rotten! My cows? Why, that meat was so good and tender, you'd give it to a nursing mother to get her strength back!'

And he began to whimper, striking his chest, crying that he was an honest man and he'd rather cut off his own flesh than sell rotten meat. He'd been known around here for thirty years, and there wasn't anyone could say he'd sold them short measures or bad quality.

'They were right as rain, sir, and if your soldiers have had belly-ache, maybe it's because they ate too much; unless some mischief-makers put poison in the cooking-pots...'

He flooded him with words, putting forward such ludicrous hypotheses that the captain, beside himself with rage, eventually cut him short.

'That's enough! You've been warned, so just watch out!... And another thing, we suspect that here in this village you're harbouring the guerrillas from Dieulet Woods, who killed another of our sentries the day before yesterday... Watch out, do you hear me?'

When the Prussians had gone old Fouchard shrugged, with a snort of pure disdain. Of course he sold them animals who'd got ill and died, he didn't give them anything but! All the carrion the peasants brought him, anything that had died from some disease or that he found lying dead in a ditch, wasn't that just what these rotten bastards deserved?

He winked, and turning towards a reassured Henriette, he murmured with mocking triumph,

'I ask you, little one—when you think that there are some round here who say I'm no patriot!... Eh? Just let them do as much, let them palm off rotten old nags on them and line their pockets in the process... Not a patriot! Good God, I'll have killed more of them with my sick cattle than most soldiers will have done with their rifles!'

When Jean heard about it, though, he was worried. If the German authorities suspected the villagers in Remilly of harbouring guerrillas from Dieulet Woods, they could well order a search at any moment, and discover him. The thought of putting his hosts at risk and causing even the slightest trouble for Henriette was something he couldn't bear. But she begged him and made him agree to stay for a few more days, for his wound was healing slowly, and his legs weren't yet strong enough for him to rejoin one of the regiments in the country, in the north or along the Loire.

And the days up until the middle of December were the most frightening and distressing they had spent alone together. The cold had become so intense that the stove wasn't enough to heat the large, bare room. When they looked out of the window at the thick snow covering the ground, they would think of Maurice buried somewhere in that icy, dead Paris, from where they'd heard nothing they could depend on. The same questions came up again and again: what was he doing, why didn't he give them any sign of life? They didn't dare voice their dreadful fears for him, his being wounded, or ill, or maybe even dead. The few vague bits of information which continued to reach them via the newspapers were not designed to reassure them. After some supposedly successful sorties, which were constantly proved untrue, there had been rumours of a great victory won by General Ducrot on 2 December, at Champigny,* but then they found out that the very next day, abandoning the positions he had just conquered, he'd been forced to cross back over the Marne. Each hour, the noose around Paris grew tighter, with famine beginning to set in: first the cattle and goats and now potatoes were requisitioned, gas was already unavailable to ordinary people, and soon the streets would also be in darkness, furrowed by the red trails of flying shells. Neither of them could warm themselves, or eat a thing, without being haunted by the vision of Maurice and the rest of the two million people living there, shut up inside that giant tomb.

As well as that, the news from all over the country,* from the north as well as the centre, was getting worse. Up north, the 22nd army corps, made up of militia, companies from supply depots, and soldiers and officers who'd escaped from the disasters of Metz and Sedan, had been forced to abandon Amiens and withdraw towards Arras; and Rouen in turn had fallen into enemy hands, without this handful of routed, demoralized men having had a chance to defend it properly. In the centre, the victory at Coulmiers won by the Loire army on 9 November had generated a blaze of optimism: Orléans reoccupied, the Bavarians put to flight, a march on Étampes, and the siege of Paris lifted. But on 3 December Prince Friedrich Karl suddenly reoccupied Orléans, cutting the Loire army in two, three corps of which withdrew to Vierzon and Bourges while the other two, under the orders of General Chanzy,* began retreating as far as Le Mans, a heroic withdrawal involving a whole week of marching and fighting. The Prussians were everywhere, from Dijon to Dieppe, from Le Mans to Vierzon. After that, nearly every morning the distant crash could be heard of some stronghold which had surrendered to shelling. Strasbourg had succumbed as of 28 September, after forty-six days under siege and thirty-seven days of shelling, its walls hacked down, its monuments riddled by nearly two hundred thousand missiles. The citadel in Laon had already blown up and Toul had surrendered; after which came a long, sorry list: Soissons and its hundred and twenty-eight cannon, Verdun with a hundred and thirty-six of its own, a hundred at Neufbrisach, seventy at La Fère, and sixty-five at Montmédy. Thionville was in flames, and Phalsbourg was opening its gates only after putting up nearly twelve weeks of furious resistance. It seemed as if the whole of France was burning, collapsing, to the sound of raging cannonfire.

One morning when Jean was absolutely set on leaving, Henriette took his hands and held him back, gripping him in despair.

'No, no! I implore you, don't leave me on my own... You're too weak still, just wait a few more days, just a few more... I promise to let you go, as soon as the doctor says you're well enough to go back into battle.'

CHAPTER FIVE

On this frozen December evening, Silvine and Prosper found themselves alone with Charlot in the large farmhouse kitchen, she sewing, he in the process of making himself a fine switch. It was seven o'clock, and they had dined at six without waiting for old Fouchard, who must have been held up at Raucourt, where there was a shortage of meat; and Henriette, whose turn it was to keep watch at the hospital that night, had just left, advising Silvine to make sure Jean's stove was well stoked up with coal before she went to bed.

Outside, the sky was very dark above the white snow. Not a sound came from the village, buried beneath the drifts, and the only noise in the room was the scraping of Prosper's knife as he concentrated on carving diamond and rose decorations into the dogwood handle. Every now and then he'd pause and look at Charlot, whose large, blond head swayed, heavy with drowsiness. When the child eventually fell asleep, the silence seemed to grow louder then ever. His mother gently moved the candle away, so that the bright light wouldn't be in her little boy's eyes; then, still sewing, she fell into a deep reverie.

It was then, after further hesitation, that Prosper made up his mind.

'Listen, Silvine, I've something to tell you... I've waited until I was alone with you...'

Already worried, she looked up at him.

'Well, it's this... Forgive me for causing you pain, but it's better that you should be warned. This morning in Remilly, at the corner of the church, I saw Goliath, as sure as you're there in front of me now, oh! quite clearly, no mistake about it!'

She grew deathly pale, her hands shook, and all she could do was give a muted cry.

'Oh my God! Oh my God!'

Prosper went on, choosing his words carefully, telling her what he'd learned during the day by questioning people here and there. No one was left in any doubt that Goliath was a spy, who had established himself in the area beforehand so that he could get to know the roads, resources, and how everything was organized. They recalled his stay at old Fouchard's farm, the abrupt manner of his departure, and the places he'd visited after that, over by Beaumont and Raucourt. And now, here he was back again, in some undefined post at command headquarters in Sedan, once again doing the rounds of the villages, apparently with orders to denounce some, tax others, and see to it that the crushing requisitions imposed on the locals went smoothly. That morning he'd been terrorizing Remilly about a delivery of flour which had been too slow and incomplete.

'You're forewarned,' repeated Prosper as he finished, 'and that way, you'll know what you have to do when he comes here...'

She interrupted him with a cry of terror.

'You think he'll come here?'

'Lord! Seems likely to me... He'd have to have very little curiosity not to, seeing as how he's never seen the baby, although he knows he exists... And besides, there's you, you're not at all bad-looking, and I'm sure he'd want to see you again.'

But she gestured pleadingly to him to stop. Woken by the noise, Charlot had raised his head. His eyes unfocused, as if waking from a dream, he remembered the insult some joker in the village had taught him, and with all the seriousness of a little chap of three years old, declared,

'The Prussians are pigs!'

His mother took him wildly into her arms, sitting him on her knees. Oh, the poor thing, her hope and her despair, whom she loved with all her soul, and whom she couldn't look at without weeping, this son of her flesh for whom she suffered, when she heard him called the Prussian by the other kids his age, when they played with him in the street! She kissed him, as if to put the words back into his mouth.

'Who's been teaching you such nasty words? I won't allow it, you mustn't repeat them, my dear.'

Then, in that stubborn way children have, Charlot, choking with laughter, immediately went and said it again,

'The Prussians are pigs!'

Then, seeing his mother burst into tears, he began to cry too, clinging to her. My God! What fresh misfortune was threatening to strike her? Hadn't it been enough to have lost the only hope left in her life with Honoré's death, and with it the certainty of being able to forget and live happily again? Must the other man now come back to life, to complete her unhappiness?

'Come on,' she murmured, 'time to sleep, my dear. I love you very much, even so, for you don't know the pain you cause me.'

And she left Prosper alone for a moment, who, so as not to embarrass her by his gaze, had pretended to go back to his careful sculpting of the switch-handle.

However, before putting Charlot to bed Silvine usually took him in to say goodnight to Jean, with whom the little boy was great friends. That evening, as she entered, candle in hand, she saw the wounded man sitting up in bed, eyes wide open in the shadows. What, wasn't he asleep? Goodness, no! He was daydreaming about all sorts of things, alone in the silence of this winter's night. And while she stoked up the stove with coal, he played for a moment with Charlot, who rolled about on the bed like a young cat. Jean knew Silvine's story, and he felt affectionate towards this brave, submissive girl who had been so sorely tried by misfortune, in mourning for the only man she'd ever loved, the only consolation she had left this poor child, whose birth was her torment. And so, when she had covered the stove and came over to take the child from his arms, he noticed from her red eyes that she'd been crying. What? Had someone given her yet more cause for worry? But she wouldn't answer: later on, she'd tell him about it, if it was worth it. My God! Wasn't her life just one long string of sorrows now?

Silvine was finally taking Charlot out, when the sound of footsteps and voices came from the farmyard. And Jean listened in surprise.

'What's all that about? That's not old Fouchard coming back, I didn't hear the wheels of his cart.'

Deep within his remote room, he'd come to be acquainted with the life of the farm, and the slightest noises had grown familiar. Straining his ears, he said at once,

'Oh! Yes! It's those men, the guerrillas from Dieulet Woods,* coming for supplies.'

'Quick!' murmured Silvine, swiftly leaving the room and leaving him in darkness once again. 'I must hurry and get them their bread.'

In fact, they were already banging on the kitchen door, and Prosper, uneasy at being on his own, hesitated, negotiating for time. When the master of the house wasn't there, he was seldom happy to open the door, for fear of being held responsible for any damage. But he was in luck, for just then old Fouchard's cart came down the hill, the trotting of the horse's hooves muffled in the snow. And it was the old man who greeted the men.

'Ah! Good, it's you three... What have you got for me in that wheelbarrow?'

Wiry as a bandit, hunched inside his blue woollen shirt, Sambuc didn't even hear him, he was so infuriated with Prosper, his Honest Joe of a brother as he put it, who was only just deciding to open up.

'Hey, you! D'you think we're some kind of beggars, leaving us out here in such weather?'

But while Prosper calmly shrugged his shoulders without answering, and led the horse and cart into the stable, it was old Fouchard who stepped in once again, leaning over the wheelbarrow.

'So, you've brought me a couple of dead sheep, have you... Good job it's freezing, otherwise I'm sure they wouldn't smell at all nice.'

Cabasse and Ducat, Sambuc's two lieutenants who accompanied him on every outing, cried out in protest.

'Oh!' said the first, the typical Provençal loudmouth, 'they're no more than three days old... They're from the Raffins' farm, there's a nasty bout of sickness going round the animals.'

'*Procumbit humi bos*,'* declaimed the other man, the former bailiff whose penchant for little girls had resulted in him being struck off from the profession, and who liked quoting in Latin.

Shaking his head, old Fouchard went on disparaging the merchandise, which he pretended was too far gone. And entering the kitchen with the three men, he concluded,

'Well, anyway, they'll have to make do with that... It's a good thing they haven't got two cutlets to rub together in Raucourt. Eh? When you're hungry, you'll eat anything.'

Deep down he was delighted and summoned Silvine, who was coming back from putting Charlot to bed.

'Fetch some glasses, we're going to drink a toast to Bismarck kicking the bucket.'

This was how Fouchard kept up good relations with the guerrillas from Dieulet Woods who for the past three months had been emerging from their impenetrable thickets at dusk, prowling round the roads, killing and robbing any Prussians they could take by surprise, and when enemy game was scarce falling back on local farms and fleecing the peasants. They were the terror of the neighbourhood, all the more so because, with every new convoy that was attacked and every sentry found with his throat cut, the German authorities took it out on the nearby villages, accusing them of conniving with them, slapping fines on them, taking the mayors away as prisoners and burning down cottages. And if the peasants didn't give up Sambuc and his gang to the Germans, in spite of their sincere desire to do so, it was simply through fear of meeting a bullet round the corner of some lane if things didn't go according to plan.

But Fouchard had had the extraordinary idea of doing business with them. Tramping up and down the land, through ditches as well as stables, they had become his suppliers of dead meat. There wasn't a cow nor a sheep could drop dead inside a three-league radius without them coming at night to remove it and bring it to him. In return he paid them in supplies, particularly bread, whole ovenloads of loaves that Silvine baked especially. In any case, even if he didn't really like them, he had a sneaking admiration for the guerrillas, clever rascals who got their business done by thumbing their noses at the lot of them; and even though he made a fortune out of his dealings with the Prussians, deep down he would laugh, in a savage sort of way, whenever he learned that yet another one had been found dead by the side of the road somewhere with his throat cut.

'Your very good health!' he said, clinking glasses with the three men.

Then, wiping his mouth on the back of his hand,

'Look here, you know they've made a right old song and dance about those two headless Uhlans they picked up near Villecourt... You do know that the village has been burning since yesterday: they called it meting out a sentence to the locals, to punish them for taking you in... You ought to be a bit careful, you know, and not come back right away. We'll bring your bread to you.'

Sambuc snorted violently, shrugging his shoulders. Oh, right! Well, the Prussians could go to hell! Then all at once he lost his temper and thumped his fist on the table.

'Jesus Christ! Uhlans are fine, but it's that other one I'd like to get my hands on. You know the one I mean, the spy, the one who used to work for you...'

'Goliath,' said old Fouchard.

Frozen to the spot, Silvine, who'd just begun sewing again, stopped and listened.

'That's him, Goliath!... Oh! The bastard, he knows Dieulet

Woods like the back of his hand, he could get us nicked one of these days; particularly since he was boasting today at the Hôtel de la Croix de Malte that he'd deal with us before the week was out... He's a nasty sod, it has to be him guided the Bavarians, the day before Beaumont—eh, you lot?'

'As sure as that candle there!' confirmed Cabasse.

'*Per amica silentia lunae*,'* added Ducat, whose quotations were sometimes a little off the mark.

But Sambuc gave another hefty thump on the table, making it shake.

'Judged and sentenced he is, the bastard!... If you ever happen to know whereabouts we might find him, let me know, and his head can go join those of the Uhlans in the Meuse. Oh, yes! Christ alive, you can take my word for it!'

There was a pause. Silvine stared at them, very pale.

'These aren't the sort of things we should be talking about,' cut in old Fouchard prudently. 'To your very good health, and a good evening to you!'

They finished off the second bottle. Prosper, coming back from the stable, helped to load the loaves of bread, which Silvine had put into a bag, on the wheelbarrow, in place of the two dead sheep. But when his brother and the other two men left, he turned his back and didn't even answer as they disappeared with the barrow, through the snow, calling out,

'Good evening, till the next time!'

The following day, after dinner, when old Fouchard was alone in the house, he saw Goliath himself come in, tall and broad and pink-faced, with that tranquil smile of his. If Fouchard was at all shocked by this sudden apparition, he didn't let it show in the least. He just blinked, while the other man stepped forward and shook him briskly by the hand.

'Hello, Fouchard.'

Only then did he seem to recognize him.

'Well! It's you, my son... Oh, you've filled out a bit—just look how fine and plump you are!'

And he examined him closely: dressed in a sort of cape in a coarse, blue material, with headgear made of the same fabric, looking well-off and pleased with himself. Apart from that, he had no trace of an accent and spoke with the slow, thick cadences of the local peasants.

'Why yes, it's me, Fouchard... I didn't want to come back to the area without popping in to say a quick hello.'

The old man remained on his guard. What did he want, coming here? Had he found out about the guerrillas visiting the farm the day before? He'd have to wait and see. In any case, seeing as he was being so polite about it, the best thing was to be polite back.

'Well, well, my son, seeing as you've been so kind, why don't we have a drink.'

He went to the trouble of going to get two glasses and a bottle. All this wine they were drinking was making his heart bleed, but you had to know how to be generous when it came to business. And the scene from the night before began again, they clinked glasses in the same fashion, said the same words.

'To your very good health, Fouchard.'

'And to yours, my son.'

Then a complacent Goliath made himself at home. He looked around him, like a man recalling past times with pleasure. However, he didn't talk about the past, any more than the present for that matter. The conversation turned to the sharp cold spell which was going to get in the way of the farm work; luckily there was a good side to the snow, because it killed off pests. He showed only a flicker of sadness as he alluded to the deep hatred and fearful disdain that he'd encountered in the other houses in Remilly. Wasn't that right? Each man has his own country, and it's only natural to serve your country as you see fit. Only in France, there were certain things that they had funny ideas about. And the old boy watched him, listening to him talking so reasonably, in such a conciliatory tone, with his broad, jovial face, telling himself that this fine man before him surely hadn't come here with bad intentions.

'So, you all by yourself today, Fouchard?'

'Oh, no! Silvine's out there, feeding the cows... Do you want to see her?'

Goliath began to laugh.

'Goodness, yes!... To be perfectly honest with you, Silvine's the reason I came.'

At once old Fouchard stood up, much relieved, and shouted at the top of his voice,

'Silvine! Silvine! Someone's here to see you!'

And off he went, quite unafraid now that the girl was there to protect the household. When something like that keeps hold of a man for so long, even after years and years, then he's done for.

When Silvine came in, she wasn't surprised to find Goliath there, still seated, looking at her with a kind, if somewhat awkward smile. She'd been expecting him, and once across the threshold she merely stopped, her whole body tensing up. Charlot, who came running up to her, threw himself at her skirts, astonished at the sight of a strange man.

There was a pause, a few seconds of embarrassment.

'So, this is the little one?' Goliath finally asked, in his conciliatory voice.

'Yes,' replied Silvine coldly.

There was another pause. He had left in her seventh month of pregnancy, he'd been well aware that there was a child, but this was the first time he'd seen him. And, him being a practically minded fellow who was convinced he'd acted for the right reasons, he wanted to explain why.

'Look, Silvine, I can understand you must still be feeling bitter towards me. But it isn't really fair, you know... If I left, and caused you such pain, you should have told yourself that it was because I wasn't my own master. When you've got commanders to obey, you have to obey them, don't you? Even if they'd sent me a hundred leagues away, I'd still have gone, even on foot. And obviously I couldn't say anything: you don't know how it broke my heart to leave like that, without so much as a goodbye... Today, my God! I won't say I was sure I would come back. But I did hope I could—and you see? Now I'm back again...'

She'd turned away from him, and was watching the snow in the yard through the window, as if determined not to hear him. Troubled by her disdain and stubborn silence, he broke off his explanations to say,

'Do you know, you've grown even more beautiful!'

She was indeed very beautiful, all pale, with her magnificent huge eyes lighting up her entire face. Her heavy black hair fell around her head like some eternal mourning bonnet.

'Come on, have a heart! You ought to know that I don't wish you any harm... If I didn't still love you, I wouldn't have come back, would I?... But now, seeing as how I'm back and everything's worked out, we can see each other again, can't we?'

She suddenly shrank away, taking a step back, and looked him straight in the eyes.

'Never!'

'Why not? You're my wife, aren't you? This is our child, isn't it?'

She kept her gaze fixed on him, and spoke slowly.

'Listen, it's best to get this over and done with right now... You knew Honoré, I loved him, I've never loved anyone but him. And he's dead, your lot killed him, back there... I will never, ever be yours again. Not ever!'

She had raised her hand and swore this oath, in a voice so full of hatred that for a moment he was quite dumbfounded, and dropped his familiar tone, murmuring,

'Yes, I knew about Honoré being dead. He was a very kind person. But what's to be done? Others died, too, that's war... And well, I thought, once he was dead, there wasn't anything left to stop us; for after all, Silvine, I must remind you that I didn't force myself on you, you did consent...'

But he didn't finish, for he saw what a distressed state she was in, hands covering her face, ready to tear herself apart.

'Oh, yes, that's right! That's right, and that's what drives me so insane. Why did I consent, when I didn't love you at all?... I can't remember, I was so sad, so sick at heart because of Honoré leaving, and maybe it was because you talked to me about him, and you seemed to like him... Oh God! The number of nights I spent crying just thinking about it! It's a terrible thing to have done something you didn't want to do, and not be able to explain afterwards why you did it... And he'd forgiven me, he'd told me that if those Prussian bastards didn't kill him, he'd marry me in spite of everything, as soon as he was back from the army... And now you think I'm going to get back with you? Oh, I tell you, even if you hold a knife to my throat I'll say no, no, never!'

This time, Goliath became morose. He'd known her as a submissive girl, but now he sensed that she was unshakeable, fiercely determined. Easygoing fellow that he was, he nonetheless wanted her, by force if necessary, now that he was master; and if he desisted from using violence, it was out of an instinct for cunning and patience. This colossus, with his huge fists, didn't like hitting people. And so he thought of another way to make her submit.

'Right! Well, if you don't want me, I'll take the child with me.'

'What do you mean, you'll take the child?'

Charlot was still there, forgotten, hiding in his mother's skirts, doing his best not to burst into tears in the middle of this quarrel. And Goliath, finally getting up from his chair, approached him.

'Isn't that right? You're my little boy, aren't you, a little Prussian... Come here, so I can take you with me!'

But Silvine, shaking, had already gathered him swiftly into her arms and was clasping him to her breast.

'Him, a Prussian! No, he's French, he was born in France!'

'French! Just look at him, will you, and then look at me! He's the spitting image of me. Does he look at all like you?'

All she could see then was this tall, blond man, with his curly hair and beard, his thick, pink face with blue eyes shining like the glaze on pottery. And it was absolutely true, the little boy had the same yellow thatch of hair, the same cheeks, the same light-coloured eyes, the whole of that race was in him. Even she felt how different she was, with her black tresses escaping from her chignon onto her shoulder, all dishevelled.

'I made him, he's mine!' she said furiously. 'This is one Frenchman who'll never know a word of your foul German language. Oh yes! This is a Frenchman who'll kill the lot of you one day, to avenge the ones you killed!'

Charlot had begun to cry and sob, clinging to her neck.

'Mummy, Mummy, I'm scared, take me away!'

Then Goliath, no doubt wishing to avoid any sort of scene, drew back and merely declared, in a harsh voice, returning to the intimate tone from before,

'Just you remember what I'm about to say, Silvine... I know everything that goes on here. You receive visits from the guerrillas from Dieulet Woods, with that Sambuc, who's the brother of your farmhand, a bandit you provide with bread. And I know, too, that this farmhand, Prosper, is an African Chasseur, a deserter who should be in our hands; and I also know that you're hiding a wounded man, another soldier; one word from me, and he'll be sent straight to a German fortress... Eh? You see, I'm well informed...'

Now she was listening to him, mute, terrified, while Charlot, his face buried against her neck, repeated, stammering,

'Oh! Mummy, Mummy, take me away, I'm scared!'

'Right then!' said Goliath. 'I'm not an unkind man, and I'm not exactly fond of quarrels, you know that; but I swear to you I'll have them all arrested, old Fouchard and the others, if you don't agree to let me into your bedroom, next Monday... And I'll take the boy, too, I'll send him back home to my mother, she'd be more than happy to have him; because the minute you decide it's over, he's mine... You do understand, don't you, that all I'd have to do is come and get him, because by then there'd be no one left here. I'm the master, and I'll do as I please... So, what's it to be?'

But she didn't answer, she just held the child more tightly than ever, as if she were afraid someone might snatch him from her there and then; and dread and loathing began to show in her huge eyes.

'Fine, I'll give you three days to think about it... You'll leave your bedroom window open, the one overlooking the orchard... If I don't find that window open at seven o'clock on Monday evening, I'll have them all arrested the very next day, and I'll be back for the boy... Goodbye, Silvine!'

He calmly left, and she stayed rooted to the spot, her head churning with such huge, horrible ideas that they left her like some idiot. All day long, the same storms raged inside her. At first, her instinctive reaction was to pick up her child and just start walking straight ahead, anywhere; the only thing was, what would she do once night fell, how would she earn a living for him and herself? Not to mention that the Prussians out on the roads would stop her and maybe bring her back. Then it occurred to her to talk to Jean, and warn Prosper and even old Fouchard; but again she hesitated, drew back: was she sure enough of people's friendship to be certain that they wouldn't sacrifice her in the interest of a quiet life for the rest of them? No, no! She wouldn't say anything to anyone, she'd get herself out of danger on her own, since it was her doing alone, by her stubborn refusal. But God! What could she come up with? How could she prevent this misfortune? For her integrity revolted at the idea, and she would never have forgiven herself as long as she lived if, through her doing, such dreadful things happened to so many people, especially to Jean, who was so kind to Charlot.

The hours passed and the next day went by, without her finding a solution. She went about her work as usual, sweeping the kitchen floor, tending the cattle, making the soup. And in her silence, a terrifying silence she wouldn't break, her hatred for Goliath built up inside her like poison, hour upon hour. He was her sin, her damnation. If it hadn't been for him, she would have waited for Honoré, and Honoré would have been alive, and she would have been happy. What a tone he'd used to tell her he was master! Anyway, it was true, there were no longer any gendarmes or judges to go to, might alone was in the right. Oh! To be the strong one, to be able to take him when he came, this man who was talking of taking away others! For her, only the child was of her flesh. This accidental father didn't count, he'd never counted. She was no one's wife, all she felt was a rising tide of anger and the bitterness of the vanquished when she thought of him. She would have killed the child rather than hand it over to him, and then she would have killed herself. And she'd already said it to him, she wished that the boy, the child he'd given her like some sort of gift of hatred, could have been grown up already, capable of defending her, she could picture him in years to come, bearing a rifle, putting bullets through the hides of the lot of them over there. Oh, yes! One more Frenchman, one more Prussian-killing Frenchman!

However, she only had one more day left and must make up her mind. From the very first instant, an unthinkable idea had indeed passed through her poor, sick head in her distress: to tip off the guerrillas and give Sambuc the information he was waiting for. But the idea had remained vague and elusive, and she'd pushed it aside, thinking it monstrous, unable even to bear considering it: after all, wasn't this man still the father of her child? She couldn't have him murdered. Then the idea had come back to her, becoming more and more pervasive, more urgent; and now it was insistent, imposing itself with the winning strength of its simplicity and finality. With Goliath dead, Jean, Prosper, and old Fouchard would have nothing more to fear. She would keep Charlot herself, and no one would ever again have any claim on him. And there was something else, too, something deep and unconscious within her, rising up from the depths of her being: the need to put an end to it, to efface the child's paternity by effacing his father, and the savage joy of telling herself that afterwards it would be as if her sin had been amputated, she would be mother and sole mistress of the child, without having to share him with a male. For another whole day she turned the plan over in her mind, lacking the energy to push it away, her thoughts constantly returning to the mechanics of the ambush, thinking ahead, planning the slightest details. And now it had become an obsession, an idea which had taken root and which no longer needed weighing up; and when she eventually acted and obeyed this urge towards the inevitable, she walked as if in a dream, bending to someone else's will, someone within her whom she'd never known before.

That Sunday, an anxious Fouchard had sent word to the guerrillas that their sack of loaves would be delivered to them in the Boisville quarries, a very quiet spot two kilometres away; and as Prosper happened to be busy it was Silvine he sent with the wheelbarrow. Wasn't this Fate? She saw it as a decree of destiny; she spoke and gave Sambuc the rendezvous for the following evening in a precise voice, empty of emotion, as if she couldn't have acted any other way. The next day there were more signs, sure proof that people, and even things, wanted the murder to happen. First of all there was old Fouchard, suddenly called to Raucourt, leaving them orders to eat without him, not expecting to be home much before eight o'clock. Then Henriette, who hadn't been due on night duty at the hospital until Tuesday, was informed at very short notice that she'd be needed to replace the person on duty that evening, who'd been taken sick. And as Jean never left his room whatever noise he happened to hear, there was only Prosper left whom she was afraid might interfere. It wasn't something he agreed with, cutting a man's throat like that when he was outnumbered. But when he saw his brother and two lieutenants arriving, his disgust for these shady characters was balanced out by his loathing of the Prussians: he certainly wasn't about to save one of the dirty bastards, even if they were going to use nasty methods to deal with him; and he preferred to go to bed and bury his head in the pillow instead, so that he wouldn't hear and be tempted to act like a soldier.

It was a quarter to seven, and Charlot was obstinately refusing to go to sleep. Usually as soon as he'd eaten his soup he would slump forward, head resting on the table.

'Come on, darling, sleep now,' repeated Silvine, carrying him into Henriette's room, 'look what a nice sleepy-byes you're going to have on Auntie's big bed.'

But this treat was precisely what was making the child excited, and he wriggled and giggled fit to burst.

'No, no... Stay here, Mummy... Play with me, Mummy...'

She waited patiently, being very gentle with him, stroking him and saying over and over,

'Sleepy-byes, darling... Sleepy-byes, for Mummy...'

And the child finally fell asleep, a smile on his lips. She hadn't bothered undressing him, but covered him up warmly and left the room without locking it, for he was usually such a sound, deep sleeper.

Never had Silvine felt so calm, so sharp and clear in her mind. Her decisions were swift and her movements were light, as if she were outside her body, acting under the impulse of the other, the person she didn't know at all. She'd already let Sambuc in, along with Cabasse and Ducat, warning them to be as careful as possible; and she led them into her room, placing them to the right and left of the window, which she opened in spite of the bitter cold. It was very dark and the room was only palely lit by the reflection from the snow. A deathly silence came from the countryside, and endless minutes ticked by. At last, hearing the faint sound of approaching footsteps, Silvine left the room and went to sit in the kitchen, where she waited, stock still, her huge eyes staring at the candle flame.

They still had to wait a long time, for Goliath prowled around the farm before risking it. He thought he knew the young woman quite well, and so he'd dared to come with only a revolver at his belt. But a sense of unease put him on his guard, and he pushed the window wide open, peering inside, calling softly,

'Silvine! Silvine!'

Since he'd found the window open, it must mean that she'd thought it over, and that she consented. This caused him huge pleasure, although he would have preferred to see her there, greeting and reassuring him. No doubt old Fouchard had called her back to finish some chore or other. He raised his voice a little.

'Silvine! Silvine!'

There was nothing by way of reply, not even a breath. He swung his leg over the windowsill and entered, intending to climb into the bed and wait for her under the covers, it was so cold.

All of a sudden there was a furious scramble, feet trampling, limbs slipping, accompanied by muffled swearing and cursing. Sambuc and the others had thrown themselves on Goliath; and in spite of their number they couldn't master the colossus, the danger increasing his strength tenfold. Through the darkness came the crack of limbs and the breathless effort of holding him down. Luckily the revolver had fallen to the floor. A voice, Cabasse's, stammered out, half-strangled,

'The ropes, the ropes!' while Ducat passed Sambuc the bundle of ropes they'd had the foresight to bring with them. There followed a savage operation, with kicking and punching, legs roped first of all, then arms bound to his sides, then his whole body tied up, fumbling, haphazardly, in between convulsions, with such an over-abundance of loops and knots that the man seemed to be caught up in a net, with the mesh digging into his skin. He kept shouting, and Ducat's voice kept saying 'Will you shut your gob!' The cries ceased, as Cabasse brutally knotted an old blue handkerchief over his mouth. Finally, they could breathe easy, and carried him like some sort of package into the kitchen, where they laid him out on the large table, next to the candle.

'Prussian bastard,' swore Sambuc, wiping his brow. 'Whew! What a hard time he gave us!... Listen, Silvine, why don't you light another candle, so that we can get a good look at this nasty son of a bitch!'

Her eyes wide, wide open in her pale face, Silvine got up. Without a word she lit a candle and placed it on the other side of Goliath's head; he lay there, brilliantly illuminated, as if between two altar candles. And at that moment their eyes met: he pleaded with her, frantic, consumed by fear; but she seemed not to understand, withdrew to the sideboard and remained standing there, stubborn and cold.

'The sod's bitten off half my finger,' growled Cabasse, whose hand was bleeding. 'I'll have to break something for him!'

He was already raising the revolver, which he'd picked up off the floor, when Sambuc disarmed him.

'No, no, let's not do anything stupid!... We're not villains, us, we're judges... D'you hear, you Prussian bastard, we're going to judge you; and don't be scared, we'll fully respect your rights to a defence... You won't be the one defending you, because if we took your muzzle off you'd burst our eardrums. But I'll give you a lawyer in a minute, and a bloody good one, too!'

He went to fetch three chairs, placed them in a row and assembled what he called the tribunal, with him in the middle, flanked on either side by his two lieutenants. All three sat down and then he rose to his feet, speaking with mocking slowness which gradually rose and rose in volume, full of vengeful anger.

'I am both presiding judge and prosecuting counsel. Not exactly proper, I know, but there aren't enough of us to go round... Therefore, I accuse you of having come to France to sneak on us, so repaying us with the lowest sort of treachery for the bread you ate at our tables. For you are the primary cause of the disaster, you're the traitor who led the Bavarians by night as far as Beaumont, through Dieulet Woods, after the battle of Nouart. It had to have been someone who'd lived in the area for a long time, to know all the little lanes so well; and we're quite convinced of this, for you were seen guiding the artillery along tracks in a terrible state which had turned into lakes of mud, where eight horses were needed to pull each gun. When you see these roads now, it's impossible to believe it, and you wonder how on earth an army corps managed to get through... If it hadn't been for you, and the criminal way you got yourself pampered in our houses and then sold us to the enemy, the surprise attack at Beaumont wouldn't have taken place, we wouldn't have gone to Sedan, and maybe we'd have ended up thrashing you lot... And I won't even mention the disgusting job you're still doing, or the cheek of your showing your face here again, all triumphant, denouncing all these poor souls and making them quake with fear... You are the very basest scum, and I therefore demand the death penalty.'

There was a silence. He sat down again and finally said,

'I officially appoint Ducat to defend you... He's been a bailiff, and would have gone far, if it hadn't been for his passions. You see, I'm refusing you nothing and we're being very nice to you.'

Goliath, who couldn't move a finger, turned his gaze to his improvised defence counsel. His eyes were the only part of him alive now, eyes full of ardent supplication, beneath a livid brow, drenched in the sweat of fear, collecting in large beads despite the cold.

'Gentlemen,' pleaded Ducat, rising to his feet, 'my client is indeed the vilest of men, and I would not have taken on his defence if I couldn't point out, in mitigation, that they're all like that where he comes from... Just look at him and you'll see, by his eyes, that he is most astonished. He doesn't understand what his crime is. In France, we keep our spies at arm's length; but over there, espionage is a most honourable profession, a praiseworthy way of serving one's country... I would even go so far, gentlemen, as to say that perhaps they are not entirely mistaken. Our noble sentiments do us great honour, but unfortunately they've led to our defeat. If I dare express myself thus, *quos vult perdere Jupiter dementat*.* As you will appreciate, gentlemen.'

And he sat back down, while Sambuc began again,

'And what about you, Cabasse, have you anything to say for or against the accused?'

'What I want to say,' cried the Provençal, 'is that we're doing a lot of beating around the bush before giving this sod what he deserves... I've had my share of trouble in my time; but I don't like people larking around where justice is concerned, it's bad luck... Death! Death!'

Sambuc solemnly stood up again.

'So, that is the decision of you both, death, is it not... ?'

'Yes, yes! Death!'

The chairs were pushed back and he approached Goliath, saying,

'Judgement has been passed, you are to die.'

The two candles burned with tall wicks, like altar candles, to the right and left of Goliath's contorted face. He was trying so hard to cry for mercy, to shout out the words choking him, that the blue handkerchief over his mouth was becoming soaked in foam; and it was a terrible sight to see this man reduced to silence, already as dumb as a corpse, about to die with this stream of explanations and prayers stuck in his throat.

Cabasse began loading the revolver.

'Shall I blow his head off?' he asked.

'Oh, no! No!' cried Sambuc. 'That would suit him far too nicely.'

Then, turning back to Goliath,

'You aren't a soldier, you don't deserve the honour of dying with a bullet through your skull... No! You're going to die like the dirty swine of a spy that you are.'

He turned round and politely asked,

'Silvine, would you mind bringing me a tub?'

During the judgement scene, Silvine hadn't moved. She waited, face rigid, absent-minded, completely absorbed in the obsession which had been urging her on for the past two days. And when she was asked for a tub she simply obeyed, disappearing for a moment into the storeroom next door and coming back with a large tub which she used for doing Charlot's laundry.

'Right, put it under the edge of the table.'

She did so, and as she straightened up, her eyes again met Goliath's. In the wretched man's gaze she saw a final plea and the revolt of the man who didn't want to die. But at that moment, there was nothing of the woman left in her, just her desire for this death, which she'd been waiting for like some kind of deliverance. She withdrew to the sideboard again, and stayed there.

Sambuc, opening the drawer in the table, had taken from it a large kitchen knife, the one they used to cut the bacon with.

'So, seeing as you're a pig, I'm going to stick you like a pig.'

And he took his time, conversing with Cabasse and Ducat, to ensure that the slitting of the throat went ahead in an orderly fashion. They even quarrelled about it, because Cabasse said that where he came from, in Provence, pigs were stuck with their heads pointing down, while Ducat protested, indignant, calling this a barbaric, awkward method.

'Move him well down the table, over the tub, so we don't make a mess.'

They moved him forward, and Sambuc proceeded calmly and cleanly. With one slice of the huge blade he slit the throat from one side to the other. Immediately, the blood began pouring from the severed carotid artery into the tub, making a gentle noise like a fountain. He'd handled the wound carefully, and hardly a drop of blood had spurted out as the heart pulsed. If death came more slowly this way, the convulsions weren't even visible, for the ligatures were solid and the body remained completely still. Not a jolt, not a gasp. The death agony could be seen only on his face, on that fear-distorted mask from which the blood was draining drop by drop, leaving the skin without colour, as white as a sheet. And the eyes grew empty, too. They clouded over, then went out.

'Hey, Silvine, we could do with a sponge, all the same.'

But she didn't reply, clutching her arms to her chest in an unconscious gesture, standing bolted to the floor, a tightness round her throat like an iron collar. She was watching. Then, all of a sudden, she noticed that Charlot was there, clinging to her skirts. No doubt he'd woken up and managed to open the doors; and no one had seen him creep in with his childish curiosity. How long had he been there, half hidden behind his mother? He was watching, too. With his big, blue eyes, beneath his blond thatch of hair, he was watching the blood flow, the little red fountain gradually filling the tub. Maybe he found it amusing. Hadn't he understood at first? And did a breath of something horrible then blow over him, did he instinctively recognize the abomination he was witnessing? He gave a sharp cry of distress.

'Oh! Mummy, oh Mummy, I'm scared, take me away!'

And it made Silvine jump so violently that she was shaken to the core. It was too much for her, she crumbled inwardly, and her horror finally swept away all the strength and excitement of the obsession which had been keeping her going for the past two days. The woman in her came back to life, and she burst into tears, wildly scooping up Charlot and pressing him frantically to her breast. And she ran out with him in her arms at a terrified pace, unable to bear to see or hear any more, wishing only to vanish, anywhere, into the first hidden corner she could find.

Just then Jean decided to open his door softly. Even though he never worried about the noises on the farm, he'd been more and more surprised to hear all these comings and goings and voices calling out. And it was into his peaceful room that Silvine flung herself, dishevelled, sobbing, shaken by such a fit of distress that at first he couldn't understand her stammered words, uttered haltingly between her teeth. She repeatedly made the same gesture, as if to chase away the horrific vision. At last he understood, and he too saw the ambush, the slitting of the throat, the mother standing there, with the little boy hiding in her skirts, looking at the father whose blood was pouring from his throat; and the realization froze him to the spot, his peasant's heart, his soldier's heart, was broken in anguish. Oh! War, abominable war, turning all these poor people into wild animals, sowing terrible hatred, where the son was splattered by his own father's blood, perpetuating the quarrel between the two races, later to grow up in loathing of his father's family, whom perhaps he would some day exterminate! What dreadful harvests would be reaped from such wicked seed!

Collapsing onto a chair and covering Charlot with distracted kisses as he sobbed against her neck, Silvine went on and on repeating the same phrase, the cry from her bleeding heart.

'Oh! My poor little one, no one's ever going to call you a Prussian again!... Oh! My poor little one, no one's ever going to call you a Prussian again!...'

In the kitchen, old Fouchard had just got home. He had knocked with the master's authority, and they'd decided to let him in. And it had to be said, he wasn't overly pleased by the surprise that greeted him, finding this dead body on the table with the tub full of blood underneath. Naturally, not being a terribly patient man, he had lost his temper.

'Well, right bastards you lot are—couldn't you have done your dirty work outside? Eh? D'you think my house is a dung heap, coming waltzing in here and messing up the furniture with stunts like this?'

Then, as Sambuc made their excuses, explaining to him, the old boy went on, now overcome by fear and getting even more irritated.

'And what the bloody hell do you expect me to do with your dead body here? D'you think it's nice to go sticking a dead person in someone's house, without thinking about what they'll do with it afterwards?... And supposing a patrol comes by—I'll be in a fine mess! You lot just couldn't give a toss, could you, you didn't even bother wondering whether this would cost me my neck or not... Well, I swear to God, you'll have me to answer to if you don't take your corpse away right this minute! D'you hear me, get hold of his head, feet, whatever, but just make sure he doesn't hang around, and that in three minutes flat there's not a single hair of him left in here!'

Finally, Sambuc managed to get old Fouchard to provide them with a sack, even though it made the old boy's heart bleed to have to give away something else. He chose one of the most battered, saying that even a bag with holes in it was far too good for a Prussian. Cabasse and Ducat, though, had terrible trouble trying to get Goliath's body inside: his body was too big and too long, and his feet stuck out. Then they took it outside and loaded it on to the wheelbarrow they used for carrying the bread.

'I give you my word of honour,' declared Sambuc, 'that we're going to chuck it in the Meuse!'

'Well,' insisted Fouchard, 'just you make sure to tie two big stones to his feet, so that the bugger doesn't come back up again!'

And in the deep, black night, over the pale snow, the little procession disappeared, with only a faint, plaintive squeaking from the wheelbarrow.

Sambuc always swore on his father's grave that he had indeed attached two large stones to the feet. However, the body floated back up and the Prussians discovered it three days later, in Pont-Maugis, lying among some long grass; and when they pulled the dead man out of the sack, throat cut, stuck like a pig, they were furious. There were terrible threats, harassment, and searches. No doubt a few locals said a bit too much, for one evening they came to arrest the mayor of Remilly and old Fouchard, on charges of being too friendly with the guerrillas, who were accused of the deed. And under these dire circumstances old Fouchard cut a truly fine figure, the impassive old peasant who knows the invincible strength of calm and silence. He walked off, without panic, without even asking for an explanation. We'd soon see. In the neighbourhood, there were mumblings about how he'd already made a large fortune out of the Prussians, that he had huge bags of gold which he stashed away somewhere, one at a time, as he earned them.

When Henriette learned of all these goings on, she was dreadfully worried. Yet again, afraid of compromising his hosts, Jean wanted to leave, even though the doctor still thought he was too weak; and Henriette, once more engulfed in such a wave of sadness at the thought that they must soon be parted, insisted on him staying for another two weeks. When old Fouchard had been arrested, Jean had managed to escape by hiding at the back of the barn; but wasn't there still a danger that he might be caught and taken away at any moment, in the likely event of further searches? Apart from this, she also trembled with fear for her uncle's fate. So one morning, she resolved to go to Sedan to visit the Delaherches, who, it was said, had a very influential Prussian officer staying with them.

'Silvine,' she said as she was leaving, 'take good care of our patient, give him his broth at midday and his medicine at four o'clock.'

The servant, in the middle of all her usual chores, had once again become the courageous, submissive girl, and was now running the farm in the master's absence, while Charlot jumped and laughed around her.

'Have no fear, ma'am, he'll want for nothing... He's got me to cosset him.'

CHAPTER SIX

In Sedan, in the Delaherches' house on the Rue Maqua, life had begun again after the terrible upheaval of the battle and capitulation; and for nearly four months now, day had followed day, under the gloomy oppression of the Prussian occupation.

However, one corner of the vast factory buildings remained closed up, as if uninhabited: it was the room overlooking the street at the far end of the main apartments, the room where Colonel de Vineuil was still living. While the other windows stood open and let out the sound of constant comings and goings, the commotion of living, those of this little room seemed dead, their shutters obstinately closed. The colonel had complained about his eyes, and said that the strong daylight made them worse; and they weren't sure whether he was lying or not, but kept a lamp near him, day and night, to keep him happy. For two long months he had been confined to his bed, even though Major Bouroche had only diagnosed a cracked ankle: the wound wouldn't heal and there had been all sorts of complications. Now he was getting up, but morally he was so devastated, prey to an indefinable ill which was so persistent and pervasive that he spent his days lying on a chaise longue before a great log fire. He was losing weight, turning into a mere shadow, yet the doctor caring for him, much to his surprise, was unable to find any lesion or cause of this slow death. He was going out, just like a flame.

And old Madame Delaherche had shut herself up with him the day after the occupation. They had probably come to an agreement, once and for all and in few words, over their solemn wish to cloister themselves away together in this room for as long as there were Prussians staying in the house. Many had spent two or three nights there and a captain, Monsieur von Gartlauben, was staying there permanently. Otherwise, neither the colonel nor the old lady had ever spoken again on these matters. In spite of her seventy-eight years she would rise at dawn and come to settle herself in an armchair opposite her friend on the other side of the fireplace; and in the steady light of the lamp she set about knitting stockings for poor children, while he, eyes staring into the embers, never did anything, seeming to live and die with but one thing on his mind, becoming more and more lethargic. In a whole day they couldn't have exchanged twenty words, for he'd motion to her to stop each time that she, coming and going about the house, involuntarily let slip some piece of news about the outside world; so much so that from then on nothing from the life outside penetrated the room, and nothing reached them either of the siege of Paris, the defeats on the Loire, or the daily sufferings of the invasion. It was in vain, though, that the colonel refused to let in daylight and blocked his ears, for into this voluntary tomb, probably through the cracks and in the very air he breathed, the whole terrifying disaster, all the mortal grief must have reached him; for with each hour that passed he seemed to be poisoned nonetheless, dying little by little.

Meanwhile in broad daylight, and very much for living life, Delaherche was rushing around, trying to reopen his factory. He'd only been able to get a few looms going again so far, with both his workforce and customers in such turmoil. So he'd had an idea, to try and occupy his gloomy free time, which was to draw up a full inventory of his business and study the possibility of making a few improvements of which he'd long dreamed. Particularly since he had a young man at his disposal to assist him in the task, the son of one of his customers, who'd ended up in his house after the battle. Edmond Lagarde, who had grown up in Passy in his father's little draper's shop, had been a sergeant in the 5th infantry regiment at only just twenty-three years old, although he looked barely eighteen; he had fired away like a true hero, fighting on so fiercely that he'd returned from the battle through the Port du Ménil at about five o'clock, his left arm broken by one of the very last bullets; and Delaherche had kept him on after the wounded had been evacuated from his warehouses, out of the goodness of his heart. This was how Edmond came to be part of the family, eating, sleeping, and living there, now fully recovered, acting as a secretary to the mill owner while he waited until he could go back to Paris. Thanks to Delaherche's protection and his own solemn promise not to run away, the Prussian authorities left him alone. He was blond and blue-eyed, as pretty as a girl, and so timid and so delicate with it that he would blush at the slightest word. His mother had brought him up, bleeding herself dry for him, putting the profits of their meagre trade towards his education. And he adored Paris and would tell Gilberte how much he missed it, a wounded cherub to whom the young woman tended like a comrade.

And then the household's numbers had been swollen by their new guest, Monsieur von Gartlauben, a captain in the Landwehr whose regiment had replaced the troops on active duty in Sedan. In spite of his modest rank he was an influential person, for his uncle was the Governor-General installed in Rheims, who exercised absolute power over the entire region. He too prided himself on loving Paris and having lived there, and on there being no etiquette or refined customs of the city with which he wasn't acquainted; and indeed, he affected the correct behaviour of a true gentleman, concealing beneath this gloss his natural roughness. Forever done up tightly in his uniform, he was a tall, fat man who lied about his age, despairing at his forty-five years. Had he been more intelligent he could have been formidable; but his excessive vanity caused him to be perpetually smug, for he could never bring himself to believe that anyone could possibly be making fun of him.

Later on, he would prove a true saviour for Delaherche. How dreadful, though, were those first days, just after the capitulation! Sedan quaked, under invasion, full of German soldiers, terrified of being pillaged. Then the victorious troops headed back to the valley of the Seine, leaving just one garrison behind, and the city sank into a morbid state of peace, like a ghost town: houses forever shuttered, shops closed, streets deserted as soon as dusk fell, filled with the heavy steps and harsh cries of the patrols. There were no more newspapers, no more letters. They were walled up, suddenly cut off, left in ignorance and dread at further disasters which they could sense coming. To put the finishing touch to their misery, famine was threatening to strike. One morning, they had woken up to find themselves with no bread and no meat, the land ruined as if in the wake of a swarm of locusts, after a week in which hundreds of thousands of men had come pouring in, rushing through the town. The city had only two days' worth of provisions left, and they had been forced to seek help from Belgium, so that now everything came from the neighbouring country, across the open frontier, where customs controls had disappeared, swept away like everything else in the catastrophe. And to add to this they underwent daily harassment, locked every day into new battles between the Prussian command based in the Sous-Préfecture and the town council in permanent session at the town hall. This last, which put up heroic administrative resistance, tried in vain to argue and give in only an inch at a time, but the citizens succumbed nonetheless to the increasingly harsh demands and to the volatile and excessively frequent requisitioning.

At first, Delaherche had a hard time from the soldiers and officers billeted on him. Every race on earth would walk through his doors, with pipes clenched between their teeth. Every day, two thousand, three thousand men would unexpectedly descend on the town, infantry, cavalry, artillery; and although these men only had the right to a fire and a roof over their heads, it often meant running around trying to find supplies. The rooms they stayed in were left disgustingly filthy. Often the officers came in drunk, making themselves more unbearable than their own soldiers. However, the discipline was so strict that acts of violence and pillage were rare. In the whole of Sedan, only two women were known to have been attacked. It was only later on, when Paris refused to surrender, that they roughly made their dominance felt, infuriated at seeing the struggle dragging on, worried by the attitudes in the provinces, in constant fear of a mass uprising and the guerrilla warfare which had been declared on them by the snipers.

Delaherche had only recently played host to a major in the cavalry who kept his boots on in bed and had left the room knee-deep in filth, when, in the final half of September, Captain von Gartlauben came along, one evening of torrential rain. The first hour was fairly tough. He spoke loudly, demanding the finest room and banging his sword all the way up the stairs. However, at the sight of Gilberte, he suddenly began to behave, shutting himself away, passing by stiffly, uttering a polite word of greeting. He was constantly pandered to, for everyone knew that a word from him to the colonel in command in Sedan was enough to lighten a requisition or obtain a man's release. Recently his uncle, the Governor-General in Rheims, had made a coldly savage proclamation, declaring a state of siege and threatening to punish by death anyone working for the enemy, whether by spying, misleading the German troops under their guidance, or destroying bridges and damaging telegraph and railway lines. The enemy in question were the French; and the hearts of the inhabitants filled with fury as they read the large, white notice stuck to the wall outside Prussian headquarters, making crimes of their fears and vows. It was already so hard, having to learn about the German armies' fresh victories by the cheers coming from the garrison! Each day brought its own grief, with the soldiers lighting huge fires, singing, and getting drunk all through the night, while the inhabitants, now forced to be indoors by nine o'clock, listened from within their darkened houses, frantic with uncertainty, guessing that some new misfortune must have befallen them. It was under such circumstances, towards mid-October, that for the first time Monsieur von Gartlauben showed proof of some finer feelings. Since morning, Sedan's hopes had been rising, as rumours went round of a major success for the Loire army marching to save Paris. But how often before had the most hopeful piece of information turned into news of disaster! And as it happened, that same evening they learned that the Bavarian army had taken Orléans. In the Rue Maqua, in a house opposite the factory, the soldiers were bawling so loudly that the captain, seeing how very upset it made Gilberte, went to make them shut up, even he finding such a racket out of place.

The month went by and Monsieur von Gartlauben again found himself doing a few little favours for them. The Prussian authorities had reorganized the administrative services and had just appointed a German Sous-Préfet; not that this brought the inconveniences to an end, although the man did appear to be relatively reasonable. Among the constant difficulties which arose between Prussian command and the town council, one of the most frequent concerned the requisitioning of carriages; and a real scandal broke out one morning after Delaherche had been unable to send his barouche and two horses to the Sous-Préfecture: at one point, the mayor was placed under arrest and Delaherche himself would have joined him in the citadel, if it hadn't been for Monsieur von Gartlauben, whose simple intervention defused the angry situation. Another day, he stepped in to obtain a reprieve for the town, condemned to paying a fine of thirty thousand francs as punishment for the supposed delays in rebuilding the Pont de Villette, which had been destroyed by the Prussians, a quite deplorable business which ruined and throroughly upset the whole of Sedan. But it was after the surrender of Metz in particular that Delaherche came to owe a real debt of gratitude to his guest. The dreadful news had been like a thunderbolt for the townspeople, the quashing of their very last hopes; and in the week which followed, more masses of troops trampled through the town, rushing down in a torrent from Metz, Prince Frederick Charles's army heading for the Loire, General Manteuffel's troops* marching on Amiens and Rouen, with further corps going to bolster the besieging forces around Paris. For several days, the houses overflowed with soldiers, bakeries and butchers' shops were swept clean, right to the last crumbs and bones, and a sweaty odour clung to the paving stones, like the greasy smell of wool that lingers in the wake of large migrating flocks of sheep. Only the factory on the Rue Maqua was spared the suffering caused by this overspill of human cattle, protected by a friendly hand, marked out simply for lodging a few well-brought-up commanding officers.

So Delaherche eventually abandoned his cold attitude. The better-off families had shut themselves away in their living quarters, avoiding any contact with the officers staying there. He, however, with his continual urge to talk, to please, to enjoy life, was ill at ease with this role of sulky defeat. His large, silent, icy house, where everyone lived separately, stiff with rancour, weighed horribly on his shoulders. So one day he stopped Monsieur von Gartlauben on the stairs, to thank him for what he had done for them. And little by little it became a habit, the two men would exchange a few words whenever their paths crossed; so much so that, one evening, the Prussian captain found himself sitting in the mill owner's study, in front of the fire, where huge oak logs were blazing, smoking a cigar and chatting amiably about recent news. For the first two weeks, Gilberte didn't put in an appearance, and he pretended to be unaware of her existence, even though his eyes, at the slightest sound, would instantly flick to the door into the next room. He seemed to want them to forget his position as conqueror, and was happy to joke about some of the absurd requisitions. For instance, one day, when a coffin and a bandage had been requisitioned, these objects caused him much amusement. As for the rest of it, coal, oil, milk, sugar, butter, bread, meat, not to mention clothing, stoves, lamps, in short, anything edible and anything necessary for everyday living, he would shrug his shoulders: God, what could you do? Of course it was annoying, even he agreed that too much was being asked from them; the only thing was, this was war, and you had to survive somehow on enemy territory. Delaherche, who was irritated by the endless requisitions, was as outspoken as ever, going over them with a fine-toothed comb each evening as if he were examining his household accounts. Nevertheless, their conversation grew heated only once, over the contribution of a million francs which had just been slapped on the department of the Ardennes by the Prussian

Préfet in Rethel, on the pretext of compensating the losses caused to Germany by French warships,* and the expulsion of Germans living in France. Sedan alone had to pay forty-two thousand francs. He exhausted himself trying to make his guest understand that this was quite unfair, and the town was in an exceptional position, that it had suffered enough already without being hit by this. What was more, the two men emerged from their arguments closer than ever, Delaherche delighted to have been able to get carried away by the sound of his own voice, the Prussian happy to have displayed an utterly Parisian urbanity.

One evening, in her gay, absent-minded way, Gilberte came in. She stopped short, pretending to be surprised. Monsieur von Gartlauben rose, and had the delicacy to withdraw almost immediately. The following day, however, he found Gilberte already seated, and he took up his place by the fireside. It was the start of many a charming evening spent in this working study, rather than the drawing room, which made a subtle difference. Later on, even, when the young woman agreed to play some music for her guest, who adored it, she went alone into the adjoining room, simply leaving the door open. In this harsh winter, the old Ardennes oak blazed away at the back of the tall grate, and towards ten o'clock they would have a cup of tea and chat in the cosiness of the vast room. And Monsieur von Gartlauben had quite obviously fallen madly in love with this young woman who was so full of laughter, who flirted with him as she'd done back in Charleville with the friends of Captain Beaudoin. He began to take more care over his appearance, displaying exaggerated gallantry, taking pleasure in the slightest show of indulgence, his one fear and torment being that he would be taken for a barbarian, a coarse soldier with no respect for women.

And so they seemed to live parallel lives in the huge, dark house on the Rue Maqua. While Edmond, with his pretty, wounded cherub's features, replied in monosyllables to the uninterrupted flow of chatter from Delaherche over the dinner table, blushing if Gilberte so much as asked him to pass the salt, and while in the evenings Monsieur von Gartlauben, an ecstatic look in his eyes, sat in the study listening to the young woman playing him a Mozart sonata from the drawing room, the bedroom next door, where Colonel de Vineuil and Madame Delaherche passed their days, stayed silent, with the shutters closed, the lamp forever lit, like a tomb illuminated

by a candle. December had buried the town beneath the snow, and
the desperate news was muffled in the sharp cold. After the defeat of
General Ducrot at Champigny, after the loss of Orléans, there was
only a shadow of a hope left, that the soil of France would become
the avenger, the exterminator, devouring the conquerors. Let the
snowflakes fall more thickly, let the ground crack open where the
frost split the soil, to make a tomb for the whole of Germany! Madame Delaherche was seized by a new fear. One night when her son
wasn't there, called away to Belgium on business, as she was walking
past Gilberte's bedroom she'd heard the faint sound of voices and
hushed kisses, mingled with laughter. Shocked, she had gone back to
her room, horrified by the abomination she suspected: it could only
be the Prussian in there—she thought she'd already noticed several
knowing looks, and this final shame left her completely crushed. Oh!
This woman her son had brought into the house, against her will,
this easy woman, whom she'd already forgiven once, by keeping
quiet after Captain Beaudoin's death! So, it was starting all over
again, and this time it was the vilest infamy! What was she to do? She
couldn't allow such monstrous behaviour under her roof. The grief
of the reclusive life she led was made even worse, and she spent days
torturing herself. On the days when she returned to the colonel's
room more sombre than ever and silent for hours on end, with tears
in her eyes, he would look at her and imagine that France had suffered yet another defeat.

It was at this very point that, one morning, Henriette turned up at
the Rue Maqua to enlist the help of the Delaherches concerning the
fate of Uncle Fouchard. She'd heard people talk jokingly about the
all-powerful influence Gilberte possessed over Monsieur von
Gartlauben. And so she was a little embarrassed on finding herself
faced with Madame Delaherche, who was the first person she saw on
the stairs, going back up to the colonel's room, and thought she
ought to explain the purpose of her visit.

'Oh! Madame, it would be so good of you to step in!... My uncle is
in a dreadful situation, they're talking of sending him to Germany.'

The old lady gave an angry gesture, although she liked Henriette.

'My dear child, I have no power whatsoever... I'm not the one you
should be talking to...'

Then, despite seeing how distressed she was, she added,

'You've come at a very bad time, my son is leaving for Brussels this evening... Why don't you ask my daughter-in-law, she can do anything...'

And she left Henriette there, speechless, convinced now that she had landed right in the middle of some domestic crisis. Madame Delaherche had determined to tell her son everything before he left for Belgium, where he was going to negotiate over a large purchase of coal, in the hope of getting his factory's looms back in action. Not for a moment was she going to allow the abomination to start again, right under her nose, during this renewed absence. Before speaking out, she bided her time, wanting to be sure that he wasn't going to postpone his departure until another time, as he'd been doing for the past week. Her household would collapse, the Prussian would be sent packing, the woman flung out into the street and her name pasted ignominiously on the walls, the punishment with which any French woman who gave herself to a German had been threatened.

When Gilberte caught sight of Henriette, she gave a cry of joy.

'Oh! I'm so pleased to see you!... It seems like such a long time, and we're growing old so quickly, what with all these dreadful goings on!'

She pulled her into her room and made her sit on the chaise longue, hugging her tightly.

'Right, why don't you dine with us... First, though, let's talk. You must have so much to tell me!... I know that you haven't had any news from your brother. Hmm? Poor Maurice, how sorry I am for him, over there in Paris with no gas, no wood, maybe no bread, even!... And this man you're looking after, your brother's friend? You see, I've already heard all about it... Is it because of him that you're here?'

Henriette took her time answering, seized by a sudden sense of unease. Deep down, wasn't Jean the reason she'd come, to make sure that, with her uncle freed, no one would come and bother her precious patient? Hearing Gilberte speak of him had filled her with embarrassment, and she no longer dared admit the true motive for her visit, her conscience now troubled, finding it repugnant to make use of the dubious influence she believed the other possessed.

'So,' repeated Gilberte, with a crafty air, 'it's because of this man you need our help?'

And when Henriette, cornered, finally began to speak of how old Fouchard had been arrested, she said,

'Oh! That's right, how stupid of me! I was only talking about it this morning!... Oh, my dear girl, you were right to come, we must take care of your uncle straight away, for the last news I had wasn't good... They want to make an example of him.'

'Yes, I did think of you here,' went on Henriette, in a hesitant voice. 'I thought you might give me some good advice, that maybe you could do something...'

The young woman gave a burst of pretty laughter.

'You silly thing, I'll have him released within three days!... Hasn't anyone told you that here, in this very house, I have a Prussian captain who does everything I want?... You see, my dear, he just can't refuse me!'

And she laughed even louder, quite simply scatterbrained, full of her coquettish triumph, holding both her friend's hands in hers, stroking them, while Henriette could find no word of thanks, full of unease, tortured by the belief that what she had just heard was an admission of guilt. But how serene and full of joy she was!

'Leave it to me, I'll send you home happy this evening.'

As they entered the dining room, Henriette was surprised by the delicate beauty of Edmond, whom she didn't know. He was delightful, like some pretty object. Was it possible that this boy had fought in battle, and that someone had dared to break his arm? The legend of his outstanding bravery put the finishing touch to his charm, and Delaherche, who'd greeted Henriette like a man thrilled to see a new face, wouldn't stop praising his secretary as the cutlets and jacket potatoes were being served, recounting that he was as industrious and as well-brought-up as he was handsome. The meal, with the four of them in the warmth of the dining room, turned into a deliciously cosy occasion.

'So, you came to enlist our help in deciding old Fouchard's fate, did you?' the mill owner began. 'It's extremely annoying that I have to leave this evening... But my wife will sort it out for you, she gets anything she wants.'

He laughed, saying these things perfectly good-naturedly, simply flattered by this power, of which he was personally rather proud. Then, suddenly, he said,

'By the way, darling, hasn't Edmond told you about his little find?'

'No, what's that?' Gilberte asked gaily, turning her pretty, caressing gaze on the young sergeant.

But he would start to blush, as if overcome by pleasure, whenever a woman looked at him like that.

'Goodness, Madame, it's only that old lace, which you were so sad you didn't have to decorate your mauve gown... Yesterday, I was fortunate enough to come across five metres of old-fashioned Bruges stitch,* which is really very fine, and not expensive. The woman will be here to show it to you shortly.'

She was delighted, and could have kissed him.

'Oh! You are kind, I must reward you somehow!'

Then, as another terrine of foie gras, bought in Belgium, was being served, the conversation turned for a moment to the subject of the fish in the Meuse, which were poisoned and dying, and finally came round to the risk of plague which was threatening Sedan at the next thaw. In November, there had already been several cases of epidemic. After the battle, they had spent six thousand francs in vain to sweep the town clean and burn the heaps of kit-bags, cartridge pouches and all the suspect debris: a nauseating stench rose up from the surrounding countryside at the slightest sign of rain, so stuffed was the ground with half-buried corpses, poorly covered over with a few centimetres of earth. Graves formed a bumpy landscape in fields all around, putrefaction oozed and seeped from the ground. And another source of infection had just been discovered, the Meuse itself, even though they'd already pulled out the bodies of more than twelve hundred horses. It had generally been thought that there wasn't a single human corpse left in the river, until a local gamekeeper, looking carefully into the water, noticed white shapes beneath the surface more than two metres down, which might have been mistaken for stones: they were layers of corpses, bodies which had been disembowelled and were therefore unable to swell up and float to the surface. They had been lying there for nearly four months, in the water, among the reeds. Prodding with a hook brought up arms, legs, and heads. The current alone would sometimes pull off a hand and sweep it away. The water would grow cloudy and large gas bubbles rose to the surface, where they would burst, filling the air with a foul, plague-ridden stench.

'It's a good job there's a frost,' remarked Delaherche. 'But as soon as the snow disappears, they'll have to make thorough searches and clean all that up, otherwise it'll be the death of us all.'

And, as his wife laughingly asked if they could talk about something less distasteful while they were eating, he merely concluded,

'Lord! Fish from the Meuse isn't going to be any good for a long time!'

However, they'd finished and coffee was being served, when the chambermaid announced that Monsieur von Gartlauben was asking to be allowed in for a moment. This caused a stir, for he had never come at this time, right in the middle of the day. Delaherche immediately said that he was to be sent through, seeing it as a fortunate opportunity to introduce the Prussian to Henriette. The captain noticed that another woman was present, and was more exaggeratedly polite than ever. He even accepted their invitation to a cup of coffee, which he drank without sugar, as he'd often seen it done in Paris. As it happened, the only reason he'd insisted on being allowed to enter was that he wished to let Madame know without delay that he'd obtained a pardon for one of her protégés, some poor worker from the factory who'd been imprisoned the day before following a brawl with a Prussian soldier.

Gilberte then seized the opportunity to mention old Fouchard.

'Captain, may I introduce one of my very dearest friends to you... She would like to put herself in your hands, she's the niece of the farmer who was arrested in Remilly, you know the one I mean, after that business with the guerrillas.'

'Oh! Yes, the spy affair, that poor man they found dumped in a sack... Oh! That's a very serious business, very serious indeed! I'm afraid I won't be able to do anything for him.'

'Captain, you would make me so very happy!'

She looked at him with her caressing eyes, and he was filled with a blissful feeling of contentment, bowing to her in gallant obedience. Anything she wanted!

'Sir, I would be extremely grateful to you,' Henriette got out with difficulty, overcome by an unbearable sense of unease, suddenly thinking of her husband, her poor Weiss, shot back there in Bazeilles.

Edmond, who had discreetly left the room when the captain arrived, had just reappeared, and went over to say something in Gilberte's ear. She rose briskly and explained about the lace, which the woman had come to show her; and she followed the young man out, asking them to excuse her. Then Henriette, left alone with the two men, managed to set herself apart, seating herself in the bay of a window, while they carried on talking in very loud voices.

'Captain, would you accept a small glass of something?... Look, I'm not going to beat around the bush, I'm going to tell you exactly what I think, because I know how broad-minded you are. Well, I can assure you that your Préfet is wrong to want to squeeze another forty-two thousand francs out of the town... I mean, just think about all the sacrifices we've made since this began. First, on the eve of the battle, we had an entire French army here, all worn out and starving. Then there was you lot, and you had healthy appetites, too. The presence of these troops alone, what with the requisitions, reparation, and all sorts of other expenses, cost us one and a half million francs. Add the same amount again for the damage caused by the battle itself, the fires and the destruction, and you've already got three million. And then, I'd estimate at at least two million the losses suffered by industry and commerce... Eh? What do you say about that? There we have a figure of five million, for a town with thirteen thousand inhabitants! And now you're asking us to contribute another forty-two thousand francs, under goodness only knows what pretext! I mean, is that fair, is that reasonable?'

Monsieur von Gartlauben nodded, and merely said in reply,

'What can you do? That's war, that's war for you!'

And Henriette went on waiting, her ears buzzing, all sorts of faint, sad thoughts sending her half into a doze in the bay of the window, while Delaherche gave his word of honour that Sedan would never, ever have been able to face up to the crisis, considering the total lack of available currency, if it hadn't been for the fortunate idea of a local monetary arrangement, paper money issued by the Caisse du Crédit Industriel, which had saved the town from financial disaster.

'Captain, do have another drop of cognac.'

And he jumped to another subject.

'It wasn't France that wanted the war, it was the Empire... Oh! The Emperor's sorely deceived me. It's all over with him, we'd sooner let someone cut our arms and legs off... Look! Only one man saw things clearly back in July, and that was Monsieur Thiers!* And the travels he's now embarking on around the capitals of Europe are another great act of wisdom and patriotism on his part. The goodwill of all reasonable folk in France is with him, and may he succeed!'

He rounded off this thought with a gesture, for he would have judged it ill-placed to express a wish for peace before a Prussian, even a friendly one. But the wish was there, ardent, within him, as it was deep within the entire former democratic, conservative bourgeoisie. They were about to run out of blood and money, they had to give in; and a hidden rancour against Paris, stubbornly refusing to surrender, was building up throughout the occupied provinces. And so he concluded, in a low voice, alluding to the fiery proclamations being made by Gambetta,

'No, no! We can't take the side of these raving lunatics. It's turning into a massacre... Personally, I'm with Monsieur Thiers, who wants elections; and as for their Republic, good God! I'm not going to let that bother me, we'll keep it if we have to, until something better comes along.'

Monsieur von Gartlauben carried on nodding in a very polite manner, appearing to approve, repeating,

'No doubt, no doubt...'

Henriette, whose uneasiness had grown, couldn't stay there any longer. She felt irritated, for no particular reason, she just needed to get away from there; and softly she got up and left the room, looking for Gilberte, who was such a long time coming back.

However, as she entered the bedroom she stopped short, stunned to see her friend in tears, lying on the chaise longue, completely overcome by her emotions.

'Hello, what's all this? What's happened?'

The young woman's crying grew louder and she refused to say a word, so embarrassed that it brought all the blood rushing to her face. Eventually, hiding herself in Henriette's wide open, outstretched arms, she sobbed,

'Oh, my darling, if you only knew... I'd never dare to tell you... And then again, you're the only one I've got, you're the only one who might be able to give me some good advice...'

She shuddered, and stuttered more than ever.

'I was with Edmond... And then just a moment ago, Madame Delaherche came in and discovered us...'

'What do you mean, discovered you?'

'We were in here, he was holding me, kissing me...'

And kissing Henriette, squeezing her tight in her trembling arms, she told her everything.

'Oh, my darling, don't judge me too harshly, it would make me so very sad!... I know, I swore to you that it would never happen again. But you've seen Edmond yourself, he's so good and so beautiful! And then, just think, the poor boy's been wounded, and ill, and he's so far away from his mother! On top of all that, he's never been rich, they spent everything they had to get him an education... I just couldn't refuse, honestly I couldn't.'

Henriette listened in alarm, unable to get over her surprise.

'What! You mean, you and that little sergeant!... But darling, everyone thinks you're the Prussian's mistress!'

At once Gilberte leapt up and wiped her eyes, protesting.

'The Prussian's mistress?... Oh no, no, as if I would! He's horrible, he disgusts me... Who do they take me for? How could anyone think me capable of something so appalling? No, never, ever! I'd rather die!'

Her outrage had made her serious, her beauty full of pain and irritation, which quite transformed her. Then all of a sudden, her coquettish gaiety and careless flippancy returned, amid irrepressible laughter.

'Mind you, it's true that I do make a fool of him. He simply adores me, all I have to do is look at him to make him obey... If you only knew how funny it is, making fun of the great idiot, who always seems to think that he'll be rewarded in the end!'

'But that's a very dangerous game to play,' said Henriette gravely.

'You think so? But what have I to fear? Once he realizes that he can't count on anything, all he can do is get angry and leave... But no, not even that! He'll never realize! You don't know the man, he's one of those that women can go as far as they want with, without running any risk. You see, I've got a feeling for that sort of thing, which has always warned me. He's far too vain, he'll never be able to admit to himself that I've been making fun of him... And all that I'll allow him is to take away the memory of me, and the consolation of being able to tell himself that he acted honourably, like a true gentleman who's spent a long time in Paris.'

She cheered up, and added,

'Meanwhile, he'll get Uncle Fouchard released, and all he'll get for his trouble will be a cup of tea stirred by my own fair hand.'

All at once, however, her fears returned, and her alarm at having been caught. Her eyes began brimming with tears again.

'My God! What about Madame Delaherche?... What's going to

happen? It's hardly as if she likes me, she's capable of telling my husband everything.'

Henriette had finally pulled herself together. She wiped her friend's eyes, and forced her to rearrange her clothing properly.

'Listen, my darling, I haven't the strength to tell you off, but if you only knew how much I hold you to blame! But the stories of you and that Prussian had me so frightened, I'd feared such ugly things were going on, that goodness, this other affair comes as quite a relief... Calm down, everything can be worked out.'

It was very sound advice, especially as Delaherche came in with his mother very shortly after. He explained that he'd just sent for the carriage to take him to Belgium, and had decided to take the train for Brussels that very evening. So he wished to say goodbye to his wife. Then, turning to Henriette, he said,

'Don't worry, as he was leaving, Monsieur von Gartlauben promised to take care of your uncle; and when I've gone, my wife will look after the rest.'

Since Madame Delaherche had come in, Gilberte hadn't taken her eyes off her, her heart tight with dread. Would she speak, would she say what she'd just seen, and prevent her son from leaving? In silence, the old lady had also turned her gaze on her daughter-in-law as soon as she stepped through the door. With her rigid morals, she was probably feeling the same sense of relief which had made Henriette so tolerant. My God! If it was with this young man, this Frenchman who had fought so bravely, shouldn't she forgive her, as she'd already forgiven her for Captain Beaudoin? Her eyes softened, and she looked away. Her son could depart. Edmond would protect Gilberte from the Prussian. She even gave a faint smile, and this was the woman who had known no joy since the good news about Coulmiers.

'Goodbye,' she said, kissing Delaherche. 'Get your business done, and hurry back to us.'

And she left the room, walking slowly back into the shuttered bedroom, across the landing, where, in a stupor, the colonel was staring into the darkness, relieved only by the pale circle of light from the lamp.

That same evening, Henriette returned to Remilly; and one morning, three days later, she was delighted to see old Fouchard coming quietly back to the farm, for all the world as if he were just back from having concluded some deal in the neighbourhood. He sat down and ate a piece of bread and cheese. Then he answered all their questions without haste, like a man who'd never once been afraid. Why would they have wanted to keep him there? He'd done nothing wrong. After all, it wasn't him who killed the Prussian, was it? And so he'd simply told the authorities: 'Search all you like, but I don't know anything.' So they'd had to let him go, just like the mayor, since they had no proof against either of them. But his cunning, mocking peasant's eyes twinkled in quiet delight at having put one over on all those dirty bastards, who he was starting to have had enough of now that they were complaining about the quality of his meat.

December came to an end, and Jean wanted to leave. Now his leg was sound again, and the doctor declared that he could go and fight. This caused Henriette much grief, which she forced herself to conceal. Ever since the disastrous battle of Champigny, they'd received no news from Paris. All they knew was that Maurice's regiment, coming under terrible fire, had lost a lot of men. After that, there had just been this long silence, without a single letter, never the briefest word for them, while they knew that families in Raucourt and Sedan had received notes sent by roundabout routes. Perhaps the pigeon bringing the news they waited for with such burning impatience had encountered some voracious hawk; or perhaps it had fallen to earth on the edge of some wood, brought down by a Prussian bullet. What haunted them most of all, however, was the fear that Maurice might be dead. They waited in such dread that the great city's silence, far away, its voice stifled by the grip of the siege, had for them become like a tomb. They had given up hope of ever learning anything, and when Jean said he was set on going, all Henriette could do was give a muffled cry,

'My God! It's over, then, I'll be left all alone!'

What Jean wanted to do was go and join the Northern army, which had just been reassembled under the command of General Faidherbe.* Ever since General Manteuffel's corps had managed to get as far as Dieppe, this other army had been defending three departments which had been separated from the rest of France—the Nord, the Pas-de-Calais, and the Somme—and Jean's plan, which would be easy to carry out, was simply to get to Bouillon, then make his way round via Belgium. He knew that the 23rd Corps was being brought up to strength with all the former soldiers from Sedan and

Metz who could be rallied together. He heard people saying that
General Faidherbe was preparing to take the offensive once again,
and he set a definite date for his departure as the following Sunday,
when he heard about the battle of Pont-Noyelle, whose outcome had
been indecisive, the battle the French had almost won.

Again, it was Doctor Dalichamp who offered to drive him to
Bouillon, in his open-topped carriage. His courage and generosity
knew no bounds. In Raucourt, which was ravaged by the typhus
which the Bavarians had brought with them, he had patients in every
house, as well as the two field hospitals he visited, one in Raucourt
itself and one in Remilly. His fervent patriotism and his urge to
protest against the needless violence had twice resulted in his arrest,
then release, by the Prussians. And so the morning he came to pick
Jean up in his carriage, his face was all smiles, overjoyed to be helping another of the men defeated at Sedan to escape, another one of
these poor, brave souls, as he put it, whom he treated and helped
from his own pocket. Jean, embarrassed over the question of money,
knowing how poor Henriette was, had accepted the fifty francs the
doctor had offered him for the journey.

For their farewells, old Fouchard did things properly. He sent
Silvine to get two bottles of wine, and insisted on everyone drinking
a toast to the extermination of the Germans. He was now quite a
gentleman, keeping his nest egg hidden away somewhere; and with
his mind at rest now that the guerrillas from Dieulet Woods had
disappeared, hunted like wild animals, his one desire was to enjoy
the coming peace when it was concluded. He had even, in a sudden
fit of generosity, put Prosper on a wage to keep him on the farm,
though the lad had no wish to leave it anyway. He clinked glasses
with Prosper, and insisted on doing the same with Silvine, whom
he'd considered making his wife for a moment, seeing her there so
good, so devoted to her work; but what would have been the point?
He could see that she wouldn't be going anywhere else, that she
would still be there when Charlot had grown up and was leaving for
the army in his turn. And when he'd clinked glasses with the doctor
and Henriette and Jean, he cried,

'To the good health of us all! May each one do what he has to do,
and may no one ever be any worse off than me!'

Henriette had been absolutely insistent on accompanying Jean to
Sedan. He was dressed like a gentleman, in an overcoat and round

hat lent to him by the doctor. That day, the sun shone down on the snow in the bitter, dreadful cold. They were simply going to cross the city; but when Jean learned that his colonel was still at the Delaherche's house, he was overcome by a desire to go and pay his respects to him; and at the same time, he would thank the mill owner for all his kindness. It was his last moment of pain in this city of mourning and disaster. As they arrived at the factory on the Rue Maqua, they found that a tragic ending had turned the house upside-down. Gilberte was in a panic and Madame Delaherche was weeping great, silent tears, while her son, who had come back up from the workshops, where things had started to get going a little again, was exclaiming in astonishment. They had just discovered the colonel lying on the floor in his room, where he had dropped dead, like a stone. The ever-present lamp burned alone inside the shuttered room. Summoned in haste, the doctor had been unable to understand, finding no probable cause, neither aneurism nor stroke. The colonel was dead, struck down, without anyone knowing where the thunderbolt had come from; and it was only the next day that someone picked up a piece of old newspaper, which had been used as a book cover, and saw that it contained an account of the surrender of Metz.

'Darling,' said Gilberte to Henriette, 'just now, as he was coming down the stairs, Monsieur von Gartlauben took off his hat before the door of the room where my uncle's body is lying... It was Edmond who saw him. He really is a very fine man, don't you think?'

Jean had never yet kissed Henriette. Before getting back up into the carriage with the doctor, he wanted to thank her for the good care she had taken of him, for having looked after him and loved him like a brother. But he couldn't find the words, and opened his arms to her, kissing her and sobbing. Distraught, she returned his embrace. When the horse set off he turned round, and they waved at each other, stuttering, repeating over and over again,

'Farewell! Farewell!'

That night, back in Remilly, Henriette was on duty at the hospital. During her long vigil, she was seized again by a terrible fit of crying, and she sobbed and sobbed endlessly, stifling her sorrow between her clasped hands.

CHAPTER SEVEN

The day after Sedan, the two German armies had started moving their waves of men back up towards Paris, the Meuse army coming from the north through the Marne Valley, while the army of the Crown Prince of Prussia, having crossed the Seine at Villeneuve-Saint-Georges,* headed for Versailles, skirting round to the south of the city. And when, on this warm September morning, General Ducrot, who had been placed in command of a barely assembled 14th Corps, resolved to attack* the latter German army as it marched round to the flank, Maurice, camping in the woods west of Meudon with his new regiment, the 115th, only received the order to march when disaster was already inevitable. A few shells had been enough to sow blind panic among a battalion of Zouaves made up of new recruits, and the rest of the troops had been swept away amid such chaos that the rout didn't come to a halt until it was behind the ramparts, in Paris, where it caused extreme alarm. All the positions north of the southern fortifications were lost; and that same evening, the last thread connecting the city to the rest of France, the telegraph line along the Western Railway,* was severed. Paris was cut off from the world.

For Maurice, this was an evening of terrible sadness. If the Germans had dared, they could have camped on the Place du Carrousel* for the night. But they were thoroughly cautious people, determined to carry out a classic siege, having already set out the exact places to invest their forces, with the cordon of the Meuse army to the north, from Croissy to the Marne, via Épinay, and the other cordon of the Third Army to the south, from Chennevières to Châtillon and Bougival, while Prussian headquarters, with King William, Bismarck and General de Moltke, were set up in Versailles. The giant blockade which no one had thought possible was now hard fact. This city, with its eight and a half leagues of battlements, fifteen forts, and six detached redoubts, was about to find itself shut up like a prison. And the defence army comprised only the 13th Corps, which General Vinoy* had salvaged and brought back, and the 14th Corps, which had been entrusted to General Ducrot* and was in the process of being assembled; together they represented a force of eighty thousand soldiers, to which should be added the fourteen thousand from the marines, fifteen thousand irregulars, and one hundred and fifteen thousand mobile guards, not counting the three hundred thousand National Guards who had been spread out around the ramparts' nine sectors. Although numbers weren't lacking, experienced, disciplined soldiers certainly were. The men were kitted out and drilled, and Paris became nothing but a huge military camp. Preparations to defend it grew more feverish by the hour, with roads blocked off, houses in the military zones knocked down, the two hundred heavy-calibre cannon and two thousand five hundred other artillery weapons all in position, other cannon melted down, raising an entire arsenal from the ground, thanks to the huge patriotic efforts of the minister, Dorian.* After negotiations in Ferrières* had been broken off, when Jules Favre made known Bismarck's demands—Alsace handed over to Germany, the Strasbourg garrison taken prisoner, and three billion francs of compensation to be paid— a cry of rage had gone up, and resistance and the continuation of the war were called for as things which were essential if France was to live. Even if there were no hope of winning, Paris must defend itself, so that the motherland might live on.

One Sunday towards the end of September, Maurice was sent on fatigue duty to the other side of town, and as he walked along roads and across squares he was filled with new hope. Since the rout of Châtillon, it seemed to him that people had summoned up all their courage to carry out the massive task. Oh! Paris, this city he'd known so greedy for pleasure, so close to committing the lowest vices, now he found it simple, full of cheerful courage, accepting every sacrifice. All he could see were people in uniform—even the most uninterested sported the cap of the National Guard. Just like an enormous clock with a broken spring, all social life had come to an abrupt halt, as had industry, commerce, and business; and all that was left was a passion, a will to win, the only subject anybody talked about, which set heads and hearts aflame at public gatherings, during the watches of the guard corps, and among the continual crowds of people jamming the pavements. Now that they all had a common cause, hearts were swept along on a tide of illusions, and a feeling of tension was putting these people in danger of giving in to rash heroics. There was already an unhealthy nervousness in the air, like a fever epidemic which exaggerated both fear and confidence, unleashing the human animal into the open at the slightest whisper. And on the Rue des Martyrs Maurice witnessed a scene which gripped him: he saw a furious crowd rushing to attack a house where one of the upper windows had been seen lit up by bright lamplight all night—obviously a signal to the Prussians in Bellevue, north of Paris. Well-off folk haunted by fear were living camped out on their rooftops, keeping watch over the surrounding area. The day before, they had almost drowned some poor wretch in the Tuileries fountain, because he'd been studying a map of the city, open on the bench in front of him.

Previously an open-minded sort of person, Maurice too had now been infected by this suspiciousness, now that everything he'd believed in until then had been undermined. He no longer felt the despair that he had on the evening of the panic at Châtillon, when he'd been anxious to know whether the French army would ever be man enough to fight: his faith, that flame of hope which a single spark was enough to rekindle, and which consumed him utterly, had been completely restored by the breakout of 30 September* towards L'Hay and Chevilly, followed by that of 13 October in which the mobile guard recaptured Bagneux, and lastly 21 October, when for a short time his regiment had been in control of the park of La Malmaison. Even if the Prussians had pushed the army back at every point, it had fought bravely nonetheless, and it could still win. What caused Maurice pain, though, was to see this great city of Paris plunging from the heights of illusion to the depths of despair, haunted, in its need for victory, by the fear of treason. After the Emperor and Marshal MacMahon, wouldn't Generals Trochu and Ducrot be mediocre leaders and unconscious instruments of defeat? The very same movement which had brought down the Empire now threatened to bring down the government of National Defence, with violent men all impatient to seize power and save France. Jules Favre and the other members of the government were already more unpopular than the ministers of Napoleon III who had fallen from power before them. If they didn't want to fight the Prussians, then all they had to do was make way for the others, for the revolutionaries who were certain of victory, by decreeing a mass rising and giving free rein to the inventors who were offering to plant mines in the suburbs or wipe out the enemy in a new shower of fireworks.

On the eve of 31 October,* Maurice fell victim to the ravages of this malady of dreams and defiance. Now he readily accepted inventions of the imagination which before would have made him smile. Why not? Weren't crime and idiocy without limits? Hadn't miracles become possible, amidst all the catastrophes which were turning the world upside-down? Ever since the moment he'd heard about Frœschwiller, back there, south of Mulhouse, a long, slow rancour had been building up inside him; Sedan had left him bleeding inside, as if from a still-inflamed, raw wound, which the slightest upset was enough to reopen; the shock of each and every defeat remained with him, his body weakened and his mind enfeebled by so many days on end without bread, without sleep, plunged into the terror of that nightmarish existence, not knowing any more whether he was alive or dead; and the thought that so much suffering would end in fresh disaster, irreparable this time, made him distraught, turned this educated man into a creature of basic instinct, making him revert to childishness, forever carried away by the emotion of the moment. He would accept destruction, extermination, anything, sooner than give up one penny of France's fortune or one inch of her territory! Within him, the transformation triggered by the blow of the first battles they had lost, the destruction of the Napoleonic legend and the sentimental Bonapartist loyalty which he owed to his grandfather's epic stories, was reaching its completion. He'd already moved beyond the idea of a quiet, theoretical republic, and was tending towards revolutionary violence, believing that terror was necessary to sweep away the incompetents and the traitors who were cutting his country's throat. And so, on 31 October, his heart was with the rioters when the disastrous pieces of news came one after the other: the loss of Le Bourget, which had been so valiantly conquered by the volunteers of *La Presse* during the night of 27 to 28 October; then the arrival of Thiers at Versailles, back from his trip around the capitals of Europe, apparently returning to negotiate in the name of Napoleon III; and finally, the surrender of Metz, of which he brought back the dreadful confirmation of even greater shame, amid all the rumours already flying of this being the final hammer-blow, another Sedan. And the next day, when he learned what had happened at the Hôtel de Ville, with the rioters momentarily winning, and the members of the National Defence government being held prisoner until four in the morning, only to be rescued by a sudden reversal of public opinion—at first, the people had been furious at them, but then they grew frightened at the idea of the insurrection being victorious—on learning this, he was sorry that the uprising had come to nothing, this Commune which perhaps would have saved them, with a call to arms, to save the imperilled motherland, all the classic memories of a free nation unwilling to die. Monsieur Thiers didn't even dare enter Paris, and following the breakdown of negotiations, they were about to put the street lights back on again.

And so the month of November passed in a state of nervous impatience. There were a few minor battles, in which Maurice played no part. Now he was bivouacking near Saint-Ouen,* from where he would escape at every opportunity, devoured by a constant need for news. Paris, like him, waited in dread. The elections of local mayors* seemed to have appeased people's political passions; but practically all those elected to office belonged to extremist parties, a symptom which boded ill for the future. And what Paris was waiting for during this lull was the great breakout they were all clamouring for—victory and deliverance. Once again, no one had any doubts about this: they would send the Prussians flying and walk in over their dead bodies. Preparations were under way on the Gennevilliers peninsula, the point judged to be the most favourable for making a breach. Then, one morning, came wild joy at the good news about Coulmiers, Orléans retaken, the Loire army on the march and already, it was said, camped at Étampes. This changed everything, all that needed to be done now was to go and join up with it, on the other side of the Marne. Military forces had been reorganized to create three armies, one made up of battalions from the National Guard under the command of General Clément Thomas,* another formed from the 13th and 14th Corps, reinforced by the best elements taken from just about everywhere, which General Ducrot was to lead in the main offensive, and finally the third army, the reserve force, consisting purely of mobile guards, placed in the care of General Vinoy. And Maurice was buoyed up by an absolute sense of faith when, on 28 November, he slept overnight in the Bois de Vincennes with the 115th Regiment. The three corps of the second army were stationed there, and the rendezvous with the Loire army was said to be set for the following day, in Fontainebleau. But immediately the usual slip-ups and bad luck struck again, as a sudden high tide meant that they couldn't set up pontoon bridges, and unfortunate orders delayed manœuvres. The following night, the 115th Regiment was one of the first to cross the river; and by ten in the morning, under terrible fire, Maurice was entering the village of Champigny.* He was like a madman, his rifle burned his fingers in spite of the bitter cold. His only desire since the beginning of the march had been to keep moving ahead, right until they met up with their comrades out there in the provinces. Opposite Champigny and Bry, however, the army had just come up against the boundary walls of Cœuilly and Villiers parks, structures half a kilometre long which the Prussians had turned into impregnable fortresses. This was the limit, the moment all courage failed. After that there was nothing but hesitation and backing off, the 3rd Corps had been delayed and the 1st and 2nd, already immobilized, defended Champigny for two days before having to abandon it during the night of 2 December, after a fruitless victory. That night the entire army came back to camp out beneath the trees in the Bois de Vincennes, white with frost; and with aching feet, pressing his face to the frozen ground, Maurice wept.

Oh! The sad, mournful days which followed after that immense effort had come to nothing! The great breakout they'd been preparing for so long, the irresistible push which was to deliver Paris, had failed; and three days later, a letter from General de Moltke announced that the Loire army, in defeat, had abandoned Orléans yet again. The circle was closing in more and more tightly, and any breakthrough now became impossible. In the heat of its despair, however, Paris seemed to find new strength to resist. Famine was starting to threaten. Meat had been on ration since the middle of October. By December, not a single animal was left of the huge herds of cattle and sheep which had been released into the Bois de Boulogne, continually kicking up clouds of dust, and people had begun slaughtering horses. First supplies, then requisitions, of corn and flour would provide bread for four months. When the flour ran out, they had to build flourmills in the railway stations. Fuel was also in short supply, and was saved for grinding corn, baking bread, and making weapons. And yet Paris, deprived of gas, lit only by occasional paraffin lamps as it shivered beneath its coat of ice, with rye-bread and horsemeat on ration, still Paris lived in hope, citing Faidherbe in the north, Chanzy on the Loire, and Bourbaki* in the east, as if by some miracle they would be brought victorious to its city walls. The long queues standing in the snow outside the bakeries and butchers' shops were still cheered occasionally by the news of great, imaginary victories. After the dejection of each defeat, tenacious illusion re-emerged, burning brighter than ever among this crowd hallucinating from so much suffering and hunger. On the Place du Château-d'Eau,* when a soldier had talked of giving himself up, the passers-by had almost killed him. While the army, its courage drained and sensing that the end was near, was asking for peace, the people were still clamouring for a massive breakout, like a great flood, in which the entire population, including women and even children, would charge at the Prussians like a river bursting its banks, overturning everything, sweeping it all away.

And Maurice began to withdraw from his colleagues, feeling a growing hatred for his soldier's profession which kept him stuck out here in the shelter of the Mont-Valérien Fort, idle and useless. And so he manufactured opportunities, escaping at the earliest occasion to Paris where his heart lay. He was only at ease when in the middle of the crowd, he wanted to force himself to keep on hoping like they did. Often he would go and watch the air balloons taking off every other day from the Gare du Nord,* bearing carrier pigeons and dispatches. The balloons would climb up into the sad, wintry sky, and vanish; and fear would clutch at onlookers' hearts whenever the wind blew them towards Germany. Many of them must have been lost. He himself had twice written to his sister Henriette, without finding out whether she'd ever received his letters. The memory of his sister and Jean was so far away, back there in that vast world where nothing was happening any more, that he rarely thought about them, like some tender attachment left behind in another life. His existence was too busy now with the ceaseless storm of despondency and elation he was going through. Then, with the first days of January, he was stirred by a new sense of anger, caused by the bombardment* of the districts on the Left Bank. The delays, which he'd ended up attributing to humanitarianism on the part of the Prussians, turned out to have been caused simply by technical difficulties. Now that a shell had killed two little girls at the Val-de-Grace,* he was full of furious contempt for these barbarians who assassinated children and were talking of burning down the museums and libraries. After the first few days of panic, however, a bombarded Paris reverted to its state of heroic stubbornness.

Ever since the failure at Champigny, there had only been one fresh and ill-fated attempt to mount an attack,* over towards Le Bourget;

and on the evening that the Plateau d'Avron* had to be evacuated, under fire from the heavy artillery bombarding the forts, Maurice shared the irritation which was raging through the city. The gale of growing unpopularity which threatened to bring down General Trochu and the National Defence government gained so much strength from it that they were forced to make one supreme, useless effort. Why did they refuse to lead into battle the three hundred thousand National Guards who were forever volunteering to go, forever claiming their share of the danger? This was the torrential breakout they'd been baying for since the very first day, with Paris bursting its banks, drowning the Prussians beneath the massive flood of its people. They had to give in to this vow of courage, even though fresh defeat was unavoidable; but in order to contain the massacre, they limited themselves to deploying those fifty-nine battalions of the National Guard which had already been mobilized, in addition to the regular army. And on the eve of 19 January the atmosphere was almost festive: huge crowds on the streets and on the Champs-Élysées watched the regiments marching past, led by bands and singing patriotic songs. Children and women walked alongside, and men climbed up onto benches to shout out their heartfelt wishes for victory. Then, the following day, the entire population made its way to the Arc de Triomphe, and was filled with wild hope on hearing the news of the occupation of Montretout.* Epic accounts circulated about the irresistible surge forward by the National Guard, telling how the Prussians had been overwhelmed, and that Versailles would be taken before evening. And so how terrible was their dejection, when the inevitable failure became known! While the left column was occupying Montretout, the one at the centre, which had scaled the wall of Buzenval Park, was thwarted by a second wall inside. It had begun to thaw and the roads had been waterlogged by a fine, persistent drizzle, and the cannon, the same cannon which, with the help of contributions, had been forged from melted-down metal, were unable to get through. On the right, General Ducrot's column, sent into battle too late, remained at the rear. All effort had been spent, and General Trochu had to give the order for a wholesale retreat. Montretout was abandoned, as was Saint-Cloud, to which the Prussians then set fire. And as soon as it was dark, the only thing visible on the Parisian skyline was this enormous conflagration.

This time, even Maurice could sense that the end had come. For four hours, under the terrible fire coming from the Prussian entrenchments, he had stayed in Buzenval Park with the National Guard; and in the days which followed, after he'd returned to base, he praised their courage. The National Guard had indeed conducted itself bravely. Since that was the case, then surely the defeat must be down to the stupidity and betrayal of the commanders? On the Rue de Rivoli,* he came upon crowds shouting 'Down with Trochu! Long live the Commune!' This was the awakening of revolutionary fervour, a fresh wave of public opinion which was so worrying that, in order to prevent itself being swept from power, the government of National Defence had deemed it necessary to force General Trochu's resignation,* and had replaced him with General Vinoy. That very day, at a public meeting he'd attended in Belleville,* Maurice again heard calls for a mass attack. It was an insane idea, he knew it was, and yet his heart beat faster all the same, faced with this obstinate will to overcome. For when all else is lost, aren't miracles the only things left to try for? All night long, his dreams were filled with wondrous feats.

Another eight long days went by. Paris lay agonizing, uncomplaining. Shops had stopped opening, and the rare passers-by no longer met any carriages in the deserted streets. Forty thousand horses had been eaten, and now dogs, cats, and rats were commanding high prices. Since they'd run short of grain, the bread, made with rice and oats, had been black and sticky and difficult to digest; and in order to obtain the three hundred grams permitted on ration, the never-ending queues outside the bakeries were becoming deadly. Oh! The pain of standing there during the siege, those poor women shivering in the rain, feet soaked in icy mud, all that heroic misery of the great city unwilling to surrender! The death rate had tripled, theatres had been turned into field hospitals. At nightfall, a mournful quiet fell over what had once been the wealthy districts, plunging them into deep shadow, like parts of an accursed city, ravaged by plague. And amid this silence and obscurity, all that could be heard was the endless rumble of the bombardment, and all that could be seen were the flashes from the cannon, setting fire to the winter sky.

All of a sudden, on 28 January, Paris found out that two days earlier Jules Favre had begun talks with Bismarck* to agree an armistice; at the same time, it became known that there was only enough bread left for ten days, giving barely enough time to replenish stocks.

Surrender was being imposed brutally upon them. Mournful and numb in the face of the truth which it was being told at long last, Paris gave in. That same day, at midnight, the last cannon was fired. Then, on 29 January, after the Germans had taken possession of the forts, Maurice was sent back with the 115th Regiment to camp near Montrouge, inside the fortifications. So began for him a vague existence, full of idleness and dread. Discipline had grown much slacker and the soldiers relaxed, killing time while they waited to be sent back home. But he was as distraught as ever, nervous and touchy, displaying an anxiety which turned to exasperation at the slightest upset. He read the revolutionary press avidly, and this three-week armistice, struck with the sole purpose of allowing France to name an Assembly which would decide the terms of the peace, seemed to him to be a trap, the final betrayal. Even if Paris should be forced to surrender, he, like Gambetta, was in favour of carrying on with the war in the Loire Valley and in the Nord.* He was outraged by the disaster of the Eastern army, which had been forgotten and forced to cross into Switzerland.* It was the elections* which finally drove him over the edge: it was just as he'd predicted, with the cowardly provinces, irritated by Paris's resistance and wanting peace in spite of it, bringing back the monarchy with the Prussian guns still pointing at them. After the first sessions in Bordeaux,* Thiers, who had been elected in twenty-six departments and proclaimed head of the executive, appeared to his eyes as the monster, the man who would tell every lie and commit every crime. And his anger wouldn't die, for this peace brought about by a monarchical Assembly seemed to him to be the most shameful thing of all, and it made him mad even to think about the harsh terms,* the five million francs in compensation, Metz handed over, Alsace abandoned, France's gold and blood pouring out through this open, unhealable gash in its side.

And so, during the last days of February, Maurice made up his mind to desert. One of the articles in the treaty said that the soldiers camped in Paris would be disarmed and sent back home. He didn't wait for that to happen, for it would have been like tearing his heart out to leave the pavements of this glorious Paris, which only hunger had been able to wear down; he disappeared, and rented a room in the Rue des Orties, at the top of the Butte des Moulins,* a narrow, furnished room in a six-storey building, a sort of belvedere, from where you could see the boundless sea of rooftops, stretching from the Tuileries right across to the Bastille.* A former friend from the Law Faculty had lent him a hundred francs. Apart from that, as soon as he was settled in he put his name down for a battalion of the National Guard, and the thirty sous he received in wages had to suffice. The thought of living a selfish, untroubled existence in the provinces filled him with horror. Even the letters he received from his sister Henriette, to whom he'd written the day after the armistice, made him angry, full of supplications and desperate wishes to see him come back and rest in Remilly. He refused, he would go later, when the Prussians had gone.

So the train of Maurice's life wandered idly on, amid a growing restlessness. He no longer suffered from hunger, and he'd devoured the first white loaf, savouring it. Alcoholic Paris, where neither brandy nor wine had been in short supply, was now living it up and sliding into a constant haze of drunkenness. But it was still a prison, its gates guarded by the Germans, with complicated formalities preventing people from getting out. There was no sign of any social life again as yet, nor any work, nor of any sort of business whatsoever; and an entire population sat there, waiting, doing nothing, in the last stages of a nervous breakdown, in the bright sunlight of a burgeoning spring. During the siege at least military service had tired them out physically and kept them busy mentally; now, though, everyone had suddenly slipped into a state of complete idleness, cut off as they were from all the rest of the world. He, like the rest, hung around aimlessly from dawn to dusk, breathing the air which had become tainted by all the seeds of madness which had been rising up from the mob for months. The unlimited freedom they now enjoyed was what finally destroyed everything. He read the papers, attended public meetings, sometimes shrugging his shoulders at the worst of the rubbish he heard, but returning home with his head nonetheless haunted by violent thoughts, ready to commit desperate acts in the defence of what he believed to be truth and justice. And from his little room overlooking the city, he still dreamed of victory, telling himself that France and the Republic could still be saved, so long as the peace treaty hadn't been signed.

The Prussians were to enter Paris on 1 March,* and every heart gave a long cry of loathing and anger. There wasn't a single public meeting he attended where Maurice didn't hear accusations against the Assembly, Thiers, the men of 4 September,* accusations that they hadn't wanted to spare the great, heroic city this final shame. One evening he was so carried away that he even spoke in public, crying out that the whole of Paris should be ready to die on the ramparts, rather than let a single Prussian enter. Insurrection was springing up naturally now, organized in broad daylight among this population broken by months of fear and famine, reducing it to an idle state full of nightmares, ravaged by suspicion, faced with the phantoms of its own creation. This was one of those crises of morale observed after every great siege in history, the overflow of disappointed patriotism which, having set souls alight in vain, transforms itself into a blind need for vengeance and destruction. The Central Committee,* elected by the delegates of the National Guard, had protested against any attempt at disarmament. There was a massive demonstration on the Place de la Bastille, supported by huge crowds of people, with red flags, inflammatory speeches, and the death of some poor policeman,* who was tied to a plank, thrown into the canal, and finished off with stones. And two days later, during the night of 26 February, Maurice, woken by the call to arms and the alarm bell, saw groups of men and women dragging cannon past on the Boulevard des Batignolles,* and he even hitched himself up to one, along with twenty others, on hearing that the people had gone to fetch the guns from the Place Wagram,* to prevent the Assembly from handing them over to the Prussians. There were one hundred and seventy of them, and not enough harnesses, so people were pulling them along with ropes, pushing them with their bare hands, right to the top of Montmartre, with the wild fervour of a barbarous horde saving its gods. On 1 March, when the Prussians had to be satisfied with occupying the Champs-Élysées district for a single day, surrounded by barriers like a herd of worried conquerors, Paris didn't stir, lugubrious, its streets deserted, houses shuttered, the entire city dead, veiled in the immense crape of its mourning.

Another two weeks passed, and Maurice was no longer aware of how he spent each day, as he waited for that undefined, monstrous thing he could feel approaching. Peace had been concluded definitively, and the Assembly was to be set up in Versailles on 20 March;* for him, though, nothing was over yet, some sort of terrible revenge was about to begin. On 18 March, as he was getting up, he received a letter from Henriette, begging him yet again to join her in Remilly, affectionately threatening to set off herself if he took too long granting her this great joy. She then spoke of Jean, telling him how, after leaving her towards the end of December to join the Northern army, he'd been taken ill with a nasty bout of fever in a Belgian hospital; and he hadn't written to her until just the week before, to tell her that in spite of being still weak, he was leaving for Paris, where he was determined to go back into service. Henriette ended by begging her brother to give her detailed news of Jean as soon as he saw him. Maurice, the letter lying open on his lap, was overcome by a sweet reverie. Henriette and Jean, his much beloved sister and his brother in misery and compassion—God! How far these dear ones had been from his everyday thoughts, ever since the storm had been raging inside him! However, since his sister warned him that she'd been unable to give Jean the address at the Rue des Orties, he promised himself that he'd find him that very day by going to the army offices. But he'd scarcely got down into the street when two of his comrades from the battalion informed him of the events of the previous night and that morning, up on Montmartre.* And all of them rushed off, throwing reason to the winds.

Oh! What momentous elation carried Maurice away on that day of 18 March! Afterwards, he couldn't quite recall what he'd said or done. First, he could see himself dashing off, furious at the surprise attempt the military had made to disarm Paris before daylight by recapturing the cannon on Montmartre. For the past two days, Thiers, back from Bordeaux, had obviously been planning this coup* so that the Assembly might safely proclaim the monarchy from Versailles. Then he saw himself again, actually on Montmartre at about nine o'clock, fired up by the speeches he'd heard about victory—the furtive arrival of the army, the fortunate delay caused by the lack of harnesses which had allowed the National Guard to seize the weapons, the soldiers not daring to fire on the women and children, holding their rifles muzzle in the air, mingling with the people. Then he saw himself running through Paris, realizing by midday that the city now belonged to the Commune without there even having been a battle: Thiers and the ministers fleeing from the Foreign Ministry where they had gathered, the entire government routed,* heading for Versailles, the army's thirty thousand men quickly led away, leaving more than five thousand of their number lying on the streets of Paris. Then, at about half-past five, on the corner of an outer boulevard, he remembered being in the middle of a frenzied group,

listening without indignation to the appalling account of the murder
of Generals Lecomte and Clément Thomas.* Generals! Oh! He
remembered the ones at Sedan, incompetent pleasure-seekers! One
more, one less, it hardly mattered! And the rest of the day continued
in the same state of elation, distorting everything for him, an insurrection which the very paving stones seemed to have willed, which
was amplified by the fatal unexpectedness of its triumph, suddenly
finding itself master of the situation and finally, at ten o'clock in the
evening, leaving the Hôtel de Ville in the hands of the members of
the Central Committee,* who were astonished to find themselves
there.

One memory, however, remained very clear in Maurice's mind: his
sudden encounter with Jean. The latter had been in Paris for the past
three days, where he had arrived absolutely penniless, still gaunt,
drained by the two months of fever which had confined him to a
Brussels hospital; and coming across a former captain from the
106th, Captain Ravaud, he'd immediately enlisted in the new 124th
Company under the captain's command. There he'd once again
donned his corporal's stripes, and that evening he and his squad had
been the last to leave Prince Eugène barracks for the Left Bank,
where the entire army had been ordered to assemble, when, on the
Boulevard Saint-Martin, a flood of people had halted his men. There
was shouting and talk of disarming them. Quite calmly, he told them
to leave him alone, that all this was none of his business and that all
he wanted was to obey his orders, without doing anyone any harm.
But a cry of surprise rang out, and Maurice came up and was flinging
his arms around him, kissing him like a brother.

'What? Is it really you?... My sister wrote to me. And there was
me, meaning to go to the war offices to ask about you this morning!'

Huge tears of joy blurred Jean's eyes.

'Oh! My poor lad, how glad I am to see you again!... I've been
looking for you, too; but how was I to find you in the middle of this
enormous blasted city?'

The crowd was still muttering, and Maurice turned around.

'Citizens, please let me talk to them! These are fine people, I can
answer for them.'

He took both his friend's hands in his and lowered his voice.

'You'll stay with us, won't you?'

Jean's face showed immense surprise.

'What do you mean, stay with you?'

Then, for a moment, he listened to him speak angrily of the government, the army, recalling all the suffering they had been through, explaining that they were going to be masters at last, punish the incompetents and the cowards, and save the Republic. And little by little, as he forced himself to understand what the other was saying, the calm features of this illiterate peasant grew more and more sombre with deepening distress.

'Oh! No, no, lad! I'm not staying, if it's to do that sort of dirty work... My captain told me to go to Vaugirard* with my men, and that's where I'm going. Even if the wrath of God were to descend on me, I'd go there all the same. It's natural, you must realize that.'

He started to laugh, full of simplicity. He added,

'It's you who're going to come with us.'

With a furious gesture of revolt, however, Maurice let go of his hands. And for a few seconds they both stood face to face, one exasperated, caught up in the wave of madness which was sweeping all Paris away with it, this evil from way back, rooted in the corruption of the last reign, the other strong with his common sense and ignorance, still healthy from having grown up apart from all that, in the land of toil and thrift. Yet both were brothers, linked by a steadfast bond, and it came as a wrench when, suddenly, they were separated by a surge from the crowd.

'Goodbye, Maurice!'

'Goodbye, Jean!'

The surge had been caused by the 79th Regiment, whose compact mass, bursting out from a neighbouring street, had forced the crowd up onto the pavement. There were fresh cries, but no one dared bar the road to the soldiers, marching behind their officers. And thus freed, the small squad from the 124th Company was able to follow on without being held back any longer.

'Goodbye, Jean!'

'Goodbye, Maurice!'

They gave each other another parting wave, surrendering to the violent fatality of this separation, but their hearts full of one another.

Over the days that followed Maurice at first forgot it, what with all the extraordinary events coming one on top of the other. On 19 March Paris had awoken to find itself with no government, more surprised than frightened to hear of the sudden panic which in the middle of the night had swept the army, the public services, and the ministers off to Versailles; and since the weather was superb on this fine Sunday morning in March, Paris trundled happily out into the streets to look at the barricades. A large white notice issued by the Central Committee, calling the population to vote in the local elections, seemed very sensible. The only thing that surprised anyone was to see that it was signed by people no one had even heard of. In the dawn of the Commune, Paris was pitted against Versailles, bitter at the suffering it had endured and the suspicions which haunted it. Other than that, it was complete anarchy, a battle between the mayors and the Central Committee,* with the former trying vainly for conciliation while the latter, still unsure as to whether it could count on the full support of the federal National Guard, went on simply making modest demands for municipal liberty. The shots fired on the peaceful demonstration on the Place Vendôme* and the few victims whose blood had turned the cobbles red, sent the first shudder of terror through the city. And, while the triumphant insurrection took definitive control of all the ministries and public administration, there was immense anger and fear at Versailles, with the government hurrying to assemble sufficient military forces to ward off an attack which it sensed was imminent. The strongest troops from the Loire and Northern armies were hurriedly called up, ten days were enough to concentrate nearly eighty thousand men, and confidence returned so rapidly that by 2 April, two divisions opened hostilities and seized Puteaux and Courbevoie* from the federals.

It was only the following day that Maurice, who'd left with his battalion to conquer Versailles,* once again saw the sad features of Jean before him in his mind's eye, calling out goodbye. The attack by the Versailles forces had stunned and outraged the National Guard. Three columns—about fifty thousand men—had gone charging out that morning through Bougival and Meudon, to seize the monarchist Assembly and the assassin Thiers. This was the torrential breakout which had been so fervently demanded during the siege, and Maurice wondered where he would see Jean again, if not there, among the dead on the battlefield. But the rout came too promptly for that, his battalion had hardly reached the Plateau des Bergères, on the Rueil road, when all of a sudden shells launched from the Mont-Valérien began landing among their ranks. They were momentarily stunned, for some of them thought that the fort was occupied by their comrades, and others said that the commanding officer had promised to hold fire. And mad terror seized the men, the battalions scattered, galloping back into Paris, while the head of the column, trapped by a circular movement from General Vinoy, went on to be massacred in Rueil.*

Maurice, having escaped the slaughter, trembling from the battle, felt only hatred for this so-called government of law and order, which, crushed in every encounter with the Prussians, had only been able to find courage when it came to conquering Paris. And the German armies were still there, from Saint-Denis to Charenton, watching this fine spectacle of a nation collapsing! And so, as the sombre crisis of destruction overwhelmed him, he approved of the first violent measures, the building of the barricades blocking streets and squares, the taking of hostages,* the archbishop, priests, former civil servants. On both sides the atrocities were already beginning: at Versailles they were shooting prisoners, and Paris proclaimed that for each one of its soldiers who lost his head, three hostages would likewise; and what little reason Maurice had left, after so much turmoil and ruination, was blown away in the all-encompassing wind of fury. He saw the Commune as the avenging angel for all the shames endured, as a liberating force bringing the severing iron, the purifying flame. It wasn't very clear in his mind, simply the literate man in him evoking memories from the classics, of cities free and triumphant and federations of rich provinces imposing their law on the world. If Paris won the day, he could see it, crowned in glory, rebuilding a France of justice and liberty, reorganizing a new society, having swept away the rotten debris of the old. It was true, after the elections the names of the members of the Commune had surprised him a little, due to the extraordinary mixture of moderates, revolutionaries, and socialists from all factions to whom the great task had been entrusted. He knew several of these men, and judged them to be supremely mediocre. Wouldn't the better among them clash and wipe each other out, in the confused collection of ideas they represented? However, the day that the Commune was solemnly established* on the Place de l'Hôtel de Ville, while the cannon boomed and the trophies of red flags flapped in the wind, he'd tried to forget everything, once again buoyed up by boundless hope. And the illusions were reborn, in the acute crisis of the disease at its worst, amid the lies of some and the exalted faith of others.

Throughout the month of April, Maurice was stationed near Neuilly.* An early spring had brought the lilac into flower, and the battle raged among the tender greenery of the gardens; members of the National Guard would come home at night with bunches of flowers on the ends of their rifles. The troops assembled at Versailles were now so numerous* that they'd been able to form two armies, one of front-line troops, under the orders of Marshal MacMahon, and the other a reserve army, commanded by General Vinoy. As for the Commune, it had at its disposal nearly one hundred thousand mobile National Guards and almost as many permanently garrisoned; but only fifty thousand at most were real fighters. And every day, Versailles's plan of attack became more and more evident: after Neuilly they had occupied the Château de Bécon, then Asnières, simply to reinforce their encircling lines;* for they intended to come in through the Point-du-Jour,* as soon as they could force their way through the rampart, under the converging fire from Mont-Valérien and the fort of Issy. Mont-Valérien was already in their possession, and all their efforts were concentrated on seizing the fort of Issy, which they attacked from the gun-emplacements set up by the Prussians. Since mid-April the shooting and the cannonfire hadn't stopped. At Levallois and Neuilly battle raged incessantly, with shots ringing out every minute, day and night. Huge guns, mounted on armoured vehicles, traced the length of the railway which circled the city, firing onto Asnières, above Levallois. But at Vanves and especially at Issy,* the bombardment raged away, rattling all the windows in Paris, just as in the most terrible days of the siege. And on 9 May when, following a previous alert, Issy Fort finally fell into the hands of the Versailles army, it made defeat of the Commune absolutely inevitable, causing a panic which drove it to the worst extremes.

Maurice approved of the creation of a Public Security Committee. Pages of history* came back to him—hadn't the time come for taking energetic measures, if they wanted to save their country? Of all the acts of violence, only one had caused him a secret stab of pain, when the Vendôme column* was brought down; and he chastised himself for this as if it were some childish weakness, for he could still hear his grandfather telling him about Marengo, Austerlitz, Jena, Eylau, Friedland, Wagram, and Moscow, those epic tales which still made him shudder. But that they should raze to the ground the house of the assassin Thiers,* that they should keep hostages as a threat and a guarantee, surely these were merely fair reprisals, faced with Versailles's mounting rage against Paris, which was being bombarded and where the shells were falling through roofs and killing women? As the end of his dream drew nearer, he felt a dark, mounting desire for destruction. If the notion of justice and vengeance was to be trampled in blood, then let the earth open up, transformed by one of those cosmic, life-renewing upheavals! Let Paris collapse, let it burn like some huge holocaustal pyre, rather than be left to its vices and misery, to this rotten society full of such abominable injustice! And he dreamed another great, black dream, of the gigantic city lying in a pile of ashes, with only smouldering embers on either bank, the wound cauterized by fire, a nameless catastrophe without parallel, from which a new nation would emerge. And so the stories going round got him more and more stirred up, of districts being laid with mines, the catacombs being stuffed with gunpowder, all the monuments ready to blow up, with electric cables linking the furnaces so that a single spark would ignite all of them at once, and of considerable stocks of inflammable materials, especially oil, enough to turn the streets and squares into torrents and oceans of flame. If the Versailles army got in, the Commune had sworn that not a single soldier would get any further than the barricades surrounding the crossroads, and that pavements would open up, buildings would come tumbling down, and Paris would go up in flames, engulfing an entire population.

When Maurice abandoned himself to this mad dream, it was because of his muted dissatisfaction with the Commune itself. He despaired of its members, sensing that it was incompetent, pulled in too many different directions, becoming more frustrated, incoherent and idiotic with every new threat it faced. Of all the social reforms it had promised to bring about, it had been unable to realize a single one, and he was sure that it would leave behind no lasting achievements. What hurt it most, however, were the rivalries which were tearing it apart, the suspicion gnawing away at every one of its members. Many, the moderates, the anxious ones, had already stopped attending sessions. The rest were whipped along by events as they happened, trembling at the thought of a possible dictatorship, and they'd reached the point where groups within revolutionary assemblies start exterminating each other in order to save their country. After Cluseret and Dombrowski, Rossel* would be the next one to fall under suspicion. Delescluze,* who'd been nominated civil delegate to the forces, was unable to do anything without support in spite of his huge authority. And the grand social effort they had glimpsed began to scatter, aborting, in the isolation which spread wider hour by hour around these men smitten by powerlessness, reduced to taking desperate measures.

Inside Paris, the terror was mounting. Paris, which had at first been irritated with Versailles, still quaking from what it had suffered during the siege, now began to draw away from the Commune. Forced enrolment, the decree calling up all males under forty,* had annoyed peaceable folk and caused a mass exodus: they left by way of Saint-Denis, in disguise or with false papers claiming they were from Alsace, and on dark nights they would climb down into the ditches of the fortifications using ropes and ladders. The rich bourgeois were already long gone. Not a single workshop or factory had reopened its gates. There was no business, no work, and the idle life continued as they waited anxiously for the inevitable outcome. The people were still living entirely off National Guard wages, those thirty sous now being paid out of the millions requisitioned from the Bank of France, those thirty sous for which many fought, one of the basic causes and the *raison d'être* of the uprising. Whole districts had emptied, with stores shut and shop fronts dead. Beneath the bright sun of this remarkable month of May, the only things that passed in the deserted streets were the unflinching funeral processions of federal soldiers, killed like the enemy, priestless convoys, hearses draped in the red flag and followed by crowds bearing bouquets of everlasting flowers. Each evening the churches, which had been shut, were transformed into club halls. Only the revolutionary newspapers came out—all the rest had been banned. Paris was destroyed, this great, unhappy Paris which, even as a republican capital, still felt revulsion for the Assembly and now harboured growing terror of the Commune, impatient to be delivered of it, with all the dreadful stories going round of hostages being taken every day and of barrels of gunpowder being placed down in the sewers, where, it was said, men stood by with torches ready for the signal.

It was then that Maurice, who'd never been a drinker, found himself swept away and swallowed up by the general wave of drunkenness. Now, when he was on duty in some distant outpost, or even if he spent the night in the guard-room, he'd been known to accept a small glass of cognac. If he partook of a second he'd get excited, with the whiff of alcohol fumes in his nostrils. It was an insidious epidemic, chronic drunkenness, a legacy of the first siege which had been aggravated by the second; this population which had gone without bread, but with barrels and barrels of brandy and wine to hand, had saturated itself in alcohol, and now the merest drop made them delirious. On the evening of 21 May, a Sunday, for the first time in his life, Maurice went home drunk to the Rue des Orties, where he still slept occasionally. He'd spent the day in Neuilly again, on firing duty, drinking with his comrades in the hope that this would combat the acute, overwhelming fatigue. Then, his head swimming, with no strength left, he'd come and flung himself down on the bed in his little room, guided by instinct, for he never did remember how he got home. And the next day, when the sun was already high in the sky, it was only the sound of alarm bells, drums, and bugles which woke him up. The previous day, at Point-du-Jour, finding a gate abandoned by the sentries,* the Versailles army had entered Paris unhindered.

As soon as he was down in the street, having dressed in haste and slung his rifle over his shoulder, a terrified group of comrades whom he came across at the local town hall recounted to him the details of the previous evening and night in such a garbled manner that at first he couldn't really understand what they were saying. For the last ten days, forces in the fort of Issy and the large battery at Montretout, assisted by those on Mont-Valérien, had been bombarding the ramparts, and the Porte de Saint-Cloud had become untenable; they'd been intending to mount an attack on it the next day, when at about five o'clock a passer-by,* noticing that no one was guarding the gate, simply called over the sentries in the trenches opposite, barely fifty metres away. Without any hesitation, two companies from the 37th infantry had entered. Then behind them, the whole of the 4th Corps, under General Douay,* had followed. All through the night the army had flowed through, flooding in uninterrupted. At seven o'clock the Vergé division proceeded towards the Pont de Grenelle and got as far as the Trocadéro. At nine o'clock, General Clinchant was taking control of Passy and La Muette. At three in the morning, the 1st Corps was camped out in the Bois de Boulogne; while, at about the same time, the Bruat division crossed the Seine, took possession of the Port de Sèvres, and helped the 2nd Corps, under

General de Cissey, to enter; an hour later they would be occupying the district of Grenelle. This was how, on the morning of 22 May,* the Versailles army came to be in control of the Trocadéro and La Muette on the right bank, and of Grenelle on the left; and it was all done to the stupor, anger, and disarray of the Commune, already crying treason, frantic at the idea of their inexorable defeat.

That was Maurice's first impression, once he understood what had happened: the end had come, there was nothing left to do but get killed. But the alarm bell was clanging away, the drums were beating even louder, women and even children were at work on the barricades, and the streets were filling with the excitement of the hastily reassembled battalions, running to their battle posts. By midday, hope was again springing eternal in the hearts of the Commune's elated soldiers, determined to win, realizing that the Versailles army practically hadn't moved. This army, which they feared they'd be seeing at the Tuileries in a couple of hours, was operating with extraordinary caution, having learned from its defeats, exaggerating the tactic which the Prussians had so harshly taught them. At the Hôtel de Ville the Public Security Committee and Delescluze, the Delegate of War, were organizing and directing the defence. It was said that they'd scornfully rejected one last try at conciliation. This bolstered people's courage; once again they were sure that Paris would be victorious, that everywhere the enemy would be met with fierce resistance, just as the attack must be relentless, as hatred, fanned by lies and atrocities, burned in the hearts of both armies. Maurice spent the day near the Champ de Mars and the Invalides, slowly drawing back,* firing his gun. He'd been unable to find his battalion and was fighting alongside unknown comrades, who'd led him onto the Left Bank without his even noticing. At about four o'clock they defended a barricade blocking the Rue de l'Université where it comes out onto the Esplanade; and they abandoned it only at dusk on learning that the Bruat division, stealing along the quayside, had seized the Legislative Assembly. They'd almost been captured, and managed to reach the Rue de Lille only with the greatest difficulty, taking a long detour via the Rue Saint-Dominique and the Rue de Bellechasse. As night fell, the Versailles army was occupying a line which ran from the Porte de Vanves right up to the Porte d'Asnières, encompassing the Legislative Assembly, the Élysée Palace, the church of Saint-Augustin, and the Gare Saint-Lazare.

The next day, 23 May, a clear, spring morning with bright sunshine, was for Maurice the blackest of them all. A few hundred
federal troops comprised of men from several battalions, of whom he
was one, were still holding the district between the riverbank and the
Rue Saint-Dominique. Most, though, had bivouacked in the Rue de
Lille, in the gardens of the large town-houses situated there. He
himself had slept soundly, on a lawn, next to the Palais de la Légion
d'Honneur. Since morning he'd been convinced that the troops
would break cover from the Assembly in order to drive them back
behind the solid barricades on the Rue du Bac. But hours went by,
and no attack came. Only stray fire was exchanged up and down the
street. This was the plan of the Versailles army, taking its course
slowly and cautiously, its wise decision not to clash head-on with the
formidable fortress which the insurgents had created around the
Tuileries, but adopt a two-sided approach, from right and left, following the ramparts, so as to seize first Montmartre and the
Observatoire* then double back, taking all the central districts with
one huge swoop of the net. At about two o'clock Maurice heard
people saying that the tricolour was flying over Montmartre: the
large battery stationed at the Moulin de la Galette had been captured, attacked by three army corps at once, launching their battalions at the hill to the north and the west, and coming round via the
Rue Lepic, Rue des Saules, and Rue du Mont-Cenis; now the conquerors were sweeping down on Paris, taking possession of the Place
Saint-Georges, Notre-Dame-de-Lorette, the town hall on the Rue
Drouot, and the new Opéra; while on the left bank, the wheeling
manœuvre which had set off from Montparnasse Cemetery had now
reached the Place de l'Enfer and the Horse Market. The news that
the army was making such rapid progress was met with stupor, rage,
and panic. What! Montmartre seized in two hours, Montmartre, that
glorious, impregnable citadel of the insurrection!* Maurice was well
aware that the ranks were growing thinner, that trembling comrades
were stealing noiselessly away, off to wash their hands and put on a
smock, terrified at the thought of the reprisals to come. The rumour
was going round that they were about to be surrounded from the
Rue de la Croix-Rouge, which the army was preparing to attack. The
barricades on the Rue Martignac and the Rue de Bellechasse had
already been taken, and they were beginning to spot red breeches at
the end of the Rue de Lille. And soon only those with conviction and

doggedness remained, Maurice and about fifty others, who'd resolved to die after killing as many as possible of these Versailles men who treated the federals like bandits, shooting prisoners behind the lines. Since the previous day, their hatred and loathing had swollen, and the two factions—rebels dying for their dream, and the army fuming with reactionary passions, exasperated at having to fight on—were set on wiping each other out.

At about five o'clock, as Maurice and his comrades were retreating for good behind the barricades on the Rue du Bac, making their way down the Rue de Lille one doorway at a time, still firing, he suddenly saw a large, black cloud of smoke coming out of an open window in the Palais de la Légion d'Honneur. It was the first fire to be started in Paris; and carried away by wild fury as he was, the sight of it filled him with fierce joy. The hour had come, let the entire city blaze like some enormous pyre, let the fire purify the world! But a sudden apparition took him by surprise: five or six men had just come rushing out of the Palais with a hefty lad at their head, whom he recognized as Chouteau, his former comrade from the squad in the 106th Regiment. He'd already glimpsed him after 18 March, wearing a képi adorned by a single braid, and now he saw that he'd gone up in rank, with braids everywhere, attached to the staff of some general who wasn't engaged in the fighting. He remembered a story* someone had told him: that this same Chouteau had taken up residence in the Palais, where he lived in the company of a mistress, gorging away, lying back on the great, sumptuous beds with his boots on and shattering the mirrors with bullets, just for laughs. They'd even assured him that the mistress, on the pretext of going to the market in Les Halles, left each morning in a ceremonial carriage, taking away with her whole bales of stolen linen, clocks, and even furniture. Seeing him running off with his men, still holding a can of paraffin, Maurice felt uneasy, experiencing a dreadful sense of doubt which rocked his whole faith. Might the terrible deed be something evil, then, if it employed a man like this?

Yet more hours went by, and now he fought in a desolate state, finding that the only thing left intact within him was the sombre will to die. If he'd been deceived, then at least let him pay for his mistake with his blood! The barricade closing off the Rue de Lille, level with the Rue du Bac, was very strong, made of bags and barrels of earth piled behind a deep ditch. He was defending it with barely a dozen other federals, all of them half-lying down, accurately bringing down every soldier who showed himself. Right up until nightfall he didn't budge, exhausting his supply of cartridges, silent, stubborn, and full of despair. He watched the great clouds of smoke swell from the Palais de la Légion d'Honneur, blown down onto the street by the wind, so that the flames weren't yet visible in the fading light of day. Another fire had broken out in a town-house next door. And all of a sudden a comrade came to warn him that the soldiers, not daring to attack the barricade from the front, were in the process of coming round the back through gardens and houses, hacking holes in the walls. It was all over, they might appear right there, any minute now. And he was right, for just then a shot rang out from a window above, and he saw Chouteau again, coming up frantically with his men, running right and left into the corner houses with their paraffin and torches. Half an hour later beneath the blackened sky, the entire crossroads was on fire; while he, still lying behind the barrels and sacks, took advantage of the incredibly bright light to shoot down the careless soldiers who ventured out of doorways and into the road.

How much longer did Maurice go on firing? He was no longer conscious of time or place. It might have been nine or ten o'clock, perhaps. His loathsome task now made him choke with nausea, like some revolting wine which comes back up again when you're drunk. All around him the blazing houses were starting to envelop him with unbearable heat, scorched and airless. The crossroads, surrounded by its pile of paving stones, had become a dug-in camp defended by the fires, while burning brands rained down. Weren't these his orders? To set fire to the area as they abandoned the barricades, to stop the troops with a string of ravenous infernos, to burn Paris bit by bit as they gave it up? And he could already sense that the houses on the Rue du Bac weren't the only ones burning. Behind him, he could see the sky turning to flame with a huge, red glow of light, and he could hear a distant rumbling, as if the whole city were catching fire. To the right, the length of the Seine, other giant fires must be breaking out. He'd seen Chouteau disappear a long while back, fleeing the bullets. Even the most dogged of his comrades were now creeping off one by one, terrified at the thought of being surrounded at any moment. Finally he was left on his own, lying between two sacks of earth, thinking only of shooting on, when the soldiers, who'd made their way round through gardens and courtyards, emerged from a house on the Rue du Bac and closed in.

In the excitement of the supreme struggle, Maurice hadn't thought about Jean for at least two days. Nor had Jean, ever since entering Paris with his regiment, which was acting as reinforcement for the Bruat division, remembered Maurice for a single moment. The day before had been spent firing from the Champ de Mars and the Esplanade des Invalides. Then, today, he hadn't left the Place du Palais-Bourbon until noon, when he went to storm the barricades in the area up to the Rue des Saints-Pères.* He, calm man that he was, had nevertheless grown more and more exasperated at this fratricidal war, surrounded by comrades whose one burning desire was finally to get some rest, after so many months of exhaustion. The prisoners who were being brought back from Germany and incorporated into the ranks were constantly railing against Paris; and then there were tales of the atrocities committed by the Commune, which drove him beside himself with anger, offending his respect for property and his desire for order. He'd remained true to the very heart of his nation, the good peasant who wanted peace, so that they could start working again, earning again, creating new blood again! Above all, though, in all this rising anger which swept away with it even his most tender feelings, it was the fires which now horrified him. Oh no, not that, you didn't go burning down houses and palaces, just because you weren't the strongest side! Only scum could be capable of such deeds. And this man who, only the day before, had felt sick at heart to think of the summary executions, wasn't himself any more but a wild man with eyes popping out of his head, striking out and shouting.

Jean burst violently into the Rue du Bac with the few men from his squad. At first he saw no one, and thought that the barricade had just been evacuated. Then, down between two sacks of earth, he saw a Communard moving, shouldering his rifle, still firing into the Rue de Lille. A furious surge of fate propelled him forward and he ran, nailing the man to the barricade with a thrust of his bayonet.

Maurice didn't have time to turn round. He gave a cry, looked up. The fires lit both men up with blinding sharpness.

'Oh! Jean, my old friend Jean, is it you?'

He'd wanted to die, he was angry, impatient for death to come.

But to die by his own brother's hand was too much, it spoiled death for him, poisoning it with dreadful bitterness.

'Is it you, then, Jean, my old friend Jean?'

Transfixed, suddenly sobered, Jean stared at him. They were alone, the other soldiers had already set off in pursuit of the fleeing men. Around them the fires burned higher, the windows spewed out huge, red flames, while they could hear the blazing ceilings inside crashing to the ground. And Jean fell down beside Maurice, sobbing, fumbling, trying to lift him up, to see whether he might yet be able to save him.

'Oh! My lad! My poor lad!'

CHAPTER EIGHT

When, after countless delays, the train from Sedan finally arrived at the station at Saint-Denis* at about nine o'clock, a great red glow was already illuminating the southern sky, as if the whole of Paris was on fire. As night drew in, this glow had spread; and little by little it crept across the entire horizon, turning to blood-red a flurry of little clouds which sank towards the east, down into the gathering gloom.

Henriette was the first to jump down from the carriage, worried by the signs of burning which the passengers had noticed across the dark fields, from the windows of the moving train. In any case, Prussian soldiers, who had just taken control of the station, were forcing everybody to get off, while another two, standing on the arrival platform, shouted out in guttural French,

'Paris is burning... This train goes no further, everybody off... Paris is burning, Paris is burning...'

At this, Henriette became terribly worried. My God! Had she got here too late? When Maurice hadn't replied to her last two letters, and as the news from Paris got more alarming by the day, she'd been so mortally afraid for him that she'd made a snap decision to leave Remilly. For months now she'd been growing more and more unhappy at Uncle Fouchard's; as Paris prolonged its resistance the occupying troops had become harsher and more demanding; and now that the regiments were one by one returning to Germany, the troops continually passing through had once again drained the countryside and the towns of resources. That morning, as she was rising ahead of the dawn to catch the train from Sedan, she'd seen that the farmyard was crowded with cavalry soldiers who'd slept there, lying any old how, wrapped up in their coats. There had been so many of them that they covered the ground. Then, at a sudden bugle call, they'd all risen silently, draped in their long folds of cloth, so tightly packed together that she felt as if she were watching the resurrection of a battlefield at the peal of the trumpets of the Last Judgement. And now here were more Prussians at Saint-Denis, and they were the ones shouting out the words which so distressed her.

'Everybody off, this train goes no further... Paris is burning, Paris is burning...'

Distraught, Henriette rushed forward with her little case to ask what was happening. There had been fighting in Paris for the past two days, the railway line was cut off, and the Prussians were standing by, keeping watch. Yet she was determined to get past even so, and standing on the platform she noticed the captain in command of the company occupying the station, and ran over to him.

'Sir, I'm on my way to join my brother, who I'm dreadfully worried about. I beg you, please find a way for me to continue my journey.'

She stopped in surprise as she recognized the captain, whose face had just been lit up by a gas lamp.

'It's you, Otto... Oh! Be kind, seeing as luck has brought us face to face again.'

Otto Gunther, her cousin, was still smart and correct in his Guard captain's uniform. And he didn't recognize this slim, shy-looking woman with her pale blond hair and gentle, pretty face, hidden beneath the crape of her hat. It was only from the direct, brave light in her eyes that he eventually remembered her. He just gave a brief shrug.

'You know I've got a brother who's a soldier,' went on Henriette fervently. 'He stayed in Paris, and I'm frightened that he's got mixed up in this dreadful struggle... I beg of you, Otto, find a way for me to go on.'

Only now did he speak.

'But I assure you, I can do nothing... There have been no trains since yesterday, I think the rails have been pulled up near the ramparts. And I have at my disposal neither carriage, nor horse, nor personnel to accompany you.'

She looked at him, and could utter only muted protests in her distress at finding him so cold, so determined not to come to her aid.

'Oh, my God! You don't want to do anything... Oh, my God! Who can I turn to?'

These Prussians! They were the all-powerful masters who, at a single word, could have turned the city upside-down, requisitioned a hundred carriages, had a thousand horses brought out of the stables! And here he was refusing, with the superior attitude of the conqueror who makes a rule never to intervene in the affairs of the vanquished, doubtless judging them unclean, imagining they would soil his nice, fresh victory.

'Well then,' Henriette started again, trying to calm herself, 'at least you know what's going on, surely you can tell me that.'

He gave a thin, barely perceptible smile.

'Paris is burning... Look! Come over here, you can see it perfectly.'

And he proceeded in front of her, walking out of the station, following the rails for about a hundred paces until he reached an iron footbridge built over the line. When they'd climbed the narrow stairs and found themselves at the top, leaning on the railings, the vast, flat plain stretched before them, over a low hill.

'You see? Paris is burning...'

It must have been about half-past nine. The red glow which had set the heavens on fire was still spreading. To the east, the blood-red flurry of little clouds had disappeared, and high in the sky there remained only an inky stain, in which the distant flames were reflected. The entire expanse of the horizon was now ablaze; in places, though, they could make out the fiercer fires, with bright purple showers of sparks constantly spurting up and streaking the darkness amid the huge billows of smoke. And it looked as if the fires were walking, as if some giant forest was catching fire, igniting from tree to tree, as if the earth itself would take light, set ablaze by this colossal bonfire that was Paris.

'Look!' explained Otto. 'You see that black bump sticking out on the red background, that's Montmartre... On the left, at La Villette* and Belleville, nothing's burning yet. They must have set fire to the wealthy districts, and it's spreading and spreading... Just look! Over to the right there's another fire starting! You can see the flames, the flames are boiling up, sending out blazing smoke... And there are more and more, everywhere!'

He wasn't shouting or getting excited, and the enormity of his serenity terrified Henriette. Oh! These Prussians, watching all this! She felt the insult of his calm and his half-smile, as if he'd foreseen this unparalleled disaster and been waiting a long time for it to come. At last Paris was burning, Paris, where German shells had only managed to knock the corners off a few gutters! All his rancour was assuaged, he seemed to be avenged for the over-long siege, for the biting cold, for the new dangers which were constantly springing up and which still irritated Germany. In the arrogance of triumph, nothing—neither the conquered provinces nor the five million francs' compensation—nothing rivalled this spectacle of Paris destroyed, struck by rampant madness, setting light to itself and going up in smoke on this clear, spring night.

'Ah! It was inevitable,' he added, lowering his voice. 'It needed doing.'

Facing the immensity of the catastrophe, Henriette felt pain clutching tighter and tighter at her heart. For several minutes her own personal misfortune was forgotten, swept aside in this expiation of an entire population. The thought of the fire devouring human lives, the sight of the city in flames on the horizon, casting that infernal glow of cities damned and destroyed, made her cry out in spite of herself. She clasped her hands and asked,

'My God! Whatever can we have done to deserve such punishment?'

Otto was already raising an arm to cut her off. He was about to speak with the vehemence of that cold, harsh, military Protestantism which would cite verses from the Bible. But one glance at the young woman, meeting her beautiful eyes full of clarity and reason, stopped him short. In any case, his gesture had been enough, he'd expressed his racial hatred, his conviction that he was in France as the dispenser of justice, sent by the God of armies to chastise a perverse nation. Paris was burning as punishment for centuries of sin, for the long list of its crimes and debauchery. Yet again the Germans would save the world, sweeping away the last specks of Latin dirt and corruption.

He let his arm drop and said simply,

'It's all over... Look, there's another district going up, that other fire further to the left... You can quite clearly see that huge line spreading like a river of flames.'

They both fell quiet and a terrifed silence reigned. He was right, sudden surges of flame were rising incessantly, overflowing into the sky like fire streaming from a furnace. With every minute the endless sea of flames spread further in an incandescent swell, sending up billows of smoke and piling an enormous, thick cloud of dark copper over the city; and there must have been a slight breeze behind it, for it was slowly crossing the black night, blocking out the heavenly vault with its wicked shower of ash and soot.

Henriette shuddered and seemed to wake from a nightmare; and once again seized by anguish at the thought of her brother, she made one last, pleading request.

'So you can't do anything for me, you refuse to help me get into Paris?'

With another wave of his hand, Otto made as if to sweep across the horizon.

'What good could it do? For tomorrow there'll be nothing left but rubble!'

And that was it, she climbed down from the footbridge without even bidding him farewell, fleeing with her little case; while he stayed up there for a long time, slim and still, in his tightly buttoned uniform, swallowed up by the night, gorging his eyes on the monstrous feast offered by the spectacle of Babylon in flames.

As Henriette was leaving the station she was lucky enough to chance upon a fat lady haggling with a cab-driver, asking him to take her straight to Paris, to the Rue de Richelieu;* and Henriette pleaded so desperately with her, shedding such moving tears, that she eventually agreed to take her along too. The cab-driver, a dark-haired little man, whipped on his horse and said nothing for the whole of the journey. The fat lady, however, never stopped for a moment, recounting how, after shutting up and leaving her shop two days previously, she'd made the mistake of leaving behind some bonds hidden in one of the walls. And so for the past two hours, while the city had been ablaze, she'd been absolutely obsessed with going back to pick up her belongings, even if it meant travelling right through the fire. At the barrier there was only a sleepy guard, and the cab passed without too much difficulty, especially as the lady lied, saying she'd gone to collect her niece so that they could both look after her husband, who'd been wounded by the Versailles army. The larger obstacles started when they reached the streets, where barricades blocked their every turn, and they were continually having to make detours. Eventually, on the Boulevard Poissonnière, the cab-driver declared that he wouldn't go any further. And the two women were obliged to continue on foot, down the Rue Sentier, the Rue des Jeûneurs, and the entire Bourse district. As they were approaching the fortifications, the fiery sky had lit them up as if in broad daylight. They were surprised by the deserted calm of this part of the city, where only the faintest tremor could be felt from the distant rumbling. As soon as they reached the Bourse, however, they could hear gunfire, and they had to stick close to the houses. On the Rue de Richelieu, once they'd discovered the shop intact, the fat lady was overjoyed and insisted on showing her companion the way, down the Rue du Hasard, Rue Saint-Anne, and then the Rue des Orties.* At one point some federals, whose battalion was still occupying the Rue Saint-Anne, tried to stop them passing. In the end it was four o'clock, and the sky was getting light, by the time Henriette, emotionally and physically drained, found the door to the large house on the Rue des Orties lying wide open. After mounting the dark, narrow staircase, she had to climb up a ladder behind a door, leading onto the roof.

At the barricade on the Rue du Bac, Maurice, lying between the two sacks of earth, had managed to get to his knees, and Jean, who thought he'd nailed him to the ground, was seized with hope.

'Oh! Are you still alive, my boy? Could I be that lucky, wicked brute that I am?... Hang on, let me see.'

He carefully examined the wound in the bright light cast by the fires. The bayonet had entered the arm, near the right shoulder; and the worst of it was that it had then slid between two ribs, no doubt puncturing the lung. But the wounded man was breathing without too much difficulty. Only his arm hung down, limp.

'My poor old friend, come on, now, don't despair! I'm not sad about it anyway, I'd rather get it over with... You already did enough for me, without you I'd have died a long time ago by the side of the road somewhere.'

But hearing him say such things Jean felt another violent stab of pain.

'Will you shut up! Twice you've saved me from the paws of the Prussians! We were quits, it was my turn to lay down my life for you, and look, I've done for you... Oh! Jesus Christ! I must have been blind drunk not to have recognized you! I must have been drunk as a pig, from already having drunk too much blood!'

Tears sprang to his eyes, recalling their parting back in Remilly, when they'd taken leave of each other, wondering how and if they would ever meet again one day, and whether the circumstances would be ones of joy or sorrow. So all those days without bread they'd gone through together, and all those nights without sleep, and death always nearby, had all been for nothing? Was it all to bring them to this abominable deed, to this stupid, monstrous fratricide, that their hearts had merged during those few weeks of heroic life together? Oh no! He revolted against the thought.

'Leave it to me, my boy, I have to save you.'

First of all, he had to get him out of there, because the army was finishing off the wounded. As luck would have it, they were alone, and there wasn't a minute to lose. Swiftly he used his knife to slit through the sleeve, and then removed the rest of the uniform. Blood began to flow, and he hurried to bind the arm up firmly, using rags torn off from the lining. Then he applied padding to the torso wound and tied the arm over it. Fortunately he had a length of rope on him, and he pulled the rudimentary dressing tight, which had the advantage of immobilizing the entire affected side, and preventing haemorrhage.

'Can you walk?'

'Yes, I think so.'

But he didn't dare take him away as he was, dressed in his shirt sleeves. A sudden flash of inspiration sent him running into the next street where he'd seen a dead soldier, and he came back with a greatcoat and a képi. He flung the greatcoat about Maurice's shoulders and helped him to put his uninjured arm into the left sleeve. Then, placing the képi on his head, he said,

'Right, now you're one of us... Where are we going?'

That was the great dilemma. At once, even as his hopes and courage were reawakening, the sense of dread returned. Where could they find somewhere safe enough to hide? The houses were being searched and they were shooting any Communards caught carrying arms. And besides, neither one of them knew anyone in the area, not a soul whom they could ask for shelter, not a single hiding place in which to disappear.

'Best of all would be my place,' said Maurice. 'The house is set apart from the rest, and no one in the world's going to come looking there... Only it's on the other side of the river, on the Rue des Orties.'

Jean, wavering and distraught, mumbled and swore under his breath.

'Jesus Christ! What shall we do?'

There was no question of escaping over the Pont Royal, which the fires had lit up with a light as blinding as blazing sun. Every second, shots rang out on either bank. What was worse, they would have come up against the blazing Tuileries and the blockaded and guarded Louvre, which would have been insurmountable barriers.

'Well, then, we've had it, there's no way of getting across!' declared Jean, who'd lived in Paris for six months on his return from the campaigns in Italy.

Suddenly he had an idea. If there were still small boats moored below the Pont Royal, as there used to be, then they could give it a go. It would take a long time, and it was dangerous and uncomfortable; but they didn't have any choice, and they had to make a swift decision.

'Listen, my boy, let's get out of here at any rate, it's not safe... I'll tell my lieutenant that I got caught by some Communards and managed to escape.'

He seized Maurice's uninjured arm and held him up, helping him to get to the end of the Rue du Bac, amidst the houses blazing from top to bottom like outsized torches. A shower of burning brands rained down on them, and the heat was so intense that it singed all the hair on their faces. Then, as they came out onto the quayside, they were momentarily blinded by the terrifying brightness of the fires, sending up enormous showers of sparks on either side of the Seine.

'We're not short of candles,' grumbled Jean, bothered by the bright light.

And he only started to feel safe once he'd helped Maurice down the steps to the left of the Pont Royal, downstream. There, in the clump of tall trees at the water's edge, they were hidden from view. For nearly a quarter of an hour, they were worried to see dark shadows moving around on the opposite bank. There were gunshots and they heard a loud cry, then a splash, and foam suddenly spraying up. The bridge was obviously guarded.

'What if we spent the night in there?' asked Maurice, pointing to a wooden office of the rivers authority.

'Oh, yes, right, and get caught tomorrow morning!'

Jean still had his plan in mind. He had in fact just discovered a whole flotilla of little boats. But they were chained together, and how was he to separate one off and free the oars? Finally he discovered an old pair of oars and managed to force open a padlock, which probably hadn't been properly locked; and at once, after laying Maurice down in the bows of the craft, he carefully abandoned himself to the current, keeping close to the edge, in the shadow of the swimming baths and the barges. Neither spoke, horrifed by the dreadful spectacle unfurling before them. As they drifted downriver the horror seemed to loom larger than ever as the horizon receded. When they reached the Pont de Solférino,* they could see at a glance both banks in flames.

On the left, the Tuileries were burning.* At nightfall, the Communards had set fire to both ends of the palace, to the Pavillon de Flore and the Pavillon de Marsan; and the flames were rapidly reaching the Pavillon de l'Horloge, in the middle, where an entire minefield had been prepared, with barrels of gunpowder piled up in the Salle des Maréchaux. At that moment, whirling clouds of reddish smoke scored by blue sparks were belching from the broken windows of the buildings in between. The roofs caught fire, splitting open into blazing cracks like volcanic earth from the pressure of the furnace beneath. But it was the Pavillon de Flore, the first to be set alight, that was blazing fiercest of all, from the ground floor right up to the massive roof timbers, making an incredible roaring sound. The paraffin which had been poured over the floor and wall-hangings made the flames so intense that they could see the balcony railings twisting, and the tall, monumental chimneys, with their huge, sculpted red-hot suns, bursting open.

Then, on the right, the first thing they saw was the Palais de la Légion d'Honneur, which had been set on fire at five o'clock in the evening and had now been burning for nearly seven hours, a massive, flaming pyre which would suddenly burn itself out. Next was the Palais du Conseil d'État, an immense conflagration, the hugest of them all and the most terrifying, a giant cube of stone with two storeys of porticoes spewing out flames. The four buildings which surrounded the inner courtyard had caught fire simultaneously; and inside, the barrels of paraffin which had been flung down all four corner staircases had streamed down, sending torrents of hellfire down the steps. On the side overlooking the waterfront, the clean line of the attic storey stood out like a blackened ramp against the red tongues licking at the edges; while the columns, entablatures, friezes, and sculptures were thrown into powerful and extraordinary relief against the glow of a blinding furnace. Above all the momentum, the power of the fire was so terrible that it was as if the colossal monument was being bodily lifted up, shaking and groaning on its foundations, maintaining only the carcass of its thick walls in the violent eruption which was blasting its zinc roofing off into the sky. Then, next door was the Orsay barracks, where an entire wing was burning, forming a tall, white column like a tower of light. And finally behind this were yet more fires, the seven houses on the Rue du Bac, the twenty-two on the Rue de Lille, setting the skyline ablaze, flames standing out against more flames in a bloody, endless sea.

Jean, quite choked, murmured,

'God, it's impossible! The river's going to catch light!'

It was true, the boat floated along as if borne on a river of fire. In the dancing reflections of these enormous blazes, the Seine appeared to be flowing with hot coals. Sudden bursts of red light flickered above it, amid shimmering yellow firebrands. And they went on drifting slowly down, carried on the current of this burning water between the blazing palaces, as if down an outsized road in a city of the damned, as it burned on either side of a path of molten lava.

'Oh!' said Maurice in turn, gripped again by madness as he watched the destruction he'd wanted. 'Let it all burn, let it all blow up!'

But with a terrified gesture Jean made him hush, as if he feared that such blasphemy might bring bad luck on them. How could it possibly be that a young man he loved so much, who was so educated, so delicate, had come to have such ideas? And he rowed faster, for he'd passed the Pont de Solférino and was now in the middle of a large, unsheltered stretch of river. The light grew so bright that the water was lit up as if by the midday sun, beating straight down, casting no shadows. They could make out the slightest details with extraordinary precision, the swirls of the current, the heaps of gravel on the banks, the small trees on the quaysides. The bridges stood out particularly strongly, dazzling white, so clear that you could have counted every stone; and it was as if slender footbridges were running intact from one blaze to another, above the fiery, glowing water. At times, sudden creakings could be heard above the constant, rumbling clamour. Flurries of soot came down and foul smells blew over on the wind.* And what was so terrifying was that Paris, those other districts far away, beyond the swathe of the Seine through the city, no longer existed. To right and left, the violence of the fires was blinding, leaving a black abyss behind it. All that could now be seen was an immense darkness, a void, as if the whole of Paris had been caught and devoured in the fire, and had already vanished into an eternal night. The sky, too, was dead, for the flames reached up so high they extinguished the stars.

Maurice, buoyed up by the delirium of fever, gave a mad laugh.

'What a beautiful party at the Conseil d'État and the Tuileries... They've lit up the façades, the chandeliers are sparkling, the women are dancing... Oh! Dance, then, dance, in your smouldering petticoats, with your chignons aflame...'

With his good arm he mimed the galas of Sodom and Gomorrah, with the music and flowers and perverted pleasures, the palaces bursting with so much debauchery, lighting up the naked abominations with such a wealth of candles that they'd set fire to themselves. Suddenly there was a terrifying crash. It was the Tuileries, where the fire, approaching from either side, had reached the Salle des Maréchaux. The barrels of powder caught light and the Pavillon de l'Horloge exploded violently, like a powder keg. A huge shower of sparks rose up in a plume which filled the black sky, the flaming bouquet of this horrible orgy.

'Bravo!' cried Maurice, as if at the end of a show, when everything fades back into darkness.

Jean stammered, pleading with him again, talking frantically. No, no! He mustn't wish evil upon them! If everything was to be destroyed, wouldn't they die, too? All he wanted now was to get off the river and escape from the dreadful spectacle. However, he wisely rowed on past the Pont de la Concorde, so that they didn't disembark until they got to the Quai de la Conférence, rounding the bend in the Seine. And at this crucial moment, instead of leaving the craft to drift, he lost several minutes mooring it solidly, with his instinctive respect for other people's property. His plan was for them to reach the Rue des Orties by way of the Place de la Concorde and the Rue Saint-Honoré.* Having sat Maurice down on the bank, he climbed the steps onto the quay by himself, growing anxious as he realized how awkward it would be for them to get over the piled-up obstacles. This was the Commune's impregnable fortress, with the area around the Tuileries defended by cannon, the Rue Royale, the Rue Saint-Florentin, and the Rue de Rivoli all blocked by high, strongly built barricades; which explained the tactics adopted by the Versailles army, whose lines that night were forming an immense reflex angle, with its northern apex at the Place de la Concorde, one of its two flanks on the right bank at the goods station of the Compagnie du Nord, and the other on the Left Bank, at a bastion of the ramparts near the Porte d'Arcueil. However, it would soon grow light, the Communards had evacuated the Tuileries and the barricades, and the army had just taken control of the area, surrounded by more fires, with twelve more houses torched since nine o'clock the previous evening, at the intersection between the Rue Saint-Honoré and the Rue Royale.

Below, climbing back down onto the bank, Jean found Maurice sleepy, as if numb after his fit of over-excitement.

'It's not going to be easy... Can you still walk, at least, lad?'

'Yes, yes, don't you worry. I'll get there somehow, dead or alive.'

It was climbing the stone steps which gave him the most trouble. Up on the quayside he walked slowly, leaning on his companion's arm, like a sleepwalker. Even though daylight hadn't yet come, the reflection from the nearby fires illuminated the vast square with a livid dawn. They walked across the solitude, hearts heavy at the mournful devastation. At either end, over the bridge and at the far end of the Rue Royale, they could dimly make out the ghostly silhouettes of the Palais Bourbon and the Palais de la Madeleine, ploughed up by cannonfire. The terrace of the Tuileries, which had been battered to force an entry, had partly given way. On the square itself, bullets had pierced the bronze fountains, and the giant torso of the Statue of Lille was lying on the ground, broken in two by a shell, while the Statue of Strasbourg next to it, veiled in crape, seemed to be wearing mourning for all these ruins. And lying in a trench near the unscathed obelisk was a gas main which someone had accidentally dug through, and which had now ignited, letting off a long, strident jet of flames.

Jean avoided the barricade blocking off the Rue Royale, between the Naval Ministry* and the Garde-Meuble,* which had been spared by the fire. Behind the sandbags and barrels of earth from which it was constructed, he could hear soldiers talking loudly. In front, it was defended by a ditch of stagnant water, in which the body of a federal soldier was floating; and through a gap they could see the houses at the Saint-Honoré crossroads, in the last stages of burning down despite the waterpumps brought in from the suburbs which could be heard rumbling away. To the right and left, the small trees and the newspaper kiosks were all battered, riddled with machine-gun fire. Loud shouts went up as the firemen discovered seven tenants of one of the houses, down in the cellar, their bodies half-charred.

Although the barricade blocking the Rue Saint-Florentin and the Rue de Rivoli appeared to be even more formidable, high and cleverly put together, Jean instinctively felt that getting through here would be less dangerous. He was right—it had been completely evacuated, but the army hadn't yet dared occupy it. Cannon stood dormant, utterly abandoned. Not a soul lay behind this invincible rampart, except a stray dog which ran off. However, as Jean was hurrying down the Rue Saint-Florentin supporting Maurice, who was growing weaker, what he'd feared came to pass—they bumped into an entire company of the 88th infantry regiment, which had made its way round the barricade.

'Captain,' he explained, 'this is a comrade who's been wounded by those bandits, and I'm taking him to the field hospital.'

It was the greatcoat flung around his shoulders which saved Maurice, and Jean's heart was thumping fit to burst as they finally walked together down the Rue Saint-Honoré. Daylight was just breaking and gunshots rang out from the side streets, for there was still fighting going on all over the area. It would be a miracle if they could reach the Rue des Frondeurs without any more unfortunate encounters. Now they could walk only extremely slowly, and the last three or four hundred metres seemed as if they'd never end. On the Rue des Frondeurs they chanced on a guard post of Communards; but the latter, panicking, thinking that a whole regiment was coming, took flight. And there was only a short stretch of the Rue d'Argenteuil to go before they reached the Rue des Orties.

Oh! How Jean had been longing to see this Rue des Orties! How desperately impatient he'd been to get there, for four long hours! When they turned into it, what a relief it was. It lay dark and silent, deserted, as if it were hundreds of miles away from the fighting. The house, an old, narrow building with no concierge, slept like the dead.

'I've got the keys in my pocket,' stammered Maurice. 'The big one's the street door, and the little one's my room key, right at the top.'

Then he collapsed and fainted into Jean's arms, who found himself in an extremely worrying and awkward situation. He forgot to relock the door onto the street, and had to carry him up the unfamiliar flight of stairs fumbling his way forward, trying not to bump into anything, so as not to raise the alarm. Then, at the top, he got lost and had to put the wounded man down on one of the steps while he looked for the door with the help of some matches that, luckily, he had on him; and only when he'd found it did he go back down to pick him up again. At last he laid him down on the little iron bed, facing the window onto Paris, which he flung wide open, needing to let fresh air and light into the room. It was growing light, and he fell down sobbing by the bed, overcome, all his strength drained, as the terrible realization dawned on him that he'd killed his friend.

Minutes must have gone by, and he was scarcely even surprised when he suddenly caught sight of Henriette. Nothing could be more natural, her brother was dying, and there she was. He hadn't even seen her come in, perhaps she'd been there for hours. Dropping onto a chair, in a daze, he watched her move about in mortal grief at the sight of her brother lying unconscious, covered in blood. Finally he remembered something, and asked,

'By the way, did you close the door onto the street?'

Overcome, she simply nodded in reply; and, as she at last held out both her hands to him, craving help and affection, he went on,

'You know, I'm the one who killed him...'

She didn't understand, didn't believe him. He felt her two little hands lying calmly in his.

'I'm the one who killed him... Yes, back there, on a barricade... He was fighting for one side, I was fighting for the other...'

The little hands began to shake.

'It was as if we were drunk, we didn't know what we were doing... I'm the one who killed him...'

Then Henriette withdrew her hands, trembling, white-faced, her terrified eyes staring at him. Was it all over, then, was nothing to survive of her broken heart? Oh! Jean, whom she'd been thinking of only that evening, happy in the vague hope that she might see him again! And he had done this abominable thing, and yet he'd saved Maurice one more time, for it was he who'd brought him back here, braving so much danger! She couldn't leave her hands in his now without feeling her whole self recoil. But she gave a cry, investing it with the very last hope of her struggling heart.

'Oh! I'll make him better, I've got to make him better now!'

During her long hours on duty at the hospital in Remilly, she'd become expert at tending and dressing wounds. And she wanted to look at her brother's injuries at once, undressing him, without stirring him from his unconscious state. But when she removed the makeshift dressing which Jean had improvised, he stirred and cried out faintly, opening wide, feverish eyes. He recognized her straight away, and smiled.

'You're here, then? Oh! How happy I am to see you before I die!'

She made him hush, with a fine, confident gesture.

'Die? But I don't want you to die, I want you to live!... Don't say any more, just let me get on with it!'

However, when Henriette examined the wounded arm and ribs, her face grew sombre and her eyes became troubled. Briskly, she took over the room, managing to find a little oil, ripping up old shirts to make bandages, while Jean went downstairs to find a bowl of water. He didn't say another word, but watched her bathe the wounds and deftly apply dressings, incapable of helping her, utterly worn out since she'd arrived. Nevertheless, noticing her concern, when she'd finished he offered to go and look for a doctor. But she had all her wits about her: no, no! Not any old doctor, who might betray her brother! They needed a man they could be sure of, they could wait for a few hours. Eventually, as Jean was talking about leaving to rejoin his regiment, they agreed that, as soon as he could get away, he would come back and try to bring a surgeon with him.

He still didn't go, apparently unable to resign himself to leaving this room, full of misfortune that was his doing. The window had been closed for a while, but was now open again. And from his bed, head propped up, the wounded man looked out while the other two also gazed into the distance, in the heavy silence which had come over them.

From this high position on the Butte des Moulins, at least half of Paris stretched out before them, first the central districts, from the Faubourg Saint-Honoré right up to the Bastille, then the entire length of the Seine, with the distant signs of life on the Left Bank, a sea of rooftops, treetops, steeples, domes, and towers. The day was growing lighter, and the abominable night, one of the most terrible in history, was over. But in the clear, pure rays of the rising sun, beneath the rosy sky, the fires burned on. Opposite, they glimpsed the Tuileries still ablaze, the Orsay Barracks, the Palais du Conseil

d'État and the Palais de la Légion d'Honneur, whose flames, paled
by broad daylight, seemed to send a shudder across the whole sky.
There must have been other houses on fire, too, beyond those on the
Rue de Lille and the Rue du Bac, for columns of sparks were rising
up from the Carrefour de la Croix-Rouge, and even further away
still, from the Rue Vavin and the Rue Notre-Dame-des-Champs. On
the right, close by, the fires on the Rue Saint-Honoré were burning
themselves out, while on the left, at the Palais-Royal and the new
Louvre, fires started late, towards dawn, were now petering out. But
there was something they couldn't at first work out, a thick, black
cloud of smoke, which the westerly wind was blowing right under
the window. Since three in the morning the Ministry of Finance had
been burning, not giving off any tall flames, but being eaten up by
thick swirls of soot, so smothered were the prodigious masses of
paperwork packed beneath the low ceilings of the plaster framework.
And even if, as the great city awakened, the tragic impression of that
night no longer prevailed, with the terror of total destruction, the
Seine flowing on fire, all four corners of Paris aflame, yet a sense of
sad, mournful despair drifted over the spared districts in an endless
cloud of thick smoke, spreading wider and wider. Soon the sun,
which had risen clear, was hidden from view; and all that was left was
this mourning, in the tawny sky.

Tracing a hand slowly across the boundless horizon, Maurice,
who must have been getting delirious again, murmured,

'Is everything burning? Oh, what a long time it's taking!'

Tears came to Henriette's eyes, as if her unhappiness had been
made even worse by these huge disasters in which her brother had
got mixed up. And Jean, who didn't dare take her hand again or
embrace his friend, rushed out wildly.

'Goodbye, see you later!'

He wasn't able to come back until about eight o'clock that evening, after nightfall. In spite of his acute anxiety, he was happy: his
regiment, no longer engaged in the fighting, had been moved back
from the front line and had been given orders to guard the district;
which meant that, bivouacking with his company on the Place du
Carrousel, Jean hoped to be able to come up every day for news of
the sick man. Nor did he return alone, for he'd bumped into the
former major from the 106th, and, having failed to find any other
doctor, had brought him back with him as a last resort, telling him-

self that whatever else, this terrible man, with his lion's head, was a decent one.

Unaware who the wounded man was that this pleading soldier was bothering him about, and grumbling about having to climb so many stairs, when Bouroche realized that the man before him was a Communard he at first flew into a violent rage.

'Jesus Christ! Are you having me on?... It's one of these bandits who've had enough of robbing, murdering, and setting fire to buildings!... I know exactly what's wrong with this hooligan of yours, and I'll take it upon myself to heal him, oh yes, I will, with three bullets to the head!'

The sight of Henriette, however, so pale in her black dress, with her fine, loose, blond hair, suddenly calmed him down.

'He's my brother, sir, and he's one of your soldiers from Sedan.'

He didn't reply, but removed the bandages and examined the wounds in silence, took phials from his pocket and reapplied the dressing, showing the young woman how it should be done. Then, in his rough voice, he suddenly asked the wounded man,

'Why did you go over to the side of those scum, what made you do such an appalling thing?'

Maurice, whose eyes were glittering, had been watching him wordlessly since he came in. Ardently, through his fever, he replied,

'Because there's too much suffering, too much unfairness and shame!'

At that, Bouroche threw up his hands, as if to say that you'd go a long way, with ideas like that. He was about to speak again, but thought better of it. And he left, adding simply,

'I'll be back.'

Out on the landing, he declared to Henriette that he didn't dare give any guarantees. The lung was seriously affected and haemorrhaging could result, which would finish the patient off.

When Henriette went back inside, she forced herself to smile, in spite of the blow which had just struck right to the heart of her. Wasn't she going to be able to save him, wasn't she going to be able to prevent this horrific thing from happening, prevent the three of them being separated for ever, when they were all there, reunited once more by their fervent desire to live? She hadn't left the room all day, an old lady in the building had obligingly taken care of the shopping. And she went back and took up her place on a chair, near the bed.

However, giving in to his feverish excitement, Maurice was questioning Jean, eager to know what was happening. Jean didn't tell him everything, and avoided recounting the tales of anger and fury mounting against the failing Commune in liberated Paris. It was already Wednesday. For over two days now, since Sunday evening, the inhabitants had been living down in their cellars, sweating with fear; and on the Wednesday morning, when they'd finally been able to venture out, the sight of the ripped-up streets, the rubble, the blood, and above all the terrible fires, had given them a raging thirst for vengeance. The punishment was going to be savage. Houses were searched, and scores of men and women under suspicion were picked up and flung to the summary execution squads. From six o'clock that evening, the Versailles army had been master of half of Paris, from the Parc du Montsouris as far as the Gare du Nord, along the boulevards. And the last twenty or so members of the Commune had been forced to seek refuge on the Boulevard Voltaire, in the town hall of the eleventh *arrondissement*.

There was a silence, and Maurice, eyes gazing far away into the city, through the window which was open onto the warm night air, murmured,

'Anyway, it's still going on. Paris is burning!'

It was true, the flames had appeared again as soon as the light had faded; and once more, a wicked glow began to turn the sky to purple. In the afternoon, when the powder-keg of the Palais du Luxembourg* had exploded with a terrifying bang, the rumour had spread that the Pantheon had collapsed right into the catacombs. Moreover, throughout the day, the fires from the previous day had continued to burn, the Palais du Conseil d'État was still on fire, and the Ministry of Finance was still sending up great whirls of smoke. They'd had to shut the window at least a dozen times to shut out the menacing cloud of black butterflies, pieces of burning papers continuously flying past, borne up into the sky by the violence of the flames, falling back down to earth as fine rain; the whole of Paris was covered in them, and they were found as far away as Normandy, over twenty leagues away. Now it wasn't just the western and southern districts which were burning, the houses on the Rue Royale and at the cross-roads between the Rue de la Croix-Rouge and the Rue Notre-Dame-des-Champs. The entire eastern side of the city seemed to be in flames too, with the immense pyre of the Hôtel de Ville blotting out the horizon like some gigantic bonfire. There, too, blazing like torches, were the Théâtre Lyrique, the town hall of the sixth *arrondissement*, and nearly thirty houses in the neighbouring streets; not to mention the Théâtre de la Porte Saint-Martin to the north, a red glow set apart, like a haystack standing deep in shadowy fields. Individual acts of vengeance were also at work, and perhaps criminal elements were persisting in the hope of destroying certain dossiers. It wasn't even a question any more of using fire as a means of defence, to stop the victorious army. It was just madness blowing on the wind with the Palais de Justice, the Hôtel-Dieu, and Notre-Dame spared entirely at random. It was destruction just for the sake of it, to bury the old, rotten human race beneath the ashes of a whole civilization, in the hope that a new society would spring up happy and innocent, in the middle of an earthly paradise out of some primeval legend!

'Oh! This war, this loathsome war!' half-whispered Henriette, looking at the city of ruins, suffering, and agony.

For wasn't this the final, fatal act, the madness in the blood which had germinated on the fields of defeat of Sedan and Metz, the epidemic of destruction born of the siege of Paris, the paroxysm of a nation in mortal danger, amid all the killing and ruination?

But Maurice, his eyes never straying from the burning districts beyond, stammered slowly and painfully,

'No, no, don't curse the war... The war's good, it's doing its work...'

Jean cut him short with a cry full of hatred and remorse.

'Jesus bloody Christ! When I see you there, and to think it's all my fault... Don't keep defending it, war's a foul thing!'

The wounded man gestured vaguely.

'Me? Oh, what do I matter? There'll be others!... Maybe this bloodletting's something which needed to happen. War's life, and life can't exist without death.'

And Maurice's eyes closed, wearied by the effort these few words had cost him. Henriette signalled to Jean, asking him not to say any more. She herself felt a surge of protest inside her, of anger at human suffering, which belied her calm, frail, feminine bearing, so full of courage, with her clear gaze where the heroic soul of her grandfather lived on, that hero of Napoleonic legend.

Two days passed, Thursday and Friday, with more fires and massacres. The boom of the cannon was unceasing; the Montmartre batteries, which had been captured by the Versailles army, kept up a relentless bombardment of those which the federals had set up at Belleville and Père Lachaise; these fired randomly on Paris, and shells had fallen on the Rue de Richelieu and the Place Vendôme. By the evening of the 25th, the entire Left Bank had fallen into the army's hands. On the Right Bank, however, the barricades on the Place du Château-d'Eau and the Place de la Bastille were still standing firm. These were two real fortresses, defended by terrible, incessant gunfire. At twilight, as the final members of the Commune scattered, Delescluze had picked up his cane and strolled calmly over, right up to the barricade closing off the Boulevard Voltaire, where he fell, shot down like a hero. At daybreak the following day, the 26th, the Château-d'Eau and the Bastille were taken by storm, and now the Communards occupied only La Villette, Belleville, and Charonne,* and there were fewer and fewer of them, reduced to a handful of brave men prepared to die. And for two days they would keep up their resistance, and fight on furiously.

On the Friday evening, as Jean was slipping away from the Place du Carrousel to return to the Rue des Orties, he witnessed a summary execution at the bottom of the Rue de Richelieu which left him deeply shocked. For the past two days, two courts martial had been in operation, one at the Palais du Luxembourg, the other at the Théâtre du Châtelet.* The men condemned by the first were shot in the garden, while those found guilty by the other were dragged as far as the Lobau barracks,* where firing squads in continuous session dispatched them in the inner courtyard, almost at point-blank range. It was here, above all, that the butchery became terrifying: men and children condemned on the strength of a single piece of evidence, that their hands were black with gunpowder, or merely that they happened to be wearing army boots; innocents falsely denounced, victims of private vengeance, screaming out explanations, unable to make themselves heard; hordes of men flung pell-mell before the barrels of the guns, so many wretched people at one time that there weren't enough bullets for all of them, and the injured had to be finished off with rifle butts. Blood flowed freely, and bodies were carried off by the cartload, from morning until night. And all over the conquered city, at the whim of sudden outbursts of vengeful rage, other executions were carried out, in front of the barricades, up against walls on deserted streets, on the steps of monuments. This was how Jean came to see the local inhabitants taking two men and a woman to the guard post outside the Théâtre-Français. The bourgeoisie were proving more ferocious than the soldiers, for the newspapers which had begun appearing again were openly inciting extermination. A huge, violent crowd was having a go at the woman in particular, one of those arsonists* who haunted their hallucinating imagination, and who was accused of roaming the city at night, slipping past rich houses and chucking cans of burning paraffin down into the cellars. They were shouting that she'd just been caught crouching down at a basement window on the Rue Saint-Anne. And in spite of her sobs and protests they threw her, along with the two men, down into the bottom of a barricade trench which hadn't yet been filled in, and there they shot them, in this black pit, like wolves caught in a trap. Passers-by watched, a lady stopped to look with her husband, while a baker's boy, delivering a pastry tart nearby, whistled a hunting tune.

Jean was hurrying to reach the Rue des Orties, cold creeping through his heart, when he suddenly remembered something. Wasn't that Chouteau he'd just seen, the former soldier from his squad, wearing the honest worker's white smock and watching the execution, waving his approval? And this was the man who'd played the role of bandit, traitor, thief, and murderer! For a moment, Jean was on the verge of going back there and denouncing him, and having him shot on top of the bodies of the other three. Oh! How sad it all was, when the guiltiest of all escaped punishment, parading their impunity in broad daylight, while the innocent rotted in the ground!

Henriette, hearing the sound of footsteps coming up the stairs, had come out onto the landing.

'Be careful, he's terribly over-excited today... The Major's been back, and he's made me lose all hope.'

In fact Bouroche had shaken his head, still unable to make any promises. Perhaps, in spite of everything, the patient's youth would triumph over the setbacks he feared.

'Oh! It's you!' Maurice said feverishly to Jean, as soon as he caught sight of him. 'I've been waiting for you, what's happening, where have things got to?'

Then, propped up against the pillow, facing the window he'd forced his sister to open, to show the city submerged in darkness again, lit up by the glow of a renewed flame, he said,

'Well? It's starting again, isn't it, Paris is burning, this time the whole of Paris is burning!'

With the setting of the sun, the fire which had started in the Grenier d'Abondance* had ignited the distant parts of the city, north of the river. At the Tuileries and the Conseil d'État, the ceilings must have been collapsing, causing the timbers to catch light, for in places the fires were flaring up again, and every now and then sparks and flashes of flame shot up into the air. Many of the houses where the fire was assumed to have gone out were also beginning to burn again. For three days, darkness had been unable to fall without the city appearing to blaze again, as if the shadows had blown onto the still-smouldering embers, bringing them back to life, sowing them on all four corners of the horizon. Oh! This hellish city which glowed red as soon as dusk fell, aflame for seven whole days, its monstrous torches illuminating the nights of that bloody week! And that night, when the docks burned at La Villette,* the light over the immense city was so bright that one could truly believe that this time, every single corner had been set on fire, overrun and submerged beneath the flames. In the bleeding sky, the red parts of the town created a flood of burning rooftops seeping off into infinity.

'This is the end,' repeated Maurice. 'Paris is burning!'

He grew excited at these words, repeating them a score of times over and over again, from a feverish need to talk after the heavy sleepiness which had kept him practically mute for the past three days. But the sound of muffled sobbing made him turn his head.

'What! You, little sister, brave girl that you are?... Weeping because I'm going to die...'

She interrupted him, crying out,

'But you're not going to die!'

'Yes, I am, it's better that way, it has to be so!... Oh! Come on, it's not as if anything worth much will be dying with me. Before the war I caused you so much pain, I was such a heavy burden on your heart, and on your purse!... All those stupid, crazy things I did, I'd have come to a bad end, who knows? Prison, or the gutter...'

Once again, she cut him off vehemently.

'Don't! Don't! You've made up for all that!'

He fell quiet, and thought for a moment.

'Maybe when I'm dead, yes, maybe I will have done... Oh! My old friend Jean, you certainly did us all a favour when you got me with your bayonet.'

But Jean, too, protested, his eyes full of tears.

'Don't say that! You'll have me banging my head against a wall!'

Fiercely, Maurice went on,

'Just remember what you told me, the day after Sedan, when you claimed that it wasn't always a bad thing, to get a good slap... And you said, too, that when something somewhere started to rot, like a gangrenous limb, then it was better to see it lying on the ground, lopped off with an axe, than let it kill you, like cholera... I've often thought about what you said, since I've been on my own, shut up in this insane, wretched Paris... So there we are! I'm the rotten limb you've lopped off...'

He was getting more and more excited, he wasn't even listening to Henriette and Jean any more, who were terrified and begging him to stop. On and on he went, heated and full of fever, overflowing with symbols, bursting with images. It was the healthy part of France, the reasonable, level-headed part, the peasant part, the part which had stayed closest to the soil, which was now suppressing the insane part, the frustrated part, spoiled by the Empire, unbalanced by dreams and decadence; and so it had had to cut right into its very flesh, and tear out its whole being, without really knowing what it was doing. The bloodbath, though, was necessary, and it had to be French blood, this appalling holocaust, this living sacrifice amid the purifying fire. As of now, the calvary had been climbed right to the top, to the most terrifying of agonies, the crucified nation was expiating its sins and was about to be reborn.

'Jean, my old friend, you're the simple, solid one... Go on! Go and pick up your spade again, pick up your trowel!... Plough the field and rebuild your house!... As for me, you were right to lop me off, for I was the ulcer clinging to your bones!'

He went on raving, he tried to get up to go and lean out of the window.

'Paris is burning, there'll be nothing left... Oh! This flame which removes everything, heals everything, I wanted it to happen, oh, yes!

It's doing good work... Let me go down, let me finish the work for humanity and freedom...'

It was all Jean could manage to get him back into bed, while Henriette, in tears, began talking to him about their childhood, begging him to calm down, for the sake of their love for each other. And above the huge city of Paris, the fire's glow had swelled larger still, the sea of flames appeared to have gained the distant shadows of the horizon, the sky was like the roof of some gigantic oven, heated white-hot. And in this smoky, fiery light, the thick black fumes from the Ministry of Finance, which had been obstinately burning for two days without a single flame, went on drifting past in a slow, sombre cloud of mourning.

The following day, which was Saturday, Maurice's condition showed a sudden improvement: he was much calmer, and the fever had subsided; and Jean was overjoyed when he found a smiling Henriette, picking up once more the dream of the three of them living in harmony together, living in a happy future which was still possible, a future she didn't want to spell out. Would Fate be merciful? She spent her days and nights without ever leaving the room, which her Cinderella-like gentleness and constant activity and her silent, subtle attentions filled with a sort of continuous caress. And that evening Jean lingered, sitting with his two friends, with a surprised, trembling feeling of pleasure. During the day, the army had taken Belleville and the Buttes-Chaumont. Only Père Lachaise cemetery still resisted, transformed into a fortified camp. As far as he could see, it was all over, he even claimed that they'd stopped executing people. He simply talked about the flocks of prisoners being driven to Versailles. That morning, he'd encountered one which stretched the entire length of the quayside, with men in smocks, overcoats, shirt-sleeves, women of all ages, some with furrowed, shrewish faces, others in the flower of youth, children barely fifteen years old, an entire flood of misery and revolt which the soldiers were driving on beneath the bright sunlight and which, so it was said, the bourgeoisie of Versailles greeted with jeers and jabs from sticks and parasols.

On the Sunday, however, Jean was terrified. It was the last day of the atrocious week. From the moment the sun rose triumphant on that clear, hot, festive morning, he felt the shudder of the final agony in the air. The renewed massacres of the hostages* had only just come to light: the Archbishop, the curate of the Madeleine, and others, shot on the Wednesday, at La Roquette; the Dominicans of Arcueil shot down as they ran, like hares, on the Thursday; and then more priests and a total of forty-seven gendarmes felled at point-blank range, in the district of the Rue Haxo, on the Friday. It had rekindled furious reprisals, and the army carried out mass executions of the final prisoners they took. For the whole of this fine Sunday, the squad never once stopped firing in the courtyard of the Lobau barracks, accompanied by death cries, blood, and smoke. At La Roquette,* two hundred and twenty-seven poor sods, pulled in at random, were machine-gunned down in a heap, the bullets slicing through their bodies. At Père Lachaise cemetery, which for four days had been under bombardment and was finally captured tomb by tomb, a hundred and forty-eight men were shoved up against a wall, and the plaster streamed with huge, red tears; and when three of them, only wounded, tried to escape, they were caught again and finished off. How many good people were there for every villain, among those twelve thousand wretched souls* who had lost their lives because of the Commune! It was said that the order had come from Versailles to stop the executions. But still they were killing. Thiers would remain the legendary butcher of Paris, for all his honest glory as liberator of the land; while Marshal MacMahon, the man who'd been beaten at Frœschwiller, whose victory proclamation was plastered all over the walls, was now simply the conqueror of Père Lachaise. And sunny, Sunday-best Paris seemed to be in festive mood, with an enormous crowd thronging the reconquered streets, people strolling down the roads, happily meandering along to look at the smoking ruins of the fires, mothers holding laughing children by the hand, stopping and listening with interest for a moment to the muted sounds of gunfire coming from the Lobau barracks.

On the Sunday evening, with daylight growing dim, as Jean climbed up the gloomy staircase of the house on the Rue des Orties, a terrible sense of foreboding closed in on him. He entered the room and immediately saw the inevitable end of it all, Maurice lying dead on the little bed, choked to death by the haemorrhage of which Bouroche had been so afraid. The sun's crimson farewell seeped in through the open window, and two candles were already burning on the bedside table. And Henriette, dressed in the widow's mourning she'd been wearing since she arrived, was kneeling down, crying silently to herself.

Hearing someone come in, she looked up, and shuddered when she saw that it was Jean. Distraught, he went to rush forward and seize her hands and join his grief with hers in an embrace. But he felt her slight hands tremble and her whole being draw back from him, shaking and revolted, tearing herself away, for ever. Wasn't it all over between them, now? Maurice's grave, fathomless, separated them. And he too could only fall to his knees, sobbing quietly.

But after a pause, Henriette spoke.

'I had my back to him, I was a holding a bowl of broth, when he gave a cry... All I had time to do was run over to him, and he died, crying out for me, and you, too, in a pool of blood...'

My God! Her brother, her Maurice she'd adored since before they were born, who was another part of herself, whom she'd raised, whom she'd saved! Her one and only love ever since, back in Bazeilles, she'd seen the body of her poor Weiss lying riddled with bullets at the bottom of a wall! And so the war had finally taken everything dear to her, she would be left alone in the world, widowed and left with nothing, no one to love her!

'Oh, Christ!' cried Jean, sobbing. 'It's all my fault!... My poor, dear boy, I'd have given my life for him, and look, I've gone and slaughtered him like some animal!... What will become of us? Will you ever forgive me?'

And just at that moment, their eyes met, and what they were finally able to read quite clearly in each other's gaze left them both overcome. The past rose up before them, the room hidden away in Remilly, where they had spent such sad, sweet days. He found his dream again, the dream that had at first been subconscious, then only faintly sketched out: a life back there, marriage, a little house, a field to cultivate that would yield enough to feed a family of decent, humble folk. Now he felt it as a burning desire, a keen certainty that, with a woman like her, so gentle, so busy, so brave, life would have become a true paradise. And she, who hadn't even been touched by this dream before, so chastely and unknowingly had she given him her heart, she too now saw it clearly, and suddenly understood everything. So, she'd wanted it too, that distant marriage, without even realizing it. The germinating seed had suddenly and imperceptibly grown, she truly loved this man who at first had been merely a source of comfort to her. And this is what their eyes were saying, and it was only now that they openly loved each other, as they were about to bid one another farewell for ever. They had to make this one last, dreadful sacrifice, this final wrench, and see their happiness, which only a day ago had still been possible, foundering along with the rest, being swept away on the tide of blood which had carried off their brother.

Jean got slowly and awkwardly to his feet.

'Farewell!'

Henriette stood motionless on the tiled floor.

'Farewell!'

But Jean went over to Maurice's body. He looked at him, with his high forehead which now seemed even higher, his long, slender face, his empty eyes, which once had held a spark of madness, a spark which had now been put out. He would have liked to kiss him, kiss that dear boy of his, as he'd called him so many times before, and he dared not. He saw himself covered in his blood, he recoiled before the horror of destiny. Oh! What a death, when an entire world was falling apart! On the last day, among the final remains of a dying Commune, this victim had had to be added to the pile! The poor soul had gone, starved of justice, amid the final convulsions of the great, black dream he had dreamed, this monstrous, grandiose conception to destroy the old society, burn Paris, turn the soil, and purify the field, so that the idyll of a new, golden age might spring up from the earth.

Filled with dread, Jean turned back towards Paris. At the end of a beautiful Sunday, on such a fine, clear evening, the slanting rays of the sun, skimming the horizon, lit up the immense city with a burning, red light. It looked like a bloody sun over a boundless sea. The panes of the thousands of windows glowed as if fanned by invisible bellows; the rooftops blazed like beds of hot coals; yellow walls and the tall, rust-coloured monuments were licked by flames like flickering fires in the evening air. Wasn't this the final burst of sparks, the enormous, purple bouquet, the whole of Paris burning like some giant sacrificial fire, a dry, ancient forest suddenly flaming sky-high, in a sparkling, crackling whirl? The fires burned on, there were still great clouds of russet-coloured smoke rising up into the air, and a huge noise could be heard, perhaps the last cries of those being shot in the Lobau barracks, or perhaps the joy of the women and the laughter of children, as they dined in the open air after their happy stroll, sitting outside the cafés. From the devastated houses and buildings, from the gutted streets, from all the ruins and all the suffering, life was stirring once more, amidst the flames cast by this regal sunset, by whose light the fire of Paris was finally burning itself out.

It was then that Jean felt an extraordinary sensation. As the day slowly faded above the flaming city, it seemed to him that a new dawn was already breaking. And yet this was the end of everything, fate working relentlessly, an accumulation of disasters greater than any nation had ever known: endless defeats, provinces lost to the enemy, the millions they had to pay, the most terrible of civil wars engulfed in a wave of blood, ruins and bodies lying right in the middle of the capital, no money and no honour left, an entire world to rebuild! He himself left behind a heart torn in two, with Maurice, Henriette, and his happy future life swept away in the storm. And yet, beyond the still-roaring blaze, life was springing up again, indestructible, far away in the wide, still, supremely clear sky. This was the sure rejuvenation of eternal nature, of eternal humanity, the renewal of life promised to the man who hopes and toils, the tree which sends out a new, strong shoot after the rotten branch, whose poisonous sap has been turning the leaves yellow, has been cut off.

With a sob, Jean said again,

'Farewell!'

Henriette didn't look up, her face hidden between her two clasped hands.

'Farewell!'

The devastated field lay fallow, the house had been burned to the ground; and Jean, the humblest and most suffering of men, walked away into the future, off to the great, and difficult task of rebuilding France.

EXPLANATORY NOTES

While they do not contain every single village mentioned in *La Débâcle*, the Maps (pp. xl–xliii) will allow the reader to identify the principal towns and battles referred to in the novel.

7 *this August evening*: i.e. of 6 August 1870.

General Félix Douay: commander of the 7th Corps. In 1871, he would lead the first Versaillais troops into Paris (as described on p. 480).

Frœschwiller: see Introduction, p. viii. The French had decided to establish their position around this half-timbered village on the eastern slopes of the Vosges mountains. But the disposition of their four divisions was so clumsy that the Germans won a battle they could well have forfeited. The French lost 11,000 killed or wounded, in addition to surrendering 200 officers and 9,000 men. It was the first battle of the War in which heavy artillery took its deadly toll, leaving the fields and woods so littered with bodies that it took a week to bury them all.

Wissembourg: see Introduction, p. viii. Town at the foot of the Vosges mountains, a strategic death-trap for the 6,000 French troops surrounded there on 3–4 August by 50,000 Germans; the town, with its hopelessly antiquarian fortifications, fell on the 4th; as the French withdrew, they left a thousand prisoners and another thousand dead or wounded, including their divisional commander, Abel Douay (Félix's brother), killed by a shellburst. The anger at the news of this defeat misdirected French strategy, as they rushed to confront the 270,000 men of the German army of the Rhine.

8 *Rognes . . . the drama which had taken his wife from him*: cross-reference back to Zola's *La Terre* (1887), set in the Beauce, around Chartres; Jean's wife Françoise dies after being attacked by her brother-in-law.

Solférino: after the bloody but indecisive battle of Solférino against the Austrians, on 24 June 1859, Napoleon III proposed an armistice to Emperor Francis Joseph, thus bringing this campaign to an end.

10 *death of his brother*: cf. note to *Wissembourg*, above.

Brigadier-General Bourgain-Desfeuilles: almost certainly modelled on the commander of the 5th Corps, General Pierre Louis de Failly (1810–92), universally judged the most incompetent of all the French generals in the Franco-Prussian War.

Napoleon's Grande Armée: i.e. the force whose legendary sequence of victories under the command of Napoleon Bonaparte had resulted in the conquest of most of continental Europe (cf. note to p. 21).

14 *France of the plebiscite*: held on 8 May 1870 in response to growing

opposition, this referendum retrospectively approved the reforms to the constitution since the emergence of the 'Liberal Empire' in 1860; a massive government majority seemed to have restored Napoleon III's fortunes.

14 *claim to the Spanish throne by some German prince*: see Introduction, p. viii.

15 *land in Denmark*: Denmark, attacked by Prussia in 1864, had held exploratory talks with France about the possibility of her shipping a force of some 40,000 men to Germany's North Sea coast, to which Denmark would add another 30,000 men and march jointly on Kiel and Hanover. It was a threat which the Prussians themselves took very seriously, but beyond such talks no preparations for a seaborne invasion had been made.

16 *ailing Emperor*: Napoleon III had been in increasingly poor health since the early 1860s, often in visible pain caused by bladder problems. By 1868, medical writers were called in by the opposition press to regale their readers with intimate details of how he would die. On 28 July 1870, he arrived at Metz to take command. The 1859 campaign against Austria, however, had already shown his total incapacity for generalship even when in good health; now he was suffering agonizingly from a huge kidney stone, in constant pain and virtually unable to mount a horse.

Saarbrücken victory: the occupation of this frontier town, to provide French control of the lateral communications between the Moselle and the Bavarian Palatinate, was achieved on 2 August; with six divisions concentrating on one regiment and a handful of cavalry, it would have been more extraordinary if this limited objective had *not* been realized; the French lost eleven men killed, and nobody who had taken part in the action could have been under any illusions about its significance, magnified proportionately to the distance from it. By the time it reached Paris, news of the 'victory' included the surrender of three Prussian divisions and tales of Saarbrücken being razed to the ground!

the Prince Imperial: i.e. Napoleon III's 15-year-old son and heir Eugène-Louis (sometimes referred to as Napoleon IV, though he never reigned as such), uniformed as a second lieutenant, who accompanied his father to Saarbrücken where they both watched from a suitable distance as French troops went into action. Much was made of the story of him pocketing a bullet which had landed close to his feet 'no more moved than he would be on a walk in the Bois de Boulogne' – a sang-froid which had sceptical Parisians snorting incredulously (a song went round to the effect that the bullets had been deliberately laid before him to pick up). On 27 August he was sent away for his own safety to Belgium, and thence to England. He died in 1879, fighting as a volunteer with British troops against the Zulus in South Africa.

MacMahon: supreme commander of the left wing of the French army of the Rhine, Marshal MacMahon (1808–93) was the hero of the Crimean War (1854–5), a former Governor-General of Algeria and later President of the Republic (1873–9). The soldiers' faith in his putting everything 'right' is fatally misplaced. Virtually every strategic decision he took in 1870 was the wrong one.

17 *murdered by the Cossacks in 1814*: reference to the Tsar's army's role in the invasion of France in 1814 by the allied forces ranged against Napoleon Bonaparte.

19 *Sadowa*: the sudden and complete victory of the Prussians over the Austrians in this battle (3 July 1866) announced to the world the emergence of a new military power; it was also a bitter defeat for French policy based on mediating between hypothetically exhausted belligerents.

Italy and the Crimea: Napoleon III's foreign policy adventures of the 1850s.

routine of the African school: France had been engaged in fighting in North Africa almost continuously since 1830, but in colonializing encounters very different from the techniques of modern warfare honed by the Prussians.

20 *the Limousin*: region of western France, with its main city, Limoges, approximately 200 km. north-east of Bordeaux.

Sebastopol: long and costly siege of the Crimean War, ended when the Russians abandoned it in September 1855, sinking their ships and blowing up its forts.

down there in Africa . . . Laghouat: all sites of the Algerian campaigns (cf. note to *routine of the African school*, above).

21 *Austria . . . Prussia . . . Russia thrashed*: evocation of Napoleon's famous victories at Castiglione (1797), Marengo (1800), Austerlitz (1805), Wagram (1809), Eylau (1807), Jena (1806), Lutzen (1813), Friedland (1807), Smolensk (1812), and Moscow (1812). The last of these, however, is perhaps ironic, given how soon the French were then forced to retreat.

Spain and England thrashed all over the place: in fact only in the Peninsular War (1808–14), notably at Corunna (1809).

22 *Crown Prince*: Frederick, son of the Prussian King, succeeding him in 1888.

Wörth: down from Frœschwiller (cf. note to *Frœschwiller*, p. 515), in the valley. French counter-attacks above Wörth initially swept the Germans back down the slopes, Bavarians and Prussians alike crumbling away before the bayonet-charges of MacMahon's Zouaves (cf. note to p. 69). But, far from being 'taken prisoner', the Prussian Crown Prince ultimately triumphed, riding through the shambles of Frœschwiller to receive the acclamation of his men, with the road through the Vosges to the Lorraine now open before him. Zola's preparatory notes here underline his view that this prelude to Sedan was the decisive moment in France's overall defeat.

24 *Frossard at Spickeren*: it was at General Charles Frossard's suggestion that Saarbrücken had been occupied (cf. note to *Saarbrücken victory*, p. 16). He subsequently fell back to defend the Spickeren heights, some 6 km. east of Forbach, abandoning his position on 5 and 6 August as the German armies advanced towards Metz.

26 *Les Halles*: district of Paris at that time the location of the central markets which are the setting for Zola's *Le Ventre de Paris* (1873). The Rue de la Cossonnerie still exists in this first *arrondissement*.

Picardy: region of France stretching eastwards from the English Channel through Amiens, 130 km. due north of Paris.

Sologne marshes: the Sologne is the region south of Orléans (cf. note to *news from all over the country*, p. 418).

37 *No one was punished*: Zola followed his sources here in noting that not a single soldier was shot for military indiscipline between the start of the War and Sedan.

38 *all the fighting would be done on German soil*: the fact that the French only had maps of Germany is testimony to such arrogance.

41 *Württemberg troops*: i.e. from the south-west German state of that name (extending into the Black Forest area) which had retained its distinct military identity while adopting Prussian regulations and equipment for its army.

43 *Bismarck kipping down in the Tuileries*: Prince Otto von Bismarck (1815–98), architect of German unification under King William, and Chancellor of the latter's Empire. The Tuileries palace, site of the extended present-day Louvre, was the seat of French imperial power.

44 *Badinguet*: nickname given to Napoleon III by his political opponents as a result of his having disguised himself in the clothes of a workman of that name when he escaped from the fortress of Ham (50 km. south-east of Amiens) on 26 May 1846, where he had been imprisoned since 1840 after an abortive attempt to seize power.

47 *Porte de Pantin*: Paris was a walled city at this time; the Porte de Pantin métro stop, in the north-east of the capital, marks this former point of entry.

49 *canal from the Aisne to the Marne*: running, between these two rivers, in a jagged line up from Châlons, through Rheims, to a point a few kilometres west of Neufchâtel-sur-Aisne.

Garde Mobile de la Seine: army reserve force established in 1868.

50 *General Steinmetz*: maverick commander of the German First Army; on 15 September he was transferred to honourable retirement as Governor of Posen, leaving Moltke's supremacy in the German armies unchallenged at last.

Prince Frederick Charles: see Introduction, p. viii.

Bazaine: Marshal Achille Bazaine (1811–88), responsible for the army of the Lorraine before taking over from Napoleon III on 12 August as Commander-in-Chief of all French forces; see Introduction, pp. viii–ix.

the fall of the liberal minister: i.e. that of the Prime Minister, Émile Ollivier (1825–1913), forced to resign on 9 August. See Introduction, p. xii.

Prince Napoleon: cousin of Napoleon III, instrumental in changing the leadership of French forces at the emergency Châlons meeting of 17 August.

General Trochu: Louis Trochu (1815–96) was at the time the commander of the newly formed 12th Corps of the French army of the Rhine. His appointment as Military Governor of Paris, in anticipation of its defence, did not bolster confidence in the collective hopes of conquering Berlin.

51 *attitude of the Empress Regent*: Napoleon III's wife Eugénie (1826–1920) had been appointed Regent when her husband and son had left for the front on 26 July. It suited opposition journalists to embroider the truth of the Emperor being under the thumb of this Spanish-born aristocrat with dynastic pretensions.

General Palikao: the hard-line General de Montauban, Comte de Palikao (1796–1878), was appointed President of the Council (i.e. Prime Minister replacing Ollivier) and Minister of War on 10 August.

52 *Monsieur Rouher*: Eugène Rouher (1814–84) had been Minister of State 1863–9; he enjoyed such power that he was referred to as 'Vice-Emperor' by those keen to create jealousies in government ranks. On 21 August, as President of the Senate, he went to Rheims to convey to MacMahon the Council of Ministers' decision that Bazaine had to be rescued at all costs. He is one of the principal models for the figure of Eugène Rougon, the protagonist of Zola's most closely focused study of Second Empire politics, *Son Excellence Eugène Rougon* (1876).

Épinal engravings: Épinal (366 km. east of Paris) had been famous for these since the end of the eighteenth century.

54 *the holy phial*: used for anointing the kings of France at their coronations in Rheims cathedral.

Clovis: legendary King of the Francs (481–511), the founding father of the French monarchy.

55 *upsurge of heroism and genius*: there follows a fuller evocation of Napoleon Bonaparte's famous victories (cf. note to *Austria . . . Prussia . . . Russia thrashed*, p. 21), here eulogizing his generals: Louis Desaix (1768–1800); Michel Ney (1769–1815); Pierre Augereau (1757–1816); Joachim Murat (1767–1815); and André Masséna (1758–1817).

62 *African Chasseurs*: the cavalry of the French army in North Africa.

63 *Médéah*: town some 155 km. south-west of Algiers.

64 *Toulon*: French naval port on the Mediterranean.

large battle there on the 14th: the battle of Borny, indecisive (there were 5,000 German and 3,500 French casualties, and territory was neither won nor lost) except in so far as Bazaine lost twelve vital hours in trying to escape from Metz.

64 *Uhlans*: the term applied by the French to all German cavalry.

On the 16th, they had fought again: at the double battle of Rezonville-Gravelotte, with huge numbers of casualties on both sides (over 15,000 French and nearly 14,000 Germans). The French let victory slip by failing to follow successful defence with resolute attack.

the dance began again on the 18th: at the battle of Saint-Privat, engaging the bulk of both forces for the first time in the War (188,332 Germans and 732 guns against 112,800 French and 520 guns). After crippling losses on both sides, the French retreated.

65 *General Margueritte*: the admiration for him expressed here anticipates the heroism of his exploits at Sedan (cf. note to '*Oh, how brave!*', p. 292).

67 *embroidered with bees*: emblem of the first Napoleonic empire, deliberately adopted by Napoleon III to reinforce the legitimacy of his own.

69 *Zouaves*: Berber name for the indigenous troops of the French army of North Africa who were to gain a reputation for their fierceness and bravery during the military campaigns of the Second Empire.

74 *Turks*: like the Zouaves, the *turcos* were native troops formed into French regiments.

76 *Chasseurs*: French cavalry.

82 *Saint-Cyr*: military academy, the French equivalent of Sandhurst and West Point.

89 *in the same affectionate tone*: at this point in the original French, the changed relationship between Maurice and Jean is signalled by the use of 'tu'.

92 *Prince of Saxony*: in order to maintain sufficient forces to deal with both Bazaine and MacMahon, the German Second Army was split into two (thus explaining the reference here to 'a Fourth Army'). The regiments pared off constituted the army of the Meuse, under the command of Crown Prince Albert of Saxony, with the aim of pursuing MacMahon. The remaining four corps of the Second Army would stay at Metz with the First Army, with Frederick Charles assuming command of the whole investing force.

118 *Angoulême*: some 440 km. south-west of Paris.

127 *the night which the Emperor and Marshal MacMahon had spent there*: i.e. that of 29 August. Zola was furnished with an eyewitness account of the movement through Raucourt by a local doctor's widow who came to see him on 2 May 1891.

138 *Beaumont*: this battle, on 30 August, was another disaster, with the French losing nearly 7,500 men. Although Zola took notes on it, he skips over this prelude to Sedan in his narrative.

143 *a black invasion*: the second Bavarian Corps (part of the Prussian Third Army) took over Raucourt on the afternoon of 30 August.

152 *Turenne*: legendary French hero (1611–75) of the Thirty Years War, born in Sedan.

154 *Louis XV's reign*: from 1715 to 1774.

Baybel farm: Delaherche's climb up to this point, which overlooks the whole of the valley of the Meuse, is based on Charles Philipotteaux's (the mayor of Givonne), with whom Zola had long discussions during his research at Sedan. He also annotated Xavier Raspail's *Napoléon à Baÿbel, le 30 août 1870* (Paris, 1875), having planned from the beginning that the Emperor should be seen here.

157 *leafy green Sommauthe hillock on the right*: Zola had noted that the King of Prussia being here meant that Napoleon III was looking directly at his opposite number.

173 *the day was only barely beginning*: the battle of Sedan began at first light on the morning of 1 September. By sunset it was effectively over.

174 *General Lebrun*: had taken over from Trochu (cf. note to *General Trochu*, p. 50) on 17 August as commander of the 12th Corps.

178 *They're just keeping you distracted, in Bazeilles*: Weiss's role as all-knowing military strategist is underlined by the fact that these were the very words used by General Ducrot (cf. note to p. 186) in his warning to both Lebrun and the Emperor's staff-officer.

they'll see how distracted we are: precisely General de Wimpffen's (cf. note to p. 186) retort.

185 *the life painted back into his cheeks with vermilion*: see Introduction, p. xxi.

186 *The Marshal—wounded!*: MacMahon's leg was pierced by a shell-fragment while riding out towards Bazeilles. He was then taken back to Sedan (as described on p. 220). He designated as his successor General Auguste Ducrot (1817–82), the most competent and experienced if not the most senior of his corps commanders. Ducrot was in charge for barely three hours. For MacMahon was unaware that General Emmanuel-Félix de Wimpffen (1811–84) had already been nominated to replace de Failly (cf. note to *Brigadier-General Bourgain-Desfeuilles*, p. 10) in response to the news from Frœschwiller (cf. note to *Frœschwiller*, p. 7).

189 *The hundred thousand men*: a German figure much disputed by the French who estimated the numbers from the original Châlons army of 110,000 to have been reduced by this stage to only 70,000 men.

196 *Colonel de Vineuil*: at this point modelled on the real-life General Doutrelaine.

212 *the Hôtel de l'Europe*: Zola would stay at this very hotel in April 1891.

232 *Toulon, Rochefort, or Brest*: France's principal naval bases; for Toulon, cf. note to p. 64; Rochefort is on the Atlantic coast approx 500 km. south-west of Paris; Brest is on the tip of Brittany.

238 *Bazeilles was ablaze*: of the 423 houses in the town, thirty-seven were set ablaze by German shells, while 363 were deliberately torched.

292 *'Oh, how brave!'*: historically authenticated as the Prussian King's gasp of admiration at the sight of the famous cavalry charge of the Margueritte division. The original French words ('Ah! Les braves gens!') are still carved today on their memorial above Floing. With his artillery shattered and his infantry nearly overwhelmed, Ducrot had turned to General Margueritte to act as a battering-ram to force a breakout towards the west. Margueritte was himself terribly wounded while reconnoitring the slopes towards Floing and the Meuse down which the charge was to be made. This duly provided a spectacle of anachronistic courage which lives on in the annals of French military history, as volleys of German breech-loading rifles cut down the thundering horsemen.

294 *letter . . . to the King of Prussia*: cited here verbatim, the letter borne by General Reille, an officer of the imperial suite, was in fact studied by both William and Bismarck, the latter drafting the reply at the end of this fateful day. Zola's exclusive focus on the weary interchange between reigning 'brothers' has the effect of putting the human cost preceding it into a fraternally tragic, rather than geopolitical perspective.

300 *Tuileries*: cf. note to *Bismarck kipping down in the Tuileries*, p. 13.

303 *Fantassins*: infantry soldiers.

319 *desperate situation the French army found itself in*: surrounded by a German army 250,000 strong, armed with 500 guns. De Wimpffen found himself 'negotiating' with (in Moltke and Bismarck) the most brilliant military and political strategists of the age.

along with weapons and equipment: the Germans had taken 21,000 prisoners during the battle, and to these 83,000 were now added. In addition they captured over 1,000 wagons, 6,000 horses, and 419 guns. Their own losses came to 9,000 officers and men.

320 *any officer who promised*: 550 officers took advantage of this 'concession'.

332 *He wanted to see the King of Prussia*: Bismarck only allowed him to do so once the terms of the French capitulation had been agreed.

333 *Hôtel de la Poste in Bouillon*: see Introduction, p. xxi. The Emperor had secured German agreement that he might avoid his angry troops by heading through Belgium towards the palace of Wilhelmshöhe above Cassel, formerly the residence of his cousin Jérome when he was King of Westphalia, which he reached on 5 September. Zola made a sketch of the Emperor's overnight room when he visited it in 1891 during the preparation of *La Débâcle*.

334 *Rouget de l'Isle*: author (1760–1836) of the 'Marseillaise', composed in 1792 for Napoleon Bonaparte's army of the Rhine, but adopted by revolutionaries from Marseilles marching on Paris.

349 *predators*: in view of the long-standing debate about traces of anti-Semitism in Zola's work, it is worth pointing out that the original French

expression here is 'une basse juiverie de proie', with its suggestions of ghetto, community, or cabal.

401 *Henriette, reading from old newspapers*: this device allows Zola to recapitulate the chronology of the major developments of the War of which his fictional participants had only fragmented knowledge (see earlier notes, to pp. 7–64, for references repeated here).

404 *Bazaine . . . must be planning to deal them a hell of a blow*: Even after the French First Army had ceased to exist, there was still a misplaced confidence that the Second, under Bazaine, would escape from Metz and change the outcome of the War. Henriette nurses Jean 'during the first days of October'; by the end of it, Bazaine had surrendered (see Introduction, p. ix).

405 *the second thunderbolt had struck Paris on 3 September*: that morning a Havas agency telegram from Brussels announced the capitulation of the French army at Sedan; it was not believed; but, at 4.30 p.m. the Empress received a telegram from Napoleon III himself, confirming the disaster. Paris was stunned, but more concerned about the consequences for the imperial regime than the strategic implications of military news nowhere equated with national defeat.

Favre, Gambetta . . . proclaim the Republic: Jules Favre (1809–80) was the implacable left-wing opponent of the Second Empire. In accepting the popular acclamation of the Republic voted by the Legislative Assembly as the impatient mob invaded the Chamber, he had cried that it should be proclaimed not in the Palais Bourbon but at the more appropriately populist location of the Hôtel de Ville. He took over the Ministry of Foreign Affairs in the government of National Defence, nominally under Trochu's presidency, but with Léon Gambetta (1838–82) in the key role of Minister of the Interior.

the Empress Regent: making her way through the communicating door between the Tuileries Palace and the Louvre, she was eventually smuggled out of Paris by Dr T. W. Evans, an American court dentist. She made her way via Trouville to England, where she was reunited with her son (cf. note to *the Prince Imperial*, p. 16) in Hastings on 8 September. The following March, her husband joined her at the country house she had found in Chislehurst. He would die there on 10 December 1873, while she survived until 11 July 1920.

Wilhelmshöhe: cf. note to *Hôtel de la Poste in Bouillon*, p. 333.

406 *government for National Defence was being set up in Tours*: 237 km. southwest of Paris, from which Gambetta made his way to the Delegation of the provisional government there by balloon on 7 October. On arrival he also took over as Minister of War, calling the nation to arms and organizing new forces to continue the fight. Even with the capture of the armies of Châlons (at Sedan) and the Rhine (at Metz), France still had over 1,000,000 men serving, training, or liable for military service.

406 *they had seen them east of Paris*: the German advance on the capital had
      begun on 7 September; by the 15th, Moltke's headquarters had been
      established at Château-Thierry, some 60 km. east of Paris on the Marne.
      On the 20th, his cavalry patrols joined up with those of his Third Army
      at Saint-Germain-en-Laye, to the west, thus encircling the city.

412 *carrier pigeons*: ingenious solutions were found during the War to main-
      tain communication across the German encirclements, not only through
      the use of balloons, but also by using an extensive pigeon service central-
      ized at Tours and by reducing messages to such microscopic size and
      newspaper format that a single bird could carry 30,000 of them.

      Bazaine has just betrayed us: see Introduction, p. ix. After the War,
      Bazaine was put on trial for his life, charged with such treason for which
      historians can find no evidence.

413 *the defeats ... at Chevilly, Bagneux, and Malmaison ... and ... at Le
      Bourget*: all failed attempts to break the German stranglehold by seizing
      these village outposts. The most significant encounter was at Le Bourget,
      at first taken (during the night of 27 October, and hailed in Paris as
      a potential turning-point in the War) but subsequently recaptured
      (30 October) by the Prussians who took 1,200 prisoners, thus exacer-
      bating the increasing lack of confidence in the government of National
      Defence's ability to live up to its name.

      a real insurrection: on the morning of 31 October, indications that France
      would have to seek a humiliating armistice (following Thiers's return, cf.
      note to p. 453), together with official publication of the news of the loss of
      Le Bourget and the capitulation at Metz, provoked agreement among the
      delegates of the twenty *arrondissements*, meeting in the Place de la Con-
      corde, to march on the Hôtel de Ville to proclaim the downfall of the
      government and the inauguration of the Commune. On this occasion, a
      Parisian revolution was averted by a mixture of luck, concession (cf. note
      to *the elections of local mayors*, p. 464) and waning enthusiasm. The pol-
      itical situation nevertheless remained so volatile that Thiers, escorted
      from Versailles to the Pont de Sèvres by Bismarck's troops, was not
      allowed to enter the city; and the armistice negotiations he was
      encouraging were broken off on 6 November.

416 *a confused vision*: see Introduction, p. xxvi.

418 *Champigny*: Ducrot had escaped from Sedan during the chaotic evacu-
      ation of the Châlons army to internment in Germany. The battle of
      Champigny was one of several attempts he led to break out of Paris, in
      this case to the east, in the loop of the Marne between Champigny and
      Bry. His 80,000-strong force attacked on 29 November, initially securing
      a bridgehead but ultimately repulsed by German reinforcements. By
      4 December, Ducrot had lost some 12,000 officers and men and urged
      Favre and Trochu to sue for peace.

      news from all over the country: this paragraph summarizes the vicissitudes
      of French resistance to the invasion after Sedan and beyond the fall of

Metz. As the Germans swept westwards in arcs to the north and south of Paris, the French assembled the army of the Loire around Orléans, 116 km. south of the capital. In the region of the Forest of Orléans on 5 October, this had forced enemy cavalry outposts to fall back on Étampes. At the battle of Coulmiers, on 8 and 9 November, the French secured the victory necessary for them to reoccupy Orléans. But, by the first week of December, they were forced to abandon it again, a fatal blow to the hope that the Loire would provide an impregnable line of defence against the German advance on Paris.

419 *Chanzy*: General Antoine Chanzy (1823–83), retaining command of the second army of the Loire after the fall of Orléans (cf. note to *news from all over the country*, p. 418) and distinguishing himself in the subsequent campaign through December and into January, if not by victory, at least in staving off or mitigating defeat, thereby slowing up the German advance.

422 *the guerrillas from Dieulet Woods*: the so-called *francs-tireurs* numbered some 60,000 men, organized by the government of National Defence, effectively harassing German lines of communication all over France throughout the autumn of 1870, but bringing terrible reprisals against the rural population accused of harbouring them.

423 *Procumbit humi bos*: the ox falls to the ground.

425 *Per amica silentia lunae*: i.e. 'through the friendly silence of the moon' (from Virgil's *Aeneid*, 2.7 255, and almost apposite given its context of the 'treacherous' Greeks making their way into Troy).

435 *quos vult perdere Jupiter dementat*: i.e. 'Jupiter drives mad those he wishes to destroy', popular saying and incomplete variation on *quem Jupiter vult perdere dementat prius*, based on a seventeenth-century French commentator's note on Sophocles, *Antigone*.

445 *General Manteuffel's troops*: Edwin von Manteuffel (1809–85) had been appointed commander of the German First Army and, after the capitulation of Metz, assigned the task of advancing westward to the Oise to break up the French forces which were assembling in the north. At the beginning of November, he was dispatched by Moltke towards Amiens and Rouen, the latter falling without resistance on 5 December.

447 *French warships*: although French squadrons in the Baltic and the North Sea had cruised uneasily off the German coast in an attempt to maintain a blockade, until the government of National Defence summoned them back to France, this was indeed merely a 'pretext' without substance.

451 *Bruges stitch*: this Flemish city had been famous for its textiles and embroidery since the Middle Ages.

453 *Monsieur Thiers*: the veteran Adolphe Thiers (1797–1877) had not accepted office in the government of National Defence, but set out on a European tour to enlist the sympathy and, if possible, the aid of the neutral Powers for the new regime. He was respectfully received in

Russia, Austria, Italy, and England. On 30 October he returned (virtually empty-handed save for an offer from the British to mediate between the belligerents). He advised ministers to accept any German terms for an armistice (cf. note to *a real insurrection*, p. 413) so long as elections could be held which would return a government authorized to make peace.

457 *General Faidherbe*: previously Governor of Senegal and a highly skilled administrator, Louis Faidherbe (1818–89) succeeded in forging an army of the North from the remnants of French forces defeated elsewhere. His attempts to recapture Amiens on 23 December, at Pont-Noyelle, were not sufficient to break the German lines cutting off Lille from Paris.

460 *at Villeneuve-Saint-Georges*: just to the east of the present-day Orly airport, on 17 September.

Ducrot . . . resolved to attack: on 19 September, he attempted an offensive movement towards the Versailles road, but his inexperienced forces disintegrated; he had to abandon the fortifications of the Châtillon redoubt and retreat to Paris.

telegraph line along the Western Railway: at Saint-Germain-en-Laye, where the meeting of German cavalry patrols on 20 September completed the encirclement of Paris and signalled the beginning of the siege.

Place du Carrousel: in the first *arrondissement*, in the very heart of the capital.

General Vinoy: the aged Joseph Vinoy (1800–80) would in due course take over from Trochu as Military Governor of the capital (cf. note to *General Trochu's resignation*, p. 468). His 13th Corps contained the only regular regiments still at liberty—the 35th and 42nd, which had formerly garrisoned Rome. This corps, dispatched to join MacMahon, had been at Mézières when the army of Châlons surrendered at Sedan. Vinoy had extricated it with some skill from under the noses of the German cavalry, during the night of 1 September, and brought it back via Laon to the capital, together with about 10,000 refugees from MacMahon's forces.

the 14th Corps, which had been entrusted to General Ducrot: this is slightly misleading to the extent that while Ducrot, on 16 September, had been named commander of both the 13th and 14th Corps, the latter was under the orders of General Renault, Vinoy having been unwilling to serve under Ducrot on the grounds of his own seniority.

461 *Dorian*: formerly an industrialist, Pierre-Frédéric Dorian (1814–73) was the vigorous new Minister of Public Works.

negotiations in Ferrières: on 19 and 20 September, between Favre, as Foreign Minister, and Bismarck, at the Rothschilds' huge palace at Ferrières, where the Germans had established their political and military headquarters, just to the east of Paris. Favre burst into tears on learning that German terms for peace involved huge reparations and France ceding the city of Strasbourg, as well as the province of Alsace and part of that of Lorraine, including Metz and Château-Salin. He returned to Paris in despair.

462 *the breakout of 30 September*: when the 13th Corps sprung an attack from Moulin-Saquet and Hautes-Bruyères towards Thiais, Chevilly, and L'Hay, taking a few houses only to abandon them having sustained heavy casualties. On 13 October, 20,000 men of this same corps, together with units of the mobile guard, moved from the forts of Montrouge and Vanves to briefly occupy Bagneux, Clamart, and part of Châtillon (all these villages beyond the fortified walls of the capital are today incorporated within its southern suburbs). On 21 October, 10,000 men of the 14th Corps captured Malmaison and its park, to the west of Paris, before retreating to the safety of the city walls.

on the eve of 31 October: cf. note to *a real insurrection*, p. 413, with which Maurice is now associated, preparing the ground for his participation in the 1871 Commune.

464 *Saint-Ouen*: at that time a small village just north of the city walls.

the elections of local mayors (cf. note to *a real insurrection*, p. 413). Previously these had been appointed by the Ministry of the Interior. The elections on 5, 6, and 7 November resulted in the success of Commune candidates in the heavily working-class eleventh, nineteenth, and twentieth *arrondissements*. So Zola exaggerates here in writing that, symptomatic of the impending crisis, 'nearly all those elected to office belonged to extremist parties'.

General Clément Thomas: an unfortunate choice in so far as he was detested by the left for his brutal repression of the uprisings of 1848 (cf. note to *the murder of Generals Lecomte and Clément Thomas*, p. 473).

465 *Champigny*: cf. note to *Champigny*, p. 418.

Bourbaki: General Charles Bourbaki's (1816–97) audacious strategy was to draw the Germans away from Paris by transferring his army from the Loire to the Saône Valley at the end of December, and drive up through Dijon and Besançon to relieve Belfort. The gamble failed. Poor organization and winter conspired to transform the plan into the humiliating retreat of 80,000 men into Switzerland on 1 February, with Bourbaki himself relieved of his command after a botched suicide attempt a week earlier.

466 *Place du Château-d'Eau*: in the tenth *arrondissement*, now the Place de la République.

air balloons . . . from the Gare du Nord: by 1870 the development of coal-gas had made these a viable proposition. From 26 September onwards, there was a regular postal service, balloons leaving Paris two or three times a week (cf. note to *carrier pigeons*, p. 412).

the bombardment: the German bombardment began on 5 January. The range of the new siege-guns allowed them to throw a shell some 8 km., from the Châtillon heights to the Île Saint-Louis in the very centre of

Paris. Between three and four hundred fell daily on the city, most of them exploding harmlessly in open spaces. Public buildings which suffered some superficial damage included the Panthéon and the Sorbonne. Parisians who flocked curiously to the Left Bank, which bore the brunt of the bombardment, were disappointed to find how little could be seen. But it both strengthened Parisian resolve and shifted European public opinion against the Germans.

466 *Val-de-Grace*: military hospital, formerly a convent, built between 1645 and 1665, and situated in the Rue Saint-Jacques, in the fifth *arrondissement*.

one fresh and ill-fated attempt to mount an attack: on 21 December, again with the intention of retaking the village of Le Bourget (cf. note to *the defeats . . . at Chevilly, Bagneux, Malmaison . . . and . . . at Le Bourget*, p. 413). Trochu had rightly predicted that renewed failure would be politically intolerable.

467 *the Plateau d'Avron*: overlooking the Marne, this position (taken during the breakout to Champigny) had to be evacuated on the night of 28 December as German guns started pounding the eastern ring of forts.

news of the occupation of Montretout: three army columns had been formed: on the left flank of the Mont-Valérien, Vinoy's headed for Saint-Cloud and Montretout; in the centre, General de Bellemare's for Buzenval; on the right, Ducrot himself made for Malmaison and Longboyau. The French lost a total of 3,000 men.

468 *Rue de Rivoli*: in the first *arrondissement*, alongside the Tuileries and the Louvre, and heading past the political nerve-centre of the Hôtel de Ville. Following these demonstrations in the wake of so many abortive attempts to break the German siege, the government of National Defence was fighting ever more desperately for survival. Zola omits important developments between 20 and 29 January such as the springing from captivity of leaders of the aborted coup of 31 October, the arrest of prominent radicals, and other measures designed to repress incipient revolution.

General Trochu's resignation: faced with Trochu's refusal to do so, the government took the step of suppressing the governorship of Paris altogether; and while Trochu was persuaded to remain as President of the Council, it offered the command of the armies, which Ducrot refused, to Vinoy (cf. note to *General Vinoy*, p. 460). Maurice's perception of such decisions is necessarily simplified.

Belleville: the most radical working-class area of Paris, in the twentieth *arrondissement*.

talks with Bismarck: informal talks had begun on 1 October, followed by various other opportunistic attempts to break the stalemate reached at Ferrières (cf. note to *negotiations in Ferrières*, p. 461). Formal negotiations were reopened on 23 January, Favre meeting Bismarck at Versailles, now the centre of German civil and military administration. Two days later he was authorized to sign an armistice lasting three weeks, to enable the National Assembly to meet at Bordeaux and finally resolve the question of peace or war. This armistice of 28 January provided for an immediate war-indemnity of two hundred million francs from Paris itself, yielding the perimeter forts and dismounting the guns from the city walls.

469 *the Nord*: the department of which Lille is the regional centre.

Switzerland: cf. note to *Bourbaki*, p. 465.

the elections: i.e. those for the National Assembly. Held on 8 February, the results proved a decisive rejection of Republican policies to continue the War rather than submit to German terms. While Paris and the great cities returned representatives of the left, the more conservative provinces generated a huge monarchist majority in favour of peace at virtually any price. Thiers, who had been publicly arguing for this course of action since October, was the obvious choice to head the new government (Gambetta having resigned on 6 February).

first sessions in Bordeaux: from 13 February onwards, the date on which Zola started his parliamentary chronicles for *La Cloche* (see Introduction, p. x).

harsh terms: agreed by Thiers and Favre when they resumed negotiations with Bismarck on 21 February. The latter was now able to dictate the price to those mandated to seek peace. It included not only reparations and the whole of Alsace, but also the northern area of Lorraine, including Metz, which had already been organized by the German administration as 'the new department of the Moselle'. The south of the province, round Nancy, would remain French. The only point ceded by the Germans was France's retention of Belfort, of far less military importance than Metz. The terms were ratified by the National Assembly on 1 March by 546 votes to 107.

Butte des Moulins: on the heights of Montmartre.

470 *from the Tuileries . . . to the Bastille*: i.e. a panorama stretching from the centre to the eastern fringes of the city.

The Prussians were to enter Paris on 1 March: the unexpectedly speedy implementation of the peace terms (see note to *harsh terms*, above) deprived the Kaiser of the three-day triumphal entry into Paris of 30,000 men prior to an evacuation which it had been agreed would take place immediately after formal ratification. A contingent from the Third Army marched down the Champs-Élysées on 1 March under the gaze of a curious and intermittently jeering crowd, but the Kaiser had to be content with reviewing his troops at Longchamps on 3 March as they left the city—instead of leading in his Guard with a splendour designed to match that of the victory parade following Napoleon Bonaparte's defeat in 1814.

the men of 4 September: i.e. those who had assumed power after the demise of the imperial regime (cf. note to *Favre, Gambetta . . . proclaim the Republic*, p. 405).

471 *The Central Committee*: the *Comité Central de la Garde Nationale* was elected following the decision by delegates of the National Guard, at meetings on 15 and 24 February, to create a federation of their units (from which derives the French term *fédérés* used for the combatants of the Commune). The Committee wielded huge potential powers, in charge of the most powerful armed force in France by virtue of Bismarck having accepted, against his better judgement, French warnings that attempts to include the National Guard within the demilitarizing clauses of the peace terms would lead to civil war. By 26 February it had some two hundred cannon at its disposal, recovered from artillery parks at various points in the city in order to prevent them falling into the hands of the Germans when they entered Paris under the terms of the armistice.

death of some poor policeman: there were huge demonstrations in the revolutionarily resonant Place de la Bastille on 24, 25, and 26 February. The victim of the crowd's anger during the last of these was a certain Vincenzoni who (it was claimed) was spotted noting down the identification numbers of units of the National Guard taking part in the march of some 300,000 people.

Boulevard des Batignolles: in the seventeenth *arrondissement*, on the way up to Montmartre.

Place Wagram: at the northern end of the Avenue de Wagram, which leads up to the Arc de Triomphe.

in Versailles on 20 March: see Introduction, p. ix.

472 *the events . . . up on Montmartre*: while riots had broken out on 3 March, as the Germans were leaving the city, the declaration of the Commune was catalysed by the government's attempt to retrieve the cannon (cf. note to *The Central Committee*, above) which had been dragged up to the heights of Montmartre. Early on the morning of 18 March, regular troops took them over but found that there were no horses available to move them. During the confrontation with the members of the National Guard alerted by tocsin, many of these troops refused to fire on the assembled mob. The building of the symbolically white Sacré-Cœur after the Commune was designed to erase this inaugurating site of 'Red Paris'.

Thiers . . . had . . . been planning this coup: as early as 8 March, he had foreseen that his government's authority would be fatally compromised if he allowed the cannon to remain in the hands of the National Guard, with only 6,000 of its 400,000 strength reckoned to be loyal. It was only on the 17th, however, that he and Vinoy elaborated the abortive military operation at Montmartre.

the entire government routed: as the revolutionary movement spread through the city, Thiers, his ministers, and the few regular army units in Paris decided to withdraw to Versailles.

473 *the murder of Generals Lecomte and Clément Thomas*: the former had been

dragged off his horse and captured during the encounter at Montmartre; but his fate was really sealed by the fortuitous presence of the hated Thomas (cf. note to *General Clément Thomas*, p. 464). After being kept prisoner for most of the day, the two old generals were savagely butchered on the afternoon of 18 March.

the Hôtel de Ville in the hands of the members of the Central Committee: the government had originally considered holding out here, but by 7.30 p.m. those manning it had melted away. Virtually spontaneously, revolutionaries entered it and unfurled a red flag from its belfry. By the morning of 19 March, 20,000 men of the National Guard were camped outside it.

474 *Vaugirard*: part of the fifteenth *arrondissement*, staging-post for regular troops withdrawing to Versailles.

475 *a battle between the mayors and the Central Committee*: who began a series of meetings on 19 March, the mayors of the twenty *arrondissements* arguing unsuccessfully for a return to constitutional authority. On 26 March, the Committee organized the election of a new Municipal Council to run the city. In the strictest sense, this related the 1871 Commune to variants of municipal independence since the French Revolution, whatever the social and philosophical mythologies with which the term had been invested by bourgeois fears and proletarian ideals. From its first meeting on 28 March, however, it was clear that the majority of those present wished the Commune to arrogate to itself more than purely municipal functions.

peaceful demonstration on the Place Vendôme: outside the National Guard headquarters, on 21 March, by a motley of anti-revolutionary citizens. As they turned into the Rue de la Paix, they met a detachment of trigger-happy National Guard who opened fire. About a dozen of them were killed, marking the end of any hope that the rift between Versailles and Paris could be repaired without further bloodshed.

Puteaux and Courbevoie: just across the Seine from what is now the western suburb of Neuilly (cf. note to *Neuilly*, p. 477).

conquer Versailles: the intention of the disorganized force which set out from Paris on 3 April, but which succeeded only in recapturing the Pont de Neuilly. It was no match for the heavy guns of the Mont-Valérien fortress overlooking them or the Versailles cavalry. Vinoy ordered all National Guard prisoners to be shot out of hand. Civil war had begun.

476 *Rueil*: i.e. Rueil-Malmaison, in what are now the western outskirts of Paris. It was here that the first of the Commune leaders, Gustave Flourens, was killed.

the taking of hostages: notably the President of the Court of Appeal and the Archbishop of Paris. A notorious 'Law of Hostages' was passed on 5 April in direct response to Versaillais treatment of National Guard prisoners.

476 *the day that the Commune was solemnly established*: on 28 March, with a spectacular display of revolutionary triumphalism.

477 *Neuilly*: it is not by chance that Zola stations Maurice here. For what was then a village (now part of the western suburbs, but still as prosperous) was at the interface of the opposing forces and progressively reduced to a shambles as it repeatedly changed hands.

The troops ... at Versailles were now so numerous: inflated by Bismarck's acquiescence that the size of the army should be increased to 170,000 men, and that the return to France of 400,000 prisoners of war should be speeded up, including MacMahon himself who, after seven months of internment beyond the Rhine, was urging for an opportunity to erase the humiliation of Sedan.

to reinforce their encircling lines: Versailles troops occupied Neuilly on 6 April, the Château de Bécon on the 17th, and Asnières on the 19th.

the Point-du-Jour: the Porte du Point-du-Jour was at the extreme south-western point of the city (just to the east of the present-day Porte de Saint-Cloud), close to where the Seine flows out towards Sèvres.

Levallois ... Vanves ... Issy: the modern reader may recognize these sites as terminal points on métro-lines, located as they are on the western periphery of the city. It was on 13 May that the fortress at Vanves fell to MacMahon's troops. But Thiers's capture of the one at Issy was far more significant, with immediate consequences for the unravelling of the Commune's military leadership (cf. note to *Cluseret and Dombrowski, Rossel*, below).

Pages of history: the creation, on 30 April, of the *Comité du Salut Public* (with a membership of only five in order to reinforce executive direction) inevitably recalled the body of the same name established on 6 April 1793 which exercised dictatorial power (under Robespierre) during the Terror.

Vendôme column: 44 m. high, it was made from 1,200 bronze cannon captured from the Austrians and Russians, erected in 1810, and dedicated to the veterans of the battle of Austerlitz (1805). As an emblem of Napoleonic glory (it originally had a statue of Napoleon on the top), it was a target for the Commune which decreed, on 12 April, that it should be pulled down. On 16 May, in a major ceremony, it came crashing to the ground. It was rebuilt in 1874.

the house of the assassin Thiers: in the Place Saint-Georges, in the ninth *arrondissement*. Its destruction was decreed on 11 May and implemented a few days later. Thiers's belongings were confiscated and distributed among the city's libraries and museums. His personal bitterness was limitless.

478 *Cluseret and Dombrowski, Rossel*: Gustave-Paul Cluseret was appointed military commander of the Commune on 2 April, but arrested by the end of the month as a result of the failure to regain the initiative, and put on trial for dereliction of duty. He had appointed Jaroslaw Dombrowski as

Commandant of Paris. When his former Chief of Staff, Louis Rossel, succeeded the disgraced Cluseret (but with the new title 'Delegate of War'), Dombrowski was initially placed in direct control of the Right Bank, but subsequently given command of all the Commune forces, at which point (on 6 May) Rossel resigned. He escaped imminent arrest by his own side on the 9th (coinciding with the fall of the Issy fortress), but was executed after the Commune. Dombrowski himself was later accused of betraying the revolutionary cause, before being killed defending it.

479 *Delescluze*: Charles Delescluze (1809–71) was a former radical journalist who became one of the most prominent leaders of the Commune, and ultimately one of its martyrs, killed on the barricades on 25 May (evoked on p. 506). Earlier, on 21 April, he had tried to bring some sort of order to its affairs by replacing its Executive Committee by a kind of war cabinet formed from the Delegates of its Commissions. In practice, this reorganization made as little difference as his succeeding Rossel as 'Civil Delegate to the Ministry of War'.

the decree calling up all males under forty: this included the 31-year-old Zola who left the city on 10 May (see Introduction, p. x).

480 *a gate abandoned by the sentries*: as a result of continuous bombardment by the powerful battery established by the Versaillais at Montretout (cf. note to *news of the occupation of Montretout*, p. 467).

a passer-by: a civil engineer named Ducatel, who felt no love for the Commune, out on a stroll near the battlements on his afternoon walk on Sunday, 21 May.

General Douay: cf. note to *General Félix Douay*, p. 7.

481 *on the morning of 22 May*: by 3 a.m., 70,000 troops had entered the city.

slowly drawing back: Maurice's movements can be retraced eastwards from the esplanade of the Invalides, in the seventh *arrondissement*, back towards the Rue de Lille, at the rear of the present-day Musée d'Orsay. Across from the latter is the Palais de la Légion d'Honneur (built in 1786), next to which Maurice sleeps, which has its main entrance on the Rue de Lille.

482 *Montmartre and the Observatoire*: i.e. from north and south, respectively, the Observatoire being at the edge of the fourteenth and fifth *arrondissements*.

impregnable citadel of the insurrection!: (cf. note to *the events . . . up on Montmartre*, p. 472). At this symbolic site, the famous guns were unserviceable and the barricades half-built, and the defenders who had not slipped away during the night were overwhelmed by the full division of troops launched up the northern slopes by General Ladmirault who ordered all survivors to be shot.

483 *a story*: based on that of Émile Eudes, formerly in charge—at least nominally as well as unwillingly—of the Issy garrison, ensconced with his mistress in the Palais de la Légion d'Honneur since 22 April.

485 *Rue des Saints-Pères*: dividing the sixth and seventh *arrondissements*, this runs towards the Seine. At this point, Jean is barely a hundred metres or so from the intersection of the Rue du Bac and the Rue de Lille to which Maurice has retreated.

487 *Saint-Denis*: now part of the industrial suburbs north of Paris.

489 *La Villette*: to the north-west of the Buttes-Chaumont, in the nineteenth *arrondissement*. Looking from the north, as here, it is to the left of Montmartre.

491 *Rue de Richelieu*: in the second *arrondissement*.

492 *Rue du Hasard, Rue Saint-Anne and then the Rue des Orties*: the Rue du Hasard is now the Rue Thérèse, running between the Rue Saint-Anne and the Rue de Richelieu; the 'Rue des Orties Saint-Honoré' (to restore its full name) was destroyed in 1876, to make way for the south-western end (and final part) of the new Avenue de l'Opéra. This is one of the few points in the novel where Zola takes liberties with his urban geography: the Rue Saint-Anne, running parallel to the Rue de Richelieu, is a very considerable distance from Montmartre (cf. note to *Butte des Moulins*, p. 469) where we are originally told Maurice is living. It seems likely that Zola, wishing to place him on the Right Bank, affording him the necessary view of the burning city, then realized that Montmartre would be inaccessible once in the hands of the Versaillais. It is made explicit at the end of the detailed itinerary later followed by Jean and Maurice that the Rue des Orties is reached along the Rue d'Argenteuil, very near the Rue Saint-Anne (cf. note to *by way of the Place de la Concorde and the Rue Saint Honoré*, p. 497). On p. 501, it is again stated that it occupies 'a high position on the Butte des Moulins' with 'Paris stretched out before them', but the perspective is foreshortened to include 'close by, the fires on the Rue Saint-Honoré'.

495 *Pont de Solférino*: built in 1858-9, opposite the Palais de la Légion d'Honneur, this bridge (beautifully decorated to celebrate the victories of the Italian campaign) was demolished in 1961, to make way for the Left Bank *voie express*, and replaced by a footbridge, itself subsequently removed in anticipation of the new 'Passerelle de Solférino' currently (1999) being completed.

the Tuileries were burning: set on fire at 10 p.m. on 23 May. In the Salle des Maréchaux, the Communards had stockpiled gunpowder and indiscriminately smeared the fine hangings with tar and petroleum. Subsequent references to the various *pavillons* will be familiar to modern visitors to the Louvre.

496 *wind*: conditions for arson were perfect to the extent that a wind of virtually hurricane strength began blowing on the night of 23 May, after weeks of abnormally hot weather.

497 *by way of the Place de la Concorde and the Rue Saint-Honoré*: having rowed away from the city, Jean and Maurice come up from the river on

the western side of the Place de la Concorde, cut across the latter (looking right to the National Assembly and left up the Rue Royale to the Madeleine) and then head north up the Rue Saint-Florentin which itself meets the Rue Saint-Honoré, down which they walk towards the Rue d'Argenteuil (cf. note to *Rue du Hasard, Rue Saint-Anne and then the Rue des Orties*, p. 492).

498 *Naval Ministry*: the Ministère de la Marine et des Colonies occupied the two monumental buildings forming an entrance to the Rue Royale on the north side of the Place de la Concorde.

the Garde-Meuble: repository of the equivalent of the Crown Jewels, once in the Palais Bourbon, but more recently (earlier in 1870) occupying a new building in the Rue de l'Université. Zola's memory and sources serve him false here.

504 *Palais du Luxembourg*: adjoining the well-known Gardens.

506 *Charonne*: near the Père Lachaise cemetery, in the twentieth *arrondissement*, one of the last remaining strongholds of the Commune and against the eastern wall of which (and thus known to this day as the *Mur des Fédérés*) 148 captured Communards were summarily executed on 28 May.

Théâtre du Châtelet: facing the Place du Châtelet, in the first *arrondissement*.

Lobau barracks: behind the Hôtel de Ville.

507 *arsonists*: the so-called *pétroleuses* remained, in Zola's day and beyond, one of the most abiding legends of the Commune, no less provocative than the term itself (used here in the original French). Historians have since dismissed the Versaillais claim that there existed veritable brigades, 8,000-strong, of these fiendishly amazonian creatures. What is certain is that, on the basis of possibly a few incidents, any woman carrying a bottle of any sort was shot on sight.

508 *the Grenier d'Abondance*: vast grain reserve established by Napoleon I and moved in 1837 to warehouses at La Villette (see below); the reference here is to the original building on the Boulevard Bourdon, near the Arsenal.

docks . . . at La Villette: otherwise known as the Bassin de La Villette, the arrival point for traffic along the Canal de l'Ourcq to the east and the communicating one which rejoins the Seine to the north-west of Paris and towards the sea.

510 *massacres of the hostages*: (cf. note to *the taking of hostages*, p. 476). Archbishop Darboy, being held at La Roquette Prison, was shot on 24 May, together with the ex-Empress's confessor, Abbé Deguerry, Judge Bonjean, and three Jesuits. On the 26th, fifty further hostages removed from the prison were executed in the Rue Haxo, having been trailed through jeering crowds up what is now the Avenue Gambetta, in the twentieth *arrondissement*. The incident in which the priests tried to make a run for

it seems to have occurred on the 27th (the Saturday rather than the Thursday).

511 *At La Roquette*: some 1,900 prisoners are said to have been shot in two days; at the Mazas Prison, another 400. Firing squads worked mercilessly all over Paris, executing without trial anybody who had fought for, or even sympathized with, the Commune.

twelve thousand wretched souls: Zola follows contemporary sources here in underestimating the number of dead. Reliable French historians today seem more or less agreed on a figure of between 20,000 and 25,000 during 'Bloody Week' alone.

A SELECTION OF   OXFORD WORLD'S CLASSICS

GEORGE ELIOT	Adam Bede
	Daniel Deronda
	Middlemarch
	The Mill on the Floss
	Silas Marner
ELIZABETH GASKELL	Cranford
	The Life of Charlotte Brontë
	Mary Barton
	North and South
	Wives and Daughters
THOMAS HARDY	Far from the Madding Crowd
	Jude the Obscure
	The Mayor of Casterbridge
	A Pair of Blue Eyes
	The Return of the Native
	Tess of the d'Urbervilles
	The Woodlanders
WALTER SCOTT	Ivanhoe
	Rob Roy
	Waverley
MARY SHELLEY	Frankenstein
	The Last Man
ROBERT LOUIS STEVENSON	Kidnapped and Catriona
	The Strange Case of Dr Jekyll and Mr Hyde and Weir of Hermiston
	Treasure Island
BRAM STOKER	Dracula
WILLIAM MAKEPEACE THACKERAY	Barry Lyndon
	Vanity Fair
OSCAR WILDE	Complete Shorter Fiction
	The Picture of Dorian Gray

	Oriental Tales
WILLIAM BECKFORD	**Vathek**
JAMES BOSWELL	**Boswell's Life of Johnson**
FRANCES BURNEY	**Camilla**
	Cecilia
	Evelina
	The Wanderer
LORD CHESTERFIELD	**Lord Chesterfield's Letters**
JOHN CLELAND	**Memoirs of a Woman of Pleasure**
DANIEL DEFOE	**Captain Singleton**
	A Journal of the Plague Year
	Memoirs of a Cavalier
	Moll Flanders
	Robinson Crusoe
	Roxana
HENRY FIELDING	**Joseph Andrews and Shamela**
	A Journey from This World to the Next and The Journal of a Voyage to Lisbon
	Tom Jones
	The Adventures of David Simple
WILLIAM GODWIN	**Caleb Williams**
	St Leon
OLIVER GOLDSMITH	**The Vicar of Wakefield**
MARY HAYS	**Memoirs of Emma Courtney**
ELIZABETH HAYWOOD	**The History of Miss Betsy Thoughtless**
ELIZABETH INCHBALD	**A Simple Story**
SAMUEL JOHNSON	**The History of Rasselas**
CHARLOTTE LENNOX	**The Female Quixote**
MATTHEW LEWIS	**The Monk**

The Oxford World's Classics Website

www.worldsclassics.co.uk

- Information about new titles
- Explore the full range of Oxford World's Classics
- Links to other literary sites and the main OUP webpage
- Imaginative competitions, with bookish prizes
- Peruse *Compass*, the Oxford World's Classics magazine
- Articles by editors
- Extracts from Introductions
- A forum for discussion and feedback on the series
- Special information for teachers and lecturers

www.worldsclassics.co.uk

American Literature

British and Irish Literature

Children's Literature

Classics and Ancient Literature

Colonial Literature

Eastern Literature

European Literature

History

Medieval Literature

Oxford English Drama

Poetry

Philosophy

Politics

Religion

The Oxford Shakespeare